ON THE OCEANS OF ETERNITY

S. M. Stirling

A ROC BOOK

ROC
Published by New American Library, a division of
Penguin Putnam Inc., 375 Hudson Street,
New York, New York 10014, U.S.A.
Penguin Books Ltd, 27 Wrights Lane,
London W8 5TZ, England
Penguin Books Australia Ltd, Ringwood,
Victoria, Australia
Penguin Books Canada Ltd, 10 Alcorn Avenue,
Toronto, Ontario, Canada M4V 3B2
Penguin Books (N.Z.) Ltd, 182–190 Wairau Road,
Auckland 10, New Zealand

Penguin Books Ltd, Registered Offices:
Harmondsworth, Middlesex, England

First published by Roc, an imprint of New American Library,
a division of Penguin Putnam Inc.

First Printing, April 2000
10 9 8 7 6 5 4 3 2 1

 REGISTERED TRADEMARK—MARCA REGISTRADA

Printed in the United States of America

To my father, Alfred Bruce Stirling

ACKNOWLEDGMENTS

Many thanks to the cadets and staff of the Coast Guard Academy, New London, Connecticut, for their hospitality and interest; special thanks to Professor Faye Ringle of the Academy; and to the officers and crew of *Eagle*, for the guided tour.

My apologies to her captain for the unspeakable things I did to his cabin.

"Wenlock Edge" by A. E. Houseman, *A Shropshire Lad*, 1887, XXI

Excerpts from "March of Cambreadth," Heather Alexander, *Midsummer*, copyright © 1997 Sea Fire Productions

Thanks to William Pint and Felicia Dale for permission to quote from their beautiful songs in *Hearts of Gold*, © 1994, *Round the Corner*, © 1997, *When I See Winter Return*, © 1997, Waterbug Records; available at *http://members.aol.com/Pintndale/*

And to Tony Goodenough, for permission to use lyrics from "Pump Shanty."

Thanks also to Ms. Margarita Booker of Ronald Wharton Rifles, and to Mr. Geoffrey Boothroyd.

My thanks to Bobby Hardenbrook for his help with the website www.av.qnet.com/~fourls/island/island.htm

All errors, omissions, infelicities, and lapses are purely mine.

PROLOGUE

August, 1240 B.C.
August, 10 A.E.—Neayoruk, Kingdom of Great Achaea

"**B**ut Lord Cuddy, *why* does the interior of this furnace have to open out?" Augewas asked. "It made the construction much more complex than the earlier ones."

William Jefferson Cuddy, onetime corporal in the United States Marine Corps, onetime machine-tool operator with Seahaven Engineering, and currently *ekwetos* and Master of Engineers to the High King of Great Achaea, stopped his thoughtful pacing. Production scheduling for something as big as a steel mill was a nightmare, even for this miniaturized antique . . . especially when even the executives he had to rely on were mostly ex-peasants who could barely comprehend that "on time" didn't mean "in a while, maybe."

Even if you explain twice about the big hand and the little hand, with diagrams and a boot up the ass, Cuddy thought. A simple technical question was a relief.

"Ummmm," he said, racking his brain and looking up. The interior of the furnace was dimly lit by a shaft of light from above, more brightly by the kerosene lamp the slave behind them held. It smelled of rock and fresh brick and mortar, and the special firebrick and calcinated limestone that lined it.

"Ah, stuff gets bigger when it gets hot, right?"

The Achaean architect nodded.

"So when we put the ore and flux and coal in at the top, they're pretty cold . . ."

Behind Augewas Cuddy could see the Achaean's son and apprentice Philhippos rolling his eyes, left hand resting proudly on the cased slide rule at his belt, and fought down a grin. The younger Greek was at the stage where you just couldn't believe the ignorance of your old man . . . just about the age Cuddy had left home in Milwaukee to enlist in the Crotch with parental curses and a flung beer bottle following him.

Of course, Philhippos had grown up in the new world Cuddy and the other Americans of William Walker's band were making of this Bronze Age kingdom. He really *did* know a lot more about this stuff than his dad. Hard to remember they'd been here most of a decade now.

The young man spoke: "And this *coal*"—he used the English word, there being no equivalent in Mycenaean Greek—"is it better than charcoal because it burns hotter, or because it is a stonelike ore and can support more weight, or what?"

However grimly the *telestai* might cling to old usage on their baronies, language had grown less formal among the new elite of Great Achaea under the influence of twentieth-century English. Philhippos's father disliked that particular trend; he raised a hand, and the boy added hastily: "Lord Cuddy."

"Both, and because there's more of it," Cuddy said. "Now that we've got the mines up in Istria going, we can ship it down by sea cheaper than burning charcoal up in the hills; and besides, eventually we'd run out of trees."

He whistled, and the workers at the top let down the inspection platform. The overlords stepped onto it, and it rose smoothly up to the summit and the heavy iron-coated collar of timbers around it. From there Cuddy could look down on the raw, brawling town of Neayoruk, down to the smoke and thronging masts of the harbor enclosed by a mole running out to an island half a mile from shore, and to the hammered-metal brightness of the Laconian Gulf beyond. Sweat sprang out on his forehead and he turned gratefully to a cooling wind from the water, bringing the tang of salt, coal smoke, the hot metal of the forges whose hearths sent trails of smoke up to the azure Mediterranean sky.

"We're on schedule," he said with relief, taking in the activity below with an experienced eye.

"That is good," Augewas said. "The Wolf Lord will be pleased."

"Yeah," Cuddy said, shivering slightly at the thought of William Walker, King of Men. "That's *real* good."

CHAPTER ONE

**September, 10 A.E.—Babylon, Kingdom of
Kar-Duniash
October, 10 A.E.—Severn valley, Alba
October, 10 A.E.—Walkeropolis, Kingdom of
Great Achaea
October, 10 A.E.—Irondale, Alba**

Dr. Justin Clemens—Captain, Republic of Nantucket Coast
Guard (Medical Corps)—sipped at the thick sweet wine,
mouth dry. It was never easy to tell someone about the Event.
Much else about the Twentieth had faded, but that memory of
terror remained far too fresh. He'd been a teenager then . . .

His fiancée picked a date from the bowl on the low table
that stood between her and the Islander medic. He went on:

". . . and then the glowing dome of light was gone, and our
whole island of Nantucket was . . . here. Back in this age. More
than three thousand years before our own time."

The platform beneath them was the terraced rooftop of a
section of The House That Was The Marvel of Mankind, The
Center of the Land, The Shining Residence, The Dwelling of
Majesty—in short, the palace of King Kashtiliash son of Shagarakti-Shuriash. It sprawled around them as a city within the
greater city of Babylon; crenellated outer walls where sentries
paced with the late-summer sun bright on their steel and
bronze, whitewashed adobe and colored brick and tile, courtyards, gardens, audience halls, workshops, storerooms, hareem,
barracks, shrines, and archives, faint sounds of chanting, talk,
feet, wheels, hooves, a whiff of cooking and a stale draft of
canal-water . . .

The two doctors sat on cushions beneath an awning, amid
potted plants and flowers and dwarf trees brought from all over
these lands.

Justin watched the woman as she frowned and thought, noticing again how her face turned beautiful with the mind within,

despite thinness, big hooked nose, receding chin, and incipient mustache. The huge dark eyes had depths to them. It made him painfully aware of his own round-faced near-plumpness, kept under control only by the necessities of campaigning and twelve-hour workdays.

Here's hoping she gets it, went through him. *So many just can't grasp the concept.* Plain bewildered, or lost in superstitious terror. But Azzu-ena was extremely bright, and practical, to boot. Her doctor-father had had no sons, and brought his daughter up to his trade, which was unusual but not completely outlandish in Babylon. These archaic-Semitic peoples weren't what you'd call feminists by a long shot, but they weren't as pathological about it as many of their descendants would . . . would have, in the original history . . . become.

Well, there's the Assyrians, he reminded himself. *They shut women up in purdah like Afghans in the twentieth. But they're just nasty in every conceivable way.*

Of course, *asu* was not a very prestigious occupation among the Babylonians regardless of whether the doctor was a man or a woman. Medicine and surgery were just treating symptoms, to their way of thinking; the *ashipu,* the sorceror/witch doctor, had the real power.

As one of the physicians on call for the King's women, Azzu-ena had been given the run of the Palace after her father died, including its huge library of clay tablets; she had talked much with foreigners, here where merchants and embassies from all the known world sought the court of the King; otherwise, she had been left mostly to herself and her thoughts.

"I see," she said at last. "Everything you have shown and told me in this past year has been true, so this must be also. I knew when I saw you cut the child from the womb—and yet the mother lived!—that your arts must be beyond ours . . ."

The doctor winced a little. Someone as intelligent as Azzu-ena would *think* about the implications of the Event:

Your world is dead three thousand years. In most places that means that nothing, nothing of what you love and what makes up your inmost soul remains; your people, their poets and Kings, their Gods and their dreams, their hates and fears, the words your mother sang you to sleep with, all gone down into dust and shadow—

A little more of Babylon would endure, which perhaps would be worse; to have those parched bones dug up and studied by an academic curiosity equally dry.

"That's why we have arts that you don't," Justin went on

aloud. "We have three thousand years more history . . . more time to learn things."

The concept of development through time puzzled her at first; Babylonians thought of history as decline from a previous Golden Age, not of progress. They did know that there had been a time before metal or agriculture, though; he reminded her of that, and went on:

"And it's why we command so few of the arts we had before the Event."

Her eyes went wide. "I . . . don't understand. You have thunderbolts to knock down city walls, you can fly, your ships of the ocean sail about the earth as if it were a pond, you really *know* what causes diseases and how to cure them . . ."

"What we've shown is just the shadow of what we had. Think of it this way. If this palace—the palace and its dwellers alone— were to be thrown back to the time before men knew how to cultivate the earth or make bronze or write on clay, what would happen?"

Her brows knitted in thought. "The palace artisans—there would be none to bring them food, without peasants to grow the barley. So they would have to go into the fields with plow and hoe and sickle themselves . . . and there would be no traders to bring tin and copper and hard woods when those in the storerooms were used up . . . and no work for all the scribes, without a kingdom to administer . . . too many priests . . . they would all have to go to the fields or make bricks."

Smart girl! Clemens thought admiringly. It was a *long* time before Adam Smith's observations on the division of labor, but she'd grasped the principle that specialists depended on a big population.

"Exactly," he said aloud. "*We* were faced with starvation, because almost none of us were farmers or fishermen; and very few were even artisans, because Nantucket had few . . . places-of-making, workshops." That was as close as he could get to *factory* in this language; they were speaking Akkadian, to improve his command of it.

"We had—have—the *knowledge* to make, oh, carts that run without horses or oxen, or flying ships much larger and faster than what you've seen, or—" He shrugged. "But not the skilled workers and special machines, or the machines that made the machines, or the smelters and forges to make the metal, or to find and refine the fuel, or the farmers to grow the food and the roads to bring it to us. What we were able to make and maintain was only a shadow of what our whole realm, the *United States,* was able to do.''

A buzz of voices rose from city and palace, a snarling roar echoed from the sky, and a long teardrop shadow fell over them. They looked up, leaning out from beneath the awning and shading their eyes with a hand. The orca shape of the Republic of Nantucket Air Service's *Emancipator* was passing over Babylon. Five hundred feet of canvas, birch plywood, and goldbeater's skin, the dirigible droned along with six ex-Cessna engines pushing it through the warm Mesopotamian air, the Stars and Stripes on its cruciform tailfins and the Coast Guard's red slash and anchor on its flank.

Azzu-ena shuddered. "*That* is but a shadow of your arts?" she said.

"A faint shadow," Clemens said. "We have to hope it's enough. It's more than the rebel Walker has."

To himself he added: *We think. So far.*

"Then how can he hope to stand before you?"

"He'll be fighting close to the lands he's made his own, near to *Ahhiyawa,* Greece. The lands of our strength are far, far away from here."

> "On Wenlock Edge the wood's in trouble;
> His forest fleece the Wrekin heaves;
> The gale, it plies the saplings double,
> And thick on Severn snow the leaves."

"That's Wenlock Edge," Commodore Marian Alston-Kurlelo went on, pointing to a looming darkness in the south, an escarpment beyond the river they sought. Her hand swung westward toward a conical shape. "And we're on the slopes of Wrekin hill. An English poet named Housman wrote that, a little before my time."

Adventure, bah, humbug, she thought. *A Shropshire Lad I could read back home in front of the fire, with a cup of hot cocoa.*

She gripped the hairy warmth of her horse more tightly with her thighs, as rain hissed down through the tossing branches above. It ran around the edges of her sou'wester and rain slicker into the sodden blue wool of her uniform, leaching her body's warmth. If you absolutely had to be out in weather like this, nine hundred pounds of hay-fueled heater were a comfort.

Marian Alston had joined the Coast Guard at eighteen, a gawky bookish tomboy furiously determined to escape her beginnings on a hardscrabble farm in the tidewater country of South Carolina. She was in her forties now, a tall slender ebony-black woman going a little gray at the temples of her close-cropped wiry hair, with a face that might have come from a Benin bronze in its high-cheeked, broad-nosed comeliness.

They paused at a slight rise, where a fold in the ridge gave them a view over swaying forest and the country that fell away before them. She went on:

> *'Twould blow like this through holt and hanger*
> *When Uricon the city stood:*
> *'Tis the old wind in the old anger,*
> *But then it threshed another wood*

"It's a good poem," the younger woman riding beside her said.

Swindapa, Dhinwarn's daughter, of the Kurlelo lineage, lifted her billed Coast Guard cap and shook her head. Droplets flew off the clubbed pigtail that held long wheat-blond hair in check, save for a few damp strands that clung to her oval, straight-nosed face. Her smile showed white even teeth, and her English-rose complexion was tanned by a decade of sun reflected off the ocean.

She went on: "But why are so many Eagle People poems sad? Don't you ever make poems about beer? Or roast venison and playing with babies and making love in new-mown hay on warm summer afternoons?"

One of the Marines riding behind them chuckled, barely audible under the hiss of rain, the soughing and wind-creak of branches, and the slow *clop-plock* of hooves in wet earth. Alston smiled herself, a slight curve of her full lips.

"I've got gloomy tastes," she said. "If we're benighted out here and we can find anything that'll burn, we can at least arrange the venison." An extremely unlucky deer was slung gralloched across one of their packhorses. "Still, he catches the area, doesn't he?" she went on, waving.

She'd visited here as a tourist before the Event—even now her mind gave a slight hitch; English tenses were not suited to time travel—and the bones of the land were the same.

And the weather's just as lousy, she thought, sneezing.

But there were no lush hedge-bordered fields here, no half-timbered farmhouses or little villages with pubs where you sat with the ghosts of cavaliers and highwaymen, no ruined castles and Norman churches, no shards of Roman Viroconium—Uricon, in Shropshire legend. No Iron Age hill forts, either, on the "blue remembered hills." Not yet, and now not ever, here. Sometimes back on Nantucket among the buildings and artifacts of that future you could forget, or your gut could forget. Forget that an entire history—three millennia of people, being born and living, fighting and building and bearing children and dying—had . . . vanished . . . when the Event happened.

The little party rode their horses down narrow rutted trails made by deer and wild boar and aurochs as much as men and men's herds, beneath towering oaks and beeches, ash and chestnut and lime, tangled thorny underbrush to either side. Wind whipped through leaves turning sere and yellow with early autumn, scattering them downward with a steady drip and drizzle following behind. The air above was thick with wings, many on their way southward for the year, and their cries drifted down with the rain; redpolls and siskins chattered anger at the humans from the boughs. The trail veered down from a ridgeback, through a marsh-bordered stream edged with alders; water lapped her stirrup-irons and mud spattered on her boots and trouser legs with a cold yeasty smell. The storm mounted, moaning through the branches and ruffling the surface of the puddles. It was good to speak into the teeth of the whetted wind:

> Then, 'twas before my time, the Roman
> At yonder heaving hill would stare:
> The blood that warms an English yeoman,
> The thoughts that hurt him, they were there.

"Roman?" Swindapa asked.

In the decade they'd been together the young woman of the *Fiernan Bohulugi* had acquired a fair modern education to add to the lore of an astronomer-priestess of Moon Woman and hunter of the Spear Mark, but not much of it concerned the details of a history that would never happen.

"A people that invaded . . . would have invaded Alba a long time from now. About . . ." *Let's see, this is year 10 A.E., which makes it 1240 B.C., Claudius invaded Britain in the 40s A.D., so . . .* "Call it thirteen hundred years from now. They would have built a city thereabouts." She nodded off to the northwest, to where Wroxeter stood in her birth-century.

"Like the Sun People," Swindapa said with a slight shiver.

Alston leaned over and squeezed her shoulder for an instant. The Event had dumped her command—the Coast Guard training windjammer *Eagle*—into the early spring of 1250 B.C., along with the island of Nantucket. The first thing they'd done besides catching a few whales was make a voyage to Britain, to barter steel tools and trinkets for desperately needed food and seed corn and livestock; they'd ended up making their first landing among the Iraiina tribe, the latest of many *teuatha* of the Sun People to invade the White Isle. Among the gifts those proto-demi-Celts had given Alston was a girl they'd taken prisoner from the Earth Folk, the *Fiernan Bohulugi*, the megalith-building natives of Alba. Swindapa, who still sometimes woke screaming from nightmares of that captivity.

"That's a long time gone, sugar," Marian said. "Lot of water under the bridge, and the Sun People are pretty quiet, nowadays."

> *"There, like the wind through woods in riot,*
> *Through him the gale of life blew high;*
> *The tree of man was never quiet:*
> *Then 'twas the Roman, now 'tis I.*
>
> *The gale, it plies the saplings double,*
> *It blows so hard, 'twill soon be gone:*
> *Today the Roman and his trouble*
> *Are ashes under Uricon."*

"Yes," Swindapa said quietly. "Would you, would *we* have made war on the Sun People, if Walker hadn't come here and tried to be a King among them?"

Ouch. That's a toughie. "I think we'd have helped the Earth Folk defend themselves," she said. "I was pushin' for that, as soon as I got to talking with you."

A brilliant smile rewarded her, and Marian felt the familiar but always startling warmth under her breastbone. *And personal matters aside, we needed something like the Alliance.* Nantucket was too small in area and numbers to keep even the ghost of civilization alive on its own.

"You were so shy in those days," Swindapa said. "I *knew* Moon Woman had sent you to rescue me and put down the Sun People, and that Her stars meant us to be together always, but I had to *drag* you into bed," she went on.

"Well, whatever else the *Fiernan Bohulugi* are, they aren't *shy*," Marian agreed. *Lordy, no. Got me out of the closet, for starters.*

Swindapa sighed again. "I thought once the Sun People were beaten, we'd have peace. Sailing, work, and the children."

Marian's expression turned grim. "Not while William Walker's above-ground, I think." Her fist hit the saddle horn. "Damn, but I should have finished him off!"

"You were nearly dead with wounds, yourself. And he was prepared to flee if he lost."

Alston shook her head. There were no excuses for failure. "A rat always has a bolt-hole. All our problems since, they're because he got away."

"When I was a fighting-man, the kettle-drums they beat;
The people scattered roses before my horse's feet.
And now I am a mighty King, and the people dog my track;
With poison in the wine-cup, and daggers at my back."

"Self-pity, Will?" Dr. Alice Hong asked mockingly.

"Robert E. Howard," William Walker replied. "*Kull the Conqueror,* specifically."

He turned from the tall French doors and their southward view over the palace gardens and the city of Walkeropolis. The valley of the Eurotas reached beyond, drowsing in a soft palette of green and brown and old gold, up to the blue heights of Mount Taygetos. The city's smoke and noise drifted in, mixed with flower scents from the gardens, and a warm hint of thyme and lavender from the hills.

The King of Men smiled at her. "I thought it was appropriate."

He was a little over six feet, tall even by twentieth-century standards, towering here in the thirteenth century B.C. Broad-shouldered and narrow-hipped, he moved with an athlete's quick, controlled gracefulness; reddish-brown hair fell to his shoulders, confined by the narrow diadem of royalty wrought in gold olive leaves. The face it framed would have been boyishly handsome yet, even in his thirties, if it had not been for the deep scar that cut a V across his cheek and vanished under the patch that hid his left eyesocket; the level green stare of the surviving eye glittered coldly. He wore loose trousers of black silk tucked into polished half-boots, and a gold-trimmed jacket of the same material cinched by a tooled-leather belt that bore revolver and chryselephantine dagger. A wolfshead signet ring of ruby and niello on the third finger of his right hand was the only other ornament.

"Or to put it in American, babe," he went on in a voice that still held a trace of Montana, "the Greek VIPs liked it better when I was the wizardly power in the background and not Supreme Bossman. Planting my own lowborn outlander ass on the throne of the Kings of Men has seriously torqued them out."

"Rational deduction from the information available," Helmut Mittler agreed, running a hand over his close-cropped gray-and-yellow hair. "The disaffected Achaean nobles haff little grasp of sophisticated conspiratorial politics, but they are not stupid men—not the surviving ones. They haff support among the more reactionary elements of the population . . . and they learn quickly."

He pronounced that *und zey learn kvickly;* the Mecklenberger accent was still fairly strong. His Achaean was better, but for small conferences like this Walker preferred English. There was something about the sonorous formalities of Mycenaean Greek that wasn't conducive to quick sharp thought, in his opinion.

"Evolution in action," Walker agreed, nodding to the ex-*Stasi* agent.

Who managed to get out before the Berlin Wall went down, with a fair amount of money and some extremely good fake ID, he reminded himself. It wouldn't do to underestimate his security chief. Aloud he went on:

"We caught the dumb ones first." A chuckle. He'd introduced crucifixion, along with the other innovations. "Those who cross me get crossed." It impressed the wogs no end.

"I get a lot of information through the Sisterhood," Hong said. "Yeah, there are still a lot of the *telestai* and *ekwetai* . . . mmmm . . . unhappy—especially since Agamemnon . . . ah . . . died."

"Shot while attempting to escape," Mittler chuckled. "Classic."

"Jumped off a fucking cliff calling on the God-damned Gods," Walker grated. *Which gave him major mojo among the wogs.*

The "given sacrifice," they called it. Walker'd had years of clear sailing, while Agamemnon imagined the foreigner he'd raised up was *safe,* because he didn't have the blood-right to the throne that too many of Mycenae's endlessly intermarried vassal Kings and nobles could claim. Fortunately, dead men had trouble taking advantage of their own *baraka,* especially when their heirs died with them.

Dumb bastard, trying to break out like that. Hell, even at the

*end I was treating him well, and pretending that the orders came
from him . . . in public.*

Now . . . he had the New Troops and their firepower, yes,
and the crawling terror of Helmut's secret police, not to mention the supernatural dread of the Sisterhood of Hekate, but
raw fear was a chancy basis for power. Frightened men were
unpredictable. He'd take force over legitimacy any day, if he
had to choose one or the other, but it would be nice to have
both. Presumably his kids would—legitimacy meant staying on
top until nobody could remember anybody else, when you came
right down to it. Dynastic immortality wasn't the type he'd have
picked, given options, but it was the only kind going.

"And that's why I have to get back to Troy," he said, returning to his swivel chair behind the desk.

The other two looked at each other. "Sir," Mittler said,
"your position here in Greece is still unstable. Particularly with
many troops being required abroad."

"That's what I've got you and your Section One for, Helmut," Walker said genially. "How did the old saying go? A
secure throne needs a standing army of soldiers, a sitting army
of bureaucrats, a kneeling army of priests, and a crawling army
of informers."

Alice looked at him and gave the faintest hint of a wink; he
replied with a smile that barely crinkled the skin around his
eyes. *And, of course, I have Alice and her little cult to watch
the watchmen.* Mittler's cold gray eyes caught the byplay, and
the ash-pale brows rose slightly.

Dr. Alice Hong was a complete nutter, a sadist in the literal
clinical sense of the word—she couldn't get it off without in-
flicting or feeling pain, preferably both—but very smart. And
fully conscious that a woman could never rule *Meizon Akhaia*
in her own right, not in this generation, which made her the
safest of all Walker's American followers. Mittler didn't have
that drawback in plumbing design . . .

Of course, Mittler was also smart enough to see that a power
struggle at the top might well bring down the whole jury-rigged
structure of Great Achaea. And Helmut Mittler wanted to defeat the Republic of Nantucket, wanted it very badly. Partly to
keep the wealth and power he enjoyed, and partly to satisfy an
old and bitter spite against the people who'd ruined his country
and cause. The Nantucketers were the closest thing to the
United States around, here in the Bronze Age.

Walkerian Age is more appropriate now, he thought absently,
considering, then came to a decision.

There were times when the mushroom treatment was useful, but if you kept your top-flight people in the dark and covered in horseshit *all* the time you couldn't expect them to make sound decisions. And an operation this big *required* delegation, absolutely, however much it went against his personal inclinations. So . . . he'd fill them in.

"I don't have *Zeus Pater* for a great-granddaddy," Walker said genially. "What I do have is the prestige of victory. Momentum. That keeps a lot of mouths shut and minds obedient that wouldn't be, otherwise. So I need a big, conspicuous win, particularly since we're up against guys with guns now, not just pumping out grapeshot at bare-assed spear-chuckers. So it's back to Troy for the last act there."

"Sir," Mittler said, clicking heels and bowing his head. "I must therefore begin preparations. When Troy falls, we can at least deal with that damned Jew, Arnstein; he has been the brains of their intelligence apparat. Stupid of them to let him be caught there. If I haff your permission?"

"Certainly, Helmut. Keep up the good work," Walker said. *You pickle-up-the-ass kraut,* he thought behind the mask of his face as the other man left.

There were times when Mittler's eternally punctilious Middle European *Ordnungsliebe* got on the American's nerves; it was like being trapped with a Commie/Nazi villain from a bad fifties war movie. *Ve haff vays to mak you talk.* But he was a *useful* kraut.

Of course, he's built up quite a local cadre who're loyal to him *and not me or the kingdom, but it's an acceptable price. For now.*

Besides, everyone knows who Helmut is and what he does. That made him too unpopular to rule himself, like Beria, or Himmler.

Alice stretched in her chair, arms over her head and small breasts straining against the thin white silk of her tunic. Walker watched with detached appreciation; sex with Alice was like fucking a humanoid cobra, but it had its points as an occasional diversion.

"If dear, dear Helmut ever has to . . . go . . . you really *must* let me handle it," she said. "He doesn't know nearly as much as he thinks he does about what the human body can endure."

Walker cocked an eyebrow. "I'd have thought you had some things in common," he said.

"Really, Will! The man has no sense of *artistry*. He might as well be adjusting the bolts on a tractor." She looked at her watch. "Well, I have to run. We're holding an initiation to-night—quite important. Girls only, I'm afraid . . . unless you want to watch through the spyhole again?"

"Thanks, but business calls. See ya, babe."

The cult she'd established was a hobby with Alice, and another chance to engage in the sadomasochistic *Grand Guignol* she adored, but it had tentacles throughout *Meizon Akhaia*, among women of all classes, and in the medical service she'd organized and taught. These Gods-besotted wogs took religion very seriously indeed, and after the perversions and atrocities of the initiation process the new members felt completely committed, as if they'd severed all links to everyone except the Dark Sisterhood. He vaguely remembered reading that the Mau Mau had used the same tactics. Some of the Haitian *bokor* brotherhoods, the darker side of Voudun, did that, too—it had been in the Coast Guard briefing papers, when he was stationed down in the Caribbean watching for drugs and refugees coming out of Port-au-Prince.

"Education is a wonderful thing," he mused, pulling another pile of reports toward him.

Crops, roads, factories, schools . . . there was a hell of a lot more to being an emperor than "inventing" gunpowder, or even just commanding armies. Right now he was sweating blood trying to get a banking system established. Turning this Bronze Age feudal mishmash into something worth running had been like pushing a boulder uphill, even with twenty carefully picked American helpers and the fifty tons of cargo—machines, metals, tools, books, working models—that he'd liberated from Nantucket along with the schooner. And the earliest stages had been hardest.

Satisfying, though, he thought. How had Jack London put it?

"It is the King of words—Power," he quoted to himself, remembering a boy reading in the rustling scented solitude of a hay barn, alone with his savage, bright-colored dreams. "Not God, not Mammon, but Power. Pour it over your tongue till it tingles with it. Power."

And there was no road to Power that didn't involve hard work; that made the work satisfying in itself, fun, worthwhile. He bent back to his task.

"Lord King," a soft voice said a few hours later; he noticed that, as he hadn't the noiseless slaves who'd turned up the kerosene lanterns.

Walker looked up. It was his house steward, the chief of the residential staff. "Yes, Eurgewenos?" he said.

"Lord King, shall I have the kitchens send a meal here? And do you wish a particular girl for the night?"

"Mmmm, no."

He looked out the window; almost dark. Dinnertime, by the wall clock; they'd finally gotten those to work well enough for everyday use and were closing in on chronometers good enough for navigation. When he'd arrived, Mycenaean Greek had used *a moment* for all times less than their vague conception of an hour. . . .

"Inform the Lady Ekhnonpa that I'll be dining with her and the children."

"The King commands; we obey."

A hareem was very pleasant, but he had a certain nostalgic affection for Ekhnonpa and he'd kept her around. She'd borne him three children, and put on a good deal of weight, but her undemanding adoration was relaxing, sometimes. Her father, Daurthunnicar, had been a chieftain up in Alba, his first base of operations after he'd cleared out of Nantucket; he'd won the daughter and heir-apparent status by beating the tribal champion . . . to death, with his hands and feet. The Nantucketers had upset that applecart—he touched the scar and the patch over the empty eyesocket Alston's sword had left, and his lips curled back from his teeth for a moment.

Time to settle that debt, he thought. *In full. With interest.*

Swindapa raised her head, took a long breath through her nose, cocked an ear. "Not long now," she said. "That's hearth smoke, and a dog barking."

The deer track widened and turned into a rutted mud road as it wound upward; that made the forest less gloomy, but it also let in more of the rain coming in from the Welsh mountains. A clearing appeared, and little thatched clusters of round wattle-and-daub huts with sheepfolds and cattle corrals around about; the cold breeze ruffled rain-dimpled puddles. Smoke came leaking out of thatch in tatters that ran down the wet driving wind—or in a few cases from chimneys of brick or sheet iron, nowadays. A noisy dog brought some of the inhabitants out to the side of the road. They were wrapped in sheepskins and blanketlike cloaks of raw wool, looking like hairy bundles with feet.

A few carried weapons—steel-headed spears or crossbows handed out to the Republic's Fiernan allies during the Alban War a decade ago, and a couple of trade muskets with waxed leather wrapped around the flintlock and pan. They relaxed and pointed the business ends skyward when they saw the Nantucketer gear and uniforms, and the standard-bearer that marked an embassy. The Stars and Stripes hung limp and wet on the pole socketed into the bearer's stirrup, but the gilt eagle above was a bright flash in the rainy dimness.

Marian glanced backward out of the corner of her eye; the khaki-clad Marines were sitting their horses easily, reins in their right hands and Werder rifles riding in the crook of their left arms, eyes wary even here among friendlies. She had her eye on their sergeant, Zena Ritter, for possible promotion—a slender, wire-tough young woman with cropped dark-red hair and an implausible number of freckles, who'd been taking correspondence courses from Fort Brandt OCS via Westhaven HQ. The Republic's military needed people who could function out on their ownsome without undue hand-holding, satellite links, or a Pentagon to do their thinking for them.

As she watched, Ritter tossed a bar of ration chocolate to a clutch of children. The waxed paper wrapping came off to squeals of delight.

Generous, Marian thought. Even back on Nantucket chocolate was still expensive, gathered wild in Central America and traded to Islander schooners working the Main. *And they recognized it. Must be a fair bit of trade through here . . .*

Swindapa reined her horse aside and spoke to the locals in the purling glug-glug of the *Fiernan Bohulugi* tongue, a language that had vanished a thousand years before the birth of Christ in Marian's history. She dropped the knotted reins on her saddlebow to let her hands move in fluid accompaniment to her thought. When she rode on she was shaking her head in amazement.

"Sugar?" Marian asked. *Lord, if you tied a Fiernan's hands, they'd be struck dumb.*

"It's . . . these people are out in the . . . what's the word, the *sticks*? They talk a dialect I can barely follow."

The black woman smiled to herself; Swindapa's lineage, the Kurlelo, lived by the Great Wisdom—Stonehenge—far south of here in Wiltshire on the open upland downs. By Fiernan reckoning, that made them the center of the world; the Kurlelo Grandmothers were the high priestesses of Moon Woman and students of the stars that revealed Her will. Those dry and sunny hills were thickly peopled and closely farmed as well, very different from these middle lands of Alba; here human habitations were still islands amid swamp and a wildwood-jungle of giant oak trees on heavy clay. Not until the Age of

Iron brought better tools and plows would settlers make much progress against the King trees and the thick fertile low-country soils that bore them. In the original history at least . . .

"In the sticks, yes," Swindapa went on, in pleased wonderment at how far the changes had gone. "And yet look at all they have! Ten years ago, they would have made most of their tools of wood and bone and stone, shared one bronze blade with the whole family. Now they have steel axes, pans, spades, scythes, Nantucket plows . . . even iron *stoves*. And yes, they say we're getting near Irondale. Right where you thought we were."

"Glad of it, 'dapa. Gettin' old and creaky for riding in the rain like this, much less a God-damned week of it."

She kept herself in shape as conscientiously as she worked at any other duty—a certain bleak inner honesty made her admit that *compulsive* would be a better description—but today creak and click and joint pain told of the teeth gnawing, quiet and relentless. The Event had sent thousands back through time, but every one of them still slid down the slippery slope of entropy at a minute per minute on their own personal world-line.

Oh, hell, this is nothing compared to standing a quarterdeck watch in the Roaring Forties.

Wet wool clung and chafed against her skin, and the raw clammy chill had sunken in toward her bones. The cleared fields grew and spread out to the edge of sight, muddy plowland and pasture with treelots, and then the terrain rose slightly, hills deep in forest once more. The road climbed with it, becoming broader and better-built as it did, then snaked down a dry gully toward the Severn, winding its way from the mountains of Snowdonia to the estuary far southward.

She looked up to where the sun would have been, if the sky weren't the color of wet iron. It was getting on toward evening; somewhere a wolf called to its pack and the sobbing howl echoed through the gathering dusk. The crossbred Morgan-chariot pony mounts scarcely flicked an ear at it; their shaggy coats were wet and mud-streaked, and their heads drooped. One blew out its lips in a blubbery sigh, and Marian slapped her mount's neck in reassurance.

"Warm stable and oats soon enough, boy. We all need it."

"I'd rather have some roast pork and a bed, myself," Swindapa said, her urchin grin bright. "*And* a bath, nice and hot."

Marian suppressed an involuntary groan at the thought of sinking into a steaming tub. Irondale's lights showed bright through the wavery murk ahead as they came down onto the road along the narrow riverside flat. By the roadside was a man-tall granite boundary-marker. On one side were Fiernan geometrics; the other bore the Republic's eagle, with an olive branch in one claw and a bundle of arrows in the other.

"It's grown," Swindapa went on thoughtfully, looking at the town's lights. They'd last visited in 04, when the new settlement was nothing but mud, stumps, tents, and construction-yard litter. "Three thousand four hundred residents, according to the latest report."

Her slight singsong accent grew a little stronger, as it did when she used the mnemonic training she'd received as an apprentice to the Kurlelo Grandmothers at the Great Wisdom.

"When I saw the numbers I thought that was many," she continued after a moment. "But I hadn't realized that three thousand four hundred was *so* many."

Which was natural enough; the whole of Alba hadn't had a single town, before the Event. As near as they could tell, there were fewer than half a million people in the whole of the British Isles. Possibly *many* fewer. By the standards of this era that was a dense population; the best estimate the Republic's explorers and savants had been able to come up with counted around fifty million for the entire planet.

"Halt! Who goes?"

She nodded approval as the sentries stepped out from neatly camouflaged blinds on either side of the road and raised their rifles. One had a bull's-eye lantern as well, and snapped it open to shine the beam on their faces. Marian raised her right hand to halt the little column.

"Commodore Marian Alston-Kurlelo and Lieutenant Commander Swindapa Kurlelo-Alston and party," she said.

That flustered the militiaman a little, and he stammered and flushed before stepping back with a salute. "Pass, friend!"

Marian returned the gesture; she could hear him chattering excitedly in Fiernan as they heeled unwilling horses into a walk again and passed on into Irondale. *Fame,* she thought. Her mouth twisted ironically as they rode into the scattering of buildings, several streets of them on either side of the main road. A few were round huts and wood shacks from the early days, more small brick cottages with tile roofs and chimneys, with a scattering of big houses in what she thought of as the Nantucket Georgian style.

Half a mile up the S-shaped valley of the tributary stream a dam penned back the flow into an artificial lake, and sluicegates released it in a torrent of white foam onto the tops of half a dozen thirty-foot overshot waterwheels; they turned with a constant groaning rumble and splash, a querning undertone to the other noises. As the riders watched, a blade of fire lanced skyward from a blast furnace, white at its core and framed in red where it left the top of the sooty pyramid of brick, shedding a long plume of spark and cinder downwind. It was accompanied by an enormous shrill scream, like a wounded horse the size of a mountain. The living horses beneath them shied and skittered, then quieted as the sound stopped and their riders soothed them. A smell of hot iron and coal smoke drifted down through the wet along with the clangor of the works and multicolored volcanos of sparks from the Bessemer converters.

Their horses' hooves clopped hollow on asphalt pavement; they passed schools, Ecumenical Christian church, public baths, library in a corner of the town hall, medical clinic where a pair of doctors from the Cottage Hospital healed and taught. Then the inn, a rambling brick structure two stories high, wings added on to an original modest core, with yellow lamplight showing behind its windows. That brought an inner groan of relief. She threw up her right arm, hand palm-forward.

"Halt and dismount!" Swindapa called crisply beside her, and the hoof-clatter died.

Alston swung down out of the saddle with a creak of leather, conscious of a little more stiffness than she would have felt a few years earlier. Despite the rain and raw chill, people were thick on the sidewalks here, under the bright gaslights of the cast-iron streetlamps. It was a mixed crowd, Nantucketers born and naturalized, Fiernan Bohulugi and Sun People from scores of lineages and tribes, plus little dark hillmen from the mountains to the west who were neither. Plenty from beyond Alba, too; a burly redhead covered in swirling tattoos from the Summer Isle—Ireland-to-be—a pale giant from the Baltic in a shaggy bearskin cloak, gawking about him in wonder . . . More and more, in wildly varying costume although sensible Islander-inspired overalls and jackets and boots predominated; many wore miner's helmets with lamps, or hard hats; there were even umbrellas. A round score of languages sounded, with weirdly accented *lingua franca* varieties of English the most common and the smooth pleasant singsong of Fiernan a close second.

If clotted cream could speak, it'd sound like Fiernan, Alston thought as she arched her back and stretched muscles stiffened by a long day in the saddle. *Too bad a commodore can't rub her ass in public* . . . Alder-wood clogs rattled on the brick, almost as loud as the clop of shod hooves and the rumble of steel-rimmed wheels.

"Stand easy, Corporal," Swindapa said.

"Ma'am! Squad, stand easy. Unload," Sergeant Ritter echoed.

The Marines raised the muzzles of their rifles, thumbed the cocking levers on the right side to the safety position; then came a chink-*ting* as the triggers were pulled. The grooved blocks that closed the breeches snapped down and the shells in the chambers ejected, to be neatly caught and returned to bandoliers.

The inn's sign creaked above her. She could make out a gilt low-relief eagle—modeled on the figurehead of her *Eagle,* the Coast Guard training windjammer she'd sailed a little too close to Nantucket the night of the Event. Beside it was the crescent Moon that had become the Fiernan national sigil. An open door swung a waft of warm air and light and cooking smells in their faces.

"Commodore Alston-Kurlelo!" the innkeeper said. He walked with a limp, and snapped off a salute to her as he came, then advanced with the hand extended and a wide white grin.

The name and face popped up out of the officer's retrieval system at the back of her brain; he'd been a first-year cadet on the *Eagle* at the time of the Event, and with the expeditionary force in the Alban War, the year after. Badly wounded at the Battle of the Downs, when they broke Walker and the Sun People war-host. Plus blacks were rare enough in the Republic to be notable.

"Cadet Merrithew," she said, shaking his hand. "Wayne Merrithew." He was a stocky man in his late twenties now, his dark-brown skin a few shades lighter than hers, wearing an apron and holding a towel and a glass he'd been polishing.

"I thought you were working over in Fogarty's Cove on Long Island, back the other side of the pond?"

He shook his head, still grinning. "Not since 05. Decided to get my savings and gratuity out of the Pacific Bank and set up here, ma'am, once my in-laws sent word how well things were going in Irondale," he said.

He'd married an Alban, as had many of her original cadets—they'd been over two-thirds male, which had upset the gender balance back on Nantucket considerably, in the beginning. She'd been relieved when so many war brides turned up.

Not that I could have complained even if I'd disapproved, she thought with an inner smile, glancing at her partner as she stroked the nose of her horse. *Seein' as I did pretty much the same.*

"How is Amentdwran, Wayne?" Swindapa asked.

'Dapa remembers him, too, Alston thought. Not from any particular effort, but the Grandmothers made a science of memory; they'd had to, with an astronomy-based religion and no way to store information except in living brains.

"Fine, fine—expecting again, that'll be number four, after the twins. But come on in out of the wet, for God's sake! No, my people will take care of the horses."

Two came at a run, agog at seeing the living legends; they bobbed heads and made the Fiernan gesture of reverence, touching brow and heart and groin, then led the horses around to a laneway at one side of the building. Alston cocked an eye at her escort, but the Marine noncom had her squad well in hand—they'd taken their rifles and gear first, and she was telling off one to go check that the stabling was all right. It would be, but you had to make sure. Horses were equipment, and if you took care of your equipment, it took care of you.

"The deer's yours, Mr. Merrithew," Alston said, indicating it with a lift of her chin. "Dumb beast walked right out in front of us yesterday and stood there in plain sight of God and radar."

"Well, I'll take that, but the rest is on the house," he said, and raised a hand to forestall protest. "The skipper doesn't pay in any place I own. And Pete!" An eight-year-old boy came up, face struggling between awe and delight; the café-au-lait skin and loose-curled hair left no doubt who *his* father was, in this world of palefaces. "Run up to the Manager's house and tell them all who's here!"

They walked through into the main room of the Eagle And Moon, shedding rain slickers in the hallway and feeling their bodies relax in the grateful warmth. That also brought out the odors of wet wool and leather and horse sweat and everything else that went with a week's hard travel and camps too muddy and wet and cold to do much washing. Marian Alston-Kurlelo wrinkled her nose slightly; there was no point in being squeamish in the field, but she liked to be clean when she could, especially in civilized surroundings like these.

She looked around; the inn was whitewashed plaster on the inside, with flame-wrapped logs crackling and booming in an open fireplace, and a less decorative but more effective cast-iron heating stove burning coal in a corner. A long bar with a brass rail stood on one side, swinging doors let a clatter and the savory smell of roasting meat and onions and fresh-baked bread in from the kitchens, and a polished beechwood staircase with a fancifully carved balustrade led upward. Coal-oil lamps were hung from oak rafters, bright woven blankets on the walls along with knicknacks that included crossed bronze-headed spears over the mantel, and a sheathed short sword modeled on a Roman *gladius* and made from a car's leaf spring. They hadn't had many firearms, that first year . . .

"Kept my ol' Ginsu," Merrithew said, slapping the sword affectionately. "Okay, Sergeant, you and your squad, the beds're up the stairs thattaway, bedding, robes and towels, bathroom's at the end of the corridor."

"Very well, Sergeant; carry on," Swindapa said; her responsibility, as Alston's aide-de-camp.

All to the best, Alston thought. Ritter's air of hard competence tended to turn to blushes and stammering when addressing the commodore directly—there were drawbacks to being a living legend.

"Settle your people in, and then dismissed to quarters until reveille tomorrow," Swindapa went on.

"Ma'am!"

"Sue, show 'em." Another brown-skinned child, this one with enormous eyes of hazel-green; she grabbed the sergeant by the hand and led her away. "Commodore, Ms. Kurlelo-Alston, your room's at the end of the corridor here. The bath's ready, too, and we'll have your kit unpacked by the time you're finished, and hot robes. I recommend the roast pork tonight; it's acorn-fed, and damned good."

He bore them on, chattering, and thrust thick ceramic mugs of hot mulled cider into their hands. Alston closed grateful fingers around hers, and met the cerulean blue of Swindapa's eyes. The Fiernan spoke her thought for her.

"We may live, after all."

CHAPTER TWO

September, 10 A.E.—Upper Euphrates, 3000 ft.
October, 10 A.E.—Irondale, Alba

I'm getting peopled out, Lieutenant Vicki Cofflin thought.
The long gondola of the airship RNAS *Emancipator* had
few places where privacy was possible, except the little cubicle
that held the head. The great orca-shaped hull above was much
larger, but the gasbags filled it.

And I'd like to see some stars, she thought. Although the
downward view from the commander's chair at the nose of
the gondola was grand, a huge sweep of moonlit plateau and
mountains three thousand feet below, and she still felt a thrill
sometimes when she realized *Emancipator* was *hers*. They were
heading for the passes of the anti-Taurus now, and they'd be
in Babylon by late afternoon. A routine voyage . . . which was
exactly what you wanted. Excitement meant adventure, and
adventure meant bad luck or somebody screwing up.

"Take the com, Alex," she said to her XO. "I'm going topside." Then aloud—not too loud, most of the crew and passengers were asleep in the Pullman-style bunks behind her: "Mr.
Stoddard has the deck."

"Mr. Stoddard has the deck, aye."

Wicker creaked as she unstrapped herself and rose, turning
to let Alex Stoddard by in the narrow space. She took her
sextant from the rack beside the ladder, although there wasn't
really any need for a navigational fix, with the Euphrates right
there below them like a river of silver through the huge tawny
spaces of Anatolia. It couldn't hurt, though, and it gave her an
excuse for taking a break topside. Besides, it was procedure,
and if you made procedure a habit it was there when you really
needed it.

She put hands and feet to the rungs, unsealing and resealing
the flap-door on the roof of the gondola, then went up further
through the creaking dimness of the hull, throbbing with the

sound of the engines. A few of the duty watch were on their
endless round of checking—for frame stresses, cracks, evidence
of chafing that might lead to leaks as the bags surged about
within their nets. The maintenance crew carried rechargeable
flashlights, jerking and spearing through the gloom of the
Emancipator's interior. More pre-Event technology that
couldn't be replaced as yet, incongruous against the balsa-and-
plywood frame of the airship.

*We know how to do so much more than it's possible to do,
goddammit!* ran through her with a familiar frustration, like a
toothache that had been with her since the Event had crashed
into her world a few weeks past her eighteenth birthday. *The
problem is all the things we know about and need but can't
make,* she thought.

Councilor Starbuck thought that the whole United States
would have been just barely large enough to maintain one mi-
crochip factory. As it was, they could just barely maintain the
recycled Cessna engines that pushed *Emancipator.*

In her more pessimistic moods, she thought that they'd have
done worse without Tartessos and Great Achaea to goose and
terrify the Sovereign People into forgoing current consumption
for investment. On good days, she concentrated on how much
better the Republic could do this time around once those nui-
sances were put down.

*Someday we'll have everything they did in the twentieth, and
more. We'll hit the ground running and not stop this side of the
stars, and we'll do it without screwing the place up.* That would
take generations, though. She'd planned on Colorado Springs,
before the Event, and dreamed of eventually joining the astro-
naut program. . . .

With a sigh she unlatched the rubber-rimmed wooden hatchway at the top of the ladder and stuck her head into the observation post.

"Oh," she said. *Oh, damn. Must have come up here while I
was in the head.* "Good very early morning, Colonel Hollard."

"Couldn't sleep, Captain Cofflin," the other woman said.
"Nice view up here, too."

It would be impolite to duck right down. There was plenty
of room for two; the observation bubble was domed with what
had started life as a shopping-center Plexiglas skylight, and
rimmed with a padded couch. It was cold, but not as draughty
as the wickerwork-sided main gondola below, and, anyway, her
generation had gotten used to a world where heating was often

too cumbersome to be worth the trouble. You put on another layer of clothing or learned to live with being chilly, or both.

A continuous low drumming sound came from outside, under the whistle of cloven air, the sound of the taut fabric of *Emancipator*'s outer skin flexing under the 60 mph wind of her passage.

Well, you've got reason to be sleepless, Vicki thought as she sat and looked at the other's impassive face. She didn't know all the details, but everyone had heard something—mainly that somehow the Mitannian princess Kenneth Hollard had saved from the Assyrians had managed to seriously torque off King Kashtiliash . . . the local potentate Kathryn Hollard had married in a blaze of publicity and gossip that had them talking all the way back to Nantucket Town.

I thought we had culture clash in our family, Vicki Cofflin thought. Her father had come from the piney woods of east Texas. *I didn't know the meaning of the* word, *back then.*

"Cocoa?" Hollard asked, holding up a thermos. Those *were* within Nantucket's capabilities, if you didn't mind paying three weeks' wages for it.

"Thanks, ma'am." The cocoa was dark and strong, sweetened with actual cane sugar from Mauritius Base.

"You're welcome . . . let's not be formal. I was just looking at the stars, and thinking about the Event," Hollard went on meditatively.

"Oh? Nothing better to do?"

Vicki grinned, glancing up herself. Thinking about the Event had become a byword for useless speculation and idle daydreaming; they just didn't have any data to go on. There was also what amounted to an unspoken rule against talking about it at all, among the older generation.

The stars were enormous through the dry clear air, a frosted band across the sky. *Skyglow's one thing I don't miss about the twentieth,* she thought.

"It occurred to me," Hollard went on, looking up and sipping, "that we may be wrong about what happened up in the twentieth when we . . . left. That they got the 1250 B.C. Nantucket swapped with us, that is. That's what most people assume, but there's no reason to believe it."

"Oh?" *Well, a fresh hypothesis, anyway.* "What else could have happened?"

Everything uptime of us could have all vanished the moment we arrived here, like a stray dream. She didn't mention that; it was another unwritten courtesy rule. The thought that they'd unwittingly wiped out billions of people and their own country and kin was just too ghastly to contemplate. Those inclined to brood on it had made up a goodly portion of the rash of post-Event suicides.

"Well, I don't think the Event was an accident," Hollard said. "The transition was too neat—a perfect ellipse around the Island, for God's sake!—and we arrived too smoothly. No earthquakes, no tremors even, no tidal wave. . . . I mean, there must have been differences in sea level, the temperature of the land underneath the wedge that got brought along with us, air pressure . . . and despite a subsoil of saturated sand and gravel ready to turn to liquid jelly at the slightest quiver, every-damn-thing was so stable that nobody noticed until they checked the star patterns. That and the rest of the world being 1250 B.C.'s. Accidents just don't happen like that."

"Well, chunks of land just don't get displaced three millennia, either," Vicki said, but she nodded. That was the reasoning behind one of the major schools of thought about the Event. No way to *check,* of course. "Whoever or Whatever it was that did it could have integrated the ancient Nantucket into our slot just as easily," she pointed out.

"Yes, but a technology *that* advanced—not just raw power, but subtlety—could as easily have not moved Nantucket at all." At Vicki's expression she grinned slyly. "They could have scanned Nantucket, right down to the positions of every atom, and then *re-created* it here and now. Then we'd get the two separate histories, the way Doreen Arnstein says—she's the scientist, I never could get my head around that quantum mechanics stuff. And our doppelgangers—our *original* selves—would go on up in the twentieth without even noticing."

Vicki gave a low whistle. "You know, that's a really clever idea. And completely, utterly useless!"

"It beats thinking about my family problems," Hollard said, with a wry twist of her mouth.

"Mmmmm, if you don't mind me asking . . ."

Hollard shrugged. "Everyone else is going to know, soon enough. You know Ken—Brigadier Hollard—rescued Raupasha while he was mopping up the Assyrians north along the Euphrates, just south of the Jebel Sinjar?"

Vicki nodded. "Way I heard it, she'd killed the Assyrian King."

"Tukulti-Ninurta, yes. *His* father killed *her* father—that was when the Assyrians took over what was left of the Kingdom of Mitanni, which wasn't much by then—and Raupasha was smuggled out by loyal retainers. In the original history, she probably married some local squire and vanished from sight."

"Yeah. Then we came along and retumbled the bingo-balls."

"Mmmm-*hmmm. This* time around, Tukulti-Ninurta showed up there with some odds-and-sods of his guard and court, after we and the Babylonians smashed their army. Made her dance for him, then he was going to drag her off and rape her. She got him first, knife in her sleeve and slit his throat neat as you please when he grabbed her. Then Ken arrived, just before they lit the fire under her feet."

Vicki nodded. Even by the ungentle standards of the ancient Orient, the Assyrians were first-order swine; the locals all hated them. That didn't make the memory of bombing runs over Asshur much more comfortable, though. She went on, pushing aside the thought of burning rubble collapsing on kids like her Uncle Jared's:

"Yeah, I've seen the princess a couple of times. Smart girl, charismatic as all hell. Asked a lot of questions the time we had her up in *Emancipator,* and I got the feeling she really understood about atmospheric pressure and buoyancy."

"Mmmm-*hmmm,*" Hollard said. It was a verbal trick Vicki had noticed Commodore Alston use. "Learned English fast, and all the rest of it—well, she had a pretty good education by local standards, already spoke and wrote four languages."

"Was it the Babylonians' idea to make her queen of Mitanni, or ours?" Vicki asked curiously.

Officially, it had been Kashtiliash's father's notion all the way, but that was diplomacy for you. *Limp as an official explanation* wasn't a proverb for nothing.

"Oh, ours, but Kash and his father liked it. As a vassal kingdom, they'd get tribute and troops from Mitanni and without the bother of garrisons and officials. It was Princess Raupasha who shoveled the manure into the winnowing fan, right after the battle with those Hittites, the ones Walker talked into rebelling against their King."

Vicki nodded. She'd ferried wounded from that fight back to Ur Base. "Offered your brother the crown, or something, wasn't it?" she said.

"Damn, I knew we couldn't keep it under wraps for long. No, not *quite* that bad," Kathryn said, and gave the details of Raupasha's offer. "She *is* only seventeen, still . . ."

"Ouch," Vicki Cofflin said. Local politics weren't her department, thank God, but—"Ouch, ouch, ouch."

"Mega-ouchies," Hollard agreed. "Yeah, Kashtiliash hit the

God-damned roof. Akkadian is a great language for swearing in, and he nearly blew out the circuits on the radio set we were using . . . I don't blame him for that, or for suspecting that Ken or the Arnsteins put her up to it."

"Yeah. My sympathies." She hesitated. "How does your brother feel about it?" Kenneth Hollard wasn't married, except to the Marine Corps. She'd had the odd daydream about him herself. . . .

This time Kathryn Hollard's laugh was long and loud. "Oh, he *thinks* he's horrified, and he *thinks* she's a sort of unofficial kid sister," she said. "You know how men are."

"Ayup. Emotional idiots."

A nod. "Well, with some exceptions, some of the time. Kash, for instance."

Vicki hestitated again. *Damn, but I've got a bump of curiosity bigger than the Elephant's Child,* she thought. You couldn't pick up a copy of *People* magazine these days to find out details, either. The monthly *Ur Base Gazette* was a feeble substitute.

"He's not exactly what I'd have expected, for the son of one of these absolute monarchs," she said cautiously. "Of course, I've only met him a couple of times. Lots of . . . ah . . . presence." They both knew what she meant; a maleness that blazed.

Kathryn grinned. "Oh, yes indeed; smart, too, and likes new ideas. Did you know that his family have run Babylonia for nearly four hundred years? They foster their kids out with their kinfolk who stayed in the highlands, and then put them in the House of Succession—sort of like a strict boarding school, with other grandees' kids, where they get used to hard work and people saying 'no.' Not a bad system."

Vicki nodded. She couldn't imagine marrying a local herself, King or no King, but tastes differed. "What about your kids, if you don't mind me asking?"

"Oh, we agreed on a Nantucket tutor, and a spell on the Island with my relatives." She sighed. "Not that I'm going to have time to be pregnant until this damned war is over, probably."

"Yeah, it is inconvenient," Vicki said. She'd been thinking about a family of her own . . . False dawn showed in the east; time to get back to work. "Best of luck, then."

"It's all such a monumental distraction from the real war," Hollard said.

"Or at least our part of it," Vicki replied.

Hollard chuckled. "Yeah. At least we don't have the chief's worries, or the commodore's."

"Good to find you on this side of the pond, Ron," Marian Alston-Kurlelo said.

It was also good to be full, dry, dressed in a warm kaftan and slippers instead of a sopping uniform and wet boots, eating something because of the way it tasted, not because you were so hungry that hardtack and jerky went down easy.

"That's why I dropped by," she went on. "Didn't want to pass up a chance of settling some details with you in person."

She looked down at her half-finished dessert and pushed it away with a sudden memory of what her older sisters had looked like after forty-odd years of chitterlings, ham hocks, and sweet-potato pie. Swindapa snagged the dish and began to finish it off; it was baked apples with honey and cream, one of her favorites. They were sitting in the snug, a booth by the fire, with Councilor Ron Leaton and the manager of the Irondale Works, Erica Stark. She was a competent-looking woman in her late thirties, with the pale bony face and faded blue eyes of an old-stock Nantucketer. Leaton was as abstracted as ever, despite more gray in his light-brown hair and beard. The long pianist's fingers with their ground-in patina of machine grease toyed with a cup as he spoke.

"I was up on Anglesy, some problems with the drainage engines in the copper mines, then dropped down to troubleshoot the *Merrimac* project with Erica. I was surprised to hear you were coming," he said. "I expected you and the fleet to be off by now."

Alston nodded and glanced over her shoulder. Over at one of the long common tables the Marine escort were enjoying themselves with food, drink, and local company caught by the glamor of the uniform. She caught Swindapa conscientiously checking in that directon occasionally as well. They were good troops, but young, and only Ritter was actually something approaching a native Islander—she'd been a ten-year-old orphan adopted by an elderly couple in Nantucket Town, right after the Alban War. The rest of her squad were foreigners enlisted for pay, adventure, and the promise of citizenship at the end of their hitch, like much of the Coast Guard proper and most of the Marine Corps these days. Four of them linked arms over shoulders and sang, fairly tunefully:

"When you see the Southern Cross for the first time,
You'll understand why you came this way—"

Nobody was getting too loud, and nobody minded. *OK, that's well in hand,* Alston thought, then sighed as she replied to the engineer-entrepreneur. "I expected to be away by now myself, but the first casualty in any war is your battle plan," she said. "Sometimes even before the war starts . . . Two clans of the Uarwasorii *teuatha* started another round of one of their God-damned blood feuds on their way to the muster point."

"And none but Marian could deal with it," Swindapa said pridefully.

Alston smiled a crooked smile. "I do have the *baraka*, the *keuthes*, they call it," she said. "Or the Sun People *think* I do, which is 'bout the same thing."

"So they could surrender to you without losing too much face," Stark said shrewdly.

To the Sun People, *keuthes* was rather like having Fate putting a finger on your side of the scales, or a big spiritual battery pack full of capital-L Luck. The way the charioteer tribes looked at it, she, Alston, had a monstrously unfair amount of war-*keuthes*, giving her an unbeatable edge in anything involving fighting, raiding, or plundering. They called her the *Midnight Mare*, and it was a title of high respect and fear, which were much the same thing in their terms, invoking both the feared black-hued demons of the night and the wild power of *Hepkonwsa*, the Lady of the Horses.

Ron Leaton nodded. "You're the one who beat their war-host and wizard chief on the Downs. They believe in legends and heroes, not institutions and governments."

Marian shrugged. *What I'm needed for here is to keep our local allies together, and convince them we'll win. Luckily, I've got a good general staff, who can handle things at home under Jared.* A moment of worry: *Do the enemy? It wouldn't necessarily be obvious to our agents.* She didn't think so. Walker would be too suspicious of possible rivals, and the concept would be alien to Isketerol of Tartessos.

Instead she went on: " 'Dapa and I had to take a company of Marines from Portsmouth Base up north to kick ass and take names. We had a radio along, heard Ron was here, sent most of the party back, and dropped over ourselves to consult after the shouting was done."

The actual slaying that started the whole mess had been a fair enough fight, which helped.

Alston was glad they hadn't had to actually open fire; she'd gone armed and in uniform all her adult life, but not from any love of combat. *I leave that to maniacs and Sun People warriors, which is much of a muchness.* Killing human beings was a disgusting incident of her real job, which was winning safety for her children, partner, friends, people.

Now, William Walker and Alice Hong, a few of their collaborators, I'll make an exception for them, yes. I'll have to repress an impulse to swing on the bastard's ankles when we hang him.

"Short form"—leaving out days of knife-edge tension amid hair-trigger barbarian tempers and alien weirdness of belief and custom—"it went fairly smoothly, but somebody with less *keuthes* might have had to kill some of them, and that might have screwed up the whole muster, so it was worthwhile doing it myself, even at the cost of some delay."

Everyone nodded; that sort of thing could get very ugly very quickly. Every clan of the eastern tribes had a feud with *somebody* waiting to flare up again, and everyone was related to everyone else by descent or marriage or blood brotherhood, so a single killing could sprawl out into an uncontrollable free-for-all of ambushes and lethal brawls like a sweater unraveling from a single tug. When things got to that stage you had to send in a punitive expedition, which nobody liked.

"Swan-eating savages," Swindapa said, in her own language; that was a vile insult, to a Fiernan.

Stark nodded agreement. "We get a fair bit of that sort of trouble," she said. "There are a lot of migrant laborers from the Sun People tribes working here." A grimace of distaste. "Had to hang a couple for this and that."

"Mmmm, this is extraterritorial, isn't it?" Marian said. Places like Irondale were usually under the Republic's legal system. Fiernan law and custom had no provisions for towns, for any settlements of individuals who weren't related to each other; or any real conception of government or the State, come to that.

"We bargained for a perpetual lease on the land from the Telukuo lineage," Leaton said. "They got a lump sum and a one-fifth stockholding in the Irondale Company, and a lot of them got in on the ground floor as employees, so they're foremen and skilled workers now—we've trained some really good machinists—they're getting rich, hardly bother to farm anymore." He grinned and rubbed his hands. "Everyone concerned with this little baby is getting rich."

"I hear Sam Macy is complaining about that," Alston said.

She and Swindapa had gotten a fair bit of cash last year; prize money from some ships taken in a skirmish with the Tartessians before open war was declared, and they'd put much of it into Irondale Company stock. Money wasn't extremely important to her, but she'd been born ain't-no-doubt-'bout-it-grits-every-day *poor,* and disliked it. And there were the children to think of.

"Cheap-labor competition undercutting Nantucket industries, Sam says," she went on.

Leaton flushed. "I talked to him just before I came over, two weeks ago. Don't get me started!"

"Oh, by the milk of Moon Woman's flowing breasts, don't get him started," Swindapa said—in Fiernan—and rolled her eyes.

"Macy's not so bad," Alston said. "A representative government has to have an opposition party—better him than, say, Emma Carson."

The engineer snorted. "Nantucket's an *island,* for Christ's sake, and not a very *big* island, either—fifty square miles of sandbank, and the water supply's limited to shallow wells. Way things are going, Nantucket Town alone will have twenty thousand people in another decade and we'll be running out of space to live, much less for factories. Whereas this place . . . it was the Silicon Valley of the Industrial Revolution."

Alston raised her eyebrows; she'd read a good deal of history, but mostly in the military and maritime fields. Leaton had run a computer store before the Event; more importantly, he'd operated a machine shop out of his basement and studied the history of technology as an obsessive hobby. The hobby had turned into Seahaven Engineering, and those lathes and milling machines and gauges, the library of technical works and hard-won personal skills, had saved them all and gone on to grow and multiply and mutate in the years since. Making Leaton the most powerful of the Republic's new merchant princes along the way, if also the least worldly.

I like him. Usually do, with someone who really knows their work and is proud of it.

He continued: "Well, if you want to get technical, this"—he tapped his boot on the stone floor—"is where they first used, would have used, coal to smelt iron, and where the first iron steam-engine cylinders were cast, and where the first iron bridge was built—Coalbrookdale and Ironbridge Gorge. First railroad, first iron boat . . . Not by accident, any of it! The seams in these hillsides, they've got iron ore, coal, and fireclay in the same strata—some of the hills around here ooze bitumen. It's finest low-sulfur coking coal, too, no impurities, sweet enough to eat with a spoon. Plus abundant waterpower that's easy to tap and a navigable river at our doorstep and plenty of good timber, limestone, big area of farmland upriver to supply food, lead mines . . . If I were doing it over again, I wouldn't have built a Bessemer plant back on the Island at all, we should concentrate on high-value-added stuff there—"

Alston saw Erica Stark put an affectionate hand on the engineer's arm. *Well, well, perhaps the inveterate bachelor has met his match.* Or at least someone who could stop one of his lectures in its tracks. When Leaton said "if you want to get technical," strong men blanched.

"You don't have to convince *me,* Ron," the Guard commander said. "Save it for the Council sessions, or the Town Meetin'. Just tell me about what I ordered."

"Oh." Leaton cleared his throat. "Well, yes, it's about ready. All the plating, three-point-five inch and ready for assembly, edges milled and holes for bolts drilled. That"—he nodded northwards, toward the faint muffled sound of the forging hammer—"is the crankshaft being finished off; we turned the propeller shaft last week. Erica did, rather."

"The lathing-shed team did, rather," she said. "For once, everything was on schedule."

A Fiernan in Nantucketer clothes that didn't hide six months of pregnancy came with thick clay steins and a small glass on a tray: three beers, a mead, and a whiskey. Alston sipped at the liquor; wheat-mash bourbon, not quite Maker's Mark, but smoothly drinkable. Then she blew froth and took a mouthful of the beer, crisp hop-bitter coolness to follow the love-bite of the spirits.

"Not bad," she said.

Particularly compared to the flat, spoiled-barley bilgewater she'd tasted on her first trip to Alba. Someone who'd worked at Cisco Breweries on-Island had come back here with a bag of hop seed and a head full of tricks.

"Scheduling trouble?" she went on.

"Mostly Alban workforce," Stark said, in a tone that was half groan. "Back on Nantucket they're the minority and work our way. Here . . . There's a festival, they stop working to dance for the Moon. Their second cousin twice removed visits, they get drunk, then stop working. The salmon are running, they stop working to fish. They feel like going off and hunting wild pigs for a while, they stop working and hunt. It's haying time on their sister's farm, they stop working here and work there. A swan flies over the plant, they stop working and pray all day—"

Swindapa set down her mead, scowling. "Swans are sacred," she said, her tone unusually clipped.

Marian Alston-Kurlelo winced slightly; not only that, but they carried the souls of the dead to the afterlife and back to be reborn, in the faith of Moon Woman—she'd wondered sometimes if that was the far faint source of the legends about babies and storks. One of the few things that could get Fiernans into the mood for a really murderous riot was harm done to one of the big white birds. They were as bad that way as Hindus were with cows.

Would have been with cows, she reminded herself. Right now, the Aryan ancestors of the Hindus were beef-eating, booze-swilling charioteer barbarians not much different from their remote cousins here in Alba.

"And people aren't machines, Ms. Stark," Swindapa went on. "Fiernan aren't *zorr'HOt'po,* either." The word meant something like "maniacs" or "obsessive-compulsives." "Who in their right mind would spend all their days in a coal mine, or a factory full of heat and stink? You've told them that working for pay isn't like being a slave, and that's how they behave—like free people."

"Oh, no offense meant," Stark said soothingly. "But it *is* inconvenient, sometimes. Machinery *costs* the same whether it's working or not. We're having trouble just getting *enough* people, too; we're importing labor from as far away as the Baltic—got two hundred in from Jutland just last week, they're having a famine or war or something over there."

Alston nodded and took another mouthful of the beer. It wasn't that these Bronze Age peoples were lazy. They went after seasonal jobs like planting and reaping at a pace that would kill most people from the twentieth. The problem was that they were burst workers; much of the year they loafed, or worked a long day at a slow pace with frequent breaks as whim took them. The sort of steady, methodical, clock-driven effort that post-industrial Western urbanites put in was alien to them, and usually profoundly distasteful. That prompted a thought.

"How did those, mmmm, 'Silicon Valley' types you mentioned deal with the problem?" she asked. "They must have been getting their miners and forge-workers straight off the farm, too."

Leaton and Stark glanced at each other, and she caught similar looks of distaste. "Unpleasant ways," the man said. "Nearly as bad as the ones Walker uses."

Alston's lips pressed together. *Flogging and terror,* she

thought. The reports from the Councilor for Foreign Affairs' agents were gruesome. Stark took up the story:

"And Britain had millions of people then, most of them day laborers. It was take any work they could get or starve, for a lot of them."

Good point, the Guard commander thought. It would take generations for Alba to get crowded, even with the medical missionaries at work. By then birth control might have caught on.

She shrugged. "The factories exist for us, not us for the factories," she said.

Specialists tended to forget that. *Just as I occasionally need Jared to remind me that the Guard exists for the Republic, not vice versa.* "You got what I needed done, and in time—just."

"Right," Leaton said. "It'll all be aboard the *Merrimac* by the end of the week along with the technicians, and she ready to sail from Westhaven to join the fleet at Portsmouth Base."

"Most excellent," Marian said. "Isketerol of Tartessos is making far too much progress for my taste. I want to have an ace up my sleeve besides the *Farragut.* 'Dapa and I will ride downriver with the cargo and around Cornwall with the ship. Faster, and I want another look at the *Merrimac* anyway."

Swindapa sighed. "I don't understand how Isketerol's done so much so quickly," she said. "Walker had twenty helpers from Nantucket."

"My fault," Alston-Kurlelo said with bitter self-accusation. "It was my idea to bring him back to Nantucket, when we came here right after the Event to trade for seed corn. I wanted him to teach the languages he knew, and about conditions in the Mediterranean. He *learned* far too much, far too fast."

"He got half of all the stuff that Walker stole," Leaton pointed out gently. "Which was a cargo *intended* to set up a self-sufficient base and included a pretty complete technical library. Plus what Walker made here, and training for his crew from Walker's gang while they were in Alba, and the ship they took as a model. Plus he's snookered us more than once since then—remember when he bought all those treadle-powered sewing machines, and we found out he was taking them apart and using the gearing for machine tools? Plus he had a whole kingdom to draw on once he got back to Iberia. Southern Spain's a rich area—coal, minerals, timber."

Marian Alston-Kurlelo shook her head; there were no excuses for failure. "Well, have to do the best we can with what we've got."

Swindapa touched her arm. "Moon Woman will send us a fortunate star," she said, smiling gently. "Heather and Lucy are depending on it."

"Everybody is," Marian said, putting down a slight twinge of pain at the thought of their daughters. They grew and changed so quickly at that age . . . "And a lot of them are going do die before we set it all right."

CHAPTER THREE

September, 10 A.E.—O'Rourke's Ford, east of Troy
October, 10 A.E.—Nantucket Town, Republic
of Nantucket

Colonel Patrick James O'Rourke (Republic of Nantucket Marine Corps) threw up his hand to halt the column and reined in his horse. The little dapple-gray tossed its head and snorted; he soothed it with a hand down the neck.

"Steady there, Fancy," he said, bringing out his binoculars.

The horse was one of the Oriental chariot ponies they'd bought locally and broken to the saddle. Some laughed at him for riding an entire male, but there were times when you wanted a mount with some aggression, though. The animal was small, barely thirteen hands, but O'Rourke wasn't a large man himself; a stocky carrot-haired five-foot-eight, which he'd been pleased to find put him well above average in most of the Bronze Age world.

"There they are," he went on, pointing to the smoke of cookfires.

The little outpost below stood in the middle of a valley flanked on either side by rough hills—shrubby maquis of dwarf oak and juniper and tree heather below, real oaks and then tall pines further up their sides, rising to naked rock. Further south loomed Mount Ida; southwestward the rumpled valley dropped down toward the not-quite-visible Aegean Sea, and the plain of Troy beyond. The valley floor was farmland, richer than the rocky plateau to the eastward; it was tawny-colored now at the end of the summer dry season, dust smoking off stubblefields, between drystone walls, turning the flickering leaves of the olive groves a drabber green and coating the purple grapes that hung on the goblet-trained vines. A scatter

of stone and mud-brick huts dotted it, clumping around the
line of a stream and the rutted track of dry mud road that
wound down toward Troy. The sheepfolds and pens near them
were empty, and the smokeholes in the flat roofs were cold;
like sensible peasants anywhere or -when, the locals had headed
up into the hills when the armies came near, driving their livestock ahead of them.

The air was hot and buzzed with the sound of cicadas; sweat
trickled down his flanks under the khaki uniform jacket as he
scanned the bright openness of the great landscape. There was
a strong smell of rosemary and thyme crushed under the hooves
of the animals. There were two dozen of those; his staff gallop-
ers, trumpeter, a radio tech with her equipment on pack mules,
and two sections of mounted rifles.

The Nantucketers and their allies were camped around a larger
building on a slight rise, a bigger version of the huts; he could
see where the poles that held the thick earth-and-brushwood roof
poked through the peeling brown mud-plaster of the wall. A
few tall poplars near it hinted at a water source; a row of
wagons and herd of oxen with a few hobbled horses grazing
nearby marked the transport they'd brought with them. Another rectangular building stood some distance away, a storehouse by the look of it, and there were a couple of rough
stone paddocks.

O'Rourke's eyes caught a flickering brightness on one of the
high hills to the south of the valley. *Heliograph,* he thought.
Good that they're keeping on their toes.

He chopped his hand forward again. The group rocked into
motion, a column of twos threading its way downward at a trot.
The wind was from the east, blowing their own hot dust onto
their backs; even at the head of the column O'Rourke could
feel it seeping gritty down his collar and getting between his
teeth. There were a lot of birds in the sky. This was the season
northern Europe's flocks left for their winter quarters, crossing
over from Thrace via the Dardanelles; eagles, herons, storks,
in clumps and drifts and singly.

For a moment he wished they'd bring some of their weather
with them, then crossed himself to avert the omen. The fall
rains would start soon enough. Dust was bad. Mud was worse
when you had to move, especially if you had to move in a
hurry. Nobody in this part of the world built all-weather roads.
Nobody except William Walker . . .

A line of Marines covered the eastern approach to the Nantucketer base, waiting with their rifles ready behind low *sangars*

of stone. O'Rourke nodded approval. Beyond that the little base was bustling; several Conestoga wagons and native two-wheel oxcarts, pyramids of boxed supplies, of barley in sacks and wicker baskets and big pottery storage *pithoi*. Working parties bustled about, Marines in khaki trousers and boots and T-shirts, Hittite auxiliaries in kilts and callused bare feet.

A wiry twentysomething woman with a brown crew cut came up and saluted; he'd have thought her indecently young for the rank, if he hadn't rocketed up from captain to colonel in about two years himself. Between the breakneck expansion of the Corps in the last couple of years, casualties, and officers getting siphoned off for everything from training local allied troops to running crude-oil stills, promotions were rapid if you had what it took. He was a little short of thirty himself, and Brigadier Hollard only a few years his senior, and this baby captain wouldn't have been twelve when the Event hit—he couldn't remember if she was Island-born or an adoptee.

"Captain Cecilie Barnes, Colonel. First Combat Engineers," she said; the bare skin of arms and neck glistened with sweat, her cotton T-shirt stuck to what it covered, and she was as dirt-streaked as her command. "Is the battalion close behind? We're about ready to start on the bridge, the river's nearly breast-deep already, and once the rains get going . . ."

He returned the salute, then swung down from the saddle and stripped off his gloves. A Marine from the escort came up to take the bridle; before the man led the horse away O'Rourke stroked Fancy's nose and fed him a couple of candied dates to keep him out of a snapping-and-kicking mood.

"There'll be no battalion, Captain," he said. "And no bridge."

"Sir, we were told to get ready for—"

"I know. The enemy got frisky a little north of here, and we had to put the battalion in to stop them—quite a shindy. The siege of Troy isn't going well. Not enough weapons or supplies in the city. That's freeing up enemy forces to probe inland. If the city falls, the fertilizer hits the winnowing fan for true."

Barnes frowned. "Sir?" she said hopefully. "We've seen the *Emancipator* taking in equipment for Troy . . ."

"Only a few tons at a time, and we can't risk any more flights—too much else for it to do and too hard to replace. Walker's been bringing in more of his troops, and more of those Ringapi devils. Giving them more guns, as well, which is how he's getting them here. I dropped by to—"

The heliograph blinked from the hillside again. O'Rourke

could read the message as well as any . . . *enemy force in sight, numbers several hundred.*

"—to give you a hand setting up the defenses," he said. This base had just gone from a forward supply depot to the penultimate front line.

The garrison in Troy was supposed to be buying time for the First Marines; the First was in the westlands to buy time for the expeditionary force as a whole. He only hoped the people back home were doing something valuable with it.

"Heather! Lucy!" Chief Executive Officer Jared Cofflin yelled. "Marian! Junior! Jenny! Sam!"

You had to be specific; just "kids!" didn't get their attention. The children had burst into the Chief's House, home from school, and were in the middle of some game that involved thundering up and down stairs and whooping like a Zarthani war party doing a scalp dance, with a couple of barking Irish setters in attendance. Cold autumnal wind blew through the opened door, along with a flutter of yellow-gold leaves and a smell of damp earth, damp dog, woodsmoke, and sea-salt.

"Quiet, I said!" he bellowed, and snagged one setter by the collar. It wagged its tail and looked sheepish, trying to turn and lick his hand, hitting his elbow instead, putting a wet muddy paw on his leg. "You too, you fool dog."

"Yes, Uncle Jared?" Lucy asked sweetly.

She looked like a picture of innocence carved from milk chocolate, dressed in jeans and indigo-dyed sweater, twisting a lock of her loose-curled black hair around a finger as she rubbed a foot on the calf of the other leg. Her sister Heather stopped beside her with an identical angelic expression, red-hair-and-freckles version. They were both adopted from Alba, of course. Heather's parents had been villagers killed by one of Walker's raiding parties—Swindapa had found her crying in a clump of trees not far from their bodies. And Lucy's Alban birth-mother had died in childbirth; *her* father had been one of Walker's renegades, a black Coast Guard cadet from Tennessee. The Islanders had found her in the remains of Walker's base after the Battle of the Downs; by now he had to remind himself occasionally that they weren't really twins.

Both brought their school satchels around and hugged the strapped-together books and lunch box and wood-rimmed slateboards with studied nonchalance, a gesture aimed at his subconscious, where the memory of their excellent marks presumably hid ready to float up and restrain his temper.

Might have fooled me, he thought, trying to school his face into something formidable. *Fooled me back before the Event.* Back then he'd been a widower, and childless. Here he was married and father of four, two of them also adopted from Alba. *I should be insulted. They don't try this act on Marian or 'dapa, much.*

"What did I say about running around inside the house?" Cofflin asked.

Usually sternness came naturally to him; he had the dour Yankee visage common among the descendants of the seventeenth-century migrations that had settled Nantucket, bleak blue eyes, long face on a long skull, thinning sandy-blond hair streaked with gray. But it was hard to look po-faced at a kid having fun, especially with a close friend's daughter who'd been in and out of your house all her life.

"Sorry, Uncle Jared," they said together; and yes, they'd seen the twinkle he'd tried to bury. "Sorry, Dad," his own added, in antiphonal chorus—ages ten to six, but they played together and stuck together.

Good kids, he thought, and made his voice gruff for: "Well you should be sorry. You especially, Lucy and Heather. You don't get to run wild because your mothers are away."

"Can we go over to Guard House and play till dinner?"

Cridzywelfa, the Alston-Kurlelo's housekeeper, was looking after it while Marian and Swindapa were off with the expeditionary force. Which was fine, but . . .

"All right, as long as you don't wheedle too big a snack out of her and spoil your supper. Be warned!"

Cridzywelfa had been a slave among the Iraiina, back before the Alban War. Many of the newly freed had moved to Nantucket, after the founding of the Alliance and compulsory emancipation; entry-level jobs here looked good to people from that background, without kin or land. She'd learned English and settled in well, and she spoiled her employers' kids rotten, but wasn't what you'd call self-assertive.

On the other hand, her own two, they might as well be American teenagers. Or Nantucketers, to be more accurate. The melting pot was bubbling away merrily around here, of which he heartily approved, but not all the seasoning came from the local shelves.

The pack of them took off, with the dogs bouncing around them. The door banged shut, and the sound of children's feet and voices faded down the brick sidewalk.

"Sorry," he said to his two guests as he led them down the hallway.

Sam Macy grinned and shook his head. "Heck, I've got five of my own, Jared."

Emma Carson smiled politely—it didn't reach her eyes, which were the same pale gray as her short hair—and accompanied the two men into the sitting room. The Chief's House had been a small hotel before the Event, and long before that a whaling skipper's mansion, back in the glory days of Nantucket's pre–Civil War supremacy in the baleen and boiled-blubber trades. Given a few modifications, that had made it ideal for his new job; among other things, it had a couple of public rooms on the first floor that did fine for meetings, business and quasi-business and the sort of hospitality that someone in his position had to lay on.

Being chief of police was a lot simpler than being Chief Executive Officer of the Republic of Nantucket, he thought, something that had occurred to him just about every day since the Event landed him with the latter position.

The meeting room had a fireplace with brass andirons and screen; he took a section of split oak from the basket and flipped it onto the coals. For the rest, it sported the usual décor that antique-happy Nantucket had had back when it was a tourist town: oval mahogany table and chairs, sideboard and armoire, mirrors, flowered Victorian wallpaper, pictures of whaling ships. He felt a small glow of pride at the thought that by now anything here could be replaced from the Island's own workshops, at need; and there were souvenirs dropped off by Marian and a dozen other Islander skippers. A wooden sword edged with shark teeth, a three-legged Iberian idol, a boar's-tusk helmet plumed with a horse's mane dyed scarlet . . .

One of the paintings was post-Event, of him signing the Treaty of Alliance with Stonehenge in the background.

Not Stonehenge. The Great Wisdom. That was a better name, for a temple still whole and living. *And O'Hallahan left out the rain halfway through the ceremony, and all the umbrellas. And the Grandmothers looked a lot more scruffy than that—opinionated old biddies—and the Sun People war chiefs were scowling, not smiling—God-damned gang of thugs—and a lot of them looked pretty beaten-up, still bandaged from the Battle of the Downs. And Marian would eat kittens before she'd look that self-consciously Stern & Noble. Oh, well . . . Washington probably didn't stand up when he crossed the Delaware, either.*

People needed legends. Nations were built on them, as much as on plowland and factories, or gunpowder and ships.

The oil lanterns over the mantelpiece were quite functional now, too, and he lit one with a pine splinter from the fire before joining the others at the table. Martha came in with a tray bearing cookies, a silver pot of hot chocolate, and cups. She set it down and sat, opening her files; she was General Secretary of the Executive Council, and one of the Oceanic University directors, as well as his wife since the Year 1. She'd been a librarian at the Athenaeum before the Event, back when he was police chief—Navy swabby and fisherman before that, to her Wellesley and amateur archaeologist.

Odd, he thought happily. *Beer-and-hamburger vs. wine-and-quiche.* It had turned out to be a good match. She was still rail-thin despite bearing two children and helping raise four, a few more wrinkles and more gray in the seal-brown hair, a long slightly horselike face on the same model as his own. *And we make a good team.*

The necessary greetings went around, few and spare as local custom dictated. "Ayup, business," Cofflin said.

God-damn all political wheedling, he thought, with a touch of anger he kept strictly off his own features. *You'd think with a war on and good men and women dying, everyone would pull together.*

He knew how Martha would react to that; a snort, and a sharp word or two on the subject of his being too smart—and too old—to think anything of the sort.

"Well, they're not wasting time," Patrick O'Rourke said.

He watched the impact footprints of the mortar shells walk up the broad valley toward his position, each a brief airborne sculpture the shape of an Italian cypress made from pulverized dirt and rock. It hadn't been more than half an hour since he'd arrived to give Captain Barnes the bad news and gotten caught in it himself.

Whoever was on the other end of that mortar wasn't very good at it, but they'd get the shells here eventually. . . .

His staff gave him an occasional glance, as if to wonder when he was going to notice the approaching explosions. *Time to take pity on them,* he thought, and went on aloud:

"Take cover!"

The base's garrison were already in their slit trenches. Everyone else dived for a hole once he'd given the signal, and he hopped into his after them, with a whistling in the sky above to speed him on his way.

Whonk!

The explosion was close enough to drive dirt into his clenched teeth. He sneezed at the dusty-musty smell and taste of it and grinned. *There's one thing to be said for a war; it teaches you things about yourself, it does.* One thing he'd learned was that physical danger didn't disturb him much; some, yes, but not nearly with the gut-wrenching anxiety that, say, being afraid of screwing up and giving the wrong commands could do.

In fact, sometimes it was exciting, like rock-climbing or a steeplechase on a wet raw day. Whether that said something good or bad about his own character he didn't know.

Or much care, he thought. Horses screamed in terror in the pen beyond the field hospital. That was one thing he *did* regret about being back here; the poor beasts were still caught up in the quarrels of men. There were human screams, too, fear mostly—he'd become unpleasantly familiar with the sounds of agony—from the throats of locals.

One of those shells could land in here with me, he thought. *Of course, if we're to be playing that game, I could have stayed in Ireland the year of the Event.*

A safe, sane year in the last decade of the twentieth century. PCs, parties, Guinness on tap, girls, cars, trips to England or Italy, himself an up-and-coming young prospective law student in an affluent family. Nothing to bother him but boredom and a nagging doubt he really wanted to follow the law for the rest of his life.

One more year I'll work the summer on Nantucket, said I.

He'd done it the first year for the money and travel, and the second for fun; it was a wild young crowd on the island during the summer back then, one long party. When you were nineteen, working three jobs and sleeping in a garage *could* be classified as fun.

Just for old time's sake, to be sure. Then I'll stay in bloody Dublin and study for the final exams. One more year can't hurt, though, and the next thing I know I'm back in the fookin' Bronze Age with no prospects except farming potatoes, the which my grandfather moved to Dublin to avoid.

"*Or* goin' fer a soldier, which ye've doon, at that, ye iijit," he muttered under his breath, mimicking his grandfather's brogue before dropping back into his natural mid-Atlantic-with-a-lilt. "Maybe the English are right, and we're so stupid we don't even know how to fuck without arrows sayin' *this way* tattooed on the girl's thighs . . ."

On the other hand, not even the English ever claimed that the Irish weren't hell in a fight. It was just a bit of irony that nearly half the soldiers under his command were some sort of Alban proto-Celts from the dawn of time, who'd been in the process of conquering England when the Nantucketers arrived. Ireland itself was still populated by tattooed Moon-worshiping gits not yet up to the chariot-and-tomahawk stage. Even the *Fiernan Bohulugi* who made up most of the rest of the First Marine Regiment thought they were backward.

"Oh, well, at least Newgrange is there in the now," he muttered, shivering a little inwardly. The great tomb-temple by the Boyne River was already millennia old in this predawn age, as old now as Caesar's Rome had been to the time in which he was born.

He levered himself back up and looked about, shaking clods off his cloth-covered coal-scuttle helmet—what the Yanks called a Fritz. No real damage and it didn't look as if there had been any casualties. Except among the Hittite auxiliaries; some of them had been caught in the open, and all two hundred hale enough to run were taking to their sandaled heels, except for their officer. *He* was trying to stop them, poor soul, striking at fleeing men with his whip. At least they were so terrified they were just dodging rather than stabbing or clubbing the man. Discarded spears and bows marked their passage back up the valley toward the high plateau and at least momentary safety.

"No surprise *there,*" one of his aides said sourly. "Here we are, outnumbered twenty to one and our allies are running like hell."

"It's a typical Marine Corps situation, to be sure, Sally," he answered, replacing the helmet and dusting off his uniform instead. "Don't be too hard on the locals, though; it's a bit alarming, the first time under fire." Probably they wouldn't stop this side of Hattusas.

O'Rourke unsnapped the case at his waist and leveled the binoculars westward; clouds piled high in the sky there, hiding a sun just past noon. There had been rain a few days ago, and might be more soon.

He heard a sergeant's familiar rasp: "Nobody said *stop working!*"

The khaki-clad Marines went back to building the wall the company commander had laid out, using mud brick and stones from a livestock enclosure nearby, and sacks of grain and boxes of supplies. More manned the parapet, but the enemy were just beyond effective rifle range.

The mortar stayed silent; probably the crew had just noticed that it could only reach the Islanders at extreme range, which was wasteful. He watched the men who crewed it lifting it bodily, baseplate and all, into a chariot fitted with floor-clamps to receive it. These weren't Walker's uniformed troops; instead they wore plaid-check trousers and wraparound upper garments, their hair and mustaches long, and some of them were blond or red-thatched. Auxiliaries, then, that migrant horde from the Hungarian plains Walker had enlisted, the Ringapi they were called. He scanned back and forth. Five or six hundred of them. A few firearms, amid more spears and bows, axes and swords and gaudily painted shields. Flintlock shotguns, and some rifles. Impossible to be sure at this distance, but he thought that the rifles were muzzle-loaders, probably kept in store after the Achaeans learned to make better and then handed out to allies. . . .

"We'll risk it," he said.

"Sir?" Cecilie Barnes said.

"Can't let them set that mortar up just as they please, Captain," he said. *Because never a piece of artillery have we here, yet.* "Let them get into range, position it in a nice piece of dead ground, and they'd hammer us to flinders with it. Sergeant! Saddle up the Gatling. And someone get my horse from the pen."

"Ah, sir, I should—"

"Stay here and hold the fort, Captain."

He swung easily into the saddle; Fancy sidled restlessly under him and tossed its head, still nervous from the explosions. The Gatling-gun crew were mounted as well, on the horses that drew it or the ammunition limber. As machine guns went the six-barreled weapon was big and heavy, but it had the supreme virtues of simplicity and ruggedness.

O'Rourke drew his revolver, and checked that the *katana* over his shoulder was loose in the scabbard. He was playing platoon commander, but he was young yet, not thirty years, and willfulness was a perogative of command.

Besides, it's my fault they're in this trouble here. Or my responsibility, or whatever.

He'd sent them here. He had to plug the exits from the coast inland toward the Hittite heartlands, and he didn't have enough troops to do it—too many valleys led down to the coastal plain.

What would happen if Troy fell and freed up most of Walker's army, God only knew; they couldn't plug every hole. *He who defends everything, defends nothing, as old Fred said.* It had been his decision to strip this valley nearly bare, and to visit at this precise hour, and now . . .

"Let's go!" he shouted, and gave the horse some leg. "Come on, Fancy."

Bouncing and rattling on its field-gun carriage, the machine gun and its crew followed. The boiling knot of Ringapi tribesmen grew closer with frightening speed. A couple of them fired their shotguns at him; he could hear the flat *thump,* see the double spurt of smoke from firing pan and barrel, but they might as well have been firing at the moon that hung pale over the peaks to the east. A few knelt and took careful aim with long weapons . . . yes, the distinctive *crack* of rifled arms, and the nasty whickering *ptwissssk!* of bullets overhead. Firing high—not estimating the range right or adjusting their sights, the idle bastards. There they went, biting open cartridges, priming the pans, pouring the rest down the barrel and ramming the bullet on top; muzzle-loaders for sure. Minié rifles, much like those of the American Civil War, except that they were flintlocks. That would make the extreme range about a thousand yards, which meant they were just getting into dangerous territory. There was a clump of olives at just the right distance.

"There!" he cried, pointing. Then: "Halt!"

His mount reared and thrashed the air with its forehooves. The Gatling crew reined to a stop as well, wheeling as they did to bring the business end of their weapon around to face the enemy, leaping down and unfastening the hitch that connected trail to draught-pole, catching hold and running the weapon forward to the edge of the olive grove. One private held the team; the sergeant stepped into the bicycle-style seat on the trail, bending to look through the sights.

More of the tribesmen were firing, and more of the big lead slugs kicked up spurts of dirt around O'Rourke's horse. His stomach tightened, breath coming a little quicker as cut twigs from the twisted olive trees fell on his helmet and the shoulders of his uniform. The odd drab-green olives joined the twigs, brought down a little unripe.

"Got it," the sergeant in charge of the Gatling said. His hand worked the crank on its right side, back half a turn and then forward . . .

Braaaaaapp.

Smoke poured from the muzzles as each rotated up to the

six o'clock position and fired, a dirty gray-white cloud pouring backward with the light afternoon breeze. Glittering brass dropped out of the slot at the bottom as each passed the extractor, like the metallic excrement of death. O'Rourke raised his binoculars again. Men were down, scythed off their feet by the heavy .40 caliber bullets, some screaming and writhing like broken-backed snakes.

Brave enough, he thought: the Ringapi were clustering, coming together for the comfort of a comrade's shoulder, clashing weapons on their shields and shouting defiance. *Doing exactly the wrong thing, poor fools.* Perfectly sensible with the muscle-powered weapons they'd grown up with, sure death now.

"Whatever modern training they've had is pretty sketchy, then," he murmured to himself. One of their bullets went *ptank-whirrrr* off the gun-shield of the Gatling and wickered past him, a lethal Frisbee of flattened lead.

"On the mortar and the other chariot, the one with the ammunition," he said aloud.

"Yessir," the sergeant on the Gatling said tightly, his hands adjusting the elevating screw. "Here goes—"

Braaaaaappp. This time horses went down, kicking and screaming, louder and more piteously than the wounded men. O'Rourke winced slightly; the beasts had no idea of the point of politics they'd been killed over. *Braaaaaaap.* Hits on the other chariot, the one with the ammunition. Sparks flew as rounds slammed off metal, the barrel and baseplate of the mortar, the iron bands around a box of finned bombs.

Some of the Ringapi knew enough to run, because any second now . . .

BADDAMP. A globe of red fire for an instant, dirt gouting up, with bits of men and horses and chariot mixed in, raining down for scores of yards around. O'Rourke whooped with glee as he controlled his mount's plunging alarm.

"See 'em off!" he shouted, and the sergeant swung the muzzle of the Gatling back and forth, stopping only for his crew to slap another drum-shaped magazine onto the top of the weapon.

More Ringapi fell, the armored chiefs in their gaudy trappings and the bare-chested madmen sworn to the death-gods in the front row. The rest were farmers in drab wool, and took to their heels . . . except for a few with rifles who settled behind rocks or trees, and sent unpleasant reminders cracking overhead. The Gatling-gun crew waited for the shots, then sent a burst at each puff of smoke. O'Rourke let them have their fun for a few moments, then waved a hand.

"Cease fire." *We're not that well supplied with ammunition,* he thought but did not add. "Back to base."

The crew ran the Gatling back, clipped the trail to the harness of the four-horse team and mounted up. O'Rourke backed his horse a few paces and looked around. His breath went out in an *ooof,* as if he'd been punched in the gut. More of the Ringapi were swarming out from the stone walls and brush-tangles all about, running down the hillsides . . . many of them east of him, between here and the fortlet. The westering sun flashed off their metal, and the hillsides echoed with their wolf howls.

Either they're smarter than I thought, and set this as an ambush, or more stubborn, and just hid until the Gatling stopped instead of running away. Bad news either way.

"Too many!" he shouted, as the Gatling squad went for their rifles. "Get moving—*go!*"

They heeled their horses into a gallop. The Islander officer felt his lips skin back from his teeth; this was going to be too God-damned close for comfort. He went after them, keeping Fancy in hand and well below its best pace; horses in harness pulling loads could never equal a rider's pace. Instead he turned a little aside at an easy trot. He felt an odd calmness, somehow hot rather than cool. His eyes darted about, methodical and quick.

"You first, boyo!" he snarled.

A man hurdled a stone wall, screeching. His body was naked except for the glittering ring of twisted gold about his neck, and he carried a big round-cornered shield painted with a black raven on red; a long leaf-shaped bronze sword swung in his other hand, blurring as he loped forward. His face was twisted into a gorgon mask of fury, a white rim of foam around his lips, penis erect and waggling as he leaped, lime-dyed hair standing out in waving spikes around his head.

O'Rourke waited until he could see the mad blue eyes, white showing all around them, before he brought the pistol down. *Kerack,* and a jolt at his wrist. A puff of smell and the stink of rotten eggs that came with burned sulfur. The Ringapi had enough experience of firearms to bring the shield up as O'Rourke aimed at him. The barbarian was close enough for the Islander to see a tiny dark fleck appear on the red leather of the shield and the man went down, screaming what might be curses or possibly incoherent bellows of rage as he clutched at a broken thighbone; even a berserker couldn't move with a major bone gone to flinders. Blood jetted from around the clutching fingers.

Something went through the air far too close to O'Rourke's head with an unpleasant *swissssh*. He turned in the saddle, fired three times, saw another Ringapi double over and fall as the egg-shaped basalt stone in his sling flew wild. *Damn.* A good slinger had almost as much range as a pistol, and more accuracy when the pistoleer was on a horse's moving back. Two more shots sent another ducking behind a wall.

"Faster!" he shouted to the Gatling crew.

Unfortunately, if they went *much* faster the weapon or the ammunition cart was likely to overturn. He had a sudden, vivid memory of a childhood nightmare in which he'd been menaced by monsters and yet couldn't run, moving in slow motion like someone trapped in honey. Another sling-bullet went through the air close behind his horse's rump, striking a stone near its left rear. The animal bounded forward and then went crabwise, trying to crane its head around to see what had stung it.

"Watch where you're goin', Fancy," he warned it, with a taut grin.

The leap had put him close behind the Gatling; some of the crew had their personal weapons out, but you might as well spit at someone as try to hit him with a rifle from a jouncing gun carriage. He took a moment to let the reins fall on his saddlebow, opening his pistol and letting the spent brass spill. Two crescent-shaped speedloaders and the cylinder snapped back in.

"Keep going, Sergeant," he called to the head of the Gatling crew. What he had to do was quite clear. Quite insane as well, but that was war for you. He turned his horse back toward the enemy and clapped heels to its flanks with a yell.

Not really *suicidal,* he thought. There wouldn't be more than a dozen or so scattered foemen he'd have to knock back on their heels—given a good horse, momentum, a revolver, and luck it was just possible.

Brave and obedient, Fancy bounded forward with jackrabbit acceleration. The clump of Ringapi pelting up right behind the Islanders gaped for a second; they'd been focused on pursuing someone who ran. Their war howls turned to yells of surprise as he bore down on them, their heads swelling from dots to the faces of men with rushing speed. Chariots didn't teach you how nimble a single horseman could be, with a well-trained mount—and he'd spent some time teaching Fancy a few gymkhana tricks.

The first two warriors pivoted on their left heels, shields swinging out to balance the javelins they threw with their right. O'Rourke judged the trajectory, then ducked and brought his face against Fancy's mane. The sweet musky smell of horse filled his nostrils, and the whetted bronze heads of the spears whipped through the space he'd occupied a second before. As he'd guessed—to these men horses were a mighty prize, one of the things war was fought *for,* and it would never have occurred to them to aim at his mount. Then they sprang aside with yells of fear as the horse thrust between them, knocking one arse-over-teakettle with its shoulder. O'Rourke leaned far over, and for an instant the muzzle of his Python was inches from a face screaming hatred.

Kerack. The Ringapi's head snapped back as if he'd been kicked in the face by a horse. A round blue hole appeared over the bridge of his nose, and the back of his head flew off in a spatter of bone fragments and pink-gray brain. The horse staggered beneath O'Rourke. Something had landed on its rump, and an arm went around his throat, jerking him back upright in the saddle. He could sense the laurel-leaf dagger rising. His right hand moved, pointing the heavy pistol back under his own left armpit, jamming the muzzle into the other man's torso before he jerked the trigger twice. The hot flare scorched him through the linsey-woolsey of his uniform jacket, and the weight fell away behind. Something had hurt Fancy as well, and the stallion bugled out his own battle cry, rearing and milling with his forehooves. They came down on the face and shoulder of a Ringapi who was trying to aim a bow, and he fell with an ugly crunching sound. Fancy danced over him, stamping, then lashed out at another with his hind hooves. They hit a shield; O'Rourke could hear the wooden frame break, and probably the arm behind it.

"*Quiet,* ye git!" he snarled—hitting anything from atop a horse was difficult; a bucking horse made it impossible . . . but it wasn't at all impossible for someone on the ground to spear him out of that saddle. Some remote corner of his mind was surprised at his tone, that of a man mildly annoyed in the middle of a difficult task.

Fancy quieted somewhat, less at his voice than at the familiar feel of thighs and the hand on the reins, and spun nimbly about. A barbarian was getting up, a scrape raw and bleeding across one cheek, blood dripping from his nose and his long droopy mustaches and his stubbly-shaven chin. The spear he drew back to throw didn't look to be made for javelin work; it was six feet long and had a broad flame-shaped bronze head. It didn't have to be a purpose-made throwing spear, with the thick-muscled arm of the northern savage behind it and only ten feet between them. O'Rourke fired the last three rounds in the revolver as fast as he could squeeze the trigger and bring the muzzle back down. The hammer clicked at last on an empty chamber, but the Ringapi did not throw. Instead he sank down to his knees, looking puzzled, blood welling from nose and mouth. Then he pitched forward on his face, spear dropping in the dust.

O'Rourke was already wheeling his horse, slapping the pistol back into its holster and his heels into Fancy's flanks. *No time to reload,* he thought, as the stallion sprang forward again, glad to be allowed to gallop at last. He was familiar with the rubber duration of combat—it felt like twenty minutes or so since the Ringapi sprang their ambush, but it was probably less than five by the clock. *And if they'd waited just a bit and hit us all together I'd have been dead the first minute,* he thought, leaning forward into the speed of the horse's rush.

He'd moved fast enough to distract the barbarians. The Gatling crew were safely past them, bouncing back up the dusty, rutted track toward the Nantucketer outpost. Most of the enemy were behind him, too, but there was one standing in the roadway between him and safety—or at least between him and such safety as the improvised base-cum-field-hospital promised. A quick glance right and left showed that all that solitary Ringapi had to do was delay him a few moments and he'd be swarmed under.

The man ahead looked a little out of the ordinary run of savage. He wore a bowl-shaped rimmed helmet of polished bronze with a tall scarlet-dyed horsehair plume and hinged cheek-guards; there were crossed gilt thunderbolts on the face of his black round-cornered rectangular shield, and gold rings around his arms and his neck. The chain-mail shirt above his flapping checked trousers was from a workshop in *Meizon Akhaia,* and so was the bright silver-glittering steel of the long spearhead. He held the shield up and slammed the butt of his spear into the ground, bracing his right foot against it for further strength and slanting the point forward—probably his folk's way for a man on foot to face a chariot.

"Damn," O'Rourke muttered. *This lad's been to school, he has.* A slinger and archer were running flat out to join him, too, and they'd be there far too soon.

The Nantucketer reached back over his left shoulder and drew the *katana* as the rocking speed of the gallop increased.

The sharkskin wrapping of the hilt was rough against his hand as he raised the sword; he'd likely get one and only one chance at this, and the enemy was also likely to be far more experienced with cold steel—well, with edged metal—than he was. Suddenly he didn't much care.

"Lamh Laidir Abu!" he shrieked, and braced his feet in the stirrups, rising slightly.

He could see the Ringapi chief's bared teeth now, and the spearpoint pivoted to follow him—it would be in his side, or Fancy's, if he turned wide; or if he turned further than that, it would put him in range of the men running through the fields on either side, clambering over fieldstone walls—it wasn't the ones yelling he was worried about, it was the grimly intent, running as hard as they could. A few premature slingstones and arrows came his way, and the odd bullet.

Everything fell away, except the spearpoint and the fearless blue eyes behind the helmet brim. *Now, he's used to chariots, which can't shift all that fast, so—*

A press of his right leg, and Fancy crawfished at the last instant. The steel head of the spear flashed by, close enough to strike the stirrup-iron that held O'Rourke's right boot with a tooth-grating *skrrriinng*. The *katana* came down, and he felt the edge jar into meat. He ripped it upward with a banshee shriek, upward like a polo mallet and into the jaw of the slinger taking aim five yards behind the fallen chief. The man beyond him was drawing a long yew bow, but wasn't quite fast enough. He threw himself down with a yell, and Fancy gathered himself and took to the air in a soaring leap that would have cleared a six-bar fence.

O'Rourke whooped as he came up the slight slope to the base, drops of blood flinging back from the sword as he pulled the horse back to a canter and then to a walk. The Marines stationed on the wall cheered and waved their rifles in the air, the ones who weren't taking long-range shots at any Ringapi unwise enough to show himself. He was still grinning as Captain Barnes came up and snapped a salute.

"Sir, that was the most amazing thing I've ever seen!"

"Ah, wasn't it, though?" O'Rourke said with a laugh, returning the gesture.

"And it was about the dumbest thing I've ever seen, too—sir."

"No, no, just Irish," he chuckled, then nodded to the man beside her as he cleaned and sheathed the sword.

Hantilis son of Tiwataparas was a Hittite; his title translated roughly as *Overseer of One Thousand,* or Colonel, in English; a short heavy-boned muscular man, big-nosed and hairy and stocky and swarthy, with dark eyes under heavy eyebrows. The short sword at his side was steel, a diplomatic gift, as was the razor that kept the blue-black stubble on his chin closer than bronze had ever done; most Hittites of the upper classes were clean-shaven, in vivid contrast to Babylonia. He wore a bronze helmet with a crest that trailed down his back like a pigtail, a belted tunic, and a kilt, with calf-boots that had upturned toes, standard military dress for his people.

"Bravely done," he said, in slow accented English; King Tud-haliyas had set a number of his officer-nobility to learning the Nantucketer language, as well as a corps of scribes. "Like . . . how say, old stories."

He mimed plucking a stringed instrument, the sort of thing a bard would accompany an epic with. O'Rourke nodded a little smugly; it *had* been a little like something out of the *Cattle Raid of Cooley.* He smiled to himself: as far as Nantucket's little band of scholars could tell, the Ringapi were some sort of proto-Celt themselves, or else close cousins to the earliest Celts, if distinctions like that had any meaning this far back. They came from what would have become Hungary and Austria in the original history, lured by Walker's promises of south-land loot and help against predatory neighbors; warriors and women and children and household goods in wagons and Uncle Tom Cobleigh and all. *Volkerwanderung* like that were common enough, and getting more so; this was an age of chaos and wars and wanderings, even before the Event.

"What is . . . Irish?" the Hittite went on

"Ah . . ." *Christ, how to answer that in words of one syllable.* "A different . . . tribe," he said. "Not important."

The Hittite scowled and glanced eastward, where the mercenaries he'd been commanding had gone.

"Kaska dogs—they run like coward sheep," he said.

He dropped into Akkadian to do it, which he spoke far better than he did English; O'Rourke had a fair grasp on that ancient Semitic language as well, from the year he'd spent in Babylonia. It was the universal second language of the educated here and of diplomacy as well, like Latin in medieval Europe, and so doubly useful.

"I bow in apology," the Hittite went on, and did so.

O'Rourke shrugged; they'd have fought well enough, against the weapons they understood.

He looked around the enclosure. Walls were being built up

to six feet with sacks and baskets of barley, with a fighting platform on the inside for the troops to stand on.

"How many effectives?" he asked.

"Sir," Brand said. "Lieutenant Hussey and eighty-seven enlisted personnel in my engineering company; another ten from the clinic personnel. About thirty-five sick and wounded from various units that've been operating around here; mostly they're down with the squirts of one sort or another. Plus the sixteen rifles you brought."

He nodded; dysentery happened, no matter how careful you were about clean water and food. Then he dictated a message for reinforcements—and as a wish rather than a hope, a request for air support—to Hattusas HQ. The ultralights were overstretched as it was.

"Sir, should you be staying here?" Barnes asked. "We may be cut off."

"It's where the action is," O'Rourke said absently, looking around again. "Hmmm . . . Captain, how are we fixed for these barley sacks?"

"Tons of it, sir. This *was* a forward supply collection center. The storehouse is full of boxed dog biscuit, too."

He looked around, scowling. *The hospital's got to be inside the perimeter. That leaves us with this goddamned east–west rectangle of wall to hold—inefficient.* The walls were very long relative to the area within.

"Then run another breastwork, *here*"—he drew a line in the dirt with the tip of his boot, extending it across the last, eastward third of the rectangle, the one that included the storehouse. "We'll need a fallback position. And a last-stand redoubt in the center of the space it encloses, using all the barley sacks you have left over—nine feet high, with a firing step."

"And the Gatling, sir? There?"

"No, plunging fire isn't effective against a massed attack," O'Rourke said, shaking his head. "We'll use it to cover the largest field in front of the gate here and shift the rifles to . . ."

After he'd finished, he noted Hantilis staring at what the Marines had accomplished, working on the field entrenchments. It *was* fairly impressive; they'd turned an enclosure that might have done a good job of keeping goats out into something resembling a miniature fort.

"How they work!" the Hittite said, in a mixture of English and Babylonian, amazement clear in his tone. "I have never seen even slaves beneath the overseer's lash toil so!"

"And you won't," O'Rourke said dryly. "A slave—his tools are his enemies and he delights in idleness; to destroy your goods is his pleasure. On the Island, a free man's pride is in the work of his hands, and all honest work is counted honorable—to employ such a one is to profit, even if the wage be high. A slave just eats your food and dies."

Hantilis frowned, something his heavy-boned face made easy; the Islander could see him turning the thought over in his head. Then he shook it aside for now.

"Can we stop the enemy here?" he asked. "My King prepares for war, but he must have time."

"We're *buying* time," O'Rourke said. "That's what expendable means, boyo."

"Sam, we needed that ship," Jared Cofflin said. "Sorry, but there *is* a war on."

Emma Carson stayed quiet. *Quiet as a snake,* Jared thought. *Heard a snake bit her once. The snake died.* A little off-balance here in the Chief's House, though; she wasn't a frequent guest.

Sam Macy nodded unwillingly. "Wish you could have taken something besides the *Merrimac*, Jared," he said. "Or given me some warning. The Republic's paying fair compensation, but I had a buyer lined up"—who was confidential information, of course—"and it isn't going to do my reputation any good having to back out. Reputation's my stock-in-trade, as much as plank and beam."

Macy was a short thick-bodied man of Jared's age, most of it muscle despite an incipient pot. His gray-shot black hair was still abundant, though, and he'd added a short spade-shaped beard back when shaving got difficult, and kept it after hot water, soap, and straight-edge razors became available again. Before the Event he'd been a house-building contractor; since then he'd become something of a timber baron in the limitless forests over on the mainland, that leading his firm naturally to interests in shipyards and ships, and occasionally to operating ships until the right price was offered.

"It was there, and the less warning, the less likely word is to get to the enemy," Jared said. "The Arnsteins are pretty sure they've still got some eyes here. We can move information more quickly, Tartessos doesn't have radios, thank God. Yet. But there are ways for them to communicate."

Macy nodded. "Well, if you let the *Inquirer & Mirror* have the story eventually, so everyone knows it was . . . what's the word . . ."

"*Force majeure*," Martha supplied helpfully.

"Right."

"Mmmmn-hmm," Cofflin said, nodding an affirmative.

"What the hell did you want her for, anyway?" Macy said. "She's a good ship, weatherly and fast—but I thought there were ample transports? The buyer was looking into opening a regular private trade with Anyang."

"State secret," Cofflin said. "We need her; leave it at that."

It made him a little uneasy to use phrases like that, but it worked. The abortive Tartessian invasion this spring past had frightened and enraged the entire population. It was also a pity he had to put a spoke in the wheel of those plans for trade. Policy was to encourage private enterprise, wherever possible. He'd detested the period of absolute emergency right after the Event when he and the Council had to run everything, handing out rations and assigning work. Each step toward normalcy since had been a relief, and his greatest ambition as head of government had been to become as irrelevant as he could to as many people as possible. He didn't like the way the war was making them lose ground.

"Filthy war," Macy said, as if echoing his thought, and everyone nodded.

Emma Carson cleared her throat. "Now, Chief, I'm on the board of Chapman, Charnes & Co.," she said.

Jared nodded noncommittally. The Carsons *were* Chapman and Charnes nowadays; they'd bought in with profits made in the mainland trade and managed the firm shrewdly. Those initial profits hadn't been too scrupulously made, and there had been trouble with the Indians over their habit of including free firewater as a bargaining tool; the mainlanders were fully capable of realizing they'd been diddled when they sobered up. The Carsons had loudly demanded that the Republic's military enforce those debts; he'd refused and got the Meeting to back him. Neither of them had enjoyed the clashes over that.

Carson went on carefully: "We were the buyers for Sam's ship—wanted to see how she'd do on a shakedown cruise across the pond to Alba, before we sent her really far foreign."

Macy snorted. "Emma, you wanted to take possession in Westhaven because you could sign up a crew cheaper there than you could here in Nantucket Town or the outports," he said. He looked back at Jared. "Chief, I still say we should have a law saying that the crews of Nantucket-flagged vessels have to be citizens. Registered immigrants, at least."

"Sam Macy," Carson said, exasperation showing in her

tone—they had this argument every time they met in public—
"I *don't* think we should be copying . . . what were they called?
The Navigation Acts, the ones the British had before the
Revolution."

Jared and Martha caught each other's eyes and nodded
slightly. "Let's save that for the Town Meeting," Martha said
dryly.

Carson's reply was equally pawky-cynical: "Ms. Cofflin, you
know as well as I do that if all four of us agree on something,
we can get it through the Meeting. I presume that's why we're
all here now."

"Mebbe. Do we agree on a wartime compromise on the immigration laws and the income-tax rate?" Jared Cofflin said,
leaning back; the delicate cup and saucer looked absurdly small
in his big gnarled fisherman's hands. *I suppose it was inevitable
we'd get political parties.*

The unity they'd had right after the Event was lifeboat politics. That didn't keep him from being nostalgic about it. He'd
been a small-town boy too long to imagine that Nantucket
would ever be without its share of homegrown gullible idiots
and nosy-parkers. Or smart bastards like the Carsons untrou-
bled by excessive ethics and ready to manipulate both types of
natural-born damned fools.

Carson shrugged. "We all want the war won," she said. "That
needs money, and trade's how we get it. Now, we were buying
the *Merrimac* for the China trade. There's a big market there
for furs and ginseng, as well as the usual tools and trinkets,
and they've got jade and silk and tea. Plus it would be an
alternate source for raw cotton, now we've given them the
seeds. Hemp, too, maybe metals . . . well, never mind."

"All of which," Martha said, "would be nice replacements
for your prewar trade to Tartessos."

"Well, yes," Carson said. "But all that needs ships, ships
need crews, and the shipyards need workers to make the ships.
Not to mention the cost of improvements like the new piers
and wharves, which take tax money, which means taxes would
be lower if we had more hands."

"I *thought* we'd get back to the immigration quotas," Macy
said, and his fist hit the table. "Yes, taxes might be lower . . .
but so would wages. That's fine for you and me, Carson—we're
employers, and big ones. Good enough for people who own
their own farms, or fishing boats, or stores or workshops or
whatever. Bad news for people who live off their paychecks."

"Any citizen can claim a land grant," Carson said piously.

"We've got the whole of Long Island to settle, and more besides."

"Sure! But how about staying alive until enough's cleared to live off? And not everyone wants to be a farmer; *I* sure as hell wouldn't. Or knows how to go about it."

"Well, I'm not so sure it would be a bad deal for our citizens if labor were cheaper," Carson said. "Think about it, Macy. We've got far too many people with priceless pre-Event skills hauling nets, hunting seal, hoeing potatoes, and chopping down trees. With more labor, a lot more of them could move up, become employers themselves. Those who couldn't are the sort who couldn't find their own butt cheeks with both hands anyway."

"And I can see damned well where *that* would end, too, Carson—with Walker's setup. I don't want my children growing up in a slave state."

"Wait a minute, you son of a bitch, you can't accuse me of—"

"People!" Martha Cofflin's voice cut through the rising anger. "Quietly, please."

"The present quota's not *enough*," Carson said, more calmly. "A thousand a year is far too few for what we need." An arm waved towards the windows. "There's a whole *world* out there waiting for the Republic!"

"If you were thinking about the Republic, you'd have adopted some orphans," Macy said. "No quota there. Tina and I have—three. You and Slippery Dick're only interested in grown-up Albans you can put to work right away. Cheap."

Carson closed her mouth with a snap. In the long run adoption was the perfect form of immigration, producing more people who might as well be native-born, and it had become something of a tradition.

"Dick and I have put in an application for some kids," Emma Carson huffed. "It's pending right now."

Ayup, Cofflin thought. *Now that you're rich and want to get into politics to make it easier to get even richer, you want to look like a model of civic virtue. Get the Meeting to forget how many times you've been rapped over the knuckles.*

The latest had been quite a scandal; turned out Chapman and Charnes had "accidentally" dropped shiploads of horses and cattle in south Texas and the Argentine Pampas several years back—that and pigs, all sorts of animals suited to taking care of themselves. The stock had gone feral and were breeding like crazy. The Conservation Board would never have gone for it, but now it was a *fait accompli,* and promised to be a little gold mine in the long run.

"Let's not rehash that stuff," he said aloud. He'd deal with the Carsons, because he had to, but one important reason he let himself be talked into staying with this lousy job was keeping people like them away from the levers of power. "We've chewed all the Chiclet off that gum a long time ago. Let's concentrate on wartime needs."

Martha took up the argument: "Now, Sam, you know that generally we—Jared and I—more or less agree with you on the immigration issue. Haven't we worked together on the Council on that? *And* we persuaded Ron Leaton to go along with us."

Carson ground her teeth behind a bland smile. She hadn't enjoyed it when the Cofflins split Leaton off from her block. Executive Council seats weren't elective, either; they were appointed by the Chief. Leaton was on the Council; she wasn't, and wouldn't be while Jared Cofflin was in office.

"Yeah," Macy said. "And okay, I agreed that we should keep granting ex-Marines citizenship, and the ones who enlist in the Guard. Doesn't that satsify you, Carson?"

"No," Carson said bluntly. "We need the extra labor *now,* not after the end of the war or six years from now or whatever." —

"We're on the horns of a dilemma," Martha said. "Yes, we need more people; but we also need them to pick up our ways—not just the three R's and English, but our habits of thought. That takes personal contact. Otherwise, in a democracy"—and the Republic was very emphatically that; major issues were settled by the Town Meeting—"the consequences could be . . . drastic."

"Oh, not necessarily drastically *bad,*" Carson said thoughtfully.

Ayup, Emma would *see that.* She wasn't the nicest person in the Republic, but she was nobody's fool. Albans didn't understand representative government, much, but they *did* comprehend patron-and-client relationships, right down in their bones. *Which is perfect for someone who wants to build up a Tammany-Hall-style political machine.*

"God-damn Walker." Jared sighed. "If it weren't for him, and this war he's forced on us, we could take everything more slowly. But . . . needs must when the devil drives."

"All right, Jared, what do you want?"

"An equality of dissatisfaction, Sam. You let us raise the quota a bit more and recruit a bit more. Ms. Carson, you go along, even though it's not nearly as much as you want. You both agree to our building up overseas capacity the way Ron Leaton wants, but not as much as he wants."

Macy checked himself with a visible effort and knotted his brows in thought. Emma Carson glanced lynx-eyed at him, then at the Cofflins, then steepled her fingers and waited.

The bargaining went on for hours. *And the worst of it is,* Jared Cofflin thought, as darkness fell, *I'll have to invite* Emma *to dinner along with Sam. I'd a hell of a lot rather it was Ian, say. Even if he did beat me like a drum at chess after the plates were washed.*

With an effort of will he pushed worry for his friend away; Ian Arnstein was in Troy, and Troy was under siege from Walker's men. Instead he murmured to Martha as they left for the dining room:

"What was that thing you told me—something Elizabeth I said about why she didn't like to pick a fight?"

Martha closed her eyes in thought for a moment, then quoted in the same low tone: "*I do not like wars. Their outcomes are never certain.*"

She'd once remarked that "Bright Beth" or "Smart Lizzie" would have been a much better nickname than Gloriana.

Jared sighed. *Marian,* win *this damned war, and win it quick. I don't like the feeling I'm getting of things spinning out of control.*

CHAPTER FOUR

September, 10 A.E.—Tartessos City, southwestern Iberia
October, 10 A.E.—Severn estuary, Alba
September, 10 A.E.—Tartessos City, southwestern Iberia

Ersibekar artakerka akoltistautenkar eribekau
Uortakerkar burlterkar saldulakogiar saldulakogiau—

"Lord King, the embassy of *Meizon Akhaia* requests audience," the court messenger said.

Isketerol of Tartessos broke off the silent prayer, lowered his arms, and turned away from the edge of the palace rooftop, scowling at the messenger. Beyond him the Greek herald bowed in his sea-stained tunic and fringed kilt, a tall brown-haired young man with a warrior's supple strength, looking around with bright-eyed interest despite the haste that had brought him up from the docks without pause, and his ships all the way across the Middle Sea from Great Achaea to Iberia. He went to one knee for a moment, then stood and met the Tartessian ruler's eyes:

"Rejoice, my Lord King. I am Telemakhos son of Odikweos, who is *wannax* in Ithaka and *ekwetos* to the King of Men in Mycenae," he said. "My father brings the word of your blood brother the High Wannax William Walker to you, and will take your word to the King of Men."

"Rejoice, prince," Isketerol of Tartessos said in fair if accented Greek. "My guest-friend King Odikweos is always welcome at my hearth, but the embassy of Great Achaea must wait on the Gods of the land. This is the day when the King weds the Lady of Tartessos."

"My father honors the Gods of his guest-friend, and the High Wannax honors the Gods of his blood brother," Telemakhos said, bowing again. "The embassy will await the King's word."

Isketerol nodded regally. *In truth, I doubt that William greatly honors any gods at all.* The thought was frightening even to a man as well traveled as the King, but William Walker hadn't suffered any ill luck from his lack of piety. Quite the contrary, in fact. With an effort, he cleared his mind of such matters; even of the fear of the Nantucketer attack both spies and his own mind told him was building on the other side of the River Ocean, looming over his folk like an avalanche of anvils. Today was for the Gods.

"Come. My people await me."

The procession formed in the main courtyard of the New Palace as the sun sank westward. Despite that location the rite was in the manner made sacred by long custom, lest the Lady be offended by breach of ancient ways. The King came first, in a simple kilt of soft-tanned goatskin, but glittering with the metal that was the tears of the Sun—a round crown of sheet gold embossed with studs about his brows and set with tall feather plumes, pectorals of gold shaped like miniature oxhides over his chest, a necklace of gold disks around his neck, a belt of worked gold plates making a broad band about his stomach.

"Behold the Sun Lord!" cried the Lady's Lady—by tradition the senior wife of the King was high priestess of the City's patron goddess. She stood in a long blue robe hung with silver and turquoise, her sleek raven hair braided and bound in two disks on either side of her head. "Behold the Sun Lord, come to do honor to the Lady of Tartessos!"

"Behold him!" cried the crowd around the colonnaded court; his other wives, his children, wisemen, war-captains, *their* families and retainers . . .

Their finery was a shout of color, saffron and indigo and cochineal-crimson, sparkling with silver and turquoise, polished steel and bronze. The uniformed Royal Guards who kept a corridor open for him to the gates snapped to attention and brought their flintlock rifles to present arms.

Isketerol nodded slightly. The gates swung back, and the roar of the crowd beyond struck him like a blow to the face, along with the scent of sweat and flowers and wine, garlic and olive oil and hot stone. More soldiers lined the route ahead, facing away with rifles held level before them, pushing against the surging crowd; it was the greatest of good luck to touch the King on such a day. That had been possible before Isketerol seized the throne from his distant kinsman and began the changes, for Tartessos had been smaller then. What was left of Old Town lay southward, to his left, in a tangle of little thatched mud-brick houses across the bottom slopes of the hills.

There he had managed to touch the King's heel himself once, so long ago.

Not so long ago, he thought stoutly, stepping forward. *And it did bring me luck!*

The Lady's Lady paced on his left, and the others of the royal household took their places behind—the family, the retainers, the great carved and painted and gilded carts with their images of the Grain Goddess and Arucuttag of the Sea, and their attendant priests and priestesses, that the others of the Great Gods might witness this rite. There was no need for an image of the Crone, of course—She was present everywhere, ubiquitous as shadow, for wherever life went, there Death was also. Musicians beat on drums, plucked harps, played bone flutes, sounded bronze trumpets in peal after peal of sound; warriors followed in the panoply of his youth, bronze disks over their chests secured by leather cross-belts, helmets of sinew sewn with bronze scales, sword and spear and bow. Attendants behind flung handfuls of dried figs, raisins, and olives to the crowd, symbols of luck and abundance. A chorus of girls in white robes, virgins of the best families in the kingdom, came behind them singing of the land's longing for the Lady's return with cool winds and fruitful rain after the dry death of summer. Their hands had woven the rich gown his priestess-wife wore, the sacred dedication of their last year of maidenhood.

He'd hidden behind the Year-Maidens, when he was a boy, then rushed forward to touch the King and gotten rapped with a spear shaft for his pains . . .

Not so long ago. I'm not forty winters yet. A young forty winters, only a few strands of gray in his bowl-cut hair, and all his teeth still sound. For the rest the King was a man of the type common here in southern Iberia, olive-skinned, black of hair and eye, of medium height, slender and lithe and quick-moving. His shoulders were broad for his height, his arms strongly muscled, his hands bearing a sailor's callus from rope and steering oar, spear and sword.

The road under his feet was part of the New City, broad and straight and covered in asphalt, with sidewalks of brick on either side, flanked by buildings of two and even three stories. Many of them were built of pale-rose sandstone barged down the Rainbow River, and those of adobe brick were whitewashed to brilliance; both had sloped roofs of fine red tile, some with doorways of fanciful wrought-iron or cast-bronze fretwork opening onto interior courts where fountains played. Isketerol's heart swelled with pride at the sight, at the wealth and might and knowledge he had brought to his native city. More Tartessians crowded the windows and balconies, dressed in their best, wreaths in their hair, throwing flowers and handfuls of grain before his feet.

"*The King lives! The King lives!*" they shouted. "*Seed the field! Seed the field! The King lives!*"

Isketerol came at last to a special ramp built downward into the water of the river; Tartessos stood on a triangle of land where two streams met after their long journey southward from the mountains. Here he looked out over a broad bay, intensely blue beneath the late-summer sun, over to green marshes where birds rose ten thousandfold to add the thunder of their wings to the thunder of voices from behind him. The wharves and city walls and shore were black with his folk; a silence fell on them as the King removed his ornaments and flung them one by one out into the waters.

"Oh Lady of Tartessos, giver of life, You who are the rain and the river and the soft autumn fields that welcome the plow, receive my gifts! By my gifts, know that the King and Your people remain loyal unto You!"

Beside him the Lady's Lady did the same, murmuring her own invocation—that was not a thing for men's ears—until they stood naked side by side. Then they waded out, amid the flowers floating on the waters, and swam to a raft anchored some fifty feet beyond. Isketerol turned to the south, toward the place where the fresh water met the salt on the edge of sight. Boats bobbed and dashed about, the sunset ruddy on their sails, turning the foam at their bows to blood-color as well; a few lights already starred masthead and bowsprit in the falling dusk.

"Oh Arucuttag of the Sea," he prayed, raising his arms high and hands palm outward in the gesture of reverence. "Hungry One, Lord of Waves, Storm Lord, remember my gifts unto You." Those had been made yesterday, beyond sight of land—gold, and the blood of a strong young warrior. "Remember, and grudge not that Your sister comes to wed with me, for the renewal of the land. Whelm not our ships with Your anger, but give us swift voyaging and good winds, full nets and victory. Wait in patience until the grain grows gold, when She shall return unto You and Her sister of the ripened corn rule the summer."

He turned, and his wife did as well to face him. This once in all the year he went to his knees before her, because this was not only the mother of his sons but the Lady Herself come in the flesh for this hour. Again he raised his hands in the attitude of prayer.

"Oh Lady of Tartessos," he called. It was as if Someone else spoke through his lips; now he *was* the Sun Lord. "You have been in Your brother's hall all the long summer while the land grew dry. My longing has called the grain from the moist soil and given it My gold, and I have lain with Your sister to bring forth the harvest for the reapers. Yet You came not, and now the dry land perishes for Your rain, that the grain may be sown once more. Without You, My light cannot make the Grain Goddess's earth fruitful. Do You hide Your face in anger from Your people? Do You come from Your brother's sea in anger, with the waves of the salt flood?"

"No!" she called. "The Lady comes again in love, bringing the rain that gives Her people life, swelling the rivers as a mother's breasts swell with milk. Come to me, Sun Lord, as the Sun sinks beneath the River, and together we will bring rain and cloud, sowing and reaping!"

She sank gracefully to the heaped wool blankets, opening arms and legs to him. The deathly silence broke into cheers as he went in unto her, and cannon roared all along the city walls and from the ships anchored in the harbor, rockets flaring up to burst in multicolored splendor overhead.

The fall weather of the Year 10 had cleared, down near the reaches where the Severn gave into the Bristol Channel. The day was bright, brisk, a chill wind whipping the blood into your face; the coal smoke from the steamboat's stack tattered away south and west, losing itself over smargadine waters and white-crested waves. Marian stood on the deckhouse that spanned the curved boxes that held the vessel's paddle wheels, behind opened windows, Swindapa beside her. Froth churned white behind them, surging against the first of the train of four barges on their tows behind. The craft's blunt bows sledged their way into the waves, and spray on her lips tasted of salt now. There was a new roll and swing to the craft's movement, infinitely familiar, paradoxically reassuring with its hint of accustomed danger. Now and then water would show green over shallows, or throw spray skyward from a rock. The captain of the tug stood beside the wheel, a stocky middle-aged man in sweater and sea boots and the shapeless remains of what had been a peaked yachtsman's cap, scratching in his close-clipped gray-yellow beard now and then and occasionally raising his binoculars. From time to time he gave an order, in English or Fiernan or a mishmash of the two tongues. When he spoke to Marian Alston, it was in a cornhusker Indiana rasp.

"Tricky navigation in these parts, ma'am. We missed the tidal bore you can get around here this time, mostly, thank God, but there's rocks and shifting sandbanks most of the way from here to Westhaven." He looked over his shoulder, down at the water, then unplugged a speaking tube, whistled into it, then shouted in a good-humored bellow:

"More steam, goddammit! Or I'll come *wo'tuHuma ssoWya* and fry my bread in your drippings! *N'wagHA tobos!*"

Wonder how he ended up here? Marian thought. *Knows his work, obviously, though.*

"Left two, Cindy," he went on to the young woman at the wheel, then put his hand on it. "Good—smooth, not too fast, don't try to force it."

"Aye aye, Dad." A chuckle. "And Dad? It wasn't really nice to say you'd stuff them in the furnace."

"You don't have to hire 'em," he said, and rumpled her hair with rough affection. To Marian: "Hard to get stokers, Commodore. Even harder to keep 'em. Black Gang work ain't what you'd call popular."

"Understandable, Captain Bauerman," she replied, clasping her hands behind her back and rising slightly on the balls of her feet. Keeping balance against the movement of the deck was something a life at sea had made wholly automatic.

He grinned, respectful of her rank but not in the least intimidated by it. "Oh, hell, Captain's a little too fancy for a tugboat skipper," he said. "Good to get home, though."

Westhaven was a little west of the site of Bristol in the twentieth, not far from where the Lower Avon joined the Severn estuary. *Or where the Hillwater joins the River of Long Shadows,* she thought, with a quirk of her mouth. First landfall near Portsmouth, right after the Event, where she'd rescued Swindapa; then here the following spring to deal with Walker. Pentagon Base, they'd called it, after the shape of the fort they built.

She turned her head and saw Swindapa looking at her, smiling, knew that she was remembering the same days. *Lot of water under the bridge,* she thought, with a warm lightness that hadn't changed. It always made her want to break out in a silly grin, too. . . .

"Lot of changes," she said aloud instead, nodding toward the land.

The shoreline passed, in stretches of reddish sandstone cliff

or low salt marsh; inland were rolling fields and woodland turning to blue hills in the distance. The air was full of wings,
raucous gulls following lug-sailed fishing boats, waterfowl from
the seaside swamps, sea eagles; seals in the water and a spray
of fish jumping to flee the liquid grace of their rush, a whale
spouting not too far away.

I never knew how . . . empty of life . . . the twentieth was,
Alston thought, not for the first time. With luck and good man-
agement, they'd see that things stayed that way. *If we win the
war,* she thought grimly. *I doubt Walker would give a damn.*

As they watched, one of the deep-ocean ships cast off from
the steam tug that had brought it out of Westhaven harbor and
hoisted sail—it was a three-masted schooner, about two hundred tons, a whale among the minnow-tiny coracles and sewn-
plank fishing boats around it. *Maybe Alban-built,* she thought,
as it heeled and the sails bellied out into taut beige curves, a
white bow wave surging back from its sharp prow. They knew
wood, cloth, and rope well enough and could afford to buy
what they couldn't make. Certainly mostly Alban-crewed; Fiernans, or at least Fiernans who'd studied with the Grandmothers, picked up the math needed for practical navigation fast
enough.

There were changes ashore, too; progress had gone furthest
and fastest in this area, near the largest of the Islander bases
in Alba. A decade ago the land had been strewn with widely
scattered hamlets of round huts, small fields about them worked
with hand-hoe and scratch-plow; beyond broad rings of scrubby
second growth and rough pasture. Now most of the brush had
been cleared, stubblefields and pasture edged with fences or
new-planted hawthorn hedges; even the primal wildwood had
retreated a bit, though nobody had found it worthwhile to drain
much of the vast swamps.

Alston leveled her own binoculars. A puffing steam road-
hauler pulled a threshing machine; harvest was well past, the
wheat and barley in thatched stacks, and the thresher was on
its rounds, doing in a few hours what would take scores of
workers all winter with flails. More wagons piled with sacks of
grain waited beside a dammed stream and its mill, the big
wooden wheel turning briskly under the white water pouring
from the sluice. *That* represented about a thousand women who
didn't have to spend three hours every morning kneeling to
grind their families' daily grain on a metate-like arrangement
of two stones.

Among the Sun People further east grain-grinding had been

the primary work of slave women, that and carrying buckets of water on a yoke across the shoulders, and gathering firewood. The Earth Folk had been more humane about distributing the toil, but it still meant endless hours of backbreaking monotony for somebody.

"Many changes," Swindapa said, leaning her elbows on the edge of the window before them. The breeze of their passage cuffed locks of wheat-colored hair backward around her tanned face, and she squinted into the wind. Fine lines appeared beside her eyes as she did, the beginning of the sailors' wrinkles that were more deeply grooved in Marian's skin.

Lord, 'dapa's going on thirty now, Marian thought with a sudden shock. One reason she'd resisted the younger woman's determined attempts at seduction back on the Island those first few months had been the difference in their ages.

Well, nobody can accuse me of cradle-robbing anymore.

"Are you happy about what's changed?" the black woman asked.

Swindapa turned her head and smiled. "Oh, mostly, *bin'-HOtse-khwon,*" she said, and nodded toward the shore. "Some of the Earth Folk grumble, not most. Who'd watch their children die, when they didn't have to? Half did, in the old days. And we have peace, at least in our own land."

"Mmmmm-hmmm, I've heard complaints about everything being done the Eagle People way."

"Bread together," Swindapa said, and at her raised brows went on: "Haven't I told you that saying? Well, you take flour and water and yeast—none of them rules the others, and together they make the bread. Together we're making something new, and the Fiernan Bohulugi are the yeast, I think."

If we win this war, Marian thought; and knew from the shadow in the other's eyes that she had seen that thought, too.

"Odikweos, my friend, it is good to see you," Isketerol said.

His part in the autumn rites was done for now, with the Sacred Wedding. He had bathed, dressed himself in a saffron-yellow tunic trimmed with purple dye of Ugarit, thought carefully and consulted a few advisers. He clasped hands with the other man in the *Amurrukan* fashion that Walker had made common in Great Achaea, then received a kiss on the cheek as from a near equal; the other man was a ruler himself, after all, if also a vassal of the King of Men in Mycenae. This was not the first time he'd come to Tartessos as envoy and negotiator.

"You are well, and your women and children, your flocks and fields, all those beneath your rooftree?"

They exchanged the necessary courtesies, while outside bonfires and torches and kerosene streetlamps made the streets nearly as bright as day for the festival that would continue for three days and nights. Here in the upper chamber the lamps were also bright, bringing out the murals of dolphins and squid and bright birds that rioted in crimson and umber and blue against the green background. That was a subtle compliment to the Achaean underking, for artists from Mycenae had made them, sent with many other craftsmen as part of the alliance between Walker and his blood brother. The ebony table with its inlay of ivory and faience had been made in Pi-Ramses beside the Nile; it showed that Tartessians had long fared widely. Besides native dishes of tunny baked with goat-cheese and squid fried in garlic-laden olive oil, the golden dishes bore chickens on spits, roast potatoes, salads that included such exotics as tomatoes and avocados; there was chocolate cake for dessert. The foreign delicacies from west over the River Ocean were a reminder that like Great Achaea, Tartessos also commanded the New Learning. The air smelled of the good food, of fresh bread, wine, perfumed resin that sent tendrils up from worked-bronze stands, and of the jasmine that grew in stone troughs by the windows. Cool evening air bore a reminder that summer was past and awoke appetite.

The Greek poured wine—they dined without servants within earshot, for their talk was of statecraft—and added water to his cup. Isketerol winced slightly; that was no way to treat a fine mountain vintage.

Oh, well, to each land its customs.

"That was a fine sacrifice you made," Odikweos said, smiling and showing strong white teeth.

He was no taller than the Iberian King and of much the same years, his hair black with reddish glints and his eyes hazel, but more broad-built, his arms and legs thick with knotted muscle, battle scars running white under heavy body hair.

"The King is the land," he went on. "We have a similar rite to *Gamater* on Ithaka."

Isketerol nodded noncommittally; he knew Achaeans tended to assume that any foreign deity they met must be much the same as the one of theirs He or She resembled. Himself, he felt that was . . . what was the Achaean word? Hubris?

"The Gods send luck," he said. "It's up to us to seize it." They both poured a small libation into bowls left on the floor for that purpose and the King continued: "In the time of my grandfather's grandfather, legend has it that if the King could not raise a stand to plow the Lady's Lady, she sacrificed him there and then to bring the rain—spilling his blood rather than his man-seed in offering," he said. "That was a favorite jest of the Jester."

Isketerol nodded to a grinning clay statue of the Jester at the foot of the table and tossed a pinch of sweet-smelling resin onto the coals that smoldered in a bowl before it, giving the Lady's favorite son His due. The smoke rose in a blue coil, hiding the disquieting smile. As the saying went, the Jester slew men as boys threw stones at frogs, for sport . . . but frogs and men both died in earnest.

Odikweos shuddered. "The thought alone would be enough to make a prick of bronze go limp!"

Isketerol chuckled. "And in ages before that, the King was *always* sacrificed for the autumn rains; some of the inland villages still give the fields a man every year."

"I've seen much like *that* in Sicily, after we brought it under Great Achaea and I was made viceroy," Odikweos said.

Isketerol nodded; he'd watched that conquest carefully seven years ago, since Sicily was half the distance across the Middle Sea from the Achaean lands to Tartessos. He'd been greatly shocked at how little time it took the Achaeans under Walker to overrun the huge island, and a little shocked at the methods William used to pacify it; the Eagle People, the *Amurrukan* of Nantucket, had struck him as a soft lot, in the months he'd lived among them. But William was a hard man, and no mistake . . .

He plunged his fork into the tunny, savoring a mouthful. "Years ago, when William and I made war in the White Isle, I remember pledging gold to the gods for a taste of tunny with cheese, or olives, or a salad . . . or *anything* besides boiled meat and black bread," he said.

His face grew grave. "Now we make war again, and against the same foe—Nantucket."

"May the gods grant a better outcome this time, for Tartessos and Great Achaea," the Greek said, and poured another libation. "Nantucket stands between both of our realms and the desires of our hearts."

Isketerol joined him in the gesture of sacrifice—it could not hurt—and waited in silence. Back then he'd been a mere merchant and of a house richer in honor than goods or power, adventuring in the northlands in hope of profit. It was there he'd met William . . .

"My High King has heard of the repulse of your attack on

Nantucket," Odikweos said gravely. "He grieves with his blood brother."

Isketerol nodded. *And I can believe as much of that as I wish,* he thought. He and the High Wannax had been allies, blood brothers, and friends of a sort for a good ten years now, since they met on Alba. That didn't mean either trusted the other overmuch. After all, Walker had begun his climb to power by betraying his superiors and his oaths to them. . . .

"How will the High Wannax show his grief?" Isketerol asked pointedly. "I could use more boring machines, and help with the converter to make steel. If the Islanders attack, I will need better artillery."

He glowered a little at that; it had been his spies in Nantucket who told him of the *manganese* that was necessary if the steel was to be good and not a spongy mass of air-holes, not his blood brother in Mycenae.

Back on Nantucket William had bought his help with promise of the great ship *Yare* and half its cargo of treasures—books and tools and machinery that the Islanders had put aboard to establish a base of their own in Alba. He'd helped William to pirate it; stood at his side while he conquered a kingdom in Alba with it; stayed at his side when the Nantucketers broke him, and carried his fugitive band to Greece. At first it seemed that Isketerol had had the better of the deal. Walker had helped put him on the throne of Tartessos with his gunpowder bombs and those first few cannon they'd cast in Alba, and the deadly *Garand rifle*. He'd made no dispute over division of the cargo. There Isketerol was, King of his native city; and William only a foreign mercenary at Agamemnon's court, leader of nothing but his little band of Islander renegades and Alban warriors. It was only in the years that followed that he realized how much knowledge was not in the books he'd learned to read, but in the heads of that score of men . . . not only skills, but a universe of wisdom that enabled them to *understand* things in the books which Isketerol must puzzle out by himself.

He clenched a fist. *It was the Jester's gift that I met Rosita on Nantucket.* He'd brought her along only because he'd sworn to, and then she'd turned out to be invaluable. Her, and a scant handful of other *Amurrukan* he'd lured here over the years with bribes of silver and land and high rank. Bitter it was, to realize that a common laborer of the Eagle People commanded knowledge so priceless that he must make them nobles here . . .

Odikweos inclined his head, and Isketerol made a similar gesture in acknowledgment. William had selected his envoy well; this one's face showed nothing but what he intended. He changed the subject smoothly, giving news of the Nantucketers who were active in Babylon and among the Hittites, and Great Achaea's war with Troy.

"I think that the High King's gifts will make his brother glad," he said at last, when the servitors had cleared the table and withdrawn.

"Then let us go and see them," Isketerol said.

"Now?"

"What better time?"

There are few enough seasons when the King could walk through the streets of Tartessos City without ceremony and too many prying eyes—and although the Republic's embassy had left when war was declared, there would be eyes of theirs remaining. Probably with *radios* to report; the tiny but immensely powerful type they called *solid-state*.

Cloaks with hoods provided concealment, and more went masked than not on this day of festival; they took only a brace of guards each. Carnival rioted through the streets about them, masks and costumes from old story or modern fancy. Here two danced in the skin of a giant bear, or a gold-tusked boar-mask topped a naked body that capered and squealed, or deer-antlered men sported with women decked out in sheaves of wheat and little else; there a mock-Pharaoh paced, his kilt of Egyptian linen showing the waggling of a giant leather phallus, beside a would-be northern barbarian in shaggy furs, tow-flax wig and bronze ax; poetry and bawdy song echoed from walls; tables were set out with jugs of wine and rich food from the King's storehouses and those of wealthy nobles and merchants who wished to win the Lady's favor; everywhere men and women coupled, serving the Lady through Her act of generation. On these three days all the usual barriers were lowered.

"Plenty of children, next spring," Odikweos chuckled. "I don't doubt my men on shore leave are having a good time."

Isketerol nodded. "We seed our women, as the Sun Lord seeds the moist earth of the Lady. Such births are called god-children, and a foreigner brings double luck."

The guards at the entrance to the military docks were on duty and alert, though; they brought their rifles up, then stiffened as they recognized Isketerol when he flipped back the cowl of his cloak.

"Silence," he said as they bowed. "You have not seen me."

"Seen who, lord?" the young officer said brashly, grinning—this *was* the Lady's Festival, after all.

Isketerol smiled and nodded, noting the youth's face; you could always use a man who thought quickly on his feet. The little party passed through the thick seawall made of warehouses joined end to end, out onto the broad paved quayside and the long wharves with their cast-iron bollards. A leafless forest of mast and spar and rigging lifted against the bright stars and crescent moon, and that light and the lanterns atop the wall reflected from the rippling waters. A creak and groan of timber sounded through the night, wind in the tracework of rigging, call of a watchman, the sound of waves slapping like wet hands at the planking of hulls. There was a thick smell of the sea, of brackish water and tar, bilges and cargoes. Most of the ships here were large three-masters from the royal yards, well gunned, the ships that had scoured the western end of the Middle Sea clean of pirates and rivals and gone venturing to the ends of the earth.

Where the cursed Amurrukan don't forbid, he thought with a scowl.

Who were the Nantucketers to declare whole continents taboo to all but themselves? Before the war began their traders and sailors walked through the streets of Tartessos in lordly wise, looked down on his people's ways and customs, refused to trade machinery and skills he needed to build the Kingdom. As if they strove to make that lying history they'd shown him true, a future in which Tartessos was forgotten, less than legend, a few broken pots and shards. It was intolerable! He'd struck them a hard blow this spring, come close to taking the Island itself, but they'd beaten his force off with heavy losses. Now his spies said they were planning a counterstrike of their own.

Let them come, and we'll give them a warm welcome—warm as the Crone's boiling cauldron, he thought grimly. They were strong in knowledge, but few in numbers. What was that saying Will liked? *Ah, yes: "quantity has a quality all its own."* Tartessos held most of Iberia now, and the lands south across the Pillars.

Achaean guards waited at the gangplanks of the three big eastern vessels that had brought Odikweos; they cried him hail, raising their rifles. Isketerol looked keenly at those; they were the new type he'd heard of, that took cartridges of brass instead of paper and needed no flintlock or priming pan. The Greek underking saw the direction of his eyes and smiled as they took the ladder into the ship's hold.

It was a big vessel with three masts; they passed down through the gun deck into the hold. That stretched dim and shadowy as the guard lifted his lantern behind them, showing boxes and bales piled high; the air was still, with odd metallic scents under the stale odor of the bilge.

"Here," the Achaean said, and pulled back a tarpaulin.

Despite himself, Isketerol gave an exclamation of delight. The cannon squatting in a timber cradle was of the type called *Dahlgren*. They could take a heavier charge of powder, and hurl a larger ball further and harder than simple tapered metal tubes such as his makers had learned to fashion . . . as his fleet had found to its cost, in the abortive invasion of the Republic. And these were poured steel, lighter and stronger than the cast iron his makers had been forced to use until recently.

"Eighty eight-inch steel Dahlgrens," Odikweos said. "Twenty nine-inch, ten eleven-inch. Ammunition. And sample patterns and molds for all, and for the boring and turning engines, and a dozen technicians trained in the art."

He handed a printed book to the Iberian monarch. It was in Achaean—mostly in Achaean, with many words from the *Amurrukan* tongue of Nantucket, English. Isketerol spoke Greek well, and had learned how it was written in the new Islander alphabet. He flipped quickly through the volume. It held exact instructions for steel converter work, and for pouring and working heavy castings. Mingled gratitude and bitterness spread through him. If he had had this years ago . . .

Odikweos might have read his thought. "Lord Cuddy, the High King's Master of Engineers, says that much of this is the result of his own seeking," he said. "To make the . . . what's the word . . . *Bessemer converter* work properly required much *experiment*." That last word was perforce English as well. "And our third ship carries a hundred tons of the *manganese* you will need, from the mines in Messine. Also a hundred tons of sulfur from Sicily for your gunpowder mills. More of that will follow, as much as you can use."

"That is good," Isketerol said. *The sulfur will be very useful. It is not necessary that William know that my spies in Nantucket found out about the* manganese, *and the mines of it in my own Black Mountains.* "Of course, in return for such kingly gifts, I will give royal gifts in return, for my honor's sake." *What hypocrites we Kings must be.* "What is it that my brother needs?"

"Quicksilver, as much as you can spare," Odikweos said. "If you have the mines working again."

"Better than ever," Isketerol lied smoothly. *After all, William does not need to know where it comes from, so long as I can deliver it.*

"And more raw cotton."

"The harvest has been excellent—"

CHAPTER FIVE

March, 11 A.E.—Feather River Valley, California
March, 11 A.E.—High Sierras, California

The healer bowed deeply before Alantethol of Tartessos, commander of the Hidden Fort of the West—in what the Eagle People called California. He inclined his head slightly in turn; she was a woman, true, but all healers were, and they were close to the Lady of Tartessos—uncomfortably close to the Crone, as well, the bright and shadow sides of the Divine.

"Will more of the ship's crew die?" he said, shuddering slightly within.

They had found it in the river downstream halfway to the sea, aground on a mudbank; only by the favor of Arucuttag had the crew brought it that far, with so many dead or dying. Only by a for-once-merciful jest of the Jester had the ones who lived included the captain, with his knowledge of modern navigation and this secret place.

"I am not sure, my great lord," she said, frowning. "Twenty-one at least will surely live. Of the other eight, they are still very weak—and badly scarred. Perhaps none will die, perhaps half. The healer"—her tone was contemptuous; the ship's med-ico was not one of the queen's true pupils, merely one who'd had a few brief lessons—"did not recognize the sickness quickly, and she was not skilled in the understanding of *inoculation*."

Alantethol inclined his head again, in thanks for the truthful-ness not hidden behind honied lies. Best be respectful, if she was in turn. And this healer had been a pupil of the King's wife, Rosita, who had learned her art on Nantucket itself.

The commander ground his teeth at the thought. The Island-ers had humiliated him—taken his ships in that skirmish on the African coast, somehow turned his trap on him. . . .

That had been before the war broke out openly, in the spring of the year past; the King had to pay ransom and then publicly upbraid him, dismiss him, lest the conflict come too soon. In private he'd been more merciful, especially when he learned that Alantethol had kept the secret of this outpost. The cover story had held—if the captains told them it was Australia, how could the men know otherwise? Only a few of the captives knew English, anyway, and speakers of Tartessian were even rarer on Nantucket, too rare even for detailed interrogation of the officers.

Hence his appointment here. What better command to give to one who must disappear from public view than one so secret not a dozen people in the kingdom knew of it, save those sent here for life? It put him out of the way, yes—this latest ship had left the homeland only a month after the fall planting—but it was a post of honor.

Nantucket was all things hateful and vile, a land on whom he wished every revenge. Yet also the source of all power, of knowledge beyond price. The King himself owed his rise to his stay there and his alliance with the Nantucketer renegade Walker. Alantethol himself had learned En-gil-its, and read among the books copied from the King's treasure-store, the *Art of War* and *Celestial Navigation*, things of deep wisdom. Wisdom that had made the son of a fishing-boat captain a great lord, one of the New Men of the King.

The Tartessian noble stroked his gold-bound tuft of chin-beard. "So, you have this sickness of the small pockmarks under control?"

"Yes, lord," she said, bowing again. "It was very lucky that the queen's book contained that knowledge and that the cows here have the little sickness which guards against the greater, or many more of us would have died. I beg the noble commander that word be sent to the homeland as quickly as may be—"

She paused to look around. Here was nobody to overhear, not even a barbarian slave ignorant of their tongue. The commander's office was on the third story of his residence, that he might have solitude to ponder. As befitted his rank it was lined with plastered walls, with bearskins on the floor and Shang silk on the walls, and much raw gold beaten into sheets. The workers came to clean and polish only under guard.

". . . that this be done in the City and its tributaries as well, lest this new pestilence spread to our land."

Alantethol considered whether he should reveal more, then nodded abruptly. "That has already been accomplished, by

King Isketerol's wisdom," he said, bowing with hands to forehead at his overlord's name.

The healer hastily followed suit; this was a new custom since Isketerol took the throne.

"The sickness of the small pockmarks has been reported in Babylon; this ship of ours called at Meluhha on its way here, as part of keeping this base secret."

Meluhha, where traders came from all the eastern lands and men mingled. *As a sheep defecates, promiscuously, everywhere*, he thought. Undoubtedly that was where they had contracted the disease.

"Best to take no chances with the Jester's jests," he went on, in tribute to the King's wisdom.

They both made genuflection to a small eidolon of the Lady's favorite son where it sat grinning in a niche. It was solid-cast in gold, and nearly knee high to a man. That was an extravagance possible only here, where gold was like the dirt of the streams. Alantethol took a pinch of pine resin and threw it into a small brazier at the feet of the statue so that aromatic blue smoke coiled upward to please the God.

"But among the naked savages beyond our rule, the tiny daemons of this illness will spread like fire in dry summer grass," the healer said. "It will reap them as the very knife of the Crone; their flesh will seethe in Her Cauldron like a rich stew."

"This is not altogether bad," Alantethol said, pondering. "Earth must be fed," he added piously.

The savages who infested these lands—otherwise so much like home that even glancing out the window gave him a pang of longing—were not numerous by the standards of the lands of the Middle Sea, or even those of the yellow-haired barbarians of the far northern lands. They could not be, living as they did by the chase and gathering wild plants. But these were lands of amazing wealth in more than gold; well watered by many rivers, swarming with game and fish and flocks of birds, able to support a denser peopling than he would have believed possible without farming. And the Tartessians here were very few, even counting subject-allies brought from the homeland to bolster them.

And I do so count them, he thought. This far from home, differences that had loomed large in his youth became as nothing, and all Iberians were kindred. Still . . .

"We do need some of the free savages," he said. "There are

not enough of us to do all the needful work, even with the slaves we've taken. Hmmm."

He sent a small prayer to the Lady of Tartessos, and another to Her brother Arucuttag of the Sea, who watched over Tartessians abroad beyond the salt waters. *Hungry One, I will give you a strong warrior from among our captives, if you will show me a way . . . yes!*

"Let word be sent to the tribes around us," he said. "Tell them that we will give this treatment of the cow . . . but only if they cease stinting the tribute they pay for our protection." *Protection from us*, he thought; but that was the usual way. "This can be turned to much good use in subduing the savages, this pestilence of the small pockmarks."

He grinned. "You say that this illness can be transmitted by the clothing of the sick, as well as their blood and breath and sweat?"

The healer nodded. "Unless such clothing is thoroughly cleaned, with boiling water and strong soap, and exposure to clean air and sunlight. The disease may lurk therein for years, otherwise."

Alantethol laughed aloud. "Then let the blankets of those who had the sickness be preserved, in a dark warm place," he said. "If any chief is stubborn, we will send him a gift—a gift of good wool blankets."

The healer's laughter echoed his own. "A jest fit for the Jester, lord," she said. "So Arucuttag inspires the captains He favors in cunning trickery; in killing by stealth and by bold manslaying."

She withdrew with another bow, and Alantethol sprang up from behind his *desk*—the Eagle People word came so naturally now that he did not feel any jar in the rhythm of his thoughts—and paced. The King would be highly pleased if he increased the profits of the settlement without demanding expensive trade goods brought the long weary dangerous distance from the homeland—voyages took a hundred days and a score even when the winds were favorable, sometimes half as much again. The King would be *highly* pleased. . . .

No, this is not important enough for the magic talker, not in time of war. I will send the report with the next shipment, in code. Scarcely needed, given the odds of encountering an Islander vessel, but the Tartessians needed no teaching from the Eagle People in the difference between bravery and carelessness.

He stopped at a redwood sideboard and poured himself a

measured dollop of brandy, looking out the open shutters—even the commander's house did not rate window glass yet; the very goblet in his hand was a sign of privilege and luxury. Yet also a sign of how far the kingdom had come; ten years before it would have been an unimaginable extravagance even at Pharaoh's court. The only glass in Tartessos then had been beads.

Yes, the King is as fierce as a lion, but also as cunning and stealthy as a ferret, Alantethol thought with wholehearted admiration. You could tell that he had spent his young manhood as a merchant, not lolling in a palace.

Where better to hide a secret such as this than on the other side of the Eagle People's own continent? And within that wisdom, more wisdom to put it here so far from the sea. And to arrange that the supply ships remain offshore, sending in a boat to work upriver to set the rendezvous.

If a single Islander ship *did* put in at the great bay where the river flowed into the western ocean, or even one did in every year, they would see nothing except in the fantastically unlikely happenstance that they came at just the same time as the meeting between the Hidden Fort's barge and the Tartessian vessel . . . and how likely were they to come far inland, up that river and its northern tributary? Here he was midway between the gold of the mountains and the cinnabar ore of the coast ranges. Cinnabar, that precious stuff so necessary to make the newest of the new weapons, and to refining ore, and to trade with Great Achaea for powerful cannon.

He finished the brandy, relishing the bite of the spirits and the cold fire running down to his belly, but he was reluctant to return to the papers and ledgers just now. A thought tugged at him—ah. He must fulfill his oath to Arucuttag, and soon. No man was lucky who stole from the Gods, particularly that God. He would go down to the pens, and select the sacrifice.

Ranger Peter Giernas of the First Trans-Continental Expedition raised his bow, exhaling softly as he did. The arrow slid smoothly back through the centerline cutout of the weapon, wood and horn and sinew creaking slightly.

Cool morning air stroked his skin, throwing the shadows of the tall ponderosa pines behind him out onto the intense fresh spring green of the grass, starred with orange California poppies, cream-colored pasques, pink bunchberry, lavender waterleaf, golden asters, like a living Persian carpet swaying waist high. The sappy resin scent of the pines was strong, mixed with minty yerba buena, his own smells of woodsmoke and leather, and a hint of snow and rock from the peaks of the Sierra Nevada behind him.

The elk in the meadow before him raised their heads, ears flicking and jaws working as they glanced around, a few raising dripping muzzles from the little stream that ran through it. They were big reddish-brown beasts like scaled-up deer, with a pale yellowish patch on the rump and small white tails. The males had shed their antlers a while ago—it was late spring now—but they were bigger, with shaggy chestnut-brown hair on their necks like a short mane.

About thirty, he thought.

No old bulls, it was too early in the season for them to stake out breeding territories, this spring of the Year 11. A round dozen cows with their calves, some of them newborns, none more than a month or two, coming around to butt at their dams' udders or frolicking clumsily. And the ones he was interested in, adolescents of a year or two.

The whole herd was alert now, looking up into the wind from the west and away from him. Then a bristling gray-brown shape burst out of the cover at the far end of the oblong meadow, followed by two more. They seemed a whole pack as they leaped the stream and dashed about, growling, lunging, barking. The elk milled backward in dismay amid high-pitched squeals of alarm from the calves, sharp barking sounds from the cows. They faced the dogs for a moment, waiting for a rush that did not come, then turned about and surged through the flower-starred grass that came nearly to their chests, their heads thrown high and eyes wide with alarm. The pace was more a fast walk than a run, though, and the predators made no effort to close or even to cut out a calf, nipping at heels instead. One of the smaller, younger canines rolled over yelping when a cow's hind hoof caught it in the ribs with a painful, audible *thump*.

"Nice job, Perks," Giernas muttered, rising smoothly from his crouch as the herd slowed; they were more confused than frightened.

The bowstring came back to brush the angle of his jaw, and the triple-bladed steel head rested above his thumb. The elk had no time to react to his presence before he loosed, and the arrow was a long arcing streak that ended just behind the shoulder of a two-year-old cow. He could hear the meaty *thwack* of impact, and the animal staggered, ran half a dozen paces, then collapsed with frothy blood pouring out of its nose. The herd scattered in genuine panic now, the more so as the dogs abandoned their driving tactics and bored in, bellies to the ground, moving like blurred streaks with teeth. Giernas laid down his weapon and ran forward himself, drawing the long Seahaven bowie from its sheath along his right calf. He bounded past the elk he'd shot; that one was clearly dying fast. The dogs had another, a yearling cow; one gripped its nose, another a hind leg. The third, largest, had the neck, but it released its hold and backed away as Giernas came up. The man dodged a flailing forelimb, got his left arm around the animal's neck and neatly slit the hairy throat with a looping motion of his knife before leaping back.

The elk collapsed to its knees, then to its side, kicked, voided, and died. One of the dogs moved in and made as if to bite at the invitingly pale stomach; its bigger companion shouldered it away and gave a warning slash of fangs that didn't quite connect, to remind it that the humans had precedence.

"Good boy, Perks," Giernas said.

The dog was a wolf-mastiff hybrid six years old, huge-jawed and massive in a rangy long-limbed fashion; four parallel grooves down the right side of his muzzle and a tattered ear marked an indiscretion with a cougar.

And some of the other marks are from knives and spears, but nobody's done it twice, he thought.

The ranger had been training Perks since puppyhood, and the dog had walked all the way from the East Coast with the expedition. Right now he gave a canine grin, then settled in to lap at the blood pooling around the elk's throat.

Giernas turned and waved before stabbing his knife into the ground, then wiping it on a handful of grass and carefully again on the hem of his buckskin hunting shirt before resheathing it. You had to be careful about that; if blood got under the tang it could start rusting pretty fast and then snap on you at an awkward moment. As he turned he was blinded for a moment by the sun rising over the salt-white peaks of the mountains; he flung up his hand against the light, grinning and waving a hand in a beckoning gesture.

Giernas was a big young man in his twenties, deep-chested and long-limbed. The knife-cropped mop of ash-blond hair on his head was faded with sun-streaks, his close-cut beard a lighter yellow with hints of orange; his eyes were pale gray in a high-cheeked, short-nosed face tanned to the color of oakwood and roughened by exposure in all weathers.

Sue Chau led the three horses out from under the trees where she'd been on bear-watch. Like him she was dressed in worn, patched deerskin leggings, moccasins, and long hide shirt cinched with a broad belt that bore cartridge-box, flask of priming powder, knife, and a tomahawk thrust through a loop at the small of her back. Her hair was long and jet-black, eyes tilted and a cool blue; her father had been Eurasian, Saigon-Chinese crossed with Ozark-Scots-Irish, and her mother French-Canadian from a Massachusetts milltown.

In the crook of her left arm she carried a Westley-Richards flintlock rifle, and despite the friendly grin that answered his her eyes kept up their continual scan. There were a number of *un*friendly creatures in these woods on the western slope of the Sierras. Locals sometimes; most tribes and bands were eagerly hospitable to strangers, but fear or unwitting violation of some taboo or simple human cussedness could make trouble. Wolves and cougars weren't likely to be much of a problem unless it was midwinter and they were very hungry, but Old Ep—the big silvertip grizzlies that swarmed here in the Year 11—could be. The giant omnivores were appallingly numerous, they had little fear of man in an era of stone-tipped spears, and they'd far rather steal someone else's kill than take the effort to hunt for themselves.

"Good-looking beasts, Pete," Sue said, giving the dead animals an expert once-over. "They'll dress out at a hundred, hundred and fifty pounds each, easy."

"Ayup," he said. "Tender, too, and they had time to fatten on this new grass."

The two Nantucketers set to work with a silent, easy teamwork born of twenty months shared experience in everything from running battles to crossing rivers in flood. Each unlooped a rawhide lariat, snubbed it to a saddle horn, and used it to haul the elk to the edge of the woods. A convenient black oak stood there with a branch at just the right twelve-foot height; its spring leaves were tipped with fuschia and pale rose, long gold-green pollen-laden catkins hanging down from the branches. Giernas took his own rifle from the saddle scabbard, checked the priming, and leaned it within convenient reach. Then they ran a thong between the hind legbone and tendon of each elk, threw it over the branch, and used the horses to haul the beasts upward until their heads hung at knee height. That made the messy task of breaking the kills easier; they both moved their firearms as they worked, never leaving them more than a step and a snatch away.

"I hate it when I have to butcher on the flat," he said, drawing his skinning knife from the belt sheath rather than the bowie—for this work a five-inch slightly curved blade was best. He tested his by shaving a patch of hair from his forearm, then put his tomahawk within easy reach by flicking it into the oak tree at chest height.

The clear *thock* of steel in wood echoed across the meadow . . . *for the first time ever,* he thought with an edge of wonder that never quite faded.

"The meat never drains really good if it isn't hung up," Sue agreed. "Always spoils faster. Borrow your hone for a second?"

She spat on the stone and scoured a finer edge onto her knife; for butchering it was better to use a soft low-carbon steel and resharpen often. They stripped to their breechclouts before they made the first long cuts from anus to neck, and they would have shed those, too, if it hadn't been for the extreme difficulty of getting blood out of pubic hair in a soapless wash. The dogs waited, sitting panting with their tails thumping the forest floor, then falling on their portions—stomach, gut, head—with happy abandon. The major bones and the spines were chopped out with tomahawks and discarded save for a few kept to roast for the marrow; Giernas took a moment to crack the skulls so that the dogs could get at the brains, since they weren't going to take time to tan the skins with them.

A little less than an hour later the two elk were reduced to bundles of hide wrapped around the ribs, haunches, loin, heart, tongue, sweetbreads, kidney, and liver and lashed tight with lengths of tendon. The rangers carefully rolled up the broad white stripes of sinew that lay beneath the spine; it was useful for a dozen things, from bowmaking to sewing. After that they took a moment to strip off their breechclouts and wade into the stream, scrubbing each other down with handfuls of silver sand, squatting to work their hair clean and then standing hastily. This river was so clear that it was nearly invisible where the surface was calm, but it was *cold,* running down from snowmelt and glaciers.

"All clean," Giernas said, resting his chin on Sue's head and hugging her back to him with thick-muscled arms; she was five-seven, which made his six-one just the right height for that. His hands roved. "And since we've been good doobies and worked real hard . . ."

Sue laughed, stirred her rump tantalizingly against him, then broke away. "You're that anxious to get a grizzly's teeth in your ass at a strategic moment?" She laughed. "Movement attracts their eyes, you know."

"Ah, Sue, we don't have to actually *lie down,* it's such a beautiful morning, wonderful time for it . . ."

The young woman paused on the riverbank, hands on her hips and head cocked to one side. "Tell me something, Pete," she said. "I've heard you use that line while we were holed up in a cave with a blizzard outside and no firewood—"

"Hell," he said, his tone slightly hurt. "I said it would keep us *warm,* that time. It did, too."

". . . in tents while it was raining, on days hot enough to melt lead, and one time when we hadn't had anything to eat but grass soup for three days . . . so we'd forget about how hungry we were, you said. So tell me something . . . is there any time you *don't* think is just a peachy-keen wonderful time to fuck?"

"Hmmm." Giernas pulled his face into a pondering frown and stroked his chin in thought. "Now that you mention it . . . no."

Sue kicked a strategically aimed splash of ice-cold water before she turned and walked back toward their clothes. Giernas yelped, swore, and waded ashore laughing, scooping up his rifle and belt from the edge of the brook. They tied on fresh breechclouts; then they pulled on their hip-high leggings, tied them to the waistband portion of their breechclouts, shrugged into the buckskin hunting shirts, a little cold and clammy from resting on dew-wet bushes, belted on their gear, loaded their horses with the meat, and set off upstream. Giernas carried his rifle now; the bow was back on the saddle, with the quiver. He used it to hunt, saving the precious cartridges and powder, but they weren't hunting now. What he was worried about now was things trying to hunt *them;* the red-oozing bundles of elk meat were perfect bear bait.

"Perks, guard," Giernas said, as they set out, rifles in the crooks of their left arms and leading-reins in their right.

The wolf-dog was pleasantly full and plainly regarded it as time to do the sensible thing and curl up in the sun to doze, but he didn't need telling twice. A heavy sigh, and the gray shape slipped into the underbrush, moving ahead and to the flanks. The younger pair of dogs followed their sire obediently; Giernas was the alpha of their pack, but Perks ran a close second.

Seen that often enough, Giernas thought—a punishing nip on the nose, or a brief wrestle that ended with an uppity youngster on his or her back, throat caught in a warning grip. *With Perks around we've got* discipline, *by God.*

The camp was half an hour's brisk walk away, in a meadow

much like the one they'd found the elk in. They hadn't bothered to set up a tent last night, no need when they had good fires and sleeping bags lined with wolverine fur. He scrambled up a rise a half mile away and pulled out his binoculars. The others had the equipment packed and on the horses, all but one of the fires extinguished and buried, their rubbish likewise. Dogs milled around, woofing in excitement at the preparations for a journey into new country.

"Everyone looks ready, except for . . ."

"Eddie. Bet he's waiting up for us?" Sue said.

"Do bears shit in the woods?" Giernas said, looping the reins up over Kicker's saddle.

In his opinion horses were idiots every one, even by grazing-beast standards, but if you kept at them long enough they could learn. The horse rolled an eye at him, then kept moving stolidly up their own back-trail. The others, as was the nature of the tribe, followed the leader.

The humans split up, moving soundlessly into the shadows of the trees, flitting from one trunk to the next. Nothing . . . but after a moment Giernas caught a familiar sight; Perks frozen still as a statue, with his nose pointing to a big sugar pine. He moved behind the one at his back and poked the muzzle of his rifle around it.

"Peek, I see you," he called out. Playing ambush kept you on your toes. So far he was one five-gallon barrel of beer up on points, and when they got back to Nantucket he intended to collect. "Hi, Eddie. You're dead."

"It's a draw!" a man's voice said from behind the tree, aggrieved.

"No it isn't," Sue replied . . . from behind him.

Eddie Vergeraxsson stepped around the pine, shaking his head and glaring at Perks. "Not fair, when you two've got a werewolf working for you," he said.

Not entirely in jest—the slender hazel-eyed man with the queue of brown hair was a Zarthani chief's son from Alba, brought over to Nantucket as a hostage/pupil after the Alban War. He'd been a citizen of the Republic for years, but that didn't mean he thought entirely like an Islander born. He'd spent his teens in the Republic, and decided he liked being a ranger more than being heir to the *rahax* of a Sun People tribe in what a later age would have called Kent.

"Hi, Sue," he went on. "Hey, couple of elk, *eka*? I'll get it on the packhorses."

Not entirely a bad thing that he still thinks a little like a chario-

teer down deep, Giernas thought. Eddie had a bad case of what some of the older generation on Nantucket called the Spanish Toothache, particularly during his frequent quarrels with Jaditwara, but there wouldn't be any trouble over Sue. *As far as he's concerned, I'm his chieftain and she's my woman and that's it.*

Another woman ran over to him as they walked into the clearing and threw herself into his arms. He grinned, clasped her to him with his left arm, and swung her around until she squealed with glee and her blue-black braids flung out like banners. Spring Indigo was a full foot shorter than his six-one, her skin a bronze-brown-amber color, with a roundly pretty snub-nosed slant-eyed face. She was halfway to stocky . . . *but I have absolutely no complaints about that figure, nosireee.* Plenty to grab in all the right places, with the suppleness natural to a nomad in her seventeenth year. *Smart, too.* She'd learned English fast, and was picking up her letters quickly.

"Husband!" she said.

Her mouth lingered on his, tasting of acorn bread and berries. Her people didn't do lip-kissing, but she'd decided it was a good idea, during their long trek from the tall-grass prairies near where Independence, Missouri, would never be. She went on:

"You are the rising stars in the sky of my night! I am the moon to your sun! You are the greatest hunter in the world!"

"I must be; caught you, didn't I?" he said, laughing down at her face. Some of the things she said sounded a bit funny in English, but he'd learned to translate the sense of the words. "I love you too, honey. How's Jared?"

"Fed, changed, and sleeping," she said. "I think he may be starting to cut another tooth, poor thing." She turned to Sue: "Sister!"

That was a direct translation of what a second wife called the first, among the Cloud Shadow People fifteen hundred miles to the east, accompanied by an enthusiastic embrace and kiss— most grown men in Spring Indigo's tribe had more than one wife, because so many young men died early, hunting or in raids. Some things just worked out for the best, if you had luck. He seemed to have the *keuthes* where women were concerned, thank God.

Absolutely no way I was going to leave Indigo back there, with my kid. The expedition had rescued her people in the middle of a last, lost battle with enemies out to destroy them, and one of the Islanders had been injured badly enough that they decided to winter there. The Cloud Shadow tribe had a lot of amiable characteristics, one of which was that they really did believe in gratitude. The outsiders had spent the fall and winter and early spring with them, teaching much and learning a great deal, too; two of the Islanders had settled down with them for good—keeping a third of the horse-herd, among other things. Sometimes he wondered what would come of that, and of the other things Henry Morris and Dekkomonsu would show them.

They're good people, Indigo's folk, he thought; he'd considered staying himself. There were worse lives than being a hunter of the Cloud Shadow tribe. They were critically short of adult males, after their losing war, and they would have been overjoyed to make him their leader.

Yeah, I considered it for about fifteen minutes, until I finished listing all the reasons not to do it. First, no beer, ever again, he thought. *Or hot showers, and the thought of never reading another book . . .* Wilderness travel was great, if you could take some time out now and then. *But it's* damned *good luck Indigo and Sue hit it off so well.* A small party in the wilderness *had* to stick together. When they got back to the Island . . . well, they'd see. The arrangement was unconventional, true, but his people were pretty good at minding their own damn business, most of them.

Spring Indigo broke away and shoveled dirt over the last fire, then brought him and Sue their belated breakfast, cakes of fresh acorn bread and mountain trout grilled over the fire on a framework of green sticks, with a slab of bark for a plate. He squatted on his hams and ate, considering the day to come. Chuckling a little as his son Jared woke on his rabbitskin blanket—his diaper was more of the same, stuffed with soft moss—pulled himself erect, tottered two experimental steps, fell on his belly, and made a four-legged beeline for Perks.

"Perks!" It came out sounding more like *Pewks;* the boy was still having trouble with "r." "Perks!"

It was amazing what the great scarred mankiller thug of a dog would put up with, including yanks on his fur and tail and small chubby fingers poked in his ears. With no more than a look of pained resignation, or sometimes pinning the boy down with a paw and licking his face. He didn't even get up and walk away unless it got unbearable. Not at all the way he acted with adult humans who took liberties.

"Come on, *kwas'yain-daz,* strong little warrior," Spring Indigo said, scooping the toddler up. Young Jared screwed up his

year-old face and reached back toward the dog. "Ai-a, this
child thinks he is a puppy, that Perks is his uncle! When his
time comes to be a man, he will dream wolf-dreams and travel
the Other Country on four legs. His spirit animal will be the
Wolf."

"He could do worse," Giernas said.

"Dada! Dada! Fly!"

The infant scowl changed to a smile, accompanied by bab-
bling sounds that were almost words, in three languages, and
he reached for his father instead of the dog. Mixed in were
real words, also in three languages, of which his father spoke
only one; they'd made a campfire game of keeping track of
how many. The latest tally had thirty-two in English learned
from the rangers, four in Sue's occasional Cantonese, and
twenty-one in Cloud Shadow dialect. Giernas took the child,
snorting when small fingers grabbed at his nose and beard, and
whirled him around to cries of *fly! fly!* He fluttered his lips
against the bare pale-amber skin of the boy's stomach and then
handed him back, wiggling and squealing. Spring Indigo efficiently transferred him to a sling across her back, and he
yawned and went to sleep with a sudden limp finality, his cheek
pressed against the back of her neck, utterly relaxed in the
warm comfort of contact with his mother's back.

"He can ride in the horse-basket later."

Giernas nodded. *Hmm. We ought to make the next settlement
by sundown.* He splashed his face and hands with water from
the stream and dried them on grass, took up his rifle, and
walked to the head of the column. *With the elk meat for a gift.*

Most of the bands hereabout were hospitable and friendly,
but an excuse for a barbeque never hurt, in his experience.
They could lie up there for a couple of days, fix their gear and
trade for some more acorn-flour, and then another week ought
to bring them down into the lowlands and nearly to the coast.
If he'd calculated rightly, there ought to be an Islander ship
down on the coast of Peru trading for cotton and saltpeter
about now; if the radio hadn't gone on the fritz, they could
have called—but it would check in at San Francisco Bay anyway. Once a year in spring, starting last year and continuing
for four more, if there was no word. His eyes went to the
packhorses. One of them carried that equipment; there might
be usable parts, irreplaceable pre-Event stuff, so they had to
lug it along. Others bore carefully prepared hide sacks, ready
to be filled by panning the foothill streams near what the pre-
Event maps called Sutter's Mill. He didn't intend to be greedy;

just four . . . or five or six . . . or maybe a dozen . . . horseloads of two hundred pounds each. Enough to pay for the expedition, the way he'd promised the chief, and enough to give everyone who returned a good solid grubstake; that had been attractive before, and doubly so now that he wasn't a bachelor anymore.

The doing, though, the doing, that was the thing. . . .

The things we've seen and learned. My journal, Jaditwara's sketches, Sue's botanical stuff, the plants and animal specimens— He'd stood in one place on a knoll and rough-counted ten *million* buffalo going by, once. A single passenger-pigeon flock of a million and a half, crossing the Ohio . . .

The fourth member of the expedition was sitting cross-legged and leaning against a tree, sketching with charcoal on a flat piece of white pinewood. Their local guide, Tidtaway, stood a little way away from her, posing.

At least we actually know *he's called Tidtaway now.* Since he'd been visiting them for months in their winter camp and traveling with them for weeks. The name probably translated as something like "Quick Tongue."

Half the time they couldn't be sure if what a local said when he tapped his chest was really a name, or meant something like "That's me," or "I am your guide," or "Hi, and who are you?" or "Wow! Funny-looking foreigners sitting on weird deerlike creatures!"

Or a phrase might be the name of his tribe or clan or whatever they had . . . just as the "names" of local features might mean "that's a lake" or "why are you pointing at the mountain?" It was *frustrating,* not being able to stay in one spot long enough to get past gestures, grunts, and a few elementary words. But there were so *many* languages here, sometimes changing from one little band to the next, particularly up in the mountains; they'd barely got to an elementary-conversation level with Tidtaway. The ranger thought that the guide's tongue might be ancestral to the Penutian family of languages, but he couldn't be sure; the sources on the Island had been frustratingly general, and he himself was no scholar. He wished it had been practical to bring one of the pre-Event tape recorders along, so that students back on the Island could hear the actual sounds.

The Indian was a short dark man, muscular and strong, with an engaging smile showing a gap in his white teeth. Giernas suspected it was something of a salesman's smile; certainly Tidtaway had been trying to bargain with the strangers from the moment they arrived, and hadn't stopped since they decided to winter near his band last fall.

Jaditwara of the Teluko lineage of the *Fiernan Bohulugi* finished the drawing and shook back her long yellow mane, slipping on a beaded headband she'd gotten in trade for another drawing six months before, and picking up her rifle. Giernas chuckled silently to himself; among other things, the guide had tried to buy Jaditwara with three strings of oyster-shell beads, a volcanic-glass pendant, and a bundle of wolverine pelts. Now he exclaimed in wonder at the drawing, wrapped it carefully between two pieces of bark secured with thongs, and added it to his bedroll—a large woven mat that also served as a poncho or cloak at need, rolled into a tube with a bearskin lashed around it. The lashings also held one of the grooved throwing-sticks with a hook at the end the Aztecs had called—would have called—an atlatl, and four feathered darts with wickedly sharp obsidian points that must have come from far away in trade. For the rest he wore sandals, a breechclout with panels falling fore and aft, and a belt that carried a steel trade knife and a stone-headed hatchet; his hair fell to the shoulders, confined by a headband sewn with plaques of bone.

"Let's go," Giernas said.

Tidtaway picked up a quiver of arrows and a short recurve bow; that had been a major part of his pay, that and showing him how to make and repair and use it. He trotted up to take point with the Islander leader, making a respectful circuit around Perks, who didn't like him. Eddie fell back to walk rearguard; Jaditwara led the horses, all traveling single file. After the first mile or so Spring Indigo judged Jared asleep enough and transferred him to a fur-lined wicker basket on one of the pack saddles. It was shaped like a recliner version of a child's car safety seat, complete with leather crossbelts; versions of it had held the boy for better than two thousand miles of travel. She shrugged into a haversack arrangement that put another openmouthed basket on her back and ranged alongside the pathway with a digging-stick, stopping now and then to collect a handful of clover or bulbs, or early flowers gone to seed, and toss them over her shoulder. When she saw something unfamiliar she'd call Sue over, and the handy little *Field Guide to Western Plants* would come out. Once or twice what they saw wasn't listed at all, and a specimen would be carefully transferred to the drying press. The only problem were the colts, who had a tendency to wander and dash about. When

Jared woke up, he'd point and say *dis? dis?*, his current all-purpose word for "information, please."

The pace was easy enough, easier on the humans than pack animals still a little out of condition from winter idleness; all the rangers were in hard good shape, and he'd found that Spring Indigo could walk any of them tired. If it weren't for the needs of a nursing infant they could have made the West Coast before snowfall last.

But we did *have Jared along, and weren't in a hurry,* he thought.

They'd taken the crossing of the Plains in slow stages and made frequent long stops at campsites with good water and game, particularly when they got up into the high basin desert country of Nevada. It had been late September by the time they reached Tahoe, far too late to risk the Donner Pass route. Yet still plenty of time to build good tight log cabins, cut meadow hay for the horses, and lay up supplies. They'd discovered that there were few things that ate as well as a fat autumn grizzly weighing in around half a ton—if you were carefully unsporting about shooting from a place they couldn't get at—and the brain-tanned pelts made superb coats and blankets.

He smiled reminiscently; they'd also made skis, which had been fun and had impressed the hell out of the surrounding tribes, visited far and wide to trade or for feasts and ceremonies and study, hunted, chopped holes in the ice of streams and lakes to fish, spent hours cutting wood and hauling it on improvised sleds, sometimes had daylong games of snowball ambush. Periods when they were snowbound with weeklong blizzards outside were spent resting, catching up on their notes and journals and specimen collections, playing with Jared and whittling toys for him, mending gear, entertaining visiting tribesfolk, singing, storytelling, playing chess, making love . . . not a bad winter, all in all. They'd all been glad for spring and snowmelt, though.

Today the path lay westward and downward, through pine forest and meadow, with an increasing share of black oak as they dropped, and then an occasional blue oak as well. The mountains still stood snow-fanged at their backs, but now and then the way ahead gave a clear view, and he could see down and west toward the green-gold foothills and the long blue line of forest along the rivers of the Sacramento Valley. The stream whose course they were more or less following gurgled and leaped to his right, and sometimes the foot trail was close enough that drifts of spray came through the thick growth of ferns and drifted across their faces. Near a stand of sequoia they stopped for lunch—grilled elk liver and kidneys, wild onions, and more of the acorn-meal bannocks.

"God, but this is pretty country," Giernas said, looking up into the swaying tops two hundred and fifty feet above and breathing in the cool scented air of their shadow. The thick straight ruddy-brown trunks of the grove were thirty feet around and more; he knew, because Sue had gotten out her measuring rope and sampled half a dozen. Above a pair of condors wheeled, winged majesty, their unmoving pinions spreading the width of a Coast Guard ultralight as they rode the foothill thermals.

"Rich, too," Eddie mused, biting the last of a kidney off a stick and then prying at a fragment between two teeth with a fingernail. "And I don't mean the gold; gold is good, but you can't eat it or ride it. This would be a stockman's paradise, and it's getting better as we get lower. Even better than the plains east of the mountains, more sheltered, not so cold in winter— wonderful, wonderful, wonderful grass, *Hepkonwsa* hear my word. The horses are putting on flesh, even as hard as we're working them."

Giernas snorted. "You know, back when I was a kid, before the Event, I read about a party coming west—this was long before my time, a hundred and fifty years—who starved near where we wintered."

"In the Donner Pass?"

"Yeah, the place was named for them. The Donner Party." *Donner, party of sixty-seven, your table's ready,* he quoted to himself; it would take too much effort to explain it to the ex-Alban.

Eddie looked baffled. "Starved? Even in deep-snow winter . . . that would be like starving in a stock pen."

"Natural-born damned fools can do that anywhere—"

They shot to their feet at the dogs' baying and Tidtaway's shout, wheeling and crouching. The horses began to snort and back, working their feet against the picket ropes and hobbles. Giernas snatched up his rifle and thumbed back the hammer; the others did likewise, except for Spring Indigo, who grabbed a Seahaven crossbow they had along, with a bow made from a cut-down car spring. He'd adjusted the stock for her smaller arms. The pawl-and-ratchet cocking lever built into the fore-stock was easy to handle, and since bolts were reusable she'd practiced enough to be a clout shot. She pumped it six times and slotted a short, thick bolt into the groove, moving with businesslike dispatch.

"Old Ep, sure enough," Giernas said grimly. "Perks, Saule, Ausra—back and watch! Stand!"

The humpbacked bear walked into the open shade of the great trees with a shambling arrogance, his silver-tipped cinnamon hide moving on the great bones like a loosely fastened rug. The big-dished muzzle lifted, sampling the air with its strange, tantalizing smell of cooking meat and undertone of raw bloody flesh, and then he reared to his full twelve feet of height with a grumbling bellow.

Four .40 bullets and a crossbow bolt designed to punch through armor might be enough to take him down; or they could just make him very, very angry. Since there was very little apart from another grizzly that could meet a charge, Old Ep didn't have much of a run-away-when-hurt reflex. Giernas swallowed past a dry mouth, watching the bear, watching his reaction to the unfamiliar scents and sounds, to the three dogs making little snarling rushes and bouncing about just out of range of the piledriver paws. Sometimes grizzlies ran a wolf pack off its kill. . . .

Dane Sweet ought to see this, he thought. *Hell, we're the endangered species, hereabouts.*

"I don't think he's angry, just curious," he said finally. "We'll try and see him off. Jaditwara, you and I'll fire over his head. Everyone else, yell. Sue, Eddie, Indigo, keep him covered."

Crack. Crack.

The shots blasted out, jets of off-white sulfur-smelling smoke rising from the rifles. The butt thumped his shoulder with a familiar blow. Giernas's hand went to the knob on the top of the rifle's stock, pulled it up and the lever with it, and the brass plunger attached to the underside that filled the breech. That was blocked by the greased wad from the base of the nitrated-paper cartridge; he dropped a fresh round into the slot and pushed it forward with his thumb, driving the spent wad ahead of it. A quick slap of the hand brought the lever back down; he pulled the hammer back to half-cock, brought the priming flask up and thumbed the catch to drop a measured pinch of fine-grained powder into the pan, used the flask-head to knock the frizzen back to cover it, then dropped it to dangle on its shoulder cord while he brought the weapon to full cock.

That all took ten seconds, the fruit of endless practice. Meanwhile he could see and hear the others yell, jump, howl, shriek. The bear started violently at the hammer noise of the firearms, and more at the unfamiliar scent of burned powder, falling to all fours and roaring with wide-stretched mouth, showing long wet yellow teeth in a pink cavern of mouth.

Tidtaway surprised him, turning to snatch the ends of burning sticks from the campfire in both hands. Whipping them into flame he ran forward, waving them aloft and screeching. The bear began to back up, waving its dish-faced head from side to side on the long snaky neck.

"Sue, Eddie, more shots in the air," Giernas shouted, keeping the bear's right foreleg in his sights—he was pretty certain of breaking the bone, there.

Crack. Crack. A frenzy of reloading.

The grizzly flinched, and Tidtaway ran toward it, throwing a burning stick pinwheeling through the air. It landed in dry pine duff not far from the animal. Sparks flew out, caught, and turned into crackling fire and smoke. The bear visibly decided that food wasn't worth all this trouble no matter how good it smelled and turned, hurrying away with a shambling gait that covered ground faster than a man could run, then breaking into a slow gallop, complaining gutturally. Giernas worked his mouth, whistled on the second attempt. The dogs halted, despite the almost irresistable attraction of the retreating grizzly's rump; the last thing they needed now was the bear enraged by a mouthful of fangs in the ass.

"I must be getting old," Giernas muttered. "I'm learning to leave well enough alone."

And the adventures had been a lot more carefree before Jared was born. Not just the danger of the child being injured, first and foremost and bad though that was. He found himself worrying about getting injured or killed himself and not being there to protect his son. If it hadn't been for good friends who he knew would pitch in, it would have taken all the fun out of things.

Eddie came up, laughing as he eased the hammer of his rifle back to half-cock, the safety position. "Pete, that was one beautiful rug we lost there. Did you see the size of him! That hide would be *perfect* for in front of the fire in the place I'm going to build back home on Long Island."

That was Eddie's particular dream, land of his own and fat herds and tall horses and strong sons; in that, he was still Zarthani. When the gold was in the saddlebags he could do it, and quickly, although Giernas suspected he'd be bored. The other ranger went on:

"And after I'd told her how I killed the beast single-handed as it charged, roaring like thunder, what girl could resist getting laid on it?"

Sue came up beside him. "Plenty, when they saw the scars where your face used to be before the bear ate it," she said dryly. "You're going to raise horses, so use a horsehide rug."

He glared at her for an instant, genuine horror in his look. "Kill a *horse* to make a *rug*? Are you crazy or . . ." He caught the half wink she gave Giernas. "Oh, the Lady of the Horses give you both arse-boils and bleeding piles, you scoffers!"

She shook her head as he stamped off; however assimilated in other ways he remained an obstinate pagan, convinced that Christian scorn for his tribe's ancestral gods was both blasphemy and likely to bring bad luck to boot, at least for him personally. Sue enjoyed ribbing him about it occasionally, and it usually stayed good-humored enough.

"Let's get moving, people," Giernas called, in what he thought of privately as his head-of-the-expedition voice. He chopped his right hand westward and downslope. "Yo!"

Tidtaway resumed his position after they'd extinguished the fire with earth and water, and the party passed through a rocky field of boulders, over a ridgeback, down further on the westward path.

"Good, with the fire sticks," Giernas said, in what he hoped was the guide's language. He spoke Lekkansu fluently, the tongue of the tribes who lived along the New England coast near Nantucket. That had about as much relation to the languages hereabouts as English did to Babylonian. "Strong heart." He thumped the fist of his free right hand on his hunting shirt. "Guts" didn't usually translate well.

Tidtaway shrugged. "Bears . . . with long time," he said, in atrociously accented English, and held his own hand out at waist level.

I think he means he grew up around 'em, Giernas decided. *Since he was knee high to a hopper.*

The ranger nodded; the smaller black bears were worth treating with respect, but these Western silvertips were a lot bigger and meaner. Most of the time they'd leave you alone unless you provoked them. Then again, they might suddenly decide you were edible, or just slap out at you like a man at a fly.

He snorted softly. The Lost Geezers, the way they talked about animals . . . *Hell, I* like *animals. Wouldn't want to be in a place where they were scarce. But Jesus, they're not all little fluffy bunnies that'll die if you think mean thoughts!* Time to get to business, though.

He pointed westward. "Your friends?" he said.

Tidtaway looked around at the landscape, then up at the sun that was sinking before them. When he spoke, Giernas sighed and gestured to him to slow down. After half an hour, he judged he'd gotten a confirmation of previous conversations, if they weren't just misunderstanding each other in the same way every time. The band ahead weren't of Tidtaway's people, and didn't speak his language although it was related to his. But he'd visited years ago to trade obsidian and quartz for shells and salt, and he spoke their tongue a little, and they were hospitable to traders and travelers.

Hmmmm. Tidtaway's getting to the edge of his useful range. Should we give him his stuff and pick up another guide for the rest of the way to the coast, or just pay him off and wing it?

The trail was widening, and they were in the real foothills now, growing less rocky and steep as the land flattened. The Indian looked around, increasingly puzzled.

"Where people? See hunter here, see woman here—crazy, where people?" he bust out at last, then a long sentence in his own language, and back to English: "Bullshit, man. Fuckin' bullshit."

They crested a rise and looked down into a valley bright-green with spring grass, streaked with orange-yellow drifts of California poppies. It was broad, opening out to the west into the Sacramento plain, with a river fringed by big live oaks rushing over rocks to their right, falling to a pool and then meandering down the middle of it. Here and there it spread out in shallows that reflected blue from the cloudless sky overhead, great flights of wildfowl taking off and landing as he watched. The hills to either side were low and smooth, open savanna studded with round-topped trees, huge valley oak lower down and black oak on the summits. He unlimbered his precious pre-Event binoculars and scanned; at the far western edge of the valley he could see a herd of pronghorn antelope cantering, a hundred or so of them.

Wait a minute, he thought. *They shouldn't be that close to a lair of humans.* H. sapiens was the top predator in any area, even one infested with grizzlies. Game should be a little wary, at least.

The glasses swept back to the Indian settlement in mid-valley. There were ten dwellings built amid the valley oaks for shade and shelter, circular domed huts of overlapping reed bundles bound on bentwood frames, with low doors closed by hide curtains on the southern side and smokeholes at the tops. Fairly small dwellings, six to twelve feet in diameter, easy to throw up in a few hours—the inhabitants would probably move on a set round with the warmer seasons, and shift these semipermanent winter quarters whenever the surroundings got too noisesome. One hut was larger, and thickly plastered with clay over the reeds, probably a sweat house. The site was a good one, dry even during the winter rains but near good drinking water and fishing, with marshes for wildfowl, grassland for elk and mule deer and antelope, and it looked to be good gathering country, too. Certainly there were a clutch of acorn granaries, like huge man-tall baskets woven around stout poles at their corners.

Where the hell are the people, though? There ought to be fifty or sixty in this band, from the buildings. Women grinding acorns, cooking, weaving baskets, out in the land about gathering fresh spring greens; men toolmaking, hunting, working on hides; both sexes teaching older kids by demonstration; younger children running about at simple chores or play. *There isn't even any* smoke, *goddammit.* Locals never let all their fires go out—it was taboo, and just too much of a pain in the ass to relight, when all you had was a hand-drill. They couldn't all have gone up into the Sierras already, it wasn't quite the season, and even then some of the older folks would remain at the winter base to look after their stuff.

"Doesn't look right," he said, and handed the binoculars to the guide.

Tidtaway was worried, too; he simply took the binoculars and used them, without any of the usual fulsome wondering admiration. Among his people, if you praised something highly the owner had to give it to you. He still had trouble really believing that Nantucketers didn't operate that way.

"Nobody," he said after a moment.

"War?" Giernas asked. Not likely, but . . .

Tidtaway made a gesture of negation, tossing his head, then remembered to shake it in the manner of Western civilization.

"War, kill one man one time, steal one woman one time out alone. Not whole bunch. Nobody here." His face screwed up in bewilderment.

You look just how I feel, Giernas thought. A suspicion moved below the surface of his mind. *No. Not here.*

"Sue, you come with me," he said. "Eddie—" he unhooked the binocular case and handed it over. "You're in charge here; keep watch. One shot for come running with fangs out and hair on fire, two for danger and stay put, three for run like hell. Perks, heel! Saule, Ausra, stay."

The three of them set out at a steady loping wolf-trot, slowing a little as they came down into the valley flat. Giernas kept his eyes moving; there was nothing except the usual bugs and birds, small animals; once a startled cougar standing on a rock that took one look at them and fled. The wind was steady at his back as they approached the Indian settlement.

Perks had been loping not far ahead with his usual casual alertness, panting a bit as the day grew hotter. Now he reeled in his tongue, slowed, stopped, and stood stiff-legged, growling slightly, the thick ruff of fur around his shoulders and neck bristling. Giernas stopped himself, flinging up a hand, conscious of more sweat running down his face and flanks than a mere couple of miles' run on a spring day should have brought.

"I'm going in alone," he said slowly. Sue cut off her protest at the chopping gesture he made. "Tidtaway, wait here. Same signals."

The ranger walked forward, rifle in his hands—although he had a sickening suspicion that there was nothing ahead that a bullet could protect him from. Even against the wind, the oily-sweet stink of corruption warned him at ten or twenty yards out, and the buzzing of innumerable flies. He swallowed, clenched teeth, made himself move forward at a cautious walk. The first body lay in the shadow of one of the great oaks, feet pointing at one hut and head at another. Small scavengers had been at it, and the flesh seethed with maggots, but from the dress—skirt of raven feathers, wand with a ruff of eagle feathers, necklace of bear claws centered on the skull of a falcon—this had been a shaman. He looked back along the trail; you could still see that the man had dragged himself along until he collapsed.

Probably trying everything he could to save his people, Giernas thought with a deep sadness underlaid with anger. He slung the rifle over his back and moved through the settlement, careful to touch nothing. Many of the bodies were fresher than the dead shaman; he pushed his head into one hut, then another, forcing himself not to gag, looking closely.

"Jesus," he said softly, then spat to clear his mouth of the cold gummy saliva of nausea. He raised his rifle, fired, reloaded, fired again.

Then he found an empty basket, tore it into strips, built a little tipi of dry branches, then crouched over it with the fire-maker from his belt pouch, winding its spring and checking that the flint was fresh and unworn. When he thumbed the release catch the mechanism whirred and a torrent of sparks flashed into the pan with its dried tinder. He blew softly on it, then tipped it into the basket shreds and blew again, glad of a mindless familiar task that let him distance himself from what lay about. When the fire was well set he put the ends of thick branches in it, then used more to move—scrape would have been a better term—all the remains outdoors into the huts. Then he set those on fire and stripped himself naked; everything went into the blaze that was not wood or metal, even the precious ammunition pouch and the sheaths of his weapons, even the leather sling of the rifle.

He might easily have missed the last sign as he left, skin roughened with fear. But his eyes had been trained to watch for patterns all his life since the Event, and those skills unmercifully honed as the expedition traveled west across the continent. He stopped, went to one knee, peered incredulously. The mark was old, in the shadow of a clump of knee-high bunchgrass, and nearly obliterated by the wind; a single footstep would have wiped out all trace of it. But there was no doubt of what it was. No other animal left that mark, the arched shape of a horse's hoof. His fingers brushed over it lightly. A *shod* hoof at that, he could see the marks of the nails. The expedition's horses weren't shod—carrying that many blanks would have cut too far into their useful loads, so they'd just been careful. This—

Sue and Tidtaway watched him wide-eyed as he approached, naked save for the rifle and blades he carried in both hands.

"Stand back!" he called, from twenty feet away, then thought of the flies. Unlikely that they could come upwind, but . . . "*Get* back—get back a mile, then wait for me. Do it! Now!"

Neither hesitated. Giernas turned and ran for the river, found a spot where water curled clean over rocks and sand, checked carefully that no victim had crawled this way in the grip of fever, then washed himself and his tools again and again, gripped Perks by his ruff and forced the dog through the same despite whinings and squirmings and the occasional growl.

I hope this works, he thought desperately. *God, I wish I knew more about smallpox.*

All he knew for sure was that if it hit people who hadn't been vaccinated, most of them would die. That was what the books said, and he'd seen far more proof than he ever wanted.

CHAPTER SIX

*September, 10 A.E.—Babylon, Kingdom of
   Kar-Duniash
September, 10 A.E.—O'Rourke's Ford, east of Troy
October, 10 A.E.—Westhaven, Alba*

King Kashtiliash—Great King of Babylon, King of the Four
Quarters of the Earth, King of the Universe, viceregent of
the great god Marduk, overlord of Assyria by right of conquest
and of Elam by treaty of vassalage, and ally of the Republic
of Nantucket in this the Year 10—slept with a Python revolver
beneath his pillow.

His hand clenched on the smooth checkered wood and metal
of the butt as he woke. The gesture was instinctive, although
for most of his twenty-seven years it had been the hilt of a
dagger he grasped on waking. It was no less necessary this last
year since his father died and he took the throne; more so,
if anything.

The royal bedchamber was large and dim, and thick brick
walls and cunningly contrived vents in floor and ceiling kept it
cool even in the summers of the Land Between the Rivers.
That slight breeze sent a ripple through the rich hangings on
the walls amid a scent of musk and incense, as well as a welcome breath across sweat-slick skin. For a moment his sleep-
dazzled eyes thought that that was what had awoken him. An
animal alertness brought him fully alert. A shout would bring
guards with sword and rifle . . . but if an intruder had come
this far, it might well be that the guards had been corrupted.
He did not think so, but he did not intend to risk his life on
the question, either. And Ku-Aya was gone from her place
beside him . . . His thumb drew back the hammer of the
weapon, softly, slowly, still beneath the muffling pillow, all to
mute the distinctive *click*.

The bed was raised on a low platform, with tables of inlaid
sissu-wood on either side. One of those held a kerosene lantern,

its flame turned down to a slight red glow. He let that be, and took instead a steel fighting knife of the kind his *Nantukhtar* allies called a bowie in his left hand. The pistol in his right felt absurdly light after the bronze swords he had borne since toddlerhood, but intensive practice had made him adept with the Islander weapon. His bare feet touched silently on the tile and soft rugs of the floor—an advantage of royal rank, for mats of reed or straw would have made a sound, rutching under his weight. Kashtiliash son of Shagarakti-Shuriash was tall for a man of Kar-Duniash, broad-shouldered and thick-armed, his hairy muscular body compact and strong, tanned to bronze on face and limbs, fading to his natural dark olive on his torso. Waving blue-black hair fell to his shoulders, loosed for the night from its usual bun at the nape of his neck, and his curled beard was thick and dense, growing up to the edges of his high cheekbones, framing a beak-nosed, full-lipped face and eyes of a catlike hazel.

They quickly found the source of the disturbance that had troubled his sleep, and grew wide at the sight. A sliver of light was showing beneath the doors that led to the private rooms of the Lady of the Land, Queen of Babylon, Lieutenant Colonel Kathryn Hollard. Who was hundreds of miles away this night—

His feet moved with a hunter's silence, despite the solid weight of muscle and bone they upbore. Slowly, carefully he moved his left arm until the knuckles of the hand that held the knife touched the slick inlaid cedarwood of the door. He slitted his eyes—it would not do to be blinded by the sudden wash of light—and pushed sharply, wheeling to bring the Python up.

He froze, as astonished as the figure in his sights—more so. It was his concubine Ku-Aya, naked as he, her plumply pretty face going slack in astonishment, then pasty-white with terror. She cowered back against the spindly *dressing table,* nearly overturning the lamp. Then she dropped to her face on the carpet; her hand moved, until he put his foot on it.

"Do not stir," he said harshly.

This was forbidden ground to all save him and a few servants. Something dark had fallen from the woman's hand. He bent and picked it up. His hand jerked as if to throw it away again when he realized what it was; a little folded tablet of lead, with a figure scratched on it, and some lines of writing.

A cursing tablet! Kashtiliash thought, stomach crawling with the sickness of horror.

He recognized the scorpion-tailed, four-winged, lion-pawed drawing. In his studies in the House of Succession he had read the mighty collection of incantations known as *Utukku Lemnutu,* The Evil Demons. The lines pressed into the lead were crude, but there was no doubt that they showed *Pazuzu,* the Lord of the Demons of the Waste—master of sandstorms and bringer of all ill fortune for travelers. But the words inscribed below were not a prayer or spell to foil the demon's wickedness. They were an invocation, a *summoning.*

"The punishment for sorcery directed at the King's person is flaying alive," he grated.

"Not you! My Lord King, your handmaiden lies at your feet—it is not against you! Look inside the lead, and my lord will see!"

She *did* lie at his feet. He carefully bent the soft metal back, and a fine dusting of hairs fell into his palm. They were the color of desert sand, light and fine—hair such as was almost never seen in the land of Kar-Duniash. Cropped short, in the manner of the Nantukhtar warriors; Ku-Aya must have plucked it from a hairbrush of the queen's. He raised the pistol then, rage washing red across his vision. A curse against someone traveling . . . as the queen did this night, in the Nantukhtar ship of the air, over the deserts where Pazuzu had most power. Memory made him lower the pistol; Kathryn would not thank him for such a deed. She did not believe any curse of this land held power over her, either.

"You conspire against the queen, the Lady of the Land," he said. "For that also the punishment is death."

Ku-Aya surprised him, wrenching her wrist free and hunching backward, hissing like an Egyptian cat. "The queen! The sorceress who has bespelled our lord!" Her voice rose to a shriek. "The unnatural bitch, not even a woman, a man with breasts—the doer of evil, they plot against my lord and he will not *see*—"

"Silence!"

Kashtiliash controlled himself with an effort, his breath slowing. He dropped the knife and pistol on the table, grabbed the woman by her neck, and pitched her into the royal bedchamber. Then he belted on a light kilt—it was unlawful, unlucky, for ordinary men to see the King's nakedness, at least here in the palace—and shouted for the guards. They came, along with a *sa resi,* an eunuch chamberlain.

The armed men bristled at the sight of the anger on his face, facing outward and bringing their rifles to port-arms as they glared about for intruders.

"Stand easy," Kashtiliash said, gesturing impatiently. "There is no enemy here." He nudged the woman with his toe. "Captain Mar-biti-apla-usur."

"Command me, King of the Universe!"

"This woman has gravely displeased me," he said. "She is to be expelled from the palace. As she is, taking nothing."

The guard captain bowed. "What shall be done with her then?" he asked.

"I do not care. She is become a weariness to my spirit."

The guardsman bowed again, grabbed the blubbering woman by her hair, and pulled her out of the chamber as she scrambled to rise. The officer would probably add her to his household, or sell her—Kashtiliash had spoken truth when he said he was indifferent.

"Oh King, live forever," the eunuch said, rising from his prostration. "Do you wish another woman?"

"At this hour? Leave me, go, go," Kashtiliash said.

His sigh was half groan in the silence as the chamber emptied. *There is only one woman that I wish were here, and I am angered with her.* Or at least with her brother, the general of the allied Nantukhtar forces here in Kar-Duniash.

Raupasha had claimed Kenneth Hollard for her consort. Did that mean a plot to sieze Mitanni from his control, or could it be only the foolishness of a besotted girl?

"Officer on deck!"

Private Kyle Hook swung his legs down from the bunk and came to attention. Sick call beat lying on the hospital bunk looking out the window—though it was pleasant enough to watch everyone else working for once. The colonel had arrived, red-haired little I-am-at-God's-Right-Hand O'Rourke himself, and everyone was running back and forth like ants in a hill someone had poked with a stick.

Prancing around on that fancy horse of his like he's something special, Hook thought. *Dumb mick was working as a fucking waiter when the Event happened. I should be out there, not him.*

The doctor made her rounds, small and neat in a blue Coast Guard uniform and white coat; most of the ones in this room were ambulatory cases, but there were a few pale and drawn with fever that she stooped over as they lay. Her face hardened when she came to Kyle Hook.

"So," she said, looking him over. She was a slight gray-haired woman with pawky blue eyes that made nothing of his extra inches of height. "Malingering again, eh, Hook?"

"No, ma'am," he said, working his left arm slowly and cautiously. "Shoulder hurts something awful, ma'am."

"Take off your shirt, then," she said briskly, and put her black bag down on a window ledge.

"I'm not well, Dr. Wenter, really I'm not, ma'am," Hook said, muffled by the T-shirt he was cautiously removing.

"You're a malingerer, a liar, and a thief, Hook," the doctor said briskly, yanking it free and bringing a yelp from him.

He kept himself meek; if you shaved a gorilla and stuffed it into a blue sailor suit, it would look a lot like the orderly behind the medic.

"Turn your ugly face to the wall, and shut up. How you ever made it through Camp Grant mystifies me. Even the Marines . . ."

Because I didn't have any choice, bitch, he thought, bracing his hands against the mud brick.

It had been Camp Grant or Inagua Island Detention Center and shoveling salt for five years. He'd thought the Marines would be a better choice, seeing as he was an Islander born; thought he'd be sure of promotion, maybe a commission. But it was always the same story, persecution wherever he turned. *Nearly washed me out to Inagua anyway, the motherfuckers.* He'd had to bust his balls just to end up a rifleman here in the ass-end of nowhere, after a reaming-out full of threats he knew were no bluff. If there hadn't been a war on, he *would* have ended up shoveling salt.

"Ah," the doctor said, after a probe brought another yelp out of him. "As I thought, nothing but a boil. Well, I can lance it for you and the fever'll be down in a day or two."

"Lance—" he began in alarm, catching the glint of the blade out of the corner of his eye.

"This will hurt you a lot more than it will hurt me," the doctor said cheerfully. "Hold still."

He did, while the cold sting of the metal made equally cold sweat start out on his torso. *Call me a thief!* Well, yes, he'd taken things now and then, but he *needed* them. Mother and father dead right after the Event, murder-suicide, foster parents the Town assigned him doddering oldsters busy with four young Alban brats . . . what did they expect? *A good dutiful student and then a good dutiful fisherman or potato-grower.* Not Kyle Hook, no indeed. He remembered what life had been like in New York, clung to it when others let themselves forget. His father had told him he'd go to Princeton or Yale one day . . . Then the Event had come along and taken away his youth, the best years of his life; nothing but blister-hard work and school and endless boredom left.

He stifled a scream as the wound ointment was irrigated into the opened boil like burning ice over the raw flesh. You couldn't let something like that show in the Corps; too many Alban bastards who'd despise you if you did, and life would be even more hellish without some respect. Stinking savages, but there were a lot of them—and he had to kennel with them. The doctor applied a dressing and stepped back, wiping her scalpel with disinfectant.

"You'll be fit for duty in four days, Hook," she said. "You'd never have been *un*fit if you'd reported that immediately."

"Well, I couldn't see it there, could I? Ma'am," he said reasonably.

A few of the others laughed when the doctor had gone. Hook glared them into silence; he was a big young man, six feet, and strong in a lanky long-muscled fashion; few cared to meet his flat hazel eyes for long. Unarmed combat had been one of his better specialties; that and marksmanship had saved him from washing out after repeated "marginal disciplinaries" on his Recruit Evaluation Forms. When everyone was quiet he swung back onto his pallet and lay on his stomach as he looked out the window again.

"Lucky . . . the boil wasn't on your ass . . . Hook," a voice said from the lower bunk, with a strong choppy Sun People accent. "Then everyone . . . would see . . . you're a half-assed . . . excuse for a Marine."

He leaned over, glaring at the sweat-wet face of the sick man below him. "Get off my case, Edraxsson!" he said. "You've been biting my ass for a year now, and I'm fucking sick of it, you hear?"

"That's because you're . . . a disgrace to my beloved . . . Corps," the noncom said. "But I'm going to make a Marine out of you . . . yet, Hook," he said, eyes beginning to wander and then brought back by an effort of will.

"Shut the fuck up, Edraxsson," Hook barked. "You're just a useless cripple here, not a fucking noncom, so shut up!"

Edraxsson smirked, despite the fever from his infected foot— a pack mule had stepped on it, and driven filth into the wound while he was out on patrol. Hook felt something spark behind his eyes, like a small white explosion, and reached for his webbing belt where it hung on a wooden peg driven into the adobe wall.

Right across the face, he thought. *That'll shut him up, I'll give him the buckle—*

"Hey, heads up!" one of the other patients said, craning her head to get a better view through the narrow window and the thick mud-brick wall it pierced. "Something going on out there!"

Hook had a better view. The Gatling was crewed up, and the colonel leading it out at a gallop. His eyes went wider; something *was* up. When he heard the crackle of shots and then the ripping-canvas sound of the machine gun in operation, an icy trickle reached up from groin to stomach and cooled the rage there the way salt spray would a candle-flame on deck.

"Something's going down."

Marian Alston-Kurlelo ate slowly, with conscious pleasure. She loved the sea, but there were things you just couldn't expect on salt water, and a good ham-and-eggs breakfast was one of them. They were due to leave Westhaven today; touch at Portsmouth Base, and then south with the fleet. At least they'd be sailing out of Alba's late fall into the Mediterranean's mild winter. . . .

She ignored the occasional courier who came in to drop off a written message or consult in whispers with her hostess; the last thing a busy subordinate needed was their elbow joggled.

There was even tumeric for the scrambled eggs, and acorn-fed Alban hams were better than anything Smithfield, Virginia, had ever turned out. They were going to be far foreign for a good long while soon, probably eating hardtack—what the enlisted ranks called dog biscuit, with reason—and salt cod.

"What's the status on the *Merrimac*?" she asked, in a quiet moment.

"The dockside people were working all night in shifts, Commodore," Commandant Hendricksson said. "They're putting the finishing touches on stowage now, completing her provisioning."

That had had to wait until the cargo from Irondale was loaded, since stores needed to go on top to be accessible during the voyage south. Which they wouldn't, under tons of rolled steel plate, boiler, engine parts, and cannon.

"*Talbott* and the *Severna Park* finished their loading yesterday, so that's six hundred tons of coal along with it—yah, should be ample."

Alston nodded, calculations running through her head. "Plenty, if we whip the coal ashore and send the ships back for a second load as soon as we're set up," she said. "Very good work, Greta."

Hendricksson nodded; she was a tall fair woman, in her late thirties now, built with a matronly solidity and usually showing a calm, stolid reliability. "It may not be spectacular, but we do get things *done* here," she said.

The commodore inclined her head. The ex-Minnesotan had been an officer on *Eagle* before the Event. She didn't have quite the touch of the buccaneer you needed for ship command in this era, more of a routiner. Thoroughly brave, of course. She'd been one of the commando of five who went with Alston into the Olmec city-fort of San Lorenzo in the Year 1, when Martha Cofflin had been kidnapped and taken south by Lisketter's band of Save the Noble Native American imbeciles. At least, *San Lorenzo* was what the archaeologists would have called it, in a history where its lords hadn't sacrificed most of Lisketter's crew to the Jaguar God, and where it wasn't burned and abandoned after the Islander punitive expedition and the unintentional plague of mumps that followed. The jungle was growing back over the temple mounds and giant stone heads now, though the other Olmec centers were flourishing.

Martha's back in Nantucket Town . . . Pulakis is farming on Long Island, Alonski drowned on that fishing boat, poor bastard, and Greta's been in charge here since the Alban War. Hasn't been back to the Island more than a couple of times.

She'd done well, though; it was a post that suited a lover of schedules and lists and procedures. Her husband was a civil engineer of like outlook, out since the crack of dawn supervising the laying of a new water main.

"In fact, you've been doing a damned good job here overall," Alston went on, and Hendricksson glowed. The commodore didn't give praise lightly.

They were breakfasting in the commandant's residence. Fort Pentagon was garrison and civil headquarters here in Westhaven. The commander's house was inside it, built around a courtyard of its own, mostly cobbled, but with a small rose garden and a wooden jungle gym set amid grass with trampled bare spots here and there. A groom led a horse by, sparrows hopped about picking oats from the cracks between stones, someone went through the courtyard gate with a basket of laundry on her hip and laughed with a Marine who'd leaned his rifle against a wall to offer her a hand. This kitchen looked over the yard, flooded with light from the big south-facing windows; it had a pleasant austerity of flagstones and scrubbed oak, stone countertops and big cast-iron stove from Irondale. Pans and dishes were racked on the walls, sacks of onions hung from the rafters with bundles of herbs, and the ham stood in carved pink glory near the big black frying pan. The air smelled of sea and cooking.

Swindapa looked up from where she'd been dandling the commandant's youngest. "I'll go see about getting our dunnage and files down to the ship, then," she said, handing the toddler back to the housekeeper; it gurgled and stretched chubby arms at her, and she paused to give it a kiss on the nose. "It won't be in the way, now. And I can check that the briefing papers are ready, and get the requisition chits from the Pacific Bank people."

"Thanks, 'dapa," Marian said. "I had some stuff with the armorer, too—see to it, would you, sugar?"

Her Python, specifically; her *katana* and *wasikashi* she looked after herself, but something had been rattling in the pistol last time she had it on the firing range. *Goin' to need that,* she thought, with grim resignation. You wanted your tools in good shape when your life depended on them, and Westhaven had a first-rate firearms man, trained at Seahaven Engineering back on the Island.

"Let's go take a look at things in general," she went on, throwing down her napkin.

She and Hendricksson went out the front, returning the salutes of the Marine sentries, then up the brick staircase to the gateside bastions and above that to the grass-grown roof of the gun gallery and the small paved stand around the flagpole; the Stars and Stripes flapped above them in the brisk onshore breeze. Fort Pentagon's walls were sloping turf above a brick retaining wall and dry moat, and the fall wildflowers that starred them contrasted oddly with the black snouts of the cannon. She'd put the fort in on the highest ground available on the south bank, and it gave a good view.

From here she could see the whole stretch of the docks along the Avon's south bank, a dozen long rectangles stretching out into the river. Low tide left a stretch of smelly black mud between the corniche roadway with its log seawall and the deeper water where the ships rested. It also left the great timbers of the wharf exposed, black with pitch and trailing disconsolate green weed, overgrown with mussels and barnacles. Gull-wings made a white storm out over the blue-green water, stooping and diving; one let an oyster fall not far away, then flapped down to plunder the broken shell. Some of the ships were only the tips of masts over the oak planking of the warehouses stretching upstream; the wood was weathered brown near here, rawly fresh further away. Oats poured in a yellow-white stream from a grain elevator into the hold of an Islander barque as they watched, and workers with kerchiefs across their faces toiled knee-deep in the flood to spread it evenly with long-handled rakes.

"It's like watching a stop-motion film, every time we visit here," Alston said quietly.

"Damned right, Commodore," Greta said. "Even living here, it's *almost* like that for me—like waking up in the woods and finding a fairy ring of mushrooms."

Out in the blue-green waters was a lighthouse on a rocky little island, built of concrete at vast expense. A big metal windmill whirled atop it, doing duty as a wind sock and charging banks of lead-acid batteries in the structure below, handmade copies of pre-Event models from trucks. Inland from the docks was a checkerboard of tree-lined streets and squares with small green parks, shading out quickly into truck gardens and farms and round huts; she'd based the design on the original street plan of Savannah, Georgia. The public buildings were grouped around a larger central square, mostly in reddish sandstone or brick; a modest Ecumenical Christian cathedral—this had been the first bishopric off the Island—the Town Hall, half a dozen others. Between there and the docks were workshops, small factories, sailors' doss-houses and a tangle of service trades.

Form followed function; between them Bronze Age peasants and late-twentieth-century Americans had managed to spontaneously re-create most of the features of a classic North Atlantic port town.

Alston chuckled quietly at a memory; those functional features included a fair number of hookers. Until she actually went up and asked one of them, Swindapa had thought her partner was pulling her leg about that. Like most Fiernans, she found the whole concept of prostitution weirdly funny in a creepy sort of way; as she put it, it was like paying someone to have dinner with you.

All in all Marian Alston-Kurlelo liked Westhaven, though, more than any of the other outposts of the Republic. Fogarty's Cove, for instance, tended to be a little too consciously the haunt of bold pioneers, given to hitching their belts, spitting, and noting *the crops look purty good this year, ayup*. The older ones were probably modeling themselves on secondhand memories of *Last of the Mohicans* and Frontierland, and it was contagious.

"How's morale?" she said. "The civilian population, particularly." Westhaven was under Islander law and had a Town Meeting of its own, but the situation was a bit irregular, constitutionally speaking.

"Excellent, so far," Hendricksson replied. "Those posters Arnstein's Foreign Affairs people sent over really whipped up feeling. I had to have our resident Tartessians put under guard for their own protection."

Alston nodded impassively, hinding an inward wince. There were times when she felt . . . not exacty guilty . . . more like uneasy . . . about some of the things they'd been forced to introduce to this era.

Potatoes are fine, antiseptic childbirth is wonderful, democracy and womens' rights are excellent. I'm not so sure about the levee en masse, *the Supreme General Staff and systematic propaganda,* she thought.

"I'm surprised they were *quite* so effective," Hendricksson mused. "I mean, yah, yah, they were all *true*, but it was pretty blatant stuff. Maybe because they didn't grow up with TV commercials?"

"Mmmm-*hmmmm*. People here aren't . . . immunized," Alston said.

It wasn't that the folk of this era were inherently gentler than those of the twentieth; what they didn't have was the accumulated experience and examples and recorded thought of . . .

Sun Tzu, Caesar Augustus, Han Fei-Tze and the Legalists, Frederick II, Machiavelli, Elizabeth I, Maurice of Nassau, Shaka Senzagakhona of the Zulu, Timur-I-Leng, Catherine the Great, Napoleòn, Marx, Mao, Bismarck, Nguyen Giap, Lenin . . . and a lot more, Alston thought. *War and politics are technologies, too. They evolve, in their Lamarckian fashion.*

She remembered how amazed she'd been to find that the Romans had no real concept of intelligence work—it just didn't occur to them to keep contact with an enemy, or set up a network of scouts and spies and information analysts. There were a thousand examples like that . . .

"Good," she said aloud, putting a hand on Hendricksson's shoulder for a moment. "Gerta, this whole campaign depends on Westhaven. I can't operate in the Straits of Gibraltar with a logistics train stretching all the way back to Nantucket Town.

Portsmouth Base doesn't have the facilities or the hinterland to supply the fleet."

Hendricksson nodded in her turn. "The salt beef and dog biscuit will keep coming, Commodore, and the powder and shot." Then she shrugged. "Everything takes longer and costs more, yah?"

"You said it, woman." Alston smiled crookedly. The makeshifts they had to use were so damned *frustrating* at times. *On the other hand,* she thought snidely, *the squids always got the fancy stuff up in the twentieth; the Coast Guard got used to hand-me-downs and making do.*

"We'll manage here," Hendricksson repeated.

"Excellent, but keep alert." Their eyes both went up for a moment to the orca shape of the observation balloon that floated over the town on the end of its long tether. "Isketerol isn't afraid to gamble. That attack on Nantucket in the spring was a bold one . . . and just between me 'n' thee, Greta, it came far too close to success for comfort. A little less warning, or if we hadn't had the *Farragut* nearly ready to go, or if the weather hadn't turned wet and drenched their flintlocks—it would have hurt us much more badly. I wouldn't put it past him to try something else, particularly if he's desperate."

"We'll manage here," Hendricksson repeated, her face taking on a bulldog look as she glanced around the town whose building had been her lifework. Marian recognized it; people got *attached* to what they made themselves.

She sighed; now she had to go tell the captain of the *Merrimac* what they had in mind for his ship. "Speaking of which, now I've got to go and give Mr. Clammp the bad news."

CHAPTER SEVEN

September, 10 A.E.—O'Rourke's Ford, east of Troy
September, 10 A.E.—Babylon, Kingdom of
  Kar-Duniash
October, 10 A.E.—Westhaven, Alba

Colonel O'Rourke had to admit that Barnes and her people didn't waste time. The frenzy of work around the little base had died down by the dawn, barely fourteen hours after his arrival.

O'Rourke joined the line of Marines waiting for their breakfasts; regulations were that officers ate the same food as the troops in the field. For that matter, they ate much the same food at a base, save for social occasions, but in a different mess, for discipline's sake.

He took a small loaf of fresh barley bread and a chunk of hard white cheese, and held out his mess tin. The cook scooped it full of barley porridge; they'd managed to find raisins for it, and some honey for sweetener. His nose twitched at the smells; it had been a long time since dinner, and that had been a couple of hardtack crackers and a strip of jerky with everyone busy pitching in to get the defenses ready. The outer wall made a good perch; he straddled it and set the food down, tearing the loaf apart. Steaming hot from the improvised clay ovens, it was good enough to eat without butter and went well with the cheese. He spooned up the porridge, washing it down with draughts of cold water; a good tube well had been the first thing the combat engineers had put in here.

The smells went well with the fresh clarity of early morning, and he watched the purple shadows running down the slopes of the hills and lifting from the dark pines on the higher shoulders. *Now, wouldn't this be a terrible day to die,* he thought.

Captain Barnes and Hantilis came to join him. The Hittite had joined in the work readily enough, which did him credit.

"I am puzzled," Hantilis said, between bites of porridge.

"You work side by side with common soldiers, yet they obey you more promptly than my own warriors would—my *real* warriors, I mean, not those Kaska dogs. How can soldiers obey you, if they do not fear you as one placed on high above them, a man favored of the Gods?"

Cecilie chuckled. "Oh, they're afraid of their officers, all right," she said. O'Rourke helped with the translation; Barnes had no Hittite and very little Akkadian. "And even more, their sergeants."

"We're Marines," O'Rourke amplified. "We're all a band of brothers . . ."

"And sisters," Barnes put in.

"And sisters. But some of us are *elder* brothers, as it were. Everyone works, everyone fights, and everyone does what their superiors tell them to do."

Hantilis shook his head in puzzlement. They finished and scoured their pannikins gleaming clean; the noncoms were checking that everyone did likewise, which was one important way to avoid food poisoning and assorted belly complaints.

"I'm off to sluice down while I have a chance," Barnes said.

O'Rourke nodded distantly. He was going to feel rather embarrassed if nothing happened . . . but it was better to be overprepared than under.

Hantilis's head came up. A moment later the Nantucketer heard it as well.

"That *can't* be a steam engine," O'Rourke said. It was too far away, and too *big*. His head turned toward the lookout post higher up the mountain slope to the south.

"I don't think much of the soil here," Private Vaukel Telukuo said. He dug his bayonet into the turf beside him and ripped up a handful, looking critically at the dry reddish dirt that clung to its roots. "Too dry—not much weight to it, if you know what I mean."

He was a tall sallow young man, dark of hair and eye, with a big nose and long bony jaw. His companion's name on the rolls was Johanna Gwenhaskieths. He doubted that was anything her parents had given her; *gwenha* simply meant "woman" in the tongue of the eastern tribes, and *skieths* was "shield." Shield-woman probably meant something like female warrior, which was odd when you considered that among the charioteers such weren't merely rare, as they were among the Earth Folk, but except in stories virtually unknown.

Unknown until the Eagle People came, he corrected himself.

Johanna was peering down the huge sweep of hillside below them, occasionally raising the field glasses they'd been issued when they were put on outpost duty; she was several inches shorter than he, her cropped hair so fair it was almost invisible, narrow eyes a cold gray.

"Nothing so far," she said, and then dug a heel into the ground to reply to his first remark. "Not much like the fat black earth where I was born either . . . but you don't have to farm it, Vauk."

"Ah, well, I thought I was tired of farming," he said mildly. "Boring I thought it was, you know? But this soldiering, it's boring too. And I miss my cattle."

"I can stand boring," she said; where his voice gave English a singsong burbling lilt, hers was choppy and hard. "They were going to bury *me* facedown in a peat bog, with a forked hazel branch over my neck to keep my ghost from walking. So walk I did, by night, to the Cross-God mission station. The priestess there got me into the Corps." She crossed herself. "Honor to Him of the Cross, and His Father and Mother."

"Now why would anyone do such a thing?" Vaukel said indignantly. "Drown you in a bog, that is."

Johanna chuckled. "For spreading my thighs for a fine young warrior rather than a fat old man who had seven cows to give my father," she said. "And here I am, with all the fine young warriors I could want, being one myself, and nobody to send me to the bog . . . what's that?"

They both frowned and looked westward. The sound was a deep rumbling beat, echoing off the hillsides and cliffs about them. "Sounds like . . ." Vaukel said slowly. "Sounds like a *drum*, doesn't it?"

"The drum of a God," Johanna said. "Or one of those machines of steam." She brought the glasses up again, then blurted out a half sentence in her birth-tongue. In English: "Message to the base—"

When it was over and the reply came they snatched up their rifles, then the tripod with its tilt-mounted mirror that flashed coded sunlight. Vaukel put it over his shoulder, and they bounded and ran and tumbled down the steep slopes and then across the flat, running for the barley-sack ramparts of the little outpost.

"What's up?" one of the pickets called to them.

Vaukel pointed westward. "Here they come!" he yelled. "Spears like stars on water, and thicker than the grass!"

*　　*　　*

"I wish we could just elope," Justin Clemens said, dodging a rush of liquid garbage from a narrow second-story window.

The movement was a little jerky with nervousness. He consciously controlled his breathing; meeting prospective in-laws was bad enough, worse when they were foreign, worse still when you knew they and your fiancée had been feuding for years.

"Then we would not be married—not by the laws of the Land of Kar-Duniash," said Azzu-ena.

He knew that brisk tone fairly well, by now. It was eighteen months since she'd talked him into taking her on as an apprentice, and two since he'd convinced her to marry him.

And ten years going on eleven since the Event. Focus, you fool! he thought. She went on:

"I will not let my uncle and his she-demon grasp everything that was my father's in their claws; their children I would not grudge it to, the little ones who love their cousin, but *I* will settle what they receive. And those two would neglect the funerary offerings for my father. Bad enough that he had no sons to make them. Come, betrothed, come."

"Oh, all right," Clemens grumbled, wiping his face with his bandanna; weather on the banks of the Euphrates was not easy for a man inclined to plumpness, even getting on toward winter. This sun wasn't easy on the naturally pink, either; his floppy canvas campaign hat was welcome, and so was the shade of the blank-walled two-story buildings that lined the narrow twisting laneway. It didn't help that he'd had to leave off shaving for the last two weeks, but everyone told him that it would be impossible to go into a marriage-contract discussion looking like a smooth-cheeked eunuch. The resultant growth was a bit lighter than the cropped sun-streaked brown hair on his head, which made him even more conspicuous. Plus it itched and caught sweat.

Nantucketers were no longer so rare in the streets of Babylon that they attracted a crowd—small children following along, yes, and stares, pointed fingers, more than a few gestures to avert the Evil Eye and baleful magic, hands gripping amulets or small images of the gods. Clemens looked about as he walked; he was more familiar with the everyday city than most of the Islander expeditionary force, since he'd been in charge of stopping the smallpox epidemic. This was still very different from the palace quarter where he spent most of his time when not in the field or down at the Republic's outpost, Ur Base, near the mouth of the Euphrates. The street was narrow, twisting, deep in shadow and in dust at the tail end of summer, doubtless a quagmire of mud in the infrequent winter rains. An irregular trickle of sewage ran down the middle and insect-buzzing heaps of rubbish lay wherever a householder had dumped them.

Skinny feral dogs wound among the crowds, and an occasional pig even more lean and savage rooted among the offal; most Semites of this era had no taboo on hog products—though considering what the beasts ate, the Nantucketer very much wished they did. Most houses had a drain through their front walls, adding their trickle to the mess; Clemens hopped or strode over the rivulets as he walked, brushing at the omnipresent flies. The stink he'd gotten used to, mostly, but his doctor's skin crawled at the thought of the germs swarming around him like a host of the invisible fever demons the locals believed in.

Which, come to think of it, is a pretty good metaphor for the disease environment here, he thought. That was what happened when you crammed two hundred thousand people and a total ignorance of public hygiene together in a few hundred stagnant, blistering-hot acres.

The smell wasn't as bad as the horror he felt every time they brushed past a water-seller, though, bulging goatskin slung over one shoulder, cups on a bandolier over the other, crying his wares in a nasal falsetto. That water came from the canals that bisected the city, drawn directly from the same river that eventually swallowed what was running down the center of the streets.

Azzu-ena strode along nimbly beside him, one hand holding the hem of her robe up out of the road and the other pulling her shawl up beneath her chin; once she stopped to drop a packet of dried dates in the bowl of an emaciated blind beggar leaning against a wall—with no equivalent of small change, food was what you gave if you were feeling charitable. She smiled and nodded and answered greetings from passersby that were shy and awkward only because of the foreigner beside her. Her father had lived all his life in this neighborhood, the *babtum*—city-ward—of Mili-la-El, near the Eastern Gate of the great city. She'd earned most of her living in the palace, where her sex made her a favored medical attendant among the King's women, but she also tended to the needs of many of her neighbors, as her father had done before her. His ancient assistant tottered at her heels with the basket of healing tools.

So respect for his bride helped to clear a path for Clemens, as much as his alien features and uniform and the dreaded fire-weapon at his belt. Everyone knew where they were bound and why; apart from the rumor telegraph, there weren't many other reasons for a man and woman to head for the woman's relatives with a scribe in tow. Murmured good wishes followed them, and good-natured jibes at the scribe and the scribe's assistant; the portly man with the jointed waxed boards and bronze stylus of his craft nodded benignly. The skinny apprentice carrying the heavier clay just sweated.

When a train of loaded donkeys came by, everyone had to crowd the walls; their panniers nearly brushed the buildings on either side. Swaggering thick-armed toughs with cudgels and jutting curled beards flanked the robed merchant, who rode with his feet nearly touching the ground at the head of the line. When the animals passed the jostling crowd returned—pushing, chaffering, shouting, here a snatch of nasal twanging song, there a storyteller squatting at an intersection reciting the deeds of Gilgamesh and pausing until the audience tossed bits of metal or beads or handfuls of dried fruit into his bowl; a public writer waving his reed stylus above a bucket of damp clay and shouting of his skill; a hideously deformed beggar showing his sores and whining for alms . . .

Every few hundred yards the blank housefronts gave way to a clutch of tiny shops, their fronts spilling into the streets and long narrow rooms stretching back into mysterious gloom. Despite his jangling nerves, Clemens halted for a moment to watch a jeweler at work, hands tapping out a thing of beauty in gold leaf and carnelian amid trays that displayed silver cuff-bracelets, bangles, earrings, and necklaces. Terra-cotta figurines on either side of a doorway marked a chapel, where you could stop for a moment in the courtyard to pray and scatter a handful of flour for luck.

The roar of noise held few wheels or hooves in these narrow ways. Most of it was human voices, breaking into arm-waving, shouting argument and dying away into equally quick laughter, calling for alms, screaming out the virtues and incredibly low cost of their wares; near-naked laborers grunting for passage as they bent double under huge burdens of cloth or flour or cakes of dried dates, or a barefoot slave with his hair in the distinctive topknot required by law asking his way with a strong foreign accent. A drunk reeled by making attempts at song that would have been hideous even if Babylonian music didn't sound like a cat in a washing machine, priests in tassled cloaks chanted, housewives balanced the day's shopping or a water jug on their heads, scarcely a one not chattering and gesturing as she walked, squealing children ran in packs . . .

Dress for both sexes was a short-sleeved wool tunic, anything from knee to ankle length for men but always long for women. Working men wore theirs just above the knee, girded about with a beltlike sash; the odd man of wealth went robed to his sandals, with a fringed cloak wrapped about his upper body, the length of cloth and the embroidery and fringe of tassels being a mark of rank. Women always covered their legs, and the more respectable their heads as well, usually with a long cloak or shawl that might be drawn across the face. Most cloth was faded, muted grays and browns, but the exceptions were gaudily flamboyant in blue, crimson, yellow, stripes and dots and bands; jewelry was frequent, a family's store of wealth as well as display; hardly a free woman went without a clutch of lucky silver bracelets in groups of six.

And not a street sign or house number, Clemens thought, thoroughly lost. *I suppose you have to be born here to really know it.* An eeriness went beneath everything; he was watching—walking through—scenes dead and dust three thousand years and more when he was born. *And without us, it would have gone on like this for thousands of years to come.* Now *in a century or two, who knows?*

"This is my uncle's house," Azzu-ena said. Eyes peered at them over the high blank wall, then vanished hurriedly.

"Go, go, knock and require them to open," Azzu-ena went on with a shooing motion, smiling indulgently at him.

He smiled back. *God, you could drown in those eyes,* he thought.

"Go, knock," she said again, starting him out of a happy daze.

She's all ears when I'm teaching, Clemens thought ruefully. *But a lot of the rest of the time, you'd think I wasn't fit to be let out without a keeper.* Of course, he *wasn't,* when it came to the intricacies of law and custom among a people wholly foreign.

A Babylonian would have used his walking stick to knock. Clemens rapped with his knuckles on the plain rough poplar wood of the doorway, swallowing through a throat gone dry.

"Hi, I'm—"

"This is the servant of the doorway," Azzu-ena hissed in her thickly accented English. "Remember!"

"Oh, yeah," Clemens muttered.

The doorway gave into a small vestibule, cool and dim; it

was a relief when the doors swung shut behind them, closing out the noise and much of the stink of the city streets. The servant—a slave, actually, from his topknot—knelt and removed the sandals of the guests, bathing their feet in a clay basin and wiping them clean before fitting straw slippers. That was a luxury, but guests got the best any household had.

Clemens's issue boots stopped him cold, and the boy gave a shy smile when the Islander demonstrated how to undo the lacings. The socks beneath caused exclamations of wonder; he had to admit that the cool water felt good on his feet after the walk. Then the boy bowed them through another door, into the central courtyard of the house.

Hmmm. Not bad.

Uncle Tab-sa-Dayyan was a wholesale dealer in copper and other goods, who also owned houses in the city and land outside it—upper middle class, by local standards, much more respectable than his scapegrace brother the doctor had been. *Asu*—physician—wasn't a particularly exalted trade among Akkadians, although it did require literacy and hence wasn't common labor.

The house had a first story of baked brick set in asphalt mortar, and a second of adobe laid in clay; both were plastered and whitewashed. More brick paved the courtyard around the central drain. Around the walls ran a yard-wide gallery on wooden pillars, date-palm wood from the look of it. The family's chambers were on the second floor; this ground level held utility and servants' quarters, together with the little family shrine at the back—he was uneasily aware that the family's dead would be buried beneath that—and the *diwan* where guests would be entertained and spend the night, and the ablution room. These Babylonians weren't a dirty people, really. Everything was swept and tidy.

And there are my prospective in-laws. He swallowed again. *Come on, Justin, you're marrying her, not all of them. Buck up, man. Show some backbone.*

Tab-sa-Dayyan himself was a man of fifty or so, plumply healthy and looking to have most of his teeth, in flowerpot hat and densely embroidered robe, his sandals studded with bronze, his curled hair and beard mostly gray. On a family matter such as this his wife stood beside him. Her robe was even more elaborate, and she wore a heavy broad necklace and a headdress of silver and faience on her grizzled black mane; she was mostly toothless, and her lips worked over the gums as she glared at him out of beady black eyes. Beside them stood their children, from the eldest son—a solid family man himself—down to a six-year-old peeking out shyly from behind an elder sibling. Four living, which probably meant the wife had born eight or ten; infant mortality here was dreadful. Azzu-ena was the only surviving child of four herself.

"Come, be a guest beneath my roof," Tab-sa-Dayyan said, after they had invoked the gods and inquired as to each other's health, the health of their relatives, and the other matters the manners of the ancient East required; the tone was much less friendly than the words. "You will eat bread and drink beer with me, and we will speak."

The guest room was about ten feet by fifteen, undoubtedly the largest in the house; the furniture consisted of low built-in benches against the walls covered with rugs, cushions, and a low table of inlaid wood; it looked almost as pretty as the ones in the palace, except that a corner had been broken off and patched back on. A middle-aged woman brought in jugs of beer, straws to drink it with, rounds of flat barley bread like a coarse pita and bowls of oddments. Clemens found the sour coolness of the beer welcome and the fermentation ought to take care of the bacteria in the water, at that. Azzu-ena broke off a piece of bread, scooped up a paste of ground chick-peas, sesame oil, and garlic, and handed him some.

He nibbled. *Now I'm officially a guest.* That ensured at least a certain degree of courtesy.

Tab-sa-Dayyan rested his hands on the knees of his crossed legs. "So I had not expected to see this day." He shook his head; he also spoke slowly and a little loudly, evidently making allowances for the barbarian wizard's limited Akkadian. Clemens shoved down a slight irritation; he'd spent endless months drilling, and Azzu-ena told him that he was fully fluent, if weirdly and thickly accented. At least the Babylonian wasn't making protective signs.

"Irregular, most irregular. Mutu-Hadki my brother was not a wise man," the merchant said. "He should have arranged the matter of my niece's marriage and dowry before his death—she was already of marriageable age," he added sourly. A glint of hope: "You do know, honored Clemens son of Edgar, that Azzu-ena is well beyond the usual age of a bride? Most of her best childbearing time is past. She has twenty-six years—nearly twenty-seven . . ."

"Yes, I am aware of that," Clemens said dryly.

Azzu-ena tugged at his sleeve, and he cleared his throat and turned to the scribe who sat silent, smiling faintly. *Scribe didn't* mean just *clerk;* the scribal schools taught law, literature, architecture, and mathematics as well. A scribe was also the closest thing the kingdom of Kar-Duniash had to a notary public.

"Yes," the scribe said, and held out a hand without looking around. His assistant-apprentice stopped wolfing the refreshments and fumbled in his basket, handing a clay tablet six inches by four to his master. The older man took it and scanned the chicken-track rows of cuneiform, holding the tablet at a slant so that the light from the door would hit the edges of the wedge-shaped marks.

"Yes," he said again, then cleared his throat and read in a singsong, listing the regnal year at the top of the document— the second year of Shagarakti-Shuriash—and continuing:

"one sar *sixteen* gin *of built house, in the Street of the Diviners near the temple of Lugalbanda and between the houses of Igmilum the silversmith and Sallurum the leather-worker; one* sar *waste ground, one cow called Taribatum, if surviving; one chest of healer's tools, marked with the sign of Ninurta, one chest seven jars of herbs, labeled; three bushels of dry bitumen; one wooden door, of cedarwood; one wicker door; three bolts cloth of—"*

The list went on; all that her father had acquired in a not particularly prosperous lifetime. It ended with: *"—all the goods to be inherited by my daughter Azzu-ena as hers for her life and as her* seriktum-*dowry in the day of her marriage; to descend to her children or on her death childless to pass to my brother Tab-sa-Dayyan and his sons. Sworn in the temple of Ishtar, witnessed by Ah-kalla, cultic official; Lu-Nanna, priest; Uselli son of Ku-Ningal, Sig-ersetim son of Silli-Ema; and the judge Ellu-musu; 23rd day, Month of Sabatum, year Shagarakti-Shuriash King of Kar-Duniash smote the hosts of the Subartu."*

The faces of her uncle and aunt had grown longer and longer as they listened to the catalog of property they had confidently expected to inherit themselves, or at least pass to their children. At the end of the discussion they glanced at each other.

"Still, most irregular," Tab-sa-Dayyan said. "Where is the go-between, the negotiations between myself and the groom's family, the—"

"Excuse me if I, an ignorant foreigner, offend," Clemens cut in. *By local standards, he has a point.* Marriage here was a link between kindreds, not just individuals. "My parents are dead, and none of my kin reside in this city. In my own land I am an *awelum"*—which was as close as you could get to *citizen* in this language; it had originally meant nobleman, and had worked its way down to "mister," just as "mister" had—"and of age, and so authorized to deal in this matter."

The scribe nodded. "There is precedent. The law-stele of Hammurabi—"

Clemens thought for a moment as the man went on that his own Akkadian wasn't as good as he thought, until he saw that the locals were equally baffled; evidently legalese was another universal constant of civilization.

"—and so, as long as the marriage follows form, in this case the parties have the right to act for themselves. I will admit that it is unsual, most unusual, but not unprecedented, no, not by any means. Not unknown for a widow to do so, for instance." The scribe's eyebrows rose. "Unless the worthy *awelum* Tab-sa-Dayyan son of Aham-Nirsi knows of an impediment?"

Tab-sa-Dayyan's wife spoke, a minor breach of protocol in itself:

"A bride who is not a widow or divorced must be a virgin!" she said triumphantly. "If a bride is not a virgin, a contract of engagement may be broken! Is it not so? This woman"—she pointed at Azzu-ena—"it was bad enough before, when she dwelt alone like a harlot save for those useless lazy slaves of her father's that should have been sold for what they would fetch years ago and she should have lived here, respectably, weaving for her kin. But for the past year and more, she has been traveling, unescorted, in the company of this man, like a public woman of the streets!"

Clemens felt a sudden hot jet of anger, until he realized that Azzu-ena was shaking with supressed laughter. The scribe's assistant chortled audibly, Azzu-ena's father's helper hooted toothlessly, the scribe smiled, and Tab-sa-Dayyan turned an interesting shade of angry purple.

"Worthy wife of the *awelum*," the scribe said gently. "*That* argument is usually raised by the *groom's* relatives who wish to break an engagement, not thrown at the bride by *her* kinfolk."

The woman gobbled, and Azzu-ena leaned aside to take a tablet out of the satchel of the helper who had served her father, where it lay atop the bundled herbs and tools—those including a stethescope, now.

"Most learned one, if you would read this?"

"*I, Habannatum, who am naditum—nun, roughly—of Marduk in the City of Babylon, in the first year of King Kashtiliash of Babylon, the year after the plague of the small pockmarks, swear by my Lord, with my hands clasped, that the woman*

Azzu-ena daughter of Mutu-Hadki is batultu, a virgin who has not known man. I swear this by my own testimony on examination, and by that of Sin-nada the midwife, in the presence of Ninurta-ra'im-zerim the judge."

Tab-sa-Dayyan's wife sank back, glaring again. *That* gambit for disallowing the marriage wasn't going to work, obviously. Azzu-ena smiled sweetly and returned the tablet to her doctor's basket.

Her uncle spoke gravely: "I must know that this foreign gentleman is able to properly care for my niece. Has he no wife of his body in his home country, no children or household?"

Clemens sighed, and settled down to work. *Yes, I have no other wife. Yes, I am chief physician to the great general Lord Hollard—whose sister married King Kashtiliash, may the Gods grant him many years and the increase of his realm—and my wage is so-and-so many shekels weight of silver every month. In my homeland I own a house and land—*

When they got to that stage he noticed a sudden perking of ears in the Tab-sa-Dayyan family. That turned into outright respect when he mentioned that his elder brother owned six hundred and forty acres of farmland in the Republic; when you translated that into Babylonian *iku*, it sounded formidable; the sort of holding a solid minor member of the landed gentry would have; a class at least one ratchet up from Tab-sa-Dayyan's.

He didn't feel he had to mention that most of it was uncleared temperate-zone climax forest on the Long Island frontier, and that his brother and family were working it with their own four hands and an occasional hired immigrant when they were lucky.

Tab-sa-Dayyan clapped his hands. "Woman! Bring date wine and strainers!"

Oh, Lord Jesus, Clemens thought as the middle-aged servant scurried back in—the stuff tasted like alcoholic cough syrup. Still, it beat the earlier hostility. *I suppose he isn't such a bad sort. A man has to look out for his own, here.* Apart from the charity of relatives, there was no safety net short of selling yourself into slavery or starving.

The scribe opened his set of jointed waxed boards. Those could be smoothed down and overwritten, which was why they were the medium used for first drafts of documents. "This is the *riskatum*," he said. The marriage contract. "I will read the terms."

He did. Clemens swallowed, feeling his mouth dry again, and

took a long gulp of the thick sweet drink. *I'm doing it, I'm actually going through with it. Remarriage; the triumph of hope over experience. And I'm marrying another doctor again.* Enough people had told him he was being an idiot, for those and a dozen other reasons.

He glanced over at Azzu-ena. Her eyes shone in the dimness, and he fought down a grin; that wouldn't be seemly, to local eyes. He fought down an impulse to grab her and kiss her as well; that *really* wouldn't be seemly. The scribe cleared his throat, and Justin Clemens jumped.

"Oh, sorry," he said. "Here. The, ah, the *terhatum,* yes." The bride-price.

The little chamois bag was heavy, and it clinked. Azzu-ena's uncle took it, weighed it in his hand, took out one of the coins. Coined money was a novelty here, but the Republic's expeditionary force had been paying in it since they arrived. The local merchant community was thoroughly familiar with it now, and with the fact that Nantucket's money was exactly as advertised in weight and fineness of precious metal. Tab-sa-Dayyan smiled broadly as he let some of the dime-sized silver coins trickle into his palm. It was more than enough to pay the groom's share of the marriage-feast, considerably more.

"I see that my prospective nephew-in-law is a man of substance, a man of honorable means," he said. "Indeed, it would be a sad thing if my brother Mutu-Hadki's seed were to altogether vanish, or live only in his brother's sons. May you live many years, with many children—the bride-price is accepted."

"Good," the scribe said dryly, shaking the cloth back from his right arm and taking up his stylus. "My clay would be spoiled if we waited much longer."

His assistant took out a board with a slab of wet clay on it, its surface kept damp by a sodden cloth. He held the board up, turning it deftly as the scribe wrote with a wedge-headed bronze stylus. When the writing was done the scribe ran his seal across the bottom as witness and handed it to Tab-sa-Dayyan; the Akkadian merchant did the same, and handed it to Justin Clemens, who nearly dropped it. Then he fumbled in a pocket and brought out the seal he had commissioned for the occasion, a winged staff with a snake twined about it, the same as the branch-of-service flash on the shoulder of his khaki uniform.

"This is a duly executed contract," the scribe said. "My apprentice will make a copy—" The skinny youth had already formed a new tablet of clay and was writing with fluid speed, using a cheaper stylus of cut reed. "Yes. Here, we will seal this as well. Compare them, that you may swear each is identical."

Clemens could no more have read Akkadian cuneiform than he could have flown to the moon, but he examined the chicken-track patterns of wedge-shaped marks gravely. One of the few advantages of clay tablets was that they couldn't be altered after they dried; they made perfect legal documents.

"The contract is good," he said, echoed by Tab-sa-Dayyan. "I swear so, by the lives of the Gods Shamash and Marduk and Ishtar . . .

"—and Jesus," Clemens added on impulse.

"—and by the life of the King."

Then the Nantucketer took the tablet of Azzu-ena's dowry and tucked it into the haversack attached to his webbing belt, wrapped in cloth beside his copy of the marriage contract. He turned to Azzu-ena, lifted the shawl from her shoulders, draped it over her hair, then took her hand between his.

"I will fill your lap with silver and gold. You are my wife. I am your husband."

She blinked back tears; even then he was astonished, a little. He'd seen her calm while they were doing triage sorting, with an occasional stray rocket-bomb landing near the hospital tent. Her voice was steady as she replied:

"I will do you good and not evil all your days. I am your wife. You are my husband."

The witnesses cheered. The scribe nodded and quoted, this time from memory:

"If a man hold a feast and make a contract with her father and mother—or other kin, in this case—and take her, she is a wife." He smiled benignly. "So is the law laid down, from the days before the Flood. He is her husband. She is his wife."

The skipper of the *Merrimac* had guessed what was intended for his ship from the cargo delivered to her in Westhaven, the armor and steam engine and cannon. He was part-owner—about a one-sixteenth share—but from his expression it would take more than compensation money from the government to make up for what was going to happen to her. The coal smoke from the side-wheeler tug towing them out into the Severn estuary was no blacker than his mood, and the mournful steam whistle no gloomier than his tone.

"I hope you didn't pick her because of her name," he said to Marian Alston, after he'd introduced his first and second mates—son-in-law and nephew respectively. Formally, they were Reserve Lieutenants Stendin and Clammp, now that the ship and crew had been called up for military service.

"No, it wasn't the name," she said, feeling a sympathy that it would be patronizing to show. "If anything, the reverse." At his look she went on: "Macy consulted with us on the design for this class."

Historic marine architecture had been a hobby of hers before the Event; afterward it was useful in the extreme. Nantucket had also held plenty of documentation, plus experienced boat-builders whose skills could be scaled up with a little experimentation—and a few embarrassing, expensive failures. The craft that followed the fuming steam tug away from the squared-log piers of Westhaven's harbor, under the guns of Fort Pentagon, was the latest fruit of that ongoing collaboration. Alston's eye swept her long sleek lines with a pleasure that held more than a tinge of sadness, knowing her fate.

Only a single voyage across the Atlantic for you, poor bitch, she thought; the slight working of the hull against the tug's pull seemed to bespeak an eagerness to be away.

The design wasn't quite as sleek as the Guard's frigates; it was still long and lean, a smooth curve two hundred and forty feet from rounded stern to hollow-cheeked knife bows and long bowsprit, forty foot in the beam amidships, with three towering masts square-rigged save for the jibs, staysails, and a gaff mizzen. The long sweep of the ninety-foot poop was unbroken except for a low deckhouse before the wheels. In the waist were four cannon on a side, eighteen-pounders sold as surplus by the Guard when Leaton started delivering his cast-steel Dalghrens, just the sort of thing for convincing a Bronze Age chief not to try ripping off the foreign merchants. The hold was twenty feet deep.

You can go anywhere with a ship like this, she thought. Anywhere, with over a thousand tons of cargo—the *Merrimac* displaced fourteen hundred tons—and fast, as well. Four hundred miles a day with a strong following wind, and careful design had made her an economical ship. Twenty-five hands could sail her 'round the world, or fight her if some local Big Man in an outrigger canoe decided to get unpleasant, or repair any but the most extreme damage anywhere there was wood and a quiet cove.

And I feel like a murderer, knowing what they're going to do to her. Her mouth quirked in an expression that was half bitterness; sending beautiful youngsters into harm's way wasn't anything new, at least.

"Carry on, then, Mr. Clammp," she said, feeling the swell of the river mouth giving way to the harder chop of the Bristol Channel.

"Aye aye, Commodore," he said. "We'll be joining the Fleet in Portsmouth Water before the end of the week.

He turned to the rail. "Prepare to cast off," he said quietly. Then, louder: "Lay aloft and loose all sail!"

"John Iraiinanasson," the *rahax* of the Iraiina said in English, extending his hand. "An honor, Commodore Alston-Kurlelo. Lieutenant Commander Kurlelo-Alston."

"The Republic thanks you for your people's cooperation," Alston said politely, taking the hand. It was strong but soft against the sword-callus on hers, the nails neatly trimmed and clean.

Inwardly, she blinked a little. The mannerly smooth-shaven young man with his spectacles, brown crew-cut hair, pants and jacket, laced shoes and tiny silver crucifix on a chain around his neck, faint smell of soap . . . *is Daurthunnicar's great-nephew,* she remembered. A boy of eight or so when *Eagle* had arrived in Alba, right after the Event, and "guest"—hostage—in Nantucket Town for three years after that.

Invaders from the mainland only a year before the Event, the Iraiina had lost most of their land except for a patch around the Base in the post-war settlement. They'd put the advice of their mentors to enthusiastic use, though.

Now the land outside the five-sided fort that guarded Portsmouth Base was a checkerboard of neat fields colored straw-yellow, furrow-brown, pasture-green. They were divided by good graveled roads and surrounded by hedges, well-tended woodlots, houses of white-painted frame and plank or dark brick, and red hip-roofed barns. They centered on a thriving hamlet built in New England style, steepled church and four-square Meetinghouse and school around a green, houses set among gardens beside a grid of streets, workshops and warehouses under the gates of the Base and down by the docks.

In fact, the shrunken *teuatha* of the Noble Ones had become the most eager of all the Sun People tribes to learn the new ways. They'd converted *en masse* to the Ecumenical Christianity—not being pleased with how their own Gods had treated them—and in recent years had produced a number of home-grown priests and missionaries for the Church, often of a terrifying earnestness. The Iraiina had contributed more than their share of recruits for the Guard and crewfolk for Nantucketer vessels, too, and many did stints as temporary workers back on the Island. According to the Intelligence reports they'd even taken to holding Town Meetings, conducted in English with clerks of their own writing down the minutes and women allowed to vote. Perhaps the thoroughness of their defeat had helped. The Iraiina had lost most of their fighting-men during the Alban War; they'd been Walker's first followers here when he arrived in the autumn of the Year 1, and suffered cruelly for it. A fair number of the survivors had fled with Walker and his Tartessian ally after the Battle of the Downs, and some of the remainder had ended up in Nantucket, children particularly. A leaven of those had returned to settle here after years in the Republic, like yeast in bread.

Slightly to Marian's surprise, Swindapa willingly shook the young chief's hand. Only someone who knew her well could have detected the chilly edge to her smile.

"That was good of you," Marian said softly, when they'd walked past the local welcoming party and were among the uniformed Islanders beyond.

"No, it wasn't. It was cruel," Swindapa said.

Marian made an interrogative sound, and the Fiernan continued: "The men who hurt me are dead; how could hurting their children soothe my heart? But in a generation or two the Iraiina will be gone, as if they had never been—they'll be Eagle People—and they will have done it to themselves. I am *well* avenged."

There are always new depths to you, Alston thought, shaking her head slightly, then turning to look out over the base.

The tented camps were mostly down now, and there were a good thirty sail riding at anchor in Portsmouth Base's harbor. Five of them were major warships, *Lincoln*-class clipper frigates, just under a thousand tons, with twenty-four eight-inch Dalghrens each, and half a dozen smaller armed schooners. They rode at anchor in deeper water, decks shining and sails furled, the diagonal red slash and fouled-anchor symbol of the Coast Guard bright on their sea-gray sides. Beside them was the *Farragut,* the newest addition to the Republic's fleet. It was slightly smaller than the frigates, lower-slung, also with three masts but with a long slender smokestack forward of the mainmast. On either side were boxes for the paddle wheels, armored to the front by wedge-shaped timber frames sheathed in bolted steel plates, and more of the same on her ax-shaped bows; her armament consisted of two four-inch rifled cannon at bow and stern, mounted with pivots to the rear and wheels forward run-

ning on circular steel tracks set into the deck. That let them
be turned rapidly in any direction.

Good ship to have in a fight. It was a pity that she sailed like
a pig of cast iron, but you couldn't expect every design to
work perfectly the first time, the more so as this was something
genuinely new, not working to a pre-Event historical model.

The rest of the fleet were civilian ships mobilized for the
war, or hired transports for hauling troops and equipment. The
Marines had gone aboard the troopships in neat files, packs on
their backs and rifles slung, gear boxed to be swung from dock
to hold. Embarking the native irregulars was something else
again.

Marian Alston-Kurlelo clasped her hands behind her back
and rose slightly on the balls of her feet. Southampton Base
was nearly as old as Westhaven; this was near where the *Eagle*
had landed on that first trip to Alba, better than ten years ago
now. Her head turned right, northward, remembering that day.
That had been early spring, cold and windy like this, but sunny
rather than overcast. She'd been heading into the beginnings
of a war then, too, only she hadn't known it. Her eyes sought
a tall fair head among the throngs along the brick-paved waterside; Swindapa was holding a checklist, issuing curt orders to
several chiefs. One of them bridled, a backwoodsman from the
northeast by the look of his pyrographed leather kilt and forked
beard. A comrade grabbed his arm, whispered urgently, led
him aside. The rest of them nodded and scattered to obey.

Marian allowed herself a quirk of the lips, remembering how
the chief of the Iraiina hadn't even realized she was a woman,
back when the *Eagle* made its first trip up the Southampton
Water. She remembered the chaos of the Iraiina camp she'd
found, as well. The noisy sprawl of pushing and shoving around
the docks here was order itself compared to that, although it
was loud enough to scare flocks of wildfowl from the marshes
across the harbor, where Gosport would have been in the other
history. Even the Sun People could learn . . .

She watched one war band filing up a gangplank in excellent
order, the tough wood bending a little under their feet, the
sideropes moving under their hands and prompting uneasy
glances downward—few of that breed were seamen yet. They
were in no uniform, but most of them wore trousers, jacket,
and boots of Islander inspiration. The webbing harness, packs,
and bayonets *were* Nantucket-made, and so were the Werder
rifles slung reverently over their shoulders—the bandoliers were
going to stay empty until they arrived at their destination, of

course. Most of them had long tomahawks thrust through the straps of their knapsacks, a few still bronze-headed. Their leader might almost have been an Islander himself, though, a young man with cropped hair, clipped mustache, shaven chin, polished boots, a new Python revolver at his waist. And a list in his hand, from which he was obviously reading. . . .

Hmmm. On the other hand, not all progress is unambiguously positive. Not every Sun People warrior who enlisted in Guard or Marines took citizenship and stayed in the Republic after his hitch was up. Those who came back to Alba and their tribes brought their knowledge with them; many of them were the sons of chiefs, and all of them became influential men, with the skills and prestige and gold they'd earned.

Nothing like getting the hell beaten out of you to provide an incentive for learning, she thought uneasily. The Fiernan Bohulugi were genuine allies; the Sun People were that in theory, and a resentful protectorate in fact.

Teaching a barbarian can make him civilized . . . or just a more dangerous savage. You did what you had to do in the short run, but the long-term worries were killers.

CHAPTER EIGHT

September, 10 A.E.—Babylon, Kingdom of
  Kar-Duniash
September, 10 A.E.—O'Rourke's Ford, east of Troy
September, 10 A.E.—Babylon, Kingdom of
  Kar-Duniash
September, 10 A.E.—O'Rourke's Ford, east of Troy
September, 10 A.E.—Babylon, Kingdom of
  Kar-Duniash
September, 10 A.E.—Walkeropolis, Kingdom of Great
  Achaea
September, 10 A.E.—Babylon, Kingdom of
  Kar-Duniash

"**O**h Lord King, your armies are victorious!" the officer of the New Troops said, rising from his prostration and snapping off a salute he'd learned from his Nantucketer instructors.

Kashtiliash leaned back in the chair of state, elbow on the arm of the chair and jaw resting on thumb and forefinger. The officer was dressed in something similar to the Nantucketer uniform as well, boots and breeches and loose jacket with many pockets, with webbing harness of coarse double-ply canvas. He'd added an ostrich plume to the front of the cloth-covered steel helmet, though; Kashtiliash decided to check to see that nobody was wearing them thus in the field. It had been hard for him to grasp that firearms made it essential for soldiers to skulk like hunters or bandits. It would not do for them to acquire bad habits that would turn lethal when they met enemies armed likewise.

"You drove the Aramaeans before you?" Kashtiliash asked skeptically. *That* wasn't particularly difficult.

Even without firearms, it was seldom a problem to *beat* the Aramaeans . . . if they would stand and fight, which they almost never did unless they vastly outnumbered the force sent against them. Aiming a blow at the sand thieves was like driving a chariot wheel through a mud puddle; the contents spattered and flew apart in tiny globules, then ran together again and all was unchanged. So the nomads were, striking at defenseless peasant hamlets or the donkey-caravans of merchants, then fading back into the endless wastes to the west. Sometimes a King could frighten them into meekness by occupying water holes, or going after their women and sheep, but even that was difficult. Every year they grew bolder and more numerous. Villages had been abandoned in the areas most subject to their raids, and canals left to silt. Yet if the edge of cultivation moved back, then the herdsmen took those fields over and districts further east became exposed to raids.

The chronicles said the Amorites had come likewise from the western deserts long ago, and ended by ruling all the Land—Hammurabi had been of that blood. His own ancestors had been herdsmen from the other quarter, in the mountains to the eastward. The Aramaeans were only a minor nuisance so far, but a great sandstorm began with a single gust of wind.

Thus had he sent a unit of his elite, the New Troops armed and trained by the Nantukhtar, against them.

"No, King of the Universe! We did not merely chase them, we *slaughtered* them. We killed over a thousand; I have the ears in sacks, O Viceregent of Marduk. A thousand strong warriors alone; and we took over three thousand prisoners, mostly women and children, and ten thousand sheep and goats, hundreds of donkeys. The *Subartu*-tribe of Bit-Yakin will never again trouble the Land, for it has ceased to be—its flocks and its herds, its tents and its clans and its *nasiku*-sheiks."

"How?" Kashtiliash asked. "I wouldn't have thought they would stay to face our new fire-weapons."

"It was the camels, King of the Four Quarters of the Universe. The beasts are possessed of devils, but they can *travel* like devils. We went three days from water—"

"Here, show me," Kashtiliash said eagerly. There were times when he felt trapped here in the palace, but the King could not take the field for a minor punitive expedition, as a prince of the House of Succession might.

The small audience room had changed somewhat since the Nantukhtar came. The throne was the same, but one wall had been stripped of tapestries and murals and whitewashed. On it was drawn a map of the Land, as the Gods might see it. The officer took up an olive-wood pointer.

"We swung out into the deep desert—as Lord Kenn'et of

the Nantukhtar did against the Assyrians, when he pursued
them north last year. I bethought myself of that, and took the
two hundred men trained to ride the demon-beasts. While the
others came in on foot from the east, and the Aramaeans retreated before them. Even the nomads do not go so far into
the sands. They were taken wholly by surprise, between the
hammer and the anvil—and we could pursue their bands faster
than they scattered."

Kashtiliash nodded thoughtfully. The camels came from the
desert peninsula to the southwest of the Land Between the
Rivers, brought north by *Nantukhtar* ships. The southernmost
nomads had begun to use them, these last few generations, but
they knew little of saddling and harnessing them as yet, and
the northerly Aramaean tribes didn't use them at all, traveling
on foot with their possessions on donkey-back. A donkey had
to be watered every day, and could carry barely more than a
man, and no more quickly. A camel could travel up to a week
without water, eat anything that grew, carry three times the
weight of a grown man, and cover many times the ground men
or horses could. Kat'ryn had told him of how that would change
this part of the world, in the centuries to come. In her histories,
it had benefited mostly the sand-thieves themselves, the ones
who came after the Aramaeans—the Arabs, they were called,
still hundreds upon hundreds of miles to the south, in this age.

That shall not be so, here, he thought.

He had grasped whence the Nantukhtar really came, their
island adrift on the oceans of eternity. Few others in this age
could, he thought, even shrewd men, learned men. The Nantukhtar hadn't made any particular secret of it, but most dismissed
the thought with a shudder as merely more of the eldritch air
of magic that surrounded the strangers.

*But I am lucky in that my mind is supple. Perhaps because I
am young yet. It is a mighty thing, a fate laid on us all by the
great Gods, whether for good or ill.*

Aloud: "You have done well, and I say unto you well done;
the King's heart is pleased with you, Awil-Sin. Nor shall you
and your men be without reward."

Awil-Sin prostrated himself again, then bowed backward out
of the audience chamber past the motionless Royal Guards—
standing to attention was another art which the Nantukhtar had
brought. Kashtiliash glanced aside at Kidin-Ninurta, formerly
his father's chief superintendant of matters dealing with Dilmun
and Meluhha, now in charge of dealings with the Nantukhtar.
And in their pay, of course, but his ultimate loyalty was to the

kingdom. Beside him sat Bahdi-Lim, the *wakil* of the *karum*, the king's overseer of trade.

"You hear?" he said.

"I hear, O King who is without rival. Shall the prisoners be sold?"

"Mmmm, no," Kashtiliash said. For one thing, his allies would object, starting with his wife. "We shall settle them on the Elamite frontier—on the new lands watered by the canal cut by the *steam-dredges*. Well mixed with prisoners from the Assyrian war and with our own people. I have some men it is in my mind to favor with *kudurru*-grants; Awil-Sin, for one."

The two officials nodded. Land, even land next to an irrigation canal, was valueless without tenant-farmers to work it.

Kidin-Ninurta went on thoughtfully. "These camels could be of much use to us."

"Indeed. Bahdi-Lim, see that we acquire more—as many as the southern tribes will sell; inquire among the merchants who deal in Dilmun and send agents there. See that more men are trained in their handling, and see that a breeding program is put in hand." The King owned vast estates, many of them dedicated to the breeding of horses for the royal chariot corps; camels couldn't be impossibly different.

Kidin-Ninurta bowed over folded hands; he was a plump man in his middle years, beard shining with the oil of prosperity. "And when there are enough, our merchants will be greatly aided, thus bringing more wealth to the Throne. With strings of camels rather than donkeys, they could cross the wastes bearing greater loads at lower costs. Yet another thing from which we may draw wealth!"

"Yes . . . speak your thoughts, both of you."

The two bureaucrats were bubbling over with schemes to take the New Learning and make the Land rich, not to mention themselves. Kashtiliash didn't mind that; if you used oxen to tread out grain, they took an occasional mouthful. If he was to build a new standing army equipped with fire-weapons, with rifles and cannon, he would need much wealth. Even more, if he was to lift his kingdom to equality with the Nantukhtar. That would be a work of generations, though.

"It is good, and more than good," he said at last. "You will prepare a list of these projects, from the least difficult to the most, with the costs and difficulties of each. This you will bring before me, and soon. You have the King's leave to go."

His next audience would be less pleasant. He looked at his

watch, also a gift from his queen's people. The flying ship would be here late in the day. Perhaps tomorrow morning . . .

"I wish we were on higher ground," O'Rourke murmured, as the first of the enemy came into sight far down the road. *They're not wasting time; twenty-four hours after I got here.* "Or that things were more open here."

"If we were on higher ground, we wouldn't have water," Barnes replied.

The alarm had caught her washing off under the pump, and she'd come running with towel in hand; Hantilis kept sliding his eyes toward her and then away until an orderly came up with her uniform. Some corner of O'Rourke's mind not preoccupied with matters professional smiled amusement. Functional needs and Fiernan influence had more or less killed the nudity taboo in the Republic, most particularly in the military, but it always caused at least some friction when they ran into cultures that did have that sort of prohibition. He suspected that Hantilis's subconscious hadn't been registering Barnes and the others as really female in his brief exposure to the Nantucketer military, and was disconcerted when the visual evidence was unmistakable.

"Bugler, sound *stand to,*" Barnes said, buttoning her tunic and swinging on the Sam Browne harness that held pistol, sword, and belt pouches.

The clear sweet notes of the bugle sounded; few of the garrison had far to travel. Most of them had already taken up the rifles that had rested in neat tripods overnight and dashed to their posts on the walls. Others trotted out of the sunken bunker that held the explosives, each pair carrying an ammunition box by the rope handles on each end. They plumped the boxes down at intervals along the fighting platform, then used their bayonets to pry open the lids with a screech of nails.

Each lid had a label burned into its surface: *Werder .40 1000 rounds.* Within the ammunition lay in ten-round packets. The Marines on the fighting platform around the wall buckled back the covers of the bandoliers that hung from their webbing belts, revealing the neat brass rows of shells in the loops within. Barnes looked over at him, and he nodded with a slight jerk of his chin.

"Company—" she called, in a high carrying voice.

"Platoon—" It echoed through the subordinate commanders. "Squad—"

"Fix—"

"Fix—"

"Bayonets!"

There was a long slithering rasp and rattle and click as the twenty-inch blades came free and locked to the ring-and-bar fasteners under the muzzles of the rifles. One fumbled and dropped the weapon halfway through the procedure, and caught a hissed *"Sharpen up, you sloppy excuse for a Marine!"* from his corporal.

"Load!"

The same relay, and another series of clicks as the grooved breech-blocks were pushed down, a round was shoved into the breech, and the arming-piece in its curved slot at the right side of the weapon was thumbed back to full cock. A murmur, as the noncoms repeated: *"Eyes front. Set your sights at two hundred yards. Wait for the command."*

O'Rourke glanced around. *Ready for the dance,* he thought. Rifles to the walls, the Gatling between the two overturned wagons that made up the gate—that faced roughly southwest, covering the largest area of open ground. Far too many stone walls, olive groves, and shallow ravines round about otherwise, and the steep hills that pinched the valley were far too close, but that was God's lookout. Speaking of which:

"Praise be the Lord God who trains my fingers to the bow and makes my hand strong to war—"

Chaplain Smith was at it again, not a bad text. Even if the man *was* an Iraiina convert and therefore a bit of a fanatic, with a taste for the bloodier Psalms.

The enemy were coming up the road and through the fields to either side; far too many of them for comfort. O'Rourke licked sweat off his lips and took a thoughtful swig from his canteen before picking up the binoculars he'd laid on a barley sack.

Couple of thousand, at least, he thought. *Five thousand if we're unlucky. Two, three days travel from the coast—they might be able to keep them supplied, at that. But I don't think they've got the patience for a siege of the camp.*

They obviously weren't Walker's regulars; just irregular clots of footmen following chiefs in chariots. A few mounted scouts came galloping closer; and the glitter off the weapons of the host was as much steel as bronze. Presumably some of them would have learned a bit about modern warfare at Troy. . . .

The noise started again, like a giant drum, or the chuffing of a monstrous steam engine. This time he could see what it was, thousands of them beating the flats of their weapons on their shields in ragged unison. The sound boomed back from the rocky slopes on either hand as well. . . .

"Oh, for a couple of rifled cannon," Barnes said.

"Or a heavy mortar, or some rocket launchers," O'Rourke agreed.

That was a distance problem, though. Ur Base's armory down at the top of the Persian Gulf could make small-arms ammunition and some replacement parts for rifles. Every single heavy weapon and every round for them had to come by ship from Nantucket or Alba, down the Atlantic, around the Cape of Good Hope, up across the Indian Ocean, up the Gulf, unload at Ur Base, go up the Euphrates by steamboat and barge, then hundreds of miles more to the Anatolian plateau and westward to here by wagon and camel and pack mule.

Great Achaea, now . . . their factories weren't as many or as good, but being ten thousand miles closer covered a multitude of sins. Better to have a second-rate weapon that was here, rather than a first-rate one that hadn't arrived yet because the ship bringing it was becalmed in the doldrums.

The sound died out and the enemy began to spread; the nobles were getting out of their chariots, too. *Too bad. I wish they were more conservative about that.* Most of the men squatted or sat, leaning on spears or rifles. Horns blared, long upright bronze trumpets with the mouths of wild beasts, grouped around a knot of men in bright gear: gilded bronze armor, helmets topped with boars and wolves and ravens, chain mail and steel swords, guns. The knot eddied, then moved southward and up the slopes of a fairly steep hill, threading their way through terraced vineyards to the clear rocky summit. O'Rourke moved his binoculars and found himself staring at the doll-tiny figure of a man in a raven-crested helmet with long gray mustaches putting an even longer brass spyglass to his eye and looking right back at the Nantucketer. Great minds thought alike . . .

"Hmmm . . . I think the laddie with the bandaged arm beside him is the gentleman with the spear I had a bit of a brush with yesterday," O'Rourke said lightly.

The chief with the spyglass took it down from his eye and waved. Spears repeated the gesture down the hillslope, and a band of warriors five hundred strong rose and moved forward. They weren't moving in ranks, but there was an unpleasant steadiness to the way they came forward, flowing into dead ground, the shelter of groves or walls, up a long gully that sheltered everything but the tips of their spears.

"This bunch won't be spooked the first time they see guns go off," Barnes said thoughtfully. "Mother."

"This won't be the first time," O'Rourke said. "We managed to get a fair number of firearms into Troy, one way and another, and these lads have been on the receiving end."

Hantilis nodded. "I, too, was put in fear, the first time I saw the fire-weapons work their slaying," he said. "After that, I saw also that the men they killed were no more dead than those fallen to a bow or spear. Guns are better than any spear or bow, yes. They kill further, faster, more surely, yes. Still, these guns are not the thunder-club borne by Teshub of the Weather. They are only weapons. And a man with a knife or even a rock from the fields may slay a man with sword, spear, and armor, if he be brave and very lucky. A score of men with knives or rocks against *one* with a sword . . ."

Barnes and O'Rourke glanced at each other and nodded very slightly. You didn't have to have a modern education to be able to put two and two together, if the native cleverness was there.

The Hittite confirmed their thought a moment later: "That little ravine—it is a highway toward us. Only a little more than long bowshot, and the . . . Gatling . . . does not bear on it . . ."

Damn, I do wish we had a mortar, O'Rourke thought. Dropping shells right into dead ground like that was what they were made for. Then: *If wishes were horses, we wouldn't need the Town Meeting to produce horseshit, would we, then?*

"Here they come!" someone shouted from the walls.

"People can get used to anything," Kathryn Hollard said, looking down from one of the slanting windows in the airship's passenger compartment.

They'd come down the Euphrates, endless miles of irrigation canals lined with date palms, long narrow fields—about half of them flooded to soften the earth for the fall plowing, half fallow—and villages of dun mud-brick shacks. Now the shadow of the *Emancipator* passed over Babylon, slipping over square miles of flat roofs and courtyards and narrow twisty streets, cut here and there by the broader processional ways.

The sight of the dirigible overhead no longer made men scream in Babylon, or women cast themselves down in prayer. Even the donkeys had stopped bolting. Usually the craft came into a field by the river outside the northern wall; the engineers of the expeditionary force had put in basic support facilities, tanks of fuel—the engines burned a mixture of kerosene and hydrogen from the gasbag—a small steam-powered generator to crack lifting gas from water, stores of spare parts. Today the airship was coming into land at the square that surrounded the great ziggurat *Etemenanki,* the House That Is the Foundation of Heaven and Earth, near the northern gate of the city. That was the only open space in Babylon that could accommodate the *Emancipator*'s more than five hundred feet of length; it was also convenient to the main palace–administrative complex just inside the Ishtar Gate.

"Kash is not happy at all, and this is one way of showing it," Kathryn went on.

"I'm not happy either," her brother replied. "To put it mildly."

"I'm not happy—the thermals here are a stone bitch," Vicki Cofflin said.

They all glared for a second at the Princess Raupasha. That young woman folded her arms and glared back. Seventeen going on eighteen, she was tall by contemporary standards, which made her average among Americans born in the twentieth; the Marine khakis she wore showed smooth curves. Fine raven-dark hair fell to her shoulders, framing an oval straight-nosed face and dark gray eyes rimmed with green; her skin was a natural pale olive tanned to honey-brown. It wasn't quite the physical type common in Kar-Duniash, but she had been born further north, under the Taurus range, in what would be Kurdish country in the twentieth. Some of her ancestors had come from much further than that, outflung spindrift of a migration that had begun in the foothills of the Ural Mountains a thousand years before. The main stream of it had driven their chariots and horse-herds over the Hindu Kush and down into the Land of Five Rivers, where her distant Aryan cousins were compiling the *Rig-Veda* in these very decades. Raupasha's ancestors had drifted westward, to become kings at the headwaters of the Khabur and lose themselves among their Hurrian subjects.

"I did wrong," she said, in English thickly accented with the clotted sounds of her Hurrian mother tongue. "It—" For a moment a flicker of uncertainty made her seem her age. "It seemed like a good idea at the time. You had told me, Lord Kenn'et, that in your country women often take the lead in such things . . ."

"Not without warning, not in public, not in front of an army, not in a language the man doesn't speak so it looks like he's *agreeing* with it, and not when it buggers up years of work!" Kenneth Hollard barked.

My, what an interesting shade of red you turn when you're angry, big brother, Kathryn thought irreverently. She and her brother both tanned fairly well for blonds, but she could see the dark blood rising over his collar.

"I did wrong," Raupasha said again, quietly. Tears welled in the great gray eyes, but she blinked them away. "I have wronged you, to whom I owe so much. Let King Kashtiliash have my head, then, to appease the anger of his heart and bring his favor back to you."

Kenneth Hollard sighed in exasperation. His sister answered for him: "No, we won't do that. You're under the Republic's protection, and we don't withdraw that. But that's protection for *you,* as an individual, not for your people or their former kingdom. You may have to leave these lands altogether."

"And we all have to strap in," Vicki Cofflin said. "Sir, ma'am, we're coming in for a landing."

Everyone sat, in a stony silence. Kathryn Hollard swallowed a bubble of anxiety. *God, I want to see Kash again. God, I'm nervous.*

Neither of them was exactly afraid of the other but they'd both found occasion enough for irritation, differences of custom and outlook and belief that made a word or action sweet reasonableness to one and intolerable to the other. And neither of them was meek by nature.

I suppose we'd both find sweetness-and-light boring; that's probably one reason why Kash fell for me in the first place, the change from all these I-am-your-handmaiden-great-lord-please-wipe-your-feet-on-me local bimbos. This time he's got every reason to be furious with the lot of us, though.

The marriage contract specified she could leave anytime she wanted to. *The problem is, I* don't *want to.*

"Prepare for landing," Vicki Cofflin said. "Alex, I'm going to take her in heavy, on prop-lift. Landing crew ready on the ground?"

The XO was peering through heavy pintle-mounted binoculars. "Looks like it, Skipper . . . there's the signal."

"Helm, right thirty. Engines, all ahead one quarter."

The long orca shape of the *Emancipator* turned into the wind blowing out of the deserts to the west. "Altitude one thousand thirty. Off superheat!"

A hissing in the background cut off, only noticeable when it was gone. The shadow of the airship passed over the flat rooftops of Babylon, a maze of tenement and courtyard, dun-colored mud-and-timber roofs above adobe buildings. The monstrous step-pyramid shape of the ziggurat loomed ahead of them, its cladding of colored brick, glazing, and paint a blaze three hundred feet high, an artificial mountain looming against the westering sun.

"Vent hot air! All vents full."

Crewfolk spun cranks. High above, rectangular portlids in the hull swung up, allowing the heated air in the central gasbag to escape. The airship's smooth gliding passage shifted to a downward vector, and the ground swelled below them. The nose of the great craft dipped, and the uppermost level of the ziggurat *Etemenanki* rose above the gondola windows, gleaming in gold leaf. That was the House of the God, where the priestess called the Bride of Marduk awaited the pleasure of the Lord of the Countries.

"Negative buoyancy! Ship is heavy!" came the crisp call from the altitude controller. "Seven hundred pounds at ground level."

"Ballast, stand by," Vicki said. They could vent water from tanks along the keel at need and come around again. "Engines at ninety degrees."

Hands spun wheels, and outside the six converted Cessna engines on the sections of wing turned until their propellers were pointing at the ground. They were nearly over the courtyard now, coasting slower and slower as the gentle west wind pushed at the blunt prow of the vessel. Dust billowed up, and the robes of the spectators fluttered. The ground crew were from the First Kar-Duniash, the cadre unit Kathryn and a few other Islander officers and noncoms had trained as part of the alliance between the Republic and Babylon. They'd played this part before.

Emancipator's descent slowed. "Release ropes!"

Crewfolk opened ports along the keel. Dozens of ropes fell loose, to be snatched up by the soldiers acting as ground crew. They broke into teams as if for a tug-of-war, and pulled.

"All engines off!" Silence roared into the great vessel, the first since the motors were started in Hattusas twelve hours before. "Brace for contact."

The ground swelled beneath them, and a wailing chant went up as three hundred men hauled the dirigible down hand over hand and into the wind. More waited, and grabbed the oak railing that ran along the gondola on either side of the keel as it came within reach. Those ran the airship forward until it was aligned with massive forged eyebolts whose six-foot shanks had been pounded into the brick pavement of the square. Lashings secured the *Emancipator* in place; this was as safe a mooring site as any, with the bulk of the ziggurat and the enclosure walls to break any sudden winds.

"Feather props all," Vicki Cofflin said. "Ramp down! Brigadier Hollard, Lieutenant-Colonel, Princess Raupasha, you may disembark."

The main entryway to the gondola was a ramp at the rear of the hundred-foot room. It lowered with a creak of wicker and wood. A chariot stood there, the horses sweating and rolling their eyes as they shifted from hoof to hoof with a clatter of iron against brick. Around it waited mounted guards, riding with saddles and stirrups of Islander pattern, rifles in scabbards at their right knees.

"The King awaits the *Seg Kallui*," their officer said, dismounting and saluting, then going to one knee.

Kathryn nodded. "The queen hears the words of the King," she said.

"So, bet you I can make five pat hands from half a deck," Private Hook said, shuffling easily.

They might be under attack at any minute; that was no reason not to pick up a little extra cash. The best time for it, in fact, with people nervous and wrought-up. The cards poured from side to side temptingly on the gray blanket of the hospital bunk, but there wasn't time to start a poker game.

"Twenty-five cards, no more."

"By the Horned Man, I think you can do it too—with your deck," someone said sardonically.

"No, no," Hook said smoothly. "With *your* deck, and you get to shuffle."

"*Aw,* and you'll fly to the moon by flapping your arms," a Marine said.

Several who'd been recruited from the Earth Folk hissed at the blasphemy, which the scoffer answered with a jerk of his middle finger. Hook frowned carefully.

"Well, if you're not afraid of bad luck after dissing Moon Woman like that, why not put some money on it?" he asked. "Say, five dollars at five-to-one in your favor."

"I'll do that," the other man said brashly. "If you don't need beer and girls when we get back to Hattusas, I do."

"And *you'll* never get laid without paying a local for it, Haudicar," a female voice said.

The challenger scowled and pulled a Pacific Bank five-dollar note out of his pocket; that took a little work, with his right arm in a cast. Then he went over to his haversack and fished out a pack of cards. Hook waited patiently while the mark shuffled; the Fiernan woman who'd spoken caught his eye and winked behind the victim's back, moving her fingers and lips silently in the Counting Chant.

"Put up your twenty-five, Hook. Better than three weeks' pay, a gift from the Gods."

A belligerent blue-eyed stare from Haudicar, as innocent of mathematics as he was of molecular biology. Hook took the greasy, limp pack and set it on the gray blanket that covered the foot of his bunk, then split it evenly. A fair selection who were mobile enough gathered around; not many went two months in the pungent gloom of a troopship's hold outbound from Nantucket Town without learning poker.

"Which one?" he said, and the mark tapped the pile of cards on his left.

"Here we go—"

Haudicar stared as the five pat hands flowed out beneath Hook's nimble features. The onlookers yelped and hooted laughter, and a slow flush went up from the collar of his T-shirt to prominent pink ears.

"Care to try again, double or nothing?" Hook said casually, scooping up the five-dollar bill. He winked back at the Fiernan girl; he usually didn't need to pay a local when he wanted a tumble—stupid to pay, when charm could get you better sex for free—but even in the Corps it never hurt to set the mood with some beer and fancy eats on the civilian economy. With two men for every woman in most units, the competition could get a little fierce at times. Besides that, he was saving for the end of his hitch. Haudicar swore and pulled out another five-dollar bill.

"Anyone else want to go with the odds?" Hook said brightly.

A few bystanders did, but one insisted on using *her* pack, and dealing out twenty-five cards at random. Hook grinned like a shark as he arranged another five hands, ignoring the curses and stacking the bills and coins.

"Now, who'll match this pile one last time?" he said.

It looked as if Haudicar would, until he looked around and saw that all the Fiernan-born in the room were standing back, most of them grinning. Then he made the sign of the horns.

"Magic!" he spat.

The girl who'd winked at Hook laughed aloud. "Arithmetic, you dumb swan-eating sheep-shagger," she said. "The odds were fifty to one in his favor!"

The roar of laughter that followed that was cut short when a corporal looked through the door.

"You lot are pretty healthy, then," he said. A working party behind him carried in rifles, bandoliers, and a thousand-round ammunition box. Several entrenching tools were piled rattling atop it. "Get busy—knock some more loopholes in the wall there, it's only mud brick two stacks thick."

Those not too ill to work got to work, except for Hook. "Nobody want one last bet?" he asked, riffling the cards.

"At a time like this?" someone said, digging at the wall with the pick-spike on the back of the blade of the entrenching tool.

"Why not? No loss if we lose, we'll all be dead . . . oh, all right then," Hook grumbled, and picked up a rifle, wincing a bit at the pull of his lanced boil as he went to the slit window. "Holy *shit!*"

"So," Kashtiliash said, shaking back the sleeve of his robe and holding out his cup. A servant slid forward silently and poured, each movement as graceful as a reed. "You will not plead your brother's case?"

"Nope," Kathryn Hollard said, reaching for a date. "He can do that himself. You're the King here, Kash, and he's the commander of *allied* forces. It'd be a good idea to hear him out, but you decide, and I'll back you up whatever your decision is. It's going on for God-damned November; it'll be the Year 11 before we get to Walker, if we keep dicking around with this stuff."

The Kassite's thick-muscled shoulders relaxed slightly as he sipped.

Kathryn gave him a slow smile, and went on: "Actually, I had a different sort of discussion in mind for this evening."

Her eyes traveled to the arched doorway that led into the bedchamber. Kashtiliash grinned back at her.

They were dining in one of the smaller chambers in the King's private rooms—or as private as anything could be, in this ant farm of a palace. One wall was carved cedar screenwork, giving out onto a section of flat roof that in turn overlooked a courtyard planted with palms and flowers. It was still warm but not uncomfortable, especially with the overhead fan that swept back and forth above, to the pull of a cord in the hand of someone sitting in the corridor outside—she'd gotten the idea from rereading a book of Kipling's short stories. A *punkah*, they'd called it in the days of the Raj.

She and the King reclined on couches of carved boxwood,

cushioned in something remarkably like Moroccan leather, and ate from a low table set between them with lion's-paw feet done in ivory, its oval Egyptian-ebony top inlaid with lapis, ivory, and semiprecious stones. The platters bore the remains of roast chicken, a dish of beef and lentils with apricots, skewers of grilled lamb, salads, breads, pastries, spiced steamed vegetables. The palace artisans had learned to produce creditable bronze-and-gold imitations of the plain metal fork in a Marine field kit, too, which made eating a lot less messy.

"Makes a nice change from tents and dog biscuit," she said, stretching and nibbling on the fruit.

They *had* been down to hardtack for a while, when the supply lines up from the navigable Euphrates got shaky. Not to mention the grit and dirt; nothing like a couple of weeks in the field in the deserts of Mitanni—northern Syria, in the twentieth—to really work up an appreciation for a good bath and a soft linen robe. Gentle music tweetled from a corner, vivid tapestries billowed slightly along the walls, curious beasts and flowers and scenes from myths she hadn't had time to learn; the ceiling was smooth plaster set with rosettes of burnished copper. The Islander kerosene lamps made the room brighter than it would have been a year ago, but the yellow light suited the room, turning it into a fantasy of soft color amid the scents of cedarwood and incense.

"A king's wealth is some small compensation for being nibbled to death by ducks," Kashtiliash said. "I would ten times rather be in the field with my troops myself." He extended his hands. "Yesterday the *ashipu*-diviners of Nabu said that my armpits should be plucked with tweezers because a two-headed lamb was born near Nippur."

Kathryn held out her hands likewise. Servants glided in, one to pour scented water, another to wipe her hands with a towel, a third to hold the basin beneath.

Still feels a little creepy having everything done for you like this, she thought with a corner of her mind.

The rest of it was sympathizing with Kashtiliash. His administrative duties were bad enough, but there was a whole clutch of religious stuff that only the King could deal with. Kash might be absolute monarch, but the priesthoods could still tie him in knots by selective omen-reading—ignore them and the whole kingdom from nobles to peasants would expect disaster, which was a self-fulfilling prophecy if there ever was one. The queen had equivalent tasks, but so far she'd been able to plead off on grounds of military necessity and a foreigner's ignorance.

*Once the war's over I'll have to settle down and plow my way
through this stuff, dammit. Oh, well, I can study up on the religious twaddle while I'm pregnant.*

When his hands were clean, Kashtiliash clapped them together. "Leave us," he said.

"But King of the Universe—!" a eunuch chamberlain
bleated, from where he'd been standing to direct the choreography of the meal.

Eunuchs still creeped her out more than a little, but she
ignored the plump shocked face. Usually the King's retiring
was an elaborate ritual, each undoing of sandal strap or sash a
jealously guarded privilege of some official or flunky or whatever; it all reminded her of things she'd read about the court
of Louis XIV, only with oracles and diviners mixed in. At least
upper-crust Babylonians washed a lot more frequently than
eighteenth-century Frenchmen.

"Leave us! The King speaks!" Kashtiliash said, not taking
his eyes off her.

Everyone prostrated themselves and backed out. The King's
grin grew wider. "Good," he said. "It has been much too long,
my golden lioness. It would shock them, did I vault over the
table and ravish you upon the supper couch."

"You couldn't," she said. "Because I'd meet you in midair."
She stood, reached down with crossed arms, and pulled the
robe over her head.

"Golden lioness indeed," Kashtiliash said, hoarse through a
throat gone tight.

"Let's see if you can catch me, Bull of Marduk." Kathryn
laughed.

"While I am at war, I leave the realm in the hands of Odikweos son of Laertes, *Wannax* of Ithaka among the Western
Isles and *ekwetos* in Mycenae."

Walker's voice rang out across the square. Odikweos went
to one knee and bowed his head before he held out his hand
for the signet ring that would make him Regent of Great
Achaea while the King of Men was abroad.

*And I am a much safer regent than any of your own Wolf
People,* he thought. *They will watch me and I will watch them.*

Then he walked beside his overlord down the marble steps
and waited while the King poured the incense into the coals
that smoldered in the bowl of the golden tripod. The translucent grains fell on the low hot flames of burning olive wood
and then burned themselves in an upward spiral of blue smoke,

sweet and bitter at the same time. Walker lifted his hands, his voice rising in the Invocation:

> *"Hear me*
> *Lord of the battle-shattering aegis, whose power is set*
> *above Olympos*
> *Who are lord in strength above the countries, Father of*
> *All,*
> *If you are pleased that I built your sanctuary*
> *If ever it pleased you that I burn all the rich thigh*
> *pieces*
> *Of bulls, of goats, then bring to pass this wish I pray*
> *for;*
> *Let your almighty hand shield me in battle,*
> *For when the bright bronze spear stoops like the stallion-*
> *crested eagle,*
> *Then safety is hard to find and only your hand . . ."*

White-robed priests then led a garlanded bull of sacrifice up to the altar. Behind them came a chorus of handsome youths and another of maidens richly clad, flower garlands on their brows, singing as they came. The watching crowd—cityfolk, the ordered ranks of the regiments, great lords and their retainers summoned to follow the hegemon to battle—held their breath. It was the worst of omens if the sacrificial bull should bellow or fight. This one came unresisting, with a slow majestic tread. The priests gripped its gilded horns; Odikweos had to acknowledge that such things were done more neatly now, when priests were full-time specialists paid by the Throne rather than men of rank serving only for the God's honor and their own.

Behind the impassive mask of his face he shuddered. And the King had pointed out—how casually, how easily!—that priests appointed by the government could be relied on to get the omens right.

An acolyte bore the sacred basket; each of the great men taking part in the rite reached into it for a handful of barley to toss at the bull. The animal blinked in curiosity, and its broad pink tongue came out to lick up grains that stuck to its muzzle. From the basket Walker also took the sacrificial knife, long and curved and razor-sharp. First he cut a lock of hair from the bull's poll and tossed it into the holy fire beside the altar. Then he waited while Odikweos sprinkled water from the god-blessed spring over the animal's ears and eyes. It tossed its head and lowed, the symbol of its assent to the sacrifice.

The priests twisted their grip and exposed the neck. The King stepped forward and swung the blade with fluid skill; the strength and speed reminded Odikweos of his first meeting with the future sovereign, in a dark alley below the citadel of Mycenae where Walker battled assassins. He'd thought then that the foreigner was a man of his hands to be reckoned with, and he'd been right. His curiosity had led him to intervene, and that had brought him Walker's favor. From that beginning he had gained much, from that and his own wit that had also gained him William Walker's regard.

Blood flowed out over the altar, startlingly bright, smelling of salt and iron, and the bull went first to its knees and then to its side. Women screamed at the moment of the kill as the rite prescribed, long and shrill, drowning the death-bellow. A cheer went up from the crowd, deep and rhythmic from the soldiers, a chaotic wall of sound from the commons.

He felt another invisible shudder gripping his heart. The eyes of his mind remembered Agamemnon holding out his hand, wet with his own blood. *"The blood of Zeus, the blood of Poseidaion."* Then leaping from the cliff, as if into the arms of the Gods his ancestors. That blood still lay on the land.

Walker laughed at it, laughed at curses and death and fate—in the secret places of his heart, laughed at the Gods. And yet he won, and won, and won . . .

Athana Potnia, Gray-Eyed Lady of Wisdom, he prayed, in his own innermost self. *Did I do right when I gave Walker my aid?* It had raised the House of his fathers to the heights of wealth and power, but . . .

When the ritual was complete and the fat-wrapped thigh-bones smoked on the altar the square emptied, crowds surging away and troops marching in rippling unison, another thing Walker had brought to the Achaean lands. Odikweos put doubt from his mind as the King's closest gathered around him.

"The omens were good," he said politely. "The sacrifice went quiet and willing."

"Amazing what some poppy juice in the feedbag can do," Walker said dryly, and went on: "I shouldn't be gone long. I expect Troy to fall before the winter solstice."

Absently, the Ithakan noted that the last traces of the nasal whistling accent he'd once had had faded from the Wolf Lord's Achaean.

"And I'm leaving you enough troops and ships, counting your household regiment and the Ithakan fleet—keep a close ear out for news of the West, and if Isketerol asks for help, send it."

Odikweos nodded. "The Gods send you victory, King of Men, and spare your camp the arrows of far-shooting Apollo."

Walker grinned. "Thanks—and if I can teach the dumb bastards not to crap anywhere they please, like sheep, maybe they will."

The Ithakan blinked as a chuckle ran through the group. Yes, cleanliness about dung *did* seem to have something to do with the spread of sickness in a war camp, and he'd been glad to learn the rites that kept diseases of the belly away; they killed more men than bronze ever had, or bullets would. Still, it was not wise to openly taunt the power of Paiwon Apollo.

He thought of the slopes of Olympus. And striding down them a tall blackness edged with fire, like the shadow of falling night. . . .

He forced a smile himself, lest he be singled out. The only other in the circle around the King to be Achaean-born was the chief scribe, Enkhelyawon son of Amphimedes; and he was a man who'd been raised from a mere clerk to great power, not a noble born or a fighting-man. Walker's man . . .

But remember that he has *great power,* Odikweos noted mentally. There were records of everything, now. The chief scribe's office could torment a man to death and destroy his House with writs and forms. *Paper is as great a power in the land as bronze or steel, today. Greater than a bloodline descended from the Gods.*

"Helmut will keep you informed of any internal problems," Walker went on.

Odikweos bowed his head slightly. The pug-faced blond man inclined his; his countenance looked as if it had been carved from lard. *And do not underestimate this one, either,* the Greek told himself. Mittler didn't fight with his own hands, but he'd sent more Achaean nobles to the shades than a myriad of warriors; and he killed men as a housewife might rabbits, with a dispassionate briskness that ignored their squeals and kicks. In the old days a noble or vassal-ruler could give the High King a healthy piece of his mind when he wished, to his face. Now a man had to watch what he said by his own hearthside, or in the very marriage bed.

Walker's one green eye caught Mittler's. "And don't get overenthusiastic, Helmut," he went on. "I know that deep down you think corpses are the only politically reliable element in the kingdom, but please remember that dead men are useless except to the quartermasters, and mutton is much cheaper."

That brought a chuckle from Walker's closest followers, the ones who'd come with him to Tiryns so many years ago. Alice Hong's clear soprano laughter rang out, and she licked her lips.

"Oh, mutton is so greasy," she said. "Politically suspect pork now, done with noodles, or sweet and sour . . . Ragout of Long Pig à la Hannibal Lecter—even better, Long Pig *veal steak* . . ."

Odikweos looked at her and swallowed bile. *She* was not making a jest, however rough; there was no depravity beyond the Lady of Pain. *About her, I have no doubts. If ever it is in my power to slay that one, I shall. By the Kindly Ones, I shall.*

A groom brought Walker's horse; it was a tall one, three-quarter breed to the stallion he'd brought with him near a decade ago. Bastard had been the name of the sire.

The flat gray stones of Mittler's eyes were on Alice Hong as well. Walker noticed it. "My, what a happy little family," he said, swinging into the saddle. "*Hasta la vista,* and if anyone kills a rival without permission, I'll crucify them." His hand slapped his mount's neck. "Come on, Sonofabitch. There should be a big horse present at the fall of Troy, for tradition's sake."

Brigadier Kenneth Hollard drew himself erect, saluted, and bowed. Beside him Raupasha daughter of Shuttarna was flat on the ground, kissing the carpet. Even now, it still *felt* odd to see his sister Kathryn sitting on a throne one step down from Kashtiliash's on the dais, gorgeously robed and jeweled, a silk-and-gold headdress covering her cropped hair. The secondary throne was an addition to the room; ordinary Babylonian queens didn't take part in royal audiences.

Part of Kat's damned marriage contract.

He wouldn't have thought her the type to do the romantic-plunge-into-the-unknown thing, but then, she was his *sister.* She'd been an annoying brat for most of his life, then they'd become friends after the Event, but when he'd thought of her love life at all, it had always seemed sort of comic. *Until it rose up and bit us all on the ass.* Of course, it had been even more disconcerting to the Babylonians to see their prince—who then became their King—go head-over-heels for a bizarre foreigner. They had a tradition of romantic love in stories and poetry and suchlike here, but it wasn't supposed to get in the way of marriages, particularly for monarchs. It did help that a diplomatic marriage was the usual way of sealing an alliance, but there were still rumors of witchcraft bouncing about. Kat didn't have any intention of making much concession to ancient Babylonian ideas of Woman's Proper Place, either, and made no secret of it.

"Know that the King is not pleased, Lord Kenn'et," Kashtiliash said.

Hollard inclined his head in acknowledgment. Kashtiliash was making a concession by holding the audience in this lesser chamber, without the whole court looking on.

"Lord King, if I were you, I wouldn't be pleased either," he said frankly.

There were a few Babylonians present: guards, two scribes taking notes—one on paper in the Islander-introduced Roman alphabet, the other in cuneiform on waxed boards—and a couple of courtiers. They looked a little shocked at the bluntness. Kashtiliash nodded slightly; *he* didn't particularly mind, as long as the allies from Nantucket were properly respectful.

In fact, I think he finds it refreshing, Hollard thought.

"Explain this matter to me, then," the King said somberly.

"Lord King, Princess Raupasha was carried away by the heat of victory and misplaced gratitude," he said, feeling a trickle of sweat running down his flanks under the uniform jacket. "She begs the King's pardon."

Raupasha rose to her knees and threw herself down again; Kenneth Hollard kept his face impassive, but his Yankee reflexes couldn't help a small inward twinge. The Mitannian girl didn't mind, she'd been raised by a retainer of her royal father and taught the standard court etiquette.

"I most humbly throw myself on the mercy of the *shar kirbat 'arbaim,* King of the Four Quarters of the Earth, descendant of the Kings Who Were Before the King, Great King, Magnificent King, the King of Kar-Duniash, King of Assyria, King of Elam, King of Mitanni, Great Bull of Marduk, the giant unto whom the Great Gods have given rule, the Mighty, the Colossal, the Omnipotent," Raupasha said softly.

The Modest, the Humble, Hollard added to himself.

Raupasha went on: "With clasped hands, I beg that the King allow his slave to serve him as she has before."

Kashtiliash looked as if he'd bitten into something sour for a moment. *Smart girl,* Hollard thought, admiration taking the sting out of his irritation. She'd just reminded Kashtiliash that while the Nantucketers had helped him conquer Assyria—he'd been Prince Kashtiliash last year, in command of the Babylonian armies for his father Shagarakti-Shuriash—it had been

Raupasha's own hand that cut the throat of Tukulti-Ninurta. *Who, in the original history we showed him, defeated Kashtiliash and brought him a prisoner to Asshur.*

Plus she'd personally saved his father's life during an assassination attempt last spring. Some monarchs would just be angered by a reminder like that, but Kash . . .

The hard amber-brown eyes met Hollard's blue. "And if I decide that the Rivers country should not be a vassal-kingdom under Raupasha daughter of Shuttarna, but instead a province under a *sakkanakkum,* a royal governor appointed by myself?" he said.

Hollard nodded. "The land is the King's, to dispose as he sees fit," he said steadily. "The terms of our treaty of alliance are clear. The Republic of Nantucket seeks no territory in these lands, but only to make war on William Walker, the rebel and usurper who has siezed the throne of Achaea."

Kashtiliash continued relentlessly. "And if the Hurri-folk of the north rise against me, on hearing this news?"

Raupasha's fingers clutched at the carpet, but she kept a shivering stillness. Hollard answered crisply: "Then, as our treaty states, we will fight at your side against all rebels until Walker is cast down."

The Babylonian leaned back in his throne; chairs with backs were a rare luxury here, and this was carved with figures of gods and protective genii in ivory, its arms supported by gilded lion-centaurs, its feet the paws of lions with claws of gold.

"And if I demand this woman's head?" he said softly, his thick-wristed swordsman's hands gripping the carved ivory.

"That, Lord King, you must not do," Hollard said, standing at parade rest.

There was a gasp from the Babylonians; "must" was not a word used to the King of the Four Quarters, who held the life of every man in his hand.

"Before this woman was known to the King, I extended the Republic's protection over her," Hollard went on. "If her presence is an affront to the King, we will, of course, remove her from the Land of Kar-Duniash. Likewise, if my presence offends the King, he may demand that the Republic replace me as commander of allied forces here."

"You are a bold man," Kashtiliash said.

"The Republic honors its word, O King, and I am its servant—we bow to no man, but to the Law we are obedient. If the Republic broke its bond to this woman, whatever her faults, could we be trusted to keep it with you?"

Silence stretched. Then the fierce hawk-face of the Kassite monarch split in a harsh grin, teeth very white against the dense black beard.

"You are also a man of honor," he said, his fist thumping the gilded wood of the throne's arm. "Know that the word of the King of Kar-Duniash is also something that is not dust to be blown in the wind; it cannot be altered." His eyes went to Kathryn. "And if my sons are such men as you, it will be well for the realm. Approach."

Hollard did. Kashtiliash rose and gripped hands in the American gesture, then offered his cheek. *And while I appreciate the gesture,* the Nantucketer thought—it made him technically one of the Royal Kindred—*I still feel damned silly kissing a guy on the cheek.*

"There—we have regularized your bad manners," Kashtiliash said; the Royal Kindred were not required to prostrate themselves. It was a rare honor.

The Babylonian ruler sank back on his throne and fastened his eyes on the Mitannian princess. "Rise, Raupasha daughter of Shuttarna, and hear the judgment of the King." He leaned forward, one elbow on a knee.

"The King's servant awaits his word," Raupasha said, rising gracefully and standing with her head bowed under the metallic glitter of a shawl sewn with golden sequins.

"You have served my House well," he said. "In the matter of Tukulti-Ninurta my great foe, who you slew; in the matter of Shagarakti-Shuriash my father, whose life you preserved. Because of this, and for reasons of State, I am inclined to be merciful. *Once.* Do you understand me, Raupasha daughter of Shuttarna?"

"My Lord King's humble servant dares to think she understands his thought, and will strive always to do his will in the future."

Thank yoooou, Lord Jesus, Hollard thought, smelling his own sweat. *We don't have* time *for this sort of complication. Troy's under siege already.*

"Good," Kashtiliash said. He nodded regally. "You will both attend the King's feast this night. Tomorrow we will begin to plan the resumption of the war in the North."

CHAPTER NINE

March, 11 A.E.—Feather River Valley, California

"Why fire?" Tidtaway said suddenly, pointing to the columns of smoke rising from the settlement; he'd been hanging back, listening intently, but Peter Giernas had no idea how much he'd followed.

"Fire to burn out sickness," he said, and the Indian nodded.

An hour after he'd burned the dead village the expedition crouched by a fire on the ridge above. Dark smoke rose into the air from the lovely valley, and Peter Giernas shivered again as he thought of what the flames fed upon.

"Death like you can't imagine," he said. "Men, women, children . . . death."

"You've seen it before?" Jaditwara asked quietly.

"Ayup, back East, among the Sea-Land tribes, the Lekkansu and their kin, 'flu, in the Year 2—chickenpox the next year, and again the year after." He shivered again, hugging his shoulders. The soft leather of his second hunting shirt crinkled under his fingers. "I wasn't there when the measles hit, thank Christ."

That plague had traveled from band to band as far as the Great Lakes and Florida. His head came up, and his eyes caught Sue's.

"This didn't look like any of them, though. Some of the bodies were pretty fresh."

He described the marks, the red pustulent sores, skin and flesh peeling away in layers when the victims had tossed and writhed in the delirium of high fever—and probably of thirst, for there had been none to tend the last of the dying. From the looks, everyone had crowded in around the sick to comfort them, at first; most locals had that custom. Before the Event this had been a continent without much in the way of epidemic disease. Some VD, yes, and plenty of arthritis and whatnot, but not contagious fevers.

"That's not measles or chicken pox," Sue said quietly. She'd had some training, and was the closest thing they had to a doctor since Henry Morris decided to stay with the Cloud Shadow people after his leg healed. "I think . . . Pete, I think that was smallpox."

Giernas nodded, raised his eyes to meet Spring Indigo's; they were huge pools of darkness holding a terror controlled by an iron will. She hugged her child against the breast he fed from.

"I told you a little," he said. "About how our diseases can be so deadly to the people of these lands."

She nodded. "But husband . . . you said there were medicines to protect our son?" she said softly.

"And you, honey. There are in Nantucket. Not here."

They had vaccines for chicken pox and measles now, and there hadn't been more outbreaks of influenza since the Year 3; the doctors said the population wasn't big enough to keep it going, and that new strains had mostly come from Asia before the Event anyway. That didn't help people outside the regular Islander contact points much, but he'd get Spring Indigo and Jared done as soon as they reached Nantucket Town, and they ought to be all right—especially if they settled off-Island, which was what he'd planned. He'd lived in Providence Base on the mainland since it was established, anyway, right after the Event. Most of his family worked in the sawmills there.

And nobody has smallpox on Nantucket, for Christ's sake! Nobody we've run into, either. That we know of. One thing that this trip had driven home was how little they knew, though. The ones who'd set out from the Island were vaccinated; otherwise, they might have been nearly as vulnerable as the locals.

"Not everyone would have died," Sue said. "Ninety percent, maybe, if they were unlucky, from what the books said and what we've seen on the mainland near Nantucket. But not *everybody*."

Giernas nodded; that was the worst of it. In a virgin-field epidemic a lot of people would be too weak to move within hours, but some would be strong enough to travel for a week or so, and at least a few would take the disease but recover. Those who could run would have, run to neighbors and kinfolk, and the same thing would happen *there*, and—

And half the humans living west of the Sierras could die in the next six months. Maybe three-quarters or more. Nor was that all.

"Don't forget that hoofprint," he said.

"Your people?" Tidtaway asked, his face unreadable.

"No." Giernas shook his head emphatically. "No, I know all

the outposts of our folk and there are none near here . . . bringing horses here by ship would be *hard*. Not worth it for a brief visit, and I don't think our ships have even done that."

The Islanders looked at each other. Not likely to be William Walker's men, for which they all thanked their various Gods, not while he was pinned in the Mediterranean. Isketerol's would be bad enough. . . .

"Well, hell," Peter Giernas muttered very softly to himself, in the topmost branch of the valley oak that would support his two hundred pounds.

Valley oak ran to big branches; he was sixty feet up, lying on his belly with his long legs wound around the limb below him, screened behind a flickering barrier of green leaves. That was distracting while he peered through the binoculars, but much safer. He'd also taken care with the sun angles to make sure the lenses wouldn't flash and betray him. Now he handed the instrument up to Jaditwara, who could get a good deal higher.

She took them silently, sweat running down her face from the fur cap that covered her buttercup-colored hair, hair that *nobody* would think was a local Indian's if they saw it through a telescope. The Fiernan woman raised them to her eyes, hand moving slightly as she scanned, then let them drop to hang on her chest, made a correction to the drawing on the big pad before her, repeated the process with exquisite care.

Giernas stared in the same direction, although without the glasses his target was simply a dark blur in the distance, north beyond the river in the middle distance. It was the only break in the dead-flat plain ahead, until the abrupt volcanic pimple of Sutter's Buttes ten miles nortwestward, and unlike those it was man-made. Every detail was burned into his memory.

The Tartessian settlement sat north of the point where the Yuba River flowed down from the mountains and joined the Feather. Everything looked normal on *this* side of the river. The alienness started on the other shore. Furthest out from the settlement were herds of sheep, cattle, horses, sounders of swine rooting around in the tule-reed marsh by the water's edge. Mounted herdsmen directed locals on foot, and he could see enough of the riders to know that they were white men. The fort-town stood well back from the river, on a natural levee. Not very big, a couple of acres surrounded by a ditch full of sharpened spikes, a turf-sided earth wall twenty feet or so high, with corner bastions of squared logs snouting cannon—

twelve-pounders, he thought, though it was hard to be precise. There might well be rocket launchers and mortars inside, of course. There was certainly a wooden palisade all around atop the wall, black-oak logs tightly placed and trimmed to points, about twenty feet tall—probably the butts of the trunks were rammed seven or eight feet deep, with bracing and a fighting platform behind. He could see an occasional flash of metal from along the row of sharp points. Soldiers with Westley-Richards rifles like his.

All in all not very formidable, if there were any way for the Republic's armed forces to get *at* it, which at present there wasn't. Even in peacetime getting an expedition here would be a stone bitch, assuming you could get the Meeting to put up the money.

Against locals, this fortlet would be as invulnerable as steel and concrete, and it looked formidably permanent. As if to emphasize the fact, cultivated fields surrounded it, wheat and barley waist high in the warm sun, only a month from harvest; corn coming along well, alfalfa, vegetable plots, flax, a low scrubby bush that he thought might be cotton. And small orchards, vineyards showing long green shoots; they looked a little odd, goblet-trained rather than on T-stakes in the Islander manner.

Hmmm. The biggest of those fruit trees, I'd say they were seven, eight years along. But could the Tartessians have done this in the Year 3? Maybe, if they used the Yare *and started right after Isketerol's takeover, but that would tie everything up for them . . . no, wait a minute. This is a lot warmer climate than back home; trees grow faster if you water them. Cut that estimate in half . . . yeah, they could managed it* then, *sure.*

Unlike the Republic, Tartessos wasn't short of people, just people with the more complex of the new skills. The major cost for this would be tying up ships and navigators.

Hmmm. Lessee . . . The herds hadn't been very numerous, except for the pigs, which bred like flies; the sheep were in-between. So, ship in young pregnant mares and cows and ewes, a few sows, with only a bull and a stallion and ram or two—

Ayup. Say eighty in the first batch, a medium-sized square-rigger craft could do that, allowing for wastage. Two round-trips in the first year, drop down to the Canaries and across, then down the trades, and allowing for a hard time around the Horn—three trips if you had good luck running your westing down. That would give you useful locally reared numbers of horses in four or five years. If you bred all the mares as soon as possible, the herd would grow by a quarter to a third every year. Likewise, make steers of most of the male cattle to use as oxen, and in six years . . . In a generation, they'd have more than they could use, even with cougar and bear and wolf to deal with. Geometric progression started slow, but the curve went up fast.

So let's see, two hundred, mebbe three hundred acres under cultivation all up. Enough to support three hundred people say, with hunting and fishing as well.

Or to produce a surplus if there were less, but the Tartessians most *certainly* hadn't come this far for food or farmland, no matter how wonderful. Apart from sticking a thumb in the eye of the much-resented Cofflin Doctrine, which banned outsiders from trading or making settlements in the Western Hemisphere without the Republic's leave, what point was there in all this?

Fact is, I don't know yet, he thought ruefully. Decision: *We'll have to do some scouting and sneaking and keyhole listening to find out.* Gathering information was a ranger's job.

"Jaditwara," he called softly. "I don't see any real buildings outside the wall—do you?"

"Nothing but some sheds, haystacks, windmill pumps, that sort of thing," she replied. "And the boatyard by the water."

That meant everyone came back inside the walls at night. There was a jetty on the river, a mill with an undershot wheel and a boat shed, with smaller craft and a big two-masted flat-bottomed sailing barge that looked to be about eighty, maybe a hundred tons burden. Supplies must come in through San Francisco Bay, or more likely the barge took stuff *out* there, after a ship's boat had come upriver to let them know, and came back with the return load. A minimum inbound cargo, metals and manufactures, the base as self-sufficient as possible. That was crafty. Even if a ship was caught out, there would be no evidence of anything but a casual visit.

"How many—"

"Two hundred sixty-three horses, with one hundred seven two years old or older. Four hundred sixty-two cattle. I couldn't get all the sheep or swine, they're too small at this range. Lots of them, though."

"Ah."

Jaditwara hadn't had the full Grandmother training, but she'd done enough that her ability instantly to *count* things at a distance never failed to startle him. For that matter, she'd memorized his journal and Sue's, sort of a living backup system, and she had a couple of reference books stored in that long shapely skull.

"Pete," the Fiernan's soft singsong voice went on. "You notice the flagpole?"

"Hard to miss," Giernas said. "Two hundred feet if it's an inch."

"One hundred ninety-eight," Jaditwara said absently, touching her fingers together briefly in the Counting Chant. "Why so large?"

" 'Mine's bigger than yours,' " he guessed.

Tartessians thought that way, from what he'd heard of them and the few he'd met. The flagpole was made out of a whole old-growth Ponderosa pine, and the flag with the Tartessian mountain in silver on green looked absurdly small at its top. He didn't envy anyone who had to climb up the ladder of crosspieces to fix a jammed pulley. There was a platform around the top just below the flag, too. *Hmmmm.* It *would* make a crackerjack lookout post.

They dropped down the sloping trunk. Perks rose from concealment and came over, serious with the emotions he smelled on the humans. Peter Giernas took his rifle in his right hand and began to trot, careful to keep tree trunks between him and the river, although his buckskins would fade into the vegetation and all the metal on him was carefully browned. Once there was a swell of ground between him and the enemy he picked up the pace—lope a hundred yards, walk a hundred. The horses and the rest of their party were with the locals they'd met ten miles away; two hours' travel, without pushing it harder than was sensible.

Then he'd have to figure out what the hell to do.

"This is frustrating as *hell*," Sue Chau said.

Giernas nodded. The dark somber face of the chief stared back at him out of the night, from across the low embers of the oak fire. The local leader was short and lean and walnut-colored, with silver in the black hair gathered up on the top of his head through a rawhide circle; he was either called Chief Antelope, or was chief of the Antelope clan. Or "big man," "important person" might be more accurate than chief. . . . Tattoo marks streaked his cheeks beneath a thin, wispy black beard; four more bars marked his chin; bear teeth were stuck through pierced ears, and a half-moon ornament of polished abalone shell hung from his nose. He was quite naked save for a rabbitskin cloak thrown around his shoulders, a belt, a charm that looked like a double-headed penis on a thong, and several necklaces of beautifully made shell beads. An atlatl and bundle of obsidian-headed darts lay at his feet.

Tidtaway spoke a little of the chief's language; about as much as he did English. He'd been exposed to it far more often, but only in brief spells years apart, as opposed to the continuous months with the expedition. And the chief spoke Tartessian, a little; so did Jaditwara . . . also a little. Sue had made the most progress over the winter with Tidtaway's dialect, which by happenstance was a tonal language like the Cantonese she half remembered from her father's efforts to teach. Nobody was talking their native tongue, and sometimes they had to go from one badly learned foreign language through another to a third. That meant mistakes, painful misunderstandings, endless patient repetition, and no chance of conveying anything subtle or abstract.

"I think he understands that we're not Tartessians," Sue said.

Giernas sighed and worked his fingers into the deep ruff around Perks's neck. The dog was content enough, or as content as he could be around strange-smelling outsiders; he gnawed at a rack of grilled elk ribs that his master had finished, crunching the hard bones like candy cane in his massive jaws but keeping a sharp ear cocked for the start of trouble. Sparks from three campfires drifted up toward the branches of trees whose leaves were a flickering ruddiness above. Through them the stars burned many and bright in the clear dry air, like a frosted band across the sky.

"Okay, then does he understand that we can protect him from the smallpox?" Giernas said. *I hope,* he added to himself.

Sue, Jaditwara, and Tidtaway went to work again, hands moving, sometimes looking as if they were trying to throttle or pound comprehension out of the air.

"I'm not sure," Sue said at last. The others seconded her. "I'm *really* not sure that I got the idea of the percentage risk of the inoculation process across. I do know he's disappointed that we can't cure the ones already sick."

He nodded wearily. You *couldn't* get the idea of probabilities over, sometimes—some peoples just didn't have the concept, because they didn't believe anything happened by chance; if someone got sick it was the will of malignant spirits, or witchcraft, or the Evil Eye. Eddie'd thought that way as a kid; he knew better consciously these days, but deep down his gut didn't think that there was such a thing as coincidence.

The chief broke in with an impassioned speech, switching

from his own language to Tartessian now and then. Tidtaway and Jaditwara translated, sometimes overstepping each other; Jaditwara's singsong Fiernan accent grew much stronger as she drew on words learned long before she came to the Island. Giernas sighed and settled in to a job of mental cut-and-paste.

"The *Taratusus* came seven summers ago this spring."

God, Year 4, they got an early *start,* Giernas thought. *Give that bastard Isketerol his due, he's a planner.* It took malignant forethought, to start up something like this when Tartessos was just getting its first home-built three-masters and using its new guns to settle old scores with the neighbors. Or maybe he thought of it as long-term insurance. . . . *And mebbe Walker gave him the idea.*

"At first they were very few. They gave wonderful things"— he touched an iron knife at his belt—"and they helped my people in their feud with the *Sairotse* folk who dwell downstream. All they asked in return was help with hunting, some food, and a few basketfuls of the heavy rock from the streams that they showed us how to find."

He touched his necklace, which had rough-shaped gold nuggets between the abalone beads, and continued: "They killed many of the *Sairotse* men with their death-sticks and thunder-making logs. They took all the others and made them dig their ditch and build their wall, cut timber, haul earth and wood to build their great houses, or took them downriver to dig the red rock from the hills near the sea. They took the women of the *Sairotse,* but few as wives—instead they make them work like their Big Dogs."

Horses, Giernas translated to himself. It wasn't the first time they'd run into that name, among peoples whose only domestic animal was canine.

"We didn't like all that. We fought the *Sairotse* sometimes, yes, but also they were our marriage-kin. It's a bad thing that they are all gone, a whole tribe, a very bad thing. And so the spirits became angry, we knew that because there were fevers and sickness around the big houses. More and more of the strangers came—now they are more than all the people of my *Nargenturuk* clan. They rip up the ground to plant their eating grass without asking our leave. They trade like misers, making us bring more and more heavy rock for less and less; they make us bring captives of other tribes, to dig the red rock and burn it—those get the shaking sickness and die. Last year they told all the peoples here that we must bring the heavy rock, and young men and women, and furs, many other things, for *nothing*, or they would destroy us!"

"Red rock?" Giernas asked.

"Cinnabar," Jaditwara said, after searching her memory for a moment. "Mercury ore." She frowned. "The Tartessians had their own mine for that, we bought it from them before the war, but I think I heard it was damaged in a revolt just after they got it going—I know the price they asked for it went, how do you say, sky-high. The people who live near it are very fierce. The *Inquirer & Mirror* had an article about it. They thought Walker was also buying it from Isketerol."

"What's mercury good for?"

"Thermometers, barometers. Antifouling paint for the hulls of ships. Tanning furs. Medicines. For refining many ores, silver especially. Some chemical things I don't understand. And . . . explosives. Blasting caps, percussion caps for guns."

"There's a deposit near . . . San Jose, I think was the name," Sue put in. "Just south of the big bay."

Giernas grunted. *Ok. That's why they came this far. And the gold. Lots of silver in Iberia, but not much gold.* The chieftain waited out their interchange, and continued:

"And now they have brought this sickness on us. They boast that only they can halt it, by a magic of their *cows*." He used the Tartessian word for the unfamiliar animal. "They say it shows their spirit-allies are stronger than ours, their—*Gods* is the word?"

"Vaccination," Sue murmured.

"And they say they will sweep aside any who will not be their dogs. Our people who go to the big houses to trade now are beaten sometimes, kicked aside like dirt. They give us the water-of-dreams, then laugh when we drink it and act foolishly, when we give all our trade goods for another flask. When they think we do not hear, the outlanders boast that one day they will sweep aside all the peoples of this land, take it for their own! And they have some magic, that their women bear many children and all live, so they grow fast even without new ones landing from their great canoes with clouds to push them." He shook his head. "I do not understand this magic. But I can see that soon they will be too strong for us, even if all the peoples united against them."

Giernas nodded sympathetically. Hunter-gatherers like these usually had ways of keeping their birthrates low—low by the standards of the ancient world, of course. They had to, since a woman couldn't handle more than one child too young to walk;

not when she had to hunt edible plants every day, and move camp, too, and carry gear besides. So they made sure she had three or four years between kids; via a low-fat diet that lowered fertility, prolonged breast-feeding that did the same, taboos on sex for nursing mothers, sometimes abortion or infanticide, or a lot of kids just plain died of one thing or another in the hungry parts of the year.

The Tartessians had been peasant farmers for thousands of years. They bred a lot faster, since they lived in settled villages. Before the Event they'd also *died* a lot faster than hunters, particularly their children. Now they had lots of food, and pretty good preventative medicine, thanks to Isketerol and Queen Rosita, who'd been Registered Nurse Rosita Menendez before the Event. Not many of their women died of childbed fever any more, and ninety percent of their kids were going to live to have kids of their own. When the average woman had eight or nine, that added up pretty damned fast. The same thing was happening in Alba, and in the Republic. Even if they didn't get any more people from their homeland, the Tartessian settlement here in California could double in numbers every twenty years, while the locals declined.

"Tell him again that we can do something about the small-pox," Giernas said.

The chief grunted, thought for several minutes in stony silence, absently scratching at his head. Giernas sighed mentally; there would be another long siege against lice. What was the old joke? *At least our fleas and nits will mourn the passing of the human race. . . .*

"Will you fight for us?" the chief asked.

"Pete, I don't think we've got any choice," Sue said. "Unless we're going to turn around and run like hell, right now."

Giernas swallowed. *Leaving most of the people in this part of the continent to die off, and a nest of Tartessians here where nobody suspects. We might not make it back to tell anyone, either.* He looked over to where his wife and child sat.

"Honey?" he said softly. "What do you want to do?"

Spring Indigo gripped her son tightly, but her voice was steady. "The Tartessians are Eagle People enemies. How could I not stand beside my man, as my sister says?" A smile: "I know you will fight with a strong heart, Pete."

Giernas nodded. A Cloud Shadow woman adopted her husband's feuds as her own; and Spring Indigo was just plain brave besides. Throw that into the scale, then. *He* just plain didn't want to look into those dark lioness eyes and say he was going to skedaddle.

"Eddie?" he asked; no doubt there.

"I say fight, if there's anything we can do." A shrug and a grin: "They've got to have more gold in that fort than we can carry. You're the boss here, though."

Hmmm. Eddie's shed a lot of that bull-at-a-gate berserker stuff. Prudence rubbed off, evidently.

"Jaddi?"

The Fiernan-born girl nodded crisply. "Fight," she said. "It is evil, what they do here. I don't want Moon Woman to turn away from me when I ride the Swan."

Giernas sighed. "Okay, let's see what we can do. For starters, we have to make Spring Indigo and young Jared safe." *As safe as we can,* gnawed at him.

The chief spoke. Sue and Jaditwara and Tidtaway consulted.

"He says the Tartessians come to collect their tribute soon, so we have to make up our minds, or some tribes at least will be their dogs for the sake of the cow-medicine they bring with them."

Giernas started to nod, then froze. A thought struck him, like the sun rising early over the low distant line of the Sierras to the east. Slowly, he began to grin.

CHAPTER TEN

September, 10 A.E.—Troy
September, 10 A.E.—O'Rourke's Ford, east of Troy
October, 10 A.E.—Bay of Biscay
September, 10 A.E.—near Hattusas, Kingdom of
  Hatti-land
October, 10 A.E.—Bay of Biscay
September, 10 A.E.—Hattusas, Kingdom of Hatti-land
October, 10 A.E.—Off the coast of northwestern Iberia

"In the long run, I think Mesopotamia may be our Japan," Ian Arnstein said into the microphone.

He was a very tall man, towering for this era: four inches over six feet, still lanky in late middle age, with a bushy beard turning gray among the original dark russet brown—one that he'd worn before the Event, when he was a professor of classical history from Southern California. What hair was left on the sides and rear of his head was the same color. By a sport of chromosones, his face was of a type common in Anatolia even in the twentieth; beak-nosed, rather full in the lips, with large expressive dark eyes.

"Ian?" his wife said, through the earphones he was wearing, asking for clarification.

Doreen Arnstein was hundreds of miles away in the Hittite capital of Hattusas. Ian Arnstein listened to the boom of a cannon in the not-too-distant west, outside the walls of Troy, and thanked the notional Gods for that. *Now, if only I was there in Hattusas, too.* They'd about exhausted their official business, and it was a relief to talk of matters not immediately practical.

"I think I may have been too sanguine about the Babylonians," Ian said. "Yeah, it's going to handicap them not having much in the way of timber or minerals besides oil, but neither does Japan—and look how fast they picked up Western Civ's tricks. They've got a big population, a fairly sophisticated culture of their own, they're organized, and now they're run by a really smart, determined guy with a wife from Nantucket, whose kids are going to be educated in our schools. That means for the next two generations, they're going to make a *really* impassioned effort to catch up with us."

"We can worry about that after we've won this war," Doreen said. "They'll be aiming at a moving target anyway. How are things going?"

"Not so great," Ian said. "King Alaksandrus is holding steady—well, he doesn't really have much choice, now—but Major Chong isn't sure how much longer we can hold out."

"I *told* you you should have gotten out on the last flight, dammit, Ian!"

Ian sighed and shook his head. "Alaksandrus might have given up if I'd done that," he said. "Then Walker and his Ringapi would be whooping their way to Hattusas by now. You've done fine handling the Hittites." Who fortunately had institutions that didn't make dealing with a woman disgraceful. "Anyway, is David there?"

Their son was. When he had concluded the personal matters, the Republic's Councilor for Foreign Affairs sat back with a sigh.

"Bye," he said at last. "Stay well."

A hesitation at the other end of the circuit, and his wife's voice: "You too. The children need their father."

"I know—" he began; then his voice rose to a squeak. "*Children? Plural?*"

"If everything keeps on track . . . about nine months after that last evening before you got yourself trapped there in Troy VII. Serendipity."

"Why the hell didn't you tell me earlier?" he said, fighting down an irrational rush of anger.

"I didn't want to joggle your elbow with worries. Then. Now I don't want you feeling free to be a martyr."

He sighed. "Martyrhood doesn't attract me," he said. "Love you."

"You too, Ian. Come back to us."

I fully intend to do my best, he thought as he took off the earphones. Then:

"World's too damned big," he muttered to himself, pushing away personal considerations and looking at the map pinned to the wall beside the small square window. "And there's too damned few of us."

The square of heavy paper showed what would have been

the Middle East and Balkans in the twentieth. Here it bore names that had once been familiar to him only from books. Most of central and eastern Anatolia was the Hittite Empire, and points west and south were vassal states linked to it by treaty. The domains of Pharaoh Ramses II sprawled up from Egypt through what he knew as Israel and southern Syria to meet those governed from Hattusas. To the southeast was Kar-Duniash—Babylonia, an Islander ally and now including Assyria, which meant northern Iraq and chunks of the adjacent mountain country. *Babylonia's a firm ally, the Hittites a new one, Egypt's neutral . . . although there's that man of Walker's there.* The problem lay to the west.

He scowled at the black-outlined splotch on the map labeled *Meizon Akhaia*. Greater Greece, roughly translated; or Great Achaea. It left a mental bad taste; something like *Grossdeutschland*.

That hadn't existed in any of the histories he'd studied. Ten years ago it had been simply Achaea, part of it a loose confederation of vassal realms reigned over lightly by the Kings of Men in Mycenae, the rest independent minikingdoms, tribes and whatnot. Walker had been at work there for a long time now, first as henchman and wizard-engineer to Agamemnon King of Men, then as puppetmaster, for the last few years as ruler himself. Now it was a tightly centralized despotism, tied together by armies and roads, telegraphs, bureaucrats armed with double-entry bookkeeping. It had grown, too. Besides the whole of Greece proper, Walker's satraps ruled most of the Balkans up to what would have become Bulgaria and Serbia, plus Sicily, Italy, the Aegean islands. The American renegade had built up a terrifying degree of modern industry, as "modern" went in the Year 10, and as long as his Tartessian ally held the Straits of Gibraltar, the Achaean navy dominated this end of the Mediterranean.

Of course, he thought, *it's a spatchcocked modernization so far, mostly confined to a few centers. A thin film of literacy and machines pasted over a peasant mass dragooned into labors it doesn't understand by terror and the whip. Stalin's methods.*

The problem was that, at this level of technology, those techniques *worked*.

The longer we leave Walker alone, the stronger he'll get.

"The world's *far* too big," he muttered to himself, tugging at his beard. "And everything *takes* so bloody long. Sailing ships and marching feet, over half the world."

The Republic of Nantucket was trying to conduct a struggle

on a geographic scale about equal to World War I, but the forces involved were ludicrously tiny. Great Achaea probably had about a million people; Babylonia and the Hittites two or three times that each; the Republic was a couple of small towns and a fringe of farms haggled out of wilderness. Neither of the "advanced" powers could field more than a few thousand men with firearms, a few dozen cannon-armed ships, but those were the fulcrum the whole thing would turn on.

"Sure, we know the history," he mused. "Walker too—surprisingly well-read, for a complete swine. But there's nothing *in* the original history that jumbled up eras and technologies and methods like this."

He poked the the headphones with a finger and sighed; they were an example. They had some pre-Event shortwave sets, all transistors and synthetics, none of which could be allowed anywhere as dangerous as Troy. What the Republic's engineers and artisans could make instead was this 1930's-style monstrosity—five times as big and with five times the power consumption and half the effectiveness of pre-Event electronics. But they could *replace* the handblown vacuum tubes, which they couldn't do with the modern equipment. Meanwhile, the electricity came from a windmill, or squads on bicycle generators during calms.

The sound of cannon came again, louder than before, a huge heavy dull sound, like an enormous door shutting in the far distance. He rose and hurried through the corridors of the palace. They'd been opulent not long ago, before the siege; smooth gypsum floors, walls painted in a fanciful half-naturalistic style, costly embroidered hangings. The building itself was made of timber and mud brick on stone foundations, flat-roofed, two- and three-story blocks built around courtyards, all rather like a Southwestern pueblo. Now it was crowded, like the whole of the small city inside Troy's walls; here it was mainly gentry from the countryside and their immediate retainers. Most were relatives of the King, bunking in rooms normally used for storage or weaving or kept empty for guests. They looked at him with an awe that hurt, the foreign magician who would save them from the Wolf Lord of the west; a granny hunched over a piece of sewing, girl-children playing a game remarkably like hopscotch and giggling as they skipped, a proud black-haired woman with a huge-eyed child on her lap, a tall cloaked man, white-bearded, who bowed gravely. The smell wasn't too bad overall; the Republic's military medics were enforcing sanitation with fanatical determination backed up by their reputation as wizards, but there was a sour undertone to it. Those sanitary regulations were the only thing that kept this whole city from going up in a pyre of epidemics; out in the lower town below the citadel the peasant refugees were crammed in like sardines, even many of the streets turned over to makeshift shacks.

There weren't many men of fighting age in the palace. They were on the walls, or working. Ian kept his face solemn, as local manners required, and returned the greetings. Inwardly he winced a bit. They would fight to the end, now. They didn't have much choice. The original terms for surrender Walker had offered had been relatively generous, and he'd probably have kept them.

But I convinced them to fight. That was certainly to the advantage of the Republic and its Hittite and Babylonian allies. *It's only to Troy's advantage if the relief force gets here in time.* If it didn't, this whole people would be blotted off the face of the earth.

A few minutes brought him to the place he sought, the main courtyard, which had been taken over by Major Chong of the Marine Corps for his weapons, a battery of heavy mortars. Their snouts showed above the lips of the berms below, each dug into a cell of earth; for a brief moment he felt an illogical sorrow for the gardens that had given air and sweetness to this section of the great building. Now that air was heavy with the stink of burned sulfur from the black-powder propellant. The loading teams sprawled, resting. Most of them were Trojans, in tunics and kilts much like their Achaean cousins. Over the weeks of the siege there had been time to train them for most of the work, each team under a Marine or two, while the rest of the crews acted as officers elsewhere.

Ian waved to them, and turned through what had once been the queen's audience chamber. The palace and the citadel around it were on the highest ground available, and Trojan architecture ran to exterior galleries on the higher stories. Chong was there, and King Alaksandrus of Wilusia—Ilios, Troy—in full fig of bronze armor, boar's-tooth helmet, horse-hair plume, the rifle across his back looked a little incongruous. Ian exchanged solemn greetings.

It's a matter of morale, he thought, feeling a melancholy amusement at the Trojan's finery. *Like a Victorian Englishman changing into formal wear for dinner in the middle of some godforsaken jungle or a residency besieged by mutinous sepoys. Stiff upper lip and all that.*

"How's it going, Major?" he asked the Marine officer.

Chong's family had been Realtors on Nantucket, ethnic-Chinese refugees from Vietnam originally. There was a slight tinge of Yankee drawl to the man's vowels, and his handsome amber-hued face was drawn with fatigue as he shrugged.

"Exactly the way I anticipated," he said—in English, but Alaksandrus had grown resigned to his allies using their incomprehensible tongue when they wanted to leave him out of the conversation.

"That bad?"

"Take a look, Councilor."

He bent to the heavy tripod-mounted binocular telescope. The scene that jumped out at him was wearily familiar. The enemy vessels were further up the coast, just barely visible to the north, unloading new devilments; the bay that reached nearly to the wall was too close to Chong's mortars. Around Troy stretched a semicircle of siegeworks, trenches, and bunkers cut into the soft soil of the coastal flats and then over the rocky heights behind them. Beyond them stretched camps, orderly rows of tents for the Wolf Lord's men, a sprawling chaos of brushwood shelters and rammed-earth huts and leather lean-tos for his barbarian allies.

"The Ringapi don't look too happy," he said. Misery hung over those encampments as palpably as dust haze and smoke.

"Should they be?" Chong said.

"No," Ian said.

Prisoners had brought in tales of disease and hunger. He could fill in the rest for himself; the chieftains were probably wishing they'd never left the middle Danube. So far they'd gotten scant loot, and having plundered the countryside bare they were utterly dependent on Walker for their daily bread. Apparently he was doling it out in lots only slightly more generous than his allotments of second-rate firearms. You needed a long spoon to sup with that particular devil.

"Still, he's getting the work done," Chong said. "Here—"

With expert help, Ian could make out the zigzag covered ways thrust out from the encircling walls. Here and there, men toiled with pick and shovel and woven baskets full of earth to extend them, and others hauled timber and dirt forward to provide overhead cover. From two such bastions the slow bombardment came, heavy shells thudding home into the hastily heaped earth berm that the Islanders had shown the Trojans how to pile against their vulnerable stone curtain-wall.

"Dahlgren-type guns," Chong said. Ian licked dry lips and

fought for a similar detachment. "Rifled pieces would be giving us more problems."

A subordinate called the Marine officer over to a map table; he looked at the results of the triangulation, nodded, spoke into a microphone. Less than thirty seconds later a massive *whunk!* sound came from the courtyard behind them, and a plume of smoke just visible over the rooftop. A falling shriek went northwestward, and a tall plume of dirt and debris gouted out of the plain of Troy like a momentary poplar tree. The *thudump* of the explosion came a measureable time later.

"Have to be dead lucky to get a direct hit on one of the guns," Chong explained. "Especially since we have to conserve ammunition . . ."

"We've only got the one dirigible," Ian pointed out. "And it can only carry a couple of tons at a time. If we lost it . . ."

Chong nodded. The Achaeans had light cannon in yoke mounts that could swing them quickly upward, big kites with burning rags attached, and a number of other antiairship weapons. None of them had worked so far, but they kept trying.

"I don't like the looks of those approach trenches they're digging either," Chong said. "I have a suspicion they're going to use them for another mass attack on the walls. We've got nearly a thousand rifles here now, but only a hundred and twenty rounds of ammunition for each."

"God," Ian said. When the wind shifted, you could still smell the bodies from the assault three weeks ago. "I was about to complain that war seems pretty damned boring."

"Worse when it isn't, though," Chong said. "They've got those two guns in range of the walls. They'll get more. Even with the earth berm outside and heavy backing, it's not going to hold."

Hurry up, Hollard, Ian thought. *You too, Marian.*

"Here they come!"

Patrick O'Rourke had been stripping and cleaning his Python revolver, as an aid to thought. At the cry his fingers automatically snapped it back together, checked that the cylinder was full, and clicked it home.

A man in a peaked bronze helmet with a gilded wheel on the top had been haranguing the enemy in the ravine three hundred yards to the northwest, never quite exposing himself enough for a sharpshooter to get him. The responses grew louder and louder, until all five hundred of them there were shouting. Voices rose in an ululating shriek . . . followed by a second of ominous silence.

Then they slammed their spears against their shields three times in unison. A final united hissing shriek of: *SssssSSSSAA! SA! SA! SssssSSSSAA* and the Ringapi surged up out of the ravine and charged, screaming. O'Rourke blinked, squinting into the setting sun; they weren't holding anything back, coming on at a flat-out sprint to get over the killing ground as fast as they could—but the rest of the barbarian host wasn't moving. Could they be trying something clever? Or was it just bare-arsed backwoods stupidity?

"Sir?" Barnes asked.

"By all means," he said.

"Volley fire—*present*!"

Along the wall rifles came to shoulders with a single smooth jerk, sunlight flashing off the blades of the bayonets. He could hear the sergeants and corporals repeating over and over: *"Pick your man. Aim low. Pick your man. Aim low."* Not to mention: *"Eyes front!"* on the other walls.

"Fire!"

BAAAAAMMMM. The north wall disappeared in an instant fogbank of dirty-gray smoke, stinking of rotten eggs and fireworks. O'Rourke blinked again as the spent shells tinkled to the ground and the smoke blew clear; hardly a bullet had missed—it was a clout shot, and you couldn't graduate Camp Grant without being able to hit a man-sized target at that range nine times out of ten. Some of the heavy Werder slugs had punched through a first man and killed the one behind him.

But they're not stopping for shit, as the Yankees say, he thought. Speeding up, if anything; the drumming of four-hundred-odd feet on dry hard earth was like distant thunder, or a race-track when the crush was around the curve and coming up.

"SssssSSSSAA! *SA! SA!* SssssSSSSAA!"

"Volley fire—*present*!"

BAAAAAMMMM.

This time the charge wavered, ever so slightly. O'Rourke found his hand had been gripping the butt of his pistol hard enough to hurt, and he forced himself to relax it. Most of the Ringapi hadn't missed more than a step, and came right on into the muzzles of the rifles as they lifted for the third volley, leaping over their own dead.

"SssssSSSSAA! *SA! SA!* SssssSSSSAA!"

BAAAAAMMMM.

"Independent fire, rapid—*fire!*" Barnes said. Then, quietly: "By Jesus, I think they're going to make it to the wall."

"No," O'Rourke said judiciously, watching the fast steady crackle scythe into the thinning ranks of the attackers. "No, that last volley rocked them back on their heels, the saucy bastards."

Now the attack wavered, men bunching and hesitating. They were less than a hundred yards away now, close enough for him to imagine he could hear the flat smacking impact of bullets striking home, close enough to see men jerk and stumble and sprawl or a brazen helmet ring like a bell as it went spinning away from a shattered skull. They reached a low stone wall and began to climb over, until half a dozen were struck at the same instant and toppled backward. That sent them to earth, crouching behind the loose-piled stones of the field boundary.

All except a knot who came on at the same dead run, led by the chief with the gilt wheel on his helmet. A standard-bearer ran beside him, holding up a pole with a bronze boar on its top. Man after man fell, some in the sack-of-potatoes slump that meant instant death, more screaming or writhing on the ground. Bullets kicked up sudden puffs of dust around the chief's feet, or sparked off rocks, but some freak of odds and ballistics spared him even when the standard-bearer fell and the curl-tusked boar tumbled in the dirt.

"Don't kill him!" someone shouted from the firing line. "Don't kill him, Goddammit!"

A dozen others took up the cry; Barnes looked at O'Rourke and raised an eyebrow as the firing crackled to a halt. Everyone could admire courage that absolute, even in an enemy.

"Let them have their gesture," he said, and checked his watch. "Good for morale. Five o'clock . . . it's going to be a long day and night, I think."

The Ringapi chief kept coming, teeth bared and spear raised. But the end of the slamming fusilade seemed to waken him from his trance of ferocity, as much as the shouts of *Go back!* and *Look behind you!* from the line of barley sacks ahead of him. He slowed, his moccasined feet gearing down from their pounding run to a walk. The shouts continued—some of them in the Sun People dialects of Alba, close enough to his own speech to be understood for short simple phrases. He did look around, and realized that he was alone; looked back, at the ruin of his clan's war band, bodies scattered all the way to the ravine they'd jumped off from. The exaltation of the spirit that had carried him so far ran away like water from a slit sack. He turned back to face his enemies and stood, slowly raising spear and shield until they made an X against the lowering sky.

His pale eyes traveled back and forth along the breastwork. With a convulsive gesture he slammed his spear into the ground and left it quivering upright like a seven-foot ashwood exclamation mark. Then he turned and began to walk back the way he'd come, striding along at a pace neither fast nor slow, pausing only to scoop up the boar standard, until he reached the stone wall where the remnant of his followers pulled him down into shelter.

"What," O'Rourke said thoughtfully, glancing up at the hillside where the enemy commander had his post, "was the point of all that, now?"

Hantilis answered: "I think they were counting your bows . . . your guns, I mean. Testing the strength of one wall." He pointed at the enemy command post. "With the far-seeing tube he could see how you moved your men about, and plan how to strike a stronger blow."

The Islander commanders nodded. *Well, that's a cool one, then,* O'Rourke thought. *When he puts things together, look out for fair.*

"Heads up!"

The cry came from sentries stationed on the flat roof of the hospital. They were pointing southward.

"Mind the store, *macushla,*" O'Rourke said, and jumped down from the firing platform. He nodded in passing to Chaplain Smith, who was helping organize the stretcher-bearers.

"The hand of the Lord fell heavy on the enemy," Smith said. "But Colonel, I must protest that many of the troops are given to blasphemy in the heat of battle. No luck can come of taking the name of the Lord in vain, or that of His mother. I do not speak of naming heathen Gods," he added sourly, acknowledging the regulations about religious tolerance without approval. "Only of my own flock."

O'Rourke stared at him for a second, before he could force himself to believe the man was deadly serious. "Reverend Smith, you may tell your flock that I'm firmly opposed to blasphemy in all forms," he said finally.

The young ex-Iraiina smiled and drew the sign of the cross. "Bless you, my son."

The Islander colonel was shaking his head as he trotted on through the open space. *Mary Mother of God, but sometimes I wonder if sending those missionaries to Alba isn't going to come back to haunt us,* he thought to himself, and went up a rough pole ladder to the roof of the hospital. The lookout there pointed southward and a little west.

"They're moving there, Colonel," she said. "Fair number of 'em, but pretty scattered."

He trained his own binoculars and hissed. Yes, Ringapi for sure; moving by ones and threes and little groups, into the hills that made the southern wall of the valley and into the open forest above that. There they promptly disappeared into the shadowy bush, settling down behind trees or rocks. That was probably a hunting skill where they came from—mostly prairie and forest and wooded mountains, from the Intelligence reports—but useful here nonetheless. The first puff of smoke came as he watched. The crack of the rifle sounded a perceptible fraction of a second later; he couldn't see where the bullet landed. That was the signal for more; he scanned the mountainside, trying to count the guns as muzzle flashes winked at him out of the shadows. Now he could hear bullets going by, or going *thock* into the hard mud-brick walls of the hospital building, or making a peculiar crunching *shrush* into the sacks of barley.

"Lieutenant Hussey," he called, as he dropped down the ladder again.

"Sir?"

The boy was even more painfully young than his captain, thin and dark; O'Rourke decided that either he was getting old himself, or this one had lied about his age to enlist.

"Hussey, pull me out twelve Marines and a corporal—all of them good with a bayonet. Include—" He named four from the escort that had ridden in with him. "Form them up by the wellhead over there. Take charge of them, and use 'em as a flying squad, to plug gaps. Oh, and marksmen on the south wall are to reply to those riflemen on the hill."

Barnes had come up while he was speaking, and raised an eyebrow. "They won't be able to see them, sir," she pointed out.

O'Rourke nodded. "But it will keep their heads down. They aren't what you'd call good shots—lousy, I'll wager, the lot of them—but there *are* a lot of them."

"And we're what you might call a large target," Barnes said grimly, tapping her fingers on her holstered pistol.

As if on cue, one of the Marines on the north-facing wall dropped back and cried out, clutching at his leg, and yelling: "Corpsman, corpsman!"

The stretcher-bearers trotted over and lifted him onto the stretcher, trotting off to the hospital building, ignoring the occasional bullet kicking up a pock of dust in the open space they had to cross.

"That we are, *macushla*," O'Rourke agreed, his voice equally ironic. He pointed westward, past the hospital building. "Droopy Gray Whiskers up there, his dispositions make sense now. He'll send his men in like this"—he clenched his fist, put the first two fingers out in a fork, and pushed them forward— "at the hospital; it's where we're weakest because the firing line is narrow, and the sun'll be directly in our eyes. Then the most of them will come around the north side, along the building's wall, and then the breastwork."

"Not the south at the same time?"

"Not in force; they'd get in the way of those gentlemen up there." He jerked a thumb at the snipers on the hillside above them. "If we last until dark, then yes."

"Pray for dark, then—except that then the rest will be able to get closer."

She looked southward, frowning slightly; he noticed how feathery-fine her eyebrows were, above the dark-blue eyes. "I'll take every second rifle off that wall when the attack comes in."

He nodded. "Until then, they're safer there. But a last thing . . . put your eye to one of those rifles up there, and tell me what you see."

Barnes did; her eyes went a little wider, and she looked down at her watch. "That's a damned fast rate of fire, if they're using the sort of muzzle-loading abortion Walker was supposed to be handing out. Westley-Richards model at least," she went on, naming the first flintlock breechloader Seahaven had turned out for the Republic's armed forces. "Or even Werders."

"I doubt Walker is handing out the latter; he doesn't have enough of the copies he's made to arm his own forces yet. So either he's giving the savages there first-rate . . . or at least second-rate . . . rifles, or they captured a good many recently."

Their eyes went down the road to Troy, until a voice called them back: *"Here they come, the whole fucking lot of them!"*

The flagship of the Islander fleet shipped a surge of black water across her starboard bow, shrugged it off, raised her long bowsprit into the storm.

"I don't like the look of this," Marian Alston-Kurlelo said, legs flexing to keep her upright as the stern of the ship went through its cycle of pitch . . . roll . . . rise . . . heel . . . fall.

"No, ma'am," Commander Jenkins said, voice pitched loud to carry through the rumble and hiss of the sea, the creak and groan of timbers working with the rushing speed of the ship. "Dirty weather, and a filthy night."

She was standing on the quarterdeck of the *Chamberlain,* not far from the ship's newly promoted captain. He had sailed on her as Alston's XO while the commodore was acting as captain-aboard as well as C-in-C, and was still a little nervous about the three broad gold stripes on the cuffs and epaulets of his blue jacket that marked his promotion to commander and captain of the frigate.

I have no intention of joggling your elbow, she thought but did not say. The OOD probably felt just as nervous having the godlike authority of a captain and commander on the same quarterdeck on her usually lonely vigil; it was just after two bells on the midwatch, one in the morning to civilians.

"I think it's coming on to a really stiff blow," she said thoughtfully, instead.

The sky was pitch-black and the sea reflected it, with the wind making out of the west and a nasty cross-chop, a chaotic surface of waves crashing into each other in bursts of off-white foam. Sheets of cold rain blew in with the wind mingled with spindrift whipped off the surface of the waves, making her want to hunch her right shoulder; she did nothing of the kind, of course, standing erect with her hands clasped behind her, letting the wind slap the oilskins and sou'wester against her. The only light was from the big stern-lanterns and what leaked from the portholes of the deckhouse behind her, and the riding lights at the mastheads; she could see others spaced out across the heaving waters to her west, the rest of the Republic's south-bound fleet. There were four hands on the benchlike platforms on either side of the frigate's double wheels, wrestling with the tension that flowed up through the rudder cables and drum to the wooden spokes. Plenty of it, with this cross-sea and the heavy pitch it imposed.

They're probably thinking about their reliefs and a hammock, Alston mused. Although the crew's hammocks on the gun deck would be swaying like branches in a gale, and it would get worse—they'd have to fasten the restraining straps across themselves. *I should go below, get some rest. If only we'd been able to get the politics finished and get away earlier in the season!*

If there hadn't been so much riding on this fleet—if she'd been commanding a single ship, say—she might well have been enjoying herself. This was *real* sailing. The burden of worry made that impossible.

"There are times I badly miss satellite weather pictures," she said.

"Ma'am."

Jenkins nodded for politeness' sake; he was barely thirty, and they were a fading memory of the CNN National Forecast to him. They'd been an essential tool of the sailor's life to *her*, for better than a decade. You developed a sixth sense about weather, if you studied it carefully all your life, but it just wasn't the same as that godlike eye in the sky.

The Bay of Biscay was always risky, and the winter storms were coming on, raging down out of the North Atlantic and funneled into this giant cul-de-sac. She could feel it in her gut, the terrible ironbound coast of northwest Iberia lying off her lee, waiting there to port. Reefs growling in the surf like hidden tiger-fangs, sheer cliffs and giant waves breaking on them like the hammer of Ogun until mountains trembled, a graveyard of ships for millennia. And the Lord Jesus pity any fisherman out tonight in a Bronze Age coracle, or a boat of planks sewn together with willow withes.

The spray on her lips wasn't quite icy, but it was rawly cold, with the mealy smell of snow in it somehow. Anyone who went overside in this would be dead in half an hour, even if they didn't drown first. Looking up she could see the masts nearly bare, furled sails with doubled gaskets, the remaining sheets of canvas drum-taut and braced sharp as the *Chamberlain* heeled to the wind coming in on the starboard beam. Everything else was as secure as it could be, too; deadlights on the stern gallery, guns bowsed up tight, extra lashing on the boats. Glancing at Jenkins she could see his gray eyes slitted and peering upward, then reaching out to touch a stayline—feeling the forces acting on his ship, the messages in the heave and jolt as she cut into every wave and rose, paused, swooped downward.

Much heavier and we'll have to come about into the wind and heave to. Can't run before it, or even scud. Christ, no, she thought, as a wave came across the forward third of the ship's starboard side, swirled across the waist deck and poured out of the scuppers. Not nearly as much sea room as she'd like.

Another glance to starboard. Thirty ships, counting every transport. As many as Nantucket could spare, with a minimum to keep essential trade running and patrol the oceans near home—trying another invasion would be suicidal for the Tartessians, but you never knew what a desperate man would do.

It was far more than the Republic could afford to *lose,* that was for certain.

And then there was the *Farragut.* She thought again about the design of the steam ram's bows, a nagging concern. They'd had to mount the heavy steel plates before they left, with action in the offing on arrival at Tartessos. The steam ram was a bad enough seakeeper without them. With the added weight forward she sailed the way a whale swam—always rolling about and inclined to dive unexpectedly. Bad luck, to run into a storm with that bastard designer's compromise along. . . .

At least she can claw off to windward under power, if need be, she thought.

In a sailing ship the only thing you could do with a lee shore was go aground on it, when you started to lose more in leeway than you made in headway won on each tack. And when a storm mounted past a certain force, even the most weatherly ship sagged more and more to leeward with each extra knot of wind speed. Her mind drew the parallelogram of forces for each ship in the fleet, varying with their depth of keel and their ability to point to windward, correlated it with their positions relative to the coast to the southeast and what she knew of the set of the oceans around here.

Safe enough, so long as it doesn't get much worse. Or if it waits more than six or eight hours to get worse. Otherwise, we've got a marginal situation here.

"Mr. Jenkins, I'm goin' below," she said. "Please have me woken if there's a substantial change in the wind, or any important messages from the fleet." At least every ship had a well-maintained pre-Event radio this time, and Guard or Marine techs to maintain it.

"Aye, aye, ma'am!"

She turned and rounded the low deckhouse, one hand lightly on the safety line strung beside it, water swirling calf high around her sea boots as the ship took a black wave edged in white froth. She waited until it had run free through the scuppers and then opened the hatch and went down the companionway. The *Chamberlain* had forty-six feet of raised quarterdeck and this space beneath; the companionway ended in a bulkhead, with corridors to either side lined with the little cubicles of officers' quarters, the galley, and officers' mess. Right ahead was a tub made from a large barrel split lengthwise. It had a couple of inches of water sloshing around in it, and wet-weather gear hanging from pegs above. She added her own. In a gale, it mainly served to break the force of the wind; her uniform was sopping, and her skin crinkled beneath it.

Someday I'll be too old for this shit, she thought. *It's the only good thing I can think of about getting old. Of course, I intend to get as much fun as I can out of being a crotchety old lady, and if I can think of some way to shock the grandchildren, so much the better.*

Her own quarters were to the rear, the stern cabin of the ship—what would have been Jenkins's, if his frigate weren't also the flagship. She returned the salute of the Marine sentry, who looked sleepily alert, and went through into the darkness. The heavy plank deadlights were secured over the broad stretch of inward-sloping windows to the rear, and it was pitch-black. A heavy fluffy towel lay over the back of a chair whose legs were bolted to the deck at the central table; she smiled gratitude as she stripped and dried herself off. Her teeth were still nearly chattering in the raw chill of the cabin. Wooden ships and central heating didn't go together, nor could they ever be completely dry in heavy weather—oak beam and plank just weren't steel girders and welded plate.

The *Chamberlain* was a dry ship by those standards; there weren't any drips or spurts of water, just a pervasive dampness.

And I'm a tropical bird, she thought. *Say what you like about South Carolina, it isn't usually like this.*

That made the bed's dry warmth doubly delicious as she slipped under the covers. She carefully stayed on her side of it, though. Normally Swindapa didn't wake if Alston came to bed late, just rolled over and grappled in her sleep like a semi-conscious octopus, but contact from an expanse of sea-chilled flesh . . .

Might as well drop ice cubes down her spine. Instead Alston pulled the covers to her chin and lay on her left side, with her knees braced against the padded six-inch board that rimmed the cabinward side of the bunk in rough weather.

The Farragut *should be all right,* ran obsessively through her mind. *So, she doesn't have as much reserve buoyancy as I'd like, particularly with the armor and ram reinforcement fitted. She's still tight, and she can still maneuver under power. She* will *be all right. Go to sleep, Goddammit!*

It wasn't only that there were a hundred-odd crewfolk aboard her, or that Trudeau was an officer she'd shaped and a friend besides. That all mattered, but Alston also had to *fight* when she got where she was going. *Farragut* was a boar-hog beside the deadly gracefulness of the clipper-frigates, and barely seaworthy in the deep oceans, but she was a good third of the fleet's fighting power. *I need that ship, dammit. For Tartessos, and afterward.* Of course, the Coast Guard fleet had superior guns, not to mention gunnery—the Tartessian vessels in the attack last spring had been carrying fairly crude stuff; cast-iron or bronze eighteen-pounders at most, the sort of thing Nantucket had been turning out in the Year 3, and it had cost them heavily against the poured-steel eight-inch Dahlgrens of the Islanders. Far heavier shot and greater range and accuracy, for about the same weight on the gun deck.

Now, will it be better to engage at a distance, try to keep them off and pound them? Then again, if we close we have the—

"You're *freezing*," a voice said in her ear. Warmth pressed against her, along back and legs, as her partner curled near spoon fashion. Arms wrapped around her, slender and strong, and she smelled the clean familiar scent of healthy skin and Nantucket Briar shampoo.

"Didn't want to wake you, sugar," she murmured in the darkness.

"I can feel your spirit," Swindapa said. "*And* the knots in your back. There's nothing you can do about the weather that you haven't done! Turn around so I can get at it, then let all the thoughts go, and *sleep*."

She obeyed, sighing slightly as slender fingers kneaded her neck and shoulders and down along her spine, then up to massage her scalp through the inch-long cap of tight wiry curls. When they had finished she felt as if her head was floating on the pillow, instead of being tied to her shoulders with heated iron rods.

"Sleep, *bin'HOtse-khwon*," her partner's voice murmured in the darkness. The lack of light was like black velvet pressing against her eyes now, and the other's breath went warm across her cheek. "Sleep now."

Damn, Alston thought, on the soft creamy edge of unconsciousness. *But it's nice to be . . . settled. Gives a center to your life. And you can feel really close snugglin'.*

Baaamm.

Princess Raupasha of Mitanni swayed backward slightly as the shotgun punched at her shoulder. The sharp *thudump* of the second barrel's buckshot was nearly lost in the hammering of hooves, the crunching whir of the tires over sandy dirt, the creak of wood and leather and wicker.

"*Aika-wartanna!*" she cried. *One turn.*

Her driver pulled the horses into a turn so tight that the right wheel came off the ground. The whole crew leaned in that direction, to put their weight against the force trying to overturn the war-cart. The wheel thumped back down and she snatched out the next weapon from the leather bucket fastened to the chariot's side and turned to keep the target in view. It was straw lashed to a pole amid a forest of others, each shaped roughly like a man and each with clay jugs of water inside. That leaked out where the lead balls had scourged the straw, making a dramatic stain on the dried grain-stalks.

Thudump.

"Tera-wartanna!" Three turns. *Thudump.*

Straw and pottery and water flew out. She handed the shotgun off to her loader with a show of nonchalance. Inwardly she exulted as the driver pulled the team aside, slowing them from the pounding gallop to a trot and then to a walk, soothing them as he reined in.

As I dreamed, Raupasha thought, looking behind her at the watching teams of her squadron. *As I dreamed, but never hoped . . .*

Her foster father Tushratta had hoped the child beneath the heart of King Shuttarna's wife would be a son, to avenge his lord; that was why he'd smuggled her out, rather than dying by Shuttarna's side in battle with the Assyrians. Instead the royal woman had borne a daughter and died herself. In the lonely desert manor to which he'd fled he had raised Raupasha much as he would have that longed-for son, and her bedtime stories had been of Mitanni's ancient glories. How often in the chariot beside him, hunting gazelle or lion in the wastelands, had she dreamed herself as a great King like Shaushtar or Parsatatar in the epics! Bending the bow and scattering the enemies of her people like the lightning bolts of Indara Thunderer.

I do not have the strength of arm to bend the bow of a mariyannu *warrior,* she thought. *But I can pull the trigger of this gun as well as any. True lightning, as I dreamed.*

The other chariots gathered around at her gesture. She looked at them with pride. Such a little while ago her Mitannians had come to war in creaking chariots with warped wheels, relics hidden for a generation from the Assyrian overlords. The hand of Asshur had lain heavy on the Hurrian folk, and still heavier on their onetime lords. The artificers and silver of the Eagle People had given her two hundred sound chariots—with iron-rimmed wheels, and collar harnesses and iron shoes for the horses themselves. Each war-cart held three, Hittite-fashion; a driver, a warrior, and a loader for the firearms that replaced the horn-backed bows of old. The foot soldiers now had rifles, and drilled under the critical eye of Marine *noncoms*.

"You see," she said, when they were gathered around. "The *shotguns* and the *rifles* hit further and harder than bow or javelin."

Just then a young spotted hound leaped into her chariot; she ruffled its ears absently, and it put its paws on the railing, waiting eagerly for a run to drive the wind into its nose.

"Down, Sabala," she said sharply.

The dog let his ears droop and curled up out of sight on the wicker-and-lath floor of the chariot with a deep sigh.

A warrior spoke; a lord named Tekhip-tilla who had much gray in his black beard, a man who had fought in the last wars of the old kingdom. "Princess, they do." He looked at the fire-weapons racked snugly in leather scabbards on the rail of his chariot. "But I have already seen that this means a man on foot with a *rifle* is a much smaller target than a chariot . . . and he can shoot more steadily. Can chariots go near such, and live?"

Raupasha nodded. "But most of the enemy host will not have rifles," she said. "Only the . . ." She thought, searching for a Hurrian phrase that would match the English concept of a standing army. "Only the . . . *household troops* of the Wolf Lord. His barbarian allies, the Ringapi, they will fight mostly with spear and sword and bow, in chariots and afoot. Them we will strike. Also, there are other weapons that our allies the Eagle People will give us—stronger weapons."

A murmur of awe at that; everyone here had seen the *Nantukhtar* ship of the air and their other wonders.

"Here is a handfast man of the *Nantukhtar* lord Kenn'et. He will tell you of the *mortars* and *rocket launchers* . . ."

When explanation was finished and the cheering had died down, Raupasha flung up her arms. "Yes, we shall have weapons of great power—like the Maruts of Indara Thunderer—or the sons of Teshub," she added, switching the metaphor to a God more familiar to ordinary folk. "But no weapon is mighty without the skill and courage of the warrior who wields it! Are your hands skilled to war, your hearts full of Agni's fire?"

"Yes!" they roared.

"Good, for this is not a war of a day, of a week, or a season. This is a war where only men fit to bestride the universe may hope to conquer. Our allies—those who freed us from the yoke

of Asshur—fight across the wide world and call us to fight at
their side. Shall they call in vain?"

"No! No!"

When they left the practice field for camp, it was as a proud
column of twos, stretching back in a plume of dust and a proud
glitter of arms. Sabala stood proudly, too, basking in her reflected glory, paws on the forward railing of the chariot and
ears flapping as arrogantly as the banner above her.

Now, if only you were Kenn'et, she thought a little desolately,
resting her hand on the hound's skull and looking northward;
it would be weeks before she could rejoin the Nantukhtar lord.
His tail beat happily against her leg and the side of the chariot.
Never would she forget the sight of Kenn'et, bending above
her; when she'd lost conciousness dangling by her thumbs with
her feet six inches over the Assyrian preparations for a hot
low fire.

I did not know, then, she thought. Then she had only thought
him handsome, and brave, and a warrior-wizard. *But now I
know. Whatever King Kashtiliash thinks, you are my lord. And
I will have you for my man as well, though I die for it.*

Something woke the commodore. Not the pendulum-bob way
she and Swindapa were sliding back and forth in the bunk; they
were thoroughly used to that. Perhaps a different note in the
scream of the wind in the rigging, or in the endless groaning
complaint of the ship's fabric. Her first thought was:

Blowing harder. Goddammit, wish I'd been wrong.

She disentangled herself from arms and legs and sat up. Swindapa could blink alert in a second, when she had to. When she
didn't she preferred to come awake slowly, drifting up from
the depths. Marian put one hand on a grip-loop bolted to the
bulkhead and worked the sparker on the gimbaled lantern by
the bunk with the other. The sparks cascaded like miniature
lightning inside the thick wire-braced glass of the chimney, and
then the cotton wick caught. She turned it up, and the yellow
kerosene light ran off the polished curly maple and black walnut of the commander's cabin, and the gray steel of the two
stern-chasers lashed down near either rear corner. Otherwise,
it was austere enough, a couple of chests and cupboards, family
pictures, a shelf of books secured with hinged straps above her
desk and the rack for her sextant, the semicircle of seats below
the shuttered stern windows and the big central table with the
map still fastened down in its holder, and Swindapa's desk on
the other side. That was flanked by filing cabinets; even a Kur-

lelo Grandmother's art of memory was stretched when it came to the logistics of a force this size, and Lieutenant Commander Swindapa Kurlelo-Alston handled most of those details.

Thank you for Swindapa, Lord Jesus. Or Moon Woman, or fate, Alston thought, not for the first time. *But usually it isn't her genius for paperwork that I'm thinkin' of.*

The cabin also had a chronometer and barometer set into the wall. She looked at those and raised her eyebrows. Three hours' sleep, and after all that time the glass was *still* falling. This was going to be a bad one. Then she looked up at the repeater-compass that showed as a dial above the bunk, slaved to the main instrument in the binnacle at the wheels. *Uh-oh.*

Swindapa was yawning and stretching behind her as she pulled on wool longjohns and a fresh uniform. It was a cold-weather pattern, the wool unfulled. That made the dye a little patchy, but it also shed rain almost as well as oilcloth. She was nearly dressed when the knock came at the door.

"Commodore! Message from the *Farragut!*"

"Thank you, yeoman," she said to the signals tech, opening the door and taking the transcript.

Shipping heavy water, violent roll, engines stressing hull frames but pumps keeping pace. Alston winced. Boilers were *heavy.* She read the rest: *Striking all sail and heaving to under paddles alone. Captain Trudeau.*

"A reply, ma'am?"

"Acknowledge, *luck be with you,* and hourly updates," she said.

"And ma'am, the captain sends his compliments, and he's bringing her around into the wind. The storm's strengthening."

"Tell Commander Jenkins that I'll be on deck presently."

Swindapa clubbed her long yellow hair into a fighting braid at her nape and shrugged into her uniform. Alone, they gave a moment to a fierce hug and then put on their official faces, plus their oilskins and sou'westers, tying the cords under their chins as they went up the companionway to the fantail deck. Water crashed into their faces as they came on deck, flying in hard sheets over the port bow of the ship and tearing down the two hundred feet to the quarterdeck through pitch-dark chaos. Each of them put an elbow about the starboard safety line as they ran forward in bursts to the wheel and binnacle, struggling to keep their feet as the wind tried to fling them backward like scraps of paper in a storm. The gale from the north was cutting across the long Atlantic westward swell, creating a chaos of waves that had the bowsprit following a corkscrew pattern, heaving the ship in what seemed like three directions at once.

Lower topsails, she noted, looking up into the rigging for what the ship's commander had set. *And foretopsail staysail.*

Good. The *Chamberlain*'s bows were pointing northwest now, up into the wind. Theoretically they were tacking, but there was no chance of making any real forward way in weather like this. You didn't want to; the object was to keep the ship moving as slowly as possible and still have steerageway, so that she rode the incoming waves rather than cutting into them. They were probably drifting a little to leeward, overall—the mass of ocean beneath her was too—but *Chamberlain* should come through all right if nothing important gave way.

There was a group around the wheels; Commander Jenkins, his XO, and the officer of the deck as well, with a couple of ensigns and middies looking on anxiously.

"You have the wheel lashed, I see, Captain," she said to Jenkins.

He nodded, exaggerating the gesture to be seen in the chaotic darkness. "Foretopsail's braced sharp and staysail's sheeted flat!" he yelled, his face indistinct under the flapping brow of his sou'wester except for a white flash of teeth. "You showed us that trick on *Eagle,* Commodore!"

Braced like that, the square sail slowly forced the *Chamberlain*'s bow up into the wind, until it started to luff; then she fell away to the east pushed by the staysail and helped by the pounding waves crashing on her port bow, until the topsail filled again and the cycle repeated. Everything would be fine if they stayed far enough away from the cliffs somewhere behind them, unseen in the night. They were moving forward a bit, but the ship slid a little more sideways and to the rear every time, and the whole mass of water it sat in was making a couple of knots eastward.

"Lieutenant Commander!" Marian said. "Order to the fleet, *Heave to* and *Report status.*"

"Aye, aye, ma'am!" Swindapa replied, before she turned and made her way to the deckhouse that contained the radio.

Marian looked out into the blackness, where only the white tops of the great waves heading toward them were visible before they broke in frothing chaos across the forecastle and waist of the ship, feeling the vessel come surging up again each time to shrug the tons of water overside. *And if I'm any judge of weather, it's going to get worse,* she thought grimly.

It did; the next few hours brought what was technically dawn, but without any lightening that she could see. Breakfast was flasks of coffee brought up by the wardroom steward, hard-boiled eggs, and sandwiches made of pitalike flatbread wrapped around cold corned beef. By that time they had to duck their heads to breathe, or turn around for an instant; there were more dimly seen oilskinned shapes on the quarterdeck, as officers relieved by the next watch stayed to keep their eye on the ship's death struggle with the sea. There wasn't much point in going below, to pitch about wakeful in their bunks. There wasn't much conversation either, when you had to scream into someone's ear with hands cupped around your mouth to be heard at all.

The radio shack abaft the wheels was a little better, since it rated some of the precious electric lights, running from the same bank of batteries and wind-charger that powered the communications gear and the shut-down computer and inkjet printer. When Marian pulled herself through its hatch the ensign on watch threw his weight beside hers to close the oak portal; most of the spray had been caught by a blanket-curtain hung before it for that purpose. The absence of the full shrieking roar outside made it seem quiet, until she had to talk.

"Let me see the latest reports from the fleet," she said to the technican on radio watch.

Quickly she ruffled through the sheaf of papers. The tone of a few was increasingly panic-stricken, but nobody had actually started to founder, or lost masts or major spars yet. She frowned over one from the *Merrimac;* the ship was riding far too low and rolling sluggishly. *Captain Clammp to flag: I suspect cargo is shifting on its pallets and increasing the working of the seams. All pumps manned continuously. Heavy rolling threatening masts and standing rigging. Am attempting to rig preventer-backstays.*

Marian Alston shaped a silent whistle. Putting crews into the tops in weather like this to rerig meant Clammp was *really* worried. And if the rolling was that bad, he was right to worry; losing a sail in weather like this could be catastrophic. Losing a mast didn't bear thinking about.

"Ma'am, message coming through from the *Farragut.*"

There was a spare headset. She put it on, and immediately winced at the blasts of lightning-static that cut across it. The voice blurred behind it, every second or third word coming loud and clear. *Masts . . . boiler . . . buckle . . . hatchway . . . port paddle . . . repairs.*

"*Farragut,* this is Commodore Alston. Repeat, please. I say again, repeat!"

Nothing but more static. *God-damn. If she had a hatchway staved, got cold water pouring in and dousing her boiler, losing power in this . . .*

"Inform me if there's anything more from either *Farragut* or *Merrimac,* please, Ensign."

"Aye, aye, ma'am!"

Back out into the darkness, but just as she left there were a series of lightning flashes that cast the whole ship into stark black-and-white. There were four crewfolk standing by the wheel, with safety lines rigged from their waists; most of the rest of the deck watch were huddled under the break of the quarterdeck. Those around the wheel were catching the full fury, and it struck her breathless; either it had worsened in the last ten minutes, or she'd been unable to remember just how bad it was. On the transports, with hundreds of panic-stricken, seasick landsmen belowdecks, things must be indescribable. She was profoundly glad she'd had at least a couple of platoons of the Marine regiment shipped on every keel that carried Alban volunteer auxiliaries.

She rejoined Swindapa and opened her mouth to speak. Then her head whipped up, alerted by some subliminal clue, a hint her conscious mind couldn't have named. Several others did the same; and without the slightest warning the wind backed and turned ninety degrees. The lunging twist of the ship turned into a heel that had crew clutching for the safety lines or rigging or the circle of belaying pins around the masts.

With a screech the lines holding the staysail gave way, and it bellied out and filled to splitting. That pulled the ship's head violently around dead into the wind and jerked her forward into the oncoming wave, accelerating fast enough to be felt as a surge. Alston's eyes went wide as she watched the frigate's knife bows ram into the oncoming wave, not rising to it at all, no time to ride up the cliff-steep face of the wild water. She clenched her hands into the brass rail around the binnacle and watched the whole forecastle go under, as if the *Chamberlain* were running downward on rails. The wave broke across the waist of the ship, struck the break of the quarterdeck, and surged across it even as the whole hull tilted to the right until the starboard rail was under.

As the surge knocked her feet from under her, she could see the faces of the hands at the wheel, shocked and pale in the binnacle lights, sharing her own certainty that the ship would never come up again, that the monstrous weight of seawater would crush her like a barrel in the grip of a giant. There was something like a pause, and then she saw the forward end of the ship coming up, rising like a broaching whale from the depths.

"Mind your helm!" Jenkins roared in a fine sea-bellow, cutting away the lashings on the wheel; blood from his nose ran down his face, whipping away in the blasting spray. He sprang to the steering platform, and the others heaved with him to spill wind from the sail. "Keep her so! Mr. Oxton, turn out the watch below—all hands! Ms. Tauranasson—"

A quick glance around showed her Swindapa on the starboard line. Tauranasson was hanging limp from her safety line, probably slammed headfirst into something, and in no condition to do anything much. A middy and hand were hauling themselves toward her to take her below to the sickbay.

"Clew up the topsail—man the fore clew-garnets! Take the way off her!" He fumbled for the speaking-trumpet slung over his shoulder.

Not even a powered megaphone would do any good at present, much less an ordinary speaking-trumpet, and it had to be done *now.* "I'll see to it!" Alston shouted into his ear, then turned and plunged forward.

Another surge took her as she grabbed for the railing of the companionway that led down from the quarterdeck to the waist. Her feet went out from under her again, the base of her spine struck something hard, and sensation vanished in a wash of white-hot ice from stomach to feet. Then Swindapa was hauling her upright; she forced paralyzed lungs to work, saw the watch still clinging to the safety lines, moved forward.

"The fore clew-garnets!" she shouted into a CPO's ear, grabbing him by the shoulder. *"Come on."*

They fought their way forward, gathering up a few more dazed crewfolk. By the time they reached the foremast the petty officer had his teams moving like sentient beings and not stunned oxen. Wet hemp rasped her palms as everyone tailed on to the line, coughed sea wrack out of their lungs, scrabbled for footing on the wet, slick deck . . .

"Heave—" A trained scream that cut through the wind for a few yards at least.

"Ho!"

Alston waited until the work was well in hand before dropping out of the line team; she could feel the way coming off the ship, the bow once more rising lightly to the oncoming waves. More hands were pouring topside; few had been asleep anyway, and one of the advantages of a ship with a full fighting crew—far larger than necessary for mere sailing—was that there were always plenty of hands and strong backs around in an emergency.

Now, she thought. *We actually may live out the night.*

There was something to be said for a direct, physical risk. It took your mind off things you couldn't do anything about. Like the rest of the fleet; or the rest of the war, for that matter.

I always feel ridiculous riding in a chariot, Doreen Arnstein thought. "At least this one has springs and seats," the Assistant Councilor for Foreign Affairs murmured to herself. "*And* a sunshade. With gold tassels, yet."

The springs were from a Honda Accord, the tires solid rubber on steel, the body was wood inlay with a gilded brass rail 'round about to hang on to. It was more of a two-wheeled wagon than a copy of the war-carts the Nantucketers had encountered in the Bronze Age world. They'd run it up for purposes of swank—or public relations, if you wanted to get formal; there was plenty of room for her, the driver, and Brigadier Hollard. The horses pulling it were two precious Morgans shipped in from Nantucket, sleek black giants by local standards, drawing gasps and stares on their own. A leather-lunged Hittite herald went ahead:

"*Make way! Make way for the honored guests of the One Sun, the Great King of Hatti! Make way for the honored emmissaries of his brother, Great King Yhared-Koff'in! Make way!*"

Some of the crowd made way for the herald's voice, some for the ram's-horn trumpets blown by the two men behind him, still more for the reversed spears of the troop of Royal Guards. A guard of Marines rode behind, the butts of their rifles resting on their thighs; their saddles and stirrups still drew pointed fingers and murmurs of amazement.

Doreen fanned herself; it was a fairly warm day for late autumn, and still more so in the ceremonial robe she was wearing, fairly crusted with gold and silver thread and gems until she blazed and glittered when a ray of the bright upland sun struck her, the more so from her diadem and earrings.

Wearing this sort of thing makes me feel like I'm acting in a bad historical drama, she thought. Glittering jeweled robes looked perfectly natural on, say, Princess Raupasha. On herself they just . . . well, *I'm no princess. Not even a JAP. I'm a thirtysomething, former astronomy major from Hoboken, New Jersey.*

And the roundish, curve-nosed, full-lipped face with the dark eyes and curly coarse dark hair that looked out of her mirror *really* didn't go with this getup.

"But it impresses the yokels no end," Kenneth Hollard said, looking indecently comfortable in his Marine khakis.

"That's why we're taking the long way in," Doreen replied. "It impresses the nobility, too." *And when the cold weather hits, pretty soon, it's going to be worse than the heat. Oh, well.* "They're even more status-conscious here than they are down in Babylonia."

"*That's* saying something," Hollard muttered.

He had a look she recognized—extreme frustration. Getting anything done in these ancient Oriental kingdoms was difficult-to-impossible. Getting it done quickly . . . *Oi. But fretting about it just gives you heartburn.*

"And the people are spooked by what they've heard about Walker and the Ringapi," she said. "Letting them know they've got wizard allies of their own bucks them up."

She shoved the constant nagging worry about the situation in general and Ian in particular and took in the scene about her. Even after weeks in Hattusas, the capital of the Hittite Empire could still thrill her. It wasn't as big as the largest Babylonian cities, and there was nothing as hulkingly massive as their ziggurats. Cruder and rawer; cyclopean stone walls outside, shaped beside the gates into figures of brooding warrior-Gods and pug-faced lions. The Islander party had been directed through the Gate of the Sphinxes, on the southern edge of the city. A massive rampart a hundred and fifty feet thick and twenty high supported the city wall, its earthen surface paved to make a smooth glacis. The ramp led upward past a man-high outer wall, then straight to the foot of the main ramparts; those were of huge stone blocks longer than she was tall, rough-fitted together without mortar and smoothed on the outside, thirty feet high and nearly as thick. Towers studded it at intervals of a half-bowshot, squatly massive; the crenellations on top were like teeth bared at heaven. Metal gleamed on spearheads and helmets on the walls, blinking back blinding bright in the morning sun.

"Impressive," she said to Kenneth Hollard.

"I'll say," he replied; but he was weighing them with a slightly different eye. "Still, that's really two walls with cross-bracing and the cells filled with rubble. You could knock it down into a ramp with some of our five-inch rifles. Take a while, though. A lot longer than with a brick wall and mud-brick core, the way the cities down in the Land Between the Rivers have. They really know how to use rock here, and they've got a lot of it. It'd take forever to force a breach if they had concrete to use to consolidate the rubble fill . . ."

"Ken," she said, a slight scolding tone in her voice, "it's not really polite to speculate in public on how you'd destroy the capital of an allied power."

He grinned; it turned his naturally stern face into something charmingly boyish. "Professional reflex, Madam Councilor," he said.

"I was thinking of how much work it must have taken," she replied.

The ramp came to the rampart and made a sharp turn to the left, throwing them into the shadow of the city wall.

"Well laid out, too. Spear side," Hollard said, and continued at her raised eybrows: "With the ramp this way, your right side—spear side—is to the wall and you can't use your shield to stop the sharp pointies they're raining down from up there."

He tossed his helmeted head to the right. Doreen looked up, and tried to imagine a roaring crush of men where she was, wrestling with battering rams as arrows slammed down in sleet-ing clouds like hard, hard rain . . . There were scorch marks on the massive stones going by at arm's length from her. She knew from chronicles in the twentieth confirmed here that Hat-tusas *had* fallen at least once about a century before, sacked and burned by the Kaska mountain tribes from the country just to the north.

"Determined bastards, they must have been," Kenneth Hol-lard said, reading her thought. "You'd pay a real butcher's bill taking this with scaling ladders and handheld log battering rams, against any sort of opposition."

That was one way to put it. Her mind shied away from giving her a picture of what the words meant; she'd gotten case-hard-ened, somewhat, since coming here, but there were limits she didn't want to cross. Even more, she didn't want to imagine what was happening under the walls of Troy right now, or inside them.

"And look at the pavement," he went on.

She did. It was made of the heavy flat rocks as well, and some of *them* were scorched, too.

"How?" she said.

"Olive oil," he said. "Possibly naphtha, but probably olive

oil, heated—great big boiling tubs of it, maybe mixed with tallow or lard. Wait until the attackers are really packed in here"—he looked up and down the long ramp, estimating the space—"say fifteen hundred of them. Pour the mixture down from the wall along here, and it'd run all down this ramp and onto the glacis, under the feet of the men packed in shoulder to shoulder and nose to tail, spattering on the clothes and faces of a lot of 'em, or running under their armor—make the road surface damned slippery, too. They'd be immobilized. Then toss down a torch."

God, she thought, fighting down queasiness. *Crisco Extra-Virgin Instant Hell.* There were times—watching the *Emancipator* bombing the Assyrian cities, for instance—when she'd felt a little guilty about helping to introduce modern weapons here. Then again, when you saw what human ingenuity could manage with low tech, did it matter? *When people want to be atrocious, they'll find a way, even if it's labor-intensive.*

Sphinxes flanked the gate, carved into enormous masonry blocks that ran all the way from the entrance back through the thickness of the wall. The man-headed lions had little of the Egyptian grace, but plenty of power. The crowds thinned out here, no room for them, but a line of Royal Guards lined the tunnel-like way between the inner and outer gates. Those were bronze-faced wood, under arched gateways straddled by great square towers. The pointed arches themselves were something to see, each half-carved out of a block of granite that must have weighed thirty or forty tons—they didn't know how to build arches or domes here out of blocks, but this served the same purpose.

As they moved into the streets the crowds were dense once more, and she put the scented feathers of the fan to her nose again; the stench wasn't quite as overpowering as, say, Babylon in August, since Hattusas was both smaller and at the moment cooler, but it was bad enough—sewage, animal droppings, garbage, and old sweat soaked into wool, all activated by the fresh sweat of crowding and excitement. She swallowed; her stomach had gotten a lot more vulnerable to this sort of thing since she'd gotten pregnant. That had happened the first time, too, but she'd been back in safe, comfortable, clean Nantucket then.

The thought made her snort a little with laughter. Anyone fresh from the twentieth would find Nantucket odorous enough and to spare, these days; land tons of fish and shellfish every day, and no matter how the gulls scavenge and how zealous the recycling collectors are about potential fertilizer, the air will take on a distinct tang. Rendered whale blubber didn't help either, or factories driven by wood-fired steam engines, or . . .

It still smelled a lot better than this. There weren't as many flies, either. She waved some of the flies away, swallowed again, and to take her mind off her stomach admired—rather dutifully—a blocky temple of dark-gray limestone. Unlike the Babylonian kind, this had big rectangular windows in the outer wall, reaching nearly to the ground. Through them she could catch a bright sideways glimpse of the Holy of Holies, where a burnished man-high silver statue of the God flashed and glittered on a pillar that rested on a golden lion. The figure was shown with shield, club, and helmet . . . *That's Zababa*, she reminded herself. *I think*. The Hittites had so *many* damned Gods, and most of them had at least two names—here they threw every pantheon they came in contact with together, in a *mispocha* of celestial miscegenation and cheerfully incoherent syncretism.

The road inside the city was paved, which was something of a relief even if the pavement was lumpy and uneven; they worked their way up toward the stark citadel that crowned the eastern lobe of Hattusas's figure-eight layout. They passed more temples, dozens of them; hundreds upon hundreds of blocky stone-and-timber houses and others of unplastered mud brick or combinations; carved slabs graven with rows of scimitar-wielding Gods; crowds staring or cheering or making gestures of aversion; one bunch cut the throat of a lamb over an improvised altar as the Islanders passed, and Doreen had a horrible intuition that it was to *her* . . .

The King's residence was a fortress in its own right, even more impressive than the southern wall when you factored in the steep rocky scarps below. There was another ramp for the horses to climb, more ceremonial to go through before and after they passed through the gates; there were two great Kings present and the representatives of a third, Jared Cofflin being granted that status since nobody in the ancient East knew what the hell to make of an elected head of state. Plus vassal Princess Raupasha, now that her little *faux pas* was forgiven if not forgotten. Doreen sighed as she tucked her attaché case under her arm and Hollard offered her an arm down from the chariot. Even in the Bronze Age, you couldn't escape going to meetings. . . .

Quiet fell once they were within the throne chamber; it was big and dim, with spears of light coming from windows and openings in the flat roof above. Other pillars of vividly painted wood upheld the high ceiling; Royal Guards around the edges of the room stood motionless as the idols in their wall niches and the painted figures of dead Kings making offerings. The soldiers' weapons and bronze-scale armor glittered, and so did the images, their eyes seeming to move and follow her with a glisten of onyx and lapis lazuli. Tudhaliyas sat motionless on his throne, with *Tawannannas* Zuduhepa beside him.

Doreen sent up a silent prayer of thanks that Hittites had that institution. Zuduhepa was queen in her own right; if she outlived her husband, she'd carry the title and very real power that went with it into the reign of her son until her own death. That made them more accustomed than most peoples in this era to taking a woman seriously. Her predecessor, Tudhaliyas's mother, had been a holy terror all her long life, and had hand-picked her successor; that young woman had even taken Zudu-hepa as a throne-name on her accession.

Of course, local custom was getting a bit bent out of shape, just lately. Kathryn Hollard was there, too, beside King Kashtil-iash, and in Marine khakis that clashed horribly with the Oriental-rococo splendor of the chair; by the terms of her marriage contract she was commander in chief of the New Troops of Kar-Duniash.

And she's looking disgustingly sleek and satisfied, Doreen thought with friendly amusement. *I guess the Bull of Marduk lives up to expectations.* She couldn't imagine sharing a husband with the hareem as local custom required, or for that matter marrying a local at all, but those two were apparently happy enough with the relationship. Princess Raupasha sat to one side on a lower, slightly plainer throne; *she* was wearing trousers and boots, set off by a gold-washed tunic of chain mail.

Must have had some local artisans do that, Doreen thought. The polished Fritz helmet with the gold diadem around the brows and the purple-dyed ostrich plumes was rather striking, too. *Say what you like, that kid has style.*

The two Islanders drew near to the throne, saluted and bowed respectively, and repeated the gesture to the other monarchs. *God, I'm getting good control of my facial muscles,* she thought, fighting down a giggle. Court dress for a Hittite King looked very much like a gaudily embroidered mid-Victorian dress with a flounced skirt, combined with a skullcap . . . Like everything else here, the greetings involved endless ritual, mostly religious. Hierophants set out tables before each of the participants in the conference, with dishes covered in embroidered linen cloths. Doreen's nose twitched—it was lunchtime, by her clock—but she waited patiently.

Musicians in ragged motley came in. They carried instruments; *arkanmmi, huhupal* and *galgaturi,* none of which could be described in terms of Western analogues, except that they involved blowing, plucking, and percussion. The *thump-tweedle-plink* sounded low and not unpleasant. Other ragged men *danced* in, holding their hands above their heads and twirling gently in circles until the skirts of their robes flared out and clinking finger-cymbals sounded. Doreen's eyes went wider; evidently the tradition of the whirling dervish was a lot older in this part of the world than anyone had suspected.

At last the various rituals were completed (the dish turned out to be strips of beef with onions in a garlic sauce) and the Kings and principals were seated around a table in a smaller room. Doreen recognized it with a twinge of nostalgia; it was where Ian and she had had their first audience with the Hittite rulers . . . *God, only a few months ago. Ian . . .*

"I and the *Seg Kallui* have brought forward as many of our troops as we can," Kashtiliash said at last. "More await the command in Babylon. Lord Kenn'et, when do we strike the *Ahhiyawa*?"

"We don't," Kenneth Hollard said. "We wait for them to strike us."

Kashtiliash looked unhappy, or possibly angry. "You did not wait for the Assyrians to strike," he pointed out. "We advanced together and crushed them, *thus.*"

He was speaking Akkadian; everyone in the room understood it, more or less. Absolutely everyone understood the gripping, mangling gesture of his great scarred hands.

"That was in Kar-Duniash," Kenneth said. "In Kar-Duniash, we had the Land of the Two Rivers to draw on for food—land more fertile than any other in this part of the world except for Egypt. And we had the Two Rivers themselves, and the canals, and our steamboats. Rarely did we operate more than a week's travel from water transport."

He went over to a map drawn on a whitewashed wall; a light well in the ceiling above made it seem to glow.

"Here, we are six hundred miles as the bird flies from the head of navigation on the Euphrates. More than a thousand as the roads go, and they're very bad roads over mountains. On good roads with our wagons, the practical limit on hauling food by animal traction is about one hundred and twenty miles. On these roads, with your wagons, it's sixty miles. After that, the wagoneers and their animals have eaten all the cargo. All our transport capacity has to go to weapons and supplies, because we haven't had time to teach the Hittite—Nesite—folk how to make anything we need. It's been hard getting in enough rifles and ammunition to reequip your Royal Guards."

Tudhaliyas nodded somberly, rubbing his fingers over the arms of his chair. He was an able man, in Doreen's opinion, but something of a worrywart. He'd also insisted on getting at least a few thousand rifles and some cannon as a condition of the alliance; which made sense, when you looked at it from his point of view, but was an infernal nuisance.

"I can summon a hundred thousand men to my banner," he said. "If I call in all my garrisons, all my own troops, all those of my nobles and Royal Kin and holders-of-land-on-service, and the contingents of my vassal rulers. But if I call them all to the same place, they will starve to death in short order."

Kashtiliash looked at him somberly, tugging at his curled beard. "Surely you have royal storehouses in each region," he said. "Surely your city-governors and provincial overlords and the nobles of the lands each have their own reserves of food. In my land, there is never less than three years' supplies for court, armies, and cities in storage, at least of grain and dates, onions and salt fish."

The Hittite nodded. "Oh, yes; we too take precautions. But remember, every *iku* of my lands yields perhaps half of what yours does, my brother, yet takes as much labor of men and oxen to cultivate. And I cannot ship the grain of that *iku* of land from place to place by barge, as you do; our rivers are rivers of rock and spray, not broad paths. If I call too many beasts and carts and men from the fields, the harvest will fail and we will all starve. Then most of the soldiers must be home for planting, and still more for the harvest. Our harvests have been poor for four years, as well—not enough rain in most of Hatti-land. Stores are low."

Kashtiliash tugged at his beard again. "How is Walker better-suited than we?" he asked the Islander commander.

"He can bring in his supplies by water, as you can in your land, my kinsman," Kenneth said, moving his hand down the western coast of Anatolia. "Water transport is quick and cheap. And he can draw on the whole of Great Achaea's surpluses, which are greater than Hatti-land's, because he has had years to spread new methods and crops and tools, and to build roads and grain stores."

"But he cannot sail his ships inland . . . ah, my kinsman, I see," Kashtiliash said, grinning in his blue-black beard. "That is what you mean."

"Yeah," Kenneth said, nodding. "We've got to get him away from his base of supply and closer to ours." A grim smile. "Let's call it the *Attaturk Plan*. We've been stockpiling food and fodder in selected locations since the harvest"—he tapped points marked on the routes inland from the coast toward Hattusas—"and we've got to be prepared to deny him local replenishment."

"You mean we must be prepared to burn my own lands and turn my own people out onto the roads of the winter," Tudhaliyas said. "Lest Walker feed from their storehouses and flocks."

"Yes, Your Majesty," Kathryn Hollard said gently. "Or they will be Walker's lands and Walker's people—his slaves, rather."

Kashtiliash gave her a fond glance and went on: "What I can do for you after this war, my brother, I will do. As my allies say, we cannot move grain enough to feed many from Kar-Duniash to Hatti-land, but silver, plow oxen, seed-grain, cloth, these I will send."

"The Republic will help all it can as well for rebuilding after the war," Doreen said. "We can ship in, and show you how to make, new tools for farming—how to build better roads to spread harvests around, and how to preserve food better. We can show your healers how to stop epidemics. If we can get command of the sea, we can help feed the coastal zones, as well."

Tudhaliyas nodded, looking as if his stomach pained him. "Silver and cloth are well, but we cannot eat them, and if we eat the seed corn now and do *not* get more . . ." A deep sigh. "Let it be so. You have given me the head of the rebel Kurunta, and Walker was behind him. More, the Wolf Lord is all that you say in the way of greed and evil, from what the refugees tell."

Doreen put her hand on her stomach. They were talking about deliberately creating famine.

She shivered. A hell of a lot of people were going to die because of what was decided in this room, without ever knowing why. An anvil from orbit falling and shattering their lives without purpose or cause they could see.

No, she scolded herself. *A hell of a lot of people are going to die because of what* Walker *decided to do. He's responsible, nobody else. Self-defense is self-defense, even if it means . . . drastic measures.*

"Perhaps only troops equipped with the fire-weapons should

be called up," Tudhaliyas said. "That would help in the matter of supplies."

Kathryn shook her head. "O One Sun, we need troops of the old kind as well. They can checkmate Walker's savage allies, and they can harass his men when they spread out to forage. And the chariots can also be useful, if they are used in a new way with new weapons."

She looked at Princess Raupasha. The Mitannian girl began to speak, growing enthusiastic, her hands tracing accompaniment through the air. Tudhaliyas grew thoughtful.

"That would please my nobles," he said at the end. "They have seen the power of the new weapons, but a landed man grows with his feet in a chariot; it is not meet or seemly for him to go to war like a peasant spearman."

Kenneth Hollard gave a grim smile. "In the Republic, we have a saying: 'The flies have conquered the honey.' We want Walker's conquests to be like that." His hand moved west. "Our fleet is moving to the Pillars, here, as well. If they can break the Tartessian hold on the straits, they can move into the Middle Sea. Much of Walker's supplies come from Sicily, this large island here. Denying it to him will strike him a heavy blow."

"*If* is a word like a pig covered in olive oil, tasty if you can pin it down and set it on fire," Zuduhepa said, tilting her elaborate, golden-bedecked headdress as she turned to watch Kenneth Hollard. "Let us speak further of that which your fleet can do."

"Here, ma'am," the steward said. "Galley stove's working again."

Marian Alston-Kurlelo took the cup and sipped cautiously through the drinking hole in the cover. The storm was over, technically, although the sky above was covered in scudding gray tendrils and the light of noon was a muted glow, like being inside a giant frosted-glass globe. The wind was strong out of the northwest, but no longer a gale; still cold and raw, though, and she was grateful as she felt the aching need for rest being driven back by the strong harsh coffee, and a welcome warmth spreading in her stomach.

"Thank you, Seaman Puarkelo," she said, and the boy blushed. Alston gave an inward sigh. Commander Jenkins was forward, surveying the damage. There was a fair amount of it, the bowsprit rolling loose, foretopsail yard carried away, dangling ends of broken rigging, but none of it was fundamental.

One of the ships scudding along southward in company had lost her foremast just above the tops, and Alston's eyes narrowed as she saw the busy chaos on her foredeck. Then it settled down, and a long spar began to rise needlelike through the rigging—a jury-rig, but a sound one. Jenkins was deep in conversation with his XO and the ship's carpenter as he came back to the wheels, sounding remarkably cheerful.

Well, he didn't lose any of his people, she thought. *Do Jesus, it would be nice to have only one ship to worry about again.*

"Ma'am," he said, saluting. She returned the gesture. "There's nothing up ahead that we can't have fixed in a day or two."

"Very satsifactory, Captain," she said. Raising her voice slightly: "A very satisfactory piece of seamanship last night, in fact, Mr. Jenkins. The *Chamberlain* showed very well indeed. Well done."

The exhausted, red-eyed face flushed with pleasure. Then he grew grave: "Anything from the rest of the fleet, ma'am?"

"I was just expecting—ah." Swindapa came up; she looked wearied as well, with a bandage across her forehead where a flailing line had lashed her. "Any news?"

"Total casualties are twenty-seven dead, confirmed," she said.

Damn it to hell. To be expected, in a blow that violent, in a fleet that included thousands of troops packed in like sardines. Light casualties, really. *And I hate losing every God-damned one.*

"Two hundred seven seriously wounded, mostly broken bones and concussions," the Fiernan went on seriously. "Not counting walking wounded fit for duty." She looked up, the cerulean-blue eyes sad. "That's from ships in contact. All ships have reported except for the *Farragut*, the *Severna Park*, and the *Merrimac*," she said.

Alston's belly clenched. The steam ram, a collier, and their secret weapon . . . and nearly two hundred souls.

Swindapa went on: "We're still trying for—"

A rating from the radio shack ran up. "Ma'am!" he said, thrusting a paper at her. "Ma'am!"

"Report from the *Merrimac*!" Swindapa said.

A sound something like a cheer went up from some of the middies and hands on the quarterdeck, and the officers smiled. Alston allowed herself a slight curve of the lips as well, as she took the transcript.

It didn't quite die as she read it. *Nearly doomed* wasn't as bad as *actually dead*. Or so she thought until they came in sight of the stricken vessel . . .

"Damn," she said mildly, lowering the binoculars.

"Right on the mark," Jenkins said, impressed. "Where you said the winds and current would throw them."

The maintop was a little crowded, with captain, commodore, and a couple of other officers standing on the little triangular railed platform; the usual lookout was out on the yard.

"From the description, it could only be these shores," Alston said absently. "*They* certainly didn't have much idea where they were. The only good thing about it is that we're here now—and that there's deep water all the way to the cliffs."

She raised the binoculars again. The storm had died down, there were streaks of blue overhead, but the enormous swells still came pounding in from the west, out of the deep reaches of the Atlantic that ran landless from here to the Carolinas. There was already white on the tops of some of the mountains landward; down from there the land ran steep, densely green forest below the moors, then dropped sheer into the sea battering it from the northwest. No sign of human habitation, although she'd give odds that eyes were fixed on her ships from somewhere up there. The wind had shifted to a steady westerly, strong enough to make the rigging drone a steady bass note, and to send the *Chamberlain* slanting southeast with her port rail nearly under, white foam breaking from her bows. The mast swayed out, over the rushing gray water, back over the narrow oval of deck, out again in a wide warped circle. She ignored it as she focused on the wounded ship to leeward.

"*Merrimac,* all right," she said. "Badly beat up."

Nearly destroyed might have been a better way of putting it. All three masts were gone by the board, the foremast nearly at deck level, the main about twenty feet up; the mizzen was still there about to the mizzentops. Standing rigging hung in great swaths and tangles; the deck looked as if there was scarcely a foothold free of fallen cordage and spars and sails. The pumps were going, a steady stream of water over both rails, and a set of pathetic jury-rigged sails were up, triangular swatches that looked as if a bunch of small sailboats were sitting on the big Down Easter's decks.

"I wonder Clammp hasn't got his boats out towing," Jenkins said.

"Take a look at her stern davits," Marian said grimly. A boat was dangling there, or at least the rear third of one. "Ms.

Kurlelo-Alston, what boats do we have with the frigates still sound? Six-oared or better."

"Eight, ma'am," Swindapa said instantly. "Three more under repair and ready within a few hours."

"Good . . . all right. Those boats to the *Merrimac.* Ship's doctor from the *Chamberlain,* medical supplies, stretchers, cordage. Portable pumps, four of 'em. She'll need hands . . . besides the boat crews, fifteen hands and a middie, ensign, or lieutenant from each—good riggers, sailmakers. And ship's carpenters with their mates and kit from, hmmm-mmm, *Lincoln* and *Sheridan.*"

"Yes, ma'am." Swindapa repeated the order and leaned out, grabbed a backstay, and slid the hundred feet to the quarterdeck with her feet braced against the hard ribbing of the hemp cable to control her speed.

"A tow, Commodore?" Jenkins asked quietly.

Marian Alston looked beyond the laboring hulk of the *Merrimac.* Close, far too close, the great swells surged and roared against sheer rock, throwing foam mast high. Even across several miles of sea she could hear the sound, and through the binoculars see the grinding snarl where the huge mass of water pushed eastward by the long storm met the immovable object of the Cantabrian Mountains, where the Pyrenees slid down into the Atlantic. There was clear water beyond that last finger of granite reaching out to sea . . .

. . . and the *Merrimac* wasn't going to make it, not under that miserable jury-rig; if she was doing two knots, it was a miracle. The swell and drift eastward would cut her off long before; she was making a yard eastward for every one she made south. *Close, but no cigar.* Anything that hitched on would be dragged to leeward as well by fourteen hundred tons of dead-in-the-water inertia.

"No, Commander Jenkins. I'm going to save that cargo if I can, but I'm not going to lose any more people for it. Rig for a tow, by all means, ready when and *if* we can get her far enough out. I'm going over to supervise recovery operations myself."

The deck had already been busy, repairs still going forward on the rigging; now it was doubly so, with lashings being untied and davits swung out. More than a few of the crew exchanged glances; launching a boat in seas this rough was gambling with a dunking at the very least, or possibly with injury and death if something went wrong halfway down. There was a scramble of orders and bosun's whistles, and deck crews formed on the lines. Jenkins murmured to his sailing master, and the voice rang out:

"Clew up!"

"Heave . . . *ho!*" The rhythmic chorus rang out, and the square sails spilled wind as the lines hauled them up like a theater curtain. The ship slowed almost instantly, swaying more toward the upright. Also rolling more, but you couldn't have everything.

The bosun's mate in charge of the boats wasn't hesitating. "Boat crew of the day to the commodore's barge! Falls tenders! Frapping line tenders!"

The commands ran on smoothly. Swindapa came up beside her. "Anything else?" she said softly, trying not to disrupt Alston's train of thought.

"Yes," she replied. "Have Captain Jenkins and . . . who's got the most left in the way of large spars?"

"Of the frigates, *Sheridan,*" Swindapa said. The stores-ships were too far out to be useful just now. "Full set—didn't lose anything."

She wouldn't, with Tom Hiller as her skipper, Alston thought. He'd been sailing master of the *Eagle* and taught Alston herself most of what she knew of handling big square-riggers. Aloud:

". . . and the *Sheridan* make a bundle of some spare spars—main and foresail—and get ready to put them overside rigged for tow." Luckily the spars were buoyant, being varnished white pine.

Fatigue and anxiety had vanished. She had a job to do; it might well be an impossible one, but all she could do was make the best possible decisions. Focus left her coldly alert, impersonal, and intensely alive.

The bosun's mate had the line team ready, and he scrambled up on the davits to give it a final visual check. A sailor brought her a life jacket; she strapped in absently, eyes still narrowed and gazing at the *Merrimac.* Swindapa came up beside her, and they both settled their billed Coast Guard caps more firmly on their heads—as usual, a few wispy strands of fine blond hair were floating free from their braid, like streamers to windward since they were both facing the port rail. Alston blinked, felt a fleeting, familiar moment of absurdly intense tenderness, a desire to smooth the strands back. Their eyes met, and spoke *later* without word or expression.

"Denniston, lay into the boat," the bosun's mate barked. A sailor climbed into it, undoing more lashings, running a final check, then gave a thumbs-up. "Cast off the gripe . . . cast off the preventers . . ." A clank as the sailor in the boat tripped the pelican hooks. "Boat crew lay into the boat!"

This time ten sailors climbed into the boat—technically the commodore's barge—in careful pairs. Two picked up oars and made ready to fend the boat off from the side of the ship; the rest of them and Denniston the coxswain grabbed the manropes that dangled from above, taking as much of their weight as possible off the tackle that held the boat.

Denniston looked over to the bosun's mate. "Ready in the boat."

The bosun's mate turned. "Ready on deck, ma'am," he said to the OOD, and received a nod. Then he went on: "On the falls!" The teams on deck took up the lines that ran to both ends of the boat, ready to control the descent. The bosun's mate took position near the rail, hands outstretched to either side. "Ready forward and aft?"

"Ready aye ready!"

"Lower away together!" A clink, and the boat sank with smooth speed. "Lively aft—easy forward—easy forward, *handsomely there, God-damn you—*"

The *Chamberlain* heeled a little more and the swell rose to meet her. The boat touched, skipped, began to throw a bow wave of its own.

"Let fall!" the bosun's mate said, stepping back; the coxswain in the boat was in charge now. From below came her call:

"Unhook aft—passengers to the line!"

Alston came to with an inward start. There was something hypnotically soothing about a well-executed maneuver like this, and the Chamberlains were a well worked-up lot; the flagship naturally stayed in full commission more than the other Guard frigates, spent less time shuttling cargo to new or remote bases, and hence less time cut back to a sailing rather than a full fighting crew. A hand was holding the line for her, and as she came up she could see one of the boat's crew below doing the same. She leaned out, took a bight of the line around her right forearm, gripped it lower between crossed feet, and slid down at just short of rope-burn speed. Two of the sailors caught her and she stepped forward to a place in the bows of the boat, grabbing a thwart.

Seen from the surface the swell was like the surge of a giant's muscle beneath them, infinite power enclosed in a silk-smooth skin, dangerous and beautiful. The bitter kiss of foam blew onto her face, and she could feel the living heave of the ocean through the thin inch of oak that made up the cutter's planks.

Swindapa came down the line next, then the rest of the hands being sent across, while the tools and cordage and sailcloth came down on whiplines.

"Let go forward!" Denniston said.

The coxswain was a short woman, thickset and muscular, with cropped black hair and bright green eyes, in her early twenties. Alban, from an eastern tribe, but she'd taken an Immigration Office name. Some of the Sun People tribes had sent in fairly bitter complaints about girls running off for this reason or that—being married to suitors they didn't like was the most common—and their fathers having to repay the bridewealth and swallow public shame.

If they don't like it, they can change their God-damned customs.

"Fend off," the coxswain said. Oars pushed the longboat away from the heaving wooden cliff of the *Chamberlain*'s side; other boats were being lowered even as they moved. "Out oars and stroke . . . stroke . . . stroke . . ."

That was awkward in the crowded barge; it was even more so when they stopped to raise the mast, step, and brace it. That gave her something to do; she shifted over to the windward rail, along with everyone else except the coxswain at the tiller, sitting on it to fight the heel and make the boat stiffer as it raced across the wind toward the stricken *Merrimac*.

Under the urgent focus on the task ahead ran the sheer exuberant satisfaction of the cutter's racing speed, the sea hissing past six inches away—less when they crested one of the huge waves and white water burst around them. She fought down an urge to whoop and grin as the bow went up . . . up . . . up; then the great jerk of acceleration on the crest as the sail caught the full force of the stiff wind and cracked taut. And the long roller-coaster swoop down the skin of the gray-blue swell, with goose-wings of spray flying higher than her head from the boat's bows and the curving wake racing aft.

For a moment she was a skinny black girl in faded cutoffs and a T-shirt again, dancing with excitement in a little dinghy as it tossed in a yachtsman's wake off Prince Island.

Swindapa *did* whoop, and the coxswain gave an exultant tribal screech, half-standing at the crest to get another sight of the *Merrimac*'s sails, leaning expertly into the tiller and calling directions to the hands at the lines. Soon enough they could see the mountain peaks ahead to the southeast, and then the stumpy tops of the ship's mutilated masts.

"Ready to let go!" Denniston called. The hull came up beside them, looming a dozen feet overhead. There were plenty of ropes overside, and a few of the *Merrimac*'s hands waving and calling. "Ready to fend . . . let go the sail!"

The cutter turned up alongside the ship, and the sail rattled down. Alston moved to take one of the ropes and secure the bows with a running bowline knot. "Denniston, I'm going to rig for tow," she said crisply. "When I do, tail on to the line and haul away; I want her head about five points up and as much way as you can."

"Yes, ma'am." A hesitation. "Ma'am, we're not going to tow this bitch free—not even with all the boats."

"I'm aware of that, Petty Officer Denniston," Alston said. "Every bit helps, though."

"Ma'am. Aye, aye, ma'am!"

She nodded, gripped the rope, braced her feet against the slick heaving planks of the ship's side, and swarmed up hand over hand. The others followed, and the gear; she was looking about, taking in the details. Not much was recognizable of the trim, neat new ship she'd boarded in Westhaven. *Hmmm. Wheel's still functional.*

"Where's Captain Clammp?" she said, striding over to a young man she recognized as one of his officers. "I need a report on the status of the ship."

Red-rimmed eyes blinked at her from behind thick spectacles. "Thank God you're here, ma'am," the young man said. His face worked for an instant, as if he was about to burst into tears, then stiffened. "Ma'am, Captain Clammp was injured when the foremast gave way—knocked down—when the wind shifted. He's been unconscious ever since. We . . . ah, we lost five hands, including Lieutenant Stendins." Which had left this teenager in command, probably on his first voyage out of home waters. "Several more were injured. We . . ." he made a helpless gesture toward the chaos of the ship.

Marian Alston put a hand on his shoulder and squeezed gently. "Son, you kept the ship afloat through as bad a blow as I've seen," she said. "Now help's on the way. I need to know everything."

While he told her, Swindapa was directing the unloading of the boats arriving from the frigates. The Merrimacs staggered away from the pumps, and fresh hands began plunging the levers up and down; a tow cable with an empty hogshead on the end for a buoy went overside and the boats made fast, strung out and began to pull the *Merrimac*'s prows to the west of south. Captain Clammp came by, bandaged like a mummy and lashed to a stretcher, to go overside into boats and be rowed out to the warships.

"You've done a fine job," Marian said to young Clammp. "Now rest."

He staggered off. The new hands at the pumps were swinging the levers vigorously, and there was a perceptible increase in the jets of water going overside. One of them started a chanty, and the others took it up:

> *"They say life has its ups and downs;*
> *That really now, is quite profound!*
> *I'd like to push the captsan 'round,*
> *But it's pump her mates, before we drown!"*

More men and women came running to gather around her as she made a high beckoning gesture with the fingers of both hands; the motion of the ship changed beneath her feet as the added thrust of sixty or seventy strong backs swinging ashwood oars came on to the towline. She looked around at the circle of faces; a couple of ensigns, a lieutenant, and half a dozen experienced petty officers and chiefs—ship's carpenters, rigging specialists.

> *"Pump me mates*
> *Pump her dry;*
> *Down to hell, up to the sky—*
> *Bend your backs and break your bones*
> *We're just a thousand miles from home!"*

"All right, people, we need to lighten this ship and get some sail on her," Alston said briskly. "Guns overside. Get the auxiliary pumps started; once you've made some headway in the hold, start her fresh water overside as well—stores, this clutter on deck, everything that can be heaved to the rail except her main cargo." Most of which was far too bulky and heavy to move anyway. "Chips?"

The *Lincoln*'s master carpenter jerked a thumb westward to where two more boats were towing bundles of white pine spars, seventy feet long and a foot and a half thick in the middle.

"With those spars, ma'am, we can do jury masts on the main and fore—scarf and wold 'em. That'll give you something. It'll take a while."

> *"Sometimes when I am in me bed*
> *And thinkin' of the day ahead;*
> *I wish that I could wake up dead—*
> *But pumpin's all I get instead!"*

"Get it done in the next fifty minutes or there's no point," she said over the sound of the chanty. "I want the rigging ready to go up and the sails, too." She pointed ahead, to where the breakers made a white line to their south and east. "The swell, tide, and wind are all shoving us toward that. We need to bring her head around five points, and get some real way on her— five knots, more would be better—and the wind's not favorable." Not dead in their teeth, but coming in over the starboard quarter.

She tapped a fist into a pink palm. "We need what's on board to win this war; to keep it, we have to save this ship, so that's exactly what we're going to do, people. Let's do it; let's go."

They gave a short, sharp cheer and scattered to their work at a run. Alston watched them go, fighting down a ferocious impatience. Who knew what devilments Isketerol might be up to, might get up to in the future, if they gave him time?

Swindapa came up and handed her a piece of hardtack. She looked down at the hard gray-brown crackerlike rectangle, puzzled for an instant, then ahead at the cliffs they'd be passing— hopefully passing, and not running into—in an hour or two.

"If Jack Aubrey could get close enough to those rocks to hit 'em with a ship's biscuit, why not me?" she said, matching Swindapa's grin for a brief instant. It was good to remember that there was more to the world than their present trouble.

The chanty went on, pounding to the rumble and splash of the pumps:

> *"Yes how I wish that I could die,*
> *The swine who built this tub to find;*
> *I'd drag him back from where he fries,*
> *To pump until the bitch is dry!"*

CHAPTER ELEVEN

October, 10 A.E.—Hattusas, Kingdom of Hatti-land
October, 10 A.E.—Troy
November, 10 A.E.—Northeastern Carpathian foothills
September, 10 A.E.—O'Rourke's Ford, east of Troy
October, 10 A.E.—On the coast of northwestern Iberia
September, 10 A.E.—O'Rourke's Ford, east of Troy
October, 10 A.E.—Achaean encampment, near Troy

"I like this game," Raupasha said. "But it will be long before I fight to a draw even with your son, much less you,
my sister."

Doreen Arnstein looked down at the chessboard, shivering
a little in a way that had nothing to do with the cold that was
sending fingers through the thick robe wrapped about her. She
was playing her son David and Raupasha simultaneously, with
a time limit on her moves. That made it a challenge, enough
to keep her mind off Ian; the news from Troy wasn't good. In
fact, it was desperately bad, and only desperation would have
driven Ken to order the last-chance maneuver that was taking
place this night.

David had made his move, and went back to the little three-
inch reflector she had mounted on this flat rooftop. Originally
she'd put that up as a sort of homage to her beginnings; she'd
been a student astronomer at the time of the Event, interning
at the little observatory on Nantucket run by the Margaret
Milson Association. Tonight her son wasn't studying the stars;
in between moves, he had the telescope trained to the
southwest.

The Arnsteins had been given a royal villa outside the walls
of Hattusas; the Islander military had set up around it, sinking
wells and installing rudimentary sanitation and getting doctors
and their equipment ready. That had been the first priority,
even before starting to shuttle in troops and weapons; *then* they
could move westward toward Troy and the Aegean Sea.

Now the campfires and lanterns twinkled about the building in orderly rows, and a long rectangle off to the west marked the *Emancipator*'s landing ground. The chill of autumn fought with the warmth from wood burning in two bronze baskets, and there were fewer bugs splatting themselves there, or against the kerosene lantern on the table beside them. A kettle of sassafras tea kept warm near one brazier; mugs and a platter of cookies stood beside the chessboard.

Doreen fought to keep her attention on the chessmen; there was something reassuring about the feel of the pre-Event plastic, like an old teddy bear. It was a reminder of a world where your husband wasn't threatened by sadistic surgeon-torturers, or mad ex-Coast-Guard warlords, or barbarians with bronze axes. . . .

No, just by cancer, muggers, drive-by shootings, and LA drivers, she thought. *Plus if it hadn't been for the Event, you'd never have met Ian, not really—never even have considered marrying him, at least. No David then, or Miriam. I'm going to call her Miriam, by God, and Ian's going to be there to help with the diapers!*

"You shouldn't done that," she said to her son. "Look—I'm in a position where you're going to lose this castle, to save your King. In fact . . ."

The boy came over and scowled, knotting his brow in thought. Doreen felt her heart turn over; he looked so much like his father when he did that. He was tall for his age, with hands and feet that promised something like his father's inches, but his face and build were more like hers. The Middle Eastern sun had burned him brown over the summer and brought out a few russet highlights in his dark curly hair. The scowl turned into a shrug as he reached out and tipped over his King.

He's worried, too, she thought, giving him a quick hug before he turned back to the telescope. *Or he'd fight to the death, the way he usually does.* And he'd be his usual one-question-after-another self, instead of so quiet.

"Now you will beat me like, how you say, the big bass drum," Raupasha said.

When Doreen was silent for a long moment the Mitannian girl reached out a hand and touched her arm. "I pray to Hebat . . . Arinna, they call her here in Hattusas . . . that your man will return and hold the son you bear in his arms," she said gently. "My father died while I was in the womb, and that is a heavy thing."

Doreen found herself blinking back tears, and gave the

younger woman's hand a moment's squeeze. "Thanks, kiddo," she said.

"I hope it's a daughter, though," she went on. "One of each."

Raupasha looked a little baffled; *many sons* was a common goodwill wish in this part of the world. Doreen went on, smiling a little: "Now Ken, he'd be a little disappointed if *you'd* turned out to be a boy, for instance."

Raupasha's face lit up as if a lamp were burning behind it. "Do you think so? Really?" she said, flushing. "Oh . . ."

Doreen chuckled. "But there are difficulties. Not least, there's Kenneth. He . . . feels sort of protective toward you, I think."

Raupasha looked puzzled. "Should a man not feel that he should protect his woman?"

"Well . . . that depends. I think part of your problem is that he's got this idea you're like a little sister."

Raupasha snorted. "He will have to learn I am not a little girl!" A sigh. "But there are more difficulties than that." She paused and changed the subject. "Doreen, what is a Jew?"

Doreen's eyebrows arched. "Well, it's sort of—" *hmmm. Can't say "religion," because Ian and I aren't believers, much. And religion's a nearly meaningless word here, where you can mix'n match your deities.* "—sort of like a tribe."

"But you are all Eagle People, all *Nantukhtar,* aren't you?"

"Well . . . yes. It's a little more complicated than that . . . why do you ask?"

"Because I heard someone say that the Jews are clever, and I wondered what they meant." She chuckled. "If you are a Jew, then playing this game with you makes me think it must be so."

Doreen laughed with a sigh in it, and looked down at the chessboard. "Yes, I think you could say 'clever.' Part of it's that we've usually been few compared to our neighbors and not much liked, so we had to outsmart those who had more . . . weight of fist than we did. And part of it's that our God made us some fiendishly complicated laws, and we spent a lot of our time studying and arguing about them. Or we made the laws fiendishly complicated so we *could* spend our time arguing and studying them. That got to be a habit—so we ended up arguing with everybody and studying everything; like me with the stars, or Ian with ancient times."

Raupasha nodded. "It's good to be clever," she said. "It

helps when you're not strong, and when you are it makes your strength more—"

"It's the ship!" David squealed. "Dad, it's *Dad!*"

Doreen dashed over and pushed the boy aside, peering through. The *Emancipator,* right enough. *Why haven't they radioed?* she thought furiously. Was that a good sign, or a bad? *What's been happening in Troy?*

"They're over the wall in the lower town," Major Chong said.

"That mean what I think it means?" Ian Arnstein asked.

The air was thick with smoke drifting up from the lower city, smoke that stank of things not meant to burn. Through the narrow window he could see the flames, under an overcast sky darker than the inside of a whale's gut.

And I'm Jonah, in the belly of the beast, he thought, as a red spark arched out from the darkness into the maze of flat-topped buildings. The spark snapped with a vicious quickness, flying dirt and timbers showering skyward, then the shadows fell again. Slightly further away a line of orange fire traced across the night. *Flamethrower,* he thought. Simple to use; one man on the hose, two working the pumps . . . and the attackers would be under the stream of burning oil as they fought their way through the narrow twisting streets.

Chong coughed and grimaced; a bandage hid most of the left side of his face, crusted dark. "It means that they're going to be here and damned soon. We cut it close, Councilor."

"I'm not altogether happy about leaving." King Alaksandrus was down there, defending the city. *And I talked him into fighting to the last,* he thought with a sharp stab of guilt. A wave of sound came with the flicker of the fires, a distant screaming brabble of voices, punctuated with explosions and a growing crackle of gunfire.

"Sir, you've got your orders and I've got mine, and the war isn't over yet. There are Marine units only three days' march away."

"That isn't going to do the Trojans much good," Arnstein said, unfolding himself from the chair.

"Neither is getting yourself killed, sir," the Marine said. "You know what the commodore says."

"Yeah, the Light Brigade got what they deserved, like Custer." Ian sighed. "All right." *It'll be good to see David again, and Doreen. Even though she's going to ream me out like a Roto-Rooter for getting caught here in the first place.*

"Wait a minute," he said. "I thought it was too risky for the airship to set down here?"

"They're not," Chong said. "We've got a big net set up on the highest roof, fastened to a hook on a pole. They're going to snatch us off with a slow approach."

"Oh, *joy*."

The offices of the Islander mission were as bright as the kerosene lanterns could make them. As he watched the radio operator gave a last tap at the key, flipped open the casing of the radio and began methodically smashing the interior with the butt of her rifle. He winced again, at the waste; at least this was one of the post-Event models, not the irreplaceable pre-Event printed circuits. Others went by with armfuls of documents, throwing them onto the fire in the courtyard outside.

"Let's do it," Arnstein said.

"Right," Chong replied. "I've got the explosive charges ready on my mortars, with all the remaining ammunition."

The palace-citadel of Troy was like a set of adobe sugar cubes piled three stories high around irregular courts; there were gleams off colored shapes on the walls as they passed, a glimpse of hands raised in prayer, a boar turned at bay, a great-eyed goddess leaning on a long sword. Humans were few, palace servants huddled in corners clutching at each other, once a man running by with a golden vase in his arms. A slave, from his skinny shanks and ragged tunic; where he thought he was going with his loot was a mystery, given what Walker's barbarian allies were rumored to do in a captured town. Others lay sodden and unmoving, breached amphorae of wine spilling like blood beside them. That was a lot more sensible, all things considered.

"Up through here, Councilor," Chong said, looking over his shoulder as they came through into a broad upper chamber—part of the queen's suite, he remembered.

The Islander party broke into a trot—mostly Islanders, there were a couple of locals along with the Marine escort, both girls; there had been enough time for that. One of the office staff had snatched up a toddler from somewhere, and the child was making a steady, thin wail. The vanguard of the escort vanished up the next staircase; Ian turned to take a last haunted look at the dying city outside the broad unshuttered windows.

Something happened. Ian Arnstein never remembered exactly what; in the next moment of clarity he found himself lying on his back, with his head twisted up against the wall. An inlaid griffin-footed table lay against his body, but he could see around the edge of it. Things were happening in the darkened room—the kerosene lantern was burning in a corner, the liquid from its reservoir spreading slowly over the gypsum slabs of the floor. Gunshots were strobing, the vicious repeated snaps of revolver fire, the heavier red blades of rifles, a bloom of white-red from a shotgun. But the sounds were distant, muffled; his ears hurt, and he raised a hand to paw feebly at one. His fingers came away red and wet from his face, but he felt no pain.

I should help, he thought.

The words were distant, with an unhuman calm. There was a Python .40 at his waist, but his hand was too weak to do more than touch the checkered walnut of the butt.

The firing had stopped as weapons emptied and cold steel's unmusical clash and rasp took its place. Figures were fighting, figures in Marine kakhi and Coast Guard blue and others in form-fitting black. The black figures were hard to see in the dimness, as if shadows had come to life to kill their creators. He blinked. *Hoods, too,* he noted in a daze; like ski masks, leaving only a strip across the eyes bare. They carried swords, like Japanese swords, except that they were straight-bladed, and blackened except for a strip along the single cutting edge. The swords wheeled and flashed, blurring through the air, clashing against bayonet and rifle butt.

He saw a Marine drive the twenty-inch blade of his bayonet through the stomach of a black-clad figure, then stagger backward and fall with a spiked disk in his throat. Major Chong was backing unwillingly up the stairs, his *katana* clashing with the blades of two attackers, the swords flickering like beams of light in a dance of killing beauty.

Then something fell with a soft heavy weight across Arnstein's legs. He looked down and kicked in reflex as he realized it was a body; one of the dark-clad figures, eyes open and staring. There was a soft heavy resistance as the corpse flopped free. The dark clothing was some snug knitted fabric; there were boots and webbing harness of soft black leather as well, and black-enameled metal buckles. The belt bore a pistol holster, empty, and a sword sheath was strapped across the back, slanting to put the hilt over the left shoulder. A hand twitched, glittering; over it was strapped a tiger-claw arrangement of steel blades, more a climbing tool than a weapon.

There was another explosion, up the stairway leading to the roof. This time he could hear it, more or less. The glassy barrier separating him from the world lifted, enough for him to know that he hurt and that his head was a throbbing ache.

Enough for a jet of fear; Chong wasn't supposed to allow him to be taken alive . . . *but the last he could have seen of me was a limp, bloody body lying against the wall.*

Then came a snarling roar like nothing else in the post-Event world; the roar of internal combustion engines, close at hand overhead. Another explosion, and the two dark-clad figures who'd pursued Chong tumbled back down, one crawling and dragging the other.

"Grenades," she gasped—the English word, thickly accented. Then more Greek, also with an accent and in gasps as she fought for breath: "Kleo is hurt—wounded me—the thing that flies—with the Red Sword mark, the Lady's enemies, it comes—"

There was a heavy thump from above, a chorus of yells, and a rushing mist of water down the staircase like heavy rain—the net being snatched up by the hook, the ballast dumped from the dirigible's tanks for emergency lift, he realized. Freedom, safety, life.

That penetrated the muzziness about his brain a little. He scrabbled with feet and hands, trying to push himself erect. A blade flashed to rest near the tip of his nose, close enough for him to smell the blood on it. He stared up along the length of it, past the gloved hands holding the long hilt in an *iajutsu* grip, up to the eyes visible through the slit of the mask. They widened slightly.

"This is the one the Goddess told us of!" a light voice said, speaking the archaic Greek of this era.

Arnstein stood as the blade tapped under his chin, shakily raising his hands. He towered over the black-clad fighters. More than he should have. His eyes sharpened; the attackers were short even for Bronze Agers, and slim with it, for all the speed and ferocity of their movements. Women.

Ninjettes, he thought dazedly. *Well, I'll be damned.* The Republic's military was about a third women, jealously maintained Coast Guard tradition, but he'd never heard that Walker had bothered to upset local taboos that way. Not even the Nantucketers had all-female units.

He licked his lips, trying to nerve himself to fight and force them to kill him. Before he could hands gripped him, ran him back against the wall, plucked the pistol from his belt, searched him with expert skill. A loop of cord was thrown around his hands and jerked tight, a one-way knot. The fresh pain brought him more to himself, and despite fear and hurt he gagged a little at the thick feces-and-blood stink of death, with the sharp acid odor of stomach acids under it.

Others were finishing the Islander wounded; Ian averted his eyes from the knife strokes. They were seeing to their own hurt, sorting them, laying out the dead, bandaging and—it seemed incongruous even now—giving injections from the medical kits some of them carried.

One who seemed to be the leader stopped at a slight figure whose hands cluched at a belly that welled blood, black as the cloth in the darkness. She bent to meet the eyes of the wounded one.

"You are sped beyond healing," she said, after a moment. "How?"

"Here," the wounded girl gasped. She pulled down the mask, exposing her throat and tilting her chin. "So . . . I go . . . less disfigured . . . to Her."

"As you will," the leader said. "You will have your pyre and your ashes will go to Her temple."

She put the point of her sword to the offered spot below the ear, holding it with her left hand. Her right came back, and she slammed the heel of that hand down on the hilt. The victim gave one convulsive jerk and lay still. When the leader came to Arnstein, he was astonished to see a track of tears sparkling down from the eyes to soak into the fabric of her mask.

"You will await the Lady of Pain," she said.

Uh-oh. This is bad, this is very bad.

He knew who she meant. The *Despotnia Algeos,* the Lady of Pain, Avatar of Hekate. Alice Hong, Walker's bitch-queen, sadist and surgeon. This must be some weird special-operations branch of her lunatic cult. Silence went on, in the thick smell of death and the dimness. The whatever-they-were cleaned their weapons, reloaded their revolvers and shotguns—modern-looking break-open breechloaders much like the Republic's—and kept watch. The noise from the streets was changing, more screams, then a crescendo of firing, light cannon, a strange *braaaaap . . . braaaaaap . . .*

"Can I have some water?" he croaked.

The one who'd been guarding him hit him three times in less than two seconds, with her elbow, with the ball of her foot, and the third time with the pommel of her sword. Pain flooded through him, like white light along his nerves. He was conscious of his own gaping mouth, but for long moments too paralyzed to breathe.

"The Goddess-on-Earth said you must be taken alive," his captor said. "She didn't say you had to be happy." He couldn't see the expression on the face behind the mask, but the eyes were suddenly avid. "You will feed the Dark Goddess well. If I am lucky, I will help with that."

It was several hours before the noises in the city died down. Ian's tongue felt thick, dry, and fuzzy; his head felt fuzzy, too, and he supposed this must be what shock felt like, combined with extreme fear and weariness. He was a scholar of sedentary habits who'd never see sixty again, even if it was three thousand years before he was born, and this sort of thing was *not* his speciality. Unwillingly, because it would be so tempting to sink down into a fog of apathy, he flogged his mind back to a semblance of alertness. The *fighting* noises had died down, at least. From the city came the pulsing roar of fires, and underneath that a huge brabbling murmur that poured like a cataract of white noise into the palace windows. *Screaming and shouting,* he realized. There were nearly thirty thousand people packed into the fifty acres or so of the miniature city below the heights of the palace-citadel. Thousands of Walker's troops were probably pouring into the city, possibly tens of thousands of his barbarian allies. The tribal confederation of the Ringapi had had a rough time since they left the middle Danube, and they had a bad reputation in a sack even when they were in a good mood. That was the death agonies of a whole people he was listening to, a threnody of agony and terror and despair larger than worlds.

Then firing sounded closer; the dull thumps of the flintlock shotguns Walker had handed out to his barbarian allies, and then the crisper bark of rifles. His guards came tensely alert at door and windows. The noise ceased, and there were crashing and screams of pain, laughter and exultant tribal screeching, while the smoke grew thicker. Then:

"The King comes! The King of Great Achaea! The King of Men!"

The harsh male shout cut through the background noise like a knife. The dark-clad women drew their swords and went to one knee facing the door, heads bowed and the blades across the outstretched palms of their hands. Soldiers came into the room, riflemen in gray patch-pocketed tunics and trousers, laced boots, leather webbing harness, and helmets like flared round-topped buckets with a cutout for the face and straps leading to a cup at the chin. An officer with a pistol in his hand

and sword at his waist followed, added his quick scan to theirs, then stepped aside.

William Walker strode through, Alice Hong at his side. Ian struggled a little more upright, pushing his back against the blood-speckled, bullet-pocked painted plaster of the wall, smearing red across griffins and lions and proud nobles in chariots. The renegade looked around, raising a brow over his single cold green eye. A smile blossomed as he looked at the captured American.

"Not bad work," he said in English. "Not bad at all, Alice. I must admit I didn't think this Sailor Moon Platoon of yours would be any practical use, but they came through big-time." He switched to Achaean: "You have done well, Claw Sisters. Very well; the King is pleased."

"Never underestimate the power of faith, Lord Enabler," Hong said lightly, as her followers rose and sheathed their blades. "Or of deep *manga* scholarship."

She wore a stylish version of her cultists' gear, picked out here and there with silver studs. Walker was in something like a loose karate *gi* of a coarse black silk, with the pants tucked into polished calf-boots and a black-leather belt to hold *katana, wazikashi,* and revolver. The only touches of color to highlight the piratical elegance were the massive ruby signet ring on his right hand and the crimson wolfshead picked out on his eye-patch. When he grinned the scar that ran up under it moved, and his face went from boyishly attractive to a caricature of evil.

All hail the Demon King, Arnstein thought, surprised at the sardonic note his mind could still muster. *Although I've seen something awfully like that . . . where . . .* That was it; the black outfit Luke Skywalker wore when he walked into Jabba the Hutt's palace in the third Star Wars flick, *Return of the Jedi.*

Oh, Jesus, he thought. *I've been captured by psychotic media fans.*

Walker took three quick strides, still smiling, and jerked the older man half-erect with a hand wound into his beard.

"What, Professor? No witty repartee? No crushing pop-culture put-downs? I'm disappointed, Dr. Arnstein, I really am."

Arnstein set his teeth against the pain in his face. *Well, I did think about saying:* I have no use for these two 'droids, *but under the circumstances, that would probably be indiscreet.*

Alice Hong sauntered over, smiling. "I can take it from here, Will," she said. "Rest assured, he'll give you chapter and verse, *very* soon."

The wall behind him made it impossible to shrink backward. He wanted to, though.

"Alice, Alice," Walker said, giving a reproving click of his tongue. "You *still* haven't noticed something."

"What, Will?"

He released the older man and turned, holding up his index finger. "You can only torture a man to death *once*." He turned back to Arnstein and put the fingertip near his right eye. "But keep in mind, Professor, that you *can* always do it once. So strive to be useful."

He turned to the gray-uniformed officer and switched to Achaean: "Captain Philowergos, this man is to be taken to the ships under close guard, and shipped to Walkeropolis at the first opportunity."

"Yes, Your Majesty," the man said, saluting and inclining his head. "To Section One?"

"No, no." Walker glanced at Arnstein and winked. "I don't think Operations Minister Mittler *likes* you, Professor. You've put sticks in the spokes of too many of his wheels—and he's prejudiced. He was a commie in this life, but I think he wore those flashy double-lightning-bolt runes in a previous existence. Hmmm."

A snap of his fingers brought paper and pen. He scribbled quickly. "Category One confinement. You'll be quite comfortable, Professor . . . physically at least. And when I have the time, we'll have a nice long chat, hey?"

"Oh, Will, really now—are you expecting to turn him to the Dark Side of the Force, or something? Let's interrogate him and kill him. Simpler, safer, more *fun*."

"Not *now*, Alice!"

The soldiers clamped hands that felt like iron in gloves of cured ham on Ian Arnstein's upper arms. As they hustled him out the door, he could hear Alice Hong's voice raised in mocking song:

> *"Jedi get angry—oooo, Jedi get mad—*
> *Give him the biggest lickin' he's every had!*
> *Jedi you can be the Dark Looooord of the Sith . . ."*

Ohotolarix son of Telenthaur, born a warrior of the Iraiina *teuatha*, frowned and dusted sand across the paper of his latest report. He shook his right hand, clasping and unclasping his fingers to rid them of a cramp that his clutch on the quill pen had brought. His hands had taken a while to learn the arts of pen and ink; his first twenty years had been taken up with the skills of a *wirtowonnax,* spear and axe, rope and rein, plow and spade and sickle. Life as the Wolf Lord's handfast man and chief henchman and Commander of the Royal Guard had taught him more, though. The use of letters was a weapon, and one as deadly as any sword—as any cannon, even. He shook the sand off the paper, folded it, and sealed the triangle with a blob of wax from the candle on his desk, then rose.

A trick of the lamplight showed him his face in the thick wavy window glass. It looked younger than the thirty winters he bore, for he had taken up the King's habit of shaving his face. His yellow hair was cropped above his ears as well; beside his eyes and grooved between nose and mouth were the marks of life, of knowledge and power. He was no more the glad boy the Eagle People had rescued from a coracle swept out to sea during the Iraiina *teuatha*'s crossing from the mainland to Alba. Each dawn was not a wonder now, nor each battle a blaze of glory where he would win a hero's undying name, and he did not see in each woman the promise of a fresh garden of delights.

He snorted softly to himself. *Winter thoughts.* He was in his prime, more skilled in a dozen ways, more deadly than that boy could have dreamed, wiser than he could have imagined.

I have journeyed far by land and sea, gained much, lost much, seen and done things dark and terrible. These are the deeds and rewards of manhood.

"Time to finish the work of the day," he muttered. He took up a folder, then walked out past the gray-uniformed guards, returning their salute; down the stairs and through the residence hall to the main exit.

Days were short here in this season, shorter than they ever grew in Greece; it was not night just yet despite the overcast, but you could tell it would not be long. The air was cold, the sky dark-gray with cloud out of which a scatter of white flakes fell, and the lanternlights lay bright across the wet brick of the pavement. Beside the train of goods waiting to go southward guards stamped and swore and blew on their gloved hands. He grinned to himself as he pulled the cold air deep into his lungs; the Achaeans among Fort Lolo's garrison were like wet cats when the weather was like this, stalking around in affronted amazement. Ohotolarix found the cold charming, much like the winters he remembered from his tribe's first home, the lands along the Channel and the River Ocean in the far west. Woodsmoke blew pungent from brick chimneys, mixed with the smell of supper cooking and the damp mealy scent of the snow.

"Hey, Otto," a voice said.

"Henry," Ohotolarix said in reply; he'd long since ceased resenting how Walker's folk mispronounced his name.

They meant it as a compliment, in any case; and Henry Bierman was high in Lord Cuddy's service. He handed the commander a sheaf of papers of his own, bound in leather and secured with tapelike ribbon. "Here's my latest for Bill Cuddy and the bossman."

"All goes well?" Ohotolarix asked. "I'd have been happier to get them off earlier today."

"Sorry; some things can't be rushed, and the King's Council wanted these figures complete. Things are going great, actually. That iron ore's even better than we thought, seventy-eight percent metal and no impurities; they didn't call these the 'Ore' mountains for nothing."

Ohotolarix juggled languages in his head for a moment, and then smiled a little at the pun. Bierman was a fussy little sort, with thick lenses before his eyes. No shadow of a fighting-man, but able at his work. He went on:

"The second charcoal blast furnace'll be functional before Christmas. Plus the silver-lead and zinc outputs're up, and we're getting useful quantities of gold from the sluice . . . well, you know."

Ohotolarix nodded, glancing northward. The peaks of the Carpathians were already snow-covered, glimpses of white through the clouds. Mountains fascinated him; he'd been raised in flat country, along the ocean shore, where folk lived on hills to avoid the floods of the marshland. There was a power in those great masses of rock, beyond the wealth of metals in the stone, and the usefulness of them.

And they are far from the sea, easy to fortify at uttermost need. "Let's get them moving, then," he said. "Light enough for a few hours travel, the channel's well marked."

Fort Lolo proper—the place was named for a *ruathauricaz* in the King's homeland of Montana—had been built on the site of a native stockade; quite an impressive one, no mere line of tree trunks on a mound, but a cut-off hill topped with timber-framed ramparts of rubble and stamped earth. The folk had been much like the Ringapi to the west in speech and customs, but not part of that tribal confederation; long-standing enemies of theirs, rather. The Ringapi lords had been delighted to point his expedition in this direction, back last spring. Nowadays they were a little less pleased, but not in a position to object.

Survivors of the valley's population had been put to work building a proper moat-and-earthwork fort under Achaean engineers, with cannon and quickshooters in well-sited bunkers, and a covered fighting platform for riflemen. Inside were barracks for the two companies of troops and their womenfolk and children, the commandant's house, armories, outbuildings, emergency quarters where the townsfolk and rural colonists might flee in the unlikely event of a siege. The buildings were of squared timbers on brick foundations, with steep-pitched tiled roofs; brick paved the streets between them, and the central square. Many of the dwellers had gathered to watch the departure of the southern caravan.

The guards moved down the long coffles, shoving and shouting at the slaves, who responded with a stunned, sheeplike obedience. Only a dozen of the men who'd oversee the slave drive were rifle-armed Achaean troops. Most were natives in check trousers and plaids or wolfskin cloaks, armed with steel-headed spears and swords that were part of price of their hire. There was no use wasting his elite on such work when most of the journey would be quiet river passage through allied lands, until handover at the White Fort, the northernmost border of Great Achaea on the Danube. The slaves were shaven-headed and linked neck to neck with chains between their collars, handcuffed and hobbled as well, with heavy packs of hardtack and jerked meat on their backs; three in four were males.

Two wagons followed. One held bales of fine furs, and little casks of raw amber—traded from the forest tribes north of the mountains, like most of the slaves; the other boxes of silver and gold ingots. They passed through the dogleg entranceway with its squat guard towers, and then down the gentle slope to the river wharves. The river—natives called it the Growler— was broad but shallow here, running southward until it met a larger stream and that flowed into the *Danau*, the Great River.

Lady Kylefra finished her inspection of the stock as they went by, yawning as she came to stand beside him. There was careful respect in Ohotolarix's nod; the young woman had been among the first taken as Alice Hong's pupils, back in Alba, before they had to flee to the Middle Sea; that meant she had been brought up to it since childhood. She was a full doctor now, and high in the cult of Hekate of the Night, as the badge at her shoulder showed—sun and moon, entwined by a darkly glittering niello serpent with two heads meeting at the top. Black sun, black moon.

"They're ready to go," Kylefra said, brushing back a lock of ruddy-brown hair.

She spoke in English, which Ohotolarix thought an irritating affectation, as if she were of the royal family or Hong herself. *If she won't speak in the kingdom's language, why not the tongue of home?* he thought. The dialect of her *teuatha* wasn't much different from his. *You are no more of the Eagle People than I.*

"I've vaccinated them all and checked for anything communicable," she went on; he had to admit that sentence would have needed a couple of English words anyway. "And deloused them, and given the guard corporal instructions on keeping them healthy."

"Good," he replied in official Achaean, although his English was better than hers. "As the King says, a dead slave is a dead loss."

"If we'd waited a bit, I could have gelded the males in this lot, the way I did the ones we're keeping for the mines here," she said. Her tongue came out to touch her upper lip. "They're more docile that way . . . and the Dark Lady would appreciate so . . . tasty . . . an offering."

He'd become quite good at concealing his thoughts and keeping the feelings of the heart away from his face—necessary for a man of position in *Meizon Akhaia*. He still thought she saw—and inwardly smiled at—his hidden shudder. He'd gone boar-hunting in the mountains all *that* day, and the endless moaning and sobbing from the pens had still given him a sleepless night. The Horned Man knew Ohotolarix son of Telenthaur was no milksop nor behindhand in manslaying and feeding the Crow Goddess, but . . .

Bierman didn't bother to hide his disgust, with the insane excess of self-confidence Ohotolarix had noted among the Eagle People followers of Walker at times. Not so much heedless courage such as an Iraiina or Ringapi might show . . . more an unconsciousness that saying what you felt could be dangerous. As if they had to deliberately remember the risk, like someone who'd grown up in a land without wolves absentmindedly petting one he met in the woods. The man muttered *bitch* under his breath, too.

"We need to get the coffles off south soon," the Guard commander replied hastily to the healer-priestess. "In full winter, too many would die on the road, or the rivers may freeze.

Besides, not all of them are going to the mines—some may be selected for skilled work, or become freedmen eventually or even go into the army, and those need their stones."

Kylefra shrugged and sighed. Attendants brought their horses, and they swung into the saddle. More of the curious were watching as they came down into Lolo Town. A group of schoolchildren halted to watch as well, until the collared slave woman shepherding them along gave a cluck and sent them crawling like unwilling snails toward their lessons. Presently hooves and wheels boomed hollow on the boards of the long pier that bridged the broad marshy edges of the Growler. Upstream of it were booms of logs floated down from the mountains; tied up or anchored were flat-bottomed barges. The smell of their cargoes came across the cold water, faint but pungent; beeswax, honey, sacks of potash, piles of leather or rawhides. Others bore the products of Fort Lolo's domains, ingots of copper or dull-shining lead or zinc.

Ohotolarix oversaw the loading of the slaves, the most troublesome cargo, and the amber and precious metals—the riflemen would be sitting on those all the way to the White Fort, in case one of the Ringapi chieftains let greed overcome good sense.

Ah, you're not that youth of nineteen summers anymore, and Sky Father's Mirutha witness it! he thought, chuckling a little. The Iraiina had never been a forethoughtful folk. Even more than their distant Ringapi cousins they were headlong warriors, men with fire in their blood and little in their heads but bone. *How I have changed, and how much my* wehaxpothis *has taught me!* In his heart, the homely Iraiina word for *chief* still carried more power than the Achaean terms.

When the work was finished he hesitated where the road forked on the way back to the fort; the southward path lay down-valley toward the farms and manors the men of Great Achaea had set out when they took this land. The valley itself widened like a funnel from here, falling away to the vast flat plains southward. Most of it had been open when the Achaeans arrived, some farms and villages, more land left rippling in chest-high grassland, with copses of oak trees here and there, and marshes along the waterside. The snags of sacked native garths still stood in a few places, blackened timbers and crumbling wattle-and-daub, the lumpy remains of a sod roof. Squares of dark earth showed a fuzz of blue-green, winter wheat peeking up ready for its blanket of cold-season snow; dry maize-shooks rustled in others, or the stubbled remains of sunflowers and flax. In a few workers toiled to lift the last potatoes, or watched over the herds.

His own hall was there, and despite its raw newness—only this spring past had they laid out their own fields, after reaping the natives' harvest the first year—it was already his favorite estate, even more than the Sicilian ranch. He had broad acres in many of Great Achaea's provinces, ably managed by stewards, but this one reminded him more of the old homeland; his youngest wife kept the house, with their new son by her. It would do his soul good to spend a day seeing to the fields and new-planted orchards, and most of all looking over his herds in the pens and pastures. Full-fleeced sheep and fat cattle and tall deep-chested horses, the only wealth that was really real, the delight of a man's heart, second only to strong sons. It was just a half hour's ride and the paperwork was mostly done. . . .

Thus he was looking southward and was among the first to see the party riding up toward Fort Lolo. For a moment he knew only angry astonishment that the sentries hadn't raised the alarm. Then he raised his binoculars; there wasn't any dust from the graveled roadway with the wet weather of the last few days, so he could see clearly. A column of horsemen in the gray uniforms and flared steel helmets of *Meizon Akhaia,* with the red wolfshead banner at their front. A coach behind it, and a train of light baggage wagons—horse-drawn, hence fast but expensive—with a herd of remounts. He had enough time to note that they were of unusual quality before he noticed one rider curving out ahead of the others and then spurring to gallop. A small figure in black on a big slim-legged horse, riding like a leopard, with long loose hair bright gold . . .

"Princess Althea!" he cried, bowing in the saddle as she drew up.

"Uncle Ohoto!" she replied, leaning over in the saddle to embrace him and kiss his cheek.

"You've grown, daughter of my chief," he said happily, hands on her shoulders. *Was it more than yesterday when I came growling across the nursery floor, playing bear for you?* "You're almost a woman now—will be, in another few winters."

She'd shot up, and no mistaking; she'd be as tall for a woman as her sire was for a man. The outfit—loose jacket, sash, full trousers in fine black cloth edged here and there with gold, polished boots, long dagger and pistol on a studded belt—didn't look quite so much like a child's dress-up in imitation of her father anymore. Her face had begun to lose puppy fat, and yes, there was something of her father in her eyes as well, for all they were blue rather than green. Something of her mother, too, who had been a chieftain's daughter Walker had captured in a raid.

"But what are you doing here, Althea?"

The girl drew herself up solemnly and waited until a crowd had gathered. "Rejoice!" she said, slightly louder. "The High King is victorious—Troy is fallen!"

They all cheered; the soldiers first, and those from the Achaean lands who knew what it meant, and then the generality. Ohotolarix was as loud as any, although he fought down bitterness; obedient to his lord's orders, he was here in this backwater and not fighting by his side as a handfast man should. He obeyed, but it was hard, hard . . .

Althea threw up her left hand and a ragged silence fell. "Hear the word of the *wannax,* the King of Men—sent by him through his own blood, the Princess Althea of the House of the Wolf."

The silence was complete now. "His word to Ohotolarix son of Telenthaur is, *Well done, you good and faithful warrior!* As the Wolf Lord pushes forward the boundaries of Great Achaea on the plains of Wilusia, among the proud horse tamers of Troy, so his right-hand man Ohotolarix, the *lawagetas* of his Royal Guard wins him lands and subjects here in the far northland."

She gestured grandly at the herd. "From the plunder of Troy he sends the horses of Wilusia, said to be sired by the North Wind."

Ohotolarix looked them over; not bad at all, especially after a trip like this. Not big, by comparison with Bastard, Walker's steed, but he already possessed a three-quarter-bred stallion of that breed. For a moment a horseman's instincts possessed him, and his mind dwelt on what he could do with these by cross-breeding and breeding back.

"He also sends gold and fine goods—" The guardsmen pulled back covers and the lids of chests; the audience cheered. "—slaves of Troy, bronzeworkers and carpenters and masons, and a daughter of the Trojan King, Alaksandrus."

A girl stepped down from the carriage, auburn-haired and richly dressed in a foreign way. Althea leaned forward and whispered in his ear, giggling slightly: *"She looked terrible when we caught her, all skinny. But we fattened her up on the road so you could have fun bouncing her around."*

Then she cleared her throat and called a man forward, opening a long rosewood case and handing Ohotolarix a double-barreled rifle, its smooth-polished butt inlaid in ivory and gold with hunting scenes, the barrels gleaming with damascene patterns.

"See how the King of Men honors the greatest of his warrior chiefs! Honor to Ohotolarix, favored of the Wolf Lord!"

Ohotolarix grinned at her and waved to the throng who cried him hail, and felt himself blinking back tears of joy. *I might have expected it,* he thought. *From the best of lords.*

It wasn't that he lacked gold cups and fine cloth and jewels, or splendid weapons, or horses, or a girl to give variety to his nights. It was the honor, publicly bestowed. That no matter how far he was from his lord's sight he was never far from his mind or heart, never forgotten.

"Never—" He cleared his throat and continued. "Never shall the House of the Wolf lack for a strong sword at their side, wise counsel, and a life to be laid down for theirs. From me and my sons, and the sons of my sons," he said.

Ohotolarix raised his voice in his turn. "All hail to the Princess Althea and to the Wolf Lord. Tonight we feast!" The gathering broke up in cheers.

That was a feast to remember, although he kept himself moderate, since the princess was there. If something like this had befallen back in the days when Daurthunnicar was High Chief of the Iraiina and Walker new-come to Alba, he'd have gotten roaring drunk before the meat was done, there'd have been a death-fight or two, and he'd have finished by taking the Trojan girl on the tables to cheers and rhythmic thumping of drinking horns and hands slapping knees. Instead he contented himself with wine enough to make the light mellow and all men his friends.

Yes, manners were more seemly now, particularly where the commanders sat. That was at the elevated base of the great U-shaped table set pointing its open end toward the feasting-hall's doors. Glass-globed lanterns shed light, and two big stone hearths on either side held crackling log fires in firedogs of massive wrought iron, burning wild apple wood that scented the room. Carved shutters were closed over the glass windows; between them massive wooden pillars rose from the smooth stone floor past the second-story gallery that ringed the feasting-hall and up to the rafters. He'd brought in Ringapi craftsmen to do the pillars in the shapes of Gods and heroes but the tapestries against the wall were southland, bright fabulous beasts and battles and sea creatures, ships and cities. The tables, chairs, and silverware were in the style of *Meizon Akhaia,* colorful with inlaid work of ivory and semiprecious stones, silky with polishing.

Ohotolarix looked around as he cracked walnuts in his fist and sipped at heated apple wine, thinking of the smoky turf-walled barns Iraiina chiefs had called their great halls when he was a young man, and how they'd awed him. If he could have seen this then . . .

I'd have thought it was Sky Father at feast, in the hall beyond the Sun, with the ancient heroes and warrior Mirutha *at his board!*

A bard had come with the party from Walkeropolis and the plain of Troy. He sat in the space between the tables when the roast pigs and beefsteaks, the fried potatoes and steaming loaves and honey-sweetened confections were done, plectrum moving on the strings of his lyre as he sang:

> *Planting his cannon right in front, mouths gaping wide,*
> *Double-shotted the blow, to give it heavy impact,*
> *Wannax Walker hurled hot iron at the gates, full center, smashing*
> *The hinges left and right and the cannonballs tore through,*
> *Dropped earth and stone with a crash and walls groaned and thundered*
> *And our lord burst through in glory, face dark with fury*
> *As the sudden rushing night, and our men blazed on in steel*
> *And terrible fire burst from the godlike weapons that they carried,*
> *Rockets and rifles in their fists. No one could fight them, stay them,*
> *None but the Gods as Walker hurtled through the gates*
> *And his eyes flashed fire . . .*

That had them hammering fists on the tables, and Ohotolarix gave the man a gold chain; he could see it himself, the cannon belching red fire in the night, and the roar of onset as the assault began . . . Then two of Hong's followers, the select ones known as the Claws of Hekate, gave a demonstration of swordwork.

Not bad, he thought; they were supple and very fast. *I could take either or both, though. I'm just as quick, and weight and reach count for a good deal, in the end.*

He signaled an end to the public part of the feast by a show of gifts of his own to men stationed here—horses, ox-teams, silver, bronze, a fine sword, a grant of early discharge and land to one who'd become betrothed to a Ringapi chief's daughter.

At last most of the guests and all the women were gone—except for Lady Kylefra and the princess, both of them exceptions to the usual rules, for different reasons. The commander of the escort company was a man he'd fought beside many times, Iraiina-born like Ohotolarix; his second was an Achaean from Thessaly. They talked of the siege of Troy, feints and counterstrikes and raids, boasting genially of men killed and goods plundered and women raped. He took away an impression that casualties had been higher than anticipated, but not disastrously so.

"You won't find it dull here while the princess is visiting," he said after a while, leaning back in his chair and holding out his cup to a slave. "The hunting here is as good as any I've ever seen—no lions or leopards, but deer, auroch, wolves . . . bears, bears beyond number. Every once in a while we have an expedition against the natives, or pitch in to help the Ringapi against their neighbors. Just dangerous enough to be real sport, and then we can collect something—slaves and cattle, at least. Something a bit different, before you return to the real war."

The Achaean sighed—he went by the name Eruthos, "the Red," although his hair was dark-brown, so he'd probably shed a lot of blood. He and the Iraiina, Shaukerax, exchanged glances. "We're here until recalled, and so's the princess," he said. "Brought a whole raft of her things, you'll find—boxes of books, servants, and tutors."

"That's right," the girl said; she'd been drinking wine cut with two parts of water, and slowly, but she still spoke with care. "Damn, Harold's still with Father, getting to see all the fun stuff." Then she brightened. "But I forgot to tell you; when we took Troy, we captured I-an Aren-stein."

She pronounced the name slowly and carefully; they'd been talking the Achaean of the court, salted with English words and the Eagle People accent, and it didn't clash that much.

"Hmmm, that *is* news," Ohotolarix said, rubbing his chin thoughtfully.

That had been his first sight of the Eagle People, after he woke on their great iron ship; the bearded face of that tall old man, a thing of sanity amid alien madness. It had been Arnstein and his woman who learned the first words of his tongue, too. Later word had come that Arnstein had risen very high among the enemy, become wiseman and adviser to the Islander King, Cofflin, and his emissary to the great rulers of the East.

"A great blow against the enemy," he said.

Althea nodded. "It was Auntie Hong's ninjettes who captured him, the Claws of Hekate," she said eagerly. "They climbed right up into the citadel, the night the city fell—caught him and held him until the Guard got there."

The officers nodded sourly. Kylefra's eyes sparkled at their discomfiture. "And so the two Claws you saw were among those sent with the princess, to help instruct her," she said proudly. "They bore messages from the Daughter of Night for me." She looked at Althea fondly. "In a year or so, Princess, you will be eligible for initiation—there's much they could teach you."

"How to climb up walls and use those cool throwing stars, sure," Althea giggled, then touched a hand to her mouth. "But I'll worship as my father does. And now I should go to bed. May the sweet rest of drowsy night be yours, lords, Lady Kylefra."

Hmmmm, Ohotolarix thought. *Now, there goes one who will be as bad to cross as her father, in her time. And afraid of nothing, nothing at all.* Odd to think that of a girl, but things were different now . . . *Oh, well, Harold will inherit.*

The scar-faced Achaean officer had been exchanging glances with Kylefra. After a moment they excused themselves. Ohotolarix waved the slaves away and poured for himself and Shaukerax, dropping back into their birth-tongue. The speech of the *teuatha* of the Noble Free Ones sounded a little rusty and strange in his own ears, but it was pleasant to speak it again.

"*He'll* get more than he bargained for," he said, jerking a thumb after Eruthos, and they laughed together.

"Oh, you know these Achaean stick-at-naughts," Shaukerax half joked. "They'll put it in a girl, a boy, a goat—anything that's handy, even a black-sun witch."

"Surely you do them an injustice," he replied solemnly. "They'll take a sheep before a goat, and an ewe before a ram." Ohotolarix shook his head as their mirth died down. "This Eruthos, is he capable?"

"A born killer. He fought very well indeed before Troy. A friend of his fell in a sortie, while Eruthos was off the field, and he went berserk—slew the enemy commander and dragged his body around as if he couldn't bear not being able to kill him again and again. That's when we named him. His father called him Ach . . . Akhil . . . too much wine, I can't pronounce the damned thing, one of those *-eus* names. He's of good birth, though, his father a petty King and his mother a high priestess. From Thessaly; the Greeks there aren't quite as oily as the southern ones."

Ohotolarix nodded. Shaukerax went on: "It's good to see the work you've done here, too. I remember the first years after we came to Achaea from Alba, and you've done better, faster, by *Diawas Pithair*. Especially since it's been only, what, barely a year and a bit?"

The Guard commander shrugged. "I had a lot more to work with than the King did to start with," he said. "And I had Great Achaea to draw upon whenever I found something lacking, man or machine. And I didn't have to break the trail or deal with all that tricky Achaean intrigue—if those faithless dogs didn't have lords and kin, they'd betray each his own self for the joy of it."

"These Ringapi do seem more our kind of men."

"That they are. The King told me he'd considered coming here, rather than Mycenae. Sometimes I wish he had."

Shaukerax shook his head violently. "Too far from the sea. Sitting here, how could we take revenge on the cursed Eagle People for breaking our tribe?"

"We could have fought them at a time of our choosing, not theirs. This is a richer land than Achaea, in many ways. And there's a pleasure to building that's as great as raids and wars, I find. But . . ." He sighed, drank, shrugged.

"A man's fate is as it is," Shaukerax agreed. "I do hope the rest of this war is more entertaining than the siege of Troy; that was more like being a mole than a warrior, and they held out until the men weren't worth selling or the women having."

He grinned and punched Ohotolarix on the shoulder. "Speaking of which, you have that Trojan to prong; she's still a virgin, and if you knew how difficult *that* was to arrange, with the stallions-on-two-legs I have to command . . ."

Ohotolarix rose, laughing and slapping the other on his thick shoulder in turn. "We can find you a virgin—a girl, not an ewe—if you want, even if she isn't sired by the ruler of a great city."

Shaukerax finished his wine and wiped his mouth with the back of a hairy ham-sized fist. "*You're* the one who's been sitting on his arse like a great chief taking his ease, brother," he said cheerfully. "*I've* been traveling hard for weeks. I want a woman, not a wrestling match. You'll need the exercise."

His host snapped fingers for the steward of the house and

gave instructions; the two men parted, promising to meet for a boar hunt soon. He paused on his way up the stairs, looking back over the feasting-hall of the commandant's house as the slaves cleaned and swept and polished. A man's fate was as it was . . . but the thread could take some strange twists. From the hut of a common warrior-herdsman of the tribe to this! What might have happened if Walker and the Eagle People had not come?

You would have died of thirst in that coracle, fool, he told himself. *And many another man who's died in those years since might yet live.*

Private Hook heard the cry. *"Here they come, the whole fucking lot of them!"* from the lookouts on the roof above. He heard it with a little difficulty, because Sergeant Edraxsson was raving in his bunk, calling commands to an imaginary platoon. There was no time to get an orderly now, either, to give him a shot and quiet him down.

"Oh, shut your bloody hole!" he snapped, and threw some water from a jug on the sick man; his wounded foot was giving off a bit of a smell, too, under the sharp aroma of the disinfectant on his bandages.

The raving died down to mumbles. The thunder-rumble of the approaching Ringapi host was much louder; five thousand men made a good deal of noise, walking in a group. Hook had taken over the slit window that had been here before the Islanders came; it gave him a better view and field of fire than any of the improvised loopholes. Right now the view was uncomfortably good. Not good enough, though; the sun was nearly in his eyes, making him squint and making them water.

"Shit on it," he said, and pulled a chest near.

Then he dumped packets of shells on it, ripping them open with his teeth and tossing the heavy paper aside. Wearing the webbing hurt too much, with the left strap pressing on the open sore on his back.

Best place in the station, he thought, with a little sour satisfaction; all those dumb bastards out in the open on the breastworks were exposed to the enemy firing down from the hill, nothing but a ditch and six-foot wall between them and hand-to-hand combat with the enemy's spears and swords. He had three foot of rock-hard mud brick. If you had to be here at all, this was the place to be. *I wonder if I could get out after sundown?* No, better not, unless things got really desperate. He didn't want to be out there alone in the dark with the fucking locals, either.

Bugle calls and shouts sounded outside. "Set your fucking sights," he said to the other walking wounded. "Four hundred."

He wanted as many of those locals killed as far away from his precious pink buttocks as he could arrange. Hook thoughtfully licked a thumb and wet the foresight of his rifle, watching the approaching host. They weren't just marching up the road from Troy; splitting up into columns, rather, and flowing forward from wall to wall, grove to grove, pausing to build up in little hollows where they couldn't be seen. Chiefs directed them, with horn calls and waving spears.

"Okay, buddy, let's see you manage this," he snarled.

The foremost figures were close enough to distinguish arms and legs from bodies. That meant . . . he carefully adjusted the sights of his Werder, rested his left hand beside the window, and clamped the forestock to the mud brick with the thumb it lay across. His right snuggled the butt into his shoulder. Lay the sights on that big, confident-looking bastard with the tanned wolf's-head over his helmet and a belt with gold studs, waving a steel longsword and shouting. Breathe out, stroke the trigger with your finger . . .

Crack. The recoil punched back at him. *One hundred and—* The big local doubled over, clutching himself as if he'd been kicked in the groin. Hook laughed as his finger continued the pull. The trigger came all the way back and hit the little stud behind it. The block snapped down and the shell ejected, a sharp fireworks smell in his nose. He reached down without taking his eyes away, picked up a fresh round, pushed it home, then transferred his thumb to the cocking lever on the side of the breech. It slid back with a smooth resistant softness and a double *click-clack;* the breech came up and tension came on the trigger again.

Hook shifted his aim, chuckling softly. There weren't many things he liked about the Marine Corps. One of them was that they'd pay him to kill people.

The Republic's fleet had folded its wings and come to rest in the Groyne, off what another history would have called the city of La Coruna, in the far northwest of Iberia. A fishing village huddled at the end of a long peninsula, amid a few scattered fields. The inhabitants had fled in terror when the Islander ships appeared; this was an ancient stop on the trade routes to northern Europe, but they had seen nothing on this scale before. Coaxed back, they sold provisions and stored wood, very sensibly made no objection to working parties on shore, and for modest payments in coin and trade goods provided all the information they could through Tartessian-speakers who'd learned that tongue from the numerous south-Iberian traders who passed this way. In fact, the headman of the village bore a Tartessos-made musket with immense pride undiminished by the fact that it was missing a trigger and several other essential parts, and his tribesmen walked in awe of it.

From the quarterdeck of the *Chamberlain* Alston could see liberty parties moving around, working parties stacking firewood on rafts or towing it out to the ships, and the brown canvas of the field hospital they'd set up.

Her lips quirked almost invisibly. Some of the Sun People auxiliaries had gone on their knees and kissed the solid earth when they were set ashore, and then flung up their hands in the gesture of thankful prayer. They'd clubbed together to buy a cow and some sheep to sacrifice, and it would have been military horses—or men—without the Islanders watching. Mass seasickness on the transports had been no joke; several of them still had hatch covers off and ports open, water pouring over their sides from the pumps as the bilges were repeatedly flooded and pumped out. The smell was no longer perceptible at distance, thank God; just a clean scent of sea and damp forest from the mainland, tar and hemp, paint and wood, and cooking from the galley.

It was good to see the ships in order again; after a week of hard effort they looked nearly as trim as they had setting out from Portsmouth Base. *And no word of the* Farragut, *or the* Severna Park, *either.* Still, only two lost out of nearly forty . . .

The frigates lay in a line, their battleship-gray hulls with the red Guard slash rocking slightly at anchor beneath furled sails, a slim lethal elegance. Two of the schooners—*Frederick Douglass* and *Harriet Tubman*—were on patrol well out to the west, invisible against the setting sun, and an ultralight buzzed through the sky above, tiny against the fading blue and the few sparse white clouds. The rest of the fleet were closer in to shore, at last with the full complements of masts, spars, and sails.

It was just chilly enough to make the wool of her uniform jacket welcome, and the thought of dinner enticing. They deserved one day of rest before putting to sea again.

"Ma'am, the captains will be arriving soon," a middy murmured.

"Thank you, Mr. Rustadax," she said quietly.

She glanced over to the quarterdeck gangway, where the flagship's accomodation ladder led down to the water. The captain's gigs from the warships were standing in toward it, oars rising and falling. The first of them slid out of sight, and the bosun's pipe twittered. The immaculately uniformed side boys—*and girls,* her mind prompted wryly—came to attention. There were five of them, the number due to a commander. In the first age of sail senior officers had come aboard in a bosun's chair, and the number needed to haul on the line had been an indication of rank . . . and hence physical weight, which in those days tended to grow with age and importance.

There was a rattle of rifle butts on the deck as the Marine guard snapped to attention. The quarterdeck bell began to sound, a measured bronze *bong-bong . . . bong-bong . . .* four strokes in all as the visiting officer walked up the ladder.

"*Lincoln* arriving!" the bosun barked, saluting with his left hand and bringing the little silver pipe to his mouth with the other.

At the weird twittering sound the Marine guard near the rail moved in a beautifully choreographed *stamp-clack-clash* as they brought their rifles to present arms, the twenty-inch blades of their bayonets glittering like polished silver. Alston gave a slight nod. Although compulsively tidy herself she had no use for spit and polish, not when it was just for its own sake. But ceremony had a very definite, very necessary place in any military organization. It taught—at a level well below the conscious mind—that they weren't a collection of individuals, but a community with a common purpose more important than any single member. And *that* was as functional as a bayonet or eight-inch Dahlgren; so was the habit of obedience. Both were particularly needed in the Republic's military, where so many members were only a few years—months, sometimes—from a Bronze Age peasant's hut. Constitutional government was pretty abstract to them, but ceremony and ritual were the warp and weft of their lives.

Commander Victor Ortiz looked a little peaked still as he came to the top of the accommodation ladder, a bandage wound around his head where a falling block had laid it open during the storm, but he moved alertly as he answered the side boy's snapping salute and the Marines' present arms, then turned to salute the national ensign at the stern.

"Permission to come aboard," he said, his XO waiting behind him.

"Sir! Permission granted," the OOD said; she led him to Commander Jenkins, and the captain of the *Chamberlain* to the commodore; they exchanged salutes.

"Hello, Victor," Alston said. "All in order?"

"Ready for tomorrow's tide, Commodore," he said, smiling.

The ritual was repeated as the other captains came aboard; there was a slight variation for the last, a thickset, middle-aged black man in Marine khaki rather than Guard blue. Six bells, six side boys, and:

"Brigadier McClintock, Second Marine Expeditionary Force!"

McClintock was moving a little stiffly, legacy of helping put down a panic riot among the auxiliaries when they thought the ship they were on was going to sink in the storm—how they thought rioting would keep them from drowning was a mystery, but such was human psychology.

She estimated that the Marine officer's glum expression was probably due to McClintock's own personal problems, not the pain of a pulled muscle; his partner and he had split up rather messily over the summer, one reason he'd pushed hard for this position. He'd gotten it because he'd done so well during the Tartessian invasion last spring, of course. Alston felt a certain sympathy for him, but . . .

Well, fidelity is hard enough to maintain in a relationship with only one *man in it. With* two, *do Jesus, you might as well expect ducks to tap-dance. One reason among many I'm damned glad to be female* and *gay.*

No matter, he was a professional—he'd been a Marine DI before the Event—and did his job regardless. If she was any judge, he'd probably go right on doing the job if gut-shot, until the blood pressure dropped too low to keep his brain functioning.

"Brigadier," she said, shaking his hand. "Your people have been doing a crackerjack job ashore—and they probably saved several of the transports."

His ship hadn't been the only one with a riot aboard. A rioting mob composed of hysterical Sun People warriors could get . . . interesting. She was deeply glad there had been Marines aboard all of them.

"Ma'am, it was a welcome distraction," he said, in a soft North Carolina drawl. "That-theah blow was *somethin'*."

The sound gave her a pang of nostalgic pleasure. Not that it was identical with the Sea-Island Gullah that she'd grown up speaking, but it was a lot closer than the flat Yankee twang which had been coming out on top in Nantucket and the outports over the past decade. That was the prestige dialect these days, carefully copied by newcomers who wanted to fit in and shine in reflected social status, the way she'd striven to speak General American most of her life.

Assimilation, she thought.

The wardroom stewards circulated with glasses of sherry—or a fairly close analogue, ironically imported from Tartessos before the war—until the sun almost touched the horizon. There was a fair crowd; all the Guard's ship captains, their executive officers, McClintock and his chief of staff, the colonels of the Third Marines and First Militia. The conversation and circulating died down as the ship's bugler sounded *first call,* five minutes to sunset. Glasses went back on trays, and everyone turned to face the national flag. The Marine band struck up the "Star-Spangled Banner"—various proposals to replace that with "Hail To Nantucket" had been shot down by overwhelming votes of the Town Meeting, including her own—and the flag slowly descended, to be folded as the last note died; by then the sun had nearly disappeared, leaving only a band of crimson fading to deep purple across the western horizon. Bonfires blossomed on the beach, and after the band laid down their instruments she could hear *retreat* sounding on bugles from across the anchorage as the other ships of the fleet went through their less elaborate ritual.

"Gentlemen, ladies," she said, and led them down the companionway. Set up for a dining-in, the table filled most of the cabin; she made her way to the top of it, flanked by the stern-chasers on either side. Silver gleamed on crisp linen, reflecting the flames of the lanterns; the stern gallery windows were slightly open, bringing in the smell of salt water to mingle with the odors of roasted meat. Stewards wheeled in trays.

One of the minor benefits of being the first head of the Island's military—the equivalent of head of the Joint Chiefs and Secretary of Defense and a Founding Mother, all in one—was that she'd been able to set most of the traditions as she pleased while things were still fluid. Some of that had been very satisfying, in a petty sort of way; for instance getting rid of the old Coast Guard habit of handing out medals and ribbons for everything, starting with breathing and working up to really tough stuff like brushing your teeth regularly. Others had been more important. She'd been a mustang herself, and it had been a minor miracle that she'd ever ended up commanding the *Eagle,* otherwise known as the Guard's floating recruiting poster. After the Event, she'd made sure that everyone's career path started before the mast.

Some changes were more aesthetic, like the ones she'd established for military-social affairs such as this.

She raised her glass in the first toast. "Gentlemen, ladies— the Republic which we serve. A government of laws, not of men."

A murmur of "The Republic" as wine glistened in the firelight. That had been one custom founded with an eye to the future, when more officers were locals born. *Got to get them used to the concept of loyalty to institutions, not just particular people.*

Then she looked at the XO of the *Tubman,* the junior officer present.

"Fallen comrades," the young man said.

"Fallen comrades," everyone replied; perhaps a little more emotionally than usual, with their recent casualties.

There was a clatter of chairs and rustle of linen as the officers seated themselves. Alston looked down the table three places, to where Swindapa was in animated discussion with the XO of the *Douglass;* that young man was a Kurlelo, too . . . although there were thousands in that lineage. They were speaking English, of course; that was the compulsory service language. Swindapa's accent was noticeably lighter than her kinsman's. *Hmmm,* she thought. None of the captains was Alban-born yet, but three of the XO's were. *Coming along there.*

She'd have preferred to have her partner seated beside her, but there was a certain precedence involved. The food came in; boiled lobsters, salads of local greens and pickled vegetables out of barrels put up in Alba, roast suckling pig from the forests inland, fresh bread from field ovens set up ashore. Alston had long ago decided that the Republic's forces wouldn't follow the ancient military tradition of lousy food. There would be plenty of times when they'd all be living on salt cod and dog biscuit, but when the cooks had something better available they'd by-God know what to do with it.

If I have anything to say in the matter, and I do, she thought, and sipped at a Long Island merlot. Martha Cofflin, née Stoddard, had given her and Swindapa a palate education over the last decade or so, as wine became available again. *Educated Jared as far as she could, too,* she thought. The chief had had blue-collar beer-and-whiskey tastes like hers before the Event,

and was more set in them. Cooking had been her hobby since
her teens, along with the martial arts, and that inevitably meant
at least a little exposure to the grape. Leaning back a little she
studied the faces of the commanders over the rim of her glass.

Victor Ortiz was telling a story about an expedition to the
Far East, to Sumatra—one of those odd local cultures; in this
one everything inland was holy and everything that came from
the sea debased. One of his crew on a party sent into the
interior swore they had spotted what sounded like an ape-man
of some sort . . .

*And the dawn came up like thunder/out of China 'cross the
bay,* she quoted to herself. She'd never done more than touch
on those islands, in the *Eagle*'s early round-the-world survey.
She'd read the logs and reports—

Good bunch, she thought, weighing faces and souls. *Hard
workers, smart, plenty of guts. This war's different from anything
else we've done post-Event, though. We're not skirmishing, or
giving some local chief a thrashing for getting nasty with a trader.*

They'd already had a staff briefing, and conversation was
more general than shop—everyone here knew the others well.
The officer corps of the Republic's miniature military was too
small for anything else.

"I'd like to leave a force here," she said after a while. They'd
be leaving the *Merrimac* and her collier anyway; the big ship
was too badly damaged to be allowed anywhere near a fleet
action, and her cargo wouldn't be useful until they had a secure
base near Tartessos. "Pass those peas, please . . . Say a platoon
of your Marines, Jim." The brigadier nodded thoughtfully.

"I'd assumed you would, Commodore," he said. "Hmmm.
Walking wounded, perhaps?"

"That would do. And some volunteers from the auxiliaries."

"I don't think there will be any lack of those who'd rather
face solitude than salt water," he said, and the laugh spread
around the table. "With a couple of heavy mortars on the tip
of the peninsula, we can interdict the entrance to the harbor.
For the landward side . . . yes, sixty or seventy riflemen, a
Gatling, and a fieldpiece would do nicely. It won't weaken our
land force 'nuff to speak of, ma'am."

The dessert brought a few exclamations; chocolate cake was
a rarity even for the well-to-do these days, and she'd sprung
for the ingredients out of her own pocket before the expedition
left. Alston hid a smile at the look of unfeigned eager delight
on Swindapa's face; that direct childlike openness was one of

the things she'd fallen in love with, and it would stay with her partner all her life.

We American-born could do with a little more of it, she thought. She hoped a dash of that Fiernan trait would survive in the bubbling cultural stew that Nantucket had become.

"Gentlemen, ladies," she said after the stewards had cleared away plates and cutlery and set out coffee, cocoa, and brandy. She took a deep breath; no sense in trying to sugarcoat it. Everyone here knew the hungry sea in all its moods. "We'll be sailing tomorrow on the morning tide. I don't think there's any point in waiting for the *Farragut* or her collier any longer."

Plenty of grim looks at that. She nodded and went on: "We'll have to assume that the *Farragut* and the *Severna Park* are lost. With them, we've lost a good proportion of our fighting power."

"Y algunos hombres buenos," Ortiz murmured.

Alston inclined her head in acknowledgment.

"Yes," she said gently. "That too, Commander Ortiz."

The wounded man raised his bandaged head and his brandy glass. "Gary and I . . ."

Yes, she remembered. *Trudeau was his protegé. And their wives were sisters.*

His mouth quirked, giving his darkly handsome face a raffish expression beneath the head-swathing linen wrappings. "There was that Javanese chief who decided he could hassle the wimpy foreign traders." A chuckle. "We strung up the *hijo de puta* by the ass-end of his own loincloth, from the gateway in the palisade 'round his village, left him yelling and screeching to the crowd, and then had quite a party . . ." The brandy swirled in the glass, glinting in the lamplight, and he brought it to his lips. "To fallen comrades."

"Fallen comrades," everyone murmured again, and there was a moment's silence.

"We'll miss the *Farragut* and her crew badly," Alston said when it ended. "However, we still have a number of advantages. This is the only chance we have this year to break the blockade of the Straits of Gibraltar; and we *have* to do that to support our forces in the Middle East."

"It's a risk, ma'am," one of the captains said soberly. "The Tartessians lost heavily this spring, but they're not short of timber or shipwrights, and for inshore work they don't need navigators. They'll have been building as fast as they can lay keels and cast guns. A big risk."

"Indeed it is, Commander Strudwick." She stood, and raised

her glass. "Therefore, I give y'all a final toast for the evening. I give you Montrose's toast."

Silence fell, broken only by the slight creak of the ship moving at her anchors and feet on the deck overhead. Everyone who went through Brandt Point knew *those* words and their maker.

"He fears his fate too much—" she began softly.

Other voices joined her, ringing louder, triumphant:

> *". . . and his desserts are small,*
> *Who will not put it to the touch,*
> *To win or lose it all."*

"Here they come again!" Private Vaukel shouted. Somewhere down the line a man raised another cry:

"Ten! This is the tenth time!"

Vaukel could feel the heat from the barrel of his Werder through the wood of the forestock, and his right thumb was scorched where it met the metal as he pushed home another round. The weapon was kicking a lot harder, too, as fouling clogged the barrel. None of that mattered, as the enemy rose up from behind a ledge of rock and the tumbled bodies of their own dead and charged, shrieking. It was as if the dead themselves arose at Barrow Woman's command, or the very earth came up in a wave to bury him. The sun was nearly down, but it lit the metal of their spears and axes blood-red, and gleamed on eyes and teeth.

"SssssSSSSAA! SA! SA! SssssSSSSAA!"

"Volley fire present, *fire!"*

The rifle kicked into the massive bruise that covered his right shoulder, but the pain seemed to be happening to someone else.

"Independent fire, rapid fire!"

His hand scrabbled at the barley sack beside him and came up empty; someone thrust a packet of shells under his hand, and he saw out of the corner of his eye that it was Chaplain Smith with a sack slung around his neck, traveling down the firing line.

He ripped it with his teeth, spilled the bright brass on the burlap, and thumbed a round home, fired, fired again, again, once every three seconds. Rifles were going off in a continuous rippling crash to either side of him, and along the south face too; ladders went up against the hospital roof and Islanders fought Ringapi along the edge. The ground ahead of him swarmed with dimly seen figures and bright edges, the air filled with yowling war cries and screams of pain. Slingstones and arrows went by overhead in a continuous stream, and flung spears; some of them had bundles of blazing oil-soaked wool wrapped around them. The air he sucked in through parched nose and throat seemed thin and insubstantial, stinking of burned sulfur and shit and blood and burning oil.

"Watch it!" someone bellowed.

The Ringapi charge struck the wall of barley sacks, and it rocked under Vaukel's feet. The attackers dropped down into the ditch—not so far this time, there was a three-deep layer of bodies there now—and leaped upward, driving spears into the sacks to stand on, clutching at the bayonets with their bare hands and striking upward with spear and ax and sword. Some stood with their hands braced against the wall and let their fellows climb onto their shoulders. Two places to Vaukel's right a Marine staggered backward with an arrow buried in his eye-socket, wailing loud enough to be overheard even through the enormous din. A Ringapi slid through the space the wounded man vacated, naked body slick with blood and a dagger in each hand, grappled a Marine, and they fell backward off the firing step together.

Vaukel fired one last round with the muzzle three feet from a man's face. Then he lunged downward with his bayonet; it went in over a collarbone and grated as he withdrew, the sensation traveling up the wood and metal and resonating gruesomely in his chest. A flicker of motion out of the corner of his left eye caught him; Gwenhaskieths was down, a Ringapi with a hand clamped around her throat and his other raising his shield to chop her in the face with the edge. Training brought Vaukel pivoting on his heel—fighting shield-armed warriors you struck at the one on your left, his unprotected spear-side. The twenty-inch blade of his bayonet caught the savage under his short rib and impaled him across the width of his torso, a soft meaty resistance and then things crunching and popping beneath the sharp point.

He twisted the blade, withdrew, slashed at another snarling face as he brought it around, punched the butt after it and felt bone break. Gwenhaskieths pulled herself erect, coughing and retching with the bruising of that iron grip on her throat, and grabbed up her rifle. The line of the north wall was surging and swaying . . .

The bugle sounded: *fall back and rally*. Long habit brought Vaukel around, as if the brassy notes were playing directly on

his nervous system; he grabbed Gwenhaskieths under the arm
and helped her along the first three paces, until she shook him
free and ran herself. Ahead of them the Marines from the south
wall had turned—behind them came the *braaaaap . . . braaaaap*
of the Gatling firing out into the gathering darkness and the
firefly sparkling of muzzle flashes from the Ringapi riflemen on
the hillside above. Captain Barnes was there in the center of
the line, steady, her face calm under the helmet as she waited
with pistol outstretched and left wrist supporting right. Vaukel
felt the sight hearten him as he dashed through the ordered
khaki line, turned, knelt, brought his hand down to the bandolier for a round.

That let him see what was happening. The Ringapi surged
over the suddenly empty wall, roaring exultation, expecting
nothing but the helpless backs of their foes. Then they saw the
line of rifles awaiting them and for one very human, very fatal
instant they stopped. The wave pouring over the wall behind
them crowded them forward, piling up in a mass of human
flesh six bodies deep, jammed skin to skin and less than thirty
feet from the line of Marines. Firelight and the last dying sun
washed across their faces with a color like blood.

"First rank . . . *volley* fire, *present—fire!*"

The Ringapi packed along the inside face of the wall seemed
to writhe in unison somehow as the volley slashed into them,
those in front punched off their feet by the heavy bullets that
slammed through to wound again in the press behind them.

"Reload! Second rank, advance!"

Vaukel took two paces forward through the Marines reloading and brought his Werder to his shoulder in unison with the
rest of those who'd been holding the north wall.

"Second rank . . . *volley* fire, *present—fire!*"

The noise inside the compound was so enormous that even
the bark of forty rifles in unison was muffled. A scream went up
from the Ringapi, and the front two ranks turned and scrabbled
backward; some threw away their weapons, and some used
them to clear a path through their fellows.

"Reload! First rank, advance! Second rank . . . *volley* fire,
present—fire!"

Three more times, and the enemy broke backward in a mass.
The Marines leveled their bayonets and charged with a long
shout, back to the barley-sack parapet. Vaukel found himself
standing there, trying to make sense of the last ten minutes.
Not far down the wall a Ringapi turned at bay; Chaplain Smith
swept him up with a grip at throat and crotch:

"Saint Michael is with us! *For the Lord, and for Gideon!*" he bellowed, hair and beard bristling, and pitched the man over the wall to crash down on two of his fleeing tribesfolk.

Vaukel felt his hands begin to shake. Gwenhaskieths staggered up, helmetless, snarling in a rasp through her damaged throat. A Ringapi came to his feet in the pile of dead and wounded barbarians ahead of her; she spitted him through the kidney from behind. At the barricade another was sitting up, until she whipped the butt of her rifle into his face, twice, and pushed the body away with a foot. A good many others were throwing aside Ringapi bodies as well, after making sure that they *were* bodies and not just temporarily out of commission; there were enough to hamper everyone's footing.

A moment later she was shaking the Earth Folk Marine by the shoulder. "C'mon . . . wake up . . . get down!"

At the touch he started and dropped down a little. Out beyond the wall it was hard to see what was happening, but voices were haranguing the enemy, the voices of their chiefs. Gwenhaskieths grinned, coughed as she drank from her canteen, spat, and offered it to him. He drank in his turn.

"Funny how close that sounds to my language," she said. "For things like *coward* and *motherfucker* and *one more time* and *take their heads,* at least. Watch it!"

Colonel O'Rourke came by, with a dried cut over one eyebrow and a bandage on his neck. "That's the way, Marines," he said, and slapped them both on the shoulder. "Keep it up, and we'll dance on their graves."

He passed on down the line. Vaukel hunched down; the galling fire from the hill behind was dying down at least. Then he heard a sharp loud *crack,* like a rifle but bigger. He turned, and saw the sergeant who'd been firing the Gatling on the south wall staggering back clutching at the ruin of a hand. Smoke poured from the machine gun where shells had hit the overheated chambers and exploded.

"Cook-off, gang-fire!" someone called.

"Oh, that's unfortunate," Vaukel said hoarsely. "Very."

"Could I have a drink?" Ian Arnstein asked, when he and his escorts had reached the Achaean encampment outside Troy.

The hour's trip between was a blur, and from things he remembered as half-seen glimpses he wanted it to stay that way. There were things you did not want to remember, or know that human beings could do to each other. They were too hard to forget.

The soldiers looked at their officer. "The King commanded that he be treated well," the Greek said.

The flask they handed him was pewter. The liquid inside was enough to take the lining off your throat, eighty proof at least; some sort of *grappa*, like the stuff Mediterranean peasants up in the twentieth distilled from the grape husks left after pressing the fruit for wine; another of Walker's innovations. He coughed, swallowed, took another long sip and wiped his mouth with the back of his hand. The cold fire burned down his gullet and hit his stomach, pushing back the chills and shaking of incipient shock. His head still hurt viciously, he'd heard that even a borderline concussion did that.

I would have been willing to believe that on hearsay, without the firsthand evidence.

"Thank you," he said, handing back the flask.

"Aye, it's not easy to face one with the god-force on him," Philowergos said with a certain rough sympathy. "Nor to see the claws of the Lady of Pain stretched out for you." His troops made gestures of aversion at the name. He offered the flask again, and Arnstein shook his head.

"Good," the guardsman said. "A little of this is strength, too much is weakness. Come."

The orderly layout of Walker's camp was disconcertingly like that of the Nantucket Marines, although the tents were leather rather than canvas. A high dirt wall enclosed a neat gridwork of graveled streets, ditches, artillery parks with rows of iron muzzles. The darkness was lit by the red glow of campfires where men cooked pots of boiling grain-mash, and by the brighter yellow of big kerosene lanterns on poles at intervals, or outside tents or rough wood-and-wattle structures larger than others. Horse-drawn ambulances clattered past them, the troops on foot giving way; here and there a mounted messenger or officers, then a mortar pulled by two mounts, the thick barrel swung up and clamped along the draught-pole. Soldiers were beginning to strike their tents as well, and they passed a broad open square where convoys of wagons were being loaded and ox-teams harnessed. There was a smell of animal dung, sweat, woodsmoke, turned earth, oil and leather, but none of the sewer reek you usually got when a large group of Bronze Agers stayed in one place for long. The prisoner and his guards halted in one corner of the square, the officer striding over to give orders and then returning to wait with them.

A mule-drawn vehicle came by, set up a bit like a Western chuck wagon, and halted to hand out small loaves of coarse dark bread, still warm from the oven, and dollops of bean soup with chunks of pork in it into the mess tins of the troops; strings of dried figs and a handful of salted olives came with it. Philowergos saw that the prisoner got some as well. Ian could feel his brain starting to work again, soaking up data like a sponge. Most likely he'd never get to use it—

To hell with that bullshit. I have a country and a family to go home to. The food helped. The body kept on functioning . . . until it didn't anymore.

The soldiers of his escort were talking among themselves. Arnstein cocked an ear at it. He was fluent in Achaean; he'd been studying the archaic Mycenaean Greek almost since the Event, and he'd been a Classical scholar before that. Captain Philowergos had been easy to understand, just some sort of regional dialect giving a roughness to the vowel sounds. What his soldiers spoke was different, almost a pidgin-Greek, stripped of many of the complex inflections, with a massive freight of English loan-words for things like *rifle* and *cannon* and *combat engineer,* and more vocabulary from languages he didn't recognize at all. They had wildly differing accents, as well.

He peered at faces. Some were olive-skinned and dark of hair and eye, like most southern Greeks here and in the twenti-eth; Captain Philowergos's swarthy, dense-bearded good looks reminded him of a waiter in a restaurant in Athens from his last pre-Event visit. Others looked like Albanians or Serbs or Central Europeans; one or two were like nothing he'd ever seen—where did the man with the white-blond hair, flat face, and slanted blue eyes come from? The rest of the army break-ing camp were just as mixed; he even saw one or two blacks. *They* must be from far up the Nile, or West Africans brought in by Tartessian merchants.

The dozen men who'd been told off to guard him squatted to eat, or sat on piles of boxes. With a little effort he could make out the conversation. Talk about the fighting, and how relieved they were at the end of the siege, of families, of places back in Greece he mostly couldn't identify. One freckle-faced rifleman complained that they hadn't even gotten a chance at the city's women; his corporal jeered at him cheerfully and slapped him on the top of the head.

"Thin like stick by now, idiot boy. Stink, bugs. Break cock on bones. Good whores in Neayoruk, clean fat ones, all you want."

"If pay," the young soldier grumbled. "No loot I see, no; not cloth, scrap silver, not a slave to sell."

The officer cut in: "The good King will see that all get a

share, recruit," he said. To Arnstein: "Wannax Walkheear is the best of lords for a fighting-man. Even if your deeds are not beneath his eye he hears of them, and the reward is swift and generous. Me, I'll save the pay and the bonus, and wait until home and my wife. I'll need it all for my farm, when my service ends."

"Walker—" the Islander paused at the scowls. "*Wannax* Walker gives land to his soldiers?"

"When they grow too old to fight, or are wounded and can't serve," Philowergos said. "Or if he wants men to hold down a new conquest. Gold is good, horses, slaves, silver—but land, land for your sons and the sons of your sons, that is best of all."

"Truth, *despotes*," the older man with sergeant's chevrons said; he had a native Greek-speaker's way with the language. "My brother lost a hand fighting the northern tribes near the . . ."

Arnstein asked a question; from the answer he thought the location was somewhere in what would have been Serbia. *Uh-oh. Leaton's people said there are zinc deposits there.* Zinc made brass, which made cartridges.

". . . and now he has land in Sicily—land like a lord, two hundred acres, good land, cropland and vines and meadow by the river, with man-thralls to till the fields, and slave girls to take the work off his wife and to warm his bed. He lives like a lord, too, drinking and hunting as he pleases; and us both born poor farmers, tenants on a *telestai*'s estate!"

The corporal who'd slapped his recruit on the head spoke: "And if a warrior shows courage and *whattitakes*"—another English phrase there, though it took him a moment to puzzle it out—"he may be raised up to a commander, become a noble and great lord."

The soldiers nodded and murmured agreement, calling the blessings of the Gods—the Greek ones, and an assortment of Pelasgian and Balkan and Danubian deities—down on Walker's head. Ian Arnstein had been a scholar most of his life, and his post-Event job hadn't been too different; they both required insatiable curiosity. The coldest attitude toward Walker he could make out in his guards was deep respect combined with fear; from there it shaded up through doglike devotion to literal hero worship. More than one dropped hints about demigodhood, or outright divinity. He suspected that only fear of hubris-bred bad luck kept that at the hint level.

Bad, he thought. *This is bad.* It looked like Walker had been taking some hints from Napoléon's bag of tricks, every soldier with a marshal's baton in his pack. *Hmmmm.* Unless that pissed off too many of the old elite of the Achaean kingdoms. *But Walker's got a lot of goodies to hand out, maybe enough to keep them all happy.* Or he would as long as he kept winning. How solid would his hold be if there were some bitter defeats to swallow?

A vehicle drew up. Arnstein blinked again. *A stagecoach, by God,* he thought, then: *no, not quite, but Walker must have been watching* Gunsmoke *when he was a kid.* His inexperienced eye could make out a few differences; steel springs and shock absorbers, for instance. The side doors bore a blazon of Walker's wolfshead logo, red outline on black. Handlers came behind, leading mounts for the escort.

"In, *despotes,*" Philowergos said, and followed him.

The seats were leather-padded; the Achaean officer sat across from him, drawing his revolver and keeping it in his lap. Ian Arnstein fought not to groan with relief at the cushioned softness, and wished he was as dangerous as the escort thought him.

"Thank you for your courtesy," he said.

Teeth flashed white in the dimness, splitting the cropped black beard. "You are of the King's people," the Greek said.

Well, Rumanian Jewish via New York and California vs. Scots-Irish-German via Georgia and Montana, Arnstein thought. *Still, you've got a point.* Although personally he didn't even like to consider himself part of the same species as William Walker, much less of the same nationality.

"And if you take service with him, you will rise high," Philowergos said. "All you Wolf People do, with your wizard knowledge. Why should I anger one who may be a high lord, especially when the King has ordered me to treat him well?" He shrugged. "And if you won't serve the King . . . well, *Zeus Pater* sends luck to those who befriend the dying."

CHAPTER TWELVE

April, 11 A.E.—Feather River Valley, California

Tarmendtal son of Zeurkenol, squadron commander in the Royal War-Host of Tartessos, of the cavalry attached to the Hidden Fort of the West, enjoyed leading a spring patrol out to trade and take tribute and show the flag.

It was a relief to be out in open prairie—what another history would have come to call the Sacramento Valley—after the dense fogs and long rains and sameness of the winter trapped within the fort's walls, and the deep mud of early spring. The ground was firm now, but the grass that waved chest high on the horses was still fresh and green, starred with unfamiliar flowers, thick with game. Off to the northwest were the slopes of the abrupt hills they had named *Duwakodeiztatun mem Mantzizetatuas*, the Piercers of Clouds, replacing the unpronounceable native gruntings. They were a welcome relief to the eye, in the tabletop flatness all about.

Yet underneath the differences of detail was a homelikeness. It reminded him of younger days, rambling about his father's estate in the country between Tartessos City and the Great River to the eastward. This whole country reminded him of home, if you could imagine home with a few brown savages, and different animals, and so much *bigger*.

He rode down the line, checking gear and bearing. They were good lads, but inclined to brood at being stuck here beyond the edge of the world, and some could never adjust to the strangenesses. Most weren't *really* Tartessians, of course; they were from the new tributary provinces in Iberia, or across the Pillars.

Today, most looked cheerful. It was a change of scene from the fort and the trodden path from there to the cinnabar mines; there had been fresh girls at the hamlet of the savages they'd stayed in last night; and hunting was excellent. He nodded to a few of the file leaders; they were of the kingdom proper, though lowborn. Older than he, too—he'd seen nine rains when Isketerol returned to take the throne and begin the changes, and seventeen when assigned this post three years ago. Then he'd been angry, sure that he was half a hostage, taken to ensure that his father remained loyal to the upstart King. Now . . .

Perhaps I'll stay here, he thought. This land was rich, rich in gold and many other things. And the dwellers so few and weak compared to the countries around the Middle Sea! More, it was much too far from Tartessos to remain tightly bound to the old country, at least a hundred days sailing and sometimes twice that. Once the settlement grew bigger and was less dependent on the yearly supply ship . . .

I could be a mighty man, here, with land to the horizon. In time my sons could be Kings. All that was needed were more people.

He pulled up beside the oxcart that carried the healer, smiling at her. She was a comely woman, perhaps eighteen winters, with olive skin stretched over high cheekbones and sharp features, but pleasantly rounded beneath her long tunic and skirt. Unwedded, too, despite being only a few years younger than he. Many men feared to take a woman dedicated to the Lady of Tartessos or the Grain Goddess to their beds, frightened by the aura of power that clung to such. But they were valued brides to men of sense and wealth, for their *mana* and connections and knowledge—especially in these days of the New Learning. Tarmendtal's own mother had been one of Her women, in her time.

"May the Lady smile on us," he said, bowing gallantly.

She raised a hand to the floppy brim of her woven straw hat. "May She smile indeed—and the Grain Goddess, who comes from the mountain to the plain in this month, as the Lady returns to the sea-halls of her brother Arucuttag."

He nodded, though he had his doubts. In Tartessos, yes . . . but did She rule here, or did some local spirit? *Yet the grain sprouts and ripens here, too, even though it was never planted before we came. Perhaps the Lady just has many names in many places.* Oh, well, the Sun Lord and Arucuttag of the Sea were a man's Gods, and they reigned in all lands—as the Sun bestrode them and the oceans encompassed them, every one.

The wagon creaked along, swaying and jouncing through the tall grass; it was the big four-wheeled kind that the Eagle People made, with a round canvas tent over it and pulled by eight yoke of oxen. It carried supplies not suitable for the packhorses, and rawhide-bound chests of hard wood, to hold the gold dust and nuggets the savages brought; baskets of beads and bundles of iron tools and bottles of fierce young brandy such as the savages lusted for; and the healer's kit. Behind it was the sacred cow of the Lady and its calf, the cow tethered to the frame of the wagon by a rope that led to its halter.

"You come among us like a cool wind in summer, lady, with your ship from the homeland," he went on. "And you guard us with the strength of your knowledge."

Guard us from the Crone, he thought but did not say—some words were unlucky.

The healer grimaced a little and took off her hat, fanning herself. "You have a real healer of the New Learning here, Lord Tarmendtal," she said. "One who even reads En-gil-its, taught by the queen herself."

She made a small protective gesture at the mention of the tongue of sorcery; Tarmendtal followed suit, although he used the hand resting on his right thigh, out of sight. He was glad of the blue faience bead on a string around his neck, that his mother had blessed for him when he left. A small thing, just hearth-magic, but comforting.

"Since I came here she has taught me—" the girl continued. A shout came from ahead, and the high silvery peal of the trumpet.

"Pardon!" the officer barked, wheeled his horse, and flicked it into a gallop with the long end of the reins.

Ahead, the scouts were galloping back toward the main body of the column. The signaler was sounding *enemy in sight,* over and over until Tarmendtal signaled him to stop—with a thump on the helmet. Ahead, northward, lay a dry gully leading east to the main river, a slough marked by a swatch of greener grass and brush; there were live oaks along it, enough to make passage difficult for the wagon. He'd been angling the column westward to cross it further away from the river, where it was merely a dimple in the grass. Figures were boiling out of it, armed men. He pulled the spyglass out of his saddlebag and snapped it open. The image was a little distorted and had a yellowish tinge, but it told him far more than his unaided eye could have done.

"The savages," he snorted.

About seventy or eighty of them, naked except for a few ornaments of bone and shell and feather, leaping and yelping out their barbarous war cries, shaking spears and darts and dart-casters, some screwing their faces up into masks of ferocity and leering with lolling tongues as they danced defiance. A few pissed in mockery, or shook their penises at the Iberians, and others turned and bent and waggled their buttocks, slapping them in ridicule.

For a moment he was incredulous. Then astonished anger awoke. The unbelievable insolence of these slave bastards! Acorn eaters! From their stirring and growls behind him, the men felt the same way.

"Sound *deploy in line*," he snapped. Then he turned in the saddle. "Second file, deploy between here and the river and keep watch." He pointed, squinting into the rising sun.

The file leader looked about to grumble, then caught Tarmendtal's eye and hastened to obey. They were three hundred yards from that stream; there were thick woods on the banks, and a deep current beyond. No sense in taking chances, and six mounted riflemen would be more than enough to see off any savages who tried a flank attack. The teamsters and porters and servants cowered around the wagon. They were natives, unarmed slaves and so not to be blamed for timidity, although if any tried to run he would feed them to Arucuttag.

"Warriors of Tartessos!" he went on; it was traditional to say something to the troops before an action, even as minor a fight as this. "Men of the war-host! Shall we let naked capering dogs make mock of us, we who are civilized men and dwellers in cities obedient to law, subjects of King Isketerol, he who has conquered from the Cold Mountains to the Great Desert and beyond?"

"*No!*" they shouted.

"We will slaughter those who fight, chase down the rest, make eunuchs of them, and put them to work in our mines, take all that is theirs and mount their screaming daughters and wives before their eyes! Arucuttag, Hungry One, to You we dedicate the slain! Sun Lord, give us victory!"

Another shout, long and full of a cheerful bloodlust; even firing from horseback, a rifleman could count on striking from several times the range of a spear-thrower, and he could simply canter out of range to reload and repeat the process as often as needful. The horses stirred restlessly, rolling their eyes and whickering at the noise and the smells of fear and aggression. He took another look with the spyglass; the natives were keeping their position, probably planning to fall back among the trees as the horsemen advanced. Tarmendtal grinned savagely. They'd soon learn the futility of that. Such places were why they had a dozen big dogs along, the kind bred in Iberia for hunting wild bull, wolf, and lion. They were equally useful for hunting wild men.

"Rifles at the ready!" he snapped. *Lord Alantethol will be pleased. An example will cow the other tribes, and there look to be some strong slaves here for the mines, when they've been caught and beaten into meekness.*

The men drew their weapons from the scabbards before their right knees and checked the priming, then buckled back the flaps of the cartridge boxes on their belts. A few added priming powder to the pans of their rifles. Tarmendtal drew his double-barreled pistol, cocked it by pushing the hammers against the side of his thigh, and gestured with it:

"At the canter—walk-march, *forward!*"

Peter Giernas sneezed softly and swore; the pollen here by the banks of the Feather River was pretty fierce. All around him the damp soil bore great oaks and tall cottonwoods, alders and willows, laced together with wild grapevines that twisted around trees from top to bottom. Mosquitoes whined, their needlelike probes going for the bare spots, hands and back of the neck. Other insects buzzed and hopped and flew, pursued by blackbirds and buntings; the clown-faced acorn woodpeckers were at work, drilling holes in trees to a demented chorus of *waka-waka-waka*. This was nesting season; scores of types of birds were doing their reproductive duty, numerous enough that their noise could be nearly painful at times. Especially when the coots in the river to his back began throwing their fits.

Good camouflage, he thought with a grim smile, training his binoculars on the Tartessian column riding unsuspectingly by. It was even better that any eyes looking this way would be sun-dazzled. Doll-tiny figures became men, close enough to see one hawk and spit, another scratch at blue stubble on his jowls, a third take a swig from a leather water bottle hung at his saddlebow. *All right, thirty horsemen.*

They all looked to be soldiers, Mediterranean types mostly, some with cropped black beards, some stubbly-shaven; a few had removed their round iron helmets to reveal bowl-cut hair, often confined with a bandanna tied at the rear. They wore tunic-shirts and loose breeches of some coarse green fabric, cotton or linsey-woolsey, boots, and thigh-length leather vests buttoned up the front. Every man had a copy of the Westley-Richards breechloader in a scabbard in front of his right knee, a short broadsword like a machete or heavy cutlass at his belt along with a bayonet; one carried a yard-and-a-half-long tube of sheet bronze flared at each end slung over his back as well. That man had an assistant and a packhorse trailing him.

Uh-oh, Giernas thought. Descriptions of those had come through before the radio fritzed. *Rocket-launcher team.* Opportunity and risk . . .

A big Conestoga-style wagon drawn by oxen brought up the rear. His chest clenched at the sight of the cow and calf walking along behind it. That must be the "sacred cow" the Indians had told him of, a walking vaccine bank. Half a dozen in ragged cloth kilts or loincloths walked by the wagon, another led the oxen, and a better-dressed one sat on the buckboard with a long-hafted goad in his hand. Those would be locals, slaves. And a Tartessian woman sat in the wagon as well; the long skirts, poncholike upper garment and big straw hat were unmistakable. Two gutted pronghorn antelope carcasses hung from the rear tilt of the wagon, and a quartered Tule elk.

"Good-looking horses," Eddie breathed from his position a little southward.

Giernas nodded, for two truths; the horses were handsome though small—dapple-skinned Barb-types, less hairy and stocky than their own Alban-Morgan crossbreeds—and it was just like Eddie to go judging horseflesh at a time like this.

"What's the woman doing here?" he asked in turn. Tartessians weren't as unreasonable about females as some locals, but they weren't what you could call enlightened either, and fighting was strictly man's work to them.

"She is a healer," Jaditwara said. "Among her people, only women do that work."

Giernas grunted. That made sense. If the enemy were using vaccination to get obedience, they'd need someone skilled in the technique. Which meant . . .

"Sue. The Tartessian woman, we need her alive, and the cow—get Tidtaway to pass the word." *For what it's worth.* Probably not much; the mountain tribesman was just as much a foreigner as the Islanders to this bunch, and had a good deal less *keuthes.* Now to get to work.

"Steady," he said, thumbing back the hammer of his rifle. Beside him Perks tensed, all taut alertness where he crouched belly-down to the ground, his nose pointed in an unwavering line to the front. No sound escaped the dog's deep chest, but the black lips were drawn back from long yellow-white teeth and his ears lay flat. "Wait for the locals."

The slough where most of the Indians were hiding formed a right angle with the river. There were seventy-three of them there, and another twenty-four near here in the riverside jungle. Their plan wasn't complex; it couldn't be, with the language barrier, and the fact that the locals had no concept of discipline. A war-leader here was anyone with a good reputation, and warriors followed him or not just as they individually pleased or their Spirit Friends whispered in their ears. It was a tribute to how monumentally terrified and pissed off the tribelets were that so many had showed up to fight. As near as he could calculate from what he'd been told by his allies, there couldn't be more than thirty thousand people in the whole of California in this era; half of them in the Central Valley, and half of that in the northern portion near enough for runners to reach. A fair number of those had been killed by the Tartessians over the last couple of years, or had died—some sort of imported lung fever had struck here long before the smallpox, and what sounded like typhus. Many of the rest were hiding in terror of the new plague that was spreading like a prairie fire.

Ninety-seven men was a big chunk of the healthy adult males left after you worked those numbers. And pretty soon *they* would have to scatter, as summer dried out the valley and they had to move up into the mountains or south into the delta marshes to feed themselves. Meanwhile half the Tartessians in the settlement were full-time fighting-men with horses and modern weapons, and they had a year's supply of stored food even if they lost this harvest.

God, listen up. I could use some help here, You know, he thought/prayed. "Right, here we go," he said aloud, as shouting broke out to the northward.

Despite the tension that dried his mouth, he grinned a little at the show the Indians were making. It would have annoyed *him*, if he'd been on the receiving end. He turned the binoculars. The Iberian commander was a young man, younger than Giernas, with a proud dark hawklike face. The ranger could see his lips curling back from very white teeth. Despite that anger, he detached a file of six troopers to screen the wagon from the river side.

All right, Giernas thought. *So he's not quite as headstrong as I hoped.* The local name for him was Bull Elk, because he liked to butt heads and yell, evidently.

"Wait for it," he said again, a little louder, looking at what he could see of his firing line. Eddie, with a grin that was a half snarl; a glimpse of Jaditwara beyond him, frowning in concentration. Sue on his right hand, relaxed and calm.

"Did you see this?" she murmured.

"See what?" he said.

"Wild oat grass," she said, pulling up a strand. "And fescue—neither should be here. They're European, Mediterranean. Must have come in in fodder or bedding, and now they're spreading, the way they did in the old history pre-Event." She nodded out to the field of waist-high native needlegrass and bunchgrass. "Come back when Jared's your age, and this'll all be gone—it'll all be these imported perennials instead. Up to your ass in feral cattle and horses, too."

Giernas blinked. There was such a thing as being *too* calm. "Let's worry about the ecology later, hey?" he half snapped.

"Waiting's hard," she said. The blue eyes were kind. "Don't worry, Pete, it'll be a cinch. Indigo and the kid will be safe as houses in a couple of hours."

"If nobody shoots the damned cow by accident," he said. "And right about now—"

Crack. Crack. The first two rifles went off, out where the Tartessians were closing on the locals' skirmish line. A chorus of whipcracking reports, followed, a long stuttering rattle. He trained his binoculars, hoping . . . *yes!* The Indians had remembered his advice; they were dropping flat as soon as the Iberians raised their weapons.

That had taken a little doing. The locals were fine hunters and trackers, but when they fought in any numbers they lined up by mutual consent and threw spears until someone was hurt. Then everyone went home and told lies about how brave they'd been while blood flowed like floodwaters. He'd harangued them about this being a hunt, not a game, but he hadn't been sure how it took.

Yes. The locals vanished in the chest-high grass. The Tartessians shouted in anger, reloading and pushing closer. Then they shouted again, in alarm; Indians bobbed up out of the tall grass, threw their darts, ran half a dozen paces and threw themselves down again. None of the soldiers had been hit yet, but one horse had a dart through its haunch and went kicking and bucking and squealing off across the prairie with the rider hauling on the reins one-handed and trying frantically to lose neither seat nor rifle. One Indian went down while he watched, punched backward with a hole in his chest and an exit wound the size of a fist blossoming out of his back in a spray of blood and bone fragments.

Puffs of smoke were blossoming out of the muzzles of the rifles, drifting northward with the wind toward the dry slough. Noise, confusion, men running and horses wheeling. Perfect.

Here we go, he thought, giving a last check that the sights of his rifle were adjusted to the right range. Breathe out. Lift the muzzle up, up, until the bead of the foresight filled the U-notch of the rear. *Squeeze* the trigger, gently, gently . . .

Crack. The butt punched his shoulder. A perceptible fraction of a second later the lead ox drawing the Tartessian wagon bellowed, half reared and then slumped, blood pouring from nose and mouth as it kicked on the ground. The woman on the seat glanced around toward it just before the cry of animal agony; she must have heard the flat smack of the bullet slapping into the ox's body behind the shoulder.

The other three Islanders fired within a second of each other. *Crackcrackcrack,* and a deep ratcheting snarl from Perks as he made little shifting motions with his haunches.

One of the Tartessian file went right back over his horse's rump, helmet flying and trailing red—a clean head shot, right through the bridge of his nose. Another cursed, jerked, then was upright again, raising his own weapon; a grazing hit on the left arm. The third shot missed clean. All in all, very good shooting, Giernas decided, as his hands moved of themselves in the reloading drill.

Sue shouted something in the local tongue, and the Indians waiting in the riverside jungle charged forward whooping and screaming; they were also dodging and jinking, making themselves as difficult a target as they could. The Tartessians did exactly what the rangers had hoped, firing by reflex at the men running toward them. Two men went down dead or wounded, but that left the enemy with no time to reload. Giernas raised his own rifle again, standing this time for a better shot. *Crack,* and the waft of burned-sulfur stink. A distant corner of his mind noted that the sulfur had come all the way from the Caribbean to Nantucket and then on horseback all across the continent; doubtless that in the Tartessians' ammunition was from Sicily, and here it was being used up in California . . .

A Tartessian screamed, dropped his rifle, and clutched at his thigh, then slid out of the saddle. Another went down as his horse did, its scream far louder than the wounded man's but equally full of bewildered agony. The three remaining dropped two Indians before they turned to gallop away; but they had left it far too late. Without the rifles firing on them from the riverbank they might have stopped the Indian charge; without the Indians they might have answered the rifles in kind . . . but now they had lost half their numbers, and a horse makes a bad firing platform.

It is also a far larger target than a man, and unlike a man it cannot hit the dirt when shot at. A shower of atlatl darts fell around the riders, hurled by experienced, muscular arms whose power was magnified by the long leverage of the throwing-sticks. One of the Iberians took a dart through the throat and slumped off his saddle in a slow-motion collapse. Another went down choking and pawing at three of the short spears sunk half their length in his chest. The third managed to get his horse around and bounding toward the main fight.

"Get him!" Giernas shouted. It was needless. All four of the Islander rifles sounded, so close together that the sound was one thick *brakk*. Horse and rider folded together and tumbled.

The rangers dashed forward toward the enemy's wagon and the precious cow, Perks running at his master's side. One of the unhorsed Tartessians rose in front of Giernas, drawing his chopping blade and raising it for a swing. Giernas ignored him. The great gray-brown shape of the wolf-dog went from an easy bounding run to a soaring leap without even breaking stride, a hundred and twenty pounds of hairy torpedo with fangs. The wide-stretched jaws snapped closed on the man's raised arm as the dog's weight crashed into his chest. The teeth clamped like hydraulic shears, and Perks savaged the arm with a twisting back-and-forth jerk of head and neck and shoulders. Bone parted with a splintering crunch as both went tumbling to the ground. Giernas jinked around the thrashing bodies and dashed on, cursing the clinging friction of the grasses. At the wagon the ragged slaves were gone, probably running for the hills at full speed. All except for one; he was wrestling with the Tartessian woman, holding her right hand by the wrist and trying to make her drop the flintlock pistol in it. Two of the locals were helping him, and/or trying to rip the woman's clothes off.

Well, just because they're being fucked over by the Tartessians doesn't make them angels, Giernas thought, and rang the steel-shod butt of his rifle off the back of the ex-slave's head. The man went down like a marionette with its wires cut; the ranger whipped the rifle butt around and slammed it under the short ribs of one local, then turned to put the muzzle under the chin of the second. It was empty, but *he* couldn't know that.

"Go! Fight!" Giernas barked, jerking his head toward the main action.

The Indians did, shrugging, one grinning and the other nursing his side and whooping to get air back into his lungs. Giernas slapped the pistol out of the Iberian woman's hand and chopped the edge of his palm into her temple with precisely calculated force. She sagged backward with her eyes rolling up, caught at the wagon wheel, and slumped to the ground.

God willing, all she'll have is a bad headache for a couple of days. She certainly wouldn't be doing anything very energetic for a couple of hours. As he reloaded he looked over her into the body of the wagon. *Ayup, hot damn—more rockets and a mortar. They must have that along for holdouts who try to hide in the hills when they come calling.*

"Four rounds," he muttered aloud. This part hadn't taken long—wouldn't have worked if it did. *Four minutes, more or less.* Time always went like that in a fight, stretching like a thread of thickening maple syrup while you waited for it to start, then blurring past once it got started.

The Tartessians' main body were just noticing what was going on behind them—as he'd thought, the noise and confusion and the sound of their own shots had concealed it from them for crucial seconds, until there was nothing they could do about it.

Plus they're overconfident, he thought with a shark grin, as he licked sweat off his lips. They'd gotten used to thinking of themselves as the Lords of Creation facing dumb nekkid savages. Underestimating the opposition always left you sorry and sore in the end.

Eddie Vergeraxsson came up, riding on one Tartessian horse and leading three more; that was a bonus, the beasts were well-enough trained to stand and be caught, and he wouldn't have to go back for theirs. Sue and Jaditwara arrived seconds later, panting but running easily with their rifles in their right hands, then throwing themselves into the saddles. Giernas took a second to lengthen the stirrup leathers on one of the horses, a gelding that wouldn't be impossibly small for a man his size.

"Perks!" he said.

The dog trotted up, head low and tongue unreeled and lapping at his muzzle. None of the blood looked to be his. He sniffed at the slumped figure of the Tartessian healer, visibly wondering if he was supposed to bite her too.

"Stay! Guard!"

The wolf-dog trotted around the wagon, then crouched in the long grass, nose and ears and eyes busy. That took care of anyone without a gun who tried to approach the wagon, and if they did have a gun they'd have to be fast and very lucky.

"What next, Pete?" Eddie said.

"Next, we make sure the ends get tied up," he said.

Over northward near the slough, the Tartessians were in

trouble. He tossed his rifle into his left hand and got out his binoculars again, stepping up onto the box seat of the ox-wagon to see better. The enemy had stayed tangled up with the first group of attacking Indians far too long. Now, just as they were turning to disengage and pepper them from a distance, the twenty-odd who'd been with the Islanders were racing to take them in the rear. Sixteen of the enemy left . . . no, make that fourteen, one took a dart in the back, and he saw two Indians leap up and tear another from the saddle like wolves at an elk, bearing him down to the ground, hands and heads and bare brown backs rising and falling above the tall grass as they hit and stabbed.

"Let's go!" he shouted, and sprang into the saddle.

The four Islanders swung southwest at a hard pounding gallop, away from the fight, out into more open country—the difference in height was invisible to the naked eye, but there weren't any trees and the grass got shorter. Giernas kept an eye over his right shoulder at the melee of horses and men, shouts and shots, edged steel and wood and chipped volcanic glass. Right about now that balls-for-brains Tartessian commander was finally going to do the only possible thing—

A trumpet sounded, high and sweet. He didn't recognize the pattern of notes. The enemy did, turning due west and spurring their horses. With no cover and plenty of room the horsemen could fire and retreat, fire and retreat, until the Indians broke and ran. The Tartessians could even ride far enough away to dismount and fire, then mount again before their enemies could come close.

The Indians gave chase, working at a tireless lope that was far slower than a horse's best, but which they could keep up much longer. Men in good condition could run down horses or deer, and most of this continent's hunters did that sort of thing on a regular basis. The Tartessians were at a full gallop now heading due west, pulling away fast; getting a little ahead of the Islanders as well, since they were on diverging courses.

"And about now, they're going to find out why we picked this place for an ambush, too," Giernas shouted gleefully, holding the unfamiliar mount on a tight rein.

The first Tartessian horse went down with shocking abruptness; it was the signaler's, right next to the commander. The *pop* of breaking cannon bone as the horse's leg plunged into the ground-squirrel hole wasn't audible at this distance, but he could see Eddie wincing in horseman's sympathy. The bugler flew half a dozen paces and hit the ground hard, not looking as if he was going to get up. Then another horse went down, and another, and the Tartessians started to rein in. You couldn't make horses run into bad ground.

"Down!" Giernas shouted, slugging his own horse to a stop.

It reared but halted, well trained. He kicked his feet out of the saddle and swung his right over the animal's head, sliding to the ground. "OK, Dobbin," he said. "Let's see if you get to live out the day."

Islander military mounts—and ranger horses—had a certain range of commands drilled in; presumably the Tartessians had copied. He pulled the horse's head around toward its shoulder and pressed down sharply on its back, pulling to the rear at the same time. It rolled eyes with white showing all around them, then obediently collapsed, hind legs first, lying down to form a living breastwork—a good choice, since he'd have had to shoot it otherwise.

The saddle, too, was copied from the Republic of Nantucket's military model, a modified Western type. He unbuckled the saddlebag's flap cover, felt around inside, and brought out a pair of ten-round cloth ammunition containers, ripping them open with his teeth while he scanned the open grassland ahead. He could see the young officer give his orders, and most of his men dismounted and put their horses down in front of them to form a defensive circle. They opened up on the Indians, steady aimed fire that stopped the charge in its tracks and sent the locals to ground.

Two others headed off southwest, moving their mounts at a rapid walk, to take word and bring help.

"Smart, but too late," Giernas said. *I hope.* "Get 'em!"

He sat, braced his elbows on his knees, adjusted the sights and aimed carefully, raising the muzzle. *Crack.* The others opened fire as well. A horse went down, then rose again, but one leg was useless, too painful for it to put weight on. The rider slid to the ground, threw the saddlebags over his shoulder, then hesitated and put the rifle behind the animal's ear and fired before running back toward his comrades. Lead slugs clipped grass around the other Tartessian. Then he reeled where he sat; Giernas could see the little cloud of dust where a bullet struck his leather jerkin.

Something went *shrrack!* through the air above Giernas's head. He threw himself down and returned the favor, reloaded, fired again. It was extreme range, nearly nine hundred yards, but they were a big target. The commander had planted a staff in the ground at the middle of the circle with the Tartessian pennant flying. As Giernas watched a group of Indians made a rush, well spread out. Bullets kicked up grass fragments and dirt at their feet, and one spun and fell backward screaming. The others went to cover again.

Another had worked his way around the circle covered by the Tartessian rifles, all the way to the stalled wagon. He flopped to the ground near Giernas; then the two men looked at each other, realizing suddenly that they had no word in common.

"Jaddi!" he called. "Tidtaway!"

Get the iron tube and its legs from the wagon, he thought, preparing for the work of translation and ducking slightly as another bullet cut a path above his head. The horse snorted, but kept still as he fired across its flank. Even a light field mortar outranged rifles comfortably. *Bring it back there—* another three hundred yards southward should make a safe firing position. And then . . .

Ahead, a faint rhythmic sound came from the embattled Tartessians. It was a moment before he realized it was singing. Jaditwara paused in her leopard-crawl through the grass, her rifle across the crooks of her elbows.

"It is, how you say, a hymn," she said. "A hymn to the Lady of Tartessos, they ask her to welcome her children home to her." Giernas's mouth quirked. The yellow-haired girl went on: "That they are brave does not mean they are not bad, Pete."

He nodded, sighing. He'd do whatever it took to win, and to win safety for his child and friends, but there were times he didn't like the taste of it.

The site of the battle was much as Peter Giernas had left it an hour ago, although the locals had gotten tired of jumping around and waving their new knives and swords in the air; a few were dressed in bits and pieces of Tartessian uniform. The captured horses were staked out to a picket line, at least, and his friends had seen that the rifles were collected. Birds were wheeling overhead, buzzards, condors, even a few hawks and eagles—none of them fussy eaters, he knew. The bodies had been piled up into a heap. He sighed as he came close.

"Yeah! Come *up* there!"

Eddie Vergeraxsson bent, gripped the central tuft of a dead man's hair, and made a quick circle with his skinning knife, wrenching and pulling as he did. The locals looked on with expressions ranging from awe through horror to fascination; scalping wasn't a widespread custom in the Americas of this era. It *was* among the Sun People of Alba, though, when they didn't have a chance to take the whole head home and nail it over the doorway.

More of the Indians were wandering around the heaped corpses, some brandishing captured swords; others were sitting by their own dead, singing quietly in a wailing falsetto, minor-key laments. They'd lost more men than the Tartessians, even in victory.

"Eddie, cut that out—you're giving them ideas, goddammit."

"Okay, Pete," the other ranger said cheerfully. "Though—I mean, hell, if you want to keep their ghosts down you have to at least . . . oh, well, sorry." He stopped, picked up one of the locals' darts, stripped off the feathers to make it look more like a spear, and ceremoniously threw it over the mound of corpses, dedicating them to Sky Father and the Crow Goddess.

Giernas nodded. *There isn't a man in the world I'd rather have at my back in a fight or beside me on a hunt,* he thought. *You can rely on Eddie, and he's fun to sit down and have a beer with, too. I love him like a brother. It's just that sometimes he's an asshole, is all.*

He rode on to the wagon. Sue and Jaditwara were inside, talking as they inventoried the contents:

". . . nucleosis you Eagle People are always on about."

"Monogamy. Mononucleosis is a disease."

"As I said."

"Little Jared's cute as a button; but raising kids sure is easier with an extra pair of hands. We'll even find a use for you-know-who—"

He could tell by the way they cut off when he reined in that they'd been talking about him. *Women,* he thought. *Grand creatures, but Lord do they like to gossip.*

He slid out of the saddle and tethered the horses, taking Jared from his mother and swinging him high until he gurgled and giggled, then handing him back.

"Everything okay?" he asked Sue anxiously.

"Hi, Indigo! Yeah, s'okay, Pete. I talked some with the Tartessian medico—slight concussion, gave her some willow-bark extract—and they're using the straight Jenner vaccination technique. That cow most definitely has cowpox, too."

She brought down a wooden box, brown olive wood marked with a device like an inverted pyramid divided by a line, and bound with brass at the corners. Opened, it revealed vials marked in the Tartessian tongue, with English translations, hypodermics, scalpels, probes.

"She's not a doctor, really, even by their standards—about equivalent to me, sort of, if Jaditwara understands what she said. This is the cowpox serum. Matter from the udder sores, egg medium." The serum was in little wax-and-cork sealed glass vials nested in individual bolls of cotton, labeled by date.

"I'm using one of my hypos, our needles are finer." She broke the seals, jabbed in the point of the hypodermic. "We want this just under the skin—putting it in a scratch would do it, but this'll be faster."

"And then we will be safe from the sickness, sister?" Indigo asked, looking at the hypodermic with interest. She'd seen them used before, mostly for administering morphia. Everyone had had an injury or two over the past year, and the expedition had doled out a little painkiller now and then to people they were guesting with.

"You may get a few days of feeling ill, light fever, maybe a bit of a rash. Then you'll be safe forever; from the smallpox, at least, sister."

Spring Indigo slipped the buckskin shirt down from her shoulder, face impassive at the slight sting, and then held the piece of cotton fluff on the spot until it stuck. When she noticed him watching her milk-full breasts, she rolled the hip she was holding Jared on a little and winked.

The toddler smiled and babbled and tried to grab at Sue as Spring Indigo brought him 'round. His cry of *Mama!* turned into a wail of betrayal as the needle jabbed his buttock.

"There, there, sweetums," Sue said. "There there—momma will make it all better."

Not from the way he's sounding, Giernas thought, amusement bubbling up under a vast wash of relief. *Nothing wrong with this boy's lungs.* Startled and angry more than hurt, but *loud*.

"You're one to tease us about monogamy," he grumbled to Jaditwara. "Hell, you stick to Eddie like glue. Even when you're fighting and you drive him crazy with that cold-shoulder act."

"I like Eddie," the ex-Fiernan ranger said. "I want to stay with him and have children together. He just needs to learn that 'my woman' isn't the same thing as 'my horse.' You Eagle People started his . . . how do you say, consciousness lifting . . . and I'm finishing it."

Young Jared's wails turned into sobs. The three women gathered around making soothing noises; he felt a little of the usual adult-male uselessness that such occasions brought out, and walked over to where Tidtaway and the local chief and Eddie were moving slowly along the line of captured rifles leaning against a log. Their mountaineer guide already had one of the rifles over his shoulder, and a bandolier and bayonet at his waist, he noted. Others of the war band were butchering the fallen oxen and horses.

"Give me a hand for a second, Eddie," he said.

They unhitched the rest of the ox-team, watching as the big red-and-white beasts lumbered out into the open grass away from the disturbing smell of blood and strange humans. They shook themselves out, milled around, and began to graze. *Won't go far,* Giernas thought; he'd worked a fair bit with oxen when he did stints as a timber runner for the sawmills in Providence Base. It helped that there was good grazing and water here. The other ranger nodded agreement.

"All looking good, Pete," Eddie said. "We've got twenty-six horses fit to ride. Six of the rifles really out of commission, but one's just a hammer sheared off. I think I can fix that from the Tartessians' kits; they have some spare parts."

"How much ammo?"

"Most of them had a few rounds left in their bandoliers, didn't get a chance to shoot themselves dry. Another fifty each in the saddlebags, and more in the wagon, with priming powder to suit. Hey, Jaddi! What's it all come to?"

The ranger woman looked up from the circle at the tail of the vehicle. "Two hundred eight rounds per weapon, Eddie."

"Yuk-huk-sau-*hau-hau-hau-hau!*" Eddie Vergeraxsson whooped and shook his own weapon southward toward the Tartessian fort two days' march away. "We've got the mortar, twenty bombs for it, and the rocket launcher and ten rockets."

"Hmmmm," Giernas said, lifting the bronze tube.

It weighed about twenty pounds. Nothing complicated, just two wooden handholds fastened to the weapon with rivets, an elementary ring-and-post sight, and brackets where a conical boiled-leather shield could be fastened to protect the user's face from the backblast. In operation a loader would push rockets up the rear and set off their fuses with a flint-and-steel lighter.

"Well, we're going to have to use up some of that rifle ammunition showing the locals how to use 'em," he said. "Say ten rounds or so."

Eddie nodded; the unspoken thought went between them: *For all the good that'll do.* It took time to make a rifleman, and a lot of practice at things like estimating ranges. These single-shot weapons weren't submachine guns, you couldn't

spray bullets in the general direction of the enemy and pray
for a hit. They were precision instruments, or they were just
noisy clubs. The locals would probably be nearly as formidable
with their spear-throwing atlatls; at least they really knew how
to use those. But having death-sticks of their own would undoubtedly do wonders for their morale.

The chief began speaking, ran into subjects beyond the mea-
ger vocabulary he shared with Tidtaway, and they called for
Jaditwara.

"These Big Dogs," he said. "Some say there are bad spirits
in them—that we should kill them all and eat them, to gain
power over this medicine."

Eddie snorted tactlessly. "Couple of them tried to get on
horseback 'cause it looked like easy fun," he said. "No bones
broken. I think."

Tidtaway had been practicing off and on for a couple of
months, and *he* still rode like an animated sack of potatoes;
these locals would be hopeless for a good long while. According
to the books he'd read back when—part of ranger training and
interesting in its own right—in the original history the Indians
had taken to horses like ducks to water. Whole tribes had given
up farming, moved onto the Plains, and become mounted buf-
falo-hunters and mobile raiders almost overnight. But *overnight*
apparently meant years rather than months.

"You already have a few dead ones to eat," he pointed out.
"And these *horses* will be very useful to you. To fight the
Tartessians, and then to carry things and carry men faster than
they can go on foot." He searched for an example. "Hunters
could ride very far and fast, and then bring meat to camp
easily."

The chief grunted, then looked at the horses staked out to
the picket line dubiously. "Maybe," he said. Then more
brightly: "We have given the Tartessians a bad defeat. Their
women will wail and put tar on their hair; their war chief will
cut his cheeks and roll in the dust. Maybe now they will leave
us alone, and everything will be as it was."

Peter Giernas sighed. "All you have done is enough to en-
rage them—as if you stamped on a man's foot, or threw one
spear at a bear," he said. "If you go home now, they will strike
again. And you will be weaker from the plague."

The older man glanced up sharply. "But now we have their
magic of the *cow*," he said. "Your shamaness says she can
protect us."

"We can protect you, here, yes. Your women and children

at your camp, yes. But not all the tribes even in the valley of this river—and none of the ones in the other land south of the delta, or in the coast valleys. Already they will begin to sicken, and when the sickness has gone past one man in two, maybe three in four, will be dead. These are the men that might have helped you fight the Tartessians. If you—all the people who dwell here—do not come together *now* and make an end of them, they will make an end of *you*. Not this year, not next, but someday, as certain as the rain in winter and the grass in spring."

The chief winced, as if the outlander had spoken in the same tones as the voice at the back of his head. His shoulders slumped.

"Then we will have to take their camp with the big houses," he said in a dull voice. "But how? The Great Camp has walls like a mountain, and they have the thunder-makers there, big logs that throw death a mile or more, and many men with the death-sticks that you call rifles."

"We need a plan," Giernas said. "For that, we need better knowledge of their fort."

He'd have to talk to people who'd been inside. The problem with that was they'd generally have only fuzzy ideas of what he wanted to know. When you put perception and language problems together, not much but noise would come out.

"And we must make sure that nobody warns the Tartessians," he went on. "So that they don't miss their men too soon." They'd caught the patrol early in its swing out into the boondocks, and it wasn't due back for weeks. "And we must gather many, many warriors. As many again as we had today, and as many more, and as many more again, at least."

At least Indigo and Jared will be safe, he thought.

When the chief went off shaking his head, Eddie Vergeraxsson laughed and shook his rifle southward again, calling out a single sentence in his mother tongue. Giernas recognized the sound, if not the meaning. Eddie had once told him that he didn't even dream in the Sun People language anymore, but now and then he used a stock phrase.

"What does that mean?" Giernas asked.

"Oh . . ." Eddie frowned for a moment, lips moving. "Near as I can render it . . . *Oh, you sorry bastards are* fucked *now!*"

CHAPTER THIRTEEN

September, 10 A.E.—O'Rourke's Ford, east of Troy

Colonel O'Rourke glared around the enclosure in an instinctive search for something more to throw into the fight. Spears and arrows lay thick on the ground or stood up from the dirt, giving it the bristling look of a hedgehog's back. More flew in continously, their heads flashing in the light of the fires that burned here and there along the barricade. The roof of the hospital seemed to have caught as well—which at least was keeping most of the enemy snipers off it; they'd brought them forward from the hillside to the south as night fell. All around the walls was a swarming melee as the Marines stabbed and smashed and cut, heaving the enemy back from the parapet and shooting whenever they got the chance to reload.

Thank God for the bayonet, a corner of his mind thought. As soon as the Republic started issuing firearms in the Year 2, they'd found to everyone's surprise that rifle and bayonet in skilled hands made a better hand-to-hand weapon than bladed weapon and shield; it combined the virtues of a spear, a quarterstaff, and a halberd.

Chaplain Smith was still doing the rounds with spare ammunition and Scripture, using a broken spear as an improvised crutch; a sopping red bandage circled his thigh. Some of the others passing out ammunition could do no more than crawl. Most of the rounds in the chaplain's sack were loose, stripped out of the remaining Gatling drums now that the weapon was useless. Even with the wind a standing fog of powder smoke ghosted around the Islander outpost, leaving everything hazed in burned sulfur; a corner of his mind estimated that every Marine in the compound must have fired something like two hundred rounds, and it was still four hours to dawn.

"We can't hold them here," he said, muttering to himself. "The perimeter's too long."

Lieutenant Hussey charged with his intervention squad to a

spot where the line bulged, their sudden ordered impact giving them an effect beyond their numbers. Hussey had managed to acquire an extra pistol from somewhere, and was shooting two-handed. Hitting what he shot at, too, a minor miracle. They fell back from the wall once the breakthrough was contained, reloaded, and headed for the next . . . but this time there were only nine of them.

Surgeon-captain Wenter threaded her way through the chaos with another group of wounded from the burning hospital, the ones who could walk helping those who couldn't, the last of her orderlies carrying one man across his shoulder and half-carrying another with an arm around his waist. She trotted over to O'Rourke and examined the bandage on his neck.

"Normally I'd say you should be on your back for a week, with that," she said. "Looks all right for now."

He nodded. "Are the wounded and sick all out of the hospital?"

"No, they aren't," she said. "Some of them are in those two rooms at the northwest corner—the Ringapi on the roof shoot at anyone who tries to get to them through the courtyard, and there's no interior corridor. All the rooms give on to the court-yard. You'll have to send in some people to get them out now."

O'Rourke looked west. "Can't be done," he said. "Get these into the storehouse." He met her incredulous glare steadily. "I'm not going to get everyone killed to rescue a few," he said. "Do it, Doctor. Do it *now*."

"Damn you, O'Rourke!" she spat, turning to obey. A glance around. "Damn all you butchers!"

He ignored her, not without an inward wince, and called Barnes over. "We can't hold," he said. "This is going to be tricky—"

"They're on the bloody roof!" someone said.

"Well, what do you expect me to do about it, shithead?" Private Hook screamed, ducking aside as a Ringapi outside the hospital's west wall thrust a rifle barrel through the windowslit.

The explosion was deafening inside the confined space of the hospital room. The bullet chipped a divot out of the pole of a bunk bed, showing the raw pinewood within. Hook stepped back before the man outside could reload or withdraw his weapon, grabbed it by the barrel with his left hand, and shoved his own rifle out until the muzzle touched flesh. It bucked in his hand as he snatched it back, reloaded, and fired again.

Sweat stung his gnawed lips. The dim lanternlit space of the hospital room was full of powder smoke, with shapes looming up out of it like rocks on the floor of hell; the smell of the diarrhea from the patients who couldn't go to the latrines anymore added the final touch. The mud-brick wall under his shoulder shook; there just weren't enough guns here to keep the enemy from dashing forward and crouching along the bottom of it. They reached up and grabbed at the rifles, or thrust spears through, or firearms of their own—more and more of those. Others were beating at the walls, cutting through with axes and spearheads . . .

Hook turned on his heel and went to the door that led into the courtyard. He opened it, and jerked back as a spear flashed down and buried itself in the floor beside his foot; he hopped back convulsively and then had to wrestle the shaft free before he could close the door and bar it again.

Edraxsson was staring at him again. "What are you looking at?" he shouted at the fever-struck sergeant. He looked around again. *We're all going to die here! Hell with we, I'm going to die here!*

Here . . .

"All right, heads up," Hook said. "We've got to get out of here."

"You sucksoul, the enemy are on the roof; they'd spit us like deer if we tried to run through the courtyard—and half of us can't walk."

Hook ignored the interruption. "They'll be through the front wall soon," he said. "Then they'll swamp us. You, you, you—cut through the interior wall there. We'll go through and down the side of the hospital that way. Come on, move it!" He picked up one of the entrenching tools. "The rest of you, keep firing. Faster, God damn you."

He slammed the pick side of the tool into the side wall of the room. The impact jarred him all the way down to the small of his back; he levered it sideways, tearing out a chunk, ignoring the pain where the bandage worked against the sore on his back.

"Come on, you lazy motherfuckers—work!"

Edraxsson laughed, high and shrill and delirious. The others looked at Hook for a moment, then moved to obey. He slammed the tool into the mud brick again and again; the stuff resisted him, bricks dried hard as iron over the years, and the mud mortar and plaster around them had been mixed with animal hair and straw to begin with. He looked through when the hole was big enough, then back over his shoulder.

"Watch it!" he yelled, snatching up his rifle and turning.

A steel spearhead probed down through the widening hole in the roof, then a bronze one. Mud and old dry bundles of reeds and twigs fell down into the room, and then the face of a Ringapi, his long mustaches dangling down to make horns below his head. Hook fired without being aware he was aiming and the man's head flew apart like a dropped melon. The body followed it, twitching and bucking like a pithed frog. Hook screamed in frustration as the ambulatory cases began dragging the ones who couldn't walk out through the hole *he'd* dug, the hole to safety and freedom.

Smoke was pouring down through the hole. The long-dry pine poles that held the whole heavy mass of the roof up must be catching as well. He coughed and fired twice more into the gap.

"Hurry up!" he screamed, and then to his horror the other two walking wounded stopped firing through the slit window and dashed out through the hole. "Cowards! Pussies!" he shrieked as he reloaded.

The door to the courtyard smashed in with a shower of splinters. Hook shot the man in the door in the belly, scrabbled in his bandolier, loaded, thumbed back the cocking lever and fired again just as the Ringapi who'd vaulted the first was drawing back his spear for the killing thrust. The heavy soft-lead slug took the other man right under the chin and flipped him backward like an anvil on a rope. The third had a long light bronze tomahawk and a shield; Hook met the descending arm with a sweep of the bayonet, gashing it to the bone. The same motion punched the edge of the butt up into the man's face, and then he turned and threw his rifle through the hole and dived headfirst after it.

The sore on his back broke open and bled as he landed, knocking most of the wind out of him. He ignored the warm trickle; it was his *ass*, now. The other two fit enough to shoot were firing through the waist-high hole into the first room.

"Leave that!" he yelled, grabbing one of them and pushing him staggering across the room. "You dig. You, get to the door into the courtyard—first thing you hear there, shoot through it, gut height."

He snatched up his own rifle just in time; a Ringapi came shoving through with a round shield held high before him and a spear short-gripped beneath. To do that he had to stick one leg through first, of course. Hook stamped down on it, felt the green-stick crunch of it breaking beneath the heel of his boot.

The shield came down and the Marine chopped his rifle butt into the bent neck before him, shoved the thrashing body back so that it blocked the hole.

Then he looked up. This room was dim and long, most of it just empty bunks. Something stung him on the neck, and he looked up to see the reeds and twigs above him blackening, little flickers of red-blue flame running along them. The smoke was thicker, choking, and he coughed. More smoke poured in through the hole from the first room, and the body moved again as hands hauled it back; he could hear them screaming in there, it must be like an oven. The fire roared like a bass undertone to the hammering crackle of gunfire outside, and the hissing, screeching war cries of four thousand men. But the ones back in there where he'd been, they were roasting by now . . .

"So *burn*, you bastards," he shouted, and threw his shoulder against a row of bunks. The pine-pole construction fell across the ragged circle cut in the mud brick, and he shot the man crawling through against that obstruction under the armpit.

Shots from behind him brought his head around. The walking-wounded case he'd pushed toward the door was backing away from it, firing through the oak boards as fast as she could re-load, and each time a hole precisely .4 of an inch snapped into existence, surrounded by long blond splinters of wood. Despite that, the impact of shoulders against the planks never ceased. Spearpoints appeared, flecking through the wood like points of red light in the smoky flame-shot darkness. More spearpoints, reaching for the bar that closed the door . . .

"You useless twat!" he shouted, running forward.

The door burst inward.

Behind Kyle Hook the last of the sick were going through the hole hacked in the wall, the final hole to the final room in this building where he was going to *die*. Something flashed behind Hook's eyes, a white light that flooded him and left him moving lightly, easily.

"Motherfuckers!"

The shouting mouths of the Ringapi were silent. That was all right, because they were—

"Bastards!"

They were the ones who'd stranded him here. They were the parents who'd *left* him on his own, gone *away* and left him in a place where suddenly nothing *worked* and there wasn't even any TV or good food or anything to do but work at things he hated. They were the foster parents always more concerned

with those Alban brats than *him*. They were the judge and
Sergeant Edraxsson and the giggling prick of a God who'd
left him here to die three thousand years before he'd even
been *born*.

And they were a bunch of homicidal locals who wanted to
kill him. He ran toward them laughing . . .

Private Kyle Hook saw the others looking at him as he came
through the hole smashed in the mud-brick wall. Their eyes
were wide and staring as he walked over to the doctor's cabinet.
The rifle in his hands was broken and bent, and clotted with
red and bits of hair and bone; he used it to smash the padlock
off the front of a supply chest and lift out one of the square
brown bottles of medicinal brandy.

"Hook—you can't do that, that's a Captain's Mast offense!"

He knocked the head off and poured the liquor into his open
mouth, sparing his bruised lips. They stung; so did his raw
throat. He laughed, drank again, threw the bottle away. "So call
me up on report—you going to put me on report, Edraxsson?"

The man with the wounded foot laughed himself, still glassy-
eyed with the fever. "I don't have to, Hook. I've won; I made
a Marine out of you, boy."

"That's not all you did," he said. He bent down and hoisted
the sick man across his shoulder, grunting at the solid weight.
"You went and sent half my pay to my foster parents while I
was in the brig." He slapped the half-conscious man on the
buttocks. "What did you have to go and do something like
that for?"

Hook glanced around at the others. "Well, come on, you
going to sit here with your thumbs up your assholes waiting
for the enemy? Let's go defend our beloved Corps."

"Well, at least the hospital's giving us plenty of light," Patrick O'Rourke said, with his back to the biscuit-tin barricade
of the redoubt around the storehouse.

"Sir?" the bugler said.

He was very young, and his voice shook a little. That was
forgivable, in this fire-shot night. The hospital at the other end
of the fortlet's long rectangle was fully aflame now, a belching
pyramid of yellow-red that sent smaller tongues licking out of
windows and loopholes. By that light he could see the backs
of his Marines, catch the flash of steel and bronze as they
fought along the lines of the barricades to either side in a
heaving, thrashing confusion. More and more clots of Ringapi

warriors were rushing in out of the darkness, and there was little long-range fire to slow them down—fewer shots at all, more shouts and shrieks, clash of metal on metal and thump of iron on wood. Arrows and flung spears and slingstones rained down out of the night in an unceasing stream. Some of them had bundles of burning oil-soaked wool attached to them, and those looked like flaming meteors and cast little puddles of light about them where they landed.

Soon, he thought, staggering a little when the shaft of a falling javelin smacked against his thigh; with a practiced effort of will he didn't think about what would have happened if the spear had come down six inches closer.

He'd briefed Barnes and all the noncoms on what they were supposed to do and told them to pass it on. The noise was enormous, stunning, and the stink nearly as bad, sweat and fear and shit and death, and the foul odor of the wrong things burning.

Now I have to ask them to run without actually running away.

"Standard-bearer," he said.

The young woman was new to the job, having only one arm usable at the moment—everyone who could fire a rifle was working, right now; even his radio tech was on the line in the redoubt. She came forward at his gesture and stood to his right.

"Bugler." He'd been sticking tight to O'Rourke's left elbow, just as he should.

"Ready," he said, flipping his pistol to his left hand and drawing his *katana.*

The sword rose, pointing to the flag and the gilt eagle topping it—he had to be seen, and if that made him a conspicuous target, that was a cost of doing business. *Now, here's where we learn whether we're certainly dead, or just probably.* If the Marines broke, they'd be overrun and swarmed under in seconds. The Ringapi didn't look as if they were in a prisoner-taking mood. *Head-taking, more likely.* Like O'Rourke's own remote ancestors, the migrants from the middle Danube were given to collecting trophies.

"Sound *retreat and rally,*" he ordered crisply.

The bugler had to take two tries—the first one ended in a strangled squeal, and he worked his mouth and spat before making a second attempt. That rang out chill and strong, cutting through the snarling brabble of battle like a knife through flesh.

For a moment, relief made his knees waver. The troops were doing it, peeling back from the walls and dashing back toward him, starting with those furthest away. It was hurried, a little ragged—and some disappeared under knots of Ringapi, spear butts rising and falling and axes glittering. But most made it back, most, the enemy still had to clamber over the wall, even if the ditch around it was full of their dead in layers often four deep.

"*To me, the First!*" O'Rourke shouted, throwing his voice from the gut. "*Rally by me!*"

The ones who lived did; he felt himself swelling with pride. They halted by the biscuit-tin barricade; not one tried to clamber over it for a moment's safety. Instead they swung into two lines, one to either side of him and one behind at the very base of the wall, forward kneeling and rear standing. The bayonets on their rifles didn't glitter in the firelight; every single one of them was colored a slick, dripping red. So was the sword of Hantilis the Hittite; he'd picked up a round Ringapi shield, now much nicked and battered, and he fell in behind O'Rourke's bugler without waiting to be told not to get in the line of fire.

Hands scrambled to reload. The whole interior of the rectangular enclosure outside the wall at its eastern end was suddenly packed solid with Ringapi warriors, every one of them rushing forward. There was no way the Marines who'd rallied to him could meet it in time . . .

. . . but the line who rose from behind the biscuit-box wall could. The space spanning the north and south walls was much smaller than either was long. Even with casualties, the rifles on the wall behind him bristled shoulder to shoulder. Cecilie Barnes's voice called out, steady and calm:

"*Volley* fire, *present—fire!*"

BAAAAAMM.

The bullets slammed into the front rank of the Ringapi, who were crammed shoulder to shoulder across the width of the enclosure, too. And packed arse to belly down the length of it, where they'd swarmed over the walls from both sides.

The Marines who'd fired ducked down and reloaded; behind them in the last redoubt another line stood and volleyed over their heads; the firing step there was a foot higher, and they were over the heads of the Marines in front of the biscuit-tin wall as well. Hot air slapped the back of O'Rourke's neck beneath the flare of his helmet, like a soft heavy hand. The noise slapped his eardrums, too, hard enough to hurt.

"*Volley* fire, *present—fire!*"

BAAAAAMM.

By then the front rank of the Marines who'd rallied to him

were ready. He filled his lungs, remembering to keep his voice in the same parade-ground tone as always:

"*Front* rank—*volley* fire, *present*—"

"—*fire!*"

"—*fire!*"

"—*fire!*"

"—*fire!*"

The volleys slashed out at intervals of three-quarters of a second, four ranks to shoot, steady as a metronome, the rifles rising and falling like the warp and weft of a loom. Islanders still fell; the Ringapi were throwing spears at close range, and they thudded into chests and bellies, gashed faces and arms. But most of the enemy were too crowded to do anything but stand or try to swarm forward. The front rank ran into an almost physical barricade of lead.

O'Rourke added his pistol's fire to the volleys. Even shooting left-handed he didn't miss, with a row of targets scarcely beyond arm's reach. This close to a Ringapi warrior with the battle lust upon him, you knew right down in your gut that this was a man who'd kill you if he could, and acted accordingly. Somewhere down deep in a very busy mind he still found a spare second to admire the way they kept coming, right into the muzzles. If this was what his ancestors were like, he wasn't surprised they'd ended up overrunning everything between Turkey and Ireland. He *was* surprised they hadn't gotten themselves massacred *en masse*.

Of course, then they'd met Roman discipline, and that was about what had happened. . . .

The wall of enemy warriors in front of him bulged, swelling upward like a wave hitting a steep beach: men falling dead or wounded; men tripping over them as they were pushed from behind by the onrush of those too stupid to realize what was happening or too brave to care; or men trying to climb right over the mass ahead of them.

"*Front* rank—*volley* fire, *present*—"

"—*fire!*"

"—*fire!*"

"—*fire!*"

"—*fire!*"

And suddenly the wave ahead of them wasn't trying to advance anymore. The volleys went on as the front rank turned and clawed at the men behind, and then they turned as well, until no Ringapi were left standing inside the enclosure.

"Cease fire," O'Rourke said, his voice sounding a little tinny and faint in his ears.

Hantilis was swearing in amazement, possibly just at being alive. Stretching across from the northern wall to the southern in front of the leveled rifles was a mound of dead and dying Ringapi; at the very front it was higher than a man's waist—nearly high enough to block the fire of kneeling marksmen, too high to remain stable, and bodies were slithering down to rest against the Marines' boots. The heaving of injured men trying to get free of the four-deep crush atop them helped that process. Where the layer of bodies thinned out behind the front of the wave the whole surface crawled and moved, amid a threnody of agony, right back to the wall of the burning hospital.

"All—" O'Rourke cleared his throat. "All right, let's get back over this wall here. See to the wounded. Move it, people, let's go!"

Barnes's voice added to his, and the surviving noncoms. He lost himself in work, waiting for the shrieks and panther screams that would herald the next attack. It was ten minutes before he realized that there was silence outside the fortlet, half an hour before he believed it. The Ringapi campfires still guttered and gleamed through the dark to the westward. Not until dawnlight caught the snows atop Mount Ida to the south was his gut convinced, and not until he heard the cries of the jackals and foxes coming close to feed.

True dawn showed the Ringapi camp struck and empty, nothing but litter and smoldering fires left burning through the tail end of night. The ruins of the hospital still smoldered as well, sending up a sour dark smoke that had everyone coughing when the wind shifted wrong. Ash came along with the smoke, more of it when brick or bits of roofing fell with thumps and crashes. Overhead there was a thick scatter of circling kites and ravens and . . .

Yes, by God, eagles too, he thought with dull amazement.

"What do they eat when there's no war?" he thought aloud.

"When is there no war in these lands?" Hantilis asked.

Barnes came up as well, with mugs of sassafras tea. O'Rourke sipped gratefully at his, trying to ignore the men calling *akawa . . . akawa . . .* from the heaps of enemy dead. Water, he suspected. And *mathair* was unpleasantly obvious, too . . .

"What's the butcher's bill, Captain?" he asked.

"Twenty-two dead, sir," Barnes said; it was as if a robot was speaking. "Including Hussey and my company sergeant.

Another forty badly injured. That's not counting the sick from the hospital."

He knew she was using the term *badly injured* conservatively; half or more of the ones still at the walls had crusted bandages. Many of them were only fit to shoot if they had something to prop them up.

"We're down to eighty rounds per rifle," she went on. "Must've shot off . . . God, forty, fifty thousand rounds. We're short of medical supplies, too; well fixed for food. Most of the transport animals are dead but we've got about six horses left."

Including Fancy; he felt a slight pang of guilt even now at how relieved that made him feel.

"We should get things policed up," she continued in the same dead voice. "Get some hot food for the troops. Clean weapons. See if we can help some of the enemy wounded, get the bodies buried or at least hauled away, strengthen the walls—they might be back."

O'Rourke looked around; most of the Marines were slumped into unconsciousness beside their rifles; the one in ten still awake on orders looked at him through red-rimmed eyes that stared out of smoke-blackened faces. He suspected he had the same fixed, flat stare; he also suspected—knew—that what everyone wanted right now was sleep.

"You're right," he said, dragging himself upright. Then, softly: "Hell of a shindy, *macushla*. Hell of a shindy, indeed." A mental shake. "First—"

"*Heads up!*" the lookout on the roof of the storehouse called, and then: "By God, it's the regiment!"

That brought a thin cheer from those awake, and woke some of the sleepers. O'Rourke dragged himself to the rooftop and confirmed the sentry's sighting; two companies in column of march, mounted scouts out ahead, and some heavy weapons in between. He walked out into the track he'd ridden down . . .

"Saints, was it only thirty hours ago?" he whispered to himself. "They must have forced the march." The base was better than forty miles away, and the roads were terrible.

He blinked in surprise when he saw who was heading up the column, and snapped off a salute. "Brigadier Hollard!" he said. "Last I heard you were in Hattusas."

"Came out to see to some things," he said.

O'Rourke looked back at the Marines who'd halted in the roadway. In normal times he'd have said they were clapped out and ready for rest; right now they looked almost indecently fresh.

"With two companies of the First and those heavy weapons, and a day to entrench, we can hold against anything outside the hosts of hell," he said.

"It looks like you already did, Pat," Hollard said softly, looking over the battlefield; he removed his helmet and ran a hand over cropped sandy hair. "Christ crucified . . . I thought you'd all been massacred, until I saw the flag still flying."

"Reverend Smith's hearing confessions right now," O'Rourke said grimly. Captain Barnes came up while he was speaking. "It didn't come cheap, I'm telling you that, I am."

"I could use some extra medics and supplies, sir," Barnes said.

Hollard shook his long head. "Of course, right away."

He turned in the saddle and gave the orders, and figures with the winged snake emblem on blue uniforms ran forward. The rest of the column seemed paralyzed, staring at the carnage around the little outpost, some of them gagging when the wind shifted.

"We can hold forever, now. Against the hosts of hell themselves," O'Rourke went on, conscious that he was repeating himself but too tired to really care.

Hollard swung down from the saddle and gave him a sympathetic slap on the shoulder. "I'm afraid that's what's heading this way," he said. "Troy's fallen, and Walker's men are pouring up from the coast—here, and up the Meneander Valley from Miletos. We're retreating."

O'Rourke nodded dully. "I'll need transport for the wounded," he said.

"*Emancipator* is making a run into the regimental HQ and she'll pick up anyone who can't march," Hollard said.

"What about the supplies here, sir?" Barnes asked.

"Take what you can. Burn the rest," Hollard said, his thin mouth and knob of a chin closing like granite. "Starting now, we don't let anything fall into Walker's hands that he can use. *Vastatio.*"

"Ah, that's the way of it, then," O'Rourke said, nodding mechanically.

"One thing," Kenneth Hollard said, looking at the barley-sack ramparts, half-visible now under the men who'd died sprawled across them. "Why didn't you dig a ditch outside the walls—no time?"

"We did dig one, Brigadier sir," O'Rourke said. "It's just full."

Hollard shook his head again. "Colonel, *this* is going to be one for the Corps history books, up there with Chosin and Okinawa."

O'Rourke hadn't thought of it in quite that way before . . . but it *was* a notable feat of arms, after all. "I'll want to see that my lads and lasses get the recognition they deserve for it, too," he said. *My one regret about that is that I'll have to recommend Kyle Hook for a medal. And there I was hopin' to send him to the punishment company.*

"And we'll have to find a name for it." Hollard's mouth quirked from its chiseled line. "How about the Battle of O'Rourke's Ford?"

Even then, they could laugh. Barnes looked at them both as if they were insane . . . which, when he thought of it, wasn't all that far wrong. Plus she'd been barely into her teens at the Event.

"Classical reference, *macushla*," he said. "Classical reference."

CHAPTER FOURTEEN

October, 10 A.E.—Nantucket Town, Republic of
Nantucket
October, 10 A.E.—Near Hattusas, Kingdom of
Hatti-land
October, 10 A.E.—Nantucket Town, Republic of
Nantucket
October, 10 A.E.—Neayoruk, Kingdom of Great Achaea
October, 10 A.E.—Nantucket Town, Republic of
Nantucket
November, 10 A.E.—Western Anatolia
October, 10 A.E.—Long Island Sound, Republic of
Nantucket

"Morning, Jared," Joseph Starbuck said.

"Morning, Joseph," Jared Cofflin replied; even in the later months of the Year 10, the government of the Republic of Nantucket remained pleasantly informal.

The Councilor for Finance and the Treasury leaned back in his chair. That was in an office of the Pacific National Bank, which was also the headquarters of the Republic's departments of finance and taxation. It stood at the junction where Main Street turned southwest and Liberty branched off from it; the redbrick rectangle with its two white pillars in front had been erected in 1818, to finance the Island's expanding whaling trade in the South Seas.

Nearly two centuries ago, or more than three millennia in the future, but once again Nantucketer ships sailed all the seas of the earth.

You need bold captains for an Age of Expansion, Jared thought. *You also need hardheaded bankers and a sound currency.*

"Good of you to drop by; I know it's supposed to be a holiday for you," Starbuck said. "But I wanted to catch you before you talked to young Tom Hollard over on Long Island. Might be I could sweeten the meeting . . . for him, at least."

Jared nodded. He could imagine Joseph on his own quarter-deck easily enough, if you ran him back a half a century or so in biological age. In his late seventies, the pouched blue eyes still reflected a mind of flinty practicality, near-perfect for *this* job.

And it's my *job to find the right people,* he thought.

About two-thirds of any leadership position was knowing how to find the right people to delegate to. The other third was knowing when they were wrong.

Of course, the fourth third is knowing when to let them fail a couple of times because it's the only way they'll believe you when you say they're screwing up. And the fifth third—

"It's a busman's holiday," he said aloud. "As for Tom Hollard, well, if you can arrange for the war to be over, and the damned income tax to be abolished, it'll make things sweet as milk. Otherwise, he's going to be unhappy. Hell, *I'm* unhappy, but we need guns and soldiers and ships and pay for the crews."

The window was open onto Main, letting in bright fall sunlight. They'd had the first frosts, and the cool salt-scented air made him glad enough of the thick raw-wool sweater he wore.

Even this early the sound of iron-shod hooves and wheels on the Main Street cobbles was fairly loud, together with steam whistles from factories and boats down in the harbor.

"I've got the estimates," Starbuck went on. "After you've read these, you can surprise him by saying he's quite right and the taxes won't be going up any more."

As he spoke, Starbuck flicked one long bony finger toward the screen of the personal computer on his desk. It was one of the two dozen or so allowed to assist vital functions at any one time; it would be a very long time before the Islanders could make disk drives, or the new Pentium the magazines had been talking about before the Event. Starbuck's work also rated one of the even more valuable dot-matrix printers, salvaged from an attic. The tapes on those could be replaced with an ink-saturated cotton that did almost as well as the woven nylon originals.

As for toner cartridges for laser printers . . . *About the time we get space shuttles.*

"End of the story, Jared, is that there's no more fat to cut into for war production."

Cofflin took the sheets and looked through them. *Ayup,* he

thought. There were times when he disagreed with Starbuck, but he'd never found him to be flat-out *wrong* yet.

"You're telling me that to get any more for Peter, we have to rob Paul?" he said. Then, deliberately provocative—Starbuck was one of those people who thought better angry: "I thought war was supposed to get economies going? World War II and all that."

"Jared, it's nonsense to think that when you take what people grow and make, lug it to the other side of the world with a lot of sweat and time, and then throw it on a bonfire, it somehow makes you well-off," Starbuck snapped. "I was a teenager in the tail end of the Depression; after Pearl Harbor, the ones who'd been idle got put to work, so everyone felt richer. That's how I got my first job."

Joseph, I happen to know you spent '44 climbing down boarding nets off very unwelcoming Pacific islands, Jared thought to himself. Not that he'd ever heard Starbuck talk about Okinawa. Or the fact that he'd lied about his age to enlist . . .

The older man spread liver-spotted hands. "Here, though? We were already using every pair of hands, tool, and machine we had *before* the war started. We can't afford to divert more."

"We can't afford to lose the war, either," Cofflin said.

Starbuck sighed. "I'm not just being cheap, Jared," he said. "With productivity so low, taxes really *hurt.* Back up in the twentieth, rich countries could afford . . . sort of, for a while . . . to pay half their incomes to the government. Half of a great deal is still a fair amount. Half of *just enough* is *not enough to live on.*"

Cofflin ran exasperated fingers through his thinning, grizzled sandy hair; he'd been fighting this particular battle since the Event, off and on.

"I know . . . but what'm I supposed to tell Marian and Ken Hollard, Joseph? When they say I'm trading the lives of their troops for money?"

"That we *can't* do any more except as a temporary last-ditch, all-out burst. Oh, I can switch things around—selling interest-bearing war bonds, things like that—but the bottom line is that we're using all our surplus. If I fiddle the books, all we'll get is inflation."

Cofflin sighed slightly again. "Well, I think we can get our new allies to contribute a bit more, but they *can't* do a lot of what we're doing; they don't have the industry."

"If they do more of the basics, we can shift around and it'll lighten the overall burden," Starbuck said. "And you could cut down on nonessential projects, like that new settlement in Argentina." He snorted. "*New 'Sconset*, indeed!"

Cofflin smiled, a slight curve of mouth. "Just planning so far, which is cheap. Got to think long-term." He held up a hand. "Not so much for the direct payoff, though we can always use more food and fiber. But when this war is over, we're going to be mustering out a lot of troops. A lot of them new citizens who'll stay here. A land grant is part of the enlistment package."

"Hmmm." Starbuck rubbed his short, white beard. "Plenty of places in the Republic to homestead already, without annexing new territory."

"Not as many as you might think. We're keeping half of Long Island in wilderness reserve. Mebbe three hundred more farms there. Besides, the Pampas aren't covered in hundred-foot-tall oak trees laced together with wild grapevines thicker than your leg. It's tall-grass prairie; Iowa by the sea, with a better climate."

"Well, that sort of decision is your department, Jared," Starbuck said. "I'm here to take the punch bowl away when your parties are half-done. You run the war."

Cofflin snorted. "At these distances? All I do is look over Marian's plans, keep the home fires burning, and go around shaking people down to pay for it all."

He paused for a moment, looking out the door. "Ever think how strange it is, Joseph, that we're giving orders here . . . and on the other side of the world, people we've never heard of are killing each other because of it?"

Starbuck snorted. "They'd be going to war anyway, Jared. We're just giving them a *different* reason."

> *The One in whose control are horses, cattle, all chariots;*
> *The One who has caused to be born the sun, the dawn;*
> *The One who is the leader of the waters;*
> *He, O people, is Indara Thunderer!*

Raupasha's voice rang out; first in the common Hurrian language, then in the ancient tongue of the *ariammanu*, the founders of the kingdom of Mitanni. Few here could speak it even in her stumbling, book-learned fashion, but holiness had ensured that the prayers survived in memory:

> *The One without whom people do not conquer;*
> *The One to whom the warriors call for help;*

The One who shakes the unshakable;
He, O people, is Indara Thunderer!

Raupasha daughter of Shuttarna raised her hands to the sky as the ancient, ancient chant echoed across the upland plain; the smell of the sacrificial blood, the fire that consumed it, the oil and pinewood, lifted her with the smoke of sacrifice to the uttermost heavens. Dawn paled the stars, and she felt as one with them—a singing exultation, like that brought by the *soma* of the oldest tales. Reluctantly she descended from that eagle-aerie of the spirt, down to the common earth of day.

That was well enough, for she liked the place of the encampment, though she had been born and raised far south of here, in the southern Mitannian borderlands. Yet still these Hittite uplands spoke to something in her soul, the vast clear spaces fringed with mountains, the spare beauty of the landscape and the thin pure upland air, even the unaccustomed chill of their early-winter nights. They went well with the sounds and sights and smells of war, barley porridge cooking over the campfires and pigmeat frying, leather, oil, horse sweat and man sweat and the leather of the tents.

Those were being struck even as she watched, the men of her chariot squadrons—hers!—fanning out from where they'd gathered for the sacrifice. She would have preferred a horse, or at least an ox, but a sheep was what they had. Orders were to hoard food jealously.

The Mitannian camp was a little away from the main Babylonian base, and that was half a day's journey southwest of Hattusas itself, for greater ease of gathering supplies. Both were laid out as the Nantukhtar had taught, in straight rows and streets; there was much digging involved in the Nantukhtar way of war, from field fortifications to latrines.

Raupasha brought herself up to attention and saluted as riders from the main camp drew rein in a spurt of dust and a few pebbles shot from under the iron-shod hooves. It was the *Seg Kallui*; as second-in-command of the Babylonian expeditionary force under King Kashtiliash, Kathryn Hollard was also in charge of the Mitannian vassal troops. Her staff and bodyguards followed her, as the noble Tekhip-tilla and Gunnery Sergeant Connor and the chiefs of the four chariot squadrons did Raupasha.

She spent a second to envy the older woman the neat uniforms of her soldiers, as the gesture was returned. The clothing was drab—khaki of a shade not much different from the Islander Marines—but uniforms were part of the New Learning. Symbols of the power of a King who could dress whole armies in his own livery.

"The sacrifice went well, I hope?" Kathryn said.

"Very well, thank you, Lady Ka"—Raupasha made a heroic effort and wrapped her mouth around the maddening *th* sound—"Kathryn."

She and Kathryn had English and Akkadian in common; they spoke the latter because many of Raupasha's followers knew the Assyrian version of that tongue.

As soon as this war is over, I must see that many of my people learn the English speech and writing, she thought. She herself worked doggedly every day at perfecting her command of it. *Perhaps even send some to Nantucket for schooling.*

Tekhip-tilla tugged at his gray-shot black beard; he was a Mitannian noble of the old school, not afraid to speak truth before his sovereign; few such had lived through the Assyrian occupation.

"Well enough," he said. "The omens were good and the smoke rose to heaven properly. Although the men might have felt better were it to a more familiar God, like Teshub of the Weather or the Ishtar of the Warriors."

Raupasha knew that, but her foster father had raised her in the most ancient traditions.

"Teshub and Indara are both among the Gods of our ancestors," she said. "Perhaps Indara is merely the older name for Teshub, since both command the storm and thunder. Yet when we worshiped Indara under that name, the kingdom was great."

"A good point, my princess," Tekhip-tilla said. "Let it be as you wish."

"To business," Kathryn Hollard said. She looked to the west. "You understand your mission?"

"Yes, Lady Kathryn." They'd gone over it exhaustively, but it was good to remind the squadron commanders. "We are to fight as the wolf does—slashing and then running swiftly."

"Good," Kathryn nodded. "Yours is not the least of tasks; the main force will be moving west behind you, and then making a fighting retreat back to the east. Eventually we'll have to make a stand. Whether or not the enemy is too strong for us at the final battle may well depend on forces like yours."

Raupasha nodded again, although she didn't altogether believe that; part of it was said to make her men's hearts strong, and to soothe their pride. These things were part of generalship and kingcraft, and she would learn all that the Hollards had to teach her. And . . .

The two women walked off a little. "Lady Kat'ryn . . ."

Kathryn laid a finger on her lips for an instant, and smiled. "Some things should not be asked. Not now," she said.

Whether King Kashtiliash will ever let Kenneth be my lord, Raupasha thought. "If not now, when?"

"Sometimes I have to make myself remember you're barely eighteen," she said, infuriatingly. "And other times it's obvious."

"I am old enough to command and rule, you thought. And in this war I may die," Raupasha said. "I feel Yama put his hand on my shoulder, and say 'make haste.' "

"And I might die, or Kash . . . King Kashtiliash might die, or Ken might die. Or the horse may learn to sing."

That startled a giggle out of Raupasha, and Kathryn grinned back, making the years between them seem to vanish.

"But after the war," Kenneth's sister said. "Then we'll either be defeated, hence dead, or the King's heart may be changed. Who knows?"

"I know," Raupasha said vehemently. "I know that it will—King Kashtiliash will see the loyalty and courage of Mitanni's troops fighting beside the men of Kar-Duniash, and his heart will be softened toward me."

"I certainly hope so. *Vaya con Dios.*" At Raupasha's curious look, she went on: "A saying. It means *go with God.*"

"And may your God be with you, Lady Ka*th*ryn."

She turned and jumped into her chariot. Her driver Iridmi and Gunnery Sergeant Connor waited there. Connor handed her the rocket launcher, and she slung the blunt flare-ended tube over her shoulder—for show's sake, to hearten the others.

"Forward!" she shouted, and Iridmi flicked the reins.

"See you later, Councilor," Jared Cofflin concluded.

" 'day, Chief," Starbuck replied; he was already turning back to his work.

Cofflin gathered up hat and jacket and ambled through the bank, nodding greetings to the clerks settling in to their jobs—there was already a click of abacus beads, a rattle of adding machines, the tapping of a manual typewriter, a scritching of quill pens on coarse paper and an occasional muttered curse as they blotted. The latest steel nibs modeled on ones found in antique shops did better . . . slightly . . . but the government made do with what the birds gave for free.

Would the extra efficiency and saving some sheets of foolscap justify springing for better pens, or would the bureaucrats just have better weapons in their campaign to drown him in paper?

The thought went into the files, along with an infinity of others. Yesterday Doc Coleman had notified him that the last Islander with AIDS had died; they didn't have protease inhibitors to keep the virus in check here and now.

Poor bastard, he thought. Smallpox they had to worry about, evidently, but at least not HIV anymore. You could *do* something about smallpox . . .

If only we could spare the people to go looking for the source of that smallpox outbreak in Babylon. Damn the war!

He went out the doors and stood for a moment on the stone steps that led down to the cobbles of Main Street. They were densely crowded, but it wasn't very much like the mob scenes the Summer People had made, back before the Event.

For one thing, there are a hell *of a lot more kids,* he thought. Better than half the people on-Island were under fourteen, the Census people told him. A population explosion, and set to get more so when the big post-Event generation, born and adopted, came adult and started having litters of their own. In the meantime . . .

Swarms of towheaded rugrats. That still stood out, even more so on a school holiday.

Although school holidays didn't mean playtime, nowadays; all the older kids were working. The board tables along the street were piled with boxes of radishes, turnips, sacks of potatoes, stacks of sweet corn, tomatoes glowing like piles of rubies, lettuce, cabbage, onions, cucumbers, melons, apples, peaches—the post-Event orchards were really starting to bear—and pies, jars of pickles and jam, cheeses, butter, homemade sausages and smoked hams, hen- and moa-eggs, baskets of live chickens or the plucked, gutted end product on ice.

The stalls stretched all the way down Main toward the harbor and into the covered market where the old A&P and its parking lot and the oil-storage tanks had once stood.

Good harvest this year. He'd read Angelica Brand's reports, but it was nice to see it firsthand as well as in the Councilor for Agriculture's antiseptic prose and columns of figures. Everyone was just a little paranoid about food supplies now.

And everything tastes so much better in season. No more wooden tomatoes bred tough for shipment. *On the other hand, nothing's available except when it* is *in season.*

The crowd was dense along the sidewalks, down to the big

clot around the Hub halfway down Main; that had gone from being a news-and-magazine store to an information exchange with rows of slate-and-chalk notice boards, and from there to a hiring hall. The usual desperate harvest-season farmers were there, bargaining for extra hands. One finally reached an agreement with an immigrant family, mother and father and four working-age children, loaded them into his buckboard and flicked the ponies into motion; his wife stood swaying in the back hefting a shovel, glaring around at anyone thinking of poaching. Cofflin snorted, eyes crinkling with hidden laughter as they rattled up the cobbles of Main and disappeared, heading westward along Orange toward the Siaconset Road and the farming country there.

His own course went in the opposite direction, over a few blocks to the John Cofflin House—an inn that'd taken over the house of a collateral relative back (or ahead) in the 1840s.

Jared's lips tightened slightly. Ian's place was just across the street in back; he'd been staying in one of the outbuildings the night of the Event, and it had become the Foreign Affairs office as well as his residence by the usual sort of happenstance.

Damn, I'm worried about them, he thought, adding a short prayer to a God he didn't think should be bothered with unimportant things. Ian dead or in the hands of William Walker and his bitch, that was important.

Broad Street, which wasn't particularly broad, ran down from there to the old Steamship Wharf, between buildings in the soberly elegant Nantucket Federal style plus a few plain Puritan saltboxes from the seventeenth and eighteenth centuries.

Meet me at the gray shingle house with white trim, he grinned to himself, remembering a pre-Event joke.

Not *totally* accurate; there were a few redbrick buildings with white trim. Nantucket's downtown was almost all pre-1860; the town had been too poor to rebuild after the whaling industry collapsed.

Broad was also crowded, as usual. Not quite as much so as it had been before the new channels and piers were opened up down the harbor, but densely enough; horse-drawn wagons nose to tailboard, a half dozen steam-haulers pulling two or three carts each. It was amazing how much noise a town of only ten thousand people could make, when shod hooves hit pavement *en masse*. This being rush hour, it also had a fair share of commuter traffic—bicycles, mainly, with the odd steam-hauler—and the sidewalks were thronged.

The breeze flickered the leaves of the big elms overhead,

letting down stabs of light that flickered off brass fittings on a horse's harness, polished metal on a steamer's frame. Businesses were opening on both sides of the street; mostly trading firms here, dealing in anything from spices to shelled corn, barrel staves, and salt beef. It paid to be near the docks, if your living depended on the sea.

Martha was waiting under the sign of the Brotherhood of Thieves. That had been a restaurant before the Event, and still was. Heating large quantities of water was a *lot* easier in big batches at a central location, with the equipment available; that helped account for all the bathhouses and steam laundries, too.

Everything was so much more convenient *with electricity,* Jared thought, not for the first time; all the alternatives were messy, dangerous, or involved far too much hard work.

The Brotherhood's carved and painted sign showed a man in antique clothing, short devil horns on his forehead; a bag of money rested on one palm and a small chained black woman on the other. Nantucket had been big in the Abolitionist movement and Underground Railroad, back before the Civil War.

Cofflin's long bony face went bleak for a moment, with an expression Robert E. Lee's men might have recognized. At Gettysburg, on the faces of the blue-clad New Englanders storming down from the Little Round Top through a hail of bone-smashing rifle fire and grapeshot to break the Confederacy's last hope at the point of their bayonets. Slavery was all too alive in the Year 10 . . .

"Morning, dear," Martha said, giving him a quick peck on the cheek. "I paahked Sam and Jenny with the Macys."

That left Heather and Lucy, and his own eldest two, Marian and Jared Jr. They weren't quite jumping with excitement, but close.

A young man in a blue Guard sailor suit and flat cap with *RNCGS Chamberlain* on its ribbon came up, slight and swarthy and impeccably neat, cutlass and revolver at his belt. He threw off a crackling salute, then stood there at ease, looking wiry and toughly competent and so damned young. . . .

Marian's idea of course, but there wasn't much point in putting someone in charge of security matters and then refusing to listen to them.

"I'm Petty Officer Martinelli, sir," the young man said. "Madam Councilor."

The chief stuck out his hand; the sailor's was strong and dry, rough with callus. "This is Jared Jr.," he said. "And Marian Deer Dancer Cofflin. And . . ."

Martinelli gravely shook hands with Jared Jr. and Marian, then exchanged hugs with Heather and Lucy.

"These two have been getting me in trouble for years, sir," Martinelli said. "Imps of Satan, as the commodore puts it."

"Only our moms can call us that, Petty Officer," Lucy said loftily. Heather stuck out her tongue, and then all three grinned.

Jared nodded, supressing a sigh. At least looking after the kids made a face-saving excuse for having a hand-holder planted on him.

"Well, make yourself useful, young man," Martha said briskly, handing over one of the suitcases.

Those and the picnic baskets were juggled from hand to hand. *At least I don't have to live in a cocoon of Secret Service agents and publicity flaks,* Jared thought thankfully. *Even so, this term is the last.*

Steamship Wharf was even more crammed than Broad Street above it, with ships two-deep on both sides where the ferries had docked before the Event and more waiting their turns out in the Great Harbor or heading down toward the new piers. Cargo-handlers and windlass-worked cranes labored overtime as bales and nets swung through the air. The smells got stronger here, too, fish from the drying sheds, whale from the rendery further southeast where a black plume of smoke tattered against the sky, tar and tarred wood, canvas, salt. A steam tug was pulling a three-master out into the harbor and up toward the dogleg passage to the sea, its paddles thrashing foam white against the blue water and sending a cloud of gulls skyward at the shrill scream of its whistle.

"The *Barbee*," Martha said, looking at the big square-rigger; she had an encyclopedic memory Jared envied, almost as good as a priestess of Moon Woman. "Clearing for Westhaven, Captain Williamson commanding, under charter to Stock and Rains Exports."

"What lading?" Jared asked. It was a good idea to keep track of things like that.

"Salt cod, two hundred and fifty tons of it," she said. "*That* we're not short of, and won't be."

Jared nodded; they'd already taken measures—minimum net-mesh sizes, quotas, a ban on dragging and drift nets—to make sure it stayed that way later. Martha went on:

"Let's see . . . spools of cotton thread, air compressors and pneumatic rock drills for the copper mines on Anglesy and the coal mines at Irondale and that new tin shaft in Cornwall; drill bits, ditto, blasting powder, ditto. Four uniflow twenty-five-horsepower steam engines from Seahaven Engineering, treadle sewing machines, glassware from the Cape Cod works, gearing, a gear-cutter, miscellaneous manufactured goods—needles, scissors, shovels, that sort of thing. Coffee, cocoa beans and manufactured chocolate, chili peppers, sugar, kill-devil rum, cochineal dye, dye-wood, indigo, Shang silk, mahogany and ebony, flamewood planks, jadeite, parakeets, furs."

Jared nodded, conscious of the children soaking it in. It seemed every kid on the Island wanted to be a merchant venturer or explorer these days, the way they'd wanted to be astronauts or fossil-hunters when he was a boy back in the early sixties.

It certainly beats wanting to be rap stars, he thought with an inward chuckle. Hard and dangerous as it was, there were aspects of the post-Event world he preferred, as a parent.

A deck crew were heaving on a line aboard the *Barbee*, roaring out in unison:

> "We will *sing* to every port of *land*
> Which *ever* yet was *known*,
> We will *bring* back gold and *silver*, mates
> When *we* return to *home*!
> And we'll *make* our courtships *flourish*, mates
> When *we* arrive on *shore*—
> And *when* our money is all *gone* . . .
> We'll *plow* the seas for *more*!"

Neayoruk, Ian Arnstein thought, as the ship that had carried him from Troy efficiently struck her sails and bent home the towrope a small galley tossed her. He pushed down the continual gut chill of fear, pushing his spectacles back up his nose and forcing himself to study the scene around him with a scholar's curiosity.

Well, it's a bit *like New York. A lot more like a scaled down Victorian Liverpool, with Mediterranean accents.*

The resemblance was heightened by the weather, gray and chill with a drizzling rain—not typical for southern Greece, but common enough in winter. He pulled the raw-wool cloak tighter about his shoulders and shivered slightly.

Barracks? Baracoons? Tenements? Ian wondered, looking at the long rectangular buildings of mud-colored adobe brick that made up most of the town; each alike, standing row upon row with a terrible impersonality that reminded him of Victorian milltowns. Many of the ships at the docks had the same look of something slapped together with a maximum of haste and no concern but pure function, boxes with blunt wedges for bows and what even his landlubber's eye saw was an almost comically simple rig, dozens of them unloading endless streams of some dark mineral. Three shoreside blast furnaces about the same height as the ships' masts belched smoke that straggled off across the water, smelling of coal and acid. More smoke trailed from smaller smokestacks around them, and across the soot-slick water came an endless thump and rattle and clangor of metal on metal.

Not everything was quite so ugly. There were bigger houses up on the slopes of the hill overlooking the town, sleek galleys oar-striding across the water with their painted eyes glaring above the bronze rams, the greyhound grace of well-built modern sailing ships, and Bronze Age craft from all around the Middle Sea. The mountains above were dark with fir and pine, and the damp air carried a breath of them over the harsh coal smoke and metallic stinks and the tar-fish-wood smells of a harbor town.

In the twentieth this was the outskirts of the Mani, an eroded limestone wasteland where a local joke said a goat would have to bring its own provisions. Here it was more like the coast of California. Parts of Marin County, say.

All in all, it doesn't look much like Gythio, he thought—he'd visited here before the Event. On an island half a mile out was the low-slung hulking shape of a fortress, and a strong stone causeway between there and the mainland. Only the looming triangular peak of Mount Taygetos and the knife-edge ridges that fell away from it were recognizable at all, and that was like looking at a skeleton and suddenly seeing it covered in flesh.

Philowergos bent to touch the stone-block pavement and murmured a prayer after they came down the gangway; Ian thought he caught a promise of a goat to Poseidaion.

The soldiers of the escort exclaimed; Ian recognized the tone if not the slang. He'd heard much the same as men settled down to watch a baseball game on either side of him. The little group stopped, standing in the thin rain and craning to see over the shoulders and slung rifles of the troops who stood in a protective box around a gangplank.

That ship had a sour sewer-and-locker-room reek even in cool weather, and was unloading coffles of filthy near-naked men with shaved heads, wearing iron collars and chained neck to neck. A helmeted officer in Walker's gray uniform stood

beside the gangplank, a man with a scar along his jawline showing white through his beard and holding a swagger stick cut
from a vinestock. He examined the slaves carefully, stopping
now and then to raise a man's chin with the stick and look into
the man's eyes.

Every tenth or fifteenth man was tapped with it, and taken
out of the coffle. The same sentence was repeated to them, in
half a dozen different languages. Most crowded forward eagerly. A few shook their heads, and were sent back to the
coffles. One man spat in the officer's face; *he* took the vinestaff
across his cheek and dropped limp as an official explanation,
drooling blood and spitting out a tooth on the dockside. The
tough wood cracked.

"Fetch me another!" the officer snapped, kicking the man at
his feet with vicious efficiency as he wiped a sleeve across his
face. A soldier hurried up with another swagger stick.

"And get rid of this carrion. The rest of you, you're the best
of a bad lot—begin! Show me if you can do something besides
scratch dirt for your betters!"

Ian blinked in astonishment as the rest of the slaves formed
pairs and began to fight. None of them had much science by
the standards of, say, Marian Alston or Kenneth Hollard, but
they all went at it as if they were fighting for their lives; he
could hear fists smack on flesh, screams of anger and pain. One
pair fell and rolled, grappling and tearing and biting, hidden
by the legs of the guards until the vanquished shrieked and the
victor rose and spat out an ear, grinning amid the blood that
ran down his chin. Laughter and cries of admiration came from
the watchers.

The hard-eyed officer went down the row of men again, tapping this one and that—not always the winner, either, although
he did take the ear-biter. The rejected were hustled away, and
a man with a bolt cutter took the collars off the dozen selected.

"What was *that*?" Arnstein asked, when they were on their
way again.

"First cut," Philowergos repeated amiably. "The Achaean
lands don't have enough youths for the King of Men's armies.
If they endure through the training camps, those men may"—
he tapped the two silver bars enameled on his helmet—"become officers, perhaps even lords with land to the horizon.
Even if they're not found worthy of the Army, they may become overseers, or police, or be trained for skilled work. Those
sent on, they'll do for the rough work of mines and fields and

forges. The chosen are men of spirit, as you saw. Such men make bad slaves."

Possibly, Arnstein thought. *Although that guy who spat in the face of* Herr Gruppenführer *there showed plenty of spirit, in my opinion.*

Past the dockyards the streets were paved with asphalt or stone blocks, with raised sidewalks on either side; there were men in green uniforms at the intersections, blowing whistles and holding up white batons to direct traffic; that was everything from Bronze Age oxcarts with solid oak wheels through rickshaws and handcarts to—he did a double take of astonishment—a Victorian-style horse-drawn omnibus. Most of the buildings seemed to be tenements, better than the row-housing he'd seen from the water, with small shops on the ground floor.

More than half the men and women who crowded the sidewalks wore collars, of iron or bronze or silver.

"I've seen the Bronze Age," Ian murmured to himself, in English. "I've seen the changes *we* make in it. Now I'm getting a firsthand look at Walker's idea of improvements."

He was lost enough in his thoughts to bump into the Achaean officer's broad back when Philowergos stopped suddenly.

Three uniformed men were blocking the way. One Ian knew immediately was from the twentieth . . . something about the eyes, or the way he stood. A blocky-square man with a square slightly jowly face, in early middle age, short blond-and-gray hair, clean-shaven face with something *wrong* about it. The uniforms were much like Philowergos's, but with a different *waffenfarbe* on the collars; a silver death's-head over a black numeral 1.

Uh-oh, his mind gibbered, with a banality that surprised him even now. The lead man's eyes flicked over him. They had none of Hong's gleeful, gloating anticipation. That was like a depraved child waiting for some monstrous Christmas present. These were like a dead man's, or a tired man looking at a fly on a hot day.

"Thank you, Captain Philowergos," the man from the twentieth said, in pelucidly pure Achaean with the slightest guttural undertone. "I will take custody of this prisoner now."

"Ah . . . Lord Mittler, I don't think . . ."

"Exactly, Captain Philowergos. You are not paid to think."

Mistake, Ian thought, watching the flush of rage come up over the Greek's collar. Telling an Achaean he was paid to obey was like calling him a slave. *That's right, Philowergos, get* good *and angry,* please, *for God's sake—*

He'd had time to recover from the shock of Troy; time to get his balance back, so he could know just how frightened he should be and to start cursing himself for thinking that getting killed was the worst thing that could happen.

"Lord Mittler," Philowergos said, "I was instructed by the King himself to take this man to Category One confinement in the palace. My head will answer for his."

"Let me see that," Mittler said, taking the orders the Achaean captain was waving. "Hmmm. Yes, these specify Category One confinement; but they don't say anything about maintaining personal custody. I will carry out the King's orders, soldier. Section One is organized for the proper supervision of prisoners. You may return to the front and fight valiantly, as I'm sure you long to do, rather than staying here with the women."

No, no, no! Ian thought. Walker's tame German was being smart again, giving Philowergos an honorable excuse for obedience. And that flush was fear as much as anger. *I don't blame you for that,* I'm *afraid of him . . . yes I do blame you for it, you cretin! He's manipulating you!* Philowergos wavered, until an iron clangor of horseshoes came near.

"Ah," another voice said. "I thought you might be here, Lord Mittler."

It was a man standing in a chariot with two others. This voice's Achaean had a distinct accent; not a foreigner's, but some sort of regional burr, archaic even by Mycenaean standards. Much like a Scotsman's English.

Ian's eyes flickered to him. He saw a stocky man, short by twentieth-century standards, medium here; old white battle scars ran up the hairy, muscular brown forearms. The Achaean was in full nobleman's gear: long crimson cloak pinned at one shoulder; tunic; checked kilt with a fringe; linen gaiters and leather boots; gold-studded sword belt bearing a long double-edged blade. A diadem held long dark hair; trimmed beard with a few strands of gray; and a shaven upper lip. There was a very modern-looking revolver at the belt as well, and the second man in the war-car rested a hand casually on the butt of a break-open shotgun.

"Rejoice, Lord Regent," Mittler said. He bowed from the waist; the others all saluted, right fist to chest and then bowed as well. With a creeping feeling that tightened the skin on his stomach, Ian Arnstein realized who this man must be.

"Rejoice, Lord Mittler," the Greek replied. "This is the awaited one, then?"

"The prisoner Arnstein, yes," Mittler said. "I was just taking him into custody."

"Forgive me—I have gray in my beard and perhaps my ears do not hear as keenly as they did. Telemakhos," he said to the younger man beside him. "What did you hear of the King's will concerning this man?"

"That he be kept in honorable detention, Father," the second Greek said. He was taller than his sire, handsomer, but with something of the same quick intelligence in his eyes.

The first man held out his hand, smiling. After a second's hesitation, Mittler handed over the written order. The regent flicked it open with a swift motion of his wrist, sheltering it from the rain with his other hand.

"Very good," he said, folding it and tucking it into a pouch at his belt. "Thank you for your efforts, Lord Mittler, Captain Philowergos, and I'll take charge of this matter now." Smiling still, he held up his right hand, where a wolfshead signet rested.

Mittler's lips tightened slightly. "Section One is charged with internal security."

"Indeed." The chariot rider's thick arm pointed toward the western mountains. "There are bands of escaped slaves up there, and they raid the settled lands. There should be no distractions from your work."

"Very well, Lord Regent," Mittler said, bowing stiffly again. He turned to go, and hissed to Arnstein: "*This is not the last you'll see of me, Jewboy.*"

In German, which Arnstein understood quite well. Ian bowed in his turn to the man in the chariot.

"Rejoice, my lord. I am Ian Arnstein, Councilor for Foreign Affairs to Jared Cofflin, Chief Executive Officer of the Republic of Nantucket."

The Greek gave him a nod. "Makhawon," he said, to the man driving the chariot. "Get down, meet me at the capital town house. You have silver? Good. Telemakhos, take the reins." The younger Greek did, with an air of quiet competence.

"Lord Arnstein," he went on. "I am Odikweos son of Laertes, *Wannax* of Ithaka in the West; this is my son Telemakhos. I say in turn, may you rejoice and live happy."

"Pleased to meet you," Arnstein said, and took the offered hand. It felt like a wooden glove inside a casing of cured ham, and helped him up into the chariot with effortless strength.

"But I really don't have much prospect of a happy life. Or reason to rejoice."

Odikweos grinned. Even then, Arnstein felt a returning touch of the glassy unreality people called post-Event-syndrome; he was talking to *Odysseus*. Or at least to another Greek King of Ithaka of the same name.

"Oh, yes, you do have reason to rejoice, Lord Arnstein," Odikweos said. "Reason indeed."

He looked after Mittler and began to laugh. After a moment, Ian joined him.

The Cofflins and their Coast Guard minder pushed through the crowds along the base of the dock.

Most were in the virtual uniform of raw-wool sweater, flat peaked cap or knitted toque, baggy pants, and sea boots that was working garb these days if you were out on the water in autumn. There was plenty of variety, though. They went past a uniformed customs agent arguing with a supercargo in blue coat and brass buttons; a woods-runner in from the mainland with a backpack of furs over his buckskins and a tomahawk slung through the back of his belt; Albans in kilt and leggings or poncho and string skirt; a Babylonian in spangled flowerpot hat, curled beard, and embroidered ankle-length robe looking about him with an iron control over a visible longing to gawk . . .

Straight Wharf was the basin over from Steamboat, for pleasure craft before the Event and the inshore fishery now, plus a few family boats like the Cofflins'. He smiled with pure satisfaction as they walked out on the creaking planks of the dock to where the *Boojum II* lay tethered. Being chief was important work, but he came of a breed with salt water in their veins. Before he went into police work he'd been a deckhand on a trawler himself, then a Navy swabby—brown-water Navy, a Mekong Delta gunboat.

The *Boojum II* was a simple enough craft, a Cape Cod catboat; the design was traditional in these parts, resurrected post-Event. From sheer cutwater to transom stern she measured twenty-eight feet, and fourteen feet of beam at the widest point, a third back from the bows; the shallow rock-elm keel was three and a half feet below the waterline when she was fully laden, considerably less now. Just a foot back from the bow was the one unstayed mast, a sturdy fifteen-foot length of scraped and varnished white pine that carried a single fore-

and-aft sail between long boom and shorter gaff spars. There was a small cabin, but most of the boat was a cockpit and tiller.

He stepped down from the dock to the smooth varnished spruce planking of the deck—not far, since the tide was full and just beginning to ebb—and handed Martha down.

"Permission to come aboard?" his son asked solemnly.

Must have picked that up from Heather and Lucy, Jared thought, hiding his grin. The Alston-Kurlelo kids used their Guard associations mercilessly in the children's scuffles for status.

"Permission granted," Cofflin said gravely.

The cockpit filled with children, somehow taking up more room than adults would have. Petty Officer Martinelli handed down their overnight bags and the picnic baskets to be stowed in the compartments under the seats. Jared leaned a hand on the tiller and looked at the small forms scrambling about.

"What do we do first?" he asked.

"Ummm . . . life-jackets?" Heather said.

"You've got it, girl," Jared said. The cloth-covered cork jackets were produced and laced on. "Next?"

"Uh, the bilges and pump, Dad?" Jared Jr. said.

"Right. See to it, son."

He ran them through the checklist; he wanted his kids to enjoy the sea, but also to remember that you didn't take chances with it. He was also conscious that Martinelli was running a surreptitious check of his own. He didn't mind, much. The boy—*young man*, he reminded himself—was about nineteen, and conscientious. At that age, sixty must seem ancient beyond conception, just a step short of drooling idiocy. He grinned inwardly, remembering how old the first trawler skipper he'd worked for had seemed.

"Right, let's get under way and out of this madhouse," he said, looking up at the sky. Blue with a slight haze; ought to hold steady, although you might get fog with that. Wind out of the north and a little to the west, about six knots; they'd have to scull clear of the dock. "Martha, you mind if the petty officer here takes the other oar?"

"Not suffering from the side effects of testosterone poisoning," she said, heading for the cabin with a basket in either hand, "I have no objection at all to leaving hard physical labor to someone younger and stronger."

Well, that's put me in my place, Cofflin thought with wry affection. "Prepare to cast off fore and aft," he said aloud.

Lucy sprang for the dock and the stern line, grabbing the

davit and casting a look of triumph at Heather. Jared Jr. scrambled to the bows; his sister Marian was kneeling on one of the cockpit seats, looking dreamily at the harbor with her elbows on the coaming and chin propped on the heels of her hands.

"Cast off."

The children freed the mooring lines and hopped nimbly back to the *Boojum*. Jared and the Guardsman picked the long oars out of their racks and pushed against the timber pilings with their collars of floating weed, then fitted them to the oarlocks and began to scull. Martha took the tiller, looking between them and craning her head a little to see past the mast. The catboat dislodged protesting gulls and sea ducks as it slid out into the millpond-still surface between the piers. He spared a glance for the vane over Fort Brandt.

"Right, sea's medium and the wind's steady," he said.

And fresh enough to raise a little froth on the long sack-shape of the Great Harbor. The lagoon ran northeastward up the Island from here; Nantucket Town was tucked away in the southwestern corner. Traffic was fairly thick . . .

"Let the centerboard go," he said. Martha did, and the wooden fin-shape slid down through the hollow box and slot to project through the center of the hull. The motion of the catboat altered as it bit water and started to resist the sideways slip of the flat-bottomed craft. They racked the oars and tied them down. The *Boojum* pitched as she lay motionless, the mast making circles against the sky.

"Cast away, loose the sail," he said.

The children were just tall enough to reach the running knots if they stood on the seats. He watched his adopted son prying at the damp hemp, a frown of concentration on his face and his sun-faded tow hair riffling in the breeze, caught Martha's eye, and grinned with the pleasure of being alive. He'd looked much the same himself, when *his* father taught him how to handle a boat, and Cofflins before *him,* back to the beginning of time or at least the settlement of the Danelaw over in the old country. Cofflins had been Lincolnshire men before the founding of New England, and fishermen since Noah.

In fact, a remote would-have-been-ancestor was probably teaching *his* boy how to handle a bullhide coracle, somewhere in barbarian Europe this very day . . . which was a bit eerie, when you thought about it. For that matter, Jared Jr.'s birth-parents had come from the part of Alba that bordered the fenland marshes, so he was probably a remote ancestor of the

American who'd raised him, which was downright *weird* when you thought about it.

"All right, everyone down, and 'ware boom," he said. Martha came to take the tiller again while he heaved. "Martinelli, lend a hand . . ."

A spatter of shots came over the low hill ahead. Raupasha nodded and smiled, more broadly as the buzzing of the ultralight grew stronger. They'd only been in the field a few weeks, but she'd grown used to air scouts and the reach of vision they gave you; the older warriors of her band still shook their heads at it, or made covert signs.

It was a bright cool day, the air smelling of damp earth and the not-too-distant sea; the grass was green, starred with some winter flowers. Trees were mostly bare now, except where distant mountains reared blue-green with pine. It would have been a beautiful country, if war had not come by; plumes of smoke scarred the sky, one from the farmstead not far behind her. The horses shied a little as beams collapsed in an acrid smell of ash, and Sabala turned his head and pricked his ears.

"Seha River Land," she read off the map; maps were wonderful things, letting your mind soar like an eagle across the earth.

They were far in the northwest of the thumb-shaped peninsula of land that held the Hittite Empire, north and east of Troy. The Seha River flowed past northward to her right, too deep to ford easily—she must remember that, not to get pinned against it. A farmhouse burned behind her, the plume of smoke one of dozens visible.

The ultralight came over the ridge and swooped downward toward them. More horses shied; some had to be fought down from the edge of bolting. Some of the men were looking more than a little apprehensive, too; Raupasha hopped down from her chariot, took the pole with the red banner, and waved it in a huge circle around her head.

The blue arrowhead drove toward her, then pulled up like an eagle—the eagle whose wings were painted on the fabric. It came by at barely head height, and a package trailing a long ribbon of cloth came down from it. Raupasha could see the pilot's goggles, grin, streaming scarf and glazed sheepskin jacket; yes, it must be cold up there. But how glorious!

One of her men ran over with the message cylinder, turning it over in his hands. Raupasha took it from him and unscrewed it, smiling a little at his gape of awe.

"Thank you, Artatama," she said.

The boy blushed and bowed with hand to forehead. Warriors liked it when their rulers knew their names—both her foster father and Lord Kenn'et had told her that. Sabala relaxed as he left; the hound was never easy when those he considered strangers approached her.

She unrolled the paper and held it beside her map. The notes were scrawled one-handed by the paper, but clear enough. She closed her eyes for a moment, called on Agni and made things clear to her inner eye. Then she called the squadron commanders to her, explaining.

"Now!" she said at last, when all was ready.

The Mitannian chariots fanned out—a hundred war-cars took up a surprising amount of space—and then surged forward. The thunder of a thousand iron-shod hooves would give the enemy some warning, but they would be swift on its heels. Reaching down, she pulled the rocket launcher from its rack, put it over her shoulder, and swung the end toward Gunnery Sergeant Connor.

"Load," she said crisply.

"Up!" he replied, sliding the rocket shell into the tail of the launcher.

She felt a click as the trigger spring took up the tension. *So many Nantukhtar things involve clicks,* she thought, mouth dry. Soon . . .

The Mitannians crested the rise, seeming to their enemies to appear from nowhere in a rattling thunder. Iridmi flicked his whip, a delicate touch that did the team no hurt but told them *time to run.*

The chariots plunged downward, over gently rolling plowland green with winter wheat, flowing around obstacles. Raupasha raised her voice as her foster father had taught her, high and pure and strong in the first note of the war-song, the ancient paean her people had brought with them from the seas of grass. The others took it up, and it spurred the horses on more than rein or whip.

Wind flew past her, and clods of turf torn up by the hooves. Sabala ran baying at the wheel, his usual gentle-foolish face turned into something altogether different, as if he were indeed Guardian of the Underworld—she had named him for that, as well as his fur.

Ahead, the enemy were strung out on a track beside a little stream lined with oleander and poplars. Part of their force was a train of wagons, some big ones of the Nantukhtar type, others commandeered from the people of this land. The rest was a working party, local peasants digging and ditching and throwing dirt and gravel from baskets onto the surface of the roadway. The two groups had fouled each other, a wagon had bogged to the hubs leaving the made section of the road, and extra teams and men had been hitched to free it. Teamsters and laborers ran about getting in the way, oxen bellowed in panic, and the escorting warriors ran for their weapons.

Connor looked back over his shoulder. "Good," he grunted.

Raupasha looked there, too, a single quick glance; yes, those men were following their orders. Hard, hard, to miss the thundering glory of this moment.

Most of the escort were Ringapi, the wild men Walker had seduced. A brace of chariots came out to meet hers, six—she had to admit they had courage, lashing their horses on and bellowing their war cries. Their foot soldiers followed, forming a ragged line to protect their charges. To one side were a half score of men in Walker's uniform, who'd been overseeing the roadwork. They went fanning out in more orderly wise, then fell to their stomachs. The dark-gray of their clothing nearly disappeared against the ground, and their rifles began to speak in puffs of off-white smoke.

She judged distance. "Now!" she shouted to Iridmi. "*Wartanna!*" Turn!

He leaned back and hauled on the reins. The horses turned, and the war-car followed. Connor and she jumped for the outside rail, their weight keeping the chariot from overturning. Despite practice, one or two of those behind did—or perhaps the bullets began to strike home, and they tumbled in disaster, broken men and horses and yoke-poles.

The chariot settled down again with a thump that resounded from her feet up her spine and clicked her teeth together. Now the Mitannian line was moving parallel to the wagon train, and only fifty yards away. She leveled the rocket launcher.

"*Clear!*" she shouted, and pulled the trigger.

SSSSSRAAAAWACK!

A tongue of pale fire lanced out, over the heads of the warriors, and behind her into the air behind the right rear of the chariot. Exultation rose beneath her breastbone as she saw that the curved white smoke trail would come down—*yes!*

The rocket landed under the front wheel of a large wagon. There was a flash—

BADAMP.

"Ammo wagon!" Connor whooped, yelling into her deafened ear.

Raupasha blinked, shook her head, blinked seared eyes. Where the wagon had been was only a smoking hole and some fragments. Bits and pieces of wagon and ox and man rained down from the sky for scores of yards all about, and the line of Ringapi foot soldiers were panicked. The galloping bar of Mitannian chariots had all opened fire—some of them were galloping very quickly indeed, as if the horses had bolted at the blast. Her men fired shotguns and rifles, pulled the pins and threw the little bombs called *grenades*. Arrows, slingstones, and a few bullets came back at them, and then she was past the end of the enemy position.

Iridmi pulled the team to the right, back up the slope, then around across it. The rest of the chariots followed, forming a *Circle of Yama*, keeping up a continuous fire on the foe. Two more chariots fired rockets; one headed over the stream to burst harmlessly, and the second struck turf near Walker's men. The noise and fire and smoke still added to the terror she wanted. . . .

"They run!" Tekhip-tilla shouted to her, his chariot pulling up level with hers. "They flee!"

"Good," Raupasha said. "But—"

A bullet went *kerwackkk* through the space between them.

"—remember the plan!"

Iridmi pulled the horses to a halt. The others did likewise, and from each car two men with firearms leaped down. Outnumbered ten to one, Walker's men died hard but swiftly. Whooping, the Mitannians descended on the supply caravan.

"Only what you can take quickly!" Raupasha reminded them, in a firm, carrying voice.

Gold ornaments were ripped free from bodies and transferred to the victors, along with the occasional silver-hilted dagger or good-looking pair of shoes. The fire-weapons were collected quickly; the Achaeans had been armed with Westley-Richards breechloaders. All others were thrown into a quickly kindled fire, to spoil them. Jugs of olive oil were smashed over boxes of biscuit, sacks of grain, sides of bacon, and soon another pillar of dirty smoke rose to the sky. Jars of flour were shattered and scattered in the rutted mud of the road. Wagons they hacked to pieces, and fed the flames that consumed bandages and medicines, cloth and leather. Most of the wine was spilt as well, although she did not begrudge the men a swallow or two.

Raupasha looked on, her joy tinged with sadness. She had spent all her life until the Nantukhtar came in a little tumbledown manor. Every family of the peasants there had been known to her, the playmates of her youth. Sweat and pain were the price of this food, as well she knew; waste meant somewhere hearths would be cold and children would hunger. With an effort, she shook off the thought.

They would hunger anyway; this was already stolen from them.

"Kill the cattle," she said when the supply convoy was wreckage or a few choice bits lashed to the sides of chariots.

"My Queen?" one man asked, aghast.

"Kill the oxen," she said. "This is true war, not a cattle raid. We cannot take them with us or leave them to work for the enemy, or to feed him."

A great silence fell, men looking at her round-eyed. Was not the ancient word for "war" the same as "to seek cattle"? And these men's families had been impoverished by the Assyrians. There was no wealth so handy as good oxen broken to the yoke . . .

She drew her pistol. A man made a halfhearted attempt to block her way, then fell back from a gray-eyed glare. Raupasha put the weapon to the beast's ear, steeling herself against the mild expression of its great brown eyes.

Crack. The animal gave a strangled bellow, tossed its head, then went to its knees and fell with a limp thud to the muddy ground.

"Butcher one," she said. "But quickly! The rest, hack them apart, slash the flesh, rub filth in the cuts. Now! Obey!"

While the grisly work went on she saw to the dead and wounded. There were only six dead; a few broken bones from the wrecked cars, to be set and splinted by the Nantucktar-trained Babylonian orderly, a flesh wound or two. It was as Kat'ryn and Kenn'et had said; surprise and speed mattered more than numbers. When they had been loaded and sent off, the destruction was near complete.

"Princess!" Tekhip-tilla said.

He pointed. Raupasha unshipped her binoculars and looked. Yes, Walker's men, several score of them. *Mounted riflemen,* in the English tongue. The reports said that several *battalions* were deployed to guard against just such raids as hers. Not very many men, for so huge a land.

"Be ready!" she called to her squadron commanders. Kat'ryn had taught her; if you sounded as if disobedience was impossible, it was. "Remember the plan—every man must act his part."

They did, doing their best to look like heedless plunderers. Walker's men were taught to despise those who fought from chariots . . . *dumb wogs*, that was the phrase they used.

The gray-uniformed men came on, deploying into line as they came. "Remember their doctrine," Gunnery Sergeant Connor murmured from close behind her. "They'll dismount at four hundred yards."

She waited, tense. Yes: now they pulled up their mounts, began to swing down. Two could play this game.

"To your chariots," she called.

The Mitannians poured back to their vehicles, slapped leather on rumps, got their mounts moving back over the ridge they'd hidden behind before the attack. They were careful to drive in a disorderly mob, careful to give no hint of stopping as they fled over the brow of the rise. Sabala was the last over the ridge, a heavy ox shank in his jaws.

"Pull up!" Raupasha ordered. Then, in an instant's tender scold: "Plunderer!" to the dog.

The chariots halted a few yards below the crestline; the two fighters jumped from each and turned back to crouch just out of sight from the valley below. The war-cars rolled on a little, waiting with the heads of their teams pointing southeast and the drivers looking over their shoulders. Connor leaped down from hers, and ran to where the mortar team were waiting, checking the elevation on their weapon. The Gatling crew had their hands on the tripod that supported their terrible weapon, ready to run it up to bear on the attackers. Raupasha flopped down on the grass herself, shotgun ready.

"Yes!" she said.

The Achaeans had remounted and were coming on regardless, leaning forward and lashing their mounts into a run. Very sure they would see only the retreating rumps of their enemies when they crested the rise.

"Ready!" she said.

The numbers were about even. With the wonder-weapons the Nantukhtar had given them, though, and the advantage of surprise . . .

Jared Cofflin kept the *Boojum* slanting away northwestward on a long tack before turning west, sailing reach with the strong fall wind a little behind his right shoulder. Nobody got seasick this time, thank goodness. Petty Officer Martinelli went forward of the mast, keeping a lookout. Once the spouts of a pod of right whales a hundred strong rose around the catboat, the warm breath-smelling fog drifting around them, and the children stood in wide-eyed wonder.

"They're traveling south from their feeding grounds in the north," Jared said. There weren't any whale-catcher boats in sight. *Quota already caught for the year*, he thought. "Down to calve in the warm seas."

The tiller bucked in his hand as one rose from the water and crashed down again, sending a wave surging beneath the *Boojum*'s keel, and he laughed aloud at the children's delighted shrieks and the sheer pleasure of the thing.

"Look!" Marian called, pointing. "Oh, Dad, Mom, everybody, *look*!"

It was one of the small islets off the western shore of Nantucket proper, a low sandy dome rising a few feet above high tide. It was dark with a ring of what looked like moving spotted gray rocks, so thick that the sands were invisible. Jared Cofflin cocked an eye at the wind, craned his head to see by the color of the water if the shoals lay the way he remembered them, and steered closer.

The rocks lifted pointed whiskered noses and their hoarse cries made a rumble of thunder through the bright air. The summer-born pups were fairly large now, their whitish bellies turning blue-gray, craning to see the boat go by with wide-eyed curiosity. Young Marian sighed, and began to recite; then to sing, a tune made recently to suit the poem as it was taught in the Natural History classes of the Republic's schools:

> *I met my mates in the morning (and oh, but I am old!)*
> *Where roaring on the ledges the summer ground swell rolled,*
> *I hear them lift their chorus to drown the breakers' song—*
> *The beaches of Lukannon—two million voices strong!*

"There aren't two million there, are there, Dad?" Jared Jr. said.

"No, son, only a couple of thousand there," his father replied. *Jesus, but standards change—a "couple of thousand" seals!* "Those are harbor seals; they don't migrate much, just like to congregate. They have their pups in summer."

Martinelli spoke up: "I've seen easy two million—heck, seven or eight, maybe ten, the experts say—up on the St. Lawrence ice, when I shipped on a catcher for the winter harvest. Harp seals—saddlebacks. That's quite a sight, but it's bitter there come February—bitter cold."

Martha got out her guitar, and the young sailor joined in with the children on the next chorus:

> *The song of pleasant stations beside the salt lagoons,*
> *The song of flowing squadrons that shuffled down the dunes,*
> *The song of midnight dances that churned the seas to flame—*
> *The beaches of Lukannon—before the sealers came!*
>
> *I met my mates in the morning (I'll never meet them more!);*
> *We came and went in legions and darkened all the shore.*
> *Among the foam-flecked offing as far as voice could reach*
> *We hailed the landing-parties—we sang them up the beach.*
>
> *The beaches of Lukannon—the winter wheat so tall—*
> *The dripping, crinkled lichens, the sea fog drenching all!*
> *The porches of our playground, all shining smooth and worn!*
> *The beaches of Lukannon—the home where we were born!*
>
> *I meet my mates in the morning, a broken, scattered band,*
> *Men shoot us in the water—men club us on the sand;*
> *Men drive us to the Salt House like silly sheep and tame,*
> *But still we sing Lukannon—before the sealers came.*

"Dad, you won't let that happen, will you?" Marian asked anxiously. "All the seals gone, I mean, Dad."

"No, I won't." He caught Martha's eye. "That is, we won't—all of us—let anything like that happen again," he said. *I hope. All we can do is our best.* "The law is that people can't take more than the seals can replace, like the rules for whales or fish, so there will always be more." *So your kids can see what you do, sweetness,* he thought.

The girl's lower lip pouted slightly. "Why do we have to take any seals?"

Unexpectedly, Martinelli spoke up: "Because we have to eat, missy; same reason the seals take fish and squid," he said. "There's plenty of working folk who're glad of a seal-flipper pie, come February. We need fur and oil, too." He shook his head. "Still, that was really something, coming over the pack ice and them stretching out further than you could see—to the end of the world, ice and seals, seals and ice. Loud, too, louder 'n cannon—Lord thundering Jesus, but there were a world of them!" He shook his head again in slow wonder. "I'd hate to think of that . . . not being in the world, that sight."

Well, there's hope for the younger generation, Cofflin thought, and joined his hoarse bass to the final chorus; he'd gotten a lot less self-conscious about singing over the past ten years. You didn't get compared to recorded professionals anymore, just to the neighbors, or at most to buskers and semi-amateurs at the ceidhles and concerts.

> *Wheel down, wheel down to southern! Oh, Goover-*
> *ooska, go!*
> *And tell the Salt-Sea Viceroy the story of our woe;*
> *For like the empty shark's egg the tempest flings ashore,*
> *The beaches of Lukannon shall know their sons no more!*

There were other things to point out; two schooners running home from the Georges Bank with their dories stacked on their decks; the unforgettably vile smell and raucous noise of a cormorant rookery on a tiny island; lobster boats and timber barges . . .

"I recognize *her*," he said with a brief grin, four hours later.

It was a smallish craft, ketch-rigged on two masts and about twice the length of the *Boojum*, with a railed crow's nest on the mainmast. There was another railed enclosure forward of the prow, out on the bowsprit. No harpooner kept station there now; the *Kestrel* was homebound for Nantucket Town, with the tails of half a dozen giant bluefin tuna hanging in triumph from the rigging. The gutted bodies would be in the hold, lying on crushed saltwater ice . . .

Cofflin felt his mouth water; it was getting on for lunchtime anyway. "Martha, maybe we'd better fire up the galley," he said. Louder, with his left hand cupped around his mouth: "Ahoy the *Kestrel*, there!"

The man at the wheel—the tuna-catcher was just large enough to make a tiller cumbersome—nodded and shouted an order to his crew. The *Kestrel* turned, slanting further south of east, then turned up into the wind in a horseshoe maneuver; her sails came down with a rush except for the jib, and she lay with her bows pitching and pointed into the wind. The gulls who'd been following hopefully made a brief white storm of wings and raucous cries around the two craft.

"Neat as ever, John," Cofflin called as the catboat came

close, and pulled on the tiller to bring her closer to the eye of the northeasterly wind.

Facing full into the wind the sail emptied and rattled, its loose edge thuttering—luffing. Two crew from the fishing craft caught the rail with hooks on the ends of long poles and held her steady. That wouldn't be safe for long.

"When're you coming back to real work, Chief?" John Kotalac said.

Cofflin shook his head. He'd spent the first harvest season after the Event harpooning bluefin; he hadn't been more ignorant than anyone else, and hadn't gotten anyone killed—not quite. Since then he'd done it most autumns, when the big fish ran up the coast. That was one of the ways you could pay Town tax, like lending a hand mining Madaket Mall, the old landfill dump, or working in some farmer's harvest gang.

"Time to let nature take its course," he said. "I'm just plain getting too slow. Not too slow to eat 'em, though. How'd it go?"

"Not bad at all," the skipper of the tuna boat said. "Got six—and Sweet can relax, not one of them under fifteen hundred pounds. Three are ton-weighters."

Cofflin nodded. Fifteen hundred pounds was the minimum legal size for bluefin; it meant they were all over thirty-five years old, fully mature and likely to have spent three decades breeding. And all taken with the harpoon. No drift nets *here*, by God. It wasn't a particular hardship, either. There were a *lot* of mature bluefin migrating up from the Carribean spawning grounds in the Year 10. He'd seen a boat about the *Kestrel*'s size knocked on its beam ends once, when it got between a school of them and the mackerel they were chasing.

"Give you a quarter for twenty-five pounds of it," he called. "That's better than you'll get from those pirates 'longshore."

Fresh tuna steak was a seasonal delicacy . . . but a glut of caviar was still a glut of caviar, in terms of what you could get in a free market. For that matter, caviar was pretty cheap nowadays. Pushcart vendors sold it. Most of the tuna would go into barrels or glass pickling jars for use in winter.

"Sounds good," John Kotalac said. Raising his voice: "Whoever's closest!"

" 'Lo, Tekkusumu," Cofflin went on, waving.

The Indian nodded courteously; he was a short broad man, looking a little incongruous in Nantucketer seagoing sweater and baggy pants and boots, since his hair was still up in a helmet-crest roach with the shaven sides of his head painted vermilion. Many of the tuna boats carried Lekkansu tribesmen from the 'longshore clans as harpooners; they learned the art quickly, since they were used to throwing things in a way few Islanders could match.

"*I greet you, elder brother,*" Tekkusumu said in his own language—Cofflin had picked up a few words of it—and then continued in good English: "The harpoon flew sweet this year."

Several of the seven-foot shafts were racked behind him, and he'd been sharpening a head when they came up, a foot-long steel shaft with a toggle-hinged blade at the tip. Now he laid it aside, drew the long knife at his belt, and jumped down into the well of the boat. When he came back up it was with a dripping chunk wrapped in coarse burlap. He leaned far out over his ship's rail to hand it down to Martha.

"From near the belly," he said to her.

Jared nodded; muscle from around the body cavity was the best. There were plenty of people on Nantucket who liked it as sushi, although barley groats had to replace the rice. *Sushi's still raw fish wrapped in seaweed to me,* he thought wryly. But lightly grilled, with just a brush of butter and salt . . . The rest of it would make a good guest-gift at their destination.

"Thanks, Tekkusumu, John! Say hello to Sally for me!"

" 'Bye!"

The crewfolk with the boathooks fended them off again, and the *Boojum*'s sail cracked like a whip as it filled and the boat paid off, turning its bow south of west. The tiller came alive in his hand again; the blunt bow surged up to the top of one of the long slow swells, then ran downward, up again . . .

A sizzle came from the little cabin, and then Martha's head came out of the door.

"All right, children; make yourselves useful."

The kids scurried around, unpacking the picnic baskets. Martha brought the tuna steaks out herself, and spelled him at the tiller while he ate; an occasional sprinkle of salt spray fell across his plate.

Funny thing, he thought. Before the Event, he'd eaten alone more often than not after his first wife died. He almost never did that now—six of them when it was just a family meal and usually more. There were times it still felt a little odd; like TV, not that he *missed* the mindless blather, just that it was something gone from the background of life.

The rest of the sail was a straight run with a stiff wind on the starboard beam and the port rail nearly under, clocking ten knots or better all the way down to Long Island Sound. Six hours later he surreptitiously worked his left arm. The adults had all taken turns at the tiller, but his shoulder was still a bit stiff and sore, where they'd taken the piece of shell casing from one of Victor C's mortars out, all those years ago. It hadn't bothered him any then, he'd had what his grandfather called good-healing flesh, like a young dog. At the time, he'd just been mad it wasn't enough to get him back to the World, although he'd enjoyed the R&R in Bangkok. The medal he'd flipped into the river the moment his feet were on the gunboat's deck again.

But these last couple of years, if it was cold or he'd pushed it beyond a certain point, the joint ached where the steel had scored bone and tendon. A ghost-pain from a war that would never happen, a memory of steel still locked unmined in Siberian mountains this fall day. Another clutch of years . . . maybe twenty if he was lucky . . . and he'd lay his bones beside so many other Cofflins in Nantucket's sandy loam. Those bones would molder away to nothingness before the year men were due to dig those rocks away and other men smelt and shape and fill them and still more launch them at an American gunboat where a bored, lonely, frightened teenager stood behind the spade-grips of an automatic cannon. . . .

I remember being that youngster, Jared Cofflin thought. *But in a way he'll never exist at all, except in my memories—I'm here and feeling a wound from a battle that never happened, never will. . . .* And that boy was as strange to him as that far-distant year.

He looked up and caught Martha looking at him, fond and dryly amused at the same time. *Act your age, then, Jared,* he thought for her, giving an imperceptible nod.

CHAPTER FIFTEEN

September, 10 A.E.—Pi-Ramses, Kingdom of Egypt

"*T*he Horus," the silver-voiced herald called, half chant and half song. "*The God is among us!*"

The Vizier of the North sank to his knees and then bent forward to symbolically kiss dirt. Beside him Mek-Andrus, Commander of Chariots, did likewise, pressing his face to the colorful glazed tile of the floor. It was cool and smooth beneath his lips, and a breath of greenery and flowers touched the skin of his back, wafting in from the pools and gardens outside into the hot gloom.

"*He of the Two Goddesses:* Protector of Egypt Who Subdues the Foreign Lands; *The Golden Horus:* Rich in Years, Great in Victories."

Spearmen in kilts, banded linen cuirasses and beehive-shaped helmets marched through the doorway and faced outward, weapons grounded and big rectangular oval-topped shields braced.

"*The King of Upper and Lower Egypt:* Strong in Right is Ra—*User-Ma'at-Ra.*"

The herald's voice grew to a shout: "*Son of Ra,* Ramses, beloved of Amun! The God is among us!"

Mek-Andrus—who had been George McAndrews in Memphis, Tennessee—saw the gilt sandals stride into view. More feet came in the background, mostly bare; fan-bearers with brightly dyed ostrich feathers on the ends of gilded poles, scribes, attendants, a couple of musicians . . . just the minimal attendants for an ordinary day's work. The hem of Pharaoh's translucent-thin pleated robe rustled across his ankles, and the sandals settled on a footstool carved with bound, kneeling Asiatics and Nubians—literally being trampled underfoot by Pharaoh.

The fan-bearers began fanning and the scribes sank into their cross-legged posture, pens poised over the scrolls of papyrus that spanned their laps.

"Rise," a clear tenor voice said.

He and the vizier came upright on their knees, raising their hands palm-forward in the gesture of worship common to most of this part of the ancient world.

"Hail to *Setep-en-Ra*, the Chosen of Ra!" McAndrews cried in unison with the official beside him.

His Egyptian was very good now. He'd been practicing hard all the years since Walker came to the Middle Sea, and he'd acquired an Egyptian servant to achieve full fluency years ago. He even had a Delta accent. His court etiquette was pretty good, too. You couldn't go far wrong here if you kissed ass upward and kicked it down.

"Rise," the Pharaoh said again. "Seat yourselves, my servants."

He did.

And with a lot less puffing and grunting than our esteemed Vizier of Lower Egypt, he thought, as the pudgy bureaucrat settled on a stool beside his. At this range, even in midmorning, he got a whiff to remind him that while upper-class Egyptians bathed twice daily, they also rubbed themselves all over with perfumed hippopotamus fat to prevent wrinkles from the dry air.

McAndrews was a big man, two inches over six feet, and at thirty biological years still in the shape he'd had as a running back at the Coast Guard Academy before the Event; broad-shouldered, with thick muscular arms, flat stomach, and long legs. That showed to advantage, since he was wearing a simple knee-length linen military wraparound kilt, vividly white against his natural dark-brown skin and cinched by a heavy belt.

By a stroke of luck, the Egyptians were among the peoples here who admired a trim figure, at least in a soldier; other men of substance were expected to have a substantial belly.

He'd shaved his head as well—fairly common, though compulsory only for priests—and wore a sphinx-type linen *khat*-headdress and high-strapped sandals with silver studs. On his upper arms were snake-shaped gold bracelets; on his chest the Gold of Valor, Egypt's equivalent of the Medal of Honor and rather more, a massive thing, rows of gold disks strung into necklaces and a spray of gold braids and flowers across his broad chest.

No sword at the belt, of course, not in Pharaoh's presence here in the capital of Pi-Ramses. He raised his eyes to Ramses's

face, feeling again the echo of the shock he'd undergone that
first time.

All right, Pharaoh is not *a brother,* he admitted.

Today the ruler wore—informally, as a mark of honor, and
probably because the daily morning meetings with the vizier
were just too frequent for the full treatment—his own short
hair with no wig, under a cloth-of-gold skullcap. That hair was
a grizzled dark auburn-brown, in this the thirty-ninth year of
his reign and sixtieth of his life; Pharaoh's eyes were hazel, his
chin knobby, his nose a scimitar beak . . . and all in all he
reminded McAndrews of a guy who'd run a really good Italian
restaurant in Memphis.

That's Memphis, Tennessee, not the place up the Nile . . .

Although Mario DeCiccio hadn't used kohl eyeshadow or
rouge on his cheeks, or gold and carnelian earrings, or a broad
collar of lapis and silver . . .

He fought down a brief, bitter stab of homesickness. *All right,
most* Egyptians aren't brothers. Not until well north of Thebes;
skin color darkened to a rye-toast-brown like McAndrews's in
Upper Egypt just before you got to Elephantine—Aswan,
where the first rapids interrupted the Nile.

In the stretch upstream of the First Cataract lived the Nubians, who were unambiguously *black,* blacker than McAndrews,
and so were Kushites south of them—but those were exploited
colonies of the Egyptian kingdom, held down by forts and garrisons. Power here lay in the lower Nile valley. Ramses was only
the second of his line to be born Pharaoh; his grandfather had
been a lucky soldier, and his family were pretty typical of the
northeastern Delta area.

Pharaoh flashed him a smile. "Still no pain, Mek-Andrus!"
he exclaimed, flicking a finger against one of his teeth. "For
the first time in twenty inundations, no pain!"

"Pharaoh is generous," McAndrews said. "Generous beyond
my worth."

And the second part of that is a lie, mutha', he thought at the
offical beside him, who was radiating wholehearted agreement
with the polite falsehood.

"I eat like a young man again," Pharaoh said happily, as a
man might who'd had abscesses and eight teeth worn down to
the nerve pulp. "I tear at meat like a lion!"

That had been another shock. He just hadn't expected these
people to be so fucking *backward* about something so simple.
Egyptians had what passed for advanced medical skills in this
era; their doctors were much in demand, or had been before the

rise of Great Achaea. What they didn't have was the slightest knowledge of dentistry. Plus their bread was full of grit.

A dentist trained by Walker's man, some bridgework and caps, ether to make it painless . . .

That was the smartest thing I ever did, the black man thought. It had won him the gratitude of Pharaoh, and a dozen other great men. *Maybe it makes up for being stupid enough to let Walker con me in the first place.*

Pharaoh leaned back on his throne. It was supported on either side by golden lions, and the back was a great golden falcon with lapis eyes, whose wings were raised protectively over User-Ma'at-Ra. The wall behind him had a mud-brick core—all secular buildings here did, stone was for tombs, temples, and the Gods. But every inch of its two-story height was covered in tilework, whose glazing shimmered like thin-sliced sapphires and rubies and emeralds in the light that streamed from the small high clerestory windows.

So were the flanking walls; the huge faience murals showed one of Ramses's favorite stories, his victory at Kadesh more than thirty years before. Bow drawn to his ear, bedizened stallions prancing before his chariot, the Pharaoh charged to victory over tumbled, fleeing Hittites. It was all busy and gaudy beyond words, like a fifties Hollywood Technicolor costume drama, and about as truthful.

Our Son of Ra got his semi-divine ass kicked at Kadesh, McAndrews knew; the city was still part of the Hittite Empire and Ramses had barely gotten out alive. You didn't mention it, if you wanted to remain healthy.

And God—my mother's God, not the God-damned things with goat's heads here—but I am so sick *of living in places where I could be taken out and killed on one man's whim.*

"So," Ramses went on cheerfully. "The reports speak well of your armory."

"Truly Pharaoh sees with the eye of Horus," McAndrews said. "The iron furnaces, the waterwheels, the rolling and slitting mill and boring machines, all the things necessary to equip the armies of Pharaoh with *rifles* continue. Ships are building in Thebes as fast as timber can be procured and shipwrights trained in the new methods. The cannon-foundry here in your city of Pi-Ramses makes more of the great guns, and will make still more if the bronze can be found."

He cast a sidelong glance at the vizier, whose responsibility it was to find the metal.

The bureaucrat coughed discreetly. "Perhaps it would be better if the powder mill and gunshops could also be transferred here," he said. "To have them so far south out of the way, near a turbulent frontier province like Kush . . ."

McAndrews shrugged. "Then they would not work, eminent Vizier," he said. "They need fast-flowing water to turn the wheels. The First Cataract is the nearest place with such rapids. And the iron ore is there, too."

Pharaoh leaned forward. "And the training of men to fire the *rifles*? How goes that?"

"Chosen of Ra, I have been working closely with Djehuty of the Brigade of Seth, and with your son the Great General of the Armies. We now have a battalion trained every month."

Ramses nodded. "It seems so swift . . ."

"Favored of Amun, a rifle not only strikes faster and harder than a bow, it is much easier to learn."

Good archers had to be virtually born at it; any peasant pulled from the plow could learn a musket in a couple of months.

"Already we have employed both the rifles and the cannon against your enemies to the southward."

Pharaoh nodded: "We have seen the reports of the damage wrought. They are all your first demonstrations led me to believe."

His fist descended slowly on his knee. "Kashtiliash in Babylon and Tudhaliyas in Hattusas have both sent to me, and this upstart from nowhere Jared Cofflin, they have all sent insolent insults, demanding that I give up your person, Mek-Andrus. To so demand you is to demand that Egypt have none of the new weapons! The weapons Kashtiliash used to conquer the Assyrians and Elamites, and which the King of Men has used to spread his power over the Sea Kingdoms. Do they think me a fool? Do they think I will leave the Two Lands bound, naked and helpless?"

That didn't seem to call for any comment. Then Ramses went on: "But now I can meet all of them on equal terms."

"Strong Bull, it is my grief that this is not so," McAndrews said, reckless of Pharaoh's frown. "At present, we have only the simpler of the new weapons."

Muzzle-loading minié rifles, basic bronze cannon, iron blades, some improvements like better chariot harness; Civil War-era matériel, or earlier.

Walker was turning out this stuff a couple of months after we arrived in Greece. He shorted me on the machine tools, all clapped-out models from the first batches Cuddy did up.

How to put it so Ramses could understand? You couldn't even *say* "interchangeable parts" in Egyptian.

"The weapons we have are to the ones the King of Men has . . . as a simple bow of wood is to the bow of a chariot fighter, strengthened with horn and sinew."

Ramses scowled again. "How long until we have the best of weapons? Nothing less is acceptable to My person!"

"Divine Horus, I have been here only one year and a few months. To make the things we need, more machines must be built and more men trained; this is not a matter of rounding up peasants to chop stone and haul dirt. It is more like training a goldsmith. Not less than one more year to produce what Great Achaea does now; perhaps as many as three. I tell the Lord of the Great House that which is true, not soothing lies."

The vizier's expression showed what he thought of *that*. Ramses was a little uncertain; but then, he'd spent his whole life wondering if people would tell him only what he wanted to hear.

"Work unceasingly," Ramses ordered. "Be vigilant for Pharaoh's interests!" And then more bowing and scraping, until he could get away.

Household slaves handed him his weapons belt, and he unhitched the Gold of Valor and handed it to one of his own retainers with a word of thanks, supressing a grunt of relief at not having the twenty-pound weight around his neck. Otherwise, Egyptian clothes made a lot of sense for the climate.

Right now the *katana* and Walkeropolis-made revolver were a lot more reassuring than a gong; there had been two assassination attempts already. Pharaoh's favor didn't necessarily protect you from a knife in the back.

Goddamn Egyptians, he thought, stepping into his chariot.

The driver flicked up the horses, wheeling them about in the broad paved forecourt. McAndrews's own retainers rose from where they'd squatted on their hams with weapons across their knees. They bowed to him and swung into the saddle, the butts of their rifles again resting on their thighs, thumbs ready to draw back the hammers and eyes wary.

They were all Nubians or Kushites or from further south, and all ex-slaves. It turned his stomach to bid in a slave market, but buying men and then treating them well, and freeing them for good behavior, was the only really quick way of getting loyal followers here. Particularly if you didn't have any hereditary clout. Many of them were from the estates in the far south

that Pharaoh had granted him, winning favor for their families
as well as themselves.

The party took off in a spurt of gravel. This end of the palace
quarter of Pi-Ramses was all gardens and pools and canals. The
great colored mass of the palace was to the northward, and
beyond that the Temple of Wadjet, the Cobra Goddess; another pile of masonry to the east honored Hathor-Isis-Astarte;
south was the Temple of Seth and west was Amun. Those two
were the primary patrons of the Ramesside dynasty, and he'd
gone to considerable lengths to pacify their priesthoods.

"*God*-damned *Egyptians*," he muttered aloud—in English, as
they passed a forty-foot-tall colossus of Ramses, carved from
Aswan granite and overlaid with sheet gold; it hurt the eyes to
look at it.

Swearing in English was a bit of a safety valve. *Will they listen
to me? No, they will not listen. What does a foreigner know?*

Oh, they'd take *some* things he offered gladly: gunpowder,
cannon, iron weapons and armor, stirrups. The Hyksos conquest still lived in memory, when they'd been caught napping
by the first horse-and-chariot army to reach the Nile valley.
Weapons they'd take, and things necessary to make the
weapons.

But, say, a wind pump to replace peasants with *shadoofs*, or
alphabetic writing? The Gods forbid! The scribes had been
even more horrified when he pointed out that twenty-six symbols from their own writing system would convey all the sounds
of Egyptian, and reduce the schooling time for literacy from
twelve years to six months. He strongly suspected some of them
were behind one of the failed assassins. Products of the scribal
schools dominated the whole bureaucracy of the kingdom; they
all had a vested interest in keeping up the value of their expensive training, and the tricks of a civil service two thousand years
old let them tie you in knots without breaking a sweat.

The Gods alone knew who the other knifeman had been
working for, which made him even more nervous. He'd taken
on a food taster recently.

Arithmetic? Rule-of-thumb worked for grandpa, so away
with outland gibberish; same for real paper, no matter how
much cheaper and better than papyrus. He'd demonstrated a
simple rotary quern for grinding grain, and met flat, blank disin-
terest, or contempt—did the dumb nigger barbarian think that
Egypt didn't have enough slave girls to rub two rocks together?

No, that's not quite fair, he made himself acknowledge. It
wasn't really his skin color they held against him; it was the

fact he wasn't Egyptian. If you tried really hard to assimilate, they'd accept a foreigner . . . or maybe his kids or grandkids. But you had to accept that Egypt was the center of everything and home of absolutely everything worthwhile.

For the first time in his life he felt some sympathy for British imperialists—at least in nineteenth-century China.

Yeah, the Confucian bureaucrats kept calling all the Brit emissaries "tribute bearers" from the "barbarian vassal Victoria." You were from the Middle Kingdom, or you were a dumb-ass barbarian—no box marked "other."

Egyptians of this era made those Manchu mandarins look like web junkie change-aholics. There were times when he day-dreamed about sailing a gunboat up the Water of Ra—the Canoptic branch of the Nile—and blowing the vizier's residence sky-high with a few shells from an eighteen-pounder, himself. Lately that had replaced strangling William Walker as his favorite fantasy.

The chariot trotted out of the high, blank, whitewashed wall that surrounded the palace complex and onto a long avenue lined with sphinxes; most bore the head of Ramses, although some had that of a curl-horned ram, the symbol of Amun, with little statues of Ramses tucked under their chins.

Yeah, the symbolism runs from I am God *to* God Really Likes Me. *Hot shit.*

Pi-Ramses was a planned city, and only about forty years old; it had many processional ways like this, as well as plenty of twisting, slimy alleys in the poorer quarters. The streets here were quiet; now and then a noble lady with her parasol-bearer sheltering her from the sun, a shaven-headed priest with a leopardskin over his shoulder, a Libyan mercenary in cloak and penis sheath, a Syrian merchant with curled beard and long striped wool robe and train of porters, or slaves from as far away as Punt or Alba on errands. Sometimes a unit of spearmen or archers or musketeers marched along to the beat of a drum. Those were like a horizontal bongo slung around the musician's neck, beaten with the hands; a glittering fan-shaped standard on a pole went before.

McAndrews's own town villa wasn't far from the palace, a mark of favor. It had a perimeter wall, too, enclosing stables, gardens, ornamental pools, pillared halls—all on a smaller scale than the palace, of course, but that must be like living in a monster hotel. This was something altogether more civilized, once he'd installed Achaean-made water filters, shower, bath, and flush johns. And given everyone a dose for worms.

He'd *almost* gotten used to the lack of privacy a great man had to endure in this era. It was still a relief when he was alone in the north loggia—alone except for Miw-Sherri. She smiled and handed him a cup of pomegranate juice, a slender brown girl in a long sheath dress banded in bright colors. That and the gold necklace set off skin one shade darker than his. She was a daughter of Ramses himself, not by a Great Wife or even acknowledged concubine, of course; informally, by a harem attendant. It was still a major honor, another sign of Pharaoh's favor . . .

"What I hadn't expected was to actually *like* her," he said to himself—again in English.

He hadn't had one woman around for long since Ygwaina died in childbirth, just before they got chased out of Alba. Even now, he shuddered at that memory. *Could Hong have saved her, if she'd given a damn?* Walker had told him Captain Alston was raising the daughter he'd never seen—told him with that goddamn half smile, half sneer . . .

His son by Miw-Sherri was going on nine months now, and both were doing fine.

"My husband?" Miw-Sherri—the name meant "kitten"— said.

"Just thanking the Gods for you, Sherri," he said, and she snuggled in against him. Egyptians didn't have the Achaean taboo on public displays of affection.

"And thinking deep thoughts," she said, poking a finger into his midriff. "Forgetting that Djehuty and Takushet are coming to dinner."

He slapped his forehead and grinned at her. "I leave all that to you," he said. "Like the wise man in the tale, I 'watch and am silent, recognizing your talents.' "

"Go then, go," she said, laughing. At seventeen she was young but a woman by Egyptian standards, and proud of her skill at managing a great nobleman's household.

He went, out into the private garden near the villa's chapel. There he stripped to his loincloth and took up the *bokken,* looking forward to burning off some of the frustration of a meeting at the palace. He'd gotten into the *iajutsu* habit during the years with Walker—relaxing, and healthy, and occasionally horribly useful. The household staff knew better than to disturb the master. He lost himself in the movements, patterned choreography of breath and will, until he looked up two hours later, running with sweat and chest heaving deep and slow. Something teased at his awareness—

Blank-faced, he took up Martins's *dai-katana,* sliding the long steel free of the sheath and raising it in both hands, right hand over left on the long hilt.

"I'll be with you in a minute," he said, without looking over his shoulder. Then:

"Disssaaaaa!"

The blade swept down, right to left, and the shoulder and arm of the papyrus-reed man-shape before him fell in a clump, the tough springy reeds sheered clear away. Another *kia,* and the return sweep bisected the whole figure.

He turned. The man leaning on his spear watching him was so black that he almost vanished in the shadow of the painted wooden pillars that upbore the portico, like a statue carved in ebony; as tall as McAndrews but a little more lightly built. His kilt was the skin of lions, and a swath of the mane lay on his shoulders; his face was marked by three parallel sets of gouges on each cheek, and by a lion's steady stare from dark eyes. Raw gold circled his arms, a necklace of lion fangs and gold around his neck, and a light bronze Egyptian army-issue fighting ax was tucked into his belt.

"You speak this language?" McAndrews said in Egyptian, going through the ritual of cleaning and sheathing the blade, his hands and face steady as rock despite the hammering of his heart.

"I learn it from traders," the other man said, and nodded. Ocher-dyed braids moved, and the ostrich plumes they carried. "And to fight the Horse Masters, the men of Khem. I am Ghejo, chief among the Marazwe, whom your messenger gave safe-conduct over the border and north to this place."

Suddenly he grinned, teeth very white. "I knew that you were rich, Mek-Andrus. I had heard that you were a wizard, and believed it, from the weapons you gave the Horse Masters. I had heard also that you were a warrior . . . and now I believe that, too."

McAndrews nodded curtly; he had a fair collection of battle scars now. *Yeah, this is a dude you wouldn't disrespect. But so am I, these days.*

"You are my guest," McAndrews said, confering semisacred status on his visitor.

He turned and dived into the tile-edged pool, swam a length, then hauled himself out. Attendants brought a towel and a fresh kilt, set out a table in the shade of the portico, loaded it with roast duck, fresh wheat bread, a salad, steamed vegetables, and a bowl of fruit. Ghejo ate the duck and bread with enthusiasm and looked at the greens as if his host were eating weeds. McAndrews hid a shudder as the Kushite smacked his lips over a jug of Egyptian beer. The stuff was brewed from a fermented mash of barley bread, and tasted like it.

"So," Ghejo said at last. "You are a warrior, a wizard, and have great wealth."

He looked around, obviously determined to be unimpressed and equally obviously awe-smitten.

"What do you wish with us poor desert dwellers?" he went on, a sardonic note in his voice.

"Because you don't build temples like the Egyptians, or write on papyrus, I don't imagine you're a fool," McAndrews said. "I'm not an Egyptian myself."

"Yes," the chief's son said, considering him. "You look more like us—and your voice is not quite a Khemite's. Tales reach us from Elephantine, at the first cataract, where you build your wizard weapons, that you are from a far, strange land. I still ask my question."

McAndrews ate a fig. "Your spear is a good weapon," he said. It was—seven feet of ironwood, with a bronze butt-spike and a long bronze head. "Have your people many like it?"

Ghejo scowled. "You know we do not," he said. "The Horse Masters take our ivory, ebony, plumes, gold dust, slaves, and give us a pittance. When we fight them, we have spears with heads of bone or stone against their bronze, and no chariots. Now we face your thunder-death-makers as well."

McAndrews nodded; with their only real trade route downstream to Egypt, the free Kushites—dwellers in what he'd known as the northern Sudan—were on the receiving end of a monopoly.

"Spearheads are made of copper and tin," McAndrews said. "Or they were, until I brought the art of iron and steel to these lands."

He clapped his hands; a guard brought a sword. It was made to a traditional Egyptian pattern, a half-moon slashing blade with a short straight section above the hilt, called a *kopesh*. This was blue-gray gleaming steel, though. The hilt was checked olive wood and the pommel gold and lapis. It was the blade that drew Ghejo's eyes; they lit as he took it up, tested the edge, stood to sweep it through a few practice slashes.

"A gift," McAndrews said grandly.

"A good gift!" Ghejo replied.

"The ore from which this iron is made," McAndrews said,

wiping his mouth on a linen napkin and eating a fig, "is common in your land."

Ghejo's head came up with a snap like a striking snake. "Say you so?" he breathed softly.

McAndrews smiled, carefully prepared words moving behind his eyes. "I do," he said. "Isn't that interesting?"

Ghejo's eyes narrowed, and he nodded. McAndrews had picked up considerable experience with barbarians over the past ten years. Most of them weren't much moved by the prospect of being civilized; civilization meant someone like Ramses hitting you up with the bill for his palaces and wars and forty-foot gold statues. He *had* found that barbarians were just as enchanted as anyone else at the prospect of wealth, and their chiefs were as greedy for power as any Pharaoh. The trick would be to make any arrangement look like a good solid exchange of value-for-value, from someone their bloodthirsty code could let them respect. They were strange, but not necessarily fools.

Meroe, he thought, as the verbal fencing went on.

The first great sub-Saharan African kingdom had been there, about where Khartoum was in the original history. It was through there that ironworking had spread to the black peoples. That was slated for five hundred years from now, though, in a history that wasn't going to happen. In *this* history, the rest of the world was getting an enormous leg up while black Africans were still just getting started. Egypt had more people than all the rest of the continent put together. Most of Africa was still pygmy and bushman country, nearly empty. His own black ancestors were a thin fringe of farmers and herdsmen along the southern edge of the Sahara. They'd barely begun the great millennia-long migration that would take them all the way to Zululand in the Iron Age, and make them masters of the tropical jungles.

It's not that Alston wants *to do down Mother Africa,* he thought grudgingly. *Or even Cofflin and the others.*

She—all the Islanders—just didn't much care. West Africa wasn't worth their while, considering the effort it would take to push through to the few Neolithic farmers of the savannahs. With so much easier and more agreeable territory open to them . . .

But if *someone* didn't do something, outsiders would take the empty parts of Africa—he'd seen how when farmers met hunters, the farmers pushed the hunters aside without even really noticing they were there. And if the Islanders were too principled to do it, others who'd learned from them would. Black folk would be confined to a little patch in the northwest of the continent, and they'd be an enclave of primitives even there, easy victims for any aggressor.

Ghejo wouldn't know what he was talking about, if he tried to explain.

"You are rich here," the chief said. "You have great power here. Why do you wish to make alliance with us? We live in little villages, or follow our herds." By the way he was looking around, Ghejo wouldn't mind an alternative lifestyle himself.

"I have wealth and power here," McAndrews said. "But I also have many enemies here. If they prevail against me, I would have somewhere to go . . . but not as a fugitive, dependent on the favor of others. And with me I could bring many others, skilled in making"—he nodded to the steel _kopesh_—"and other things besides; the fire-weapons."

"Ahhh . . ." Ghejo said. McAndrews recognized the look; it was a man seeing possibilities. "We must speak more of this—and I must consult my neighbors . . ."

"You will go from here with rich gifts," McAndrews said, smiling. "And perhaps you and many others might gain some experience with the new weapons in the war that begins soon, if you could furnish troops and workmen . . ."

There was a lot of potential around Meroe. He knew how to build dams and canals—the area south of Khartoum had plenty of land that could be watered, to support millions of people where now a few villagers scratched fields of millet and herded goats. There was iron ore nearby, and other minerals fairly close. If he wanted a better climate, the Ethiopian highlands were right there to the east, and to west it was flat open grasslands for six thousand miles to the Atlantic. Easy for innovations to spread. When the Nantucketers, or the Achaeans, landed from their helicopters, they weren't going to find nekkid savages with grass skirts, nohow.

I'm just a dumb nigger with his head full of Afrocentrist shit, hey, Walker King of Men? Didn't occur to you that if I couldn't find the black Egypt of my dreams, I could fucking build one of my own, did it?

CHAPTER SIXTEEN

November, 10 A.E.—Western Anatolia
October, 10 A.E.—Long Island, Republic of Nantucket
October, 10 A.E.—Coast of northwestern Iberia
Octrober, 10 A.E.—Long Island, Republic of Nantucket
November, 10 A.E.—Western Anatolia

"No, I don't think retreating blisters hurt any worse than advancing blisters," Private Vaukel Telukuo said seriously, glancing down at his moving boots. "About the same, they are."

"That's supposed to be a *joke,* Vauk, you great Fiernan gowk," Johanna Gwenhaskieths growled.

When she glanced aside and saw his grin she gave him a halfhearted elbow in the ribs.

"Could be worse," he said. "Could be raining."

"It *was* raining half the morning," she replied.

That was obvious enough; the track they followed to the southeast was deep in mud. That clung to boots, adding a half pound to every step, and a constant squelching undertone. Her company was near the end of the front section, two hundred and fifty helmeted heads ahead of her, then the baggage and sick-carts, then about as many more behind that. It looked a formidable host to her eyes; ten times as many fighting men as her clan had, about as many as her whole *teuatha.*

Former tribe, she reminded herself. Some might go back to Alba after their hitch, but she certainly couldn't. *The Corps is my clan and the Republic my tribe now. And this is a piss-poor excuse for a road.*

Especially compared to the watertight ones in Nantucket. It was pretty obvious that someone had driven a big herd of cattle this way not long ago; Johanna looked at the cowpats and hoofprints with envy. Driving off cattle was *fun*; besides, it meant beef.

Somebody ahead stumbled, and she cursed as she checked

and nearly stumbled herself in the slippery mud. She cursed again, silently, as she tried to get her legs back into the automatic rhythm that would carry her along without much thinking on how they hurt. It was well past the stop for the noon meal, but not nearly time to break off the day's march and make camp.

Helmet, rifle, bayonet, entrenching tool, two grenades, canteen, a hundred rounds in her bandolier and another hundred in the haversack, four pounds of dog biscuit and jerky with a couple of onions and some salt, bedroll, her share of her eight-Marine section's unit equipment, starting with a section of canvas boiled in linseed oil . . . At the beginning of a day, it didn't seem like much. When you'd been marching or fighting or both every day for a week, it began to feel like you were carrying a chief's chariot on your back.

"What I don't understand," she said, scratching, "is why we keep retreating. We beat the Ringapi at O'Rourke's Ford, we handled Walker's handfast men pretty rough seven days later at Fork Mountain—and every time, as soon as they break off we back off. All we've really done is burn farms and forage. What's the point?"

A voice from two ranks back snarled: "The point is the officers figure out what to do. We just do it."

"Yes, Corporal Hook," she said. He was a bad one to cross, doubly so now he'd been promoted. Granted he deserved it, but . . .

"We're luring them into a trap," a cheerful voice said.

She looked up, started, and almost stumbled again. Colonel O'Rourke was leading his horse back down the column.

"If you say so, sir . . . When they catch us, they try to make us run; when we run, they try to catch us. Maybe they'll be so tired from chasing us they'll be easy meat?"

O'Rourke chuckled. "Not quite, Private. Tell me, how have the rations been?"

"Fine, sir, can't complain, haven't touched my iron rations . . . oh."

She looked over her shoulder at the desolation that was in their wake. *And this miserable road to haul supplies on,* she thought.

"Oh, indeed," O'Rourke said, and led his horse on down toward the end of the column.

"And what did he mean, then?" Vaukel asked.

"That the enemy are going to get hungry before we do,"

Johanna chuckled. "Now that we've eaten the land bare, or burned it."

The weight of rifle and pack seemed lighter than they had a minute ago. She scratched again, hoping it was just sweat and that she hadn't come down with lice. Besides the medics' warnings about how they carried disease, one of the pleasures of Camp Grant—after the shock of having her head hair cropped to a quarter inch and the rest shaved—had been *not itching* for the first time in her life. You couldn't always avoid them in the field, but the knowledge that you didn't *have* to have nits all your life had been inexpressibly wonderful.

Nantucket was wonderful itself. She hoped she'd live to see it again.

"This is it, then," Jared Cofflin said aloud.

They were about a mile off the shore of the North Fork; it was a low line in the distance, lime-green of marsh and the green-gold-scarlet colors of autumn trees. He leveled a pair of binoculars.

"Well, not a bad job of navigation, if I say so myself," he said. And it wasn't, not with only a compass and logline to find his way on the map.

The wind was out of the north now, and he squinted beneath the brim of his cap as they scudded a little south of westward before it, the sun low enough on the horizon to be a nuisance. *Good boat,* he thought with a burst of affection. *She answers sweet.*

"Ready to come about," he said, busying himself with the line that ran through pulleys on the boom to a sliding track behind him along the stern. "Prepare to gybe."

Oddly enough, running before the wind was the most difficult sort of small-boat sailing. He pulled the tiller toward him, and hauled in the line with his left, to get the boom amidships; you didn't want it crashing back and forth across the cockpit.

"Gybe ho! 'Ware boom!"

The catboat was pointing due south now, and the boom swung out to starboard from the midships position. The sail thuttered as its unstayed edge caught the wind for a second, then cracked as it moved out, filled, and settled down. Time to build up just enough way on her, then—

"Lower away," he said. "Reef her."

Martinelli and Martha were on the rope, lowering the gaff and the sail with it. The children stood to the inboard edge of the boom and fastened the loose folds down with the ties sewn into the sail; they made a creditable job of it, too, if not Guard-neat.

The channel in was marked by poles with string pennants; there was a creek flowing into a shallow inlet, with salt marsh full of osprey nests perched in dead trees on the port and a spit of dry land to starboard. One of the big fish hawks punched the water not far away in a fist of spray, flogged itself back into the air with a foot of thrashing silver in its talons. He could see the mad lemon-yellow ferocity of its eye as it went by the *Boojum,* intent on its own business and ignoring him. The dock poked out into the water, a board surface on hemlock piles, with rope fenders along the sides.

He let the feel of the water and wind flow through his hands on line and tiller, up from his feet on the deck. He could smell the land now, silt and brackish water and growing things with an autumnal muskiness under it, strong even against the breeze.

"Lower away all . . . *now!*" he said.

The gaff came down the rest of the way with a run, and the two adults leaped to secure it. Martha and the petty officer took up the oars and fended off, the *Boojum* coming to rest against the wharf behind another boat that might have been its twin. There were plenty of hands on the dock to grab the lines thrown to them and make fast, not to mention a brace of excited dogs that looked to be mostly collie. They barked and dashed about until called to heel, then lay with their eyes bright and ears cocked forward.

"Afternoon, Chief," Thomas Hollard said.

The Marine commander's elder brother was in his late thirties, Cofflin knew, a little shorter and darker than Ken. He looked older than his years to pre-Event eyes, the way most people over twenty or so did nowadays; solid and troll-strong, his skin weathered and roughened by outdoor work in all weathers. The hand that shook Cofflin's was hard with callus, with knuckles like walnuts.

What Dad would have called workingman's hands, Jared thought as he shook the offered palm.

The elder Hollard's long straight nose had been broken at some time—during the Alban War, he remembered from the file he'd read yesterday—and reset a little crooked. The farmer sported a short-cropped beard, and wore dark woolen pants, white linen shirt, anorak-style jacket and high, laced boots. Probably his company clothes, and most of the rest of the farm's folk—eight adults, a dozen kids—were in clean, coarse linsey-woolsey bib overalls. Some of the kids barefoot—not surprising on a dry autumn day, seeing that a shirt cost a week's wages for a laborer, and a pair of shoes took a month's pay. One of the definitions of *affluent* in this Year 10 was having more clothes than a set to wear and a set to wash and a set for church or Meeting. Beside Hollard was his auburn-haired Fiernan wife Tanaswada, carrying their ten-month-old youngest; she was in her late twenties, had been a young widow with a baby at the breast in the aftermath of the Battle of the Downs when she met and married the Nantucketer. That boy must be the oldest child, now a red-haired, straw-hatted youngster giving the chief bashful glances, and admiring ones at Martinelli's Coast Guard uniform.

Let's see, three of their own, and another adoptee, five all up, and they're young yet—Tom here must be trying to raise himself a labor force from scratch, to be ready when his immigrants set up on their own.

"Bill, Mary, why don't you give a hand with the Cofflins' stuff?" Hollard said with an easy authority. "Chief, Ms. Cofflin, you want to see the old Alonski place now, or tomorrow?"

"Might as well take a first look now," he said. "If it's not too much trouble."

"No trouble at all," Hollard said genially. "Hey, what's that?"

"Tuna," Martha said. "We ran into a catcher boat on our way over, thought you might like some."

"Thanks; we can find some room on the grill," Hollard said. His wife gave a frank cry of delight; fish was a staple nowadays, but that meant salt cod, not this. "Neighborly of you."

Cofflin nodded acknowledgment. They'd met fairly often, since the farmer was something of a leader among the Long Island settlers and acted as delegate to cast their votes in the Meeting, but not often enough to be more than friendly acquaintances.

"Chuck, you finished the chores, didn't you?" Hollard said.

"Ayup, Dad. Checked the water troughs, an' everything."

"Why don't you show these youngsters around, then," he said.

His wife cut in: "Make sure your sister isn't left out." A slight scowl went with the boy's nod; the natural reaction of a ten-year-old burdened with someone half his age. "And don't turn up for dinner covered in mud, either!"

"Thanks, Dad—sure, Mom—you guys want to see the place?"

The children dashed off up the dirt track that led up the low slope inland, followed by barking dogs and more sedately by most of the adults. The farmer and his wife walked more slowly still with the Cofflins.

"Just through here," Hollard said. "It's a pretty enough place."

Cofflin nodded silently when they passed through the belt of trees along the shoreline. A big field had been cleared from the forest, forty acres or so, even most of the stumps gone. Shin-high autumn grass waved green-gold in the afternoon light, starred with late wildflowers, tall orange-yellow butter-and-egg plants, red-purple deer grass and hound's-tongue. A few black-coated steers raised their muzzles to glance at the newcomers, then returned to their cropping, their jaws making wet tearing sounds; only a slight ranginess in the legs and the wicked look of their horns broke the Angus look of the three-quarter-bred cattle. Across the pasture lay a house made of squared logs weathered brownish-gray, sixty feet by thirty, with a shingled roof and a fieldstone chimney in the middle of it. Several long clapboard sheds stood nearby, and a scatter of big trees left when the land was cleared, their leaves turning maple-scarlet, oak-yellow, and beech-red with autumn. They walked up to it through a neglected lawn and peered into the windows, seeing darkness and bulky shapes.

"That's the Alonski place," Hollard said redundantly. "We were partners, when he started. He wanted to do some serious fishing here, hence the drying sheds—there are oyster beds, right enough, good lobstering, and God knows plenty of fish out there in the Sound; and he thought he could start a bit of a town here eventually, inn for travelers, smithy and suchlike."

He jerked a thumb southward over his shoulder toward the Great West Road. "It's not that he wasn't a hard worker. It was the transport costs killed him—couldn't compete with the boats working out of Fogarty's Cove, and it ate his mustering-out grant and everything he could scrape together, beg, or borrow. I liked him, he was a man you'd want to have at your back. But stubborn?"

"Stubborn as a whole sounder of pigs," Tanaswanda said. "With a mule thrown in."

Her husband nodded. "His cousin Pulakis has the farm two sections east toward the Cove. When Alonski drowned in the storm of '07, his wife and kids moved in with them."

Hollard shook his head. "He was a good man."

"Indeed he was," Martha said quietly.

That's right, Cofflin thought, glancing aside at her. *He was in Marian's commando group, when they got Martha out of the Olmecs' hands.*

Hollard nodded at her. "Right you are, Madam Councilor," he said formally. Then he went on: "The parcel's one hundred sixty acres, not counting the salt marsh—it was exempted from the Coastal Reserve on the off-chance that it might actually become a town. I think in another five, mebbe ten years that might have worked, but not now. There's this clearing, I've been turning my cattle in for summer pasture, and the house— I've kept it weathertight, used it for storage—good tube well, no trouble to fit up a water system with a wind pump, and run it out to the drying sheds, they'd do fine for stables. Another thirty or forty acres fit for clearing, the rest good woodlot, and there's the dock. Nice sheltered little inlet, this here is actually sort of a peninsula between the creek and a marsh."

"Looks good," Cofflin said. "For the buyer's needs."

Martha gave a slight dry chuckle at the younger man's startlement. "It's not for us," she said. "Commodore Alston and her partner want it. For vacations, at first, and then as a retirement place. And to raise horses."

Hollard blinked; then his face split in a grin that took years off his age. "The *skipper* for a neighbor?" he said in delight, then wiped away the smile with an effort. "Well, you realize I do have to see that Betty—Alonski's widow—gets what she can . . ."

"Indeed you do," Martha said, touching him on the arm. "But we can discuss that tomorrow."

They walked up the dirt lane with its wagon-wheel ruts, through a broad belt of uncleared timber where leaves lay in drifts like old gold and scraps of crimson velvet—some still floating from the passage of children and dogs. Squirrels went up the trunks in streaks of fire, or hung from branches ratchet-chattering anger at being disturbed; a raccoon eyed them dubiously and waddled off, fat with autumn bounty. Beyond the wood lay the imperfectly graveled surface of the Great West Road that ran along the northern shore of Long Island, finishing as a forest trail opposite the lonely little outpost on Manhattan. Right now it was far from empty.

Been a while since I heard that sound, Cofflin thought. Booted feet moving in unison, crunching on gravel; his mind filled in the arms swinging, the whole like a great centipede built up of human beings. *'Bout a hundred, hundred-odd.* Camp Grant, the Nantucket Marine Corps training enclave, was five miles or so west of here. They halted; the rest of their party had, too, on the other side of the road, probably at the children's insistence.

They do love a parade, Jared thought grimly. *Wish it was the Shriners or the Fourth of July.*

A mounted standard-bearer walked his horse around the curve to the eastward, Old Glory streaming out from the staff socketed in his right stirrup with a flutter and snap. Jared Cofflin removed his hat, holding it over his heart; the others did likewise, Hollard's wife and a few of the others making the Fiernan triple-touch gesture of respect to the Republic's banner first. The fifty states the stars represented might be far away on the oceans of eternity, but the ideas it stood symbol for were very much alive. Behind the mounted man came another leading a horse, the company commander.

Walks where his troops do, Cofflin thought with an inward nod of approval.

Behind him came the hundred and thirty-two Marines, in a khaki-clad column of fours with their Werder rifles slung over their shoulders and Fritz-style helmets strapped to their heavy marching packs. The faces under the floppy canvas campaign hats were young, sweating, and tired with the day's route-march out to Fogarty's Cove and back, the bodies hard and fit with good feeding and constant exercise. Shorter by a couple of inches than a corresponding group in the twentieth would have been, because nearly everyone except the officers and senior NCOs were native to this century, but all in all a good-looking group of young men and women. The Republic could do far worse for a source of future citizens.

The company commander gave the group by the roadside a casual glance; then his eyes whipped back to Jared Cofflin's face. The chief felt himself flushing slightly, and made a slight gesture with his head, a wordless *carry on.* His: *God, but I hate this sort of thing,* he kept to himself.

"Company!" the young Marine captain barked. "Eyes"—it ran down the chain of command—"*right!*" He saluted.

The faces snapped toward the Republic's head of state, a few sets of eyes growing wide, and one luckless newly minted graduate of Camp Grant missed a step and had to skip-hop to get the rhythm back. Cofflin kept his face grave as he returned the gesture of respect, but there was a wry grin at the back of his eyes, remembering what one of *his* instructors would have done if he'd screwed up on parade when the president happened to be passing by. That rifleman was going to get one awesome ass-chewing, probably. Not that he hadn't hated square-bashing and close-order drill himself, but it had some relevance to actual fighting, here, and it maintained its immemorial usefulness in teaching solidarity.

"Fine-looking bunch," Hollard said judiciously, when they'd passed and the last pack mule was turning small with distance. "And *hungry,* thank God."

Cofflin raised a brow, and the farmer continued:

"Amazing how much a couple of battalions of recruits can eat. The Coast Guard here feeds its Marines a lot better than the Navy ever did back up in the twentieth, if *my* father's stories are anything to go on. What with taxes and all, it's at least some help when they go shopping, Chief."

"I'm not amazed," Martha said in her dry business voice. "I have to draw up the budget statements."

"We can talk about that later, too," her husband said neutrally, exchanging a glance with Hollard and seeing no surprise.

Well, the man is *a leader in the Meeting here, and a delegate.* He'd know there was more to this visit than a favor for Marian Alston. Under the Republic's constitution, the outports handled local affairs with Town Meetings of their own. They also elected representatives to the central House of Delegates, entitled to debate and vote for those who couldn't make it to Nantucket Town. The chief had to keep close track of those their neighbors looked to for guidance, perhaps especially those in the outports.

Tom Hollard was among the more successful of the farming settlers here on Long Island; if Jared hadn't read the files, it would still have been obvious as they crossed the road. Cultivated fields stretched to either side and southward to the crimson-yellow line of the woods, apples glowed red in the green of young orchards, and copper-leafed vineyards trained on T-shaped wooden stakes showed grapes in purple bunches.

It showed too as they walked up the long tree-lined graveled drive to the farmhouse. Like most, that had started as a log box on a fieldstone cellar and foundation, sixty feet by thirty, the type built by the Agriculture Department's contractors as part of the initial settlement scheme. The thick scatter of tall trees left standing around it showed what the material had been like, white oaks and shagbark hickories and tulip poplars, chestnuts and maples, beeches and elms, most of them sixty feet to the lowest branch and showing the straight vertical growth of mature closed-canopy forest. For building they need only be squared by a portable steam-driven circular saw and deeply notched at the ends to be assembled into a thick strong structure; the Department's specialized teams could throw one up in an afternoon. Over the last decade Tom had added an upper story to his, clapboards of white-painted oak plank to the outside, and an extension to one end that turned the box into an L-shape; he could just see laundry flapping on a line in the kitchen yard. A two-story verandah spanned the long southwest face.

Woodsmoke wafted from the two stone chimneys, and the mouth-watering smell of bread baking. Sheep kept the big fenced lawn smooth. A baseball diamond had been marked out in one corner of the enclosure—Tom Hollard was a founder of the local Little League, too—and there were swings and a sandbox and soccer goalposts. Quick-growing Babylonica willows drooped their branches into a pond where ducks and geese floated.

The business side hadn't been neglected either. There was a large truck garden, green rows with wheat-straw mulch between them. Off a little to the eastward—hence usually downwind—were two big hip-roofed barns, one with twin wooden silos. More besides that: piggery, chicken coops, turkey house, dairy. A thick-timbered icehouse sank nearly to its eaves in the ground, corncribs with their slatted sides bulging yellow, sheds for equipment, a small winery, a carpenter's and a farrier's workshed, two big windmills filling a water tank and bored-log pipes leading about from that. Fenced paddocks held several score of black-coated cattle, plus a couple of Jersey crossbreeds, a flock of four-foot moas who pranced in agitated alarm, and six horses. Two were half-Morgans for riding and general work. Four were the precious offspring coaxed from the seed of the single elderly Clydesdale stallion who'd been on-Island at the time of the Event, big and hairy-footed and strong.

"Two hundred twenty-five acres cleared," Hollard said with quiet satisfaction, noting the direction of his guests' gaze. His hands opened and closed in unconscious reflex, the thick callus scritching. "We could get another twenty-five this winter, and pull the stumps on fifteen in the spring—more if I can get a steam-hauler and a winch in for a couple of weeks. Costs like blazes, and powder for blowing stumps isn't cheap either."

Better than two hundred acres, with axes and two-man saws, Cofflin thought. That was reason enough for genuine pride. Cleared fields this size meant thousands of tons of hardwood removed.

They walked up a flagged path from the roadway and onto the verandah; there were roses to either side, lilac bushes, and a wisteria was making a determined effort to climb a trellis along the south wall. The ends of the rafter-beams overhead had been carved into snarling wolf-heads in the primitive, vigorous style of the charioteer tribes of Alba. Fangs from the real article grinned white in their mouths; the pelts doing rug-duty on the floor showed where they'd come from. The pillars that upheld the balcony and sloping roof above that were man-thick trunks of black walnut, polished and carved in abstract geometric designs like Fiernan spirit-poles. The work was about half-done; a basket of shavings stood by one, with a toolbox of mallets, chisels, and gouges beside it.

"That's Tanaswada and Jane," Hollard said, running a hand over the dark beauty of the wood. "They've got a knack for it. Saucarn here did the wolf-heads."

The farmworker shrugged. "It brings luck," he said, scuffing one foot against the flagstone floor. "Frightens off the *gowalun*. Easy enough, with good steel tools." Then he ducked inside and returned with a double-barreled shotgun and a leather bandolier of brass-and-cardboard shells across his chest. "Thought I'd better keep an eye on the grapes until sundown, Tom," he said, in an accent that mixed Yankee twang with Sun People choppiness.

Several of the dogs walked over to him with waving tails and canine grins and a general air of: *Hey, that's a great idea, let's go kill something, right this way, boss.*

"Yup," Hollard said. "If it has feathers or fur and comes near the vines, shoot it. Bill, you take a rifle and go with Saucarn. See the rest of you at suppertime."

The farmworkers scattered to their tasks. The head of the household and his guests seated themselves around an outdoor table made from a single yard-wide plank of curly maple, waxed and polished. The verandah had a pleasant lived-in look, with balls of wool and knitting needles dropped in a willow-withe basket, a leather-bound book on a side table with a maple leaf to mark someone's place, and a yellow brindled cat napping on a cushion. It opened an eye to study the strangers, stretched, yawned, circled, and went back to sleep with its tail tucked over its black nose. One of the dogs who hadn't gone with the armed men came over to butt its head under Hollard's palm as he sat, thumping its tail on the flagstones. Tanaswada came out with a tray of cookies and a pot of coffee, then sat and opened her blouse, unself-consciously setting her baby to nursing. That still took Cofflin a little aback—Martha had always insisted on privacy—but the Alban custom seemed to be winning out all over the Republic.

Hollard poured, added Jersey cream and maple sugar for those who asked for it, and nodded in the direction of his vineyard. "Birds love ripe grapes," he said. "So do foxes and black bears and wolves, that's why I had Bill take the rifle." His foot nudged one of the wolf pelts that were scattered across the verandah's floor. "I don't really mind the bears, they're just a nuisance, but I'm going to by-God see every wolf on Long Island shot out, and Dane Sweet can lump it if he doesn't like it."

"I don't understand why he gets so upset," Tanaswada said. "Back in Alba, we always killed every wolf we could, and they're still there and still eating our sheep. Sometimes in a really bad winter they eat humans—or did before we had guns. Children or old people caught alone, especially."

"Mmmm, it's not that simple," Cofflin said. He held up a hand to forestall the farmer's answer: "Mind you, you're right about Long Island. Sheep and wolves don't go all that well together in a place this size. He's right about the continent overall—room for everybody, even the wolves."

"As long as they aren't near my stock. I suppose you have to keep everyone happy," Hollard said, satisfied in a grumbling fashion. "Sweet repairs bicycles for a living. *He* doesn't have to worry about losing beasts he needs to make his loan payments to the Town."

"Thought you'd paid out?" Martha said.

Hollard nodded. "I have," he said. "Lots are still working on it. And I could use another loan myself—there're things the place needs, say a little steam compressor for some power tools and a chaff-cutter, and . . . There's the tax increases, too, just when most of us were starting to see the end of our settlement loans. It's frustrating."

Cofflin nodded in turn. Land wasn't worth much to a homesteader without tools and stock, and it took a good long while to make a farm a paying proposition, the more so when you were learning by doing with only books and Angelica Brand's extension officers to fall back on. Some of the settlers had failed completely, some were flourishing like the Hollards, and many more were struggling along somewhere in between.

"Good harvest this year?" he said.

Hollard and his wife looked at each other and grinned.

"Well, the wheat, rye, barley, and oats came in all right," he said. "We're finally getting a clue. Lord, the mistakes we made the first couple of years! Come Monday we're getting some seasonal people in to start on the apples, then the grape harvest. Corn's been good, so far, and the canola. We *didn't* get the apples all in last year, and had to let the pigs eat the windfalls, and you heard about the birds, bears, and grapes—every God-damned bird in creation passes this way twice a year, all hungry from their travels. Bloody migratory welfare fowl—and what those . . ." he stopped and left out a word "passenger pigeons do to a grainfield doesn't bear thinking about, thank God the kids're getting old enough to handle bird-scaring. Then there are the rest of the potatoes."

He reached out to touch wood, and Tanaswada made a geometric gesture of propitiation. "Assuming the weather holds and assuming we get everything in timely, not too bad. Prices have been reasonable this year, despite all that Alban wheat coming in."

"Then you get your easy season," Cofflin said, chuckling slightly to show sympathy. Hollard's laugh was full-throated.

"Oh, right. Nothing but the fall plowing and planting, muckspreading, shucking and shelling the corn, ring-barking trees and rolling logs and burning 'em and teaming the prime ones out for the timberyard hauler to pick up—"

Tanaswada put a cloth over her shoulder, followed it with the baby, and began patting its back. "*I've* never had it so easy as here," she said. "There, little one, that feels better, doesn't it? Tom, dear, you sit on a machine, the horses pull it, and it cuts the hay . . . I drive another machine and it turns and rakes it . . . all that's left to do is pitch it onto the wagon and take it to the barn. Can you call that *work*?"

"Yes," her husband said.

When the general chuckle had died down, he went on: "I was afraid you had bad news about Ken."

Cofflin shook his head. "Far as I know, he's doing his job well enough." He cocked an eyebrow. "Ever wish you had it, Tom?"

"Never," Hollard said promptly. "Alba was enough fighting for me, unless someone comes here." He looked at his wife and child, around at home and land. "Then we'll fight. Meantime, I'll leave it to Ken and Kathryn and the others. I've got my family and a good farm and I'm easy with my neighbors. That's enough for me; I'm content to be a . . . what's the old word?"

"Yeoman?" Martha said.

"Ayup."

Jared Cofflin sipped at the bitter-tasting coffee, pouring in more of the thick Jersey cream and wishing for the ten-thousandth time that they'd had something more than ornamental coffee plants to plant out down in the Carribean. Or that they had time to send an expedition to Ethiopia; the books said the wild coffee there was a lot better than this. Which was drinkable, if you added some chicory, but only just.

"Well, the whole purpose of this war is to make sure we *won't* have to fight on our own doorsteps again," he pointed out. "Surely your brother's made that clear to you."

"Oh, it's clear enough to *me*," Tom Hollard said. "Not everyone looks that far ahead, though. And like I said, the war taxes're hitting a lot of us just when we were finally getting out from under."

"Then it's up to us to convince 'em," Jared said, settling down to work.

A song came from the forecastle of the *Chamberlain* after the commodore's officer-guests had departed; voices in soft harmony with a flute and the strum of a guitar:

> *There is much that life withholds*
> *There is much that life denies—*
> *I am content . . . and most content . . .*
> *With seaward-gazing eyes.*

Marian Alston smiled up through the sloping windows at the frosted stars. A lot of songs had been pulled out of books and record collections that first year after the Event because there was no other way to have music besides making it yourself . . . *but the old words made more sense these days.*

"Well, that went off well," she said aloud.

She kicked off her boots, threw her jacket over the back of one chair, and sank back onto the broad semicircle of cushioned bench that ran around the rear of the cabin below the slanting windows, stretching her arms behind her head. Nothing came through the open panes but a little cool sea air; nothing showed save campfires ashore and the riding lights of the ships on the calm sea, and the crescent moon above casting a westward glimmerpath toward Nantucket and home. A single lantern turned the big room into a place of shadows, gleams from polished wood and metal, from the black-lacquered surfaces of the two sets of *katana* and *wazikashi* racked on the wall, from the glass that covered the family portraits of them with the girls. It was quiet outside, and the music came plain:

> *My dreams sail with the tall white ships*
> *My heart, it cannot bide at home;*
> *I share the blue of singing space*
> *The bitter kiss of foam.*
> *The pageantry of storm and cloud;*
> *The mystery of ebb and flow*
> *The song of water as I sleep . . .*
> *All of these I know.*

Swindapa came back from the small head that connected to the commodore's quarters portside and stopped at the sideboard to pour them both drinks. Marian watched her partner's panther-graceful nakedness with a relaxed appreciation that suddenly turned to a stab of joy so piercing that it was pain as well. Memory overwhelmed her for an instant; of a night down along the coast of Brazil, the trades steady on the port quarter in the midnight watch. The two of them had gone forward to watch the phosphorescent waters peeling aside from the bow like waves of heated metal, their wake glowing behind the ship like a mile-long streak of light across the night-dark sea. Swindapa jumped up to the rail, leaning far out with one hand on the shrouds, her loosened hair trailing to the side like a torrent of silver; turned with the wonder of it in her eyes . . .

> *No lesser joy can dim the spell*
> *Of quietly enchanted hours;*
> *When the sea wore reflected stars*
> *Upon a breast like flowers.*

She took the glass and gave a sigh of contentment as the other curled up beside her and they laid their heads together, kissing and murmuring into each other's ears.

"Yes, dinner was like a feast of kinfolk," Swindapa said, after a minute. "It's a lot like being a part of a lineage, being in the Guard."

> *Brine-scented dawns—seafaring dreams*
> *How richly these have dowered me;*
> *That I should go through all my days*
> *Companioned by the sea . . .*

"That's the way I wanted it, 'dapa," Alston replied. *Band of brothers,* she thought—a bit sexist, but traditional. "Mmmm, that's good," she added.

"The whiskey, or this?" Swindapa chuckled, as she undid the buttons of the other's shirt and moved her hands inside.

"Both," Marian said, and finished off the glass. It was due that much respect, part of her last stock of Maker's Mark. Then she pulled her partner to her, trailing lips down her neck, to the breasts warm in her hands, shadow-black fingers against pearl-white skin. The Fiernan gave a shivering cry of delight. Marian raised her head with a chuckle and said:

"The only question is, shall we make out here and scandalize the night-watch with the sound effects, or move over to the bed?"

Swindapa's hands were on her belt buckle. "Both, of course," she said, grinning affectionately. Solemnly for a moment: "It may be our last time to share ourselves."

The forecastle was silent now, and there was a harsher music in the background; one of the Sun People war bands on shore, roaring out the tune to the squeal of a primitive bagpipe and a bohdran and something shatteringly like a Lamberg drum. It was an ancient battle chant, with verses that were new since the Eagle People came to Alba:

> Axes flash, longswords swing
> Shining armor's piercing ring;
> Horses run with a polished shield
> *Fight those bastards 'till they yield!*

> Midnight mare and golden roan
> Strike for the lands we call our own;
> Sound the horn, and shout the cry—
> *How many of them can we make die?*

"Whoooooooppp!" Heather Alston-Kurlelo screeched, and let go of the rope, yodeling as she flew across the barn. *"Whoooooooo!"*

For a moment she hung suspended at the top of her arc, feeling the floating sensation of it lifting her stomach and watching the inside of the barn roof through a mist of her own red hair. Then she fell screeching in delicious fear into the soft prickliness of the hay, smelling the dried memory of flowers. It closed over her head and she swam upright in it, wading her way to the beam where the others sat and hitching herself up to sit astraddle it, kicking her bare feet and giggling.

"That was *fun*," she said.

"Yeah, but you shouldn't yell so loud," Chuck Hollard said. He looked down to the ground floor of the barn. It was mostly stalls, with the sweet-musky smell of horses; and leather, tack oil, oats, the beery smell of silage in the troughs. The horses made sort of wet crunching sounds as they munched, snorting now and then, or shifting weight from one foot to another with a *clomp* sound as the hollow hoof hit the packed dirt and straw. The newcomers had already helped him curry and feed them; grudgingly, he admitted to himself that they seemed to know what they were doing despite being townies. Jared Jr. was still down there.

"We aren't supposed to toss like that by ourselves without someone to check on us," he said. "Dad'll burn my *butt* if he finds out."

"Yeah, Uncle Jared would be mad, too." Lucy sighed. She got up and ran out on one of the narrower beams that spanned the waist of the barn and then back. "But he doesn't spank nearly's hard as our mom. Mom Marian," she added. " 'Specially when we do something we shouldn't on shipboard. Then she *really* gets mad."

"Oh, yeah," Heather said, rolling her eyes. "Like, *really* mad. ZHOtopo."

"You actually get to go *sailing*? Really sailing—far foreign?" Chuck asked. Raw envy freighted his voice.

Heather dangled her feet over the edge of the hayloft. The hay behind her had a smell that made her want to sneeze, and to throw herself into it again like they'd been doing. She picked pieces of it out of her hair and looked at the rope that ran along the pulleyway down the center of the barn's ridgepole.

"Oh, yeah," she said casually, enjoying herself. "All around the world—lots of times. Even when there's fights."

"Only once," Lucy pointed out.

I hate it when she does that. She always spoils a story, Heather thought, and stuck out her tongue at her sister, who went on maddeningly:

"And she didn't *expect* there was going to be a fight then. It just sort of happened. We stay home when she expects trouble. Like now."

"Nothing happens here," Chuck said, sick with envy. "Jesus Christ"—he sounded very like his father at that moment—"but I wish I could sail away and see all those places . . . and all the fights . . ."

"Fights are scary," Lucy said. "Looks like there are cool things to do here, though. Riding."

"Yeah," Heather said. "Ponies of our own."

"There's hunting, too," Chuck said. "Dad says I can have a hunting gun of my own soon. Dad and Mom and the other grown-ups hunt all sorts of things. Wolves, bears, white-tails, turkeys."

"We shot an elephant last year," Heather said nonchalantly.

"Oh," Chuck replied, crushed.

"We *ate* the elephant," Lucy said. "It was our *moms* shot it."

"Yeah, and then all these little brown people, locals—"

"Sort of yellow-brown—not just brown like me—"

"Real little, they were all grown-up and only a bit taller than us—"

"With funny-looking faces. They chopped up the elephant. Some of them went right *inside* it," Lucy said. "And chopped bits up."

"Like butchering a cow?" Chuck asked curiously, his eyes alight. A boy didn't grow up on a farm with any excess of squeamishness.

"Yeah," Heather said, "but it was *big*. Tall as this barn!"

"Well, tall as the place we're sitting on right now."

"Lucy, stop *doing* that! You're spoiling it!"

"No I'm not! It's better if you tell it just the way it was!"

"Hey!" Chuck held up his hands. "Hey, I want to hear about this bit."

"Oh," Heather said. "Well, then we built big fires on the beach, and the little people all put grass skirts and stuff on—"

" . . . and they painted themselves, sort of like Indians—"

"—and they put bone rattles on their ankles—"

"—and we did too—"

"And we all *danced*."

"And ate the elephant and all sorts of stuff."

"Raw?" Chuck asked in ghoulish enthusiasm.

"No, stupid. Toasted over the fires. All the grown-ups were dancing too . . . well, a lot of them. The sailors. And *that's* when the Tartessian boat came. Mom—"

"Both our moms."

"Went down and talked with them, and they got *really* mad. I could tell, even if they weren't shouting."

"That's when they had the battle?"

"No, that was a couple of days later," Heather said. She quelled a memory of cold fear. "Our moms went off into the woods with a lot of the hands. We stayed in the camp."

"We could hear the shooting, though," Lucy said.

"Yeah, and then our moms came back and then in the morning they had the big fight in the bay. That's when we . . . well, they . . . captured the two Tartessian ships. And a whole *lot* of gold. And ivory and silk and, oh, tons of wonderful cargo. I got this little cat carved out of jade, I'll show you."

"Plunder!" Chuck said. "Hey, *cool.*"

"Plundering is against regulations," Lucy said pedantically. "Only pirates plunder. This was *prize money.*"

"What's the difference?" Chuck asked, intrigued.

"We're the good guys," Lucy said. "So when we capture the bad guys' ships and take all their stuff, it's okay. And that's how we're going to buy that land down near the water."

"And have ponies and stuff," Heather finished triumphantly.

"I'm sort of busy, Doctor," Kenneth Hollard said. They were usually on first-name terms; the formality backed up the meaning of the words.

"I know, sir," Justin Clemens said. "It's about the smallpox, sir."

Hollard's long face changed from tightly reined impatience to a fear kept under equally close control. Nobody who'd been there when the disease broke loose in Babylon's teeming warrens could react otherwise.

He rose, silencing Clemens with a hand, and went to the door flap of his tent. A murmured command sent the sentries further from the tent, and posted others around it. Then he ducked back into the cooling olive-tinted, canvas-smelling gloom and turned up the kerosene lantern that hung from the central ridgepole.

"Now, let me have it, Doctor. I thought we had it under control?"

"We do, sir, in Kar-Duniash," Clemens said. He sat forward in the folding chair, knotting his hands together. "And we've got a good start on a vaccination program here in Anatolia. I thought we had reason to celebrate."

"So did I," Hollard said. "Like your wedding, Doctor."

Clemens smiled for a second; Hollard had arranged for a wedding feast in the palace, with his royal brother-in-law dropping by with a substantial golden gift. Tab-sa-Dayyan had been flabbergasted, and Azzu-ena had cried. Then his naturally cheerful face turned grave again.

"No, it's the news from Meluhha, Brigadier," he said. At Hollard's blank look—nobody could keep up with everything—

"Meluhha. India, what'll be Bombay. There's a steady trickle of trade between there and the Gulf, via Dilmun."

He moistened his lips, chapped with the long hard journey up from Mitanni. "There's been an outbreak there."

"Damn!" Hollard said, knotting his sun-faded brows. They were a startlingly light color against the teak-dark tan of his face. "How did that happen?"

"It's the damn smallpox bug, it's tough—great big mother of a thing for a virus, with a hard sheath, you can actually see it under a microscope. It'll stay infectious for *years* at room temperature under the right conditions. I think . . . I think what must have happened is that someone saw they could make a killing by stealing and selling clothing from the victims, instead of burning it. Remember how we gathered it in big heaps by the fires, toward the end there?"

Hollard nodded grimly. Thousands had died in Babylon, tens of thousands throughout the country, before quarantines and compulsory innoculation got the brushfire under control. Good cloth was valuable here, relative to most other things, because the whole process of making it from sheep to sewing was so labor-intensive. A good cloak or tunic would take a third of a year's wages for an ordinary man. A shipload was a fortune.

Clemens went on: "In a pile of wool blankets or clothes, the infection could linger indefinitely. It's a sit-and-wait pathogen, lying around on surfaces."

"Well, Jus, that's damned bad news," Hollard said, and shook his head. "After the war, we'll have to do something about it, if we can."

Clemens looked at the general, jaw dropping. "After—" His voice broke in a squeak. "Sir, they've got the disease there *right now*. This news is months old! We have to do something *now*."

The lamplight brought out the planes and angles of Hollard's bony face. "Out of the question," he snapped. The blue eyes speared Clemens's. "I have a war to run, in case you hadn't noticed, Doctor, and it's at a critical point. Every ship and sailor and Marine is needed."

The doctor looked at the general for a long moment, silent with horror. "But sir . . . Ken . . . for the love of *God,* Meluhha's a major trade center! I'm pretty sure, I've been tracing it, somehow we managed to get it to Babylon—from the African coast, or somewhere along the Red Sea, maybe. Now that it's in Meluhha, it'll spread all through continental Asia, maybe to southeast Asia as well. Virgin field epidemic—a quarter of the human *race* could die."

Hollard's face might have been rough-cast in an Irondale foundry. "And if I divert our resources, the Republic may die. I know my duty, Doctor. So should you."

"I'm a doctor, dammit. People are dying and I know how to keep them alive!"

"You're also a soldier of the Republic of Nantucket," Hollard said. "What do you think we should do? Send a fleet and a regiment to Meluhha? Because that's what it would take; they're not going to allow us to stick needles into them on our say-so. And then *another* fleet and more regiments to track down all the places people from Meluhha *might* have gone? All the Coast Guard and Marine Corps together wouldn't be enough to lock that barn door. The horse is out. That's very bad, and I'm sorry it happened, but it has."

Appalled, Clemens stared. "You're not going to do *anything*?"

"I'll recommend we step up the vaccination program at every outpost and base, and encourage all the people near 'em to come in and get it," Hollard said. "And just between me and thee, we let Walker know about the epidemic while it was on, and the Tartessians. They've got their own vaccination programs going, according to Intelligence. More we cannot do, not until the war is over. I'm sorry, Justin."

"Sorry," Clemens said. "Thank you very much, *sir*," he said.

He stood, saluted, and turned on his heel. Behind him Kenneth Hollard dropped his head into his hands, unseen.

Clemens stalked to the tent he'd been assigned. Azzu-ena was busy within, setting out their gear; she looked up at his approach and wordlessly folded him into her embrace.

"You did what you could, beloved," she said softly in his ear.

"I did *nothing*," he groaned. "I could . . . I could appeal to the chief, to the Town Meeting, launch a petition . . ."

"Would they listen, where the general would not?"

A sigh went out of him, and the rigid tension of anger. "No," he said. "They wouldn't . . . if I was them, I honestly don't know if I'd do anything either . . . *why,* dammit, *why*?" His fist struck the canvas-covered dirt where they sat.

"Ah, beloved, that is something not all the arts of your people or mine can answer," she said softly.

"What can I *do*?"

Her tone became a little sharper: "You will save those lives you can," she said. "*The regimen I shall adopt,* remember? Your patients are here. They are those you *can* assist. You will do them no good if you waste the strength of your spirit brooding on what you *cannot* do."

He sighed, straightened, ran a hand over his cropped hair. "I suppose . . . no, you *are* right." He smiled into the dark eyes. "What would I do without you?"

"I will do you good and not evil all your days," she said softly, quoting the marriage ceremony. Then she laid a hand on her stomach and her smile grew wider. "And you have already done something with me you could not do without. I was going to wait another week, but . . ."

He folded her in his arms, feeling joy blaze. The haunting thought of blankets and baskets traveling from one port to the next didn't quite fade, but it was enough. It was reason to keep going.

CHAPTER SEVENTEEN

April, 11 A.E.—Feather River Valley, California

After so long in tunic and leggings like those of the rangers, it felt a little odd to Spring Indigo Giernas to go once more in nothing more than a brief wraparound skirt of deerskin, much like what she would have worn in summer as a young woman of the Cloud Shadow people. She leaned into the tumpline that held the big carrying basket on her back, both hands gripping the rawhide just past the padded section that rested across her forehead. How quickly you got used to having horses to carry things! The burden made it natural to keep her eyes down on the graveled surface of the road. It also made it easier to hide the smile that threatened to break through when she remembered how Peter—Sue had told her the name meant "rock," which was very good—had bellowed and roared when she told him that she had to be the one to scout the enemy encampment.

Who shall go? she'd said. *My sister, with her eyes like the summer sky? Jaditwara, with those eyes and hair the color of the sun, too? You, my husband, taller than a tree and bearded like a bear—a bear whose face hair is always on fire? Even if the hair and eyes were like these people here, you all have faces like hatchets, pushed forward. Or like Eagles, of course, very handsome once it stops being strange! No, no, it must be me— didn't you say that your law was one for men and women?*

She hid a chuckle behind a decorous face. Oh, he had bellowed, yes, roared and pawed the earth like a bison in the rutting season . . . which he was like, and in more ways than on the blanket. She and Sue had worn him down though; for he was a fair man and just. It was well for a strong chief to have two wives who worked in concert—they could usually make a man see reason, which was better for everybody.

Spring Indigo licked dust from her lips, putting down fear. The fort of the Tartessians came nearer with every step, growing from a description, a shadow, to a thing like a mountain made by men.

I am just one woman of the land to them, she told herself. *They will not see my face among so many.*

To *her*, the differences between her people and these dwellers in the sunset lands were obvious, easy to see at a glance—her people were taller, with a different cast of face. But the enemy would see what they expected and no more.

Tidtaway was trudging beside her, carrying a hide sack over his shoulder. She didn't like Quick Tongue. He'd kept trying to get her to lie with him, which was bad manners if the husband did not make the offer. *Still, he is brave and has guided us well.* It would be too odd for a strange woman to come here unaccompanied; that would make them really *look* at her.

The roadway grew crowded as they approached the great fortress of the Tartessians; occasionally she stole a look at the immense log that speared up into the sky from its center. The people of the land walked to either side, leaving the center of the roadway free for riders and wagons. She glanced nervously aside at those, and up at the ramparts ahead of her.

This is as nothing before the arts of the Eagle People, who are wise and strong, she told herself. She was one of the Eagle People herself now; when they went to Pete's home she would see far stranger, far greater things. *All this the Tartessians learned from us, like a child following her mother and imitating the roots she gathers.*

For a moment it daunted her; if this was just a child's copy, a poor imitation, what was Nantucket itself like? No real picture had formed in her mind of the Island, the stories were too wild and strange. . . .

"Now I must be as a still pool, to reflect, and to remember," she muttered to herself.

The roadway rose above the crop fields on either side. Men and women were working in those, some Tartessians, some tribesfolk captives driven to work with blows. Horses pulled machines with wheels and many iron teeth down rows, and the teeth turned the soil like a digging stick but far faster. Another machine with long wooden arms that turned around and around stood and groaned, and water poured out of its base, to run off through ditches between fruit trees; workers tended the ditches with hoes, piling up earth here and tearing it down there. Beneath an open shed, men were struggling with animals—sheep, they were called—the long hair of their coats being cut off with iron shears. The near-naked beasts looked comical as they were driven away, giving bleating cries, and women carried off the hair—the wool—to great bins.

They neared the gate. She looked for the details the others had told her to observe. Squat towers bulked on each side of the massive log portal, and the snouts of *cannon*, which were like rifles but vastly larger, poked out. Lower down were long slim tubes through narrow slits in the walls. Those would be the *throwers-of-flame;* she shuddered at the thought. Many enemy warriors, all dressed curiously alike in green and brown, paced on top of the palisade above the sloping turf of the earth wall. More waited by the gates; there was a broad flat place with tables, and Tartessians sitting behind them on chairs. She recognized both from what the expedition had made for the cabins where they wintered in the mountains. The sitting men were differently dressed, in long tunics but with their legs bare, and strapped sandals on their feet. They waved and shouted, and she followed Tidtaway over to them.

A man of the land stood beside the seated official. He spoke sharply to Tidtaway, and the guide walked humbly to them and spoke. Eyes on the ground, Spring Indigo tensed. This was a dangerous part of the plan. The interpreter was of this area. Tidtaway could not pretend to speak his language anything but badly. He was to claim he came from far up the valley to the north, where the tribute caravan had passed through. They both turned so that the little round puckered scars of the *vaccination* could be seen.

It seemed the Tartessian accepted Tidtaway's story. He grunted and took the little leather bags from the guide's satchel and poured them out. Dust and nuggets panned from streams piled up, a dull yellow color against the smooth pottery on which they lay. There was a machine before the official, a metal stand with pans on either side, pivoting in the center of the arm that bore them. The seated man took one of the pans from its nest of chains, scraped nuggets and dust onto it with a spatula, replaced it, put little metal weights on the other side until they balanced. Then he consulted notes on paper; she recognized the signs, the al-pha-bet she had been learning herself, but of course in the foreign language of Tartessos. His fingers flicked stone beads strung in columns on another pottery square.

Her eyes tracked movement. The warriors in green cloth and brown leather were tensing. Very slightly, but it was the tension of men ready for a fight. They held their rifles across their chests, the sun bright on the knives clipped to their ends to make them spears as well.

They think that perhaps Tidtaway will become angry, she thought. She thought of remarks she'd heard translated as Peter and Sue and Jaditwara discussed. *Ah . . . because he will be cheated.* An angry man might forget he was alone.

The Tartessian pushed round metal disks—coins such as she'd been shown by Peter and the others—across the table. Two were of gold, but shining much brighter than the nuggets. Others were of what must be *silver,* and more still of copper, a metal she knew from small ornaments brought in trade from the far north to her birth-people. All bore fascinating pictures; of a beak-nosed man, of a woman in a fanciful headdress; of a dreadful figure with three legs and a single eye. She didn't understand how these beautiful things could be worth less than a handful of dust and heavy rock.

But I don't have to understand. Someday, yes, but not now. For now, I am a mirror.

Tidtaway carefully put the coins in a pouch at his belt, and the official signaled to Spring Indigo to put down her load. She did, and the man pawed through it in a desultory fashion. The trade goods had come from their local allies; dried smoked salmon from the spring run, together with bundles of cammas roots, red clover for teas, scraped willow bark, wild onions, dried berries, and walnuts. Her "husband's" bundles held golden beaver pelts, otter, martin, ermine, colorful feathers . . .

One of the soldiers reached out and grabbed her breast, laughing at her squeal of surprise and protest. Then he looked down and saw that some of her milk had spurted out onto his hand, and backed away, cursing and swearing, shaking the hand as if the white droplets had burned it. The other Tartessians backed away from *him,* dodging and cursing in their turn. . . .

Peter Giernas looked up scowling from the notes and map he was compiling from her story. Jaditwara laughed softly, and the man scowled at *her.* The Fiernan spoke:

"Tartessians are *so* funny. They think that if a woman's milk touches a man, and he was not the one to quicken her, he may become impotent and sterile—unclean, with his semen turned to milk." She laughed again. "He will have to undergo a cleansing ritual from their priests and priestesses. I don't know exactly what, but I hear that it's expensive. And painful, in ways that will make him not interested in women for a while."

Spring Indigo laughed aloud. So did several others; Eddie threw back his head and barked amusement, slapping his thigh.

"And it's so silly," Jaditwara added, shaking her head. "After all, how can a man ever really know who fathers a child? A mother is a mother, a father is an . . . an opinion."

Eddie Vergeraxsson stopped laughing abruptly, then gave a pained smile when the others continued. Spring Indigo hugged her knees to her, a little embarrassed but flushing with pride as all eyes waited on her, all ears listened to her. She stared into the fire, watching the low red flame over the coals, an occasional spark spitting out and drifting skyward. Her hand rested on Perks's flank, where he lay gnawing on the thighbone of a pronghorn. Jared cuddled against her, between her and the dog's back.

I am speaking at the council fire, she thought. *Very strange.* Among the Cloud Shadow folk, only strong hunters and women with living grandchildren could do that . . . formally, at least.

"Well, after that, this happened—" she went on.

The seated official snapped a command, and the soldier who had grabbed her handed his rifle to a comrade and shuffled away; then he irritably waved them on through, after marking her forehead with a daub of yellow paint, and Tidtaway's hand with a slash of red. They edged through the gateway, amid a slow stream of others. Now it was safe to gawk around, as if in wonder; many others were doing so. In fact, she *did* feel wonder. Not even the Bison Hunt Festival had ever gathered this many people together—she used the technique Jaditwara had taught her and quickly estimated that there must be at least three hundred and fifty here, not counting visitors. A broad street ran all around the inside of the wall-and-parapet defenses, covered in gravel. A network of others centered on a central plaza, where large houses stood; several were of two stories, with the ends of beams supporting floors coming out through the thick walls of adobe brick. One had a square tower three floors high, with a flat roof on top where men walked. More cartloads of sun-dried brick came in as watched, to be unloaded by sweating workers. The low-pitched roofs were of red-clay tile, and colored designs had been drawn on some of the whitewashed exteriors, showing warriors and Gods and beasts. Verandahs upheld by wooden pillars carved into grotesque colored shapes marked the grander buildings.

One structure was open to the street, with wooden doors pulled back. In it men and women toiled at benches and beehive-shaped ovens. Some took white dust, mixed it with water, kneaded and pounded. Others took lumps of beige-white stuff and thrust it into the ovens; others were taking out round loaves the size of beavers. The smell was intoxicating, bringing the water of hunger to her mouth.

Bread, she realized. Peter said he sometimes woke from dreams of eating it. *Now I know why!*

A section of the plaza had been set apart as a place where people exchanged things. She unrolled her mat and set out the goods in her basket with Tidtaway's furs beside it, knelt, sat back on her heels, and waited. Folk wandered about, looking and dickering. Soon she would be able to wander herself . . .

"Okay," Peter Giernas said, with a grin that was half relief. "*Good* job, honey."

Spring Indigo beamed back at him. Tidtaway was sitting sullen; he'd been frightened by what he saw in the Tartessian encampment, evidently putting it together with what he'd learned from the expedition, and not liking the implications.

The ranger leader spread the map on the bearhide blanket that was lying fur-side-down before him. "All right, what we've got here is a fortified square, call it three acres. Log-and-earth bastions at each corner, and two beside the gate. Each bastion has two twelve-pounders with overhead cover, and a four-tube rocket launcher on the roof. Perimeter road, then a grid, with the main road in from the gate on the north. Around the plaza are the commander's residence, the main armory, these buildings that seem to be temples or churches or whatnot—that three-legged one-eyed thing with the teeth is definitely Arucuttag. And this school, and what sounds like an infirmary."

His finger moved to the southern edge of the settlement. "Now here, this smaller building Indigo described as sunk into the ground, I'd say that's probably the main powder store. These bigger buildings along the west wall seem to be barracks for the soldiers, stables, and cottages for the married men. More of those along the south for the farmers and craftsmen, and then these workshops—smithy, carpentry shop, weaving and spinning sheds. They don't seem to bring most of the livestock inside the fort, but they could, using these open areas for pens. Honey, could you describe that machine you saw again?"

Spring Indigo frowned. "I only caught a glimpse, on my way to the jakes." The Tartessians had been *very* insistent about outsiders using those. "There was a very large stack of firewood against the wall, many cords all split very neatly—it looked like ax work. A chimney through the roof, and white vapor. Inside I saw a large wheel of iron, perhaps four feet tall, spinning fast. And an arm of iron moving back and forth, *thus*." She made a fist of her right hand and pumped her forearm back and forth.

"Ouch," Sue said. "*That's* a surprise."

"Yeah, sounds like a small stationary steam engine," Giernas said. "Pretty much like the ones Seahaven turns out. That'd be useful if they've got a machine shop, and for pumping water, maybe grinding grain and sawing wood, that sort of thing. Damn, didn't know they'd gotten that far with their mechanical stuff."

"That building was new," Indigo said. "They were still plastering the outside wall."

Giernas turned to their local guide. "What did you manage to get?" he said. Sue leaned closer to him, ready to help out with the halting tale.

Tidtaway put his palms on the knees of his crossed legs and leaned forward. "I went to a place where they exchanged the juice of the grape-bushes for *money*. There were many there— Tartessians, some of the people of this land come in to trade, even a few of the prisoners the Tartessians keep to work . . . slaves, is that the word? *Hupowah!* That juice is strong! After only one cup, I felt stronger than Bear and wiser than Raven! But I had only one, as you advised me. Others had more; some puked, or fell on the ground, or acted like they'd been eating crazyweed. I heard many talking, many in the language I know from trading here. There is a very big *boat* of the Tartessians in the river, far downstream . . . in the delta. Many things came with it. The crew was sick, the sickness of the small pockmarks, and could not bring it closer. Instead a few men came, and the big boat that lives in the house by the river there went down to it. They have hidden the great boat among the marsh reeds."

Giernas stroked his beard. He could feel the information sinking in, then stirring like seeds planted in damp earth in the spring. "Good. Now we know a lot more," he said.

Tidtaway grunted. "Now we know our enemies are very strong," he said.

"Not as strong as they would be if they knew that we knew," Giernas said, not certain that it got across. He bent his brows in thought. Easy enough to say, but exactly *how* was he going to use the information. *Oh, well, if I'd wanted a quiet life with no problems, I'd have joined the Marines . . .*

*   *   *

"I don't think cottonwood's best for this," Eddie Vergeraxsson said.

"It's not," Peter Giernas replied. He took a step back, surveyed the cut, spat on his hands and took up the adze again. "If I was building something to last. This only has to be used once, and black cottonwood works easy."

It was a hot spring day in the California lowlands, and both men had stripped to breechclouts and moccasins for the work despite the mosquitoes. Sweat ran down their bodies as they straddled the edges of the cut in the big cottonwood log, a familiar enough sensation to both of them as they swung the adzes with full-armed overhead cuts. The soft wood came free in big wedges, flying to join the piles of chips on either side. Occasionally they would pause to throw handfuls more out of the growing trough, or to touch up the edge on an adze. The air was heavy with the balsam odor of the sap in the fresh wood.

He'd decided on this spot because there was a grove of the cottonwoods near the banks of the river. They'd cut four, each with a good straight section fifty feet long and at least a yard across. The locals' eyes had gone wide at how fast the felling went with good steel axes, and even wider when the Nantucketers broke out the two-man ripsaw and used it to trim the trunks to size and give them a rough point at the front. Then they'd braced each with stakes driven deep into the soft ground and trimmed off the scaly bark; their volunteers had helped with that. Now they were cutting out the interiors of the big canoes, highly skilled work that would take months to teach anyone else to do. Both of them had learned to handle wood the hard way, working in sawmills and timber camps around Providence Base.

He worked until the strain began to throw his eye off, then stopped for a brief rest, hopping down and reaching for his canteen where it hung on one of the bracing stakes; it was a two-liter plastic pop bottle salvaged from Madaket Mall on the Island, encased in thick boiled hide molded around the shape, the best you could get. Sweat ran down into the mat of gingery blond hair on his chest, itching, and he scratched absently. The water was tepid but delicious as he threw back his head and drank, then wiped a callused palm across his face and looked around the camp. Locals were finishing off the other three canoes, smoothing inside and out with knives, pieces of sandstone and small hatchets, or arranging poles down the paths they'd take to the water. Sue and Jaditwara were over toward the camp proper, where they'd set up an improvised workbench and sawhorse, roughing the oars from red alder wood with saws and axes, finishing them with handadze, pullknife, and spokeshave before handing them over to tribeswomen to smooth by rubbing with sand and leather. For variety they trimmed plank seats from sections of split alder, drilling holes and whittling out treenails to fit from black oak sticks.

He noticed more than a few envious looks at their tools— drills, gouges, chisels—as tribesmen went by. *Well, looks like I'm doing Gardner Tool & Hardware's sales pitch for them again.* The more complicated Islander machines might appear magical and distant from ordinary life; they evoked wonder rather than a fierce lust to possess. But show people a tool that would really ease their daily work, and that was another matter altogether. You could cut down trees with a polished stone ax, and shape them with fire, flint, and obsidian, but it was *hard*. The Tartessians evidently hadn't more than scratched the surface of local demand.

Spring Indigo looked up from the main campfire and waved to him. There was a big trough there, a sort of large bucket of hide slung from a pole frame, nearly full of water. Venison and wild onions and roots and greens were cooking in it, heated by dropping in hot rocks and then stirring them around to make sure they didn't burn through the leather. It was a little more cumbersome than a metal cauldron, but a lot lighter, and easier to carry unbroken than pottery. The wind brought him a whiff of it, and his belly rumbled. He waved back to her and rubbed the ridged muscle over his stomach, grinning. She pointed up to where the sun would be in an hour and a half.

The expedition's two leather tents were set up on either side of a big live oak that offered convenient branches to hang things from, and their horses were grazing not far away; the locals were camped a bit downstream. The river to the east was the Sacramento, not the Feather, so there was little chance of Tartessians happening by, but he'd made sure that nothing was visible from the water itself—they would cut paths for the canoes at the last minute—and he had plenty of sentries about. The locals might not have much notion of consistent effort, but they understood keeping watch very well indeed.

What they didn't know, though . . . he sighed and looked at the firing range they'd set up. Tidtaway was running the eager volunteers through another round of dry-firing, doing the loading drill with imaginary cartridges and priming powder over and over again, firing with no flints in the jaws of the hammers to spare the surfaces of the frizzens. Then he would pace off the distance to the nearest target, counting loudly, run back to point out the appropriate notch on the sights, go further, and repeat the process.

Luckily most of the local hunters were pretty good at estimating range already, and they'd eliminated all the ones with bad eyesight. With only ten or so rounds each to practice real shooting with, though, he wasn't sure how much good it would all do. Every hour or so he or Sue or one of the others would go over and make sure that Tidtaway wasn't teaching anything too wretchedly wrong. The mountaineer from the Tahoe country did seem to have the makings of a good shot, if only they could let him practice enough.

They just didn't have much time, at all . . .

A cold wet nose thrust into his armpit.

"Goddammit, Perks!" Giernas hissed, blinking his eyes open into the predawn gloom of the big bison-hide tent. The air smelled of leather, sweat, and a bit of the damp chill, like the beginnings of fog.

The dog backed away, mouth hanging open in a canine grin, then turned and slipped through the opening of the tent. Spring Indigo poked her head in a second later.

"It is time to wake, husband, sister. Come wash yourself with water, drink water, make your blood thin and healthy!"

Spring Indigo's furs and blankets were already neatly rolled up. Giernas yawned, stretched and reached over to pull down the light blanket Sue was using. As usual, she was sleeping on her face and still dead to the world except for a few muffled grumbles.

"Wakie-wakie!" he cried, then administered a resounding slap to her buttocks. The resilient muscle under the thin smooth layer of female fat bounced his palm back into the air, stinging slightly.

Better move quick, he thought and bolted for the river with her curses ringing in his ears, taking the water in a long flat dive just as the sun came over the mountains to the east. Sue was a few steps behind him; he felt a strong slender hand clamp around his ankle, after which she made a determined attempt at drowning him, which was fun. When they'd rolled deep and come up snorting they surfaced, to see Spring Indigo and Perks standing on the bank looking at them. Giernas exchanged a look with her, and they waded toward the shore, mud squelching between their toes. Perks made a halfhearted attempt to dodge, and gave a yelp as the man scooped him up and whirled in a half circle, throwing him five yards out into the slow-flowing stream. The dog landed with a tremendous splash and came up with an enormous sneeze, swimming strongly with his head out of the water. When he turned Indigo was still mock-struggling with Sue.

"You take the arms," he said. "I'll take the feet . . ."

"No!" A peal of laugher. "No!"

"One—two—*heave.*"

He turned and dived back in himself, swimming deep. The water was clear for a river running through an alluvial plain, very clear once he was away from the bank, and he swam downward until he felt the strong cold hand of the current gripping him. With the young sun bright he could see waving waterweeds below him, and fish by the dozens—a huge sturgeon, some late chinook and steeleye. A river otter came by, pausing to look him directly in the face from about five feet away; he thought he saw it blink in astonishment before it curled about like a living ribbon and arrowed away, sinuous grace until it disappeared upstream.

Turning over on his back he saw the two women swimming by above. *Hell of a pleasant sight,* he thought, crouching on the bottom and driving for the surface.

By then his lungs were burning, and the first breath was almost agonizingly sweet. *Well, so's life*, he thought. He had good health, a fine young son, *two* women who liked him as much as he returned the favor, friends, the prospect of at least modest wealth and a bit of glory when he returned. *Yeah, life's been treating me damned good. Life* is *good.* Not being more given to self-examination than most healthy young men his age, the thought struck hard. *And here I am, going off to where a bunch of homicidal strangers can shoot holes in me. I must be crazy.* He couldn't even be accused of being yellow, not after the way they'd bushwacked the Tartessian patrol. Nobody would think much the less of him if he'd just taken the expedition off to the coast to hide out until the next ship arrived in San Francisco Bay.

Well, there's me, he thought wryly. *I would. Hell, okay, I'll be sensible when I'm past thirty.*

They swam ashore, passing Jaditwara and Eddie in the other direction; holding hands, this time, so they must be on the up cycle of their on-and-off personal relationship. *I wish Eddie would get his act together and settle down,* Giernas thought. *Everyone knows it's going to happen eventually—except him.*

As long as they didn't bring their split-up-make-up-repeat-cycle into business hours, and they didn't, it wasn't really his busines as leader of the expedition, and as a friend there were certain things you just couldn't say. Particularly when Eddie had taken to responding with heavy-handed jokes about how lucky Giernas was not to have to pay bridewealth *twice* . . .

"Slugabeds!" he said.

They let the slow breeze from the south dry their skins as they ate breakfast—leftover stew from yesterday, and more of the everlasting bannock-bread made from acorn meal—before getting into their buckskins. Spring Indigo brought out a spoon and fed Jared a bit of acorn mush porridge, part of the slow weaning process her people used. The toddler ate a bit, looking a little uncertain at the taste, before making a dive for the faucets. *Can't fault his taste,* his father thought. He looked around the campsite, one of . . . Lord, how many? Hundreds. In the eastern forests where the passenger-pigeon flocks wrecked forests with their weight when they landed, on the banks of the Mississipi, through the tall-grass prairies of central Missouri, where he'd intervened in a fight half on impulse and met Spring Indigo, on upland plains where buffalo herds went by for *days* at the gallop—he'd done the math and had Jaditwara check it and there had to be ten *million* beasts in that one herd—in the crystalline silences of the Nevada desert nights, by Tahoe and water so clear you could drop in a pebble and watch it fall for five hundred feet, in the Sierras . . .

Can't say I haven't had a grand trip, he thought. *And more to come, a lot more.* He hadn't seen the Great Lakes yet, or Texas or Mexico, or a Cuba that was still jungle to the tide's edge, or the Amazon or the Pampas, or . . . *Someday, maybe Africa? And I'd sure like to see a moa somewhere besides a farm, too . . .*

"Okay, let's get going," he said; Spring Indigo hugged him, wordless, as if she were trying to drive herself into his chest, then stepped back with a smile to bring luck. He whirled Jared around in a circle, holding the boy high, listening to his chuckle and cry of *Papa!* and *Fly!*, then handed him back.

"Keep the crossbow or the pistols to hand," he said, needlessly. "And always have a couple of the dogs near. Keep a horse saddled, change off so you've got one ready close by day and night."

Spring Indigo nodded: "We will be as safe as can be," she said softly. "Come home with victory."

As he slung his pack into the canoe, Perks started to follow. "No," he said.

The dog pressed his belly to the ground and looked up pleadingly. Giernas took Jared from his mother's arms and planted him before Perks's nose. "Stay!" he said sternly. "Guard!"

Perks sighed deeply and stood, moving to Indigo's side. *Guard the den, the nursing mother, and the cubs while the rest of the pack hunts* was reasoning that made perfect sense to a wolf, and to the mastiff side of his ancestry, too. He didn't have to like it, but he'd do it, and see that all the expedition's dogs did, too.

Good soldier, he thought.

That was more than you could say about the local tribesmen. They were tough enough fighting-men, but they had even less discipline than a bunch of Sun People warriors right off the boat from Alba. He could only hope that they thought Peter Giernas's *keuthes* too strong to gainsay; or his *war medicine,* or whatever they called it here.

The first problem was to get the boats into the water. A forty-foot log was heavy, even when you'd trimmed the outside and carved out most of the inside to leave a hull between two and three inches thick. The Islanders could have rigged block and tackle gear, but there were times when a hundred strong backs were faster.

"All right," he said, putting his shoulder to the rounded stern of the first dugout. The wood still smelled of balsamlike sap, and of the nut-oil the locals had rubbed into it. "Get ready . . . *heave.*"

It took a while for the Indians to get the idea, but when they did the dugout moved a little with the first shove. Another heave, and it began to surge down the pathway of smooth peeled branches they'd laid. Another, and it gathered speed, rumbling over the soft soil as feet drove ankle deep into mud, then into the water itself with a splash and final triumphant shout. Giernas held his breath for a moment, but the craft floated high and evenly—they'd left enough wood along the keel to balance it nicely. It ran out lightly into the river, then jerked to a stop when the mooring line brought it up. The others came down faster, as if knowing they could do it made everyone push harder.

Giernas stepped out to his, rolling himself over the thwart to keep his center of balance low; he wasn't a mariner by trade, but like any Islander who'd grown up post-Event he had plenty of experience with small boats. At the stern was a two-foot rounded dowel of black oak, sanded smooth and driven into a hole drilled in the wood. He picked up the rudder and tiller—

carved from a single block—and slipped it over the pivot, the
wood sliding smoothly into the greased hole. It turned easily.

"I christen thee *Mother of Invention,*" he muttered, then
called and waved.

His crew were twenty-five of the local volunteers. They came
aboard neatly enough; they all used canoes, albeit little one- or
two-man models made out of bundles of tule reeds daubed with
mud and natural asphalt. Packs and gear went into the bottom,
or up toward the bow, where Eddie had taken a little extra
time to carve a crude eagle as figurehead. They were less certain about the seats pegged to the hull, and the shape of the
paddles, but sorted themselves out soon enough.

He looked over his shoulder; the other canoes were manned,
each with an Islander at the tiller, and Spring Indigo was standing by the shore, holding Jared on one hip and waving with
the other hand. His own hand answered, and so did the other
three Islanders.

"Let's go!" Giernas said, turning his mind wholly to what he
had to do, and the few phrases in the local tongue he had
mastered.

Paddling in unison was familiar here, too, if not on quite
this scale. That was why they hadn't tried to use oars. Enough
fascinated or bewildered glances showed as the crew looked
over their shoulders at the tiller as it was. Eventually the Indians sorted themselves out, one man to a seat, twelve paddles
poised on either side. The twenty-fifth man had appointed himself coxswain.

"*Tai!*" he shouted.

An intake of breath, and the paddles rose higher. Muscle
rippled in the twenty-four strong brown backs before him, and
hands braced.

"*Hai*—tai!" from the coxswain.

"*Hunah!*" in unison from the crew, a deep multiple grunt.

The blades dipped, bit, rose dripping again. The coxswain
began tapping two sticks together, chanting as he did so:

"Hai-*tai*-tiki-tiki, hai-*tai*-tiki-tiki—"

The red-alder-wood paddles flashed, throwing bright sprays
of droplets high. Clouds of birds exploded from riverside marsh
at the sound of the chant, and from the other side of the broad
stream as well; otter and beaver plopped into the water. Far
to the east the rising sun gave the snow peaks of the Sierras a
blush of crimson, looming over the jungle of trees on that bank
and turning the horizon to a jagged line of blue and silver and
blood. He pulled the tiller toward himself, and the canoe turned

smoothly . . . until the startled paddlers stopped and looked over their shoulders again; the only way they knew of steering a canoe was with the paddles themselves.

"Paddle!" he said.

The other canoes were out as well, cutting broad circles on the expanse of the Sacramento; it was a good thing it was a couple of hundred yards wide here; they passed within a few feet of Eddie's, and the other ranger was cursing and waving his free hand, trying to kick the nearest local.

They should shake down in a few hours, Giernas thought. *And it's all downstream from here.*

CHAPTER EIGHTEEN

November, 10 A.E.—Western Anatolia
October, 10 A.E.—Straits of the Pillars, Tartessos
October, 10 A.E.—Long Island, Republic of Nantucket
October, 10 A.E.—Tartessos City, southwestern Iberia

The jolt of the colonel talking to her faded, and Johanna Gwenhaskieths's marching day dragged on; an hour of march, ten minutes of rest to swig water and gnaw a dog biscuit, another hour on the muddy road. Even in one day's march up the Seha valley, though, the landscape had begun to change; fewer trees and groves, more of them olives, a drier feel to the land. Mountains rose in the east, the edge of the high country. If it hadn't been for that change of landscape, she might have thought this the afterlife, and she condemned to a march without end.

The sun dropped behind them to the right, throwing long shadows. A bugle call sounded; Johanna found her feet stopping automatically, even before the *fall out* and *stack arms* sounded.

Good campground, she thought automatically. A nice little hill, a ruined farmstead for dry firewood . . . and she smiled beatifically at the little flock of sheep in a pen.

"Fresh meat tonight," she said happily; feast-day food.

And it wasn't her company's turn for night-watch, so there wouldn't be a four-hour chunk taken out of her sleep. That didn't mean the end of work, of course, but at least she could walk over to where her section would be in the battalion camp, add her rifle and helmet to one of the tripods, and drop her webbing harness and rucksack. Then she pulled out a bundle of stakes with a steel blade on either end—swine-feathers, to be driven into the trench outside the earthwork—and took her entrenching tool to the perimeter.

When she came back a fire was already crackling, and she

caught the smell of mutton roasting on it, enough to make her forget aching muscles, mud, and sweat.

One of her squad was frying crumbled dog biscuit in the grease that dropped from the chunks of meat; from the look, the beast had been a yearling lamb. She took some of the biscuit in her mess tin and hacked off a couple of chops from the spit with her clasp knife, blowing on her fingers as she juggled the hot food. While she gnawed the savory meat and ate the fat-rich morsels of biscuit (for once not worrying about breaking a tooth on it) Vaukel came up with two buckets of water. She hid a smile; even after this long, it was still a little odd to have someone doing women's work for *her*. Not unpleasant, she'd come to like Eagle People ways and even Fiernan more than those she'd grown up with.

"The corpsmen say the water's safe," Vaukel said.

"Ah, good!" she said, dipping up a cup that didn't have the unpleasant mineral taste of the purifying powder.

The she tossed her uniform over a branch and made for her rucksack, to fetch out a scrap of soap and half a dozen pairs of underwear and socks. A chance to clean them and herself; if she propped them on sticks by the embers of the fire they'd probably dry overnight, and if they didn't they'd be close enough to pack, or wear. When she came back the tent was up, and her squadmates were unrolling their bedding inside, and her legs were starting to tell her their tale of cooling, stiffening muscle.

"Ah, I'm getting to be a crone," she said as she slumped down.

"Legs stiff?" Vaukel said beside her. "Should I loosen them?"

"Thanks, Vauk," she said; Fiernans had a knack for that, healing magic in their fingers.

She sighed as he kneaded the knots and tension out of one leg, then another, finishing by stretching her ankles, rubbing the soles of her feet and drumming the edges of his hands up and down from heel to buttocks. *Ahh, that does feel better.* When he'd finished she looked up and caught his hopeful unspoken question, not to mention the rampant evidence of it.

"Sure," she said, with a drowsy chuckle.

A glance sideways showed the camp settling down for the night, the sun only a faint rim of light in the west. "But none of that Fiernan fancy work this time," she said, rolling onto her back. The Earth Folk could turn something as simple as fucking into something as elaborate as one of their dancing ceremonies. "I need my sleep."

Later, yawning and on the verge of slumber, she listened to a sentry's boots going past at the perimeter not far away, a wolf howling somewhere, a rustle of chill wind through the tree whose branches spread over the tent. The squad's fire was banked with earth on its outer side, to throw the warmth of the fire into the open flap of the tent. The stars were many and bright, promising dry weather . . . and dry socks, tomorrow.

War's a fine trade, she thought happily.

Even in the field like this the living was no rougher than the damp chill huts of home, parents and siblings and cousins and the livestock all sleeping in the same straw. Nor was the work harder than a croft-born girl's endless round of butter-churning and grain-grinding, cooking and weaving, walking miles under a weight of water buckets or bundled firewood; in barracks it was a good deal softer all 'round, and the company was better either way. More freedom, too; and in the uniform of the Corps nobody dared or cared to scorn you.

Then her belly tightened a little as she remembered the hissing roar of the Ringapi surging against the barricade, or the moaning scream of a mortar round from out of the sky overhead. She moved a little closer to the broad warm strength of Vaukel's back, comforted by the snores and sighs and body heat of the rest of the squad beyond as well.

At least, when you don't have a battle to fight, war's a fine trade.

"This was as close as the ultralights could get," Marian Alston said, spreading the photographs on the table. The captains crowded around, balancing instinctively against the sway of a ship under way. "The enemy have taken considerable countermeasures against airborne reconnaisance. Particularly at low altitudes."

Light cannon on counterbalanced yoke mounts designed to shoot upward, balloons with heavy pivot-rifles mounted in their gondolas and platforms on top of the gasbags, rockets. All of them crude and inaccurate, but the little motorized hang gliders weren't all that sophisticated either.

Dammit, if only we had real aircraft! Of course, while she was at it she could wish for missile boats and a nuclear-powered aircraft carrier . . . She glanced out the stern gallery windows, at the frigates following the flagship in a line that extended for miles, one ruler-straight millrace wake white across the blue of the ocean. *We'll make do.*

Still, the shots of Tartessos the City from above were fairly clear; a digital videocamera in the ultralight, run through the PC in *Chamberlain*'s radio shack and its inkjet printer.

They lay next to the maps compiled by the Department of Foreign Affairs. Both showed what would become the junction of the Odiel and Tinto Rivers in the twentieth century—*would have become*, she thought with a mental stutter so familiar she hardly noticed it now. This was considerably different from what the uptime maps recorded. The great bay was larger, the peninsula of land down its middle far narrower, and there was less in the way of swamp and marsh around its fringes. Three thousand years of human beings cutting trees in the mountains, freeing soil to erode away downstream and rivers to drop the silt on the ocean shore; three thousand years of plowed fields doing likewise. Those could change the very contours of the land.

The city itself stood roughly where Huelva would have, in a history that included a nation called *Espana*. Columbus had sailed from here, at the beginning of those fateful years when the folk of Europe broke out into the world ocean, armed with cannon and galleons, smallpox and the joint-stock company. Here it had been a glorified village barely a decade ago, mud-walled houses clinging to a few steep hills at the end of the peninsula.

Now it was a city, bigger than Nantucket. Someone whistled softly.

"Been a busy little bee, hasn't he?"

Alston nodded. "As you can see, the harbor mouth is narrow and nearly blocked by this island," she said. Her finger pointed to a long islet that divided the entrance in two. "Heavy fortifications here, here, and here—multiple cross fires. Earthwork forts with massive stone retaining walls and revetments, bomb-proof magazines, underground ways to the bastions. The landward defenses of the forts on both sides are formidable, and fronted by marsh."

"A nightmare," McClintock said. "Impossible to storm. I'm surprised Isketerol came up with it, even with the reference books."

Alston nodded again. "Heavy guns, at least forty-two pounders, with overhead protection. Rocket batteries as well. *I* suspect Walker or one of his people was consulting engineer—there's a Mycenaean look to some of that stonework. Ms. Kurlelo-Alston."

Swindapa leaned forward and pressed a control. The VCR below the TV set they'd mounted on the tabletop whirred, and images flickered across its screen, jerking and jinking as the ultralight dodged ground fire. They saw a dragon's spittle-spray of rockets rising in a sea of flame from multiple tubes mounted on wagons, soaring skyward in arches of smoke, and plunging downward toward the slender shape of a Guard scouting schooner. The white wake of the ship showed how it curved away from the coast, sailing reach at a good twelve knots.

The commander of that craft lifted her billed cap and shook her head. "They don't have as much range as the guns," she said. "Less than our rockets. More misfires, too." Some of the trails of smoke corkscrewed, or ended in ragged clouds of off-white vapor that drifted downwind to the south. "But they could swamp anyone who got close, tear a ship apart." On the screen, the rockets landed short of the ship and sent gouts of shattered water flying skyward, some close enough to throw spray on its decks. "It was . . . alarming, ma'am. I'd say seven- or eight-pound bursting charges," she finished, as Swindapa turned the machine off.

The faces stayed impassive, but Alston could feel their inner wince. So far, neither side had started using explosive shells in ship-to-ship actions. Both powers had the capacity, and some of those shells waited in the magazines of her fleet.

That presented a problem, though. The problem was . . .

. . . *two wooden ships firing explosive shell into each other are like duelists . . . where both parties start by sticking their pistol barrels into each other's mouths and then fire together on the count of three.*

She sincerely hoped the situation would result in the sort of *de facto* restraint that had kept both sides from using poison gas in World War II. For ship-to-ship actions, at least. Certainly nobody was going to show any restraint when an earth-and-stone fort shot at wooden hulls.

"So, running the harbor mouth's out," someone said in a dry tone. That brought a general chuckle.

"Ms. Kurlelo-Alston?" Marian said.

"Ma'am." Swindapa put an enlargement of a picture on an easel. "Gentlemen, ladies, as you can see the city is also strongly fortified."

And much bigger *than it was, too,* Alston thought. There must be around twenty thousand people in it now, a sevenfold increase since Isketerol came home. The old town on the rocky hills had been largely replaced by a fortified palace complex;

landward of the new city's grid of streets a Vauban-style sunken wall with bastions and deep moat ran from river to river.

A disconcerting number of buildings showed tall brick chimneys or other evidence of being manufactures. *Gardens, too. Looks like a good sanitation system . . . that's a waterworks there in the northeast corner . . . shipyards and drydocks on the northern side of the city . . .*

Swindapa moved her pointer along that shore, out toward the end of the land. "Here's the naval docks. We count twelve warcraft of five hundred tons or more."

Lips tightened. Not as powerful as the Guard's frigates, but a lot more of them.

"They're comparable to the ones we fought off Nantucket in the spring . . . but see, the number of gunports is less on each. They're probably carrying fewer cannon than they did then, but heavier metal. Certainly large shore-based crews."

Nods; operating close to your harbor you could cram in far more men than you could if you had to feed them and find them room to sleep. That would make their broadsides come faster, and give them plenty of men for boarding.

"What's this?" Thomas Hiller said, peering close at one of the sheets on the table. "They're fitting them out with some sort of . . . are those shields?"

"We think they're wrought-iron plates," Swindapa said quietly. "Not enough to give much protection from cannon shot, but useful against small arms."

"Damn," Hiller said mildly; he was a gray-bearded man, once sailing master on the *Eagle*, come out of a teaching position at Fort Brandt OCS to command *Sheridan*, the newest of the frigates. "That'll be inconvenient . . . though it might make them top-heavy in a blow?"

Alston shook her head. "Home-team advantage," she said. "They only have to be able to carry it off right outside their own harbor, and in good weather. Next is something really new. We think the Tartessians got the design from Walker. The flier took a risk for a closer shot."

Swindapa put up another enlargement. It showed a long snake-slim ship walking like a centipede across the harbor. "A galley," she said. "Three-man oars, twenty-two to a side. No mast—it's probably dismountable—with this ramming beak and two heavy guns forward and two more guns aft. They're covered with tarpaulins to keep us from getting the details on the weapons. These galleys are lightly built, mostly from pine, so they can make a lot of them. And they are very fast. With those huge crews they can't operate far from shore, but from the look of it the rowers are also armed with cutlases."

An additional hundred and sixty armed men, when the galley was fast to another ship's side. That could be very nasty in a boarding action.

"We estimate they have about thirty of them," Swindapa said. "Then there are another forty or so smaller vessels, no threat as gunships, but able to carry warriors out to a melee."

Alston leaned forward and rested her fingers on the table. "There are two options. First, they refuse to engage; then we proceed to Cadiz. Second, they come out and fight; we break their fleet, blockade the harbor mouth, and *then* proceed to Cadiz."

"What if they beat us?" the captain of the *Lincoln* said.

"Defeat is not an option, Victor," Alson said. She looked around the circle of faces. "We'll be coming up level with Tartessos's location early tomorrow," she said. "I doubt they'll try anything before sunrise—Isketerol knows we still have night-vision devices. It'll be then, or never."

Jared Cofflin woke in the darkness. He'd noticed himself sleeping more lightly, in recent years—had to visit the jakes more often, too, of course; and this was a strange bed. There was a pair of great horned owls here around the Hollard farm-stead, probably nesting in the barn; their deep feathered basso: *Whoo, whoo-oo, whoo, whoo* . . . and the answering *Whoo, whoo-oo-oo, whoo-oo, whoo-oo* seemed to go on interminably.

Some folks found it soothing. It made his thoughts turn to shotguns. He could feel that it was very late; the night had the dead stillness of the hours before dawn, the air a slight chill.

It wasn't the owls this time, at least. For a long moment he wasn't quite sure what had woken him. Martha was just stirring beside him in the big feather bed in the Hollards' guest bed-room—it was a sign of their hosts' prosperity that they could afford one, with a household that included eight adults and all those children. He yawned; Jane had brought out a fiddle after dinner, Martha her guitar, and they'd all spent some time mak-ing the night hideous with attempts at song . . . well, that wasn't quite fair; Jane and Tanaswada were really good, and Saucarn knew a huge fund of hunting and drinking songs he'd mostly translated into English, and Tom had a collection of old-time tunes, real folk material, that his mother had passed on to him.

"Uncle Jared?" a small voice said in the darkness; he could

just see the outline of the speaker against the faint starglow through the curtained window.

"Just a minute." He sighed, and reached out to flick on his lighter, touch it to the wick of the kerosene lantern, turn it up, and put the glass chimney back on. It opened up a circle of light, showing the simple beauty of polished wood, the intricate carving on the posts of the bed, the colorful throw rugs on the plank floor.

Heather Kurlelo-Alston was standing on his side of the bed; her sister was over by Martha's. They were both in their spotted pyjamas, clutching their companions—a goggle-eyed blue snake for Lucy, and a koala bear for the redhead—with a tightness that would have choked live pets. Probably they were getting past the stage where the beloved stuffed animals could offer enough comfort.

Lord, how quick they grow. Not as fast as before the Event, though, not inside. They get to stay kids while they're kids.

"I'm sorry to wake you up, Uncle Jared," Heather said in a small voice, very different from her usual brassy self-confidence.

"We were having bad dreams, Aunt Martha," Lucy said.

"We miss our moms," Heather continued.

"We're afraid they'll get hurt."

"We're afraid they won't come back, ever." A tear trickled down Heather's freckled face. "We didn't want to wake the other kids up so we came in here."

"Is that okay?"

"Of course it's all right," Jared Cofflin said; Martha seconded him in a sleepy murmur. "Come on, little'uns." He turned the lamp down to a low night-light glow.

Wish there was someone I could get to make me feel better about that, he thought dryly.

The children both jumped into the bed at slightly more than greased-lightning speed, cuddling close. Jared hugged a small flannel-clad form, feeling it relax into comfort with a little sigh. Heather nuzzled her head into the goose-down softness of the pillow, tucked a palm under her cheek, and went to sleep like a light going out. The man waited until her breathing had grown even and then gently moved her aside a bit, turning over and pulling up the covers. Lucy was snoring daintily on Martha's shoulder, and Heather curled up against his back.

Good night, he thought, and saw the answer in his wife's eyes; she touched him lightly once on the cheek. *Well, guess I do have someone, come to that. But Marian, 'dapa, you'd better come back. These two need you.* His mind unclenched, spiraling downward into the waiting soft darkness. *Hell, we all do.*

"This, too, is part of kingship," Isketerol of Tartessos murmured aside.

His son Sarsental stopped fidgeting and sat straighter on the padded stool that rested beside the carved and gilded olive wood of his father's throne. *It is not easy to sit still and listen to the drone of laws when you have only sixteen winters,* his father knew. *But it is needful.*

The audience room was large, full of courtiers, officials, and soldiers, spectators near the great doors or in the second-story gallery that ran around it supported by pillars carved in the form of heroes and monsters. Light came from glass windows and skylights between the high rafters; it stabbed on the peacock dress of nobles, the green-and-brown of army uniforms, the plain linen and wool of commoners. The walls were murals on plaster, showing the deeds of the King and the forms of the Great Gods looming over all. A smell of stone, sea-salt through the windows, city smoke, clean sweat, and dust. Isketerol fought down his own impatience—

"My Lord King!" A courier, going to one knee and saluting with fist to breast. "The enemy fleet has been sighted!"

"Where?" Isketerol said calmly, commanding his fingers not to clench on the wood.

"Passing by Cape Claw; the heliograph has carried the signal."

Isketerol nodded. That was a day's sailing away. The heliograph stations could pass that message in less than an hour, flickering light from hilltop to tower to city.

"I will hear the report in detail later," he said.

The courier looked up in surprise. "But, Lord King—"

"The *Amurrukan* must also wait on the King's pleasure," Isketerol said. "Hold yourself ready for conference with me. Now, let us continue with the case at hand."

There was silence at that, then a rising murmur of wonder. Isketerol caught the eye of a captain of the Royal Guards; that man barked an order. Uniformed men stood at parade rest about the throne, dividing the hall between those with business and those merely looking on. Now they raised their rifles an inch and slammed the steel-shod butts down on the stone pavement three times in perfect unison, *bam . . . bam . . . bam*, a gunshot sound. Silence fell, more profound than before.

Isketerol hid his smile, as he had his boredom. *Such . . .*

gestures, they are also part of kingship. It is by such things that the souls of men are governed.

He looked back at the two before him. One was a man he knew slightly, Warentekal son of Warentekal, a landowner of moderate wealth up north of Crossing; he'd conferred with him on business there, the spreading of the New Learning concerning crops and farm tools, road-tax matters, security against up-country raiders before those tribes were subdued. He was stout for a Tartessian, kettle-bellied and bush-bearded, wearing an old-style tunic that left one shoulder bare, and a studded belt; several of his sons and attendants stood behind him. The other was a woman. She was old, her gray head covered by a simple headdress, her gown faded and patched; her gimlet eyes stayed on the King's face, and her lips worked over a mostly toothless mouth. Nose and chin threatened to meet . . .

An avatar of the Crone, Isketerol thought, and made a small gesture of aversion. Only one attended her, a young man whose testicles had probably only just dropped; *he* was bandaged and leaned on a cane.

"Warentekal," Isketerol said. "It is ancient law that if a tame beast breaks down a fence and does damage to crops, then the beast shall be forfeit to the tiller of the field. This woman says that when your swine broke down the fence of her field, and her son killed and took you the hides in token as custom demands, you set your servants upon him, and drove him out with rocks and sticks. What do you say to this?"

Warentekal seemed to swell and flush. "Lord King, this woman Seurlnai and her family are the merest trash—worthless smallholders, too lazy to make a living. In former years they borrowed grain from me to live, then paid less than the debt was worth except in the eye of charity by working in my family's fields at harvest. Now they grow insolent and swollen with pride, claiming my swine when all they wish is to steal the food they are too idle to grow themselves—"

The old woman screeched an oath and shook her fist. "We paid you all our debt, in the King's good silver, you bribe-squeezing sack of pigdung, and we harvest our own land now, or did before you—"

"Silence!" the majordomo of the court said, slamming his staff down as the soldiers had their rifles. "The King will question you."

A wiseman leaned close to the King, murmured, showed a paper. "Yes," Isketerol said. "The woman Seurlnai has an elder son, who serves in the King's ships, and from his wages—sent home in filial piety—the family's debts were paid."

Warentekal glowered again, silently. Isketerol recognized the look. Doubtless the landowner was richer than he had ever been, and doubtless he could afford to hire harvest help, or rent or buy slaves enough to do it; he'd been among the first in his district to use one of the mule-drawn reapers demonstrated on the royal estates. But he also doubtless missed his petty local lordship, the loss of clientage from those who now made the King himself their direct patron.

"And then when the bailiff from my estate nearby came to judge the situation, you would not let him onto your land. Nor did you heed the order he brought from one of my judges. This is contempt of the Crown."

Warentekal went down on one knee. "To your royal person I and mine give all respect," he grated. "But Lord King, the bailiff was a man of no account, a mere freedman. Should I let him walk lordly-wise on my land, land granted to my blood by the Lady Herself, the toplofty bastard of no father? May a man of rank not do as he pleases with his own?"

"*Silence!*" Isketerol roared suddenly, a lion's menace in the tone.

Warentekal went gray, remembering too late that this was not the old King's court, and dropping to his face. Isketerol need only give the command, and he would be taken out and thrown into Arucuttag's sea with a rock in his bound hands to speed the journey to the halls of the God.

Isketerol leaned forward, and the other man flinched from his pointing finger as from a spear.

"*Your* land? The King's Law runs and the King's Peace holds on all the land in this realm. You presumed to break it—the violence you offered to this man, the brother of one of my warriors, is violence against *me*. You are not a lesser King on your estate, Warentekal, ruling there as I do here. You are my subject just as the woman Seurlnai is, and like her you hold your land of me, who am the Lady's Bridegroom."

He leaned back again, calm and remote. "Hear the judgment of the King. The man Warentekal"—by leaving off the naming of his father, he was reduced for a moment to a commoner's level—"let his stock damage the fields of the woman Seurlnai. For this, the fine is one silver dollar."

Warentekal winced. That was a moderately severe fine; several times the worth of the pigs. *You will bawl like a branded calf yourself before I am done,* Isketerol thought grimly.

"The man Warentekal ordered slaves to set upon a free subject of the King," Isketerol went on. "For this the fine is the price of two slaves." Warentekal's mouth opened and closed silently. He owned twenty, far more than was common, but two were a substantial proportion of his wealth. "Let the King's bailiff of his estate in the district select the slaves in question, a manservant and a maidservant. Let the maidservant be given to the woman Seurlnai that her labors be lessened."

He turned and questioned the wiseman again, this time about the size of the widow's holding; twelve acres, six under cultivation. One daughter lived with her yet, the others were married, and her son in the fleet was widowed.

Then he continued: "Let the manservant be put to work on the land of the woman Seurlnai until her son returns from the Royal service or her second son regains his full health, and while he labors, let his food be provided from the King's purse." A smallholding like that couldn't support another mouth, but it did need a grown man's full labors.

He sat silent for a moment. "And for the refusal of an order from one of my judges, thus spurning the King's laws, the land-tax upon the fields and flocks of the man Warentekal shall be doubled for . . . mmm, four years."

The landowner's face had gone pale. Now it turned purple. Isketerol's finger stabbed out again: "And if you break the King's Peace again, Warentekal son of Warentekal, *I will have your head*. Hear me!"

He raised his voice slightly, using a sailor's trick to pitch it to carry.

"By Arucuttag of the Sea, by the Lady of Tartessos, by the Sun Lord whose likeness I wear, by the Grain Goddess by whose bounty we live, I swear this. *That a naked virgin with a sack of gold in each hand shall be able to walk from the sea to the mountains unmolested, by the time my kingship descends to my son.*

"Let him who would threaten the King's Peace, let him who would grind down the lowly, let him who would play the bully or the bandit, know this! And he who carries the King's writ, though he be but a shaven ape or a dog walking on its hind legs, him shall you heed and obey!"

The soldiers rapped the floor again, and the clerks bent to scribble the orders, their quill pens scratching on the paper.

"This court is concluded," Isketerol went on, amid the cheers.

The old woman looked at him and nodded firmly once, then

turned and hobbled out with the rest, her hand on her injured son's arm. Isketerol snorted to himself; he knew his folk. Someone from the city might have been more effusive in their gratitude, but wouldn't have meant it as much, either.

Sarsental was glowing as they walked into an antechamber, and servants stripped the robe of state from Isketerol, bringing him the bright archaic regalia of war. *And this too I will only wear until aboard ship,* Isketerol thought wryly. *What a thing of shows and masks this kingship is!*

"You put a stick in the spokes of that one's chariot, my sire," Sarsental said.

"I showed him that the King's Law runs to his doorstep and within," Isketerol said. "To his very hearthstone and hearthshrine and ancestral graves. And I showed the common folk that the King's hand extends over a poor smallholder as well as a rich noble. Fear is a strong support for a throne; but love makes a good yokemate for it. This land of ours is a wild chariot team, my son. I hope to have them used to the bit and harness by the time I turn the reins over to you. And speaking of which . . ."

He pulled a ring from his finger. That was another thing he had learned from the *Amurrukan* books, the signet ring and seal as a symbol of the Throne. Sarsental had seen it on his hand since his earliest memories. His face went slack with surprise as Isketerol put it in his hand and folded the youth's fingers about it.

"My sire?" he said, and his voice broke in a squeak. Anger at that drove out shock, red washing the white from his face.

"While I am with the fleets and armies, I will need one to stand for me here in the city," he said.

"But . . . sire!"

"You are young, yes, but you have learned well. And you will have wisemen and war-captains of my appointment to advise you."

"Oh," Sarsental said. "Then . . . this is for show's sake?"

"No," Isketerol said flatly. "The seal is the seal."

The boy thought again, eyes steady. "Then . . . if I override the advice of those you set to counsel me . . ."

"The glory of success will be yours. Or the blame of failure."

Isketerol was not too worried; the authority would be limited to civil matters within the city walls, and he knew his son. That knowledge was confirmed when the boy stood straighter.

"Yes, my sire," he said. "You will not regret your trust."

"Good. Now, I must go to war. You are old enough to go

with me, but it would be a hard day for the kingdom if we both fell. For now, watch carefully. Think on what I do . . . and think on *why*."

"Sire!"

An hour later, Isketerol of Tartessos raised his hands in the chariot, acknowledging the cheers of his people. The horses paced slowly, prancing, their knees flashing high with every step.

"Long live the good King!" he heard. *"Victory! Victory to our King! Arucuttag fight for the King! Death to the Eagle People! Death to the* Amurrukan! *Death to the Republic!"*

The roar that followed was overwhelming, a passionate wall of sound that struck like cannonfire; the crowds pushed and heaved against the soldiers lining the roadway and holding them back. There must be nearly twenty thousand of them along the great processional way to the harbor, every free adult in the city and many from villages and farms and estates from the countryside around. Isketerol felt himself uplifted by the love and trust he saw on their faces, purified, as if his soul had been washed in a stream of mountain water. There might be reserve from the old families, and hate from foreigners, but the commons of his own people loved the King.

Had he not lifted them up, given them mastery and wealth and health, raised the burden of killing toil from their shoulders and preserved the lives of their children? Had he not written the laws down for all to see, so that a man need not accept the memory of a noble who might twist the words to his own gain? Had he not gone with gun and fire and sacrificial throat-knife against bandit and pirate and reaving mountain savage, so that every man might harvest his field and sleep easy knowing he would keep the fruits of it?

As a father they love me, he thought. *And what is a true King if not a father to the land?*

Rubber tires and steel springs made the journey down the smooth stone blocks of the road easy, which was well; he'd been too much at sea from his youth to ride easily in a chariot, and with the new stirrups and saddles it was a dying art save for ceremony. Fluttering cloak of Sidonian purple, helmet gilded and plumed, glittering gold on his chest, the snarling lion-heads on the hubs of the wheels, the silver and niello and jewels on the body of the car, all blazed like the harness of a God—made a brave show for the people, heartening them still further. He looked up; balloons were floating above the forts that guarded the entrances to the harbor, tethered by long cables. As he watched a heliograph flashed code from one to the ground, and he read it effortlessly.

Enemy ships standing off the southern coast.

Trained will kept his smile from turning into a snarl. No more than three ships had come back to Tartessos from the attack on Nantucket; if all went as he intended, not one of the Islander fleet would return from the Pillars of the Earth-House. The banners and pennants on the masts that crowded the harbor indicated the wind; a bit south of west, not the most favorable but not impossible either.

Should I make them come to me here? he mused again, for the thousandth time. Then: *No, my first thought was best. If we beat them at sea, all is won. If we are defeated, we can retire here behind the guns of the forts—that is a nut they will break their teeth on. But we will not be defeated—*

The other priests waited by the dockside, with the sacrifices for the Sun Lord and Arucuttag. For the Sky Master a fine horse, its coat yellow-gold by nature and sparkling with gold dust, like unto the horses which drew the chariot of the Sun daily across the sky. For Arucuttag a warrior in his prime; on this day of peril not a captive but a volunteer come willing to die for his people, standing proud with the ancient ax resting across his palms, its flint head crusted with old blood and deadly holiness.

"Victory shall be ours!" Isketerol cried as his charioteer reined in. "We will feast on the fish that devour the foe, and manure our fields with the bones of the invaders!"

A slow massive wave of sound rolled back, from the streets and rooftops, from the decks of the ships and from the battlemented walls of the city he had made great.

Mighty Ones, he prayed in the silence of his mind. *Take what I give, and make safe my people and the seed of my House. If the King's death is what You demand, know that I am ever willing to make the given sacrifice.*

For what was a King, if not he who stood for his folk before the Great Gods?

CHAPTER NINETEEN

October, 10 A.E.—Straits of the Pillars, Tartessos
November, 10 A.E.—Hattusas, Kingdom of Hatti-land
October, 10 A.E.—Straits of the Pillars, Tartessos
October, 10 A.E.—Long Island, Republic of Nantucket

"Dyce, keep her dyce," the young lieutenant by the wheels said, tapping his cane against the binnacle and pointing with it to remind the helm crew the heading they were keeping.

A platform put her head above the edge of the sheet-steel-and-timber barricade around the steering station; it wouldn't stop anything shot out of a cannon, but it would deflect grape-shot and rifle bullets.

"Thus, thus—very well, thus."

Marian Alston-Kurlelo clasped her hands behind her back, rising very slightly on the balls of her feet as the *Chamberlain* took the swell with a long smooth rocking-horse motion. She had spent ten years of her life building this fleet, made of wood and iron, hemp and canvas and human hearts. Now she was taking it to possible destruction, quite certain wounding and death and mutilation. Worse yet, the deeper, more atavistic fears; for Swindapa, for the children they'd left behind who might be orphaned again this day, fears of death and crippling wounds. Fear of failure worse than any, and a self-disgust at the cold exhilaration that was building beneath it all.

The flagship was leading the Guard warships in toward land, wind from the south on their starboard quarter, masts bare of all but fighting sail, with boarding nets along the sides and splinter netting overhead. The deck was nearly empty, except for the hands waiting at the lines and the Marine Gatling-gun crews crouching at the rail where their weapons snouted out from among the rolled hammocks; she looked up to the tops, where the rest of the Gatlings waited. Down again, through the deck gratings, and she could see the gun crews poised around the sleek blue-black shapes of their Dahlgrens. A few of them looked up, showed teeth that gleamed in the dark, lifted thumbs, but most waited quiet and motionless in the dimness. There was little sound beside the creak and groan of the ship working, the occasional rutch of feet on the sanded decks—sand to keep the footing from growing slippery when the planks ran with blood and body fluids—and the song of the wind in the rigging.

The faces on the quarterdeck were equally grave and quiet, except for a few middies grinning with excitement. Alston turned and looked behind her. The five frigates followed in exact line, their wakes like a single ruled line across the purple-blue of the sea. The low coastline of southwestern Iberia was less than a hint ahead, more like a line of cloud than a firm sight of land—the heights of Gibraltar and the Sierra Nevada were far off to the southeast. Swindapa came up, saluted, and handed her a folder. It held pictures, digital video shots from pre-Event cameras borne by the scouts in the ultralights, dropped onto the *Chamberlain*'s deck and run through the PC and printer in the radio shack.

"They're coming out," she said quietly; their eyes met, saying all that was needed.

Alston gave a small precise nod, looking at the picture. All the larger Tartessian ships, and twenty of the galleys. *Fangs out and hair on fire.* The enemy had fought hard during the abortive invasion of Nantucket, but they'd fight harder still here, on the doorsteps of their own homes.

What a waste.

She studied the picture. The Tartessians were forming up in a line, ragged but definitely a line, slanting down the wind to the southeast. The Islanders had the weather gauge, the wind blowing from them to the enemy, but that meant little when both sides obviously wanted a stand-up fight. The two fleets formed the acute angles of a triangle; her mind automatically extrapolated the lines. Where they met . . .

"Pass the information to the fleet, Ms. Kurlelo-Alston," Marian said.

She glanced to starboard. The transports were lying further southward, off the Moroccan coast, hull-down from her present position. Lying to the windward also meant they could move rapidly, if necessary. . . .

"On deck, there! Sail ho!"

The enemy grew from a flash of white to sails to hulls painted dark blue-gray and checked by the opening maws of gunports, as swift as always when fleets were on converging courses. The hulls were long and low, derived from the form of *Yare*, the first modern ship they'd been able to study in detail. *Six-to-one hull–beam ratio*, she noted. There were differences, though; slightly more rake on the masts, an ingenious-looking Y-fork coming up from the stem and used to set the mizzen forestays. The Tartessian shipwrights were men who understood wood and stresses and the sea, with their hands and guts if not mathematically. They'd taken the uptime carpentry tools and techniques and run with them—run far and fast.

"Carry on," she said, walked to the rail, stepped up to the ratlines, and ran up the shrouds to the mizzen top.

"Good morning," she said to the occupants—the triangular platform was crowded, with the Gatling crew and several Marine sharpshooters with telescopic sights on their rifles.

"Morning, ma'am," a sergeant said cheerfully, in a thick Fiernan accent. "Beautiful it is a morning for fight, if fight has to become."

There was something to that; not too hot, blue sky with an occasional fleecy cloud, a Mediterranean autumn on the edge of winter. She nodded back and climbed further, up the shrouds that used the top as a spreader and to the topgallant crosstrees. That narrow spreader board had room only for one, and the sailor there ran nimbly out onto the yard to give her room. She leveled her binoculars. The galleys were coming up fast behind the twelve sailing ships . . .

Now, that's cunning, she thought. *Just the thing to hit us when we're taking on the gunships.*

Like the sailing ships they had fires going in braziers on their quarterdecks next to the wheel, where the three-legged idols of Arucuttag sat in their little shrines. Her lips tightened. Turning these buccaneers loose on the world with nineteenth-century technology and Bronze Age attitudes was the Nantucketers' fault . . . hers, in particular.

The decks of the enemy ships showed plenty of other glints, the edged metal of bayonets and boarding pikes, axes and swords; as she'd expected, they'd shipped heavy crews for this action. Crowding might slow them down if they overdid it. If they didn't overdo it, it might give them a little edge because they could rotate gun crews and replace casualties. It would certainly make them harder to take by boarding. She looked up their masts, and from one came a wink of reflected light, a spyglass peering back at her.

"And they've got a smart, hard, unmerciful man to lead

them, one who's as able as any I've ever met, I think," she murmured to herself.

We gave Isketerol his chance, she mused. *If the* Eagle *hadn't turned up there in Alba, he'd have lived and died an obscure adventurer, in a people so obscure the archaeologists weren't even sure they really existed. We gave him an opportunity, and woke the fire in his belly.*

What was that phrase Doreen Arnstein had used once . . . a "mute inglorious Milton"?

Well, Isketerol was a mute inglorious Napoléon, or William the Conqueror.

He did have one weakness, or strength, that his friend William Walker lacked. To twentieth-century eyes he was ambitious to the point of madness and cruel as the sea, but he had his own standards. Walker was a solipsist, the one true love of his own life; the rest of the world was game-counters to him. By contrast, the Iberian warlord really cared about his own people; and he was a man of honor, in his way . . .

Alston leaned out, wrapped an arm and both legs around a backstay, and slid down, thinking hard as she did, as casual as running downstairs in Guard House back on Main Street. On the quarterdeck, she said:

"Ms. Kurlelo-Alston, order to the schooners. They're to move in east and west and engage the galleys. And to remember those damned things can go right into the eye of the wind."

More bitterly than ever she missed the *Farragut,* and pushed that out of her mind.

"Coming into range," Commander Jenkins said.

And we should take advantage of it, she thought. *If they've reequipped with twenty-four-pounders, six a side, they've got a broadside of a hundred and forty-four pounds each. We've got over eight hundred pounds, and the range on them.*

"Open fire as you bear on the lead ship, Mr. Jenkins," she said. "To the fleet; general engagement in line, maintain course."

A rattle of orders, from Jenkins through his subordinates, down to the gun crews. *Out tompions!* and *run out your guns!* The familiar drumming thunder as the portlids went up and the gleaming blue-black snouts came out, the grunting *hnnn-huh!,* each crew in unison as they heaved four thousand pounds of cast-steel cannon across the thick oak planking with rope and block and pulley and sheer hard sweat.

Just then the side of the first Tartessian ship vanished in a cloud of smoke; a perceptible fraction of a second later came the rolling sound of huge doors slamming echoing over the water. Marian's brows went up; wasting powder, with the guns they had available. Then she frowned. The sound wasn't quite right, too deep.

Everyone was looking northward with alert curiosity, a few faces pale and drawn. The first ball struck the water two hundred yards short of the *Chamberlain*'s bow and skipped twice like a giant's flung stone. Alston felt her teeth clench. *That's too far and too hard.*

The next two went right into a wave and vanished; the fourth skipped and struck forward, hitting the flukes of the portside anchor with a discordant metallic *clungggg* that sent shivers into the back teeth of every jaw on board as it ran up from the deck through feet to head. Numbers five and six came aboard, one with a deep wet *thunk* into the hull timbers, the last after two skips into the hammock-netting not far from where she stood. It was nearly spent, its energy wasted on the water it had grazed, but it still sent splinters and ripped canvas flying, thudded into the mizzenmast and went trundling across the deck with crewfolk hopping and cursing to avoid it.

Clunng. It struck the barricade around the wheel and compass and finally came to a halt, rolling with the pitch of the deck rather than walking itself with the gyroscopic force of rapid spin. Alston looked down at it wide-eyed as it rolled not two feet from the toes of her boots.

An expert's eye judged size and weight effortlessly. Eight-inch diameter, sixty-eight pounder. Almost identical to those the Republic's frigates used for the main armament, save that the surface was slightly pebbled rather than machined smooth. No ship of the Tartessians' size could carry a conventional gun large enough to fire that shot; it had to come from something cold-core-cast and carefully shaped by a knowledge of internal pressures. Almost certainly cast in steel, not stiff brittle cast iron.

Like the Dahlgrens on the *Chamberlain*'s gun deck, Civil War models improved by Leaton's superior steels.

Walker shipped them in, she realized. *Recently enough that our agents didn't pick it up.*

How and why didn't matter now. What did matter was that their range advantage was gone or mostly gone—that would depend on how well worked-up their crews were with their new weapons—and that their edge in weight of metal had just been cut in half. She could feel her brain working the numbers, as if she were watching some machine in Leaton's shops whirring and stretching, steel sliding on oiled steel.

"Belay firing," she said calmly. "Left to two-seven-zero. Fleet to conform. Inform all captains that the enemy mounts eight-inch Dahlgrens and repeat it. Advise schooners to employ caution."

Because at anything like close range those guns will throw a ball in one side of you and out the other, she thought, as Swindapa dashed to the radio shack.

Jenkins gave her a single startled glance, but he was already barking orders. *Chamberlain* had been sailing east on a reach, with the wind broad on the starboard quarter. Now she turned on her heel to run before the wind a little east of north, the sailors spinning the wheel and deck crews running to heave sails around from their port brace, putting the yards more nearly horizontal to the hull.

A chorus of *heave*-ho! ran across the deck, line teams bending to it with a will, sweat running down their naked backs or plastering T-shirts to skin. The change in course turned the bow toward the enemy, cutting off the gun crews' view; she could hear a muted chorus of groans from sailors who'd been ready for the crash of their first broadside. A glance behind showed the whole string of frigates turning as if they were attached to the flagship with invisible rods, heeling over to starboard as momentum pressed them down, then steadying on the new course.

The whole Tartessian line disappeared in smoke as the Islander fleet turned toward them—and therefore turned their own deadly broadsides away, cannon pointed impotently at each other or empty sea, while every gun on the enemy decks still bore right down their throats. Alston gripped her hands together behind her back; they'd have to take two broadsides without being able to reply, maybe three . . .

Iron lashed the water ahead of them; the enemy were firing at a narrower target now, perhaps a little slow to correct their aim. There was a rending crash forward, and the sound of screaming. Blocks and lines fell on the splinter netting overhead, and something came all along the deck and whirred past her close enough to whip her around like a top with the wind of its passage. That let her see Jenkins staring down incredulously at the stump where his left hand had been, and a body beyond him falling—one of the lieutenants, beheaded as neatly as a giant guillotine could have done.

She stepped forward, whipping off the lanyard from the

breast pocket of her uniform jacket and throwing the loop around his arm just above the ragged stump, pulling it taut with a hard jerk. He was going gray with shock, eyes wandering.

"You, you, get him below," she said, and they lifted the captain of the *Chamberlain* between them and dashed for the companionway. " 'Dapa, pass the word for Mr. Oxton. Ensign, give me a hand."

She was standing in a spreading pool of blood; smashing the head off lets everything out very quickly, and there are many gallons of blood in a human body. This one was that of a fairly slight woman, and they heaved it over the rail with a single convulsive movement.

"Ma'am?" Oxton said, his face set, a little pale, lips compressed, green eyes steady and level.

Good, she thought. Aloud: "Mr. Oxton, you're in command of this ship; Captain Jenkins is disabled," she said. "Keep her so."

"One minute fifty seconds," Swindapa said at her side, looking at her watch. "Two minutes . . . and ten . . ."

"Keep her so . . . dyce, do you hear?" from Oxton near the helm.

A middy came panting up from the gun deck, looked for Jenkins, ran to Oxton's side, and reported in a slightly shrill voice that number-one starboard had been dismounted, was secured, two crew dead and four wounded. There was blood spattered across the chalk-white freckled face, clotted in the short dark-red hair, and a little running from a cut over one eye.

"Very well," Oxton said. "Steady there, Mr. Telukelo."

"Yessir." He visibly took a deep breath. "The master gunner says the gun can be remounted but it'll take twenty minutes. Have to mount new ringbolts."

"Leave it secured," Oxton said. "Carry on."

"Sir!"

"Two minutes twenty seconds . . ." Swindapa said.

This time the lead Tartessian ship's guns went off in a rippling volley rather than a simultaneous broadside, firing from forward to aft with the long jets of flame raking through the fogbank of powder smoke streaming back northward across her decks.

A sailor fell out of the rigging with a long scream, one of the bosun's crew crawling aloft repairing cut lines and stays. The shriek was cut short as the man bounced off a shroud and hit the deck hard and unevenly. The *Chamberlain* shuddered and started to fall away to port as the foretopsail yard sagged, smashed clean through near the partners. More crew swarmed aloft and others went to the lines; the ship steadied as the hands at the helm wrestled with the wheel.

"Sir," someone panted. "Sir, Chips says we're hulled three places on the port bow near the waterline. He's working to plug it, two feet in the hold."

"Acknowledge. Hands to the pumps, there."

"One minute thirty seconds . . ."

Alston nodded, feeling for the right moment, eyes slitted. "Fleet to conform," she said. "Message to the transports—execute contingency C. Mr. Oxton, bring her right to three-two-zero; guns to fire as they bear."

"Right fifty degrees rudder! Haul all port, lively port!"

She raised her binoculars again as the long bowsprit swung eastward, a part of her hearing the roaring cheer from the gun deck as the crews got the order, and the cry of *silence fore and aft!* that followed it.

They were much closer now; she could easily see the Tartessian deck crews heaving to clew up the foresail and lower foretopsail to check their ship's way, taking some speed off her so their line wouldn't outrun hers and leave itself vulnerable to being broken in the middle. A hint of a bleak smile bent her full lips as the second Iberian ship was late about following suit and nearly ran its leader aboard at the stern; men were yelling at each other and waving their arms there.

Chamberlain was coming about, not to lie parallel with the enemy but to approach them at the sharpest angle that would allow her to use all her broadside guns. The Tartessians were taking the challenge, keeping their course rather than slacking off to the north to maintain their distance.

Mmmm-hmmmm. Probably they intend to let us each get tangled up with one ship, then range up and take us on the other side with the unengaged vessels. That was the rational way to use their advantage in hulls and numbers; they had about the same number of guns but twice as many ships. That made their firepower more mobile, but also more diffuse at any one point.

BAAAAMMM. The first of the *Chamberlain*'s big Dahlgrens cut loose in a spear of red fire and a cloud of smoke; the wind swept it northward like a young fogbank. *BAAAAMMM.* A steady rippling fire, each gun waiting until the turn of the ship brought the target into its sights, the gun captain shouting *clear!* and jerking the lanyard, curving his body aside like a matador to let the cannon slam backward with the recoil. Then the reloading, the swabber pushing wet sponges down the barrel with a long *sssshhhhhh* of steam to quench sparks, the powder-bag and wad, two loaders tipping the heavy steel ball in like a giant ball bearing, the rammer pushing it down, the crew hauling on the tackle to run the gun forward again and the captain slamming in a new friction-fuse, glaring over the barrel, heaving on a handspike, spinning the elevation screw and making hand signals to the crew to push the breech around and bring the gun to bear. Then *clear!*—

Brutal manual labor of the hardest kind in the stifling smoke-filled gun deck, darkness and scorching-hot cannon recoiling like the pistons of a forging hammer and as able to crush a limb or skull if one step went wrong; yet skilled labor, too, a teamwork choreographed as precisely as any dance. Automatic, endless, ignoring the heat and fatigue and dry wooden tongues, the knowledge that enemy shot could smash through the oak timbers at any second.

"One minute fifteen seconds for our first gun to repeat," Swindapa said.

That was excellent time, far better than the enemy was managing; they had heavy crews but not the long practice that gave speed and accuracy.

A gun that fires twice as fast is as good as two, she thought.

The lines of ships were less than a thousand yards apart now, cannon a continous bellowing roar, smoke choking-thick. A crackle came from the tops above her; she glanced up and saw a Marine sharpshooter leaning over the piled hammocks along the railings of the maintop, firing, slipping a new shell into the breech, picking a target, correcting her aim, firing again. The enemy were doing likewise. A young deckhand running with a bucket of sand to throw on a fire dropped and lay motionless, blood leaking from under him; another checked the body, shook her head, and helped drag it to the side and put it over. Something went *crack* overhead, hit the plates around the wheel, bounced and went off *whirrt-whirrt-whirrt*, a lethal lead Frisbee.

Only part of her attention was necessary for the business of the moment, the long waiting as the fleets ran together and hammered each other as they came. Part of her was spectator; part remembering—*do Jesus, there are a lot of things I want to live to do again . . .*

Watch an iceberg heel in the Roaring Forties, as the surf of a storm lashing around the planet broke on it in waves mountain-high, seething gray and white and green. Sea-turtles crawling up a Carribean beach turned silver under the full moon, looking like an endless field of living boulders; or a sky-full of condors over the towering painted pyramid of Sechin Alto in Peru. Hear wolves howling in the Berkshire hills on a hunting trip, with night falling and the rich yeasty smell of damp autumn leaves. Smell the clean milky scent of a baby and watch its broad toothless idiot smile as it reached for her . . . Heather and Lucy's kids. Take the pan out of the oven and feel the earthy joy of knowing she'd made a really *perfect* beaten biscuit. Sit in front of a fire at home with Swindapa on a winter's night, hearing the snow beat feather-paws against the windows, their arms around each other's shoulders and a book of Flecker propped open on their knees.

Crack. There was a cold shock in the small of her back, cold fire scoring across her flank. She spun, staggered, put a hand to her right side below the last rib. Hot wetness and torn cloth. Breath hissed out between her teeth.

Swindapa grabbed her, pushed her into the shelter of the helm barricade, knelt. A rip of cloth and cold air hit the wound.

"It needs stitches," she said.

"Can't take the time," she said, and craned her head to look. A line of red . . . not too deep, mostly in the thin layer of subcutaneous fat, not clipping the fibers of the muscle much . . .

"Bandage it," she said. "That'll have to do. No time for anything else and stitches would just rip out if I have to move."

The pain had begun, and the fire turned hot as the antiseptic powder went into the wound. *A lot easier than havin' a baby,* she told herself. Her partner wound the bandage around her waist like a sash, tying it off tight to hold the pad over the torn flesh, then tugging the jacket down over it again. She walked out, testing herself—not much loss of function just yet.

Damn, I'm getting' to be held together by bandages. There were two priceless pre-Event elastic ones on her knees as a precaution against extension injuries.

"Flesh wound," she said to Oxton's worried glance.

A ball gouged a cut out of the mainmast, neat as a cookie cutter, except that a cookie cutter would not have left a dozen sailors down with splinters through thighs and bellies and chests. No more than a hundred yards now, an endless bellowing roar, smoke stinking of burned sulfur, the copper-iron metallic taint of blood, shot crashing home like the tattoo of hail on a roof magnified to Brobdingagian size.

The two lines of battle were at their death-grapple, ton-weights of iron flung back and forth to smash metal and wood and human flesh in a chaos of fallen spars and sails and cordage like the nets of giant spiders. Through the gunsmoke she could see the two foremost Tartessian vessels. The forward one was a shambles, several gunports beaten into one, her forward mast gone above the top, blood running in thin trickles from her scuppers. But still steering, and the one behind was far less hard-hit; it yawed its bows away for a moment and raked the *Chamberlain* on its port quarter, vanishing for a moment behind a cloud of their own smoke. She could feel the heavy shot strike home, steady deliberate fire and well aimed, smashing into the left rear of the frigate and carrying across the decks below; for a moment the screams of the wounded overrode the noise of battle and the ship's fire tailed off. Then it started up again, nearly as fast, and the rudder still answered the helm. Relief felt like weakness; she forced it down.

"Ready," she said. "Two broadsides with grape and then board the leader in the smoke. Ensign Glidden. The signal now, please."

The young officer loaded his flare pistol and raised it. *Fudump.* The shell arched skyward and burst with a pop, bright crimson against the blue sky. She turned her binoculars to starboard, saw the answering blossom of sail among the transports, nodded satisfaction.

That was also the signal to the rest of the fleet, and to their own gunners. There were still two Gatling guns functional along the rail, their crews lying flat on the deck, waiting until the enemy were fully committed. Now they bounced erect, tore the covers off their weapons and began to fire. *Braaaaap. Braaaaap.* Long bursts as the Marine corporals worked the cranks, traversing the six-barreled weapons along the enemy ship's rail, across the line of gunports. They added nearly as much smoke as the cannon, but the red blade of the firing was continuous. Each had a gun-shield that turned rifle bullets with trails of sparks, leaving smears of lead across the shields. More sparks ran in trails along the line of the enemy's hull, where the thin iron plates hadn't been hammered off by the cannonade; many more must be plunging through the ports and the gaps knocked by *Chamberlain*'s guns, and she could see the scything fire hit the bulwarks and the men beyond.

Then the Gatlings in the tops opened up, two plunging fire right into the crowded deck below, another raking the enemy's tops and the riflemen and swivel guns there. A dying hand triggered one of the swivels, and some malignant chance put the one-pound shot into the barrels of the foretop Gatling and turned them into twisted wreckage.

"Ready at the helm—order will be to port the helm, hard a'port," Oxton said in a quarterdeck bellow, trained to cut through the roar of white noise. "Boarders to your stations, crews ready to follow. Starbolines to board at the peak, larbolines at the quarterdeck." In a more normal voice: "Perhaps I should lead the quarterdeck boarding party, ma'am?"

"By no means, Mr. Oxton," Alston said, grinning like a shark.

The companionways up from the gun deck grew crowded as the boarders ran from their stations by the guns. Swindapa came back, a pre-Event pump-action shotgun in either hand. She handed one to Alston, together with a bandolier of new Seahaven-made cartridges.

"The schooners report they're having trouble keeping the galleys back," she said soberly. "*Douglass* is badly damaged and the *Tubman* is sinking. They'll buy us all the time they can."

Alston nodded. Grief was a luxury she couldn't afford right now, any more than she could pay attention to physical pain. Closer, and the leading enemy ship's gunfire had fallen off, a slow halting drumroll now. The *Chamberlain*'s crew fired two more broadsides, but these had a malignant multiple wasp-buzz under the thunder of discharge—thousands of marble-sized iron balls blasting through the ten yards left between the ships, aimed slightly upward to sweep the decks already savaged by the Gatlings. You could pack a *lot* of grapeshot into the maw of an eight-inch gun . . .

"Port your helm, hard a'port!"

A crunching and grating as the flanks of the ships kissed; grapnels flew, a lurch that made everyone clutch for something to steady themselves by, rope or rail or deck; hands ran out along the yards to lash them tight to those of the enemy. She glanced over her shoulder, and saw the next Tartessian ship turning to starboard, to come alongside the *Chamberlain*'s unengaged side and flood her with men—or so they thought.

The Gatlings in the tops swiveled and began to rake the other Tartessian. Cable and line whipped free under the cutting stream of bullets; the topsail yard fell all the way to the deck, and the foretopmast toppled off to the side as the shrouds and stays were cut.

The two rail Gatlings went by Alston, each carried by six sweating, swearing Marines; they slapped their burdens down on undamaged sections of the rail and spun the clamps to seat it firmly. The gunner and assistant lowered a big five-hundred-round magazine onto its receiving rails, worked the crank a quarter turn backward, then opened fire again. The endless rippling roar merged with those from the maintop and mizzen, and bright brass shells cataracted down into the canvas bags slung beneath the mechanism as the six barrels spun.

That will keep them busy, Alston thought grimly. Aloud: "Mr. Oxton, that Tartessian will try to range up alongside and board. Have the remaining crew lie flat when she does, and give her the starboard broadside at point-blank range. I'll leave you enough personnel for that." A deep breath, and:

"Boarders away—follow me!"

A roaring cheer, bass male bellows and female hawk-shrieks, and the boarding parties swarmed forward. She racked the slide of the shotgun and leaped, first to the quarterdeck rail and then downward to the lower rail of the enemy ship. Landing, crouching to regain her balance, boot soles slipping a little before she recovered; a man came up with his face streaming with blood, drawing back for a cut with his cutlass. Rising, she lashed out with one foot, a sweeping straight-legged kick that ended with the steel-capped toe of her boot under the point of his chin. Bone crumbled and he flipped backward. Alston ignored the savage twinge of pain in her wounded side and jumped from the rail to the deck.

Her partner landed beside her, cat-steady; *Swindapa* meant *Deer dancer* in the Old Tongue, and it had been given her for good reason; ten years of training in karate and *iajutsu* helped, too.

Dead and wounded were piled thick all along the Tartessian's decks, slippery with blood and fluids and brains, piles that still heaved and screamed in places. There were still some on their feet, and more were pouring up out of the hatchways—they must have packed the holds with men, even down in the orlop and cargo spaces. With no need to carry provisions or water that was possible—

The thought took less than a second. She and her partner went to cover behind a shattered spar still tangled in its sail and raised their weapons, set their teeth and began to fire. The heavy buckshot slammed out at waist level, a rapid *thump-thump-thump-thump-thump,* twelve rounds in as many seconds. Men went down, their torsos and faces chewed to ruin, and the survivors wavered until the rush behind them pushed them on. By then Islanders by the dozen were dropping down around the leaders, firing double-barreled shotguns or Werder rifles, throwing grenades into the packed mass before them. Marian took an instant to thumb fat shotgun shells from her bandolier into the gate in front of the trigger guard and look back.

From here she could see the masts of the other Tartessian ship coming up on the starboard side of the *Chamberlain*. Then there was the roar of a broadside and the masts pitched and shivered. Alston nodded with grim satisfaction; the frigate's guns would be firing at point-blank range, their muzzles pitched up to maximum elevation—the heavy shot going through the sides and then blasting up through the decking under the feet of the enemy boarding parties in an eruption of splinters and iron. The masts pivoted away as the Tartessian paid off to get away from those gaping maws, with no way of knowing that they couldn't be reloaded.

The firing died down, almost completely from the enemy side—their weapons were slower to load. Aware of that, they rose up and charged once more instead, calling on their Gods. Behind them others were fighting the Islanders pouring onto the forecastle, and the locked ships turned into a single great sprawling brawl, blows given and received breast to breast, pistols fired with their muzzles jammed into flesh, blades short-gripped and stabbing upward.

"Up and at 'em!" she shouted.

"No, Brigadier Hollard," Doreen said, pouring the cocoa.

Kenneth Hollard looked up sharply as he reached for the cup; they were usually on first-name terms, in private, and this upper room of the Arnsteins' villa was as private as it got. The windows were closed, the lamplight soft on the vivid colors of the rugs and hangings, on books and chess set and the radio in the corner. Doreen Arnstein sat behind her desk, and her face was a polite implacable mask, her hands resting on the blotter.

"No, I don't think Ian is dead," she said judiciously. Then, before he could ask, "The Foreign Affairs department has its sources."

"Ah . . . ma'am, with Mr. Arnstein in enemy hands, they'd be compromised."

"Credit us with some intelligence, Brigadier," she said crisply. "Half the network was always my responsibility, and we had all summer to alert the others—there was always a risk that this might happen."

Her lips pressed together; Hollard nodded slightly. She'd

been after Ian to get out of Troy since just before the siege began. Perhaps the Councilor for Foreign Affairs had discounted his assistant's advice as prejudiced. Perhaps it was some sort of survivor guilt, a need to stay at the sharp end of things and share the risks of the people he had to send into harm's way.

Keeping Troy fighting was real *important,* Hollard thought. *If Ian hadn't pinned down the bulk of Walker's army—not to mention his shipping capacity—there, God knows where we'd be now. Was that worth risking one of our top leadership cadre?*

"Any information of that sort that Ian had is thoroughly obsolete," Doreen went on. "Some valuable data on our strategy and capacity, yes, but not anything that would shut down our programs."

Hollard looked at her appraisingly. He'd always admired her brains; nobody could work with Doreen Arnstein and doubt that she had enough raw brainpower to melt titanium, and a hell of a lot of information to process with it. He'd never doubted that she'd show guts at a pinch, either.

But I didn't expect her to be quite this . . . is tough *the word?* he thought.

"Ma'am . . . it might be *better* if the councilor were dead. All things considered."

Doreen shook her head. "The problem with death is that it's sort of permanent," she went on. "Don't waste that chocolate, by the way."

Hollard sipped obediently.

"If Hong were . . ." Doreen stopped for a few seconds, face absolutely still, before continuing: "If Hong were . . . torturing . . . Ian, she'd boast about it. She'd send us parts of him, or photographs. It would be an opportunity to inflict anguish on us, and she's incapable of acting otherwise."

Ken nodded. "I agree," he said gently. "But doesn't that argue that he *is* dead? Major Chong's report was pretty circumstantial."

She shook her head again. "No. Because then *Walker* would be boasting about it. He'd have Ian's . . . he'd have Ian's head on display. *He's* incapable of acting otherwise."

"Well, that's logical," Hollard said. *Not that I have an infinite faith in logic to predict how people operate.* "But Ms. Arnstein, if they *haven't* killed him and they're *not* . . . interrogating . . . him, what do you think they're doing, and why?"

"I don't know exactly," Doreen said. "I won't until I get reports—you'd be surprised at some of our agents-in-place. At a guess . . . I'd say Walker likes to keep his options open as long as he can."

"To hedge his bets," Hollard agreed. "I've studied the Alban War. He had a fallback strategy in place before the Battle of the Downs. Trouble is, he might have *won* the Battle of the Downs if he'd thrown everything into it."

Doreen gestured agreement. "And he's . . . a solipsist," she said. "Other people aren't really emotionally real to him; they're bundles of traits to be manipulated, which is one reason he can do it so well, be so objective about it. I think that's especially true of locals; they're toys he uses in his game—that may have been what pushed him over the edge into acting out his power fantasies after the Event, that and opportunity. I think—if *he* thinks he can get away with it—he'd keep Ian around so he'd have someone more, mmmm, more *real* to crow over and boast to."

"Now," she went on briskly. "I have a report from Commodore Alston and the Fleet . . ."

Damn, that is one tough broad, Hollard thought as he walked out into the corridor an hour later. He was lost enough in thought that he nearly ran into the Arnsteins' son.

"Hi, David!" he said a little awkwardly.

He'd met the boy often enough; the whole native-born Islander community in the Middle East was only a few hundred people, the top leaders far fewer. But this was the first time since the fall of Troy a few days ago . . .

Big dark eyes like his mother's looked up at the tall blond man. "Uncle Ken," he said. "Is my dad dead?"

Oh, shit. He went down on one knee to put his face more nearly level with the eight-year-old's. "Dave, I don't know. None of us know. But your mother doesn't think he is, and she's a very smart lady and she knows a lot."

The haunted eyes looked straight into his. "Have those bad people hurt him?"

Oh, shit. I know that's repetitive, but it's the only appropriate repsonse.

"We just don't know that either, Dave," he went on. "We think they've got reasons of their own to keep him safe, for now."

On impulse he hugged the slight form to him. The boy gripped him fiercely around the neck, then stifled a sob and stood back.

"And we'll get him back if there's any way to do it," Kenneth Hollard said solemnly. "I promise you that."

"Thank you," the boy said. "I know you will—you and Aunt Kathryn and Princess Raupasha and the King." A scowl. "And *kill* those bad people. All of them!"

Hollard nodded. "I intend to."

"Disssaaa!"

Marian Alston caught the boarding ax on the guard of the *wazikashi* in her left hand, grunting at the heavy impact. The Tartessian sailor grabbed her right hand as she tried to ram the muzzle of her Python into his body, and the shot went astray into the melee on the deck of the second Tartessian ship. Despite that shattering broadside it still carried enough men to be dangerous, and some quick-thinking officer had brought the crippled vessel around to the port side of the other Iberian craft. Reinforcements poured up out of its holds and into the crush.

Do Jesus, he's strong, she thought as they swayed in a stamping circle; this sort of straight-out wrestling with men was something she always tried to avoid, and her opponent was a wiry bundle of gristle and bone. *Twenty years younger to boot.* His bare chest ran with sweat and the muscle there rippled as he pushed back her arms.

She couldn't retreat; Swindapa was lying at her feet, just beginning to pull herself up, shaking her head with her left hand pressed over cheek and eye.

So cheat, she told herself and whipped up a knee between his thighs.

It impacted painfully on a boiled-leather cup, but the blow was enough to loosen his grip. She tore the wrist that held the empty pistol loose and slammed it twice into the side of his head, even as he hooked a heel behind hers and lunged forward. They fell backward over Swindapa's body and rolled, snarling; blood was pouring down the side of his face as he surged on top and pinned her legs, grabbed the right wrist again, half rose and used his weight to push the edge of the ax toward her face. Its edge was nicked and red, with shreds of flesh caught in the notched steel. The wound in her side was bleeding again, there was no way to fight without using your back and gut muscles, and the strength flowed out of her. Beyond the Tartessian's back she saw another poised with a rifle held clubbed by the muzzle, the butt rising over Swindapa's back.

Baduff!

The shotgun blast smeared the flesh off the face of the enemy

sailor who'd been about to smash her partner's spine. Alston
whipped her head aside in the moment's distraction, letting her
left arm go limp and the curved twenty-inch blade of the *waki-
kashi* snap backward. The ax slid down it with a tooth-grating
squeal of steel on steel and thumped into the decking right
next to her ear, the shaft impacting painfully against her collarbone. That left the smallsword free; her wrist traversed the
point twenty degrees and a heave of shoulder and back rammed
it up under the Tartessian's rib cage. He reared back, mouth
open in a soundless O of shock, and more blood poured down
to spatter with the rest that soaked the cloth over her torso
and hips. A heavy booted foot kicked him the rest of the way
clear, and a massive black hand reached down to help her up.

"Thanks," she wheezed, pressing a hand full of pistol over
the wound in her side.

"Sho' 'nuff mah pleasure," Brigadier McClintock said, exaggerating his drawl.

He snapped open the double-barreled shotgun and dropped
two more shells into the smoking breech, flicking the weapon
closed with a quick upward jerk of his wrist. A red-running
cutlass was thonged to his right wrist. Alston felt a brief irrational regret for the shotguns she and her partner had carried
over the rail, one smashed parrying a boarding ax, another
gone God-knew-where. Bit by bit, the pre-Event world vanished, gone down the well of entropy, and what replaced it
might be better or worse but was never quite the same. . . .

McClintock helped Swindapa to her feet as well; the left side
of her face was swelling where the flat of a rifle butt had
punched it, leaving only a slit in the puffy flesh for her eye,
but she was conscious and nothing looked to be broken. The
fight on the decks of the Tartessian craft was slowing as Marines poured across from the transport grappled to the starboard bow of the *Chamberlain*. Near her an ordered line of
bayonets stretched from rail to rail, and from behind it the
sea-soldiers poured in volley after volley of Werder bullets. A
moment of inner balance she could almost taste, and then the
surviving enemy began to throw down their weapons, going to
their knees and holding up empty hands for quarter.

"Cease fire! Cease fire!" McClintock bellowed. "Captain
Thawekulo, get theose people disarmed and under the
hatches!"

Marian went to the rail, limping, supporting Swindapa until
the younger woman was able to lean against it.

"God-damn," Alston whispered.

The four linked ships had turned under the undirected thrust of wind on masts and rigging and what sails remained, spinning slowly a hundred and eighty degrees. From here she could see right down the line of battle, now that the cannon smoke had mostly cleared. Two other frigates were in much the same state as hers, lashed to a pair of Tartessians each with transports grappled to them in turn. Khaki-uniformed Marines and blue-clad sailors and auxiliaries in everything from imitation uniforms to leather kilts to full nudity—a boastful pledge of divine favor—swarmed over them like driver ants. The third frigate, *Lincoln,* was taking its opponents under tow.

The fifth was on fire, flames licking mast high and the enemy ships frantically paying off to get away from her . . . *God-*damn, *I'll miss Hiller . . . no, wait, one of those ships that was fast to* Sheridan *is flying the Stars and Stripes . . .*

Some substratum of her mind made her throw up a hand and glance away. There was a lightning-bright red flash and a shattering roar; when the ball of smoke and fire and shattered water subsided, what was left of a thousand tons of frigate were slipping beneath the water, or flotsam on the surface or turning and flashing hundreds of feet in the air, falling again like some ghastly burning confetti mixed with parts of human beings.

"God-*damn,*" she whispered again.

From the northward came a line of polished steel beaks and pairs of heavy guns like malevolent black eyes, flanked by the flashing unison of long sweeps; behind them was a pillar of smoke, doubtless a burning ship of hers.

They broke through the schooners, she thought with heavy finality. *Just a little more time and we'd . . . if only . . . to hell with that. Let's save what we can.*

She opened her mouth to give the order to retreat; running before the wind the sailing ships could probably escape, most of them at least. Then Ensign Glidden came up, half of an ear gone under a hasty bandage and his left arm strapped to his chest. He was carefully avoiding looking what he stepped on and over, but his voice was clear:

"Ma'am! Report from the ultralights—the *Farragut,* ma'am, that smudge is the *Farragut's* smokestack!"

For a moment all she could do was stare. Behind her, Brigadier McClintock began to laugh. After a moment, Swindapa joined in, wincing at the same time but not letting the pain stop her.

*   *   *

"Well, just another rasher," Jared Cofflin said, wiping his plate with a heel of bread.

Tansawada shook a moa egg the size of a small football, took out the plug that closed a hole in it and poured more into the big iron skillet to scramble a batch. Everyone else was digging in as well, from the younglings in high chairs to the adults shoveling down eggs and sausage and bacon, biscuits and bread and stacks of flapjacks and maple syrup. Farming at this level of technology meant you had to work like a horse, but it was efficient enough that you could eat that way too.

Talk about farmhouse breakfasts . . . well, I suppose when you're used to sitting down eighteen to a meal a few more are no hardship . . . "I can always fit—"

Hooves pounded up the graveled way outside, amid shouts and a frantic barking of dogs. The sound was clear enough, but the Hollards' kitchen looked south, over fields and woodlots and the distant blue of water glimpsed through gaps between the trees. Cofflin laid down his spoon, conscious of the looks on him from around the big table, puzzled or anxious.

" 'Scuse me," he said quickly. "That's probably a courier."

He walked out into the hallway; the front door let in on another, sort of an airlock arrangement to keep warm air in in wintertime. Only when he reached for the front door's carved wooden knob did he realize he still had his checked napkin in hand, and that Martinelli was beside him, pistol inconspicuously drawn and held down by his side.

The young woman on the other side of the wood almost stumbled in as he pulled the door open; she already had the screen door propped open, and she was reaching into the leather satchel slung over one shoulder. Her horse was hitched to the rail out in the graveled driveway, blowing with wide-flared nostrils, streaks of foam on its sweat-wet neck, trying to reach the water trough. The courier might have been in too much of a hurry to walk it cool, but at least it wasn't let free to drink and founder itself.

"Chief!" the post office courier said in a thick Fiernan accent, dancing from one foot to another with excitement. "Courier message from Fort Brandt . . . they *flew* it over, Chief! Right over to Fogarty's Cove!"

The brown paper envelope was crinkly-fresh, the flap sealed with a blob of red wax. He recognized Captain Sandy Rapczewicz's seal, CO at Brandt Point station and the Republic's military commander with Marian abroad. She was a levelheaded type, so this *must* be important.

"Ms . . ."

"Mary Burns, Chief," the messenger said.

"Ms. Burns, you'd better walk that horse, then water it."

He broke the seal as she blushed, dithered, and then hurried off to obey. The summary was always right at the top . . .

He turned, to find he had an audience, some of them still clutching forks or rolls. Heather and Lucy were staring wide-eyed. As they saw his face they began to jump, their squeals an ear-piercing joy.

CHAPTER TWENTY

April, 11 A.E.—Sacramento Delta, California
April, 11 A.E.—Feather River Valley, California
April, 11 A.E.—Sacramento Delta, California
April, 11 A.E.—Feather River Valley, California

The tule-reed boat felt . . . *squishy*, that's *the word*, Peter Giernas thought. It was more like being on a living thing than a boat, or . . . a memory nagged at him, from his childhood. Yes, just after the family had moved to America, three years before the Event, when his father got a job doing plumber's work with a Nantucket construction company. He'd taken the family to the beach, and the eight-year-old Peter Giernas had gone swimming on a half-inflated rubber mattress. This felt a lot like that, except that the mattress had been smooth rather than prickly.

That was the problem with not speaking the local language; you had to do most of your own scouting, or chance some lethal surprise at the last minute . . . like the one they'd nearly had when he saw the masts of the enemy ship rising above the heads of the reeds, and couldn't make the local behind him understand what *masthead lookout* meant. He'd gotten them under the shadow of the sloughside reeds, at least.

The little craft was inconspicuous, a lot more so than a thirty-foot dugout, and just the thing for eeling through the marshes, sloughs, swamps, and shallows where the Sacramento and San Joaquin Rivers met to form a huge delta before funneling into the Pacific. Despite his compass and map, Giernas had been thoroughly lost within an hour.

There must be millions *of acres of this tule swamp here,* he thought. Plus riverbank forest even thicker and more junglelike than upstream on the Sacramento, and islands beyond counting, a demented spiderweb of channels. There was swamp, and islands of grassy prairie covered with stems twelve feet high, and

swamp shading into prairie and back into swamp and into forest, dry or with standing water around the trunks of the alders.

Mountains and features like Lake Tahoe didn't pick up and
move in periods as short as three thousand years, but this soft
muck-soiled landscape subject to annual flood was another matter.
Only the broadest outlines had any resemblance to the maps copied from a back-issue *National Geographic* for the expedition.

The smell was rank in his nostrils, full of life and death and
green growing things; just ahead of them was the mouth of a
little slough between two small islands. The lupines growing
there were four feet high and stretched along the banks on
both sides for hundreds of yards, with a band of white popcorn
flowers beyond and then masses of sky-blue Dowingia to the
water's edge.

He made a stay-here gesture to the local Indian in the canoe,
stepping ashore onto peat that yielded under his feet like wet
sponge. Going to his belly, he eeled forward until he could part
the flowers just enough for the lenses of the binoculars. The
vegetation closed over his head as well, making him invisible
to observers looking down from a masthead.

There, westward across a hundred yards of open water, was
what he sought. He'd seen the bare tips of her masts for better
than an hour, but the ship itself was still a bit of a shock.
Moored bow and stern to live oaks, on the shore of what another history would have called Sherman Island.

'Bout five hundred tons, he estimated, quickly taking in things
like the gunports to give him an accurate estimate of length.
Hundred and forty feet, he decided. *Beam, say, twenty-five,
twenty-eight feet midships.*

Schooner-rigged on three masts, big gaff mainsails, a main
topsail on the mizzen, square topsails on both the forward
masts. A rig like that would make things like beating around
the Horn into the teeth of the westerlies easier than something
square-rigged throughout, and wouldn't need as heavy a crew.
A topsail schooner, with a leering demon-mask figurehead
under the long bowsprit.

The name was picked out in gilt letters before the forward
anchor; *Hortzakadan Kaultzagurrunta,* whatever that meant.

A fish jumped just beyond his observation point, plopping
back down after its jaws closed on a dragonfly, and splashing
water on the lenses. He cursed softly, cleaned them and continued his scan. Six guns a side, bronze twelve-pounders from the
size of their muzzles; swivel guns on the quarterdeck rails—

what they called murdering pieces. Two stern-chasers, from the ports. Lighter guns, but not something you could disregard.

There were barish patches on the shore where they'd felled trees for fuel or construction, but nothing more. Giernas snorted slightly; if *he'd* been in charge, he'd have dismounted the ship's starboard guns and put them behind earthworks, to sweep the river north and south of the ship . . . oh, well, they thought they were safe enough here.

They'd certainly been hard at work. A big raft made of three layers of lashed-together logs had been secured to the ship's side, and an accommodation ladder run up the side of the hull to give easy access to the deck. The main spars had been re-rigged to act as crane-booms, swinging back and forth with loads of cargo from her holds. Giernas peered sharply at the load in a net swinging down. Bales and boxes and barrels, indistinct at this range. One of the big sailing barges was tied up to the raft, and more workers were going antlike up and down the gangplanks, stowing yet more containers in her open hold.

Okay, now, how many . . . Some of the teams hauling at the ropes looked like Tartessian sailors, although it was hard to tell—they tanned up pretty dark and worked stripped to their loincloths when the weather was good. Twenty or thirty were definitely locals, and not volunteers from the way they were touched up with the lash now and then. He saw a half a dozen leather-jerkined soldiers, but there might be more below. Slaves would mostly just get in the Tartessians' way in a fight, possibly turn on them when things got hairy.

The sailors though—they'd all know how to handle themselves come a brawl, and they could be murderously effective if they got to the ship's guns. And if the guns were kept loaded. That was standard practice at sea, but—

Hmmm, he thought. *Gunports open, but the guns aren't run out—they could have the ports open just for air 'tweendecks, it's pretty hot and humid here in the daytime already, in this damned swamp. Of course, that's assuming an awful lot . . .*

He watched with hunter's patience, occasionally shifting a little to keep muscles from going stiff. When the sun was half-way down to the line of forest on the west, the barge cast loose. Crewmen oar-walked it out into midstream, hoisted sails to the two stubby masts and slid north as the sails bellied out in the gentle easterly breeze.

Okay, subtract six for the barge crew. Lessee . . .

*   *   *

Alantethol looked at what the soldier brought. It was a spur, of the type made to strap on to a mounted man's bootheel. This was no common bit of gear from the King's workshops, though. It was bronze, inlaid with silver, the rondel larger and the blunt spikes tipped with little balls of gold. Blood drained from the Tartessian commander's face as he recognized where he'd seen it last; Tarmendtal son of Zeurkenol had been showing it off, proud of what his father sent him. He'd been so proud of it that he wore them constantly, especially when he rode off on patrol.

"It could have dropped off," one of the others gathered outside the Hidden Fort's gates said.

Alantethol restrained an impulse to lash his fist into the man's face. That would be bad for discipline . . . although right now, it would soothe his soul. "I don't think so," he said.

Decision firmed his mouth into a straight line. "Turn out a patrol," he said. "Two files—with remounts. I will take command." Twelve men should be enough. "Supplies for a week's travel, extra ammunition. And our two best trackers from the tame natives."

"Lord," the subordinate said. "That will leave few men here— there is the file at the ship, and three at the cinnabar mine."

"Little girls throwing flowers could hold these walls," he said. "Call up some of the civilians for wall duty—tell them that the King's treasury will make good any loss to them. I must find out what has happened! Doesn't this brainless savage know anything?"

There was a brief exchange between the interpreter and the native who squatted in the dust, looking up from under a tangle of black hair. At last the interpreter shook his head. "Lord Alantethol, he says that he took it from a man upriver in payment of a debt. He saw it must be ours, and that we would not trade such a thing, and ran here—he asks if his family may be forgiven their overdue tribute and his son and daughter returned to him."

Alantethol nodded. "Tell him if we find he tells the truth, his children will be returned, and rich gifts besides." *And if he lies, I will have him hung by the testicles and build a slow fire under his head.*

Meanwhile bugles had sounded within the fortress. Shouts resounded, demanding that traffic make way, and the sounds of boots striking flesh and yelps of pain. The troops he'd summoned cantered out and drew up, the sergeant who led them saluting with clenched fist. Alantethol looked over the men and ran an eye over the horses on leading-reins behind them, some carrying packs, but enough others to give every man a spare mount. If he had to make speed . . .

A cold feeling gripped his lower belly, as if the Crone were caressing him like a lover. There were another two weeks before the tribute patrol *had* to report in. This might be the Jester's laughter at a small mischief, making him look foolish for very little cause. On the other hand, he was a New Man of the King, and he had listened carefully to the King's talks about the quality called *methodical* by the Eagle People. More than once since then it had served him well. He swung into the saddle of the horse his orderly offered.

"Redouble the watch," he said. "I'll be back in three days, no more; if I'm not, button yourself in here tight, don't throw good money after bad. This may be nothing, but I've a tight scrotum over it."

By the Sun Lord, I'll be a eunuch if it gets any tighter, he added to himself.

The native trackers were stocky dark muscular men, much like any hunters of the local barbarian tribes. Their service showed only in their steel knives and hatchets, cotton tunics and bandannas tying back their hair, and the metal tips of their darts. He'd come to respect their abilities, though.

For the first day's hard riding there was little for them to do, besides interpret when they came to the initial miserable encampment that Tarmendtal son of Zeurkenol would have visited.

"Of course they're telling the truth," Alantethol snarled when the sergeant doubted it. "Look at their arms—they've received the *vaccination*. And no new cases of smallpox, either. The tracks are plain, besides. You men, leave off with those women—what do you think this is, a harvest festival? Mount up!"

The party with him had covered the distance in a third the time the tribute patrol would have made, unencumbered with a wagon and eating jerky and biscuit in the saddle rather than stopping to hunt. By then Alantethol remembered a joke that the King had told him, one Isketerol had heard from the Islander who taught him to ride horseback while he was in Nantucket. It was in the title of a book by a cavalry commander, *Forty Years in the Saddle,* by Major Assburns. It didn't seem so funny now.

He stood in the stirrups to survey a stretch of tall grass that looked much like all the others they'd seen on their ride north from the Hidden Fort. The native trackers saw something else, though. They dismounted and cast about, then came trotting back to his stirrup.

"Wagon tracks, stop here," one said, pointing about with his spear. "Whole bunch, stop there—ride about—stop there." He pointed off to the westward, toward another section of the flat plain. "Then wagon go *there*—" He pointed northward. "Most horses, they *there*."

Alantethol considered himself a fair man of the chase; his father had helped feed his family by joining hunts for wild pig in the marshes in winter. He still couldn't make hide nor hoof of the signs the trackers showed him, except for the wheel marks of the wagon.

"Wagon go slow, slow," the tracker said. After a while he pursed his lips and spat. "Not so many ox-beasts after here. And heavy, much heavy."

The Tartessian knotted a fist on the pommel of his saddle and looked around, listening to the sough and hiss of wind in grass that was drying toward summer's yellow. One of the great vultures was circling not too far up, more huge than a beast had a right to be. In the Hidden Fort you could forget how far Homeland was, how few civilized men were in this land, the sheer *size* of it. That was all too painfully apparent, out here where his soldiers were less than an ant crawling along a plank. He shivered, and promised a horse to the Sun Lord; right then he didn't feel confident enough to call the Hungry One's attention to him. Victory came from Him, yes . . . but never forever.

The other tracker came over and held up something. Alantethol took it up, smelled it, rolled it between his fingers. A ragged circle of scorched felt about the size of this thumb, greasy with beeswax, still scented with burned gunpowder. It was one of the wads that lay at the base of every cartridge, to seal the breech against the hot gas.

"Many of these?" he asked the tracker.

"Many, many," the tame savage said. "There—" He pointed to the little slough that ran down to the river ahead of them. "There—" His hand swung westward. "Many, many, many."

The Tartessian commander snarled. There had obviously been a battle here . . . but there were no signs of it, no rotting bodies and squabbling buzzards and condors. Not a scrap of gear, either. "We'll follow the wagon," he said at last. Tarmendtal might have sent the wagon on ahead and taken mounted men on a sweep westward into little-known regions, for some reason. Or . . . not.

*   *   *

"We'll go with the original plan," Peter Giernas said.

The four log canoes were gathered stern to stern so that the Islanders could confer. All of them were looking serious, except for Eddie, who was sharpening the blade of his tomahawk and whistling cheerfully. He tested the edge by shaving off one of the fringes on his hunting shirt, flipped the war-hatchet into the air in a blurring circle and caught it by the end of the two-foot handle, and slipped it onto the loop at the back of his belt.

"Sounded good to me the first time," he said. "They aren't expecting us—just go in and knock on the front door. You should let me go first, though—I'd be less of a loss to the expedition."

Giernas shook his head, slapped a mosquito and continued:

"It's not a sure thing, but it's the best chance we'll have, I think. They're not looking all that alert, from what I saw— just dull duty in a goddamn swamp. Question is, do the locals understand what we're trying to do?"

The Nantucketers exchanged looks. "I think they undersand they're not supposed to fight until we tell them to," Sue said doubtfully. "Think that'll do?"

"It'll have to." Giernas sighed. "All right, let's go. If we push it a little, we should get there for what the locals tell us is their dinnertime."

It was cooling in the branch where the canoes had lain up, as the sun set westward over an expanse like the sea. That was welcome; the swarms of mosquitoes that thickened as the sun went down were not. *I hope to hell the Tartessians haven't exposed anyone with malaria to these bloodsuckers*, Giernas thought, as his paddlers bent to their work. Birds flitted by overhead, half-visible streaks in the growing darkness, vanishing into the reeds and rank tree growth on either side. A lantern on a pole stood behind him, with the Rock-of-Gibraltar enemy flag flying beneath it. More insects bumped up against the thick pebbled glass that shielded a dim kerosene flame.

The crew of the *Mother of Invention* looked quite different now, dressed in the uniforms of the slain Tartessian soldiers, heads helmeted or wrapped in bandannas, rifles propped beside them, each with a band of hide to protect the lock from stray splashes. *God, I hope this fools them long enough*, Giernas thought, surprised by the strength of the emotion. *It's always the worst part, before the fight starts.*

The enemy would *probably* be deceived. The enemy just didn't have any *reason* to be wary. Not after six years of successful concealment. It was *easy* to hide things in the world of the Year 11. There was just so much space and communications were so slow.

They turned out into the main stream and southwest; he pushed on the tiller, keeping them close to the northeastern bank of the channel and dipping his head to let the broad-brimmed hat shade his eyes. The rest of him was partly concealed by a poncholike enemy blanket-cloak. It wasn't impossible to find a six-foot-two blond Tartessian with gray eyes and a reddish beard, he supposed; it was just so unlikely that he'd stand out like a seven-foot Chinese in America before the Event. *Just long enough, God, just for long enough.* They wouldn't recognize the canoes, either. But they obviously weren't local Indian craft, and the assumption would be they were something the enemy base had run up, especially with Tartessian soldiers crewing the first one.

"Should fool 'em long enough," he muttered under his breath. "People see what they expect to see . . ."

Out again, into the broad reach of the main channel where the Tartessian ship was moored. *"Slow!"* Giernas said, one of the words in the local language he'd memorized. He put up a hand and squinted; there were the mastheads, black against the huge red globe of the sunset notched by the distant peak of Mount Diablo.

Silence, except for the grunting exhalation of breath and the drip of the paddles, the chuckle of water along the canoe and the beat of blood in his own ears. *Christ, if I liked fighting, I'd have joined the Marines. I like to travel and hunt and see new places.* The black length of the ship showing yellow through the ports as her own lanterns were lit, a faerie glow that turned her rigging into traceries of spidersilk in the gathering darkness. A voice called sharply in the clotted tongue of ancient Iberia, all "u" and "z" sounds.

He stood carefully, gripping the tiller with one hand and waving his rifle with the other. *There. You're the only ones in this part of the world with rifles,* he willed at the sentinel who must be examining him. *Be terminally reassured, you son of a bitch.* The ranger shouted aloud the only Tartessian phrases he knew, picked up over the years on visits dockside in Nantucket Town and Providence Base and Fogarty's Cove:

"I do not understand your language!" garbling it as much as he dared. The words wouldn't carry, it was still beyond conversational distance but the *sounds* would be familiar. *"I am not interested in buying your goods! Behave yourself or I will call*

the guards! Strike sail or we open fire! Fuck your sow of a mother and your ten fathers, too!"

The voice came again; a lantern was moving on the deck, down the accommodation ladder, across the raft. Closer now, and he could see the shape of a man behind it, an armed man holding up the lantern in his left hand. He called out again, but the tone was more curious than anything else. He could smell the ship now, the gingery scents of baled cargo, a hint of sulfur, the stale-ditchwater waft of the bilges. Tar and seasoned wood and hemp from the hull and rigging themselves. And a whiff of something gaggingly foul, an oily sewer-and-old-socks reek that he'd never smelled before . . . but one he recognized from descriptions. The sound that came from his deep chest was one that would have done credit to Perks.

"Diskeletal?" the man with the lamp asked.

Giernas could see it was a sailor, in tunic and bare feet, with a cutlass at his waist and a bandolier slung over one shoulder. "Is that you?"

"Nietzatwaz," he replied—roughly *sure, that's it, correctamundo*—with a cough in the middle to hide his attempt at pronouncing the thick sounds.

He could see the man's face now, halo-lit by the lamp, framed against the ship and the dying scarlet of the sunset. He could see the exact instant when a wondering glance at the dugout turned to horror, but by then they were less than ten feet from the dock and coming in fast. The sentry juggled the loads in his hands, instinctively bending to put the lantern down—that had to be a drilled reflex for a sailor, not to spill flame. By that time Giernas had the rifle up and to his shoulder.

Crack. The man's head jerked backward as if a mule had kicked him in the face and landed full-length on his back with an audible thump. Giernas knew a moment's dismay. He'd been aiming for the gut, but the motion of the canoe had thrown him off. Shouts rose from the deck of the ship, and heads poked out of the gunports—he could see one man clearly, with a pointed black beard and waxed mustaches curling up like buffalo horns, a hunk of bread in one hand and a drumstick in the other, shouting through a full mouth. Probably asking what idiot had fired off a rifle by mistake, and was he trying to kill somebody . . .

The canoe bumped against the raft. A dozen eager hands grabbed at the roughness of the oak logs; Giernas rolled to the surface, keeping himself flat, his hands scrabbling in a wicker basket. The firepot came out; he tore off the lid, blew on the coals, and dipped in the fuses of two improvised grenades, mortar shells from the wagon that had accompanied the ambushed patrol. The nitrated cord took with a sputter of sparks and harsh-smelling blue smoke.

Just then the captured rifles went off in a ragged volley as the canoe's crew fired. From the angle of some of the muzzle flashes nothing was in danger but innocent birds passing by; but other slugs whined overhead far too close to his own precious person and he could see white flecks appear where chunks of splinter were knocked loose around the lighted gunports. While he was down he kicked the fallen lamp off into the water, but half a dozen others were being turned up on the ship, including the big sternquarter lanterns over the quarterdeck. Then he was on his feet again and rushing for the accommodation ladder, yelling *Geronimo!* in the hope that his allies would follow him. God-damn this business of fighting with people you couldn't even talk to . . .

The gunports were still open. An underarm toss sent one mortar shell into the nearest; he flipped the other into his right hand and gave it the old Providence High School Baseball Devils speedball to the next gunport ten yards further down. The oblong form of the cut-down mortar shell didn't have the same aerodynamics as one of Coach Huneck's hand-wrapped cork-rubber-and-pigskin specials, or even a rock, and it wobbled a little as it flew. His gut clenched as it hit the lip and teetered, then relaxed as it fell inside.

"Down!" he screamed. Not that it would do much good. He followed his own advice, though, with his arms crossed in front of his face.

. . . *three, two, one—*

WHUMP.

The sound was slightly muffled by the six inches of oak timber and planking, but fire and smoke belched out of four of the gunports. He winced slightly at the thought of what the grooved cast-iron casings would do in those confined quarters. Someone was screaming in there, an inhuman volume of sound. Giernas rolled, rocked back on his shoulders, brought his legs up and flicked himself back onto his feet, charging for the accommodation ladder with bowie and tomahawk in his hands. Up, up, before they recovered—

A figure at the top of the ladder, raising a gun. The tomahawk went back over Giernas's shoulder, then forward in a hard precise arc, his fingers releasing at the moment a decade's practice prompted. He would have been as astonished at miss-

ing as if his own body had disobeyed him when he told it to
take a step or pick a shoe up from the floor. The tomahawk
whirred through the twelve feet separating the two men in a
circular blur, flashing as the honed edge caught lamplight. It
landed with a dull *thock*, and the sailor stood, swaying, looking
down wide-eyed at the steel splitting his breastbone. The ranger
charged in the wake of its flight. Three long bounding strides
and he rammed the bowie in his left hand up under the
wounded man's ribs, wrenched the war-hatchet free, and
pushed the corpse aside with ruthless speed. The Indians were
pounding after him, already at the bottom of the stairway, their
shrill war cries overriding the bewildered shouts of the Tartessians. The other three canoes were plunging for the raft with
paddles flying, and he heard Eddie's baying *hau-hau-hau* under
the hawk-shrieks of the women.

Onto the deck, past a sailor who slashed at him with a cutlass
and then screamed with shock as he saw what was coming
behind. A hatchway in the deck was open, with wifts of powder
smoke coming out of it; he had to get down there before someone touched off one of the guns.

A man was coming out of the hatchway, up the steep lad-
derlike stair with a cutlass in his right hand. He cut at the
ranger, his blade sweeping like a scythe at thigh level. Giernas
shouted and turned his run into a leap head-high. The sword
whistled beneath him, and his coiled legs lashed out to strike
the man in the face with a thump that jarred up into the small
of his back. They both fell tumbling to the maindeck below,
the Tartessian dead with a shattered neck and his jaw half torn
off. The ranger lay stunned for an instant, and in that instant
something heavy landed on his stomach.

"*Uffff!*" he grunted, as the breath exploded out of his lungs.

The weight was behind a knee. Giernas caught the flash of
steel in the dimness, dropped his bowie, and grabbed. His fingers closed on a thick wrist and stopped the dagger six inches
from his face; the Tartessian soldier's other hand pinned his
tomahawk-wrist to the planks. It was the man who'd looked
out through a gunport, but now there were bleeding lines across
the spike-mustached face, and on the hairy torso that showed
through rents in his ripped, scorched tunic. The soldier was
shorter than Giernas by five inches, but he was built like a bull,
barrel chest and thick, knotted shoulders and arms; and the
ranger's lungs were empty, burning as he tried to suck in a
single breath, leaching the strength from his arms. The wrist
beneath his hand felt like living gutta-percha, and slick and wet

with sweat besides. Blood and breath stinking of garlic swept across his face, and the point of the dagger came closer, closer . . .

A loop of chain dropped around the soldier's neck and snapped taut. The chain was between the wrists of a manacled Indian, naked and thin and filthy, his eyes glaring madness in a face marked with the knotted tissue of badly healed wounds. Choking, the Tartessian kept the presence of mind to grab the chain before it could crush his larynx and to stab backward, but he had to take his attention from the Nantucketer. Giernas brought his right knee nearly back to his chest and lashed out, a heel kick that smashed into the soldier's groin with enough force to crack the pelvis. He could feel the sickening sensation of bone crumbling all the way up his leg, and there was a certain mercy in the stroke that backhanded the hammer of his tomahawk into the man's temple. Soldier and slave tumbled together on the red-wet planks of the deck as he rolled to his feet, gasping and wheezing as he forced his paralyzed diaphragm to draw in air.

Movement at the gunport turned out to be Eddie. "Sorry," the younger man said, and jerked the muzzle of his rifle upward to the beams and planks above. "More of them up there, had to deal with 'em. Sue's mopping up."

He turned and reached down, drawing Jaditwara upward with an easy wiry stength. She had Giernas's rifle across her back and tossed it to him. He took the weapon and reloaded; knife and tomahawk were more useful at extreme close quarters, but the Westley-Richards was . . . reassuring. With a moment to look around he saw that the gun deck ran most of the length of the ship, although the central half of the floor was mostly gratings that could be taken up to give access to the hold beneath. The cannon were in their bowsed-up storage position, and hanging tables had been let down for the soldiers and sailors to eat their dinner. Tables lay splintered and broken where the grenades had exploded, bodies motionless or still whimpering and twitching, food and wine and oil flowing on the deck, mingling their smells with the dung stink of death.

"Let's get these goddamned fires out—" he began. An overturned lantern could become a catastrophe very quickly.

An unearthly shriek came from the forward part of the deck, where a partition and sheet-iron chimney marked the galley. A fat man staggered around the enclosure holding his hands to his face; they could see the huge blisters spreading beneath his fingers and all down his throat and chest and belly—the sort of marks that you got when someone threw boiling olive oil on you. Giernas raised his rifle to put the man out of his misery, but before he could pull the trigger an Indian woman came after the Tartessian cook. She was naked, and they could see that some of the hot oil had spattered her here and there. That didn't affect her grip on a big iron frying pan; she swung it like a baseball bat, knocked the man down, and began to beat him with it as if she were threshing grain, hard crunching blows that went on after his head split open.

More Indian slaves swarmed up out of the hold; their local allies came down the companionways as well. The rangers pushed and shoved and showed how and ended up stamping out the small puddles of flame themselves, smothering with sand and water from the buckets. The locals were more interested in scouring the ship of the last Tartessians; it had turned from a fight to a hunt, and when a squealing ship's boy barely old enough to raise a whisker was dragged out from a cupboard in the captain's cabin and clubbed, Giernas turned aside in disgust.

Jesus knows they've got reason to hate the Iberians, he thought. *Still and all—*

"Is there something we're forgetting?" he said, then looked up at the sound of a shot. He held up a hand to mark a pause and leaned out of a gunport. "Sue?" he shouted.

"Here!" her voice came back from the deckhouse behind the wheel. "One or two of them got into the maintop with a rifle. Careful about how you come on deck—I'll keep him pinned down from here."

Jaditwara had gone into a trance of remembering. Her eyes flew open very wide, their pale blue glittering in the lamplight.

"Barrow Woman's teeth!" she blurted. The Fiernan had shipped as a deckhand before she settled at Providence Base, got her immigrant's papers, and drifted into the rangers. "The powder magazine! It'll be on the orlop deck—under the waterline—this way!"

She took off at a flying run with Eddie on her heels. Peter looked around. The locals had broken open the ship's spirit store, and they were passing bottles of wine and brandy from hand to hand; one of them even had a small cask in his hands, holding it up until the pale violent spirits ran over his face and dripped down his bare brown chest, mingling with the streaks of blood. *Be some almighty sore heads tomorrow,* the ranger thought. Or possibly some deaths—that much raw alcohol on stomachs not accustomed to it. The slaves had pulled out the food supplies from the galley and were eating with a dreadful concentrated hunger, some of them weeping as they stuffed bread and hard biscuit and dried fruit into their mouths, or gnawed on tough jerked meat. One who had learned something about blacksmith's tools had found a hammer and chisel, using them to split the soft wrought-iron rivets that held the captives' manacles closed.

Some of those poor bastards will be dead tomorrow, too, he thought sadly—burst bellies, from cramming in too much too soon on a gut shrunken by hunger.

He shook his head. The rangers were foreigners here, barely able to exchange a few sentences. They certainly didn't have any authority, and trying to exert it would only result in disaster. *With some luck, we can keep them from destroying the ship. We may be able to use her.*

Instead he turned to the aft companionway, coming up near the wheel, keeping his head below deck level where the roof of the deckhouse cut off the mainmast top. "Sue?"

"He hasn't moved for while—wait a minute—"

There was a shot from the mast, a scream from the deck, and the sharp close-at-hand whipcrack of Sue's weapon. Giernas leaped out of the companionway, vaulted the compass binnacle, and threw himself down beside the young woman. Another shot came from the top, and the bullet knocked splinters out of the planks overhead.

"Hi," she said, grinning through powder smuts. "Eddie and Jaddi?"

"Looking after the magazine," he said

"*Whoa*! Should have thought of that. One of them could have blown us all sky-high."

"Jaddi's closer to a sailor than any of us, and *hi* yourself," he answered. "How're we going to shift this bastard?"

"I don't know. There may be two, he reloads almightly fast, like it was two guns and he was handing off to someone else who was loading for him. Doesn't seem to be short of ammo, either. There are about twenty or thirty locals out there, hiding behind stuff and on the raft," she said.

"Wish we could figure out a way to use 'em before they all get at the liquor," Giernas mused, rubbing his beard. His eyes roved about. "Think you could cover me as far as the mainmast?"

The slanted blue eyes narrowed. "Maybe, but—"

"Hey, cover us!" That was Eddie's voice.

"Wait a second." Giernas took out a pocket mirror and held it up gingerly. It was hard to say in the darkness, but—

"I think he's behind those hammocks, right over to the port side of the tops. I'll go first, you on the count of two."

"Right."

"Wait for the word, Eddie. One—" He came up to one knee and fired, smooth and quick. *Crack*, and he shouted: *"Two!"*

Crack from Sue's rifle, and the other two rangers rolled into the shelter of the deckhouse. "Found the magazine," Jaditwara said. "Safe."

"One of the Tarties was trying to get in," Eddie amplified. "But the locals scragged him first." He held up a key, which nobody born around here would recognize. "Padlocked. I took a look in—we're not short of ammunition anymore. They must have been bringing it in for their settlement here."

"Right," Giernas nodded. "You three cover me. I'm going to get to the base of the mainmast and see about shifting our friend up there."

"Hey, why do you get all the fun?" Eddie said.

The other three looked at him for a second. "I'm a better shot," Giernas pointed out; which was true. Not that Eddie wasn't very good. "Get ready."

His testicles tried to crawl back up inside him for protection, and he grinned at the sensation; his bladder felt too full, too. Wait until everyone was in position, rifles primed and cocked. Blow the priming out of his own and renew it.

"Go!"

Crack!

Jaddi's gun, blasting into the rolled hammocks around the maintop. Giernas rose as he saw her finger squeeze, his soft moccasins thumping on the quarterdeck as he drove himself forward. A malignant red eye winked at him from the top, and splinters flew from the idol of Arucuttag of the Sea that stood by the binnacle.

Crack! Crack! Sue and Eddie fired.

Over the quarterdeck railing, vaulting on his left hand. *Crack!* Jaditwara firing again, and there was a hoarse cry from above. His moccasins thumped down on the main deck; it was a six-foot drop, and he took it on flexed knees and then dived for the base of the mast, sliding the last six feet over the smooth deck planks as if he was sliding for home plate. His feet touched the raised collar around the mast, and he brought the rifle up with a smooth searching motion. The floor of the main-top was a latticework. The figures moving on it were outlined against moonlight and starlight. His finger stroked the trigger, feeling a familiar light, crisp resistance.

Crack! The recoil was worse than usual, with his shoulder pinned to the deck. He'd have a bruise there, in a while.

Someone screamed. A rifle fell over the edge of the fighting platform, pinwheeling down through the lamplight and into the dark with a splash. Peter raised his legs high, flicked himself back to his feet, and sprang to the rail and the ratlines. Eddie whooped and sprang down from the quarterdeck, bounding to the other side of the ship and swarming up faster than the bigger man. Sue and Jaditwara came to one knee, covering them. Giernas reached down and drew his bowie as he climbed, then put it between his teeth—climbing was about the only situation where that actually made sense. The thick back fillet of the heavy blade filled his mouth with its unpleasant, bitter taste of oiled steel. Any second now someone would lean over the tattered hammocks around the fighting top and blow the top of his head off at point-blank range . . .

Nothing happened, except that the sound of wheezing grew stronger. The triangular basket of the fighting top was occupied by two figures. One was a man in his thirties—from the elaborate decoration on his tunic, probably the captain of the ship. He'd been wounded in one arm and patched it up with a cloth; the second bullet hole was through the upper part of his chest, just where the breastbone gave way to the neck. Blood ran out in a flood, slowing as he watched. The other was much younger, scarcely more than a boy; even in the starlight he could see the resemblance in the faces. Blood spread black in the moonlight across his torso as he struggled to lift the rifle across his lap. It wobbled, and then the muzzle sank. The boy's head slumped forward as well, and he gave a long sigh and stopped struggling for breath.

Giernas opened his mouth, catching the hilt of the bowie as it dropped and sliding it back into the sheath on his right leg.

"Hey, looks like they're both dead," Eddie Vergeraxsson said.

"Yeah," Giernas replied heavily. "They are."

Spring Indigo Giernas woke in the darkness. She knew at once that it was very late; the moon was down, and the woods by the river were quiet, the air cool and full of a deep stillness. The baby in his rabbitskin blanket was still, she could hear his breathing slow and even. It was a tickle against the soles of her feet that woke her; Perks raised his head from where he lay curled at the opening of the tent.

"Qesh'Perks'huo?" she mumbled, hoping it wasn't just the howl of some coyote. Perks was an excellent watcher and far better trained than any hound of her parents' people, but his ideas of what was important enough to wake up for weren't always the same as a man's.

She could see the outline of the wolf-dog against the lesser darkness of the tent's open flap. First his head, ears pricked; then he came to his feet and crouched, with a sound half whine and half growl. The other dogs were stirring now, too. Spring Indigo felt a cold chill at the base of her belly. A fire smoldered under its own ash outside the tent, with a low earth mound at its back to throw the heat inward; she fought down an impulse to poke it up and throw on lightwood. Instead she scrambled into her clothes—the leather kept warm and supple by lying under the blanket with her. That took an instant; snatching up the saddlebags, throwing them over a shoulder, sticking the pistols through her belt, taking up her crossbow in her right hand and her child in her left arm, scarcely longer.

A deep-chested rumble of a snarl from Perks. "Quiet!" she hissed.

He obeyed and so did his son and daughter, but suddenly there was barking from other dogs—those in the camp of the people of the land near here. Fires *were* prodded to life there, and sparks flew up among the big trees. Then a voice shouted— another screamed—and there was the flat unmusical *crack* of a gunshot.

The baby stirred in drowsy protest. She paused to give him the breast for a moment; it was worth the time, to keep him sleepy and content. *I am not as afraid as I thought I would be*, she thought as she ducked out the flap of the tent and moved northward toward the horse lines, crouching.

Yes, her mouth was dry, and her heart beat like a Summoner's drum in her ears. But it was not as bad as the fear of the Dog People, in that last hopeless flight before Peter and the other Islanders came.

I am older, she thought. *I have learned much. I will save my son, and greet my husband once more.*

Perks and Saule and Ausra—the names meant *Thunder* and *Moon* and *Dawn*, in a language that was not English—came close behind her heels as she headed through the dew-wet grass. The two horses on the picket line were stirring, throwing up their heads against the reins that bound bridles to the hide

rope stretched between two trees. Their hooves spurned the
cut grass heaped for them to eat, sending wisps of it floating
toward her. The others whickered and milled in the crude brush
corral. Closer, quick and quiet, and . . .

If I were raiding this camp, I would—

Shadow-figures stood by the corral wall. Starlight let her see
just enough of them to make out the distinctive outlines of men
raising rifles to their shoulders, and she went to the ground
with her body curled over her son. Perks froze for an instant.
Then he charged with his belly to the ground, silent as death,
a dark-gray streak in the darkness. Saule and Ausra attacked
with a good deal more noise, bounding to keep their heads
above the tall grass.

Crack. Crack. The muzzle flashes blinked like red eyes in the
night. A howl was broken by a yelping moan of pain, and then
a roaring snarl and a man's scream. Spring Indigo forced herself
to come upright on her knees—Jared was crying and struggling
against the rabbitskin wrapper that held him, but she had to
see what was coming.

A Tartessian, swearing and limping. He was looking about
for another man, something on a level with his eyes, and didn't
see her until almost the moment she raised the heavy flintlock
pistol and fired both barrels at him from less than ten feet away.

Even with her eyes slitted, the double red flash nearly
blinded her. The weapon bucked in hands smaller than it was
designed for, the hammers nearly gouging her forehead as it
recoiled. The Tartessian spun and fell, screaming and thrashing.
She tossed the weapon aside and pulled the other, scooping
up the solid weight of the toddler as she went. On, past the limp
body of a dog, and to the picket line itself. There two figures
rolled and snarled, man hardly to be distinguished from beast.
Teeth flashed in the starlight, and the bright gleam of a steel
knife blade. Spring Indigo ran over and thrust the pistol barrels
into the body of the man lying beneath Perks and pulled the
trigger; the sound of the shot was muffled, but blood and matter
blew back across her, and this time the pistol *was* wrenched
out of her grip.

Perks gave the Tartessian's face one last tear with his jaws
and then rose, trying to walk toward her. He nearly fell, then
hunched along with one foreleg drawn up to his chest; the
blood was black in the night. She hesitated for a single second,
torn . . . but Jared gave a squall, and the dog weighed more
than she did. Even if she could get him slung across one of the
horses, it would take far too long. The crackle of shots around

the encampment of the people of the land was already dying down, and she could see the ruddy light of flame there.

"Guard, Perks!" she said.

The saddle was already on the horse, loosely fastened. She quieted the eye-rolling nervousness of the animal, threw the saddlebags over its withers, and jerked the girths tight, then strapped her child into the carrying basket. Grim concentration got her into the saddle, and feet into stirrups already shortened for her. A quick slash left the lead line of the other horse free, and she wound it around her free hand.

"Hi, eeeeya *go!*" she shouted, then her heels thumped into the flanks of the horse, and it turned its head into the north and ran.

Alantethol took the pistol in his hands. It was of the type that his own folk had copied for some years, a twin-barreled flintlock, not the damnable six-shot repeaters the Eagle People had come to use lately. There were enough differences to show where it was made, though; the machining was smoother than any shop in Homeland could yet produce, the wood of the butt was one he didn't recognize, and the stamp on the locks showed the rampant Eagle of the Republic, rather than the crowned mountain of Tartessoss.

"Curse them," he whispered. "Curse them, is there nowhere in the world they will leave us in peace?"

He shook his head, looking around at the trampled remains of the camp. Two leather tents—six men, at most. Twelve horses, unshod ponies, some of them with colts at heel. Surprisingly little gear . . . except that they would have hidden most of it before they left. From the reports, only one of the *Amurrukan* had been here when his band attacked.

A scream came from the ground a little eastward, toward the river. He walked over. The captive was proving surprisingly stubborn; the file leader questioning him gave another twist to the stick in the knotted cord twisted around the native's brow. Blood ran down from the leather, and the black eyes bulged. The tame guide bent and shouted a question in the man's ear, listened to his answer, then shrugged.

"He says the Eagle People made canoes and went downstream," he said at last.

Alantethol felt the usual itch of discontent that came of working through badly trained interpreters; you might get the general sense of what someone said, but there was always a slippage of meaning—and you never got the little details that could be so crucial.

"How many? Where?" he grated.

The answers came, slow and unwilling and unsatisfactory, although they flowed a little better once the questioner had brushed burning liquid sulfur over the savage's crotch. At last Alantethol turned away and paced back and forth, hand on the hilt of the sword whose scabbard slapped at his boot. Scowling, he kicked at a tuft of the long grass and thought. The problem was that the savages here didn't *know* anything to speak of. The Eagle People had been even more handicapped by lack of the local tongues than he was. They hadn't told their allies overmuch because they couldn't.

Four of them downstream with some natives, he thought. Best send a messenger to the ship, although there were far too few of the enemy to attack there. Still, with the Eagle People . . .

"They are not more than us!" he muttered to himself. "A man of Tartessos with a rifle is the equal of any of them."

Yes, they were probably trying to make the great bay on the coast. Ships of theirs did put in there now and then. He grinned like a shark. Not for months, though, and the savages would hunt them down, given threats and rewards enough. Once they were located it would be easy enough to overfall them with numbers.

Hmmm, what of the woman they left here? he thought. Only a woman . . . but it was well to be cautious where *Amurrukan* women were concerned; they were more like men, in many respects. *But this one is a savage, the description was clear.* The Eagle People mostly looked like Albans or other northerners; this one was short, black of hair and brown of skin and flat-faced, from the descriptions. *But she did escape, probably killed two of my men. Best to track her down, and see what she knows.* Even if she was nothing but some chance bedmate-servant picked up along the way, she might know more than the local idiots. He would leave good men on it, and return to the Hidden Fort to keep his hand on things.

"There will be revenge for you, Tarmendtal son of Zeurkenol. By the Hungry One, by the Lord of Waves, I swear it."

CHAPTER TWENTY-ONE

November, 10 A.E.—West-central Anatolia
October, 10 A.E.—Cadiz Base, southern Iberia
November, 10 A.E.—Eurotas Valley, Kingdom of
  Great Achaea
October, 10 A.E.—Cadiz Base, southern Iberia

Raupasha daughter of Shuttarna tapped Iridmi on the shoulder. "Pull up here," she said.

The allied forces had been moving to an intricate dance since Troy fell and Walker sent Great Achaea's armies east into the Hittite lands. This *Nantukhtar* marching camp was on the edge of a small lake, set amid pinewoods. Mountains lay about, the broken northern edge of the Hittite lands, looming over the dry plains to the south. The cold air was full of a strong scent of pine and the smoke of fires; within was an orderly bustle, troops less clean and neat than they had been, but still showing that Islander air of purposefulness. And the weapons gleamed.

"Brigadier Hollard, ma'am?" the aide in the headquarters tent said. "He and the visiting VIPs are up at the springs . . . the hot springs, ma'am; you're the last. It's the first time in a while anyone's had a chance at a hot bath."

Raupasha flushed, conscious despite the chilly air that an odor of woodsmoke and old sweat hung about her. The Nantucketers thought the peoples of these lands repulsively filthy in their persons, she knew—if you understood their tongue, you overheard things you were not meant to. And it was important that her people be represented in such meetings, through her. And Kenn'et would be there . . .

"I have a gift," she said.

It was the the loin of a forest pig wrapped in cloth, and one of her people had even found some wild garlic and herbs to rub it with. These hills were thick with game, and there had been a little time to hunt since they'd pulled back from the valley lands to the south.

"They'll be glad of it, ma'am," the aide said cheerfully. "Sort of a picnic dinner up there. Right that way; past the *via principalis*, and just up from the edge of the lake."

The Islanders had not been here long enough to fell much of the forest; it made the gridwork of streets and tents look a little odd, among the ancient pines. Wagons rolled and working parties marched, but most of the soldiers were sprawled by their tents, cooking, working on their gear, or just catching up on sleep after weeks of grinding forced marches.

The way was pointed by a series of rough-hewn arrows on trees. The springs turned out to be a set of pools, steaming in the cold air, with a strong mineral smell about them. Some had signs on pieces of split tree trunk posted next to them, with writing in red letters: *WATER TOO HOT DANGER DO NOT BATHE* with an odd symbol covering the last word, a circle with a slash across it. Some of those were full of uniforms, being stirred by workers with wooden poles. The safer pools were full of Islander troops, splashing about in horseplay, throwing handfuls of the hot mineral-rich water and ducking each other, or simply blissfully soaking away the grime and aches.

She found Kenneth Hollard where a hot spring welled up at the top of a tiny cliff and poured down a dozen feet into a rocky pool. The path of the miniature waterfall was marked by a slick white-gold coating on the rocks, where minerals in the water had dried and plated the native granite. Wisps of steam floated above the surface of the pool; a few feet away a fire crackled in a circle of rocks, giving off sharp pops and sparks, bright against the darkening sky in the east. He was there, looking relaxed despite the dark circles under his eyes; so were King Kashtiliash, Kathryn Hollard, Colonel O'Rourke with his unforgettable blazing red hair, freckled skin red, too, where the sun had struck it, milk-pale elsewhere; and one or two others. A small yellow model of a duck floated on the water.

Everyone smiled and called greetings. She hadn't quite expected . . .

I know the Nantukhtar women are not shamefast, she thought—you couldn't walk through one of their camps and not know it. *And I know that any who presumes on it, regrets it.*

According to the stories going around the allied armies, some men who *had* made incorrect assumptions would never be interested in women again, or at least not able to do anything about such an interest.

But can I act so, stripping off in sight of all?

Her own men had gone to great lengths to preserve her modesty, which was possible because she was the only woman, camp followers aside, with the Mitannians.

All that went through her mind in an instant. The answer came as quickly: *Of course I can.* To do otherwise would be to fall from the status of comrade to that of *superstitious local* in an instant. They would still be polite to her, but . . . *And I will remind Kenn'et that I am no little girl.*

She started to go to her knees before Kashtiliash as protocol demanded; the Babylonian monarch held up a hand. "No," he said, in his deep rumbling voice. "There is . . . how do you say, my brother?"

"No rank in the mess," Kenneth Hollard said, smiling.

"Mess?"

"Where the officers eat," Kathryn said. She stood and tossed something. "Careful, this end by the stream is hot, better to get in at the bottom."

Raupasha caught it reflexively, and gulped; it was a bar of the Islander cleaning fat—soap—wrapped in a rough cloth.

"Thank you, Ka-th-ryn," she said casually; that took a monumental effort of will. Then she bent to unlace her boots.

When her clothes steamed with the rest in a nearby superheated pool she slid in quickly, soaping and then wading to the head of the pool—just bearably short of boiling hot—to stand under the fall of water and scrub down with a sponge.

"Feels good, doesn't it?" Kathryn asked.

"Yes," Raupasha said, finding a convenient ledge of rock and sitting immersed to her neck.

Did I dream it, or did I see Kenn'et's eyes widen as he looked at me? I am skinny and boyish, I know . . . but the Islanders think a woman beautiful if she does not *look plump and soft— very strange. And look at Lady Kathryn, who entranced the Great King, even though* her *body is that of a she-leopard.*

And it *did* feel good to be clean again. She sudsed her long black hair once more and submerged, scrubbing at her scalp with her fingers.

"The Mitannians have been doing very well," Kenneth said, as she surfaced. "Especially the chariot raiding squadrons. Thank goodness the front's too big here for solid lines of men; they can get in the enemy's rear and work all sorts of lovely destruction."

"I have heard," Kashtiliash said; his English was strongly accented but fluent.

Kathryn moved behind him and began to work a comb

through the sodden mass of wavy blue-black mane lying limp on his shoulders.

"Ai!" he cried, as she tugged at a knot and then used the pick on the other end of the comb. "Are you trying to scalp me bald, woman?"

"I keep telling you to cut it short like mine," she said, face intent on her work. Hers was at the regulation Marine field length, a quarter of an inch. "Then it wouldn't tangle like this, and it'd be easier to keep clean in the field."

"A King's hair and beard are his strength—my people would fear disaster, did I crop it. It is hard enough to make them see why I must travel with so little state; they complain that I move about like a bandit chief of Aramaeans."

"Well, next time you've got lice and I don't, I'm going to boot you out of my bed again."

Raupasha blinked as the King rumbled amusement, and everyone else joined in.

"Kat'ryn and I have been giving the Achaean's southern column much grief," Kashtiliash went on, with a wolf's grin. "There is only one way up the Meneander Valley."

"And their commander on the southern wing, his name's Guouwaxeus, has about as much imagination as an ox," Kathryn said. " 'Hey diddle diddle, straight up the middle' is his style. Kash and I mousetrapped the better part of a battalion last week, and got away clear before his reserves came up."

"It would have been better if my charioteers had the sense to see that they cannot mass against foot armed with the new weapons," Kashtiliash grumbled. "If they had swung around wide and then dismounted, as I instructed . . . well, that officer is dead."

He turned his leonine head to Raupasha and bowed it slightly. "You have instructed your followers better, I hear, Princess."

"The King is kind," Raupasha said, proud that her voice was steady.

This was more nerve-wracking than lying flat at the King's feet while he talked of taking her head. *Of course, my breasts and thighs were not then bared for the world to see,* she thought wryly, forcing herself not to cross her arms on her chest, and went on aloud:

"I think it may be that my charioteers had to practice in concealment if at all, while the Assyrians ruled Mitanni; they did not wish the old *mariyannu* families who survived to keep up their skills. So they are less set in their ways. Also, while the Nantukhtar are the allies of the men of Kar-Duniash, to us they are saviors, so we are more ready to listen."

Kashtiliash tugged at a mass of wet beard that bore little trace of the careful curling irons his barbers had plied in the Shining Residence. Raupasha wondered a little at his hardihood in these rough conditions, until she remembered tales of how he'd been fostered with his hill-tribe kinfolk and spent much time in the field as a soldier and hunter while his father was King.

Perhaps he finds it a relief, to be away from court, she thought. From things Kathryn had let drop, that might well be so.

And was Kenn'et looking at her with a new touch of respect?

"Hmmm," the Babylonian said at last. "I think that these are words of some worth. Men will remain with their accustomed ways of doing, so long as those are successful. They have spent much time and effort becoming good warriors in the old way; their pride is in it. Is defeat then a better teacher than victory, like a schoolmaster with a heavier switch to beat a boy's back?"

O'Rourke spoke: "Well, that would account for his lack of popularity—as the saying goes, victory has a thousand fathers, and defeat is an orphan."

Kashtiliash laughed, but went on: "And it would account for the cycles in the affairs of men; for a land raised up by fortune would grow complacent, and thus weak." He cocked an eybrow at Kenneth. "Thus your land is in great danger, now," he concluded. "From pride and sloth."

"Nantucket's not in as much danger from pride as the land of the Hittites is in from Walker, thank God," Hollard said. "It all depends on whether we can stop them west of the Halys. Beyond that, they'd be into the Hittite heartlands."

"That is the question," Kashtiliash said. He lowered his voice a little: "And whether Tudhaliyas will remain loyal if they *do* push us beyond the great river. If not, we must retreat over the mountains in winter and Mitanni becomes our front line."

Raupasha winced inwardly. *My poor bleeding country!* It would take generations to recover from the Assyrian occupation, and if in the meantime they became the battleground of contending Great Powers . . .

Everyone nodded. "It's even money," O'Rourke said. "We've slowed them just a bit, we have."

"They're not sure where our separate forces are," Kenneth said. "Tudhaliyas is building up west of Hattusas; we sent him most of those Tartessian mercenaries we captured, and they're helping train his own men. Not much in the way of artillery or Gatlings, but enough Westley-Richards rifles and mortars, and now we've got the powder mill going there's plenty of ammunition. Basic stuff, but sound."

"Ah!" Raupasha said, visualizing one of the Islander maps. "And if he advances eastward to pass us, so as to strike at the Great King of Hatti, we can descend on his sides . . . I mean his flanks."

And yes, that *was* a considering look of respect. She made herself sit up, leaning back on the rocky edge of the pool with her arms out to either side, as Kathryn had, acutely conscious of how it made her breasts stand.

"I wonder that Walker has not concentrated and struck at one of our separated forces," Kashtiliash said.

Just then an orderly came up with a basket. The tantalizing smell of fresh bread came from it. "They got the earth ovens going, sir," she said proudly. "Real risen leavened bread."

"Thanks! I get so damned sick of pita," Kenneth said, rising. "Let's eat."

The air was cold; Raupasha gratefully wrapped one of the lengths of plundered—*foraged*, she reminded herself—cloth they were using as towels around herself, knotting it by one armpit so that it covered her from collarbone to knee. The fire hissed and sputtered as a rack of beef ribs and her gift were spitted on green sticks and suspended over the coals. The basket held cheese, raisins, olives and dried figs besides the loaves. O'Rourke showed her how to cut off a slab of the bread and toast it and some cheese over the fire while the meat cooked.

"Yeah," Kenneth Hollard said, leaning back on one elbow with a handful of olives. "It *would* be logical for Walker to try and destroy us piecemeal. But only if he could find us, and move fast enough on that information. He's got more troops than we do, and his weapons are just about as good . . . but we've got interior lines, and more important still we've got radios and aerial reconnaisance, and he doesn't."

O'Rourke nodded: "It's like fighting a big, strong fellah who's half-blind and half-deaf."

Kashtiliash shrugged: "His blows are still nothing to laugh at, when he finds a target."

"It's a matter of time," Kenneth Hollard said. "He's racing the clock. The further he advances, the less fertile the country and the more time we've had to strip it . . . and pretty soon, it's going to be full winter. Rain and mud down in the lowlands. Hard snow up on the plateau."

It had grown dark, only a pink glow left on the snow peaks to the north. The firelight played over the craggy planes of his face, the light dusting of golden hair over his body, the play of long smooth muscles on long limbs and the hard V-shape from broad shoulders to narrow waist. He didn't have the bulk of thew that gave Kashtiliash a Minotaur's presence, but he shone with youth and health, strength and a leopard's deadly speed. Scars only gave him the *gravitas* of experience.

Oh, Ishtar of the Lovers, but he is beautiful, Raupasha thought, trying to keep her thought from her face. *And if some stranger were to come . . . even naked as we all are, and among so many proven fighting-men, still he would not have to ask who our leader is.*

Marian Alston stiffled a yawn with locked jaws and forced herself to listen alertly. The staff meeting was nearly finished; nobody had gotten much sleep last night, and they'd all been hard at work since before sunup. The steam ram had saved their bacon by smashing the Tartessian galleys into unthreatening splinters, but there was still plenty of damage to repair.

"*Farragut*'s still afloat," Captain Trudeau said grimly, the ointment on his face glistening in the bright sunshine. Usually he was a humorous sort, but under the circumstances . . . "And that's *all* I can say."

The Republic's fleet lay in the shelter of . . . *Cadiz, I suppose we can call it,* Marian Alston-Kurlelo thought, with its masts and spars making a spiky leafless forest for the better part of a mile along the shore that sheltered it from the Atlantic swells. Most of them were several hundred yards offshore; they'd brought the steam ram closer in, so that it would have only a few feet to settle if it finally gave up the struggle for buoyancy.

The *Farragut* was looking a bit better than it had when they first arrived, mainly because the rails weren't quite so close to the water; none of the portholes were submerged anymore, either. A trickle of black smoke came from its funnel to show that the boilers were still hot; the coal smut flowed skyward through holes punched in the sheet steel by grapeshot. The reason for keeping steam up was clear enough, as long fountains of seawater poured from the vents of the ship's pumps. There were stretches of canvas and rope along the sides, where sails had been fothered under the keel to try and seal the leaking seams between the planks of her hull, and one paddle-housing was shattered and bent. A raft floated next to it, and the sound of sledgehammers and cutting chisels working on bent steel plates rang out like discordant bells. The scent of coal smoke drifted down to the watchers on shore, mingling with the brackish salt of the shoreside marshes.

"I want to get the boilers cool as soon as I can, so we can do some real work on them," Trudeau went on. His hands were bandaged, and his naturally rather dark high-cheeked face had a reddish flushed look, with his blue eyes peering out like turquoise set in copper.

"The boiler's frame seams parted during the blow—the supporting timbers flexed under the stress—and water started dripping down into the furnaces. It was wetting the coal, keeping the temperature down so we lost steam. God *knows* what happened when we started using the ram in the battle yesterday. Plus she spewed out most of her oakum."

"What did you do about the boilers?" Swindapa asked, moving her mouth carefully. The left side of her face was a rainbow of colors from the bruising impact of the rifle butt, and a couple of teeth were still a little loose. "With the furnace, I mean."

"We had to wrap some people up in water-soaked rags and send them in to slap clay putty on the worst leaks," Trudeau said. "Nobody died, but a couple collapsed . . . that slowed us up, had to go in twice . . ."

"People went in while the furnaces were hot?" Victor Ortiz asked incredulously. "*Inside* the furnaces?"

Trudeau nodded. "Had to, Vic—*tabernac*, if we hadn't, we'd have lost power completely and been driven onto the cliffs. The masts had already gone by the board, and besides that her seams were working so badly we'd have sunk without power to the pumps, it was like trying to go to sea in a sieve. As it was we were down to six knots and barely made it here in time."

Alston spoke: "I think that was more a matter of *leading* the working party in than *sending* it, wasn't it, Commander Trudeau?"

Trudeau had been a cadet when *Eagle* was caught in the Event. He still looked much younger than the twenty-nine he was when he blushed and shrugged. "Someone had to do it," he said.

"But you did it," she said, nodding and marking it down for later reference. Ortiz was grinning through his bandage. "I take it that the *Farragut* isn't fit for duty anytime soon?"

"No, ma'am."

"Well, she did well enough yesterday, Gary. The account's in the black for a good long while."

The circle of officers nodded, silent for a second. Marian felt her soul wince slightly, remembering the rowers screaming as the steel-plated bows of the steam ram crashed into the side of a galley and rode it under in a single wallowing rush. The severed halves had each risen like broken pencils sticking out of the ocean for a moment before they plunged, and in the same instant the ram caught another of the lightly built craft with charges of canister, leaving her riddled and sinking in water that turned red. . . .

If it hadn't been for one making a suicide run to fire its Dahlgrens into the port paddle wheels, not a single Tartessian galley would have escaped. She also remembered the sheer enormous feeling of *relief* as a tactical draw and strategic defeat turned into an unambiguous victory.

Mmm-hmmm, she mused. *As it is, they got most of their galleys back, and four of their sail warcraft. Must have lost better than fifteen hundred men killed and wounded, though, and we took a thousand prisoners. That's got to hurt.*

The Islander losses had been a little over a tenth of that number, and *they* certainly hurt . . . *And we took all those cannon.*

"Well, there's no reason for the enemy to know that *Farragut*'s out of commssion for a while," she said meditatively. "We'll set up manual pumps . . . no, by God, what we'll do is put one of the stationary engines on a raft and float it out. Ms. Kurlelo-Alston, see to it." Swindapa nodded and made a note on her clipboard.

"The engines are coming ashore later today, Commodore," the blond officer said, using the clipboard to point eastward. "Captain Trudeau, I'll have to borrow your chief engineer?"

"Gladly, Ms. Kurlelo-Alston," he said.

The five surviving frigates were anchored as well; working parties were swarming over them, setting up masts and rigging from the stores-ships, repairing the upperworks, pumping hard; they'd haul them ashore one at a time to do permanent patches on the holes below the waterline, and in a week or so they'd be good as new. There were five schooners as well, but two of them would need extensive overhauls out of the water.

"Captain Galen, you'll take *Sherman* up to La Coruna and escort the *Merrimac* and the collier south," she said, picking the commander of the least damaged large warship. "On the next tide; transfer powder and shot from the other frigates' magazines to save time, and enough people to bring you up to full complement. We can keep a schooner on picket duty off Tartessos, and ultralights of course. Mr. Haddon."

The commander of the transports stepped forward and saluted, looking a little self-conscious. He was a reservist, a stocky man in his mid-forties with a gray-shot beard, a yachtsman before the Event and a merchant skipper on the Baltic run in peacetime. He'd brought his ship in to relieve the *Chamberlain* without a moment's hesitation, though.

"Ma'am?"

She returned the gesture. "Mr. Haddon, as soon as the troops and stores are disembarked, I want the troop-transports to make sail for home; except for four—all over two hundred and fifty tons—who'll be dispatched to Westhaven for another supply run. How soon?"

"Ah . . . two days, ma'am. We're really very well found now, for the most part. Four ships . . . that's more than enough."

The old custom of Marque and Reprisal had been revived with a vengeance for this war, and wherever Islander merchantmen met Tartessian, they fought. There weren't any major enemy warships abroad, though, so four big Nantucketer ships ought to be fairly safe.

"Good." She tapped two fingers on her chin; putting hands behind her back hurt, given the wounds she'd picked up. *Let's see . . .*

In her birth-century and for a millennia and more before that, Cadiz was a peninsula on the southern coast of Spain, just southeast of the mouth of the Guadalquivir River. Here it was a narrow scrub-covered offshore island nearly eight miles long, just southeast of a vast shallow bay that reached inland nearly to the site of Seville-that-wasn't. The landward side was a narrow channel a mile or two across at its northern end, with salt marsh and pinewoods on the mainland giving way to low rolling hills of oak-savanna and grass, both turning green with the autumn rains, and a few villages of fishers and farmers. The island itself was a sandbank rising to a central spine of low hills—not unlike Nantucket, some of the wags had noted—with a few smaller ones not far away. The only stone was on the western verge, where a few shallow reefs ran up out of the Atlantic swells; doubtless they were what had caught the sand drifting with the longshore current in the first place.

Now it was an instant town of thousands, streets of tents and open squares piled high with supplies. Some of the tents were huge—the field hospital had gone up first, complete with prefabricated board floors. Thousands labored, digging ditches and pit-latrines, throwing up the ramparts of earth-and-timber forts, and a steep berm and ditch around the whole camp. Others were setting up the drill that would punch deep tube wells as soon as the engine came ashore. A pontoon wharf extending out into the harbor was nearly ready, and when it was the freighters could unload directly onto handcarts and wagons; the first heavy cargo to come ashore would be steam-haulers. Off to the west she could hear the dull heavy *thudump!* of a blasting charge, shattering rock to be used to gravel the roadways, and out on the narrow channel oars flashed as boats towed rafts of oak and umbrella pine cut near the shore. A fort was going up there, too, on a point of hard land rising out of green marsh, cutting off any entry.

Alston turned her gaze to the captured Tartessian ships. Two of them were beached, drawn up ashore on the sandy mud to keep them from sinking. The others were serving as floating POW pens, their own surviving crews repairing superficial damage and working the pumps under guard until something more regular could be arranged.

"What's the status on those?" she asked.

Swindapa flipped two pages on her clipboard, but she was speaking before her eyes hit the print. "The two we ran ashore are . . . *shattered* was the word CPO Zelukelo used. The others are essentially sound, but they'll all need to be hauled up for work on their hulls before they're fully functional again."

She looked up. "Really very good ships—well built, fine seasoned wood. Composite masts, though—bound with heat-shrunk iron hoops."

The Republic used single trunks for masts, but it had access to the white pine of New England. Swindapa went on:

"We have forty-eight Dahlgrens from them, cold-core cast steel work. The armory marks read *Walkeropolis* and *Neayoruk*, which fits with the Foreign Affairs reports, and *Cuddyston*, which doesn't but I think it's up in, what's the name, Istria, where we heard they were opening coal mines. The guns are about ten percent heavier than ours, and the machining's cruder—particularly on the exteriors. But they'll throw a ball nearly as far and hard as ours, and nearly as accurately."

"Too fucking right, they will," one of the XOs muttered. "Sorry, ma'am," he went on at the Commodore's quelling look.

"Then we'll break up the two on the beach for timber," Alston went on. "That'll give us eight-hundred-odd tons of seasoned plank and beam, more than enough for our repairs and useful for construction, too. Brigadier McClintock, I want to get an accelerated training program for the auxiliaries going, starting tomorrow. We'll—"

"Is that a *railroad*?" Ian Arnstein asked incredulously.

It certainly looked like one, snaking north up the valley of the Eurotas, parallel to the two-lane asphalt road from Neay-oruk. Wooden crossties in a bed of gravel, and rails on them, shining in the sun that had emerged from the clouds at last.

Wait a minute, he thought. Those rails were wood, too, with a thin strap of iron nailed on top. Then his eyes went wide again; a train of wagon-cars came rumbling around a low hill, pulled by . . .

Elephants? he thought, feeling his mind boggle; it was an interesting sensation, a little like how your knees got after one too many.

"From Pharaoh," Odikweos said. "A man of the King's left his service some time ago, and found shelter at Ramses's court. We trade with him, and the King bought these creatures. Many men died learning the trick of taming them, but they haul like the Titans of old."

He waved a hand at the . . . *Elephant-way? Elephant-road? Whatever,* Ian thought.

"There is talk of extending it north to Mycenae, and then to Athens and beyond, as we did the road, years ago. All the changes come first to this part of the kingdom. Now, about Nantucket—"

Feeling his way, Arnstein said: "I thought I wasn't to be interrogated."

The Greek smiled. "No, only not tortured," he said.

Arnstein's eyes narrowed. Few of the Ithakan's questions had been specifically military; most of them had been about Nantucket generally, about laws and customs and governance. *Comparing my story to what he's had from Walker and his cronies,* Ian decided. *Now* that's *smart.* Of course, if this was who he thought it was, his cleverness had become a legend that lasted three thousand years . . .

He looked around at the vale of Sparta as he spoke, "hollow Lakonia" as it had been called. *I can see what he meant about the changes starting here, it being Walker's HQ. Still, they've done an awful lot in less than ten years.*

The road was crowded, troops or slave coffles or local villagers traveling on the graveled verges; trains of big Conestogas and smaller vehicles pulled by oxen or mules on the pavement, sometimes a rich man's chariot, a fair number of riders in modern saddles. Pine trunks rose beside the road at intervals, with a single strand of wire looping along; agents and merchants had confirmed that Walker was using telegraphs. Once there was a body hanging upside down from a pole as well, with a sign reading "wire cutter" spiked to it.

The Eurotas ran to their right, brown and muddy and swift over a gravel bed, lined with oleander, plane trees, and dwarf palms. The valley bottom went from flattish to rolling and back, broken here and there by escarpments and gullies thick with evergreens and aromatic shrubs. To their left the afternoon sun turned the snowcapped peaks and fingers of Taygetos to flame, casting shadows down the dark fir-forested slopes; the range loomed over the valley below like a wall, rising almost vertically. More forests clothed the gentler foothills of Mount Parnon to the east, pines standing tall in a dense blue-green bristle on the upper slopes, with traces of autumn yellow on the hardwoods mantling the lower. This was not the Greece he knew.

The valley itself was full of groves, young fruit trees, citrus—Isketerol had ordered thousands of grafted seedlings from Brandt Farms before the war, and evidently passed a lot of them on. Disc plows turned up the rich red earth in fields edged by cypresses, and gangs set out new plantings or dropped quartered seed-potatoes into the furrows. Many new olive plantings mantled slopes green and purple with lupines and vetch. Around the older olive trees workers moved, shaking the branches with long poles and throwing the fruit into baskets. Other laborers pruned and bound vines; there were many irrigated fields, watered from small dams and channels and wind-powered pumps. Most of them grew bright-green alfalfa, or vegetables, or what looked the stalks of cotton.

Mounted overseers watched them work, and there had been half a dozen armed patrols. Ian put that together with reports, glimpses of tumbledown abandoned villages, new pitched tile roofs on larger manors, rows of new-built adobe cottages looking like they'd been stamped out with a cookie cutter . . . or run up by construction gangs to an identical plan.

"Let me guess, lord *wannax*," he said to Odikweos. "A lot of the peasant tenant farmers who used to live here don't anymore."

"Yes," the Greek said, looking slightly surprised. "Many have moved to Walkeropolis or Neayoruk, many have gone into the Army, many as colonists to conquered lands."

"And to replace them, Walker . . . your King of Men, I mean . . . supplied slaves to the . . . *telestai,* isn't that the word?"

"Barons, yes."

"And so now instead of tenants they could call out to fight for them, the barons have slave gangs who'd run off or revolt without Wal . . . without the King of Men's armies and police?"

Odikweos's eyes narrowed. "Yes," he said in a neutral tone. "Some do run off, to the mountain forests, and live as skulking bandits until they're hunted down and crucified."

"Uh-huh," Arnstein said. "And I'll bet that instead of every estate being self-sufficient except for luxuries, now they couldn't survive without trade?"

"Hmmmm," Odikweos said, tugging at his beard. "Yes. Grain from Thessaly and Sicily and Macedonia; also tools and cloth from the *factories* the King of Men established." He dropped the English word into his Achaean without noticing it.

They came to the outskirts of Walkeropolis only two hours travel from Neayoruk; sixteen miles or so as the road wound—though Arnstein noted that the journey-stones beside the road were in kilometers. The small forest of crosses on the outskirts were about what he'd expected. Despite that he closed his eyes and gagged helplessly. The ravens and vultures ignored the passersby as they squabbled over tidbits, jumping back a little and waiting when a man pinned to the wood beat his head back and forth and croaked as he tried to scream past a dry swollen tongue.

Put it out of your mind, Arnstein, he thought with grim intensity. *You're trying to save your life, and maybe more. Ignore it!*

The city proper lay beyond, a mushroom growth with twice the population of Nantucket Town. His eyes went wide in surprise; the reports hadn't prepared him for how alien it looked, neither Mycenaean or modern or anything else he could quite classify. Aqueducts and smokestacks marked a considerable factory district; the buildings there were the same sort of utilitarian adobe-functional he'd noted before, but mostly whitewashed.

The layout was a grid, modified to fit the hilly terrain, with young plane trees lining the streets. Other hillsides were green with gardens and ornamental groves, red and umber tile and shining marble and neat ashlar blocks showing through, mansions and public buildings. Atop one hillside nearby was . . .

He shook his head. The Mycenaean Greeks worshiped more or less the same pantheon of Gods that their Classical descendants would . . . would have. But they did it in small shrines, or at hilltop altars, or in groves or caves. They *didn't* build what he saw there, fluted marble columns around a rectangle with a pitched roof, the stereotypical form of a Greek temple (or English bank) shining in white stone, with a big altar before it and a huge cult-statue glimpsed through bronze screenwork inside the pillars.

The sun caught out points of brightness, gilded Corinthian capitals on the columns, colored terra-cotta on the bas-reliefs of the pediments and *metopes*, the cartoon-panel-like decorations under the eves and on the triangular spaces at the front above the pillars. A complex of lesser buildings occupied the slopes below. Several other temples were under construction nearby, with a litter of blocks and concrete-mixing troughs and great timber cranes for erecting monolithic pillars.

"Let me guess," Arnstein said again. "The King of Men has set up an *organization*"—that word had also been borrowed into the Achaean of the Year Ten—"of full-time paid priests—"

"The Sacred Collegium, yes."

"—with regional over-priests in the rest of the country all reporting back to someone appointed by him."

"Yes," Odikweos said, shrugging and smiling slightly. "Many have praised his piety in bestowing these beautiful God-houses on the realm, and skilled servants to attend them. Is it any wonder that the Gods have favored him so?"

Was there a slight astringent edge to the Achaean's voice? *I hope so, but then I'm listening for my life as well as talking for it.* And he wasn't in the backwoods here. This might not be Egypt or Babylon, but it was an old and sophisticated civilization in its way.

Vulnerable, though. Writing had been a rare thing here until Walker came, used only for accounting and administration. From the number of street signs and quasi billboards, he'd put a lot of *ooomph* into teaching the three R's—and didn't this archaic Greek look odd written in the Latin alphabet! The first generation of literates in any culture tended to be pretty gullible about print. They also didn't have a word for "religion," or a concept of it as something separate from everyday life, that could be manipulated as an entity.

I'll give you any odds that Walker's got his tame priesthood working on some sort of Holy Scripture, too—a pagan Koran or Book of Oracles or something with the King of Men as the Numero Uno favored of Zeus Pater. I wonder what Odikweos would make of that?

There was no need to ask about the structure like a football stadium built into the side of a hill, with a mule-drawn trolley line running out to it. The reports had gone into revolting detail about Walker's revival . . . or premature invention . . . of the Roman *munera*. A crowd was pouring out of it as he watched, animated and brisk, many of them leading or carrying their children, and he could hear the *ooompa-ooompa* of a band that included a big water organ.

Nor much doubt about the smaller temple of gray-and-red stone on a nearby height. Instead of an exterior altar in front of the building, that had a ten-foot-high double-headed cobra making a circle in gilded cast bronze. It enclosed a sun and moon—black sun, black moon, under the flared fanged heads with their ivory teeth and ruby eyes. A party of women in rich clothing and delicately beautiful masks of black leather and silver led a man with his head covered in a sack up to it. The women stopped and bowed, then made a gesture with both fists clenched before the face, imitating the serpents, before they passed on into the temple proper.

"A few years ago it was just another snake cult," he quoted to himself in a low mutter. "And where's Conan when you need him?"

Behind the snake-sun-moon sigil was another bronze, a statue of a woman with three faces pointing in different directions—the Triple Hekate of the Crossroads. The rest of the figure wasn't at all Greek; more like Kali, multiple arms holding scalpels, bowls, knives, whips, fetters, human hearts—rendered quite accurately—and dancing in a hip-shot posture.

A tablet at the beginning of the road leading up to the building read:

> *Cold be hand, and heart, and bone;*
> *And cold be sleep, under stone . . .*

Ian Arnstein's lips quirked upward as he read; Tolkien translated quite well into Greek.

Then the ironic humor washed out of him like a candle guttering in a high wind as a long, high scream came down the hill, and he realized the man must have had the bag removed and seen his fate. The scream continued, with chanting running under it like a counterpoint. The skulls all around the temple's *metope* weren't sculpted replicas. They were the real thing, human bone mounted on polished metal disks, hundreds of them, and as many again on a pyramidal skull rack outside.

That wasn't Greek in inspiration either. Aztec, the way they'd displayed the results of their massacre-sacrifices.

It's like a theme park for demons. Walker and sado-bitch and the others have turned this place into their own multicultural sociopath's Disneyland. Except these are real *people* they're *playing with.*

He turned his eyes from Hong's temple and wished he could shut it out of his mind as well. Evil sweltered out of the very stones, like some vile metaphysical ooze that made his *soul* feel polluted, echoing with the agony within. He'd felt the same before, on a trip to Europe before the Event . . . at the gate of Dachau.

"This gift from your Island . . . some of us do not appreciate it here," Odikweos said softly.

"*That* is not something you can blame on *us*," Arnstein said. "Hong is an outlaw; were she back on Nantucket, we'd hang her."

He thought of trying to say she was crazy, but the closest you could come to saying that in this language meant literally *possessed by spirits.* The last thing he wanted to do was back up her claim to divine inspiration.

"Of course you would; she and the King are rebels against your ruler."

"No. We'd hang her for what she's done *here.*"

The Achaean gave a noncommittal toss of his head. It was nearly dark now, the sun sinking crimson on the high peak to the westward; a steam whistle hooted mournfully somewhere.

More people were spilling onto the street, but the crowds parted before the chariot and mounted guards, some murmuring or pointing after a ripple of bows and salutes. Most of the streets were lined with colonnades, with shops behind those and living quarters above; either Walker was a genuine enthusiast for the column-and-marble bit, or all this neo-Classicism was another one of his ghastly mocking jokes.

Or maybe he just read Howard Fast's Spartacus *at an impressionable age.*

There were statues here and there; *they* looked more Egyptian, with stiff forward-facing stances and hands clenched at their sides; probably because that was where Walker could get sculptors used to working in hard stone. There were fountains at the intersections, with women drawing water, and from the relative lack of smell there must be fairly good sewers as well.

No defenses ringed the city, but there was a wall topped with iron spikes and an openwork bronze gate between the common streets and the palace district. A huge rambling complex covered most of a large hill, terraces and columns, towers and bright tile and colored marble showing through gardens still fantastically lovely. His captor's guards and chariot turned aside, toward a mansion that was merely large.

"We will talk, after you have bathed and eaten," Odikweos said under the pillars of the entranceway. "There is much I have wished to learn."

Night had fallen by the time Marian Alston-Kurlelo had finished her rounds of the wounded. That was almost as hard as the battle itself.

The hospital smelled of antisepsis and pain, with an overtone of broth from the soup kettles being wheeled through for those who could use them. The first rush of emergency surgery was over, and most of the patients were lying quiet, but the lanterns in the operating theater were still burning bright. Nurses and doctors bustled by, sometimes stepping aside for a gurney with a prone patient, bags of saline drip suspended on poles.

One ward was much quieter, most of the patients there slipping quietly into the waiting darkness with their pain muffled by morphia. A priestess of the Ecumenical Church knelt murmuring beside a cot; she was just kissing the stola before lifting it over her head, and an open box beside her held a vial and wafers. Several Marines were kneeling there, too, some of them bandaged, heads bowed over clasped hands that held crucifix and rosary.

Price of doing business, Marian Alston-Kurlelo forced herself to think. It wasn't as if they'd introduced war here, and a bronze-tipped spear in the guts killed you just as painfully and just as dead as grapeshot. *At least this is about something more than a cattle raid.* Swindapa was weeping, a quiet trickle of tears from the cerulean-blue eyes, undramatic and matter-of-fact. *Wish I could do that. Wouldn't do, though. The Midnight Mare's got to keep up the image for the crews.*

Commander Arthur Jenkins was sitting propped up in bed; his left forearm ended in a mass of bandage three inches below the elbow, and other straps immobilized it. A tray was across his lap, fixed to rails on either side of the collapsible hospital cot, with a bowl of beef broth made from concentrate—what the rank and file called "Gomez soup" after the Prelate of the Ecumenical Church, because it proved the doctrine of the Resurrection of the Flesh—and the remains of a small loaf of bread. He put down the spoon as they approached and smiled, a cheerful expression that squeezed at Alston's chest below the breastbone.

"Commodore," he said. The smile went wider. "I'll have to change my name, if I'm ever promoted." At her raised eyebrows he moved the left arm slightly. "Captain Hook, what else?"

Alston found herself unable to stop a small snort of laughter. "I hope you don't think I'm going to let you off with a soft job because of this, Arthur."

"Ma'am, I'm sure there will be something useful to the Republic I can do," he said, keeping the smile on his face.

"Certainly there will," Marian said. "Commanding the *Chamberlain*, if I don't manage to get her sunk in the interim—the doctors tell me you'll be on your feet in about a month."

He looked up at her, startled hope in his eyes. She leaned forward, smiling herself, a rare flash of white teeth against her coal-black face, and laid a long-fingered hand gently on his shoulder.

"Arthur, the Republic pays you a munificent six dollars fifty cents a day—less income tax and witholding tax—to be an officer and a fighting sailor, not to play the piano, although I know you're going to miss that. And *I* set policy on disabilities, so-called. If Nelson could command an entire fleet at Trafalgar with one arm, I think you can run one ship with one-and-a-half."

"Violin, ma'am," he said, grinning as if it hurt his face less now. "I play, played, the fiddle. And hell, I can still do 'Chopsticks.'"

Swindapa leaned forward from the other side and kissed him softly on the forehead. "You are very brave," she said simply.

Alston cleared her throat. "Anyway, your family've been informed that you're alive and recovering," she said. "Standard thirty-word radiophone message back from your wife, but I thought it wouldn't hurt if I jumped the queue and brought it to you myself." He took it up eagerly. "Good luck, and listen to the doctors. I'll be in to see you now and then."

Swindapa leaned over to whisper in her ear as they left: "I don't think he was listening to that last bit," she chuckled.

They walked out the front door flap of the field hospital, their boots noiseless on the soft sand of the street outside; it would be a few days before the road team was ready to gravel it. The Marine sentries on either side slapped hands to rifles, and the officers returned the gesture of respect.

"Well, neither would I, if I was in his shoes," Alston said.

Lord, but I hate doing this, she thought, looking over her shoulder for a second at the backlit canvas of the hospital-tent complex. *Duty.* "His wife's with Brandt Farms, isn't she?"

"Plant-breeding program," Swindapa agreed. Her eyes grew a little abstracted, and her Fiernan accent went from a trace to noticeable. It always did, when she opened the doors of that memory-palace within that her training at the Great Wisdom had built. "Three children . . . she's expecting a fourth . . . they have an application in for an adoption. You know," she went on in a conversational voice, "my . . . mmm, cousin . . . at the Old Circle has a mother's-sister's-daughter, niece, who died giving birth to twins this summer, a boy and a girl. They'd be glad to put them with a good family on the Island."

"See about that," Marian said, smiling within. Her face went colder. "Now we have to do the funerals."

Most of the Guard's dead from the sea fight had gone over the side at once in the heat of action; there would be a common ceremony for them. Some had died since and would be buried ashore, and there were more from the Marines and the auxiliaries. Cremation was one of the few things the Sun People and Fiernan Bohulugi had in common, and the Ecumenical Church had no objection to it; that was a lot more practical than sending home bodies. At least they had plenty of firewood. . . .

CHAPTER TWENTY-TWO

***November, 10 A.E.—Walkeropolis, Kingdom of
Great Achaea***
October, 10 A.E.—Great River, southern Iberia

"Sam?" Vicki Cofflin said, looking at the *Emancipator*'s navigator. "Any definite idea of where the hell we are?"

"According to my calculations, the Hattusas radio beacon, and plenty of sheer guesswork, about here, Skipper," she replied.

Vicki leaned over her shoulder. *Here* was somewhere west of Monemavasia, a coastal town that didn't exist except as an Achaean base. Exactly how far west was impossible to say, with the weather like this. That didn't bother her as much as it might have a Lost Geezer; she'd grown up relying on dead reckoning guess-and-God navigation. Still . . .

"I hate bombing civilians," Vicki Cofflin said quietly.

"Don't we all," the XO of *Emancipator* replied.

"Even worse, that bastard Walker's not at home." Vicki sighed. "Well, we have to try and take out his factories." Louder: "Helm, come about to two-two-zero."

The dirigible throbbed about them; the crew were muffled in heavy wool trousers and jackets of glazed sheepskin and knitted wool caps. The thin air was damp and chilly, smelling of machine oil and wicker and tanned whale intestine. Into a patch of cloud and they lost starlight and moonlight. Darkness fell inside the craft save for a few faint lights from the instruments; then silvery light flooded them again as they broke free. The patches of clear air were growing fewer and smaller.

"Hell of a tail wind," Alex Stoddard said. His eyes flicked to the instruments. "Better than forty knots—our ground speed must be up around a hundred mph."

Damn, Vicki thought. *Too fast for comfort.*

It made her nervous, especially with a mountain range nearly eight thousand feet high to the west of the target and another one only a couple of thousand feet lower to the left. She looked down from the commander's seat onto the crumpled, mountain-strewn landscape of southern Greece, then over at the map table.

"Observers to their stations," she said.

Several of the crewfolk scattered, to point binoculars out ports in the wicker sides of the gondola. Waiting stretched; she sipped cocoa from a thermos and monitored pressure, fuel consumption, and ballast status.

"Skipper!" That brought her over to the portside observer. "That's Mount Taygetos!"

She took the binoculars herself. *Single sharp triangular peak, knife ridge running north,* she quoted to herself. That was it, snow-stark like a single fang pointing skyward through a gap in the clouds. Which meant . . .

"Goddammit, we're too far north!"

"Wind's rising and the barometer's falling, Skipper," Alex said quietly.

"How do you feel about aborting, and trying to dock at Hat-tusas, with no proper mooring tower there and fifteen thousand pounds of mixed incendiaries and gunpowder bombs racked at the keel?" she asked.

"Not very good, ma'am," the XO said. His face was underlit by the instruments, turning it half-Satanic as he grinned. "Of course, there's always the miracle of the bombs and the fishes."

Vicki grunted. *Damned if I'm going to waste all this ordnance blowing up inoffensive squid and tuna,* she decided; the thought offended her thrifty Nantucket soul.

"We'll take her in." A quick mental calculation; the airship was pointed straight for Walkeropolis, but the wind would take them well north of it. "Left fifty, rudder. Engines all ahead full. Altitude control?"

"Eight thousand two hundred seventy feet," came the crisp reply.

The drone of the engines rose to a snarling bellow. The fabric of the ship creaked and bent as the engines pushed it against the wind.

"Prepare to vent. Neutral buoyancy at three thousand feet," she said. "Vent—off superheat!"

"Superheat off—vent!"

The hissing roar of hot exhaust being funneled into the cen-tral gasbag cut off. Sharp clicking and groaning sounds followed as it cooled, and then more as hands spun the wheels that opened big flaps on the upper surface of the *Emancipator*.

There was a faint, edge-of-perception sensation like a descending elevator.

That brought a few silent winces; awfully low, with high winds, in this type of terrain. It was also the only way to get a radius-of-error less than a couple of miles when it came to aiming bombs. Walkeropolis wasn't a completely defenseless target the way Nineveh and Asshur had been, where they could loiter a few hundred feet up in broad daylight. Great Achaea had rockets, upward-firing rifled cannon, barrage balloons; and the Republic had only this one highly explosive airship, plus another knocked down in the holds of the fleet sailing against Tartessos.

"Listen up, people!" she said, a little louder.

That meant everyone could hear her, except the Gatling crew in the observation bubble topside. She pressed the button on the intercom so that they could listen too.

"We're going to make one run, straight in, and bomb whatever we can get over. The crate is going to head for the God-damned moon when we shed all that weight. Keep your hands on the valve and ballast controls, and keep your ears open for the word."

A murmur, taut readiness. She nodded and kept her eyes and binoculars scanning through the slanted windows to either side of the commander's chair. Black night outside, and the hiss of rain starting to strike the tight doped fabric stretched over the *Emancipator*'s hull.

"Vents closed—neutral buoyancy at three thousand feet."

God-damn this cloud. God-damn me; I could be back in Nantucket Town, making babies and teaching people how to fly ultralights . . . after this stinking war is over I am definitely *going to ask Alex for that date . . .*

"There!" she said, an involuntary exclamation.

Thunder rumbled above them. Lightning glinted off the Eurotas, just like the maps for one bright instant. For a while she'd been afraid they were going to end up in Italy. Or the way this damned gale was blowing, in China.

"Right fifty, helm."

The dirigible's nose turned right in a descending curve that brought her facing north as she fell. The gondola rocked, the craft pitching and rolling a little in the more turbulent air near the surface.

"She's slightly heavy, Skipper."

"That's the rain. On superheat—ten percent ought to do her."

Vicki kept her eye peeled to port, where the tree-clad mountains seemed to reach for her with crooked witch-fingers every time one of the lightning bolts struck. *Emancipator* was well below the level of the peaks now; she'd have to crane her head to see them. All her attention was focused northward. Walkeropolis didn't have a blackout; but it didn't have electric light, either. Lanterns ought to stand out, or forge-flare from the manufactures.

"Latest report from Meteorology, ma'am—HQ says a major weather system is building up clear from the Pillars to here."

No kidding; black above as a yard up a hog's arse, except for the increasingly frequent flash of lightning, as often horizontal as down to the ground below. She made herself not think about what one of those bolts into an engine or the metallic fasteners of the hull would do. The wind was picking up, too.

"Fire up the searchlight." Alex looked at her. "We'll be bombing blind, otherwise."

He nodded and unstrapped himself, lifting a hatch on the laminated-wood deck. It held a crank, and he worked that to open the doors below and lower the searchlight out into the airstream. An aluminum tube rose as he did so. Into that he thrust a metal rod with a small wheel on the end; there was a chink-*chunk* sound as it fit into the sleeve of the universal joint. Forward or back on the rod would turn the searchlight under the gondola's chin up or down; a twist on the wheel to port or starboard.

"Searchlight . . . *on*!"

Light glinted up through gaps in the hatchway. Much more poured down on the landscape below. She could see the tops of trees swaying, the slick line of a wet asphalt highway. And . . . there, ahead and to port! Buildings, a great clump of them. The stubby brick pyramids of blast furnaces against a hillside, and the courtyard-and-siding arrangement of manufacturing plant downslope of them, all neat and tiny like a model on a table.

Easier to think of it as a model, not as homes . . .

"Horizontal rudder, left ten," she said, her voice smooth and cool and remote. "Engines, ahead three-quarters." The roar of the Cessna pistons muted slightly. Over it, thunder rolled frighteningly close. "Bomb-bay doors open." The airship's ride grew noticeably rougher, as the panels opened and caught the slipstream. "Bomb-aimer, over to you."

"Ma'am," he said calmly, from his prone position behind the command section; he was using a telescope aimed through the keel. "Sir, if you could swing the light to port about fifteen degrees—yes! Right on those buildings—helm, follow that."

"Barrage balloons going up!" the observers called.

Seconds later, the same came through her headphones from the Gatling post topside. Two of the six-barreled weapons pointed out either side of the gondola as well, but they probably wouldn't get close enough to use them. She could see the barrage balloons herself now, and trained her binoculars on them—nothing else to do, unless she intervened to abort the run. They weren't blimp-shaped; more like giant letter A's made of sausages, instead. The armament was topside on a decking of light planks, they and the men who served them tiny and indistinct at this distance. Reports said it was two-pounder rifled guns on pivot mounts—useful in itself, taking up Walker's scarce precision-machining capacity.

The shape of the balloons turned them into the wind as the cables holding them payed out, a harness like a kite's leading to a single thick line on a windlass. That was no calm nosing into a steady breeze, not tonight; they pitched and tossed as they rose, fighting the ropes that held them. The buffeting the *Emancipator* was taking was bad enough; what it was like on those bare open decks, lashed by rain and lit by lightning, she hated to imagine. Particularly to a local, unused to the whole concept of flight except as something the Gods did.

Brave men, she thought unwillingly. It would be an easier world if all the villains were cowards, but nobody who'd seen Assyrians in operation would think that.

Little red lights began to snap at her from the ground as well, like malignant winks. More light cannon in counter-weighted cradles; swing the muzzle down, ram a shell down the barrel, swing it up, and fire. Her grandfather had flown B-17s over the Ruhr, and a Flying Fortress would have laughed at such antiaircraft fire. So would her great-grandfather's Sopwith Camel. Neither of those craft were five-hundred-odd feet long, or flying at less than a mile up at fifty miles an hour, or hanging under hundreds of thousands of square feet of explosive gas.

Searchlights lit on the ground as well. They were yellower than her ten-thousand-candlepower electric pre-Event model; probably burning lime in a stream of gas, in front of a mirror. Still capable of spiking her for the absurd muzzle-loading flak, though. And rockets were rising as well, glorified Fourth-of-July models, but they didn't have far to rise, either.

"Coming up on target," the bomb-aimer said.

Something burst with a red *snap* not too far away. Crewfolk scrambled up the ladders into the hull to find and patch leaks in the gasbags.

"Preparing to release bombs," the man's voice said.

And the Gatling crew screamed in her ears through the headphones: *"Jesus Christ they've got rocket pods on the balloons!"* The ripping-canvas sound of the machine gun came in the same instant.

Vicki's head came up with a snap. Her mouth opened to give an order, and then the sky to their right lit up. In that light she could see what was on the balloon's upper decking; long bundles of tubes on simple pintle mounts. Flame washed out behind the tubes, and ahead of them as the warheads raced at her.

"Valve crew, stand fast," she said. The last thing in the world they needed right now was a flood of hydrogen above the hull.

"Release bombs!" she went on, keeping her voice from rising with an effort of will that made sweat stand out on her immobile face. "Charlie, *now!*"

The *Emancipator* began to leap and shudder as the finned steel eggs nestled in her lower cargo compartments streamed down. At the same instant a dozen tracks of fire raced through the space she had occupied instants earlier. By some malign freak of ballistics, one rocket intersected the trajectory of a bomb at precisely the wrong moment. The explosion heaved the *Emancipator* upward and pitched her nose-down at the same instant, throwing everyone not strapped in flying; Vicki could hear frames cracking in the hull, and bracers along the wall of the gondola.

The rest of the rockets burst soon after, forlorn fireworks in the rainy darkness of the storm. But something also thudded into the airship, pitching her to the side with a sharp motion totally unlike the battering of the winds. Something else burst right in front of Vicki's station, and she flung up her arms to shield her face.

Another red flare, and stinging pain in her arms and chest and in her forehead. It was too dark; she pawed at her eyes and cheeks, and wiped the blood away. Rain and wind battered at her through the shattered windows. They roared, too, but not too much for her to hear:

"Fire in the hull! Fire at Ring Frame A7! Fire!"

Fire hissed through her. The worst nightmare of anyone who flew these motorized balloons. Fire below, too, as the footprint of the *Emancipator*'s bombs slashed across the landscape. More fire in the sky, as the burning barrage balloon pitched sideways, falling in a graceful arc as its gasbags burst, ignited by the backblast of its own weapons. Most of the airship's crew still standing hurled themselves up the ladders into the hull, in trained damage-control reflex, snatching Nantucket's hoarded store of fire extinguishers as they went. Nothing else mattered if the dirigible was reduced to an exploding smear across the sky of Walkeropolis.

"One and Three portside engines down!"

Vicki scrabbled clumsily at the release of her harness. "Oh, Jesus," she heard herself saying, as the ground fell away and the airship leaped upward, freed of the weight of its deadly cargo.

The slopes of Taygetos were rushing at them, faster and faster as the upper-level winds caught them and the unbalanced force of the engines slewed the *Emancipator* around toward them.

"Helm, left full rudder! Shut down starboard One and Three! Up elevators!"

"Ma'am, she won't answer! Horizontal attitude controls are jammed!"

Vicki Cofflin wiped the sopping sleeve of her jacket over her face again, trying to get the flowing blood out of her eyes.

"Valve ballast—emergency dump," she called. "All engines ninety degrees."

The problem with *that* was that most of the hands were up above. She and Alex and the helm crew rushed backward along the long gondola, heaving at the control wheels that turned the engine pods and the propellers downward, at the release levers that opened the stopcocks and let the water from the keel tanks stream out. It went with a rumbling rush that she could feel even now, but it wasn't going to be enough.

"Hold on all!" she shouted to be heard over the rain coming through the broken prow. "I'm going to drop the emergency ballast!"

The *Emancipator* was nose-up—the vertical controls were still working. All that meant was that she'd hit the mountainside keel-forward. And it made her journey back to the captain's position a climb; she ripped the wire cage off the button and hit with a reaching palm.

There was a shark *kerak . . . kerack . . . kerack* as the explosive bolts released cast-iron weights fastened into the keel. They tumbled free, and the airship leaped like a goosed kangaroo.

Vicki Cofflin had one final glimpse of the onrushing cliff face. Blackness.

*   *   *

The horse snorted and shied beneath Marian Alston-Kurlelo at the sound of a bicycle bell, moving sideways in a crablike skitter. King Isketerol had proved ready to receive a diplomatic mission, but he'd insisted on a place in the no-man's-land between the Islander base at the site of Cadiz and his own outposts, a day's travel northward.

She controlled her mount with the absentminded skill of someone who'd spent a lot of the last ten years in the saddle. The horses she and Swindapa rode were local, part of the herd they'd requisitioned from villages near their landfall at Cadiz Base over the past two weeks, and still uncertain about their new owners. The standard-bearer with the Stars and Stripes flying above a white truce-pennant was mounted likewise, for dignity's sake, and the westering sun gilded the eagle at the top of the staff afresh. Hooves clopped hollow on the hard surface, and wheels moved with a whine and crunch; the flag snapped and fluttered in the onshore breeze.

The platoon behind her were on the cycles, pre-Event ten-speed models refitted for current conditions, and a four-seater side-by-side hauling a Gatling; the Guard had requisitioned nearly every cycle on Nantucket for this expedition, giving money, apologies, and the heavier, clunkier output of Seahaven in recompense. The highway they were following ran northwest from the Cadiz area along the shore of a great inlet—what had been solid ground and marsh at the mouth of the Guadalquivir in the twentieth was open water here. A rough rectangle of sea stretched in from the coast for miles, almost to the edge of the chalk hills that had been the heart of the sherry country in Marian's birth-century.

They would eventually wear out the horses; even with solid tires cyclists covered ground six times faster than troops on foot, especially with good roads.

And these roads are excellent, she thought. *I wonder if Isketerol has thought through all the implications of that?*

The one they followed was twenty-five feet broad, with a topping of neatly cambered crushed limestone pounded to a hard smooth surface, graveled shoulders, deep flanking ditches . . . what the English of the Regency era would have called a MàcAdamized turnpike. There were even young trees planted on either side, to grow and eventually shade travelers.

Hate to think of the labor this must have taken, she thought. The day was hot enough to send trickles of sweat down her flanks under the blue uniform jacket despite the cool breeze from the water and the lingering freshness of this morning's rainfall; summer here must be like being on an anvil under the hammer of the sun. There was a scattering of clouds, growing thicker since noon, gilded now in the west where they piled mountain high above the flat horizon; she thought it would probably rain again soon. Fall and winter were the wet season here, the time of growth and life that ended as late spring faded into the dry death of summer, more or less the opposite of Alba or Nantucket.

To their left stretched the bay, green and blue and scattered whitecaps, shallowing off into a marsh of cattails and reeds close to shore. It was thick and clamorous with birds, shocking-pink flamingos and white spoonbills, greylag geese and wigeon, black-wing stilts wading about on their absurd spindly legs, red-shanks dipping their long bills for shellfish and insect larvae, although they hadn't gotten ahead of the mosquitoes, from the clouds that buzzed about. The yeasty, silty smell of marshland contrasted with the dryer scents of thyme and lavender and spice baked out of the high ground.

Out in the deeper water a column of black smoke came from the stack of a steamboat, one of the half dozen they'd brought in knocked-down form from Nantucket and assembled at Cadiz. The engine was the simple grasshopper-type that Seahaven had built for tugboats since right after the Event, its *chufff . . . chufff . . .* floating clear over the mile or so of water. The hull was a sixty-foot oval, shallow-draft; armament was two Gatlings, one on each wing of the bridge, a light three-inch rifled shell-gun forward, and a four-inch mortar on the afterdeck. For riverine and coastal work they'd proved extremely useful, and they could tow barges full of troops and supplies as well. An ultralight buzzed overhead, high enough that it was a dot of color against blue sky and white cloud.

On the right and ahead was what she'd come to think of as typical Tartessian countryside. Gently rolling right here, which was what it did everywhere it wasn't flat altogether; the mountains of the Sierra de Grazalema were just in sight to the east, and the great range of the Sierra Morena was far to the north, beyond the Guadalquivir.

Not quite forest just yet, except on some of the occasional hills; more of an open parkland with thickets and copses here and there. Near Cadiz-that-wasn't the sandy beaches were flanked by woods of resin-smelling pine; here it was oaks, cork oak and holm oak and varieties she couldn't name, clumps of gray-green wild olives, all scattered in tall golden grass with the green shoots of new growth pushing up through the natural hay. Patches that had burned off in the dry season were even more vividly green. They'd seen many herds of deer, several of them with scores of individuals, hundreds in all during the day's ride. Plus several big brown bears, a distant glimpse of wolves looking curiously back from a ridgeline, a sure-enough group of wisent, European bison, and black, bristling-fierce wild boar out grazing on fallen acorns. Cattle and horses the locals hadn't had time to drive off, too, and . . .

From somewhere ahead a deep grunting, coughing sound came: *uuuh-ooongh, uuuh-ooongh,* repeated again and again, then building up into a shattering roar. The horses shied again, laying their ears back and rolling bulging eyes, fighting the reins. Their nostrils flared wide and red; they chewed their bits, slobbering foam that dripped on the ground.

"What the hell is *that*?" asked one of the Marines nervously, his hand going to the butt of the rifle slung acros his back.

"Silence in the ranks!" Lieutenant Ritter barked, and glanced at the commodore.

"It's a lion, Lieutenant," Alston said, keeping her face straight with long-practiced ease.

There were still some in southern Europe in this era, from Iberia to Greece; it was the demands of the Roman arena that had finally wiped them out, in the other history. *A lot harder on the lions than the Christians, in the end.* Leopards, too . . .

She went on: "And I think that remark translates into English roughly as: *Mine! All mine!*"

Ritter blushed involuntarily—noticeable amid the thick scattered freckles, the same brick-red color as her hair—and smiled worshipfully. Alston hid her sigh, too, as Swindapa looked over at her with one gently mocking eyebrow raised slightly over the remains of a beautiful shiner, all that was left of her collision with the flat side of a rifle butt.

Higamous hogamous, woman monogamous, the black woman thought wryly. *Years of involuntary celibacy before the Event, and now if I wasn't extremely partnered and it weren't against regs, I could cut quite a swath.*

The problem was she'd never really had aspirations that way—the usual fruitless search for True Love had been more her style before the Event, although what she'd have done if she found it back then was a mystery considering the knuckle-dragging barbarism of the old UCMJ on the matter. Earlier, she'd even spent years trying to convince herself she was in love with a man rather than admit failure in a relationship.

The corner of her mouth riked up slightly, as she remembered a joke she'd heard in San Francisco, when she was stationed there half a decade before the Event: "What do lesbians drive on their second date?" Answer: "A moving van."

Although that's not an invariable *rule. I've known some who were complete bedhopping sluts who lost all interest the second or third time they got into your pants—Jolene, for one . . .*

She choked off the memory of the affair that had led to her divorce, nearly wrecked her career, and *certainly* cost her custody of the two children she'd borne. It didn't take much effort; time and Swindapa, and Heather and Lucy, had buried that old bitterness; she could smile at the memory now.

Well, it was stupid getting involved with a professor of Women's Studies at Berkeley, anyway. Regardless of other circumstances, when someone says things like disenchanting the hegemonic discourse of compulsory heterosexism *with a straight face, and on a* date *at that, you should* know *it can only end in tears.*

Another sound came from their right. A bellow, thunderloud, echoing across the landscape and throwing birds skyward in flocks like beaded smoke rising from tree and marsh. Again and again, a hoarse arrogant strutting proclamation to all the world.

"That's an aurochs," Swindapa said. "And it translates into English as: *This ground is yours, you mangy alley cat? Says who? You and whose army?*"

A herd of the wild cattle came over a rise. Alston brought out her binoculars to look at them; huge rangy beasts, like Texas longhorns crossed with rhinos, or Spanish fighting bulls on steroids; they were black, with long tapering horns turning to put the points forward above their eyes. If those were the originals of domestic cattle, she seriously wondered how Herefords and Jerseys had ever been produced; at the shoulder the bull stood four inches taller than the top of her head, and when he lowered his horns and tossed them high bushes went flying.

"Steady, all," she said. "Just keep moving, and don't rile him up. Scatter out of the way if they charge."

Because in a butting match between that *and a bulldozer, I'd bet on the bovine.* The herd had several young calves with it, and that and the lion's territorial announcement would make them skittish. Alston had learned their bad tempers and hair-trigger readiness to charge anything on earth firsthand in Alba and expeditions to mainland Europe.

At least in open country like this you can see them coming.

They pressed north, and the land became slightly flatter, more closely grazed; they saw cattle and sheep under the eye of mounted herdsmen, and pigs barely distinguishable from their wild cousins. At last they came to wooden fences stretching out of sight northward and to the water on the south. A tall stone pillar stood by the side of the road, crudely carved at the top in the image of a woman's face with stylized representations of breasts and a vulva below. Swindapa reined in her horse and read the lettering around the base slowly; she could speak Tartessian well, and the spelling was in the Latin alphabet and reasonably phonetic:

"Land sacred to the Lady of Tartessos and the Grain Goddess," she recited. "Let no man harm or diminish it, or let his stock or flock do so, on pain of the Cold Curse and the anger of the King."

At Alston's look, she explained: "The Cold Curse—a cold hearth and a cold womb and cold loins for all around it." A frown of puzzlement. "That's odd—the Earth Folk have that curse too . . . this must be the edge of the territory of that village the herald mentioned."

Marian Alston nodded and signaled the party forward; normally there would be guardians to keep animals out, as well. Her eyes took in the cultivated fields on either side in expert appraisal; estimating an enemy's food-producing capacity was an important part of war, in any era. The plowlands and plantations sent her eyebrows up. The olive orchards were all new, just coming into bearing; before the Event, the Tartessians simply grafted wild trees, more than enough for their limited needs. The grain was planted in large fields, ten or twenty acres each, larger than any whole farm hereabouts until recently, divided by lanes of graded dirt scattered with gravel. And the wheat and barley in them had obviously been planted with a seed-drill; that was easy to see, since the shoots were only just starting to show across the rich dark-brown earth in neat rows. Some scattered oaks had been left in the fields and young cypress trees edged many of the fields, standing like tall green candles drawing a rectilinear pattern across the land.

Mmmm-hmmm. They're using disc plows, from the look of it—six-furrow type. There were harvested fields of corn—maize—as well, chick-peas, lucerne, sunflowers, and—

"Halt," she said, and heeled her horse aside, over the ditch and up to the edge of the post-and-rail fence. "Cotton, by God!" Well picked-over, too. Nobody had raised cotton in the Sea Islands since long before her birth, but she'd seen it growing, visiting relatives up-country as a child, and since the Event in the Olmec country and Peru. This field had furrows running between the rows and cracked mud showed where water had run; there was a brick-lined irrigation ditch beyond, led in from some west-flowing stream.

A scattering of houses stood off by themselves amid the fields or nearer the road. Many were mere tents of brushwood and reed, evidently the traditional farmer's housing here. There were others made of adobe brick, rectangular and roofed in tile, all looking new, surrounded by young orchards of apricot, peach, orange, lemon, and fig. Each of the smaller buildings had an outhouse standing behind. Such a minor thing, but *important*.

One imposing structure was large enough to be called a mansion, foursquare and massive on a low hilltop in the middle distance, whitewashed, with a tower at one corner, looking for all the world like a Mexican *hacienda,* down to the row of rammed-earth cottages outside.

Leveling her binoculars she could see that the walls of the big building on its hilltop were black with the heads of people peering over, probably all the folk of the countryside round about, gathered for what protection they could find at the manor of the local aristocrat. *Mmmm-hmmm. Loopholes for small arms, looks like a light swivel gun in that tower, dry moat. Though . . . mmmm-hmmm, those adobe walls would turn to powder under any sort of cannonade.* No doubt King Isketerol wanted his local lordlings armed to stand off pirates or barbarian raiders, but not enough to get notions about independence, or potshotting royal tax collectors.

"Forward," she said.

"Walk-march . . . *walk*."

The little village at the center of the cultivation looked to be entirely post-Event, bowered in olive groves and orchards and sitting on a slight rise. Ritter halted the truce party well short of it.

"Squads one and three dismount," the lieutenant said, her eyes darting about for hidden assassins and ambushes. "Sergeant, check it out."

"Ma'am!" the noncom said, and barked orders of his own.

Marines fanned out to search, then waved the rest on when they found no human presence. It was eerily quiet with all the dwellers gone, a shutter flapping, a dog loping off as they entered, a few chickens picking through the dirt with idiot calm—and then she remembered that chickens would be a new thing here, too. In the first history they hadn't gotten this far until the Iron Age . . .

The buildings were all adobe and tile-roofed, many gaudily painted on wall and door and shutter, set well back from the road and the secondary street that ran down to an inlet of the bay and a dock. Trees shaded the houses and walled gardens surrounded them, well watered from channels in tile-lined gutters beside the streets. There were flowers as well as vegetables and herbs, she noticed with interest—roses, cannas, bougainvillea. The big wind pump filling an earthen water tank at the edge of town was a straight copy of one of Leaton's models, with laminated wood vanes that could be turned in sections to feather them in storms.

Larger buildings surrounded a square. One had tall wooden pillars brightly painted, carved in the shape of a three-legged, one-eyed monster, an armored man set about with weapons and chariot wheels all topped by a golden disk, a woman holding a sheaf of grain and another whose legs were a fish-tail, a bit like a mermaid . . . although *unlike* conventional Western representations, the wood-carver had equipped her to do more than tantalize a sailorman. Hooves clattered on rock, for the square was paved with neatly fitted blocks of pale stone in a herring-bone pattern.

Beside the fountain in the center was a stone pillar with a bronze plaque attached, rather like the historical markers you saw by the roadside sometimes before the Event.

"It's the King's Laws, according to this," Swindapa said, leaning down to read. "Mmmm . . . all free children to attend the Place of the New Learning four days in eight except in harvest season, every family to contribute food and cloth for the teacher in rotation . . ."

Alston looked around. Yes, one of the buildings had the look of a schoolhouse, long and rectangular; she heeled her mount over and sheltered her eyes with her hand to peer through thick wavy window glass. She saw rows of benches within, and a large slate blackboard; times-table in Arabic numerals on one wall, a big map of some sort on another, and a print of King Isketerol's face hanging over a teacher's table at the front.

Swindapa was still reading: ". . . then there's the Great Taboo of Shit Avoidance—that's what it says, I swear, and a good many others. Everyone to wash with *zapotikez* . . . soap? It looks like a sort of combination of public-hygiene notice and list of . . . well, there's stuff about farming—nobody to grow grain for more than two years in the same field before sowing it to fodder crops—money to be accepted for all debts, each household's public work on the roads and irrigation canals—taxes, the King's Fifth, what can be paid in kind and what in cash . . . all the Laws to be read out to the assembled people once in every moon-turning."

The Republic's commander nodded. *Well, he can't* explain *everything, I suppose.* The Nantucketers had used persuasion and example in Alba; with fewer teachers and more power, Isketerol seemed to be relying more on rote-learning.

One of the buildings off the square was a smithy, well equipped with a selection of cast-iron anvils, two hearths with piston bellows and a wallful of tools, from pincers to rasps. Even a grindstone and a simple lathe powered by foot-cranks . . . Bins outside held coal-coke as well as charcoal.

And those rafters were cut in a sawmill—probably floated down the Guadalquivir . . . machine-drawn nails, too. Mmmm-hmmmm.

Next to it was a warehouselike affair; Swindapa read the sign over the doors: "Depot of Things for Households: Let Any Who Will Buy Tools From the King on Credit."

The radio handset in Alston's saddlebags hissed and popped. She took it out, looking up reflexively for the butterfly shape of the ultralight. "Commodore Alston heah."

"Commodore, this is Scout Flight One Niner. The Tartessians under the flag of truce are approaching from the north. Thirty-one in the party as per agreement, all mounted."

"Carry on, pilot," Alston said.

She and Swindapa and the standard-bearer remained mounted, but the Marines put their bicycles on the kickstands and formed up in a rank; the Gatling crew unhitched their weapon and swung it 'round. Lieutenant Ritter reached over her shoulder and proudly drew her new officer's *katana.*

"Fix . . . *bayonets.*"

Hands flashed down to the left hip and the twenty-inch blades flashed free, rattling as they were clipped onto the Werders.

"Shoulder . . . *arms.*"

The Marines stood like khaki statues, an image a little spoiled by the peeling sunburns many of them sported. That had been one reason she wanted a fall-winter campaign; with a force made up of people from cool misty northern islands, the relatively mild and cloudy season promised less in the way of heatstroke.

That's an irony, if you like, she thought, flexing a hand on the pommel of her saddle and looking at the natural UV protection of her eggplant-colored skin.

Still, this was the best season to fight here. Summer made water scarce in these hot lowlands and likely to be bad, and sharply cut into the fodder for draught animals. The Tartessian flintlocks were temperamental beasts that didn't like the damp, too; that had worked powerfully in the Nantucketers' favor during the spring invasion.

The clatter of hooves and a low cloud of dust came down the highway from the north. Alston soothed her mount with a hand on its neck and gathered the reins a bit as well. The colors of brightly dyed cloth and polished metal came into view next, westering sun winking blinding off edged metal; then figures became distinct, mounted men . . .

And one woman, she thought, slighlty surprised; even more so when she saw it was Rosita Menendez . . . *well,* née *Menendez,* she corrected herself.

That identification took a little doing, when her hair was coiled around her ears in circles bound with silver and turquoise, topped by a flat-topped headdress of silk a little like a wimple. Square fringed earrings, rings, belt flashing with golden studs; otherwise, her clothing was a practical-enough affair of long split tunic and loose trousers.

Isketerol rode beside her, in a polished gilded helmet with purple-dyed ostrich-feather plumes at the front, saffron tunic, gold disk across his chest supported by tooled-leather straps, silver-and-leather bracers on his wrists, jewel-hilted sword . . . and a very practical-looking revolver. He must be in his early forties now but looked ageless; still lithe and hard-muscled, but with deeper lines grooved into his face from nose to mouth. Menendez had put on some weight, in a solid matronly way.

The Tartessian troops carried rifles . . . *Yes, that's Walker's imitation of the Werder.* They couldn't have all that many of them, either. Most of the weapons captured after the sea fight had been copies of the older Westley-Richards flintlock. *If he had more of those, he'd have used them.*

Isketerol's standard-bearer and a herald rode ahead, drawing rein in the square a half dozen yards from her position. The herald had a curled trumpet over his shoulder, sunlight turning the polished metal to gold; he brought the mouthpiece to his lips and blew, a long harsh brass scream, and then shouted in Tartessian:

"The King comes! King Isketerol, Bridegroom of the Lady of Tartessos and the Grain Goddess, Embodiment of the Sun Lord, Lord of the Cold Mountains and the Hot and all between, Sea-King by favor of Arucuttag Lord of Waves. Who comes to treat with the Great King, the King who admits no rival or equal within the boundaries of his power?"

Alston listened to Swindapa's murmured translation, then nodded imperceptibly, sitting with her back straight, reins in her left hand and right on the butt of her Python. The younger woman heeled her horse a few steps forward and called out in the local tongue, its harsh buzzing softened by her Fiernan accent—Tartessian and the language of the *Fiernan Bohulugi* were distantly related, but they sounded no more alike than, say, Swedish and Hindustani, which were similarly linked.

"Commodore Marian Alston, Founding Councilor, Nantucket's Councilor for War . . ." She paused and added the proudest title of all, with a slight deliberate emphasis. "Citizen of the Republic of Nantucket, comes to treat with King Isketerol."

Isketerol's hard hawklike olive-brown face showed a slight smile. When he spoke, his English was harshly accented but fluent, much more fluent than it had been the last time she spoke to him in person—that was more than nine years ago, when he'd been on Nantucket, before he helped Walker hijack the *Yare*.

Ah, she thought. *He must speak it with Menendez, and there are a few other Islanders . . . ex-Islanders . . . here, too.* Smart of him to work at achieving full fluency. Reading the books that had been part of *Yare*'s cargo, and ones he'd bought openly since, had doubtless helped as well. He'd also acquired a very slight Puerto Rican–Hispanic accent from his American wife, which was an irony, if you thought about it. As far as looks went, he could have been a brother of Victor Ortiz . . .

"Now that we have made the . . . you say . . . necessary gestures, shall we speak?" he asked.

"Yes," Alston said, surprised to feel a wry respect. *Well, he's a pirate . . . but he wasn't raised to know better.*

The leaders and their companions swung down from the saddle, handed the reins to attendants, walked a little aside. Isketerol looked up at the ultralight, westward to where the steam gunboat waited on the blue-and-cream waters of the gulf, pitching slightly with her head into the wind and paddles turning just enough to keep her so. They sent a white froth down her sides as well, and coal smoke rose night-black against the crimson disk of the setting sun.

"A not bad time to end the war, from your point of . . . perspective? View? To ah, quit while you are ahead," Isketerol said.

"We're prepared to end it, on terms," Alston said. She nodded to the flag with the truce-banner below it, her face like a mask of obsidian. "Our terms. And once made, we'll keep them. The Republic's word is good."

Isketerol nodded; the Islanders had a carefully maintained reputation of driving a hard bargain and then respecting it meticulously.

"Yes," he said. "That simplifies negotiations." A white smile, and he took off the helmet, showing a few silver hairs in the bowl-cut blue-black mane. He tossed his hair to let air blow through the sweat-wet thickness. "Unless you are waiting for the time when it *really* pays to lie."

Alston shrugged. "That's an argument without an answer," she said. "But think about this, King Isketerol of Tartessos, how far can you trust Walker's word? Did he give you every assistance he could? How hard would he fight for *you*, if he didn't stand to benefit by it?"

The olive face stayed imperturbable, but she caught a slight flare of the nostrils. Isketerol would make a good poker player, though. His fingers did not clench on the gilded helmet they were turning idly.

"He gave me enough help to become King and conquer an . . . empire, that's the term. And we have an alliance, and *my* word is good. You have won a battle, yes. You have not won a war, not against my kingdom. Still, you *have* won a battle. My word is this; if you will return home and trouble us no more, I will agree to the . . ." He turned and murmured in Rosita's ear and nodded at her reply. "To, you say, the *status quo*. Yes, things as they were before this war. Those are the terms of the King."

Alston put her fists on her hips and slowly shook her head. "Return to your closing the Straits against our ships, skirmishing with us and then calling it overzealous private actions by your captains, to your helping Walker? After you invaded our country last spring for no better reason than you wanted to take it? I don't think so."

"If you fight Walker in the east without passing through my waters, traveling around Africa and through the Gulf as your other expeditions have, I will not interfere," he said. "That much I can in honor say. No more. I will not turn on a guest-friend and blood brother who helped put me on my throne, simply because it would spare me effort and expense. And if you destroy King Walker, what check will there be on your power? How do I know you will not turn on me, next? Already you claim half the world and say we may trade and settle only in those scraps you deign to allow us."

"Do you doubt that Walker would turn on *you*, without us to worry about? Does your honor require that you see all that you've built up"—she waved about—"cast down?"

Isketerol's eyes narrowed. "You have not the strength to conquer Tartessos," he said. "I hold far more land than your Republic does in fact, claims of just nothing but words aside, and I have twenty times more people. I can afford to lose battles—you cannot. Great kingdoms are not overthrown in a single fight."

Well, he's grasped that principle, Alston thought. Wordlessly she pointed to the ultralight, to the gunboat. Isketerol shrugged.

"Yes, you have better weapons," he admitted. "But I have *more* weapons, many more. If they are not as fine as yours, still they are not spears and bows. We destroyed one of your great ships in the battle."

"You lost a dozen."

"I can *spare* a dozen, build anew, and find new crews; you cannot. If we fight and I hurt you one-tenth as much as you hurt me, I win. And you are few, and far from home, and cannot call fresh armies to you." Another shrug. "There are not enough of you to conquer Tartessos."

"Perhaps not. But there are enough of us to *destroy* the Tartessos you have made, I think." She went on to: "Tell me, King Isketerol, do the words *command and control decision loop* mean anything to you?"

Narrow-eyed, Isketerol shook his head. Rosita Menendez frowed, as if something was tugging at her memory, then shrugged. Alston's face remained a basalt mask, but inwardly something bared its teeth. *Walker* would have known—would have understood the importance of forces being able to transmit information faster, and act on it more rapidly. He was a product of Western civilization and its military-technic tradition.

Isketerol wasn't.

Yes, Isketerol's smart. He's a genius, *I think.* But he'd grown to adulthood in this world. Doubtless he'd learned a great deal from the books. It would still be filtered through the worldview built into the structure of his mind from childhood. Doubtless he'd learned a good deal from Walker, and Rosita, too, but the one would be careful not to teach too much and the other wasn't particularly intelligent or well educated . . .

Snidely, to herself: *And Rosita was a really close friend of Alice Hong, which says something about her standards of taste and judgment.*

"Why do I have a feeling," Isketerol said, an edge of whimsy in his voice, "that what you just asked me was like one of those oracles that only make sense after the disaster has happened?"

Got to be careful not to underestimate him, though. Slowly and deliberately she smiled, spread her hands.

He sighed. "Well, then, what are your terms for ending this war? I *might* pay . . ." He turned to the interpreters and fell into Tartessian. Swindapa supplied the word: she'd had ten years with Marian Alston and her tastes in reading matter.

". . . weregild for the invasion last spring, yes, blood price. Beyond that I cannot go, without violating my oaths to Walker or my duty to my folk. So, what does Cofflin offer me, in return for ending this struggle?"

Alston began to tick off points. "First, you must pay, as you said, damages—partly in cash, and partly in supplies." She held up a hand. "Not guns or powder to be used against Walker, no."

"No, food and cordage and timber that will free your shipping space for guns and powder," Isketerol said dryly.

"Of course. Next, you must be neutral in this war—and to guarantee that, disarm your war fleet and give us hostages. You must give us bases—the island my fleet's on now, the Rock of Gibraltar, and another south across the Pillars. And you must swear that in future . . ." She pulled up a phrase Swindapa had suggested, as more like the Tartessian equivalent than *noninterference in our sphere of influence* ". . . that in future you will keep your spoon out of our stewpot."

The Iberian's smile was unpleasant, and a dark flush had risen under his tan. "The world is to be yours, then; but of your gracious favor, you will allow us to keep our own homes . . . or most of them. What, do you not demand also that we free all our slaves and adopt . . . what's the word . . . an equal rights amendment and universal suffrage? As if we were naughty children who piddled on the floor, to be spanked and taught better."

"I'd like to demand just that," she said frankly; and saw him blink and nod.

This was a man who appreciated hearing what you thought, not soul-butter. *Although how long will that last, Isketerol-melad, if this absolute monarchy you're setting up continues?* She went on aloud:

"But I don't set policy, I just carry it out. First, it's not within our power to force those reforms on you. We couldn't make you *want* those things—you in the plural, your people—and it would be pointless if you didn't. By offending your people's pride, we'd make them more likely to move in the opposite direction, in fact. Second, while we may *use* our power for that sort of thing where we have it, we don't go a-conquering just so we can spread enlightenment. We certainly couldn't hold down Tartessos tightly enough to redo your . . . customs . . . without an effort which would destroy *us*. No, what I listed is the whole of our terms. Our terms *now*."

"Meaning they'll get worse, if you win," Isketerol said tightly. "So will mine, once you've broken your teeth on our defense." A pause, and he seemed to push away anger with an exhalation of breath. "The old King, the one I cast down and slew, he was my kinsman.

"Yes," he went on frankly, "I wanted the Throne for the glory and power and wealth. Yes, also to hand that down to my own sons and bloodline. But also, I struck for my people—for *their* glory and power, for the heritage of *their* sons, and the sons of their sons, that our tongue and Gods and customs would not go down into dust and be less than dust as I read on Nantucket all those years ago. Your books could not say if we even existed at all! Then I wept and raged at the Gods; yet later I came to see that this was the gift that the Gods had given me, a glimpse of a different course to be steered through the oceans of eternity. And since then I have worked and planned and fought to turn the helm thus. It was not to make my folk clients of yours that I struck that good old man down, that for years I have labored and shed blood when I might have rested in wealth and ease."

Alston nodded soberly. She understood that, well enough. Her thoughts went to ancestors of hers; and to the systems analysts of Bangalore, India, and the suit-wearing Parliamentary deputies of Taiwan, and here . . . *Mmmm-hmmm, John Iraiinanasson, for instance. You may find that you're destroying what you're trying to preserve, in the long run, King Isketerol. And that the only way you can* fight *us is to* become *us.*

Since the Event she'd come to appreciate just how weird and wide and wonderful this ancient Earth was; it wasn't altogether pleasant to think of it being remade on a single pattern, no matter how dear and much-loved that pattern was. *On the other hand, I've also learned* damned *well that all customs and ways-of-doing and thinking are* not *equal. Some are just flat-out* better *than others.* Freedom was better than slavery; the Town Meeting was better than a God-King.

You couldn't expect Isketerol to look at it that way, of course. It was a dilemma without any easy solution; one for Heather and Lucy, and their children and great-grandchildren. And Isketerol's . . .

"So this war must continue, until you see that we are not to be bent to your will," Isketerol said soberly.

"You tried to bend us to yours," she pointed out.

"Of course," he said, with another flash of teeth, genuinely amused. "And I would have ruled Nantucket well—I know that honey catches more flies than vinegar. But it didn't work—I underestimated you. And I can learn a lesson as well as the next man, when it's shot at me out of a cannon. Can you?"

"Most of the lessons life teaches us are surprises," she replied. "Usually unpleasant ones."

Isketerol nodded, and paused for a moment: "You took many prisoners this spring. What is their fate?"

"Some asked us for sanctuary," she said.

The Iberian made a gesture that Swindapa murmured was acceptance and acknowledgment. Many of the officers of that force had been from the old ruling families that Isketerol distrusted, a sentiment they shared.

"The mercenaries took service with us, and we have sent them to our allies in Kar-Duniash and Hattusas. The rest are on Long Island; they live together, lightly guarded but working as they will to earn their keep. When the war is over, we will send them home; you'll find many of them have learned useful skills."

Alston paused. "We have a number of your wounded from the latest battle; we'll return the badly hurt, if you wish. Men with limbs gone, or broken bones, deep hurts in their flesh. That would mean extending the truce, though . . . say to sundown, day after tomorrow."

"Ah," Isketerol said shrewdly. "You do not expect this war to continue long, if you return men who will fight once more in a few months."

"No, I don't," Alston said frankly.

"But in any case, that is well-done," he said meditatively, and stood in thought for a moment. "We have some of yours, who washed ashore after the battle off Tartessos—we will return them to you when you hand over our hurt men. And for this war, I will fight according to your Eagle People laws of battle—prisoners to be treated gently." A grin. "I have found this makes opponents less likely to fight to the death, in any case."

"Good." Alston cocked an eyebrow. "You'll find that many of our notions are more practical than you might think."

A long pause, and he surprised her by offering his hand. "Sundown, day after tomorrow—fighting to start again when a black thread cannot be told from a white. The war must continue, it seems."

She took it, dry and strong in hers. "It seems it must. Sundown, day after tomorrow. And may God defend the right."

"You *Amurrukan,* you are . . . how do you say . . . *weird.*"

"I've often thought so," Alston agreed.

CHAPTER TWENTY-THREE

*November, 10 A.E.—Walkeropolis, Kingdom of Great
  Achaea*
October, 10 A.E.—Great River, southern Iberia
*November, 10 A.E.—Walkeropolis, Kingdom of Great
  Achaea*
November, 10 A.E.—Cadiz Base, southern Iberia
November, 10 A.E.—Great River, southern Iberia
November, 10 A.E.—West-central Anatolia

Odikweos's mansion was a mixture of Mycenaean tradition
and Walker's innovations. Ian Arnstein thoroughly approved of some of those. There was central heating, natural
hot air from a basement stove via clay pipes in the walls and
floor; the kerosene lamps with their mirrored reflectors were a
lot brighter than the twist of linen in olive oil that the locals
had been using. And the bath suite—sure 'nuff shower stall,
hot and cold plunges—was a vast improvement over sitting in
a ceramic hip-bath and having bucketsful poured over your
head. In fact it was all about as good as a bathhouse in Nantucket Town, and far better than anything he'd had since he
left Ur Base. Flush toilets, too, and soap, and even a frayed
soft reed that made acceptable toilet paper. . . .

He turned down an offer of a massage with scented olive oil,
accepted a clean Mycenaean tunic and kilt which he suspected
a seamstress had just run up in his size. Then he sat down to
a meal of garlicky grilled pork, salad, and french fried potatoes
accompanied by watered wine in a room with big glass windows
that overlooked the town. It was growing dark outside, sunset
aggravated by thicker cloud cover.

I wonder why Odikweos is doing this, he thought. Walker
had ordered him given comfortable prison quarters, not the
quasi-sacred status of a guest. *Not that I'm objecting.* Achaean
mores had altered, and swiftly, here in Walker's kingdom, but
he didn't think they'd altered so much that Walker could just

chop him now without a major confrontation with one of his most important supporters. *But I* do *wonder why.* He was still trying to figure that out when the servants showed him into the *megaron,* the great central hall.

The old traditions of the Achaean barons remained strong here. A log fire boomed and flickered in a big central hearth rimmed with blue limestone blocks, scenting the air with pine; but a copper smoke-hood stood over it. Four massive wooden pillars supported a second-story gallery and ran up to the roof, painted red and surrounded by racked bronze-headed spears. Huge figure-eight shields were clamped to the wall at intervals. Between them ran vivid native murals; one of a man in a plumed boar's-tusk helmet shaking a spear aloft as his chariot galloped into battle; another of a boar hunt; the third of a city under siege . . . but the siege included stylized cannon, and a balloon floating at the end of a tether.

The high seat against the southern wall was empty and shadowed as he crossed the geometric pebble-mosaic of the floor. The Achaean underking was seated in a chair not far from the hearth, his cloak thrown over the chairback; a table and another seat waited, splendid with ivory and gold inlay of lions and griffins in a fashion that was centuries old.

Odikweos leaned his chin on one fist and watched as a housekeeper in a long gown showed Arnstein to his seat, set out jugs of water and wine and spun-glass goblets, a tray of bread with olive oil and honey for dipping, and departed.

Then he leaned forward, hairy muscular forearm braced on one knee, and spoke:

"You are from the days that are yet to come. You and all your people."

Ian hid his startlement by reaching for a jug and pouring wine. Unwatered, it lay sweet and thick on his tongue. *Well, here's a bright boy.* Isketerol had gone into hysterics for a day or two when he got the idea back on-Island in the Year 1; a lot of people just couldn't grasp the concept.

"How did you find out?" he asked.

"I . . . what is your word . . . *deduced* it," Odikweos went on. "Not long after the King-to-be came here to the Achaean lands. From a few things he let drop; and my guest-friend Isketerol of Tartessos is not quite as good at keeping secrets as he thinks. Now and then one or the other would say, in the *time* of the Eagle People, or 'in my *time,*' instead of 'my *land.*' "

"Pretty slim clues," Arnstein said.

A shrug. "And it was sensible. Legends tell of a time before men knew of bronze or tilled the earth, and of a time before Zeus let slip the secret of fire. Our bards sing of the days when the Achaeans were new in these lands, coming down from the north to rule the Shore Folk and mix their blood with them; and in those days we knew not the arts of writing, or of dwelling in towns or building in stone. Those we learned from Crete, before we overran it."

For a moment sheer scholar's greed overwhelmed Ian Arnstein. *Those poems I've got to hear!* Then he wrenched his mind back to present matters.

"How did you know that Walker didn't just come from a land with more arts than yours?"

Odikweos nodded. "That was my first thought, and it is what most here believe. But the King and his Wolf People lords, they knew too much of what was *here*. The mines of iron not a day's travel from this city; I saw the maps they had—wonders themselves—made of these same lands. They even seemed to know somewhat of the men of Mycenae and the other Achaean kingdoms.

"So," he went on, turning his hand palm-up, moving his fingers as if counting off points and then clenching it into a fist. "Either these men were Gods in disguise, or demigods, or seers—or they must know these things because they were from years yet unborn."

He poured wine, watered it, and spilled a few drops in libation. "And I swiftly saw that these were men as other men—weak and stupid men, many of them. Some of them were wicked men—and a wicked woman—in ways cursed by the Gods. Even Walkheear . . . yes, a great fighting-man, and of a cunning that might seem divine. But still a man, as men are."

"Perhaps not as clever as you think," Arnstein said. At Odíkweos's raised brows: "Men gather more than arts." He turned his beard toward the copper smoke-hood for a moment. "They also gather the memory of tricks and strategems of war and kingcraft. Especially in lands where everything is preserved in writing."

"Ahh," Odikweos said, nodding. "That puts in words a thought long stirring in my mind."

"So . . . what do you wish to know?" Arnstein asked.

"This," the Achaean said, his callused hand sculpting a graceful gesture through the air. "What manner of men are you? That you have many arts, that you are wise in the ways of war, this I know.

"I also know," he went on, "that we Achaeans have mounted

the lion and however much danger there is in riding, we cannot let go—too much of the knowledge from the years to come is abroad in these lands ever to return to the ways that were. Men will grow back into children and then crawl into the womb before they will sacrifice wealth or advantage in war. What I would know is what manner of men you are—are you all as Walker is, differing only in faction, or is he truly an outlaw among you for his wicked deeds?"

His hazel eyes bored into Arnstein's. "For if you are all such as Walker, then we must cherish Walker as our rightful lord, for at least he rules from the Achaean lands, and his followers of the Wolf Folk are too few to govern without many of our men at their sides in positions of honor. But if not . . ."

Ian felt his spine prickle. "You speak boldly," he said.

"I speak as I must." A grim smile. "For one thing, your mouth can be stopped. For another, you would not be believed if you accused me—a condemned man seeking safety. For a third, time snaps at my heels like a wolf indeed. In another ten years—especially with victory in this war—the King of Men will be strong beyond assailing. He will rule so many lands that we Achaeans will be but a minor part of his domains, of his followers."

His expression grew altogether harsh. Arnstein felt a trickle of fear, more immediate than the low-grade dread that had been with him constantly since Troy. This was not a man you could anger safely . . .

"I have spoken. Now *you* will speak. And you are not my only spring of knowledge in this matter. I will know if you lie; Athana Potnia is my patron Goddess, and she has given me the gift of plumbing the truth in men's words."

All right, Ian, Arnstein thought, licking his lips and running a hand over his balding head. *Now's the time to talk for your life.*

War was beginning to look like something simple and straightforward.

"You liked him," Swindapa said quietly, as the Islander truce party rode south once more.

"I'll still kill him if I can," Alston said meditatively, looking up.

The ultralight had turned southward to base, after checking that the Tartessians were headed back northwest. The first stars were out, bright light against racing scuds of cloud, clouds white-outlined by the waning moon; the wind had cooled notably.

"That's not what I meant," her partner said, cocking her head to one side slightly. "I'm surprised."

"So am I," Alston said.

One of the good things about riding a horse was that it wouldn't fall over or run into a tree if you lost yourself in thought for a few moments.

"I think he's changed," she said at last. "He's still pretty loathsome to our way of thinking—" which would apply from a Fiernan's point of view as well, although not for exactly the same reasons ". . . but being a King, I'd say it's changed him. Responsibility can do that."

"To some, maybe," Swindapa said. "I don't think so, for Walker."

Marian's face went hard. "No. Not him."

Ritter's bicycle came rapidly up from behind them. "Ma'am!" she said. "The scouts confirm the enemy delegation are withdrawing as agreed."

For an instant a flicker of regret went through Alston's mind; someone with a telescope-sighted rifle, or a long burst from the Gatling, and the enemy would be headless. . . . No. Victories won that way were poisoned fruit. If nothing else, they didn't convince the other side they were beaten the way a real fight did, and getting the other side to admit defeat was the whole reason you made war in the first place. There was no point in winning one war at the cost of laying the seeds of defeat in the next; that way lay destruction.

"We'll camp on the site we picked out on the way up here, then, Lieutenant," Alston said.

"Aye, aye, ma'am!"

Swindapa chuckled softly as the young Marine officer pedaled industriously off and spoke even more quietly: "How she jumps to please you," she teased—in Fiernan, which the standard-bearer did not speak, which gave them complete privacy.

At least she's learned some *discretion,* Marian thought with affectionate exasperation; she understood the Earth Folk language, although she couldn't speak it beyond the pass-the-salt level.

"She'd jump even more eagerly if you took a pheasant feather and tickled her on her—" Swindapa went on.

" 'Dapa!" Alston snorted, as her partner went into imaginative details, with gestures. One of the few drawbacks of having a Fiernan for a partner was her idea of a bawdy joke . . .

". . . then imagine her bursting like a ripe berry on your lips when you threw your arms about her arse and ran your—"

" *'Dapa! Stop it!'*"

. . . because in a perfectly good-natured way the Fiernan idea of bawdy tended to be luridly, awesomely explicit, even by late-twentieth-century-American standards. The Earth Folk had plenty of taboos and aversions, but few about that.

"But that would be against regulations," she finished, with a sly grin, rolling her eyes piously skyward, and making a brief steepling of fingers in the Christian manner.

That was another thing that could be annoying. The Sun People either rebelled against discipline or embraced it; Fiernans were likely to think of it as faintly silly. It was like trying to pull on a rope made of water, sometimes.

Scholarly types like the Arnsteins said it was because of their diffuse family setup, where paternity was often anyone's guess and kids were raised catch-as-catch-can, like a litter of puppies by mothers, aunts, uncles, and a score of other relatives.

Whatever, Marian thought, laughing unwillingly along with Swindapa's wholehearted mirth.

The spot the embassy had picked for its encampment was on a slight hill, where the chalky subsoil came nearer the surface as the land rose out of the alluvial lowlands to the north. It reminded her of pictures she'd seen of the Serengeti, weirdly combined with California. A scattering of cork-oak trees gave shelter, their thick, gnarled bark with its deep scorch marks showing why it had evolved in the first place; the grass fires in a dry summer here must be something to see.

The Marines set to efficiently; bicycles resting in a row, clearing the long grass—the green undergrowth was unlikely to burn but you didn't want to take chances—cutting circles of sod to make space for campfires, pitching tents, both their own eight-person squad models and smaller types for the officers. A stamping, bayonet-prodding inspection of the undergrowth produced a yelling, dodging chaos when a six-foot Montpelier snake rose and fanged the forestock of a rifle only inches from a Marine's left hand, then thrashed about hissing and striking in warning before it whipped off downhill; that set the little group of tailless Barbary apes in the trees shrieking and bolting as well.

Marian's *katana* had leaped into her hand without the intervention of her conscious mind. She ran it back into the scabbard behind her left shoulder with a hiss of steel on leather greased with neatsfoot oil.

"Damn, but I hate snakes," she muttered. "Especially poisonous ones you can't see in the grass." Her partner snorted, and Alston went on: " 'Dapa, do I mention you and spiders?"

They led their horses to the little stream at the base of the hill, watered and unsaddled and rubbed them down, checking their feet and hobbling them before setting them to graze. That would keep them happier than being tethered with a feedbag, and they wouldn't go far from the campfires with the predators about. While she tended the horses the black woman watched the Marines at work, saw Swindapa doing the same.

The officer and her noncoms paced the area around the camp carefully; she saw Ritter take a sight on a bush twenty yards off, walk a few paces, do the same, note it to the sergeant and corporals and repeat the process all around. The black woman nodded; it was a trick the Marines had gotten from the Fiernan Spear Chosen, through her—a way to identify what should and shouldn't be there. After it got dark, a creeping enemy could look far too much like a bush. They put equal care into picking a good spot for the Gatling, and a detail was already at work digging a sanitary slit trench off behind a tree. An ax rang counterpoint to the *shunk* of spade and pick, breaking fallen wood into convenient sizes.

"Squads to wash in rotation," Ritter said, when the basic work was done and deadwood fires crackled in the fire pits. "Clarkson, what do you say? Can we get some variety tonight?"

"Piece of cake, or duck, ma'am," the young Marine answered, grinning. He'd been looking over the stream that ran by the hill and into the marshes to their west.

The accent was Fiernan, Marion thought—from the west-coast area. At her slightly lifted brows Ritter went on: "You might want to see this, Commodore. He's from the Level Fens, south of Westhaven."

Swindapa nodded, then smiled and shook her head silently at Marian's inquiring look. Clarkson's section of the platoon trooped down to the river. They all stripped—soap and towels were along—but the brown-haired young man with the Immigration Office name also quickly plaited himself a headdress of grasses and reeds before slipping into the water. Even looking at him Marian had trouble following his passage down the darkened surface of the river. A minute later came a sharp gooselike *squak*— abruptly cut off. Another followed it, a minute of silence, then two more, and a thunder of wings in the darkness. Geese went by overhead, dandy-dog close, like whizzing projec-

tiles with thrashing wings and outstretched panic-taut necks,
honking in alarm. Clarkson came wading back holding four of
the big birds high; Alston realized he must have swum close
enough unnoticed to grab them by the feet and yank them
under, one after another.

"Impressive," she said. *And possibly useful,* the filing system
in her mind noted.

"Now, let me take a look at that bullet wound," Swindapa
said.

Her own bruises and nicks had faded, but there was still a
red healing weal where the slug had gouged Marian's flank.
This platoon of Marines hadn't been involved in the boarding
fight; in fact, most of its members hadn't seen combat yet—
Ritter and the sergeant and one of the corporals being the
exceptions.

In fact, Sergeant Daudrax has more scars than I do, Alston
thought, looking over at him.

Although mine show more. Scar tissue came in dusty-white,
standing out against the black of her skin. She looked down;
spearthrust in the shoulder, boarding pike along the ribs, sword
scar on the left forearm, and this would be the second bullet
mark, after the one that took off most of the lobe of her left
ear. Nothing too disfiguring yet; in fact, the Marines were casting occasional awed glances as the two senior officers soaped
up and rinsed off.

And they all hurt like hell, infants. It mystified her sometimes
why you got prestige from evidence of failure, and if letting
someone cut you wasn't failing, what was?

By the time the squad had finished washing in the river—
with much whooping and horseplay among the troops; at times
like this you remembered that many of them would be considered kids up in the twentieth—the geese had been plucked,
gutted, washed, rubbed with salt and some of the unit's precious, hoarded joint ration of Nantucket Secret Spice, and
slapped on green-stick grills over the fires. By the time the
other squads had taken their turn with the soap, the goose was
about ready, enough to give everyone a mouthful or two of the
flavorful fat-rich meat. Water was boiling for sassafras tea; that
had the added advantage that you didn't have to add the puri-
fication powder with its unpleasant metallic tang.

Two big kettles were simmering with Jesus Stew—cubes of
bouillon for stock, dried beans and peas, parched barley,
chopped-up lengths of desiccated sausage and similarly "dese-

crated" vegetables, garlic powder, and sage, that service legend claimed not only proved the doctrine of the Resurrection, but was the Life. Together with bread baked that morning at the base camp and hard crumbly Alban cheese it made a pleasant enough dinner; the Marines tore into it with the thoughtless, wolfish enthusiasm of hardworking youngsters who'd mostly been raised on Bronze Age farms where this would be feast-day food.

Despite the day's work a flute came out; the song that set them swaying and clapping was half-new, a mutation of something dug out of a book during the dark, hungry winter of the Year 1, and crossbred since with things native to this era:

> "I'll sing the base and you sing the solo—
> *Hob y derri dando!*
> All about the clipper ship the *Marco Polo*—
> *Ganni, ganni yato!*
> See her rollin', though the water . . ."

Marian Alston watched them with amused affection as she gnawed a goose drumstick, back a little around a separate fire as befitted senior officers. *There's a big part of our future,* she thought with satisfaction.

Some would go back to their birth-countries after their hitch. Most would settle down in the Republic as new-minted citizens, already English-speaking and literate, used to brushing their teeth and keeping clock-time and *not* attributing anything unusual to black magic, not to mention the males having something approaching civilized attitudes toward women beaten into their thick skulls. Then they'd become farmers or factory workers, clerks or sailors or shopkeepers, and *their* children . . .

After an hour the fires had burned low, only a few sparks drifting upward to the darkened, overcast sky; Ritter looked at her watch, nodded slightly to the platoon sergeant, and he called *lights-out* in a fine seagoing bellow:

"And this isn't a hunting trip, either. You useless bastards have work to do tomorrow, and I'm going to see that you do it! Clarkson, bank the fires. Standard watches, and keep your eyes open and your ears, too. If any of you get your throats cut I'll find a wizard to raise you from the mound and kill you again myself. Jump, you slackers!"

The sassafras tea woke her a little past midnight. She slipped on her boots—remembering that snake, and the reptiles' liking for warmth—and looped her pistol-belt over one shoulder before heading out to the sanitary trench. The air was much colder outside, but despite that she spent a long instant looking at the play of lightning to the westward, lighting up castles and palaces of cloud . . . and beyond them were the stars . . .

Someday, she thought fiercely. *For Heather's and Lucy's great-great-great-grandchildren.*

Walking past the tree she whistled softly, to let the unseen sentries know she was moving; there would be one up in the biggest cork oak, and the others were invisible even though she knew roughly where they were. Nobody in a force *she* trained was going to blunder around in plain sight of God, radar, and skulking bandits and call it sentry-go!

As she walked back, the wind from the west blew stronger, and the first drops of rain struck her skin; hard luck on the ones pulling sentry duty . . . there was a faint rumble of thunder from that direction, too.

And voices; first a low happy moan, then a sleepy, hissed grumble: "*Shut the fuck up, or at least shut up while you fuck, will you? The rest of us are* sleeping, *god-damn-it.*"

The language lessons were working well, if someone could pun in English half-awake. She slipped back into her tent, a two-person model if the two were friendly, and closed the flap. The rain beat harder, hissing on the oiled canvas above her, filling the darkness with a blur of white noise. Swindapa mumbled in her sleep as her partner sipped back under the blanket, throwing a thigh across Marian's and nuzzling into her shoulder. Alston let her mind drift; images of maps, reports, rivers, rain, marsh, swimming . . . an idle hope that the rain would be over by 0600, when they were due to break camp and get back to base. There was a thought teasing at the back of her consciousness, but forcing it would only make it recede faster.

In the morning as she woke the thought was quite clear, and Marian Alston gave a slow, hard grin at the gray overcast sky.

Ian Arnstein's throat felt sore. It had been an inspired idea to end the long night of talk with Homer; in this place, with this archaic Greek clangorous in his mouth, it was fitting. He soothed his vocal cords with more of the watered wine and went on:

> *The more she spoke, the more a deep desire for tears*
> *Welled up inside his breast—he wept as he held the wife*
> *He loved, the soul of loyalty, in his arms at last.*
> *Joy, warm as the joy that shipwrecked sailors feel*

> *When they catch sight of land . . . so joyous now to her*
> *The sight of her husband, vivid in her gaze,*
> *That her white arms embracing his neck would never*
> *For a moment let him go . . .*

Odikweos *was* weeping, leaning his elbow on the arm of the chair and his head against the hand that covered his face.

I should have expected that, Ian thought.

More than wealth, more than power, sometimes more than life itself, an Achaean noble craved undying fame—the only real immortality their beliefs allowed; their afterlife was a bitter shadowy thing, where it was better to be a hired hand on a poor peasant's farm than King among the strengthless dead. Fame was what Achilles had chosen, though the price was an early end in battle far from home.

> *Dawn with her rose-red fingers might have shone*
> *Upon their tears, if with her glinting eyes*
> *Athana had not thought of one more thing.*
> *She held back the night, and night lingered long*
> *At the western edge of the earth, while in the east*
> *She reined in Dawn of the golden throne at ocean's banks,*
> *Commanding her not to yoke the wind-swift team*
> *That brings men light, Blaze and Aurora,*
> *The young colts that race the Morning on . . .*

"So," Odikweos said when he had finished.

He wiped his eyes with his hand unself-consciously. An Achaean warrior felt no shame at tears before poetry that moved him.

"So, it is given to me to know how the men of years to come will think of me . . . three thousand years, you say?"

"Five hundred years from this night, until that poem is written down. Near three thousand more to my time."

The Achaean shook his head. "That is a number the mouth can say, but the heart cannot grasp. And my deeds will still be known! Or at least a ghost of them will be known . . . or my deeds and name *would* have been known, if things had gone forward as they did in the past your age remembers."

Brief murderous rage lit his craggy features: "And this Walker has robbed me of!"

He sat silent, thinking, before he went on: "And much of what Walker knows is the fruit of my people's minds and hands?"

"All the beginnings of it." He'd glossed over the Dark Age that had lain between this time and the glories of the Classical period. "The foundations of the house *my* people built. Every generation of ours finds fresh inspiration in it."

"And all that Walker has taken from us," Odikweos said. "I followed him for wealth, and power—and because I thought he would make our land great with his outland knowledge."

"You . . . might say he's done some of that," Arnstein said cautiously.

Odikweos shook his head violently. The fire in the great round hearth had died down; the light of the embers ran blood-red over his features and brought out reddish highlights in his grizzled black hair.

"Not so. He has made this a land of slaves—and slaves of us free Achaeans, even we nobles. What is slavery, if not to live in fear of another's wrath, obedient to his will? Do *we*, even we nobles, not live in fear of his anger, and that of his servants? Even the best among us, the men of breeding, the *kalos k'agathos*, each must guard his tongue in fear of punishment. Are we not now dependents, needing the King's favor for the very bread on our tables? At most, we are the stewards of *his* lands, not the lords of our own. As Zeus takes half a man's *arete*, his worth, away in the day of slavery, so have we fallen. The more so as it has happened inch by inch, day by day—the more so still as many do not yet realize what has been done."

"Yes, he's . . . we say *put one over on you.*"

The Greek's fist closed and came down once on the arm of his chair. "That worst of all. He *laughs* at us. He stole my glory, and sat laughing behind his hand as he did, mocking me for an ignorant savage!"

"I don't think you're really . . . real to him."

"That does not make it better."

Ian sat silent, tense. At last Odikweos went on:

"Yet all this must be borne, if Walker is too strong for you of the Eagle People. The King will not be overthrown so long as he remains victorious."

"And if he does not?"

Odikweos smiled, slow and savage. "Then . . . perhaps, we will speak more of this."

An alarm bell began to sound outside. Shrieks and screams rose under it. The Ithakan rose, cursing, and shouted for his officers and underlings.

"Your ship of the air comes again to cast thunderbolts," he

said to Arnstein. "Not as accurate as those of all-seeing Zeus, but powerful enough."

The map of southern Iberia on the commodore's table and the duplicate on the map easel still looked a little strange to eyes brought up in the twentieth. The coastal plains were much less, the courses of the rivers differing in countless details, as did the roads; the towns were utterly strange. Only the broad outline of the land remained the same, a long trumpet-shaped lowland running from a narrow tip just past where Córdoba would have been to a broad wedge-shaped base at the the sea, surrounded by mountains. Tartessos lay at the northwestern end of the trumpet's flared mouth, Cadiz Base at the southeastern. At the foot of the long chain of the Sierra Morenos flowed a great river, trending gently southwest until it reached the site of Seville-that-wasn't, then turning sharply southward into a large open bay. The map showed a major highway running from not-Seville to Tartessos City, along the line the river would have taken without its southward bend.

Alston waited while the assembled officers settled themselves around the table; the flaps were open, and the air that drifted in was rain-washed, cool and fresh, even a little chill. From outside came a distant, constant crackle of small-arms fire from the ranges—the auxiliaries getting intensive training, the Marines, militia, and Guard crews maintaining their edge—the scream of a steam whistle, the sounds of marching feet, hooves, a farrier's hammer driving home nails in a hoof, shouts and orders, a distant screech of metal on metal, a work-shanty from the piers where cargos were swung ashore.

"Gentlemen, ladies," Swindapa said, nodding as the tented room grew quiet.

"Ms. Kurlelo-Alston, the outline, if you please."

"Ma'am." She moved the tip of the ebony rod from Cadiz to where the Guadalquivir ran into the great bay. "Here— where Seville would have been—is the Tartessian forward base, at the first really firm ground. It's a town called *Kurutselcarya-duwara-biden,* and it means . . . mmmm . . . Place Where They Cross the River."

"We'll call it *Crossing,*" Alston said.

There were a few chuckles at that. Swindapa went on. "This area between Crossing and Tartessos is the heartland of their kingdom, and the most heavily populated area. Most of their mines, smelters and foundries are either here"—she tapped the mountains directly north of Tartessos City, at the sources of the Rio Tinto—"or scattered through here."

The pointer swept east and slightly north, along the foothills of the Black Mountains, the Sierra Morena as they were called in the twentieth.

"South of that is the Guadalquivir, the *Tasweldan Erriguabiden*—the Great River. It's navigable for ships under two hundred tons all the way east to here; where Córdoba is on the pre-Event maps. They've driven roads north into the mountains, and bring the products down to the water, float them down the river to Crossing, and then either by road to Tartessos—this road between them is their main highway, and it's asphalt-surfaced—or by sailing barge along the coast, since that isn't far.

"Right now, they're building up supplies at Crossing while their army masses just east of the river. We estimate their force at about seven thousand troops, a little less than double our number. The file you've been given has a breakdown on armaments."

"Thank you, Lieutenant Commander," Marian said, and rose. Swindapa handed her the pointer.

"At present, they're covering their main population and manufacturing centers, with this river to move supplies, and relying on their fortifications to protect their capital. They have more troops than we do, but they also have to garrison extensive territories. This area to the west, around their capital, is where the actual Tartessians live; around thirty-five thousand people. There's another seventy-five thousand living in the Guadalquivir Valley; closely related to the Tartessians, speaking the same language, much the same religion and customs. From our Intelligence reports, most of them are fairly happy with Isketerol's rule, apart from some of the families of their former leaders. About as many people again live in the mountains and plateau areas to the north and east of the Guadalquivir; they farm a little but they're mainly herders and hunters, seminomads, and they *don't* like the Tartessians. Neither do the people in those areas of northern Morocco they control.

"Now," Marian went on, "King Isketerol is actually in a bit of a strategic dilemma, although he doesn't realize it. We're going to point it out to him; we're also going to make clear the advantages our superior reconnaissance, mobility, and means of communication give us." She smiled slightly. "Nice of him to build these wonderful roads for us."

There was a wolfish chuckle at that, and she went on: "Our war aim here is to neutralize Tartessos, either by negotiation or by kicking them to bits and stomping on the bits; and we have to do that without damaging our own forces too much, because this is simply a prelude to the real war, against Walker and Great Achaea."

She glanced over at McClintock, who sat with his regimental commanders and staff. "Brigadier, are the auxiliaries ready to take the field?"

"Reasonably, ma'am," he said. "The more time we have to drill them, the better they'll be, of course. I've got Marine or Militia officers and noncoms in command of each group, 'advising' the locals who are nominally in charge. We're providin' all the communications and heavy weapons, of course, but they'll make pretty good riflemen. They'll hold a line."

"Excellent. Lieutenant Commander Bidden, what about the airship?"

"Five more days, ma'am. We're putting up the frames and inserting the gasbags now."

"Mr. Raith?"

The head of the Seahaven Engineering liaison spread his hands, a gesture that was a probably-unconscious imitation of Ron Leaton's. "We're setting up the slipways and rollers," he said. "Nearly done. And the machine shop will be up to speed in another day. That's all we can do until we get the *Merrimac* itself."

The Coast Guard captains looked at him. "Herself, Mr. Raith, herself," Marian corrected him. "A suggestion; look into hauling out the *Farragut* on the slipway while we're waiting for *Merrimac*. It would be a lot easier to get her back into shape that way and it'll give your team some shakedown work."

Then she tapped the end of the pointer into her palm, eyes raking the assembled officers. "What we're going to do now," she said, "is take the initiative. I intend to have the enemy reacting to what we do, and always a day late and a dollar short, with a new surprise every time he thinks he's adjusted. We're going to get inside his decision loop. Brigadier, you'll take the Third Marines and the auxiliaries north along this route . . ."

"Row soft, there." The voice of the coxswain came from the tiller. "Row soft, all."

Swindapa Kurlelo-Alston blinked under the overhang of helmet as rain came hissing down out of the night sky. That hid the Tartessian fort on the bluffs over there to the east, but she could feel its hulking menace in the part of her spirit that bore the Spear Mark of the hunter—eleven-inch guns there . . .

The darkened oars rose and fell, a low creaking of thwarts

their only sound, lost in the white noise of the rain. The water and the night hid everything, sight and sound and scent.

Marian waited quietly beside her in the bows of the launch as the fort fell away behind them and the minutes passed. To anyone else there would have been nothing in her face, nothing in the way her body waited but a tiger's patience.

Ah, you cannot fool me, bin'HOtse-khwon, Swindapa thought. *Not after all these years. I know when you worry. The dance of our souls is woven together in the moonlight.*

Inward, she counted off her heartbeats, the old technique for precise time-telling that the Grandmothers had taught before clocks; the effort of controlling your pulse helped you keep calm in danger as well, *feedback* the Eagle People called it. Worry was foolishness; Moon Woman had turned Time itself in a circle to bring them together . . .

"Now," she said, her lips beside Marian's ear. "We should be there now."

Marian signaled. The oars froze, waiting, and they coasted forward against the sluggish 'longshore flow. Reeds waved to their left, a moving blackness against the greater darkness of the land. Another boat came very close, saw the white wand in the stern of theirs, veered aside, and waited; unseen, more did behind. Then the prow of theirs grated on something heavy and hard. Her hands reached out with others, felt the links. A chain, massive, the iron links as thick as her thighs and grown with weeds and harsh barnacles. From report, it stretched from one bank of the river to the other, barring the way to anything heavier than a canoe.

"Corporal," her partner's voice said, "get to it."

Rafts of barrels towed astern of them. Figures in carefully preserved black wetsuits, flippers, masks, and snorkels rolled over the side of this and three other of the boats. Those rafts were brought forward and lashed to the chain ten yards apart; a small thick tarpaulin was draped over the middle between while divers anchored the barrels to the river-ooze. Thirty tense seconds, and a rising dragon's hiss beneath the waters. Light leaked around the tarpaulin, and a smell of scorched metal bubbled to the surface. Then all was as it had been, except that there was a gap where the chain had lain on the water. But nothing to show that at either end . . .

Marian smiled in the darkness, teeth showing in a glint of white. Swindapa felt her own glee awaken.

"Let's go!"

*   *   *

"And to think I thought I'd get away from digging when I joined up," Vaukel said.

"Shut up and dig—it keeps you warm," Johanna said.

Vaukel nodded and swung the pick, grunting as it came around and jarred into the tough, rocky earth. After half a dozen strokes he stepped back, panting, while his squadmate went at the loosened earth with her shovel. Most of their company was working in such pairs—you couldn't do both at once anyway. The rest of the army stretched off to the southward, across the broad undulating terrain, scoring it like an army of moles.

"I think that's got it," she said.

The two-person foxhole was a narrow slit a yard wide and two long, with a section running back like the stem of a T. Vaukel jumped down into it; one part was a little deeper, to give him protection equal to his shorter comrade's.

"Throw down some rocks," he said; when they came he stamped them into the wet earth, to give better footing.

Then he looked up at the sky, where the morning sun was a glow behind the gray. Back home in the valley of the River of Long Shadows he'd have said such a sky—low, wolf-colored, with wisps of fast-moving cloud—would mean rain, or snow since it was cold enough to see your breath. He took a deep breath through his nose, smelling the mealy scent. It felt a little dry for snow, but who knew so far from Alba?

Who knew the world was so big? he thought, looking westward.

While he was a boy, it had seemed that his mother's hamlet was the wide world, ringed by the forest. The sea, or the Great Wisdom, they were a marvelous far-off tale.

When his uncles and elder brothers had marched off to the Battle of the Downs he'd been green with envy . . . less so, when not all returned, but he'd listened eagerly to their tales of journeying and war and the fabulous things of the Eagle People. Now he'd seen Irondale, sailed down the river to Westhaven, and across the River Ocean on a great swan-winged ship, and walked the streets of Nantucket, which was more wonderful still. From there around the world, and past Ur and Babylon, marched from there to Hattusas and on and on, and everywhere there were different peoples and their Gods and ways.

Now men were coming across those rolling downs to the westward, coming to kill him, so he must kill them. *Very strange,* he thought.

"Good open country," Johanna said, as she looked westward.

Then she laughed. "More open, now that we've burned down or run off everything on it."

"That's a bad thing, wasting the land," Vaukel said mournfully. "Killing stock you can't eat, Moon Woman doesn't shine on it."

For a moment the two Marines looked at each other in the mutual incomprehension of culture-clash, then shrugged and set to improving their quarters with ledges or little caves to store things, and rigging a shelter-half overhead. Snow started to whisk down from the north, small dry granular flakes. They were pounding the heaped dirt and rock ahead of them down with the flats of their entrenching tools—if you left it loose a bullet might punch through—when Captain Barnes came by with a squad leading pack mules.

"Here," she said, and handed them extra ammunition and a bandolier of grenades.

"Thank you, ma'am," Gwenhaskieths said. She hefted the segmented iron egg of a grenade, her thumb caressing the pin. "We could have used some of these at O'Rourke's Ford, ma'am."

A swift grin. "Make these count. God bless."

"And you, ma'am," they both said, comforted.

Johanna jumped up to the firing step and craned her head around. "We've got backup—that's a Gatling they're digging in behind us."

Vauk nodded solemnly and pulled a dog biscuit and stick of hard beef jerky out of his haversack where it rested behind him. The hard cracker challenged his teeth as he bit a corner off and began to chew. They huddled together for the animal comfort of the warmth, and waited. He could feel his companion shivering a little beside him.

Well, that's the Sun People for you, he thought good-naturedly. *Flighty they are, sort of. But fierce as you could want when the time comes for a fight.*

It was amazing how travel broadened your perspective. Here, *dyaus arsi* and Fiernan Bohulugi and Eagle People were like a litter from the same dam.

Thunder rumbled in the west. He looked up for a moment, surprised; you almost never got thunder in a snowstorm like this.

"Guns," Gwenhaskieths said. "It's started."

CHAPTER TWENTY-FOUR

April, 11 A.E.—Feather River Valley, California
November, 10 A.E.—Great River, southern Iberia
December, 10 A.E.—West-central Anatolia
November, 10 A.E.—Great River, southern Iberia
December, 10 A.E.—West-central Anatolia
November, 10 A.E.—Great River, southern Iberia

Peter Giernas felt himself begin to shake as the canoe came to shore and he vaulted out and splashed ashore, leaving the others to haul the dugout craft onto the bank.

The campsight where he'd left Spring Indigo and Jared was empty . . . empty save for burned scraps and tattered leather flapping in the breeze. Heads remained as well, stuck on stakes; heads of local warriors, and of his dogs Saule and Ausra. No Spring Indigo. No Jared. A low bitter smell of smoke and shit wisped up from coals mostly dead with dawn dew. His eyes misted over, and he heard sounds coming from his throat as if from a great distance. The shaking grew worse. He turned in the direction of the distant Tartessian fort and took a step . . .

"Snap out of it!" Sue said, grabbing his arm. The muscle was rigid under her fingers, like carved wood. "Going berserk won't help!"

He shuddered again, like a horse twitching at the bite of flies, and shook his head. Eddie's arms gripped him from behind, and he heaved and twisted. Sue and Jaditwara joined in, wrestling him to a halt; he wasn't quite far enough gone to hurt any of them.

"Blood brother!" Eddie Vergeraxsson shouted in his ear. "Call back your spirit! We'll get them, or get revenge, but we have to *think*."

Step by step he won back to himself. At last he relaxed. "Thanks," he said, his voice harsh and unfamiliar in his own ears. "Now let's look around."

They did, keeping the locals at the shoreline. Most of the

ground around the Islander campsite was trampled too heavily for useful information, but some of it gave him a grim satisfaction that took a little of the shadow from the bright spring day.

"I think at least one of them bled out here," he announced.

"Pete!"

Sue's voice called him to the line where the horses had been picketed. "Pete, I think there was a hell of a fight here."

He came, bent low and shading his eyes with a hand. "Yup," he said. "Pawprints, lots of 'em . . . then most of the horses got led away, some of 'em broke free . . . Look, this is a blood trail."

Not much of one, an occasional brown drop. It led to the narrow band of riverside swamp.

"Cover me," he said, stripping off his buckskin tunic and taking knife and tomahawk in hand. He eeled through, the wind warm on his bare back as he followed the tiny clues—a broken tule reed, an impression in a patch of mud, tufts of brown and gray fur. A low uncertain whine greeted him.

"Perks?" he said incredulously. "Perks, boy?"

His left hand reached out through the reeds, his right ready with his tomahawk. The palm came down on a dead man's face, half–chewed away. He suppressed a startled curse and swept the tall tule rushes aside. Flies buzzed around the dead man's caked blood, and on more—his own and others'—that matted the wolf-dog's fur. Perks quivered, crawling forward on his belly, ears laid back, and licked his face and hands.

"Here, Perks. Steady, fellah."

A jet of fear went through him as the dog struggled to rise. He yelped gently as Giernas slid the tomahawk through the loop at the back of his belt and picked him up; the ranger moved carefully, but a hundred and twenty pounds was a considerable weight even for his strength.

Sue came running at his call. She ran her hands over the wounded animal. "Nothing fundamental," she said. "Except . . . yes, there's a pistol ball under the skin here on his left shoulder, must have skipped around. And this slash, and a stab here. I'll have to probe for the bullet, the rest is antiseptic and some stitches. This is one tough dog."

"He was tougher than one Tartessian, at least," Giernas said. "Do what you can."

He and Eddie and Jaddi were better trackers. He joined them, casting about through tall grass, riverside mud, beneath stands of live oak.

"Here's where the Tartessians left," Eddie said. "North— down the wagon track."

That would lead the enemy a day's hard ride north, and then they'd find the missing patrol's wagon—the Indians with it had peeled off by ones and little groups, in places where they'd be hard to trace. The wagon would be alone, destroyed, with its load of charred Tartessian bodies. *That* would drive the enemy troops absolutely bugfuck, of course.

"And they had most of our horses with them," Eddie went on, pointing. "Look."

Giernas nodded. They'd gotten familiar enough with their tracks to identify individuals by their hoofprints. Those were as individual as a man's fingerprints, when you knew how to look.

"They had a net of outriders all around," Giernas said. "Look, there and there."

Eddie frowned and nodded. "If Indigo got away, I don't think she could avoid or outrun them," he said unhappily. "Not after sunrise. They were pressing it hard, by the looks of it."

"Pete!" Jaditwara called, her voice faint with distance. "Eddie!"

They trotted over, running easily at a steady wolf trot with their rifles pumping back and forth in their right hands and their moccasins rustling through the soft ground cover. Insects and a few birds burst out ahead of them. Jaditwara was lying on her belly, hands parting two clumps of the tall grass. They circled up behind her to avoid overtreading the trail and knelt, reaching out with their riflebarrels to part more of the grass. Hoofprints, unshod ones . . .

"That's two horses . . . Shadowfax and Grimma, isn't it?" he asked.

Jaditwara nodded; those were two of hers, a mare and a gelding named after characters from some old story she liked; she'd read big chunks of it aloud to them around the fire overwinter.

"Shadowfax is carrying a rider," she said. "But a light one. Grimma is on a lead rope."

Hope blazed up in him. "Spring Indigo got away!" he said. "She must have cut west and then south, back along the Tarties' trail. That's the one way they *wouldn't* look."

The three of them jumped up and ran down the trail for a quarter hour; even through thigh-high grass you could follow it, once you knew roughly what and where to look for. Peter brought himself to a halt and scratched his head.

"She stopped and changed off here," he said.

"*Awe,*" Eddie said, and Jaditwara nodded.

"And she's pushing the horses hard," the ex-Fiernan ranger said, tossing her head in puzzlement. "Trot and gallop."

You could do that, if you had two mounts, especially if you sat light in the saddle. It was a good way to cover ground quickly, as well—better than a hundred miles in a day's journey.

Uh-oh, Peter Giernas thought, looking south.

"I think I know what she was doing," he said slowly. "She didn't know when we'd be back—everything went real quick, quicker than we thought—and she knew the Tartessians were out in force. Thirty or more, and with native trackers. Where would *you* go?"

Eddie leaned on his rifle and frowned, turning his head in a wide sweep. The fringe on the sleeve of his buckskins wobbled as he scratched his head.

"Over the river to the east?" he said tentatively. "Hide in the hills?"

"Cross two big rivers with a baby?" Jaditwara said. "And no more gear than in her saddlebags? No. She has to get shelter and food, and quickly, for her child's sake."

My son, Giernas thought, with a brief burst of fury, as quickly suppressed. *You need a clear head now, goddammit.*

"No," he agreed. "And she can't hole up with any of the locals, too much danger they'd turn her in."

"Well, she can't go west," Eddie said, waving. The land in that direction was even flatter and more open, millions of acres of grass to the foothills of the Coast Range. "So where *would* she go?"

"South," Giernas said grimly. "To the only place around here with crowds of people coming and going, strangers, where one more Indian woman with a kid wouldn't be noticed."

"Oh," Eddie said. Then: "Oh, *shit.*"

Silent, they turned and ran back along their own trail, back to the camp. The locals were setting up, looking around for evidence of what had happened to their kin, building fires. Sue had Perks beside one of the fires on a section of hide, with water boiling and gear set out beside her. She nodded at their news.

"What do we do?" she said.

Pete forced words out. "What we planned." He waved north. "There are about half the soldiers they've got left, out of touch. We've got to act before they get their act together."

"Indigo?" Sue said gently.

"The longer she's in there, the more likely she and Jared are to get caught." He took a deep breath. "We'll have to make a few changes, though."

Sue nodded, then looked down. "I've given him a shot, but I had to short it—not sure of the dose," she said. "And this is going to hurt. A little further and that pistol ball would have lamed him for life. I think it's pressing on a nerve; he snapped at me when I touched it."

Peter Giernas knelt beside Perks's head; since Sue still had both hands, the snap would have been a warning only. The dog's eyes were wandering with the drug, but the black nose wrinkled and a long pink tongue flapped feebly at his hands. He took the heavy-boned shaggy head in his arms, remembering the puppy that had looked so sheepish when it piddled at the foot of his bed. . . .

"It's okay, big fellah," he said quietly, taking the great scarred muzzle in one hand and clamping it closed, cradling the head against him firmly. "I know you did your best. You held them off while she got away. I'm sorry about your pups."

"Eddie, Jaddi, hold his paws," Sue said, washing off her hands and taking up the probe. "God, I wish I had more training for this—Henry should be here . . . All right."

She took a long breath and began. Perks whimpered, then gave a muffled howl and heaved against the hands confining him.

"Quiet, Perks!" Giernas said. "Quiet!"

The body in his arms went quivering-rigid. Sue's long-fingered hands moved; she swore, moved again . . .

"Got it!" she said triumphantly. The slightly flattened lead sphere thumped on the ground; Perks gave a long muffled whimper as she cleansed the incision and began to sew.

"He'll be all right in a couple of weeks, I think," she said, looking up and meeting Giernas's eyes.

"Thanks, Sue," he said. "And *everything's* going to be okay in a couple of days, if I have anything to do with it."

"Oh, now you sorry bastards are *fucked*!" Marine rifleman Otto Verger whispered in his birth-tongue. He grinned through the burned cork on his face; he had been born Ohteleraur son of Vargerax, far from this river in Tartessos. The inflatable craft waited where it had grounded among the reeds that swayed in the hissing rain, and he crouched on the slick wet fabric of it.

In harshly accented English: "It's me who's here the now, *and I've got my rocket launcher*!"

This little piece of Iberia was a bit like the east-country fens of Alba where he'd been born nineteen summers gone . . . except that here he had this fine piece of battlecraft in his hands, from the hands of the wizard-smith Leaton and his helpers. Verger loved the stubby weapon; his hands caressed it as he waited in the grounded rubber raft. A cammo-painted steel tube four inches around and four feet long, with flared padded ends, a shoulder stock and handgrips on the tube, a circular shield for the user's face on the left side and a simple optical sight. It was a lot heavier than a rifle, true. But with this you had the Fist of Tauntutonnarax the Horned Man itself at your command. . . .

I mean, the Fist of God the Father and Son and His Mother, he corrected himself, freeing a hand for a second to sketch a cross on his chest.

Otto Verger intended to make the Republic his home; his last leave at his father's steading had settled that in his mind, watching his kin sit on a clay floor around an open hearth, cracking fleas while the stock grunted and squealed and baaaa'ed and mooed from the other end of the longhouse. So he must make his peace with Jesus and His sky-clan.

It was always well to be in good with the particular Gods of the folk you dwelt among, even if they were so strange you couldn't understand a thing about them. They were strong; that was enough.

Their sergeant had crawled off to find the others; then he raised his head over the edge of the boat from where he lay on the reeds.

"Path's marked," he said softly. "Follow me."

Verger rolled out of the boat and wiggled forward, stopping for an instant to make sure that his loader was following them; Private Sheila Rueteklo was Fiernan, and they'd stop to look at the pretty flowers in the middle of a death-duel. A slap on his boot told him she was there, and he snake-crawled forward. Mud and cold water soaked into his already saturated uniform. There were secrets to moving through swamp. If you went flat on your belly, spread your weight, you could move across quaking ground that would suck you down to your waist if you tried to go on two feet.

The toboggans following with their gear used the same principle—the Eagle People . . .

That's we *Eagle People, fool,* he corrected himself.

. . . were marvelously clever about that, finding new ways to use old knowledge.

If you pushed reeds flat to make a mat beneath you it was even better. The sharp green smell of bruised vegetation rose up around him, mingling with the yeasty scent of the mud, the occasional earth-fart of marsh gas, and the odors of gun oil and metal. He sniffed with a hunter's caution. *Yes.* There was the smoke of many banked hearths from the shore of the river to westward. The smell could come from a town, or large village, or war camp . . . but almost certainly from the fort the briefings had described. For a while he'd been convinced they were lost on this endless river.

Dark as arm's length up a hog's ass, he thought cheerfully. *But we got here. Hard Corps!*

The rocket teams and their protecting riflemen moved in across the darkened swamp with patient stealth; every once in a while an officer or noncom would pause to look at a compass and correct their passage. At last the swamp proper gave way to mere mud, liquid beneath his body with firm ground close enough below for him to crouch and duckwalk, then come half-erect. An officer came down and led them forward along a string the scouts—those picked ones like Clarkson—had put in. A lot of fen-men in this unit . . . Verger walked silently, despite the wet ground beneath his boots and the stumps of trees. At last he came to a tangle of fallen trunks that would make a good position, and the rain lifted a little. Light, yes, there was faint yellow light from ahead. He squeezed his eyes shut and then opened them wide again. A row of squares, in a line three times the height of his head—gunport covers made from slabs of iron, with light leaking around them.

"Seventy-five yards," the officer whispered. "You start on the right gun position. Remember not to look at the flares."

She moved off into the night. *Yes, Mother,* Verger thought. He didn't mind having a woman as platoon commander . . . much, anymore. They tended to take better care of their units, less likely to get you killed to prove how long their dongs were.

He heard a series of soft grunts as Rueteklo unhitched the carrying frame from her webbing harness, and knew the feel of her hands as she lifted his free of his back. Together that was eight rockets; another eight came up from the rear, brought over the marsh on toboggans.

"Feed me," he said; it would be a while, but best to be ready. "Incendiary."

Metal touched the rear padding of the launcher, and the rocket slid home with a low *clunk-click*. The trigger on the first handgrip went taut as the tension came on the spring striker.

He could imagine the round sliding in, the egg-shaped head, the narrower body, the circle of fins at the rear with a solid rim the same diameter as the warhead. Unseen in the darkness his teeth showed. Incendiary warheads were *fun*.

Well, *all* of them were fun, but incendiaries most of all. The bursting charge scattered fire like the Christian Hell, and it burned inextinguishably, some wonderful art making it impossible to put out with water. He'd put one of those—maybe more—right through those ports.

"Up," Rueteklo said when her work was through.

"Ready," he replied, bringing his eye to the sight.

With that, he could see the clear pattern of light leaking out around the portlid of the gun emplacement; the careless bastards there didn't have any fitting to keep it light-tight. He shook his head in contempt. With a soft snort of equal scorn he remembered older men back home, saying that you had to obey like a dog to serve the Eagle People in war . . . Fools. Let them sit in their moldering dung-floored huts, wagging their gray beards and picking lice from each other's hair.

Hard Corps! he thought.

In the Corps you learned how to do things *right*. With the Empty Hand art alone he'd paid off many an old score, going back to his father's steading on leave—he was not a big man, though broad-shouldered and strong for his size. And as a Marine you could rely on the people beside you to do things the *right* way, the *Corps* way, not go off in a sulk, or rush away to grab a cow or grandstand and leave *your* arse swinging in the wind.

Oath-brothers like that gave you the strength of a *God*. More, they had the Midnight Mare and Golden Roan to lead them—*keuthes* enough to make victory sure. Just this evening before they all set off upriver he'd watched her doing some rite or other, laying a black thread and a white side by side on her sleeve and waiting until you couldn't tell one from the other. Powerful rites to put *keuthes* on your side, in the Corps.

Plus the Corps gave you weapons, finer than the *miruthas* used in the halls of Sky Father, and gold—fourteen dollars on the drumhead when you enlisted, the price of a good ox, and a dollar a day thereafter—and there was fine food like an endless feast in a chieftain's hall, healing magic like something from a tale of wizards for your hurts, the splendid uniform that all men feared, the promise of land after your hitch, the travel, the women to sport with . . .

He grinned at the memory of night before last, stealing away behind a pile of ammunition boxes with a frisky sailor-wench off one of the Guard frigates—sleep well lost. At home in the Alban lands of Sky Father's children, if you didn't have bride-wealth to offer . . . well, a girl's brothers might kick your bol-locks off if you so much as caught her by the braids and asked for a kiss. And what young man his age had bridewealth, with the price of a wife going up all the time and no cattle raids to make a poor young warrior rich?

No wife for one born like him to a common *wirtowonnax*, that he knew, not for many years. No slave women any more either for a youth to ease himself with, or captives taken on raids, not like the days before the Battle of the Downs that his uncles spoke of.

The old men got all the girls now—unless the girls ran off themselves. A young man who stayed home had nothing to look forward to except another day walking behind the arse-end of a plow ox. Watching the turnips grow and banging sheep, while the great wild world swept by on the Islanders' tall white ships.

Yes, it's good to be in the Corps, he thought, working himself into the damp earth and keeping his eyes on the target with lynx patience, ignoring the cold rain that trickled down his hel-met and fell into his sopping clothes. Good for his warrior years, and then one day he would have hall and land and herds of his own. Unless he died in battle first, of course, but all men were born doomed to meet their fate at the hour appointed. A sluggard sleeping in the straw and a hero on a bloody field reaping foemen, each died just as dead, and nobody remem-bered the sluggard's name after he was burned on his pyre.

Occasionally he stretched muscle against muscle in silent con-test, to keep limber despite the damp chill, supple for when the moment of action arrived. Rueteklo settled in beside him and to one side, a little to the rear but out of the backblast, her rifle across one of the carrying racks.

"Got a rat-bar, Sheila?" he whispered.

She handed him one and he tore off the wrapper with his teeth. He was more cautious about biting into the field ration. The slab of rock-hard biscuit inside was laced with nuggets of nut and dried fruit; it challenged his teeth, then softened as he chewed bits. Not bad. He'd heard the Islander-born moan about dog biscuit and even rat-bars, as if you could have fresh loaves and roast pig every day.

Some folk would complain if they were beheaded with a golden ax!

*   *   *

Thunder rumbled faintly to the south and east. Raupasha blinked and brushed snow from her knitted hood—what the Eagle People called a *ski mask*—and looked in that direction. High rocky hills that were almost mountains blocked her view, bare trees and fir heavy with snow and naked rock. The sound boomed on, original and echo mingling in confusion. More snow flicked into her eyes, or fell from the rear flare of her helmet down her neck.

"It has begun," she said quietly.

"Well enough," Tekhip-tilla said, from the next chariot. "Another month of campaigning and we'd all have frozen solid, so the war would be delayed until spring when we thawed."

Raupasha nodded ruefully; the old noble liked to grumble, but this was true. She was wearing a coat of wolfskin that the *Seg Kalui* of Babylon had given her, over a good tunic of the fine soft goat hair of this region, and tight drawers of the same under trousers cut down from a pair that a Ringapi chief would never need again, and Nantucketer boots. She was still cold; she and her men came from a land where snow was a rarity, and never lay long on the ground.

The land ahead barely qualified as a valley—it was lower than the rough hills to the south, and much lower than the frowning heights northward. No road ran through it, or stream, only paths made by sheep and goats. Their herdsmen had left a few square rock shelters and pens, but those were abandoned. The whole landscape looked forsaken even by the Gods, dark rocks standing up out of sparse pasture already turning white. The snow flickered down out of the north, piling up against the exposed rocks, melting a little around the stamping feet of the horses and for a little while around the steaming piles of their dung.

Raupasha tapped Iridmi on the shoulder through his double cloak, and he drew the chariot out in front of the others. She pulled up the ski mask; her followers must see her face.

"Warriors of Mitanni!" she said.

They cheered, tired and cold and hungry as they were. For a moment tears of pride blinded her; she blinked, glad of the snow that gave her an excuse to drag a mitten across her eyes. The massed chariots crowded together as closely as they could to hear her, horses tossing their heads as the snow clustered on their manes.

"Warriors of Mitanni," she called again. "You have fought

this man who calls himself the Wolf Lord—you have fought as the true wolf fights, and he has felt the sting of your fangs!"

This time the cheer had more of a snarl in it, and a few men broke into yips and howls. They'd given the Achaeans all the trouble they could with their raids, and it had been a goodly measure. Most of these men had grown up under the feet of the Assyrians, having to eat dirt before the conquerors, with only old tales to feed their pride. Now they had real victories to boast of, if small ones. They liked the taste of it, and they valued it—the more for having lacked so long, she thought.

Certainly I do. And I value what I have seen in Lord Kenn'et's eyes when we reported to him.

"Now the final battle comes," she said, and pointed westward. "The war-host of Achaea comes, slowed and lessened by our raids, hungry and cold. We must hold them here, hold them out of the Halys Gates, and the war is ours for this year. Are you ready to fight? Will you follow your princess and your flag?"

Another roaring cheer; the horses neighed at the sound, stamping their feet as if to join in. Sabala bayed, from where a groom held his collar—this was too solemn an occasion to allow the spotted clown free run, much as it grieved him. The silver chariot wheel on green that she had selected as the new banner—the *national flag*, to use the English word—of her people flapped above her head.

"Then follow!" she said.

Gunnery Sergeant Connor had picked the hill; not too high, with nothing overlooking it and a good *field of fire* from one side of the rocky cleft to the other. Nobody was going to bypass them, not with a brace of mortars dropping bombs on their heads. Raupasha's chariot rattled and bumped its way to the summit.

"Dig in!" Connor said.

Her men obeyed; the haughtiest noble had learned the wisdom of that, or had died and been replaced with picked men promoted from the Mitannian regiment of foot. Picks and shovels rang, and stones were piled up. Raupasha hopped down from her chariot and called the other leaders over to confer.

"We will send the chariots there," she said, pointing back eastward to a long cleft in the hills.

"That's far, if we need to retreat quickly," one squadron commander said.

Raupasha shook her head. "We do not retreat from this spot," she said. "We hold the flank until reinforcements come."

Her head turned southeast. Five mounted messengers had gone to Lord Kenn'et . . . *But there are still the hillmen of these part, wild with fury against us for sweeping the valleys clear,* she thought uneasily. *And in this snow, the* ultralights *cannot fly.*

Men unloaded crates of ammunition and other stores, and the vehicles clattered off again; it was an advantage of chariotry, that you did not have to carry all your gear yourself. She went about, encouraging and directing, returning the smiles of her followers. Occasionally her eyes would flick westward; an army could not come this way, it was too rough for many wagons, but a force strong enough to turn the allied army's right flank could. That was why Kenn'et had sent mobile scouting parties to secure any possible path through the northern hills, and hers had been the one which found the enemy's force. Four hundred men, to hold this place . . .

"They come," a scout gasped at last, galloping his horse up the slope.

Raupasha settled into her own slit trench, squinting through her binoculars. The short winter's day was half-gone, but the snow was heavier, and the long columns of enemy troops appeared out of it like a genie in a storyteller's tale.

"Let them get close," Connor said quietly, and she nodded.

"And ma'am?" Connor said.

Raupasha looked around, surprised. Usually Connor was all business, at least in the field. In camp he acted like an uncle, sometimes.

"Ma'am, it's been an honor to serve with you," he said.

Raupasha shook the offered hand, honored and a little chilled. *He does not think much of our chances either,* she knew, and then folded the knowledge away. It was not . . . what was the word? *Relevant.*

Instead she waited, waited until the first clumps of mounted scouts were almost at the foot of the hill. *They cannot see well either,* she thought. *And the snow is in their eyes.*

"Fire!" she said, standing.

Marian Alston pulled down the night-sight goggles. The world turned brighter, but flat and greenish, and still silver-streaked by the cold rain blowing out of the north; probably cold enough to keep natives of this southern land indoors.

And why don't I ever get to fight in decent weather? It was a minor miracle that nobody seemed to have gotten lost, doing everything by compass and dead reckoning; night attacks were notoriously chancy.

She scanned the shores. No changes from the last overflight by the air corps. Most of the buildings were on the higher eastern bank, in the bend of an elbow of the river where Seville would have been in the other history. Most of Isketerol's new town was blocky adobe buildings, built quickly for utility. Down by the river were quays, most of the retaining walls made of vertical logs, a few of stone, the surfaces paved. Huge pyramid-shaped heaps of goods there under tarpaulins, or barrels standing in the rain. There were also big sailing barges, chains of them tied up three-deep by the wharves or anchored out in the river—normal commerce, supplies Isketerol had brought up for his army, possibly both. Probably both.

Streets were empty of all but the occasional hand lantern, hurrying through the dismal murk. One larger building near the water was the *commandatura*, or equivalent; it had high blank walls and a three-story square tower at one corner to make it a minor fort. A few dim lights glowed, probably someone on watch, and another at the larger windows that ringed the top of the tower below the sloped tile roof.

All the same, there were Tartessians out on the water in this broadened stretch of river. A stretch of linked pontoons spanned across from verge to verge a little further north; past it were the stone foundation-piers of a long-arch bridge, halted with the work half-done. *Isketerol doesn't think small, that's for sure.* One set of hands trains four, four train sixteen . . . but it took a driving ruthless will to keep the process going this fast. Lanterns glowed at the bows of small galleys, patrolling with a slow pace of oars—crews probably cursing the doctrine that kept them away from dry bunks, but they mounted a couple of light cannon and swivels, and all she had were ship's boats.

Wordless, she extended a hand backward. The sailor assigned to the duty unfastened the casing and pulled out a rifle, and another for her partner. They were hunting weapons, something she and Swindapa had given each other for Christmas; each a double-barreled side-by-side .480 express ordered from Nantucket Town's best private gunsmith. Last year they'd been trapped on a game path near the African coast with nothing but service-issue to use when a bull elephant tried to convert them into toe-jam, and come out of it whole only through very good shooting combined with more than their share of luck.

The rifle was built like a break-open shotgun, the stock Mauritius ebony and the steel of the barrels blued, with a telescopic sight over the bridge. It was twice the weight of an issue Werder but so well balanced in her hands you didn't notice it for a while. She snapped the action open and dropped in two of the heavy cartridges, felt and heard more than saw Swindapa doing likewise. The breech closed with a thick oiled *snick*.

Then she pulled the handset out from cover and pressed the speaker button. "On the count of three," she said, taking off the goggles. Sight clamped down again, no more than ten yards. Trickles of cold water slid off her sou'wester and down her neck. Somewhere out there . . .

"One. Two. Thr . . ."

Fumpff. A spot of light wobbling up into the dim sky, distorted and streaked by the rain in the way. Then it swelled and burned with a harsh magnesium brilliance in the night, jerking and jinking on its parachute. The river lit up like the inside of a swimming pool. *Fumpff. Fumpff.* More of the parachute flares went up.

"Go for it!" the Marine noncom at the tiller yelled.

Alston bent her knee to compensate for the sudden heavy thrust, the crew rising and falling to the timing of their grunts, the ashwood shafts of the oars bending as they threw legs and back into the motion. The Tartessian patrol boats seemed to freeze for a moment; she could imagine them gaping slack-jawed at the boats swarming silently across their secure riverport, so tightly guarded by downstream fort and strong chain . . .

SSSSSRAAAAWACK!

The first of the rocket launchers cut loose, like a giant cat retching. The Tartessian patrol galley took the round right over its beak, just under the muzzle of the single forward-pointing cannon. Probably some hand there was reaching for the firing lanyard of a tube stuffed to the trunnions with grapeshot. That became completely irrelevant as the warhead struck metal, burst in a blossom of fire, and scattered white-hot iron razors across the foredeck. One of those must have plunged into a cartridge or powder barrel, because the whole forward third of the little ship disappeared in a globe of fire that cast reflections off the dark water and shot out a thousand red sparks in the rain. Planks and thankfully unidentifiable bits and pieces rained down as the rear part of the hull ran forward and sank with hardly a trace, leaving only a few men clinging to oars.

SSSSSRAAAAWACK! SSSSSRAAAAWACK!

Rocket-bombs lanced across the water of the river; those that missed their targets, which most did, plunged into the buildings and streets on either side. Isketerol was going to deeply regret proving that a useful bazooka could be fashioned with a tech-

nology considerably lower than Nantucket's. Once you gave
Leaton's people an idea, they tended to run with it.

The barrage had only taken twenty seconds. The launch
reached shore in about the same time; Marian gripped the
thwart with one hand as the prow grated on gravel and the
oars dropped, left to dangle in the thwarts as the Marines
snatched up their weapons and vaulted over the sides. Marian
leaped as well, came down in water barely deep enough to
cover the soles of her boots, dashed forward to the dry verge
of the riverside road with Swindapa at her side. The Marines
pelted past her; all over the river boats were pulling for their
assigned objectives. Guard sailors poured in a roaring wave
over the gunwales of the moored barges, cut or clubbed down
the scratch night-watch crews and set to work; others lay alongside the pontoon bridge. Marines landed all along the wharves.

There was a specific task for her and Swindapa. Two flicks
of her finger, and the protective lids were off the ends of the
telescopic sight mounted on the heavy game rifle; the forward
one up like a cap, to keep rain off the lens, the rear fully back.
She brought it to her shoulder and scanned up the *commandatura*'s tower. Intelligence said that Tartessians always put the
commander's quarters in the highest possible place. . . .

Make kan *primary and* ken *secondary*; Musashi's words. Ignore the irrelevant; the noise all around her, the growing chorus
of screams, shouts, shots, explosions, flashes lurid through the
downpour. Muscles relaxed but not loose, only the effort necessary to bring the weapon up. Clear lambent yellow flame light
in the scope sight, the circle bisected by the fine hairs of the
granule. Two hundred yards, a clout shot with this weapon, if
it weren't dark and *raining* . . .

Now to see if the commandant of this base did the instinctive
thing. *Yes.* A shape backlit by the lantern, against the glass.
Finger forward to set the hair trigger. Curling back to stroke
it as her breath went out in a single long smooth exhalation.

CRACK. The recoil a surprise as it always was when you
were on-target, but this gun really punished your shoulder; she
swayed backward, taking the impact rather than trying to stop
it. *CRACK.* Swindapa's a second after hers. A shape falling
limp forward through the broken glass, another behind clutching at it, trying to drag it back. *CRACK. CRACK.* The second
figure fell on the first. They lay limp and motionless, arms dangling, locked together.

No time to do more. No time to wonder if the human being
she'd just killed was a good man or bad, or if someone would

weep for him, or whether children would keep asking when their father would return. . . .

She thrust the rifle behind her; a sailor took it, and Swindapa's—the weapons would be useless in a close-quarter scrimmage. They drew their Pythons and dashed forward toward the tall gates. Seconds, less than two minutes since the flares went up. No little winking firefly lights from the parapet, not yet. Move, move, their only chance was speed and impact and purpose, cutting through the enemy's bewilderment.

"Clear!" from a bazooka team ahead of them.

The two women dived to either side with balletic grace, slapping down in controlled diving falls despite night and muddy ground. *SSSSSRAAAAAWACK!* The rocket lanced out, the backblast a wave of heat across the skin of her hands and neck. It ended against the gateway a half second later, with a hollow echoing *booooom.* Bits of hot metal flew through the air; the leaves must have been heavily reinforced with iron strapping or even plates. When she looked up and blinked the gates were leaning drunkenly, one on a single hinge and a gaping hole where they met, but they were still there. *Reinforced indeed.* Two more Marines ran forward, bundles in their hands—satchel charges. Neat as dancers they threw their burdens through the hole and then threw themselves aside, against the thick mudbrick wall and away from the gate. Another explosion, much louder this time—twenty pounds of gunpowder in each bag—and the gates disintegrated in a flurry of flying metal and splinters. The Marine platoon with them were on their feet and charging before the last wreckage pattered down; some of it struck their helmets as they pounded through.

Marian shoulder-rolled back to her feet, looked to her right, and felt a sharp stab of alarm; Swindapa was still on one knee.

"*The stars put a rock where my stomach was going to be,*" she wheezed, then took a whooping breath. "Let's go!"

A brief, nasty little firefight was spilling around the courtyard of the *commandatura* as they came through the wreckage of the gates. A two-story gallery upheld by tree-trunk pillars lined the inside of the fort's square shape. The barracks were on the other side where the tower had its base, the angry red eyes of muzzle flashes winking out from under the overhang that made its roof. A Tartessian on the fighting platform that topped the second story aimed a rifle at her; she fired, three quick shots with the pistol. It wasn't her choice of weapon—she'd been good enough to requalify as necessary, before the Event, no more—but since then she'd practiced rigorously. The third shot hit him, and Swindapa took down the man behind, and they both emptied their pistols to drive the ones remaining to cover. The enemy in the barracks were shooting, too, and the Marines were returning fire from behind the wooden posts. Marian put her shoulder behind one, felt the wood give a solid quiver as a bullet hammered into the other side, risked a look behind. Swindapa coiled ready without a trace of tension, the Coast Guard Intelligence specialist who accompanied them clutching his pistol in both hands. He was a weedy little man with glasses who'd been a clerk in a house trading with Tartessos before the war and a designer of computer war games before the Event.

Hope he doesn't manage to shoot me in the back by accident, she thought.

At the next pillar a Marine fired his Werder, then ducked back, thumbed a fresh round from his bandolier down the grooved ramp of the block and into the breech, thumbed back the cocking lever in its semicircular groove, leaned around the pillar, and fired again. There was less black-powder smoke than in an ordinary firefight, with the fine drizzle washing it out of the air.

"Covering fire!" Alston called to the Marine officer. "We've got to get to that tower room before someone destroys their files."

"Hell with that!" he called back. "You need the barracks *suppressed* to get across the courtyard, ma'am." Louder: "Everyone, load a tit." That meant filling the strip of six loops on the left breast of the uniforms. Hands transferred shells. "Everyone ready . . . rapid fire, independent . . . *fire!*"

The Werders cracked faster, mad-minute speed; trained shooters could manage a round every three seconds this way, and aim them, too. Spurts of damp adobe pocked out all around the windows in the barracks opposite as the bullets struck. More shots were going *through* the windows, and the enemy fire died down as Tartessians ducked. A pair of Marines dashed around the perimeter of the courtyard as their squadmates fired, threw themselves flat, leopard-crawled the last few yards. Grenades flew out of their hands, through the windows. Seconds later fire and shattered sun-dried brick gouted back out and the Marines all charged forward. All but the squad assigned to her.

"This way!" she shouted, drew the *katana,* and went out across the courtyard's wet stone pavement, cutting diagonally toward the rear.

Granite rutched under her boots, flickering liquidly in the

flashes of light; her sword gleamed as well. A quick glance aside showed her Swindapa's face; the same high-cheeked oval as always, but unrecongnizable with the blue eyes in a wide fixed glare and teeth bared.

Nearly to the stairs, a spiral of wooden planks around a post inside the ten-foot square of the tower's base. Men bursting out of a side door, out into the wet, *probably trying to get away out the front gate*. No time, and two had leveled their rifles at her from only five yards distance.

A shot cracked, the bullet whining dangerously off stone near her feet. The other ended in a damp fizzle as the hammer cracked the frizzen back and sparks showered into damp priming powder. The man came on without missing a beat, lunging behind the bayonet. Half a lifetime of relentless drill and the experience of far too many real post-Event encounters snapped Marian's *katana* from *jodan* up into a sweeping parry. Steel banged on wood, and the bayonet went up over her right shoulder; her left punched into the Tartessian's chest, knocking him back on his heels. Her wrists turned, hands sliding on the long hilt in small, swift, precise movements. The superb *shihozume*-forged blade swung back until the point nearly touched her left buttock, then forward with the falling stamp of her right foot. The sword flashed through an arc, all the whipping strength of arms and shoulders and gut, hips and thighs behind it.

Tense the wrists just before impact, thumping strike of sharp metal into meat and bone, rip the cut through and across, and follow through until the blade is parallel to the ground.

"*Disssaaaaa!*" she shrieked.

What had been a man flopped at her feet, neck half-severed and a great diagonal slash opening the front of his body, letting the pink-purple intenstines fall free in a sharp stink of acid stomach juices and half-digested food. The Tartessian behind saw her face clearly through some freak of sight, screamed, and threw away his weapon, turned and ran facefirst into the wall and then cowered, dazed, with his arms wrapped around his head.

Well, I guess there is *some use to this "living legend" shit, then,* she thought bleakly, vaulting over the prostrate form of the one she'd killed. Four more enemy soldiers tumbled backward through the entranceway of the tower and slammed the door behind them.

Marian and Swindapa plastered themselves to either side of the tower entrance for a brief second. Marian looked across the doorway into her partner's face; they were both panting with the exertion of close combat.

She gasped air back into her lungs, forced the quivering out of hands and arms and shoulders, then caught the eye of the Marine squad's noncom, jerked a thumb at the door to the stairwell, and raised three fingers for an instant.

Aloud, to Swindapa: "If I'm the supreme commander, why do I always end up drawing point duty in an assault commando?"

"Maybe you're punishing yourself," Swindapa replied, her teeth showing in a brief grin. "What's the word, guilt? Next time, remember you're punishing *me*, too, and I wasn't raised to do this guilt thing. It's even stupider than monogamy and a lot less fun!"

"One . . ."

"Two . . ."

"*Three!*" they shouted together.

Baaaamm. Six rifles blasted holes through the pine planks, knocking splintered holes. Two rounds came back through the boards . . . probably all the reloading the enemy had had time to do. The two women hit the door with their shoulders and burst into the room. Marian ducked and flicked her blade to the left as a rifle butt went by. It brushed across the inch-long wool on the back of her head; she pivoted and cut horizontally, uncoiling like a twisted spring. A spray of blood followed the steel as it ripped across the soldier's belly, swept upward into *chodan,* snapped down in the pear-splitter. There was a thump of steel in wood as the next man blocked the cut with the stock of his rifle. Marian snap-kicked him in the groin, rammed her knee up to meet his descending face, jerked the sword free, and lunged over his back in a two-handed thrust as he crawled away. . . .

It was too dark, cramped, chaotic for the Marines behind them to fire. For the space of twenty seconds the room was full of the deadly whirling flicker of their swords, clash and clang and clatter of metal on metal and on wood, the shrieking of *kia*-calls and the shocked screams of pain beyond what human flesh could imagine. Parry and strike by instinct and reflex with nothing clearly seen and wounded men writhing on the ground beneath . . .

Then the last Tartessians were backing up the stairs; Marian and Swindapa pressed them hard, lest they have time to reload or think up some other devilment. Bayonets stabbed down, swords licked out as the enemy climbed backward. Crash and clang . . . At last the stair came to a landing.

"Down!" someone shouted behind them.

They dropped forward, driving their opponents that last step back with thrusts at their feet. A wobbling cast-iron egg flew over their heads, rebounded off the outer wall, dropped behind the green-clad soldiers. Marian could distinctly hear the *ckkkk-ching!* as the spoon flew free of the grenade and clattered away. *Badammpp*, and a wash of heat in the damp still air of the stairwell. Up again, over the bodies—ignore them, the sight will come back too soon whether you want to remember or not, the way blood spattered in fans and arcs across the white-washed earth-brick walls, the reflex quivering of a heel beating a tattoo on the floor—and through the door. The top of the tower was a suite, a bedroom below and an office above. The bedroom was empty, but they went up the stairs cautiously. The office above was still brightly lit by a kerosene lamp.

"Oh, *hell*," Marian said.

They'd killed the Tartessian commandant with their game-rifle barrage, all right; the massive bullet had taken the top right off his head and he lay with a sprinkle of glittering shattered glass dusted over the wetness. The woman draped over him didn't look much better; the exit wound in her back was big enough to hold paired fists.

Well, the gun was *designed for elephant and buffalo,* she thought with angry resignation, as automatic reflex drew a cloth out of her belt and ran the sword through it.

It wasn't that Marian Alston-Kurlelo objected to killing women, specifically. *I scarcely could, being one myself.* What she hated was noncombatants getting injured, and the Tartessian woman obviously was no warrior. Not least because of the baby lying on the floor by the desk, still swaddled in cloth as was the custom here, screaming angrily, its face and wrappings spattered with its parents' blood and bits of their lung and brain and bone.

Cost of doing business, she thought. *Which is why I hate this business. Leave out the waste, filth, misery, wounds, pain, and death, and war would be a glorious thing.*

Swindapa snapped her sword aside with a wrist movement that flicked off excess blood, cleaned and sheathed the steel over her shoulder in a single fluid motion, and went to one knee beside the child.

"A boy," she said after an instant, an infinite tenderness in her tone. "Not hurt, just needs changing."

That's a relief, Alston thought, her shoulders relaxing. *Do Jesus, I've got enough on my conscience.*

The Intelligence specialist had fallen on the desk and filing cabinets, eyes gleaming behind his spectacles; he looked like a rabbit on pure crystal meths, giving little mewing cries of astonishment as he worked. First he stuffed his satchel full, and then he dragged Marines over by their webbing harness, cramming more files into their knapsacks.

He was literally wringing his hands when they were full; this time he reminded her of a big dog she'd seen at a barbeque once, its stomach distended like a ball and a pile of bones under its front paws. It had looked at them mournfully, moaning, longing to eat and unable to find space for another bite. . . .

She went to the window. The firing in the streets was picking up; a glance at her watch. . . . *Do Jesus, only fifteen minutes?* But at some point the Tartessians were going to get organized, even with their commander dead.

"Ortiz!" she said into the handset, and looking down toward the dockside. There were buildings burning now, and the light grew by the minute. "Report."

"Ma'am, the barges're moored with a thick chain running around the outermost train and linked to iron bollards but—"

Crack! A flash of red fire and a cheer she could hear clearly even hundreds of yards away.

"—but that's got it!" She could hear him turn his head, the voice fading a bit as he yelled: "Lay aloft there, get those sails sheeted home—Johnstone to the tiller!"

"Carry on." A switch of frequencies; Lord Jesus, but they were going to miss these things when they wore out! The post-Event equivalents were barely man-transportable, and ludicrously unreliable. "Major Stavrand."

"On schedule, ma'am! Target-rich environment here. I feel like a kid in Sweet Inspirations with a sack of gold!"

"Get it done, Mr. Stavrand," she said. "Soon."

The artillery officer liked blowing things up, which was why he doubled as a demolitions expert. He was also very good at it. *And he grew up after the Event—otherwise he'd have said "a credit card."* So the twentieth century vanished, bit by bit.

She began to turn, then staggered and threw up her hand as the tower quaked beneath her and adobe dust smoked out of the walls. One of the squat mud-brick warehouses vanished in a gout of flame and pillar of smoke, and wreckage came pattering out of the sky for a thousand yards in every direction. Much of it was burning, and no doubt it would set more fires despite the rain.

Well, Stavrand took me at my word, she thought, blinking

and shaking her head. Just then the pontoon bridge lit up, a *poca-poca-poca-poca* of small explosions sending sheets of poor man's napalm—benzene and kerosene with soap flakes—in every direction; the wood was damp and green but it caught at once, and sent a wall of flame and black smoke up across the river. Squads were moving among the piles of cargo on the wharves, sloshing kerosene about and setting yet more fires; once they danced back yelling from a pile of barrels that turned out to be full olive oil. *That* poured like a sluggish river of red lava down the streets as it burned. . . .

"Go, go, go!" Marian said to the others. The Marines went, and the Intelligence officer stumbled in their wake.

Swindapa had the baby on the desk, efficiently rewrapping it in a shawl and a section of tapestry. Without looking up she spoke:

"Before you ask what I'm doing, I'm saving the baby."

" 'Dapa . . . we just killed his parents . . ."

"Yes, and we're going to blow this place up in a minute," she said. "That just means he needs someone to look after him, doesn't he?" She jerked her tight-braided blond head at the window, and the *Walpurgisnacht* of explosions and fire and cold rain outside. "And we can't leave him in *that*, either, can we?"

"When you put it that way . . ." Marian sighed. She flicked the cylinder of her Python open, spilled the spent brass and reloaded. "Let's go."

Down the stairs, past the combat engineers setting the demolition charges and backing away, unreeling fuse from a spool they held between them. Out into the rain, Swindapa loping beside her with the squalling infant in the crook of her left arm and her pistol in her right hand. Chaos on the docks, towering pyramids of flame with scraps of tarpaulin floating up into the rainy smoke cutting the visibility even beyond what nature occluded. The bitter stink of things not meant to burn choked her until she coughed. She blinked watering eyes, wiped the back of her hand across them; the barge-trains were pulling away from the dock, the wind was light but in the proper direction, and they were operating *with* the current, thank God. Troops were pouring back to the wharf and over the retaining wall into boats and barges; some came laughing, smoke smut on their faces, alight with the thoughtless pleasures of destruction. Others limped, or staggered with comrades' arms over their shoulders, or were carried on folding stretchers. Another came grinning with a butchered lamb carcass from some Tartessian pantry under one arm and a field dressing across the side of his face.

She felt her face go grimmer, thinking of the labor that had gone into making all this, pushing plows and swinging hammers and working the heddles of looms.

Not many Islanders hurt—surprisingly few, with an operation this size. She looked at her watch again. The glowing dials of the self-winding radium face showed 0230 hours. *Less than half an hour, by God*. The Tartessians were recovering, though: pretty soon they'd . . .

Schooonk. Dozens of heads whipped up at the all-too-familiar sound.

"Medium mortar," she said quietly.

There were thousands of things the Islanders knew how to do but couldn't because the materials were too hard to find, or the tools too complicated to build. On the other end of the curve were smoothbore mortars firing finned bombs; one of those simple ideas like the stirrup or the rudder that weren't thought of until long after the technology to produce them was available. The eighteenth-century level Tartessos had achieved was more than ample . . .

Shuddump!

Dimly, half-seen, a fountain of water leaped up out of the river, hung, fell in shattered spray. "All right, people, let's get out of here before they start hitting things."

They trotted on, taking reports from the officers of various units as they went; and from the noncoms who counted off the individuals—in a few cases the dog tags of bodies—as they returned, then waiting by the boat for the final word. Once again she blessed Swindapa's faultless memory; keeping exact count of everything and everybody in a battalion-sized night raid was trivial to someone who'd been through the Grand-mothers' course. They made a good team . . . although she doubted the Fiernan system would last more than another gen-eration. When you could write things down, it was just too much damned trouble to spend a decade learning to retrieve all the data yourself.

Very damned useful right now, though. Too God-damned easy for someone to get missed in this confusion and darkness.

Marian stood with her hands behind her back on the edge of the dock; Swindapa beside her, looking out over the river because that put her body between the baby and the most likely source of high-velocity metal. There was enough light from burning supply dumps and buildings to make Alston feel horribly exposed; she relaxed stomach muscles that were drawing themselves up in anticipation of a bullet or mortar shell, forced her breath to come slow and deep and shoulders to ease. One of her elbows was aching a little, fruit of overextension past . . .

She remembered a joke current in a dojo she'd attended, long before the Event—back in her late 'teens, when she was first getting seriously interested in the Way of the Empty Hand, the real *bujutsu* variety and not the de-rated sport schools that were mostly safe:

"By the time I'm forty, I'll be the most dangerous cripple in the whole wide world," she quoted softly to herself.

But I'm a little nearer fifty than forty now, and all those years of pushing the body to ten-tenths of capacity begin to take their toll. I hurt when I've got to do things like this, and experience only compensates to a certain point.

"Uh . . . ma'am?" the head of the Marine detail said.

She looked over at him; rain-streaked soot and speckled blood ran down his face with trails of sweat. Painfully young; there was something of a gap in the age profile on the Island, a good many young adults had been on the mainland at college when the Event occurred.

He did very well indeed, there at the commandatura, she thought. *Wasn't afraid to backtalk me, either. Aggressive, but not crazy.*

"Ma'am, the brigadier will keelhaul me if I don't bring you back in one piece. As a matter of fact, he told me that if I stuck him with your job, he'd be really, really upset. Would you mind stepping into the boat now, ma'am? Lieutenant Commander?"

And let me do my job, she finished for him.

"When we're through," she said aloud. "Remember Frozen Chosin. We're taking everyone back, Lieutenant."

"Yes ma'am," he said.

A few murmurs came from the darkened figures at the oars; "Hard Corps," "fuckin' A."

Did I do the right thing, to let the Marine Corps vets who started our ground-troop training program put so much emphasis on their own traditions? Probably. Almost certainly. Fighting was an emotional thing. They'd used what they knew would work because it had worked on their own younger selves. *"A rational army would run away,"* and Montinesque was right about that. Do Jesus, I surely do feel like running away. Could have been worse, though—I could have had to work with For-

eign Legion types. "You have joined the Legion to die, and now I will send you where men die." *There's a certain bracing honesty to it, but in the long run, this is better.*

A runner came panting up. "We found them, ma'am—they got pinned when a door collapsed," he said.

"That's the last," Swindapa said crisply. "All accounted for."

"Lieutenant, you get your wish," Alston said, hopping down into the boat. Swindapa handed her down the child, and she cuddled it to her as her partner swung expertly in beside her at the prow of the launch. The formless baby face looked up at Alston dubiously, still alarmed but tired of crying for his mother, and then stuck his hand in his mouth and began to gum it in a worried fashion.

"Hell of a way to come back from a raid," she grumbled to herself. "You *do* need to be changed, little'un."

Then she looked at the river as the crew began to pull away into the central current, bright-lit through the rain by the wavery blurs of huge fires on both banks. The barge-trains were ahead of her, with the raiding force's boats around them like sculling centipedes. *Safer to have burned the barges in place,* she thought. But better for morale to take them; the troops were mostly from cultures that thought "victory" and "plunder" were the same thing. It wouldn't hurt the whole expedition's logistics if there was useful stuff in them, too.

Alston put the handset to her face with her free hand: "Commander Ortiz."

"Here, ma'am. No trouble so far."

"None on this end either," Alston said. A warbling went through the sky, and a muffled *whuddump* raised a plume of shocked white water a hundred yards behind. Spray fell across her, and the baby began to cry again, a thin reedy wailing.

"Ah . . . ma'am?" Ortiz said, bewilderment in his tone at the sound. Not at all the sort of cry you expected with a rear guard on a fire-lashed shore.

"Don't ask, Commander." She cleared her throat. "They're lobbing mortar shells into the river, but they're firing blind. I doubt they'll get any observers forward before we're out of range."

"Now all we have to do is run the guns of the fort, ma'am," Ortiz said, cheerfully deadpan.

Kenneth Hollard listened and swore. *God-damn fighting in a snowstorm. Hell of a way to spend the week before Christmas.* Something was going wrong out here on the northern flank of the allied host. The firing was still heavy, but it was dying down, which meant that the Achaeans were pushing through the narrow defile and around the edge of his command.

The snow, however, *wasn't* dying down, and he strained his eyes through it and cursed, and cursed the falling light.

But I shouldn't, he thought. *We've held them most of the day. If we can hold them until night, they'll feel it more, out in the open.*

The horse beneath him stumbled again, on a rock that turned beneath its hoof under the concealing white. He reined in and swung out of the saddle. The thunder ahead was louder than that to the south now; fewer cannon, but closer, and echoing back from the sharp cliff faces and steep rocky slopes.

"O'Rourke!" he shouted.

"Sir?"

"Officers on foot, except for couriers," he said. "Chargers to the gun carriages as spares. And the troops to the double-quick."

"Sir," the other man said, looking back at the column.

It was only thirty feet away, but still a dark indistinct mass through snow and shadow, stumbling forward into the wind with helmets bent to take the bite. The thudding clatter of boots and hooves on stone and wet earth came muffled, as if they watched an army of ghosts condemned to march forever.

"Sir," O'Rourke went on. "They're tired. We pulled them right out of the line for this. Another mile and at the double, and they won't have much left."

Robbing Peter to pay Paul and calling it a reserve, Ken agreed, behind the mask of his face.

"If we don't get there in time, there won't be anything at all left," he said. "That's the choke point. Anywhere else and they can flank us and get by."

"Sir," O'Rourke said, grinning despite the crusted snow on his eyebrows. Individual hairs peeked out, like fire through cloud. "Since you put it that way—"

Hollard walked over to the head of the column; it wound back into the rocky hills, broken here and there by the higher shape of a gun team pulling cannon or Gatlings.

"All right," he roared, and the front ten rows looked up. Hollard drew his sword; they were good for dramatic gestures, at least. "Up ahead, the Mitannians are dying to block this pass. Back there, the rest of the Corps is going to get buggered good and fair if the enemy get through. At the double—follow me!"

He turned with the standard-bearer beside him and strode forward. Behind him the whole force stumbled into a trot.

Whole force, he thought. *Four hundred rifles and half a dozen heavy weapons. About all we've got left that isn't hanging on by its teeth.*

He recognized most of the sounds ahead; the crackle of rifles, the sound of the multibarrel quick-firers the Achaeans used because Walker couldn't duplicate Gatlings yet, and the bark of cannon. Rifled three-and-a-half-inch jobs by the sound of it, standard enemy weapons. What he couldn't hear anymore was the thump of mortars, or the *braaaaap* of the Gatlings. Damn, damn . . .

Closer . . . Dense snow was certainly the thing if you wanted to surprise somebody; it hid sounds as well as blinding sight.

"Deploy into line," he said. "Heavy weapons forward as best they can—and be goddamned careful, I don't want any friendly-fire accidents here."

"Sir!"

O'Rourke gave orders; the thick column of marching Islanders dissolved, Marines running out to either side. Steel glinted bright gray through the soft dove-gray-white of the snow as bayonets rattled home, and multiple *click-clacks* sounded as the rifles were loaded. The heavy weapons deployed as well, as best they could, scattered among the infantry wherever the ground looked level enough for hooves and wheels to go forward. He had more confidence in the rocket launchers; this terrain was scattered with little gulleys and washes that would stop a cannon cold.

He drew a deep breath of air cold and damp and full of the scent of wet wool and unwashed soldier and gun oil and powder. Light flickered through the snow ahead . . . muzzle flashes.

"Charge!" he shouted, and ran forward.

Otto Verger came to full alertness when the sounds began to the northward, upriver. Very faint at first, a crackling of small arms. Then several huge soft *thuds,* like very large doors slamming shut. He turned his head, raised it slightly, strained his eyes to see through the murky dimness.

Was that a hint of fire, the red war-hawks of the *mirutha* beating their wings on a Tartessian foeman's thatch? He could hear a whispered chant from his left; it raised his hackles a little, for Rueteklo was invoking Moon Woman—or Her sister of the Barrow, who he suspected was the same as the Blood Hag of Battles. You *didn't* want to attract Her attention, and the Moon goddess was an unchancy thing . . . though to be sure, she'd be on his side this time, and wasn't that an odd happenstance? The noise from the north grew louder, and there was definitely a hint of light there . . .

"Oh, you sorry bastards are *fucked* the now," he chuckled again. "The Midnight Mare will leave hoofprints on your grave-mounds—not that you'll get graves, you'll rot unresting, your ghosts wailing in the wind . . ."

"Why don't I report you for using something else but English on duty?" Rueteklo said, equally soft, a chuckle in her voice as well.

"Oh, shut up and get ready," Verger said, switching to that language with a trace of resentment. She spoke it with less accent than he, for all his studying until he thought his head would crack.

"I wasn't talking, I was cursing the foe," he went on. It was a breach of regulations to talk anything but the Islander tongue when you were working—a fine of four days' pay and four days' KP. Most of the time he even thought in English, but it just wasn't as *satisfying* for some things, like threatening or cursing. "I'll want, mmmm, one more incendiary after the first. Then HE and frag."

"You ask, I deliver."

Gathering tension, silence save for an occasional buzz of insects—thank the Gods it wasn't summer, or they'd be eaten alive. He could feel the spirits of his fathers and their fathers gathering around him, to witness his honor or his shame; his oath-brothers were here, too, and they would see.

His training whispered at the back of his mind, cooling him. It had a voice very much like Gunnery Sergeant Timothy Welder's savage rasp: *Any dumb shit can get dead in a hurry! You're not waving a fucking brass tomahawk now, horse-boy. We don't go off half-cocked in the Corps. By the numbers, on the bounce . . .*

The light around the gunports of the fort had faded as the night grew old. The briefings had warned that Tartessians sometimes slept in the afternoon and worked late, but even these had gone to bed by now. Then a bugle blew; not any notes he recognized, but from the voices and shouts the foemen had gotten the word about their camp upstream. Their burning, devastated, plundered camp. Now the whole force would be passing back this way, and they'd need him and his brothers of the war band to shield them against a blow that could kill— him and A Company, the finest unit in the Third Marines, who were the finest warriors in the Corps—nobody outside the

Corps even counted for comparison's sake, as these Tartessian swine would find out soon enough.

He forced the quivering eagerness out of his muscles and lay in the muck, eyes pinned to the gunport. Light flared brighter around it, then faded—they were getting ready to open the port, screens rigged behind it to preserve the gunner's night sight and to stop stray sparks that might fall among ammunition.

"Just about—"

Whistles sounded in the swamp to his rear at the same instant as the rumbling squeal of iron and timber on stone. The gunports flipped up, and the long muzzles of the cannon came out.

". . . *now!*"

Behind him poles had been fitted together and supporting stakes driven deep into the muck. Now strong hands pushed and pulled the poles upright and lashed them swiftly to the frames that would hold them so. Atop each was a magnesium flare ready to burn, and a hemisphere of focusing mirror right behind it. Cords pulled, primers went *pop*, and the light speared out hell-bright across the row of gunports in the low squat bulk of the fortress wall ahead of them, painting every detail in stark relief and blinding the gunners as if they stared into the naked sun. Eyes slitted, squinting at the ground for a second to let them adjust, Otto Verger laughed aloud.

Then he pushed himself up to his knees, wide-spraddled to keep him stable. "Clear!" he shouted. The crosshairs in the sight dropped over the dark square where the cannon's muzzle showed. He squeezed the trigger, heard and felt the catch release and the striker drive down on the percussion cap. Flame spurted into the hollow core of the rocket's propellant rod, and flame spurted to the rear out the venturi . . .

"*Eat this!*" he screamed, under the *SSSSSRAAAAWACK!*

For some things, English *was* satisfying.

A dozen rockets vomited out of the wrack of brush and felled timber at the edge of the swamp. Despite the damp, reeds caught and burned behind him. He ignored them, and the harsher stink of rocket smoke. His rocket lanced out, rose, descended in a graceful arc. *There!* It struck the corner of the gunport and exploded, fire belching back out into the night, paled by the light of the flares. And doubtless belching in, washing in a cataract of fire over the wedge-shaped gun position and the men serving the cannon, leaving them wailing and dancing in the agony of burning hair and flesh. Rushing back to spread chaos and terror in the gallery behind the guns . . .

"*Feed me!*" he screamed, exultant.

"Up, up!"

"Clear!"

SSSSSRAAAAAWACK!

The second rocket followed the first to his target. He ignored the others that were lancing through the air, some through the gunports, others slamming into the wall and blasting craters or dribbling fire down it. Several of the massive guns fired, but they were unaimed, mere bellows of agony like a stricken aurochs when it plunged into a deadfall or met a line of sharp spears. Behind him came a rapid *schoonk . . . schoonk . . . schoonk* as mortars lofted shells into the courtyards of the fortress, keeping heads down there, keeping the Tartessians away from their own high-angle weapons. It was an attack that could never have succeeded in daylight, or if the enemy had had any inkling of what was being prepared for them. . . .

Another explosion, this one racking back around the barrel of the cannon. The ammunition stacked ready behind it gang-fired, throwing it forward to crash against the stone and iron of the embrasure and point harmlessly down. *Like a limp dick*, Verger thought triumphantly.

"Feed me!"

"Up!"

"Clear!"

One more cat-scream of victory from the rocket launcher, and he smashed at another gunport that might threaten his sworn brothers and chief.

"Frag round! Feed me!"

"Up!"

"Clear!"

Higher this time, at the crenellations atop the wall, where the enemy were getting riflemen into position. Their fire was wild, but it was a threat. He worked his way down it, smashing stone and men with fire and splinters of iron and granite. Body and mind and skill worked together, taking him out of himself as nothing had before, a sweetness of will and intent and action, knowing that he did better than his instructors could ever have dreamed.

"Feed me!"

"We're dry—let's get out of here, Otto. Otto, there's the recall—let's *go*."

He stood, ignoring the waves of heat from the tube of the launcher scorching his hands where they rested on the grips. He would bear it with him, and someday he would put this rocket launcher in a niche and pour out sacrifice before it as the patron spirit of the kindred he would found! He howled, ignoring everything but the wave of exultation that ran through him at the burning, blasting destruction ahead. Wonderful, wonderful destruction. This was what it felt like to be a *God*!

Sound burst from his lips, the old war yell: *"Ukasha-sa-sa-hau-hau-hau-hau!"*

"You crazy ax-kisser, there's the recall! They'll have your guts for garters!"

That cut through the red mist before his eyes. He shuddered all over as he might in the embrace of a woman and turned, heading back toward the rubber boats.

Then he was lying on his side, spitting out swampwater. He shook his head—where had his helmet gone? He tried to stand and fell over with a grunt, clamping his teeth on the scream that tried to force its way out of his mouth. The blaze of pain was hard to locate at first; one hand went reflexively to his crotch, found everything in order, traveled down his right thigh and hesitated at the ripped wetness. Light faded as the flares burned out. He made himself look. No bone ends, but something grated with near-unendurable agony as he clamped hands around the wound; the bone must be broken. Blood was flowing, but not spurting or pumping; he fumbled out a field dressing, hissed again as the antiseptic powder struck the savaged flesh, then fastened it on and tied the ends. The effort of that had him panting again.

Verger shook his head again and looked around. A crater filling with water not far away, light mortar shell probably. Rueteklo had gotten up; she still had her helmet on, but there was blood on the side of her face, and her right arm hung limp.

"C'mon," she muttered, pulling at him.

He climbed up her by the webbing, ignoring a small shriek as he jostled the limp arm. She dragged his arm across her shoulders with her good one, and they began to hobble forward. The way was muddy and dark, water rising around their calves, continually jostling his injured limb. Bullets went through the air around them with whickering cracks. His face was jammed next to Rueteklo's, her teeth showing in a huge grin of effort, tears running down through the burned cork on her face. At last the reeds stopped them, and they toppled. He blacked out again for an instant then, came to lying on his back with her fingers trying to get the carrying strap of the rocket launcher out from under the epaulet strap of his jacket.

"No," he grunted. "Comes along. *Ai!*"

That as she turned on her back and wound her good hand in

the back loop of his webbing harness, pushing them both along with her heels. Verger forced himself to push as well with his sound leg, hoping that they weren't going around in circles as the marsh grew more liquid under his back, and his heel started to slip on the slick mud-coated surface of the crushed reeds.

"Your belt . . . buckle's cutting my ear," he rasped after a moment. Something went overhead with a flat *whack* sound.

"Shut . . . *unnnh* . . . up," Rueteklo said, hitching him forward with her arm, digging in her heels and arching herself to push them further toward the river. "You've been . . . *unnnh* . . . trying to get . . . *unnnh* . . . between my legs . . . *unnnh* . . . since Camp Grant . . . *unnnh* . . . now you're there . . . *unnnh* . . . and you're still bitching."

Verger felt a bubble of laughter grunt out through his throat. It wasn't quite a warrior's laughing scorn for death . . . but it was close enough to be satisfying, despite the nausea that was twisting at his gut. Then he sensed the presence of someone else and grabbed for the bayonet on his belt; there were three dark figures—

"Calm down, Marine," a voice said—Ritter's voice. "Time for extraction."

Hard hands gripped his harness and lifted; something pricked him in one buttock, and a flood of relief went over him as the pain receded like a wave of fire rolling back from a beach. The last of the flares was burning down, but he could see Ritter stooping, taking Rueteklo over her shoulders in a fireman's lift. The man carrying him turned, and he got a twisting panoramic view of the marsh, a few fires lit by backblast still smoking-red among the reeds. Then the fortress, flames licking upward from gunports and slit windows, with a crackle of small-arms fire from the parapet despite it all. Then lines of red stabbed out from the river—the Gatlings mounted on pivots above the paddle boxes of a gunboat, the *thudump* of the light cannon on its forward deck, a red spark soaring skyward from the mortar on its stern.

Into the inflated boat again, his rocket launcher on one side, Rueteklo on the other; the rest of their squad pushing hard until they reached the few inches of water necessary to float it, then piling in and wielding their paddles.

"Thanks . . . oath-sister," he said slowly, feeling himself floating away.

"Semper Fi."

CHAPTER TWENTY-FIVE

December, 10 A.E.—West-central Anatolia
November, 10 A.E.—Great River, southern Iberia
December, 10 A.E.—West-central Anatolia

"*Charge!*" Kenneth Hollard shouted.

The bugle screamed and Marines threw themselves forward through the snow, slipping and stumbling on the muddy rocks below, still somehow keeping their order. From a height a little behind him a Gatling crew got their weapon into operation, its muzzles a continuous red flicker through the snow. Seconds later the line halted for an instant and fired point-blank into the confused mass of enemy infantry milling around the base of the hill, throwing grenades and firing rocket launchers point-blank as well; there were hundreds of them . . .

Maybe thousands, he thought.

And hundreds of their dead piled around their feet already, before the relief force arrived. They wavered; he could see the collective shudder as they tried to turn and face the new threat, saw the gray exhaustion and fear on those nearest.

"Pour it on!" he heard O'Rourke shout, and his subordinates echoing it. "Pour it on, and they'll break!"

The Islanders pushed forward, advancing by squads, throwing themselves down and firing to support their comrades moving forward. Soon the forward units were close enough to throw grenades as well, and a cannon came forward at a run with a dozen men pushing at the trail. They let it fall with a thump and jumped out of the way as the gunner jerked the lanyard. The weapon bucked back, muzzle spitting out a huge blade-shaped lance of flame. Canister whined forward, hundreds of lead balls tearing into the enemy at point-blank range.

"Sound *charge* again!" Hollard called.

The bugles cried, like the distant horns of Elfland through the blizzard. The Marines rose up like a wave out of the earth and flung themselves forward, and the enemy were running—

not retreating, running, some of them throwing away their rifles to run faster; falling, too, shot in the back or spitted with the bayonet.

Hollard ran forward with the rest. A clump of Achaean soldiers rose up in front of him, trying to buy some space for their comrades. *Crack*, and he felt the hot wind of the muzzle blast on his cheek. He fired the revolver six times and took down two men, dim figures spinning backward into the snow and rolling away down the steep ground. He had just time to slap the Python back into its holster before another was lunging at him. His *katana* slapped the weapon aside and then they were chest to chest. Hollard butted his helmet forward into the other's face, felt bone crumble, brought the sword down from its position over his left shoulder in a blurring slash, ran on over the twitching body.

The Nantucketers swept on over the crest of the hill, shooting and stabbing.

"Sound *halt*," Hollard gasped—the rest of the rocky passage ahead was a blinding whirl of snow. The guns began throwing shells into it. That and the Gatlings firing ahead ought to keep the enemy running. He couldn't send troops into that and keep any control at all.

The Mitannian flag still flew, the staff forlorn and crooked at the summit of the hill. Kenneth Hollard walked in that direction, controlling the pumping heave of his chest. Stretcher-bearers were bringing back wounded and dead; out of the corner of his eye he saw one Marine with her hand wadded in a sodden ball of fabric walking beside a figure with its poncho spread over its face.

"You great shambling Fiernan gowk," he heard her mumble, half grief and half anger. "You went and got yourself *killed*."

Then he was at the summit, amid the ruins of foxholes and the craters of a rocket bombardment—they were almost close enough to step from one to the next. The surviving Mitannians were laying out their dead as well—that looked to be half of them at least. The survivors had the stunned, distant look of men who've gone to the limit of endurance and a little beyond. One of them he recognized, Tekhip-tilla, Raupasha's second-in-command. He was kneeling beside a pile of blankets. Kenneth Hollard swallowed and closed his eyes for an instant. Then he saw that the man was holding a mittened hand between his. Sabala lay plastered to the side of her body, whining and giving the warmth that was the only gift he could.

"She lives?" Hollard said.

Tekhip-tilla looked up at him, tears freezing on his cheeks. "She lives—if you can call it that, Great General," he spat. "But I do not think she will live for long. And would she wish to, like this?"

Hollard looked down at the glistening mass of blood across the side of Raupasha's face, and swallowed again.

"Corpsman!" he called sharply. "Corpsman here."

The stretcher-bearers came at the run. Tekhip-tilla made as if to accompany them.

"No," Hollard said, barring his way with the blade of his *katana*. "You can do nothing there."

"I can be by my ruler's side!"

"You can continue the work she was hurt to do," he said sharply. "Or will you leave your countrymen in wreck? Get your men together—help us see to the wounded—everything to your chariots and pull back to base."

Tekhip-tilla nodded once, with the look of a man biting down on an upalatable truth, then stalked away and began to shout orders, shaking stunned men by the shoulder and getting them moving.

Kenneth Hollard slammed his gloved fist against his thigh. "Damn," he said. Then: "God *damn* it!"

A long breath, and he called for his radio tech. The connection was bad, but he could make out his sister's voice through the popping and static.

"Sir, the line's cracking like river ice in spring. I just put in the last of Tudhaliyas's men, and that's *it*. If they hadn't run out of rockets for their katyushas we'd be running like hell right now. The next major push is going to punch right through."

"Right," Hollard said.

He put the fingers of his right hand to his brow, squeezing the cold-numbed flesh as if he could drive answers through the bone by main force.

"Right," he went on. "The right flank's secure, I think— they're not going to put anything through here without fresh troops and with extreme caution."

"Thank God for that," Kathryn said. "We couldn't even disengage with that hanging over us. How's Raupasha?"

"Not good—bad wound," Hollard said, forcing his voice to flatness.

"Oh, *shit*. All right, sir, what are we going to do?"

"What else?" Kenneth said. "Pull back. Right to the Halys and over, if we can make it. Start right away and we'll be able to salvage something; I'll get there as fast as I can."

*   *   *

"I do not stay with a plan that is a failure," Isketerol of Tartessos snapped. "But first I must *know*. Fool, have I ever punished the bearer of bad news? Speak!"

The officer gulped, drew himself straight, then threw off a salute of fist to chest. It would have looked more impressive if he hadn't been such a drowned, scorched rat himself. The winter dawn was bright but chill; Isketerol drew his cloak around him, glad of the new-style trousers that were so much less drafty than a tunic alone, and of the warmth of his horse.

"Lord King, we lost two hundred and twenty dead—mostly in fighting the fires, and from the explosions. We do not know how many the enemy suffered, they took their wounded and dead with them."

Isketerol nodded. *Even a few years ago, he would have boasted of hundreds slain,* he thought. *And by the next seven-day, he would believe the tales himself.* That had been a difficult thing to teach, first himself and then others, the absolute importance of *accuracy*, as it was called in English. It had been easier for him because he was a merchant, used to dealing in precise quantities, so-and-so many ingots of fixed weight, interest at such-and-such a rate per year. Even better that he'd been a merchant used to foreign adventuring, where a lapse in knowledge could mean death.

He looked beyond the man who stood at his stirrup. The town of *Kurutselcaryaduwara-biden* lay in a haze of bitter smoke, tumbled blackened walls whose adobe had been half fired to baked brick, charred rafters still smoldering. Soldiers, civilians and slaves were already at work clearing rubble out of the streets, but it would be a work of months—years—to replace all that had been lost. *I should have taken more precautions,* he thought bitterly. There had been so much else to do, so many other things clamoring for attention. . . . *Now I must, though the ox is already through the broken gate and his grazing has laid waste the grain.*

Perhaps that was what the *Amurrukan* word *staff* really meant, someone to think of things the supreme commander had no time for. If that was so, it was knowledge bitter in its uselessness. There were too few who could understand the thought; he barely did himself. *I have not the time,* he thought angrily. A thousand lifetimes would not be enough.

"Do you have numbers?"

"Lord King, all the ammunition stores were lost. Over a million and a half rounds of small-arms cartridges, and—"

Isketerol forced himself not to wince as the totals were added up. Every soldier had a hundred rounds in his cartridge box and knapsack; that meant eight hundred thousand rounds with the army he had assembled, as many again with the forward bases and supply wagons—and they could shoot that off in a day or two of real fighting. Beyond that were the cannon rounds lost, and the rockets. He would have to restrict practice until more could be brought forward from the armories of Tartessos City, and that would hurt the effectiveness of the farmer-reservists he'd called up. Eventually even regulars lost skill if they could not take their rifles to the firing range. The better part of a year's output had been lost, and so he had no choice.

The officer went on, listing flints and priming powder, metal parts warped into uselessness, grain, oil, biscuit, salt fish, dried or barreled meat, preserved vegetables, uniforms and shoes, cloth and hides, rope, fodder . . . Worst of all was the wrecked engines of the base machine shop, precious lathes and boring machines.

No, even worse was the loss of trained men. At least they were not the tool and die makers—those are more than worth their weight in gold.

"We can sift the ashes for metal," Isketerol said. "See to it—particularly the lead. We'll need storage for fresh supplies brought up from the city, or downriver. Get the less damaged buildings repaired . . ."

The man hesitated again, closed his eyes for a second, then went on: "Lord King, there is also the matter of your youngest brother Prince Gergenzol . . ."

Isketerol swallowed past a thick grief, his face a mask of cold determination. *I knew he must have been struck down, or he would have been here to meet me.* Just come to a man's full years, and the command of this town had been the first great task the King had entrusted to him.

"Lord King, we have not found the body. The commander's fort was utterly destroyed; with blasting charges, I think, as well as fire. There were many bodies, but few could be identified and many were . . . fragments. No trace of his wife or son was found."

The Iberian monarch took a long deep breath, fist clenching on the pommel of his saddle. His aides and war-captains looked on anxiously; there were few ties stronger than that between uncle and nephew, for their people.

"My brother Gergenzol fell in battle," Isketerol said harshly.

"That is a fitting end for a man. And the Crone comes for us all, soon or late."

He looked about. His cousin Miskelefol waited; a sound man, if not one whose wit flashed like a sword blade.

"Lord Miskelefol," he said. "You will assume command here. We will withdraw the army to cover this area."

"Lord King—" one of his war-captains said, a grizzled man who'd been helmsman on the *Foam Treader* before the Eagle People came. "That means opening the valley of the *Tasweldan Errigu-abiden* to raids at least, and perhaps to invasion."

Isketerol nodded. "True enough, Derentersal," he said.

And perhaps even the wild highlanders will raise their heads again, he thought. To free the rich river country of the age-old terror of mountaineer raids had been the first and hardest of his works, and the means by which he had won the loyalty of the valley folk. Laying the mountains under law and tapping their treasures had been nigh as hard.

"Better to lose ground than to lose the army; that would mean the loss of the kingdom," he said.

Derentersal shook his head. "I don't see how they did it, lord," he said, looking at the ruins. "Oh, I can see how they did every *bit* of it. But to put them all together, *at the right time*, in a way so that they wouldn't be wrecked if anything went wrong . . ."

"They can talk across the air," Isketerol said. *But that isn't the whole story. To move everything as if it were the fingers of a man's hand, how?*

"Let us to our work," he said at last. "This will not be a quick war, or an easy one. But we will win it."

Miskelefol spoke, his eyes on the ruins of the commander's residence: "The new things have brought us much grief."

"And much power, and wealth," Isketerol said. "More than that, we have no choice. Now that the New Learning has come into the world, those who don't learn it will quickly become as helpless savages—then victims and slaves—to those who do. And now, we work."

The war-captains nodded; they'd seen the truth of those words themselves, in the lands Tartessos had overrun, and in the fate of those conquered by Great Achaea. They also moved briskly to their tasks. The King had never punished a man for bringing bad news, or for arguing a point within reason. The fate he brought on cowards or the lazy, though . . .

*   *   *

"But my Lord King . . . they flee! We have the victory; they run from the terror of our arms!"

William Walker looked around the command tent; his face was flatly impassive, which the more experienced among them knew was a danger signal. Outside the wind was battering at the canvas with increasing force, making the kerosene lamp over the map table sway. The men here were brigade commanders, the heads of the allied forces, his own staff . . . and his son Harold, sitting quietly in a corner and taking it all in.

First bad blizzard of the winter, he thought, as the fabric flapped. *All right.* He took control of himself with an enormous effort of will.

"No, Lord Guouwaxeus," he said with a softness that grated. "They are not *fleeing.* If they were fleeing, if they were breaking up and scattering, I would pursue them with at least part of our force. But they are not. They are making a fighting retreat, with is a very different thing."

The Achaean lord was a spare man with long black hair that was thinning on top. It brought out the starved wolfish look of his face.

"Are we not to follow up our victory?" he said.

Walker felt his will clench on his mind, like the flexing of a muscle that keeps hands clamped on a ladder over an abyss.

"Lord Guouwaxeus, has it ever occurred to you that there is a difference between *going forward* and *winning*?"

By his looks, it hadn't. About half the other men around the table looked similarly bewildered.

"Guouwaxeus, how many rounds a man does your brigade have? How many days' rations here and at the forward base? How many days' fodder for the horses?"

Guouwaxeus's lean face showed uncertainty for the first time; he looked around for the military clerk assigned to him. Walker looked instead to his chief of staff, Jack Morton. Morton had his problems—mostly trying to crawl into a brandy bottle if he wasn't watched, and a taste for humping veal—but before the Event he'd been a manager at Wal-Mart, something to do with inventory control, and a supply officer in the National Guard part-time. That made the weakness for little girls more than tolerable.

"Jack?" Walker said.

"Your Majesty, thirty-two rounds, four days' rations, no fodder," Morton said crisply, standing at parade rest.

There was a faint bruise around one eye; the best way Walker had found to keep him on the wagon in the field was to simply, personally, beat the living shit out of him every once in a while when he started to forget the previous lesson.

Walker swung around to face the others. "And that's about typical," he said. "Right now, we have just enough to get this army back to its sources of supply, *if* we're careful and start now."

He ran a hand over the map. "One-third of our forces are strung out guarding our lines of supply along these miserable mud-track roads. Every mile we go forward we get weaker and *they*"—he pointed to the east, where the dull rumble of artillery marked a rearguard action—"get stronger, falling back on their bases. And everything will get worse now that the weather's consistently bad. This army is too big to live off the land in poor country even if it hadn't been stripped, and it needs continuous resupply of ammunition and spare parts to fight at all."

About half of the dozen officers grouped around the map table looked as if they were getting it. The other half, Guouwaxeus worst of all, were staring at him as if he was reciting "Jabberwocky."

Someday, he thought, *I will watch you die on a cross, Guouwaxeus, and every last one of your wellborn shit-for-brains relatives beside you. But not yet, unfortunately.* It was one thing to teach a man how to march and shoot and dig, or even how to handle a company of riflemen, and something else entirely to teach them a whole new way to *think* about conflict. *Damn, if only I'd had another five years before this war!*

"Then . . ." one of the Ringapi chieftains said, with a speculative look. "You say we are defeated, Lord King?"

Oh, somebody give me strength. "No, Lord Tautorun," Walker said. "'Moving back' is also not the same thing as 'losing.' In fact, it's perfectly possible to move forward and win all the battles, and lose the war."

Now he got a few glances of the sort you'd expect to see on a man who'd just turned a corner and come across a hyena eating a baby. Or the way a Baptist might look if he found he'd stumbled into a Wiccan orgy.

"If we pulled back to here," he said, sketching a line on the map, "we could bring up supplies as fast as we consumed them. So we'll go a little further west, to here."

He drew a line that included most of the passes up onto the plateau from the coastal lowlands along the Aegean and Sea of Marmora.

"That means we'll be able to build up stockpiles over the winter. We'll also use the time to thoroughly pacify the areas we occupy, train new recruits, build roads and bridges, and to bring forward enough transport. Then, when we move east in the spring we can deny the enemy *his* harvests"—since grain ripened in late spring and early summer there—"and be well supplied right up to the Halys and past it. Once we've taken Hattusas, the enemy will have to fall back on Kar-Duniash. That will take another year, maybe two."

He looked around. "We'll need a rear guard, of course. Lord Guouwaxeus, I think that'll be your job."

The others drew a little aside, as if the Achaean had contracted some deadly, infectious disease.

He sat brooding over the map after the rest had left; they'd pull out tomorrow. *I hope we don't have too many frostbite cases,* he thought. Transport and shelter were very short.

Harold came up beside him. "They should not dare to oppose you, Father," he said hotly. "They are little men, without understanding."

Walker chuckled and ruffled the boy's blond mop. "Yeah," he said. "Most of the time. There are reasons to listen to them, though. First one is it makes them feel better if they think I take them seriously."

Harold scowled and clenched a small fist. "They should fear you!"

"Oh, they do. But an actively terrified man doesn't make much of a general—for that matter, if he's easy to terrify, he won't make much of a general either. Capisce?"

The boy nodded slowly. "I see, Father. They must be brave men to serve you in war?"

"Yeah, more or less. And self-confident. I can't be there to look over their shoulders all the time. Plus . . . would you like to hear a story?"

Harold perched on a chair, eyes bright; he was dressed in a smaller version of his father's black fur-and-leathers and looked comfortable in them despite the bitter cold outside the thin canvas.

"Yes!" he said.

"Okay, this happened in a land far, far to the east—China." Harold nodded; his geography lessons had taken that in. "Well, in this empire of China there was a mighty emperor, who'd put down all his neighbors and made himself ruler of all the civilized kingdoms."

"Like you, Father?"

"Sort of, but I'm smarter. Anyway, this emperor—his name was Lu Pu-Wei—"

He could see the boy silently mouthing the alien syllables.

"—had a minister named Li Ssu. Now, Li Ssu was big into punishment. He had a saying: *If light offenses carry heavy punishments, one can imagine what will be done against a serious offense. Thus the people will not dare to break the laws.* So he had pretty well only one punishment for anything—death."

"Okay," Harold said. "Yeah, I see . . . but where's the catch, Father?"

Walker laughed. "When this emperor's dynasty was overthrown, it started like this. One day, some farmers who'd been called up for military service were sitting in the mud. Rainy season, you see."

His hands sculpted the air, and Harold was bobbing up and down and grinning as his father went on:

"So one farmer says to the others: '*What's the punishment for being late?*' and the others all answer: '*Death.*'

"Then he says, '*What's the punishment for rebellion?*' and the others all answer '*Death.*'

"Then he stands up and says: '*Well, brothers, I got news for you—we're late.*' "

"Oh," Harold said. Then he laughed himself: "You mean, if they think you're going to kill them anyway, or might over some small thing, then they might as well rebel—they don't lose anything by it."

"Exactly, kid. The *other* reason for listening to the generals is that sometimes, they're *right*." He gripped the boy by the back of the neck and shook him a little. "I'm not always right. Neither will you be. If nobody tells you when they think you're wrong, you'll make more mistakes—it's like blinding yourself. Now run along; you've got some studying to do."

He leaned back and laced his hands behind his head, scowling himself, looking at the map. The temptation to try to smash them just one more time, and then they'd truly run . . . No. He might have been able to take Hattusas, but that would have been one bridge too far. Napoléon had taken Moscow, and look how much good it had done *him*.

After a moment the flap opened, and Hong came in. "You sent for me, Will?"

"Yeah," he said.

He stood and swung his arm. The open palm caught her across the face and knocked her down with a flat heavy *smack* sound and a thump as she hit the ground without any of her usual grace.

For a moment her face was fluid with surprise; then she

smiled as her tongue came out and touched the blood at the corner of her mouth, then slowly wet her lips.

"Oh, you have some *frustrations* to work off, do you, Will? I *like* that. It's been too long."

"Maybe you *won't* like it this time," he said, kneeling.

His left hand picked up a pillow and pushed it over her face with relentless strength, while his right tore her clothing open. Not until she stopped arching her body into the smothering weight and panicked, tearing at his hand and thrashing to escape, did he release the grip . . . and thrust into her in the same instant. The slight woman gasped and bucked under two hundred pounds of weight, unable to draw a complete breath into air-starved lungs.

"Bet I can make you scream," he said, drawing back a little.

Hong laughed and wrapped her legs around him. "Bet you can't," she gasped, deliberately hyperventilating; the dark flush of her face faded a little.

"And maybe I'll forget and really kill you one of these days," he said, grabbing her legs and pushing them roughly back until her knees were by her ears, rising and slamming down on her while only her shoulders and neck touched the ground.

"Oh, yeah, I know, and I *like* knowing that, too."

He set the pillow over her face again.

CHAPTER TWENTY-SIX

December, 10 A.E.—Cadiz Base, southern Iberia
December, 10 A.E.—Near Hattusas, Kingdom of
  Hatti-land
December, 10 A.E.—Walkeropolis and Rivendell,
  Kingdom of Great Achaea
December, 10 A.E.—Cadiz Base, southern Iberia
December, 10 A.E.—Black Mountains, south-central
  Iberia

*C*lack.

The *bokken* cracked together, slid free, whirled, struck. The world shrank to a strip of brightness under the helmet, cut by the bars of the face guard under it. Swindapa circled, then halted with the oak practice sword in *chudan,* the middle position, held out below the breastbone, angled up with the point at her opponent's throat level. She was motionless but not stiff; every muscle relaxed into a state where action could come immediately, weight borne by the bones rather than flesh, balance slightly forward on the balls of her feet but kept centered by the low stance.

Rigidity means a dead hand, flexibility means a living hand. One must understand this fully.

That was from the book that Marian liked so well. Very true, like most of it . . . although there was something repellent about that Miyamoto Musashi, an un-humanness. She could not imagine him dandling a baby, or carving a cradle on a winter's evening, or sitting beneath a tree after the harvest drinking beer and singing with his friends. His words felt like a man with a single huge eye who did nothing but *see* just one thing.

But he saw that one thing very clearly. . . .

Marian's *bokken* came up to *jodan no kame,* over the head with hilt forward. Her hands stood wide-spaced on the long hilt, gripping lightly with thumb and forefinger, more firmly with ring and little fingers, delicate as a surgeon's hold on a scalpel. Swindapa moved forward from bent knees, both feet pushing at once as the sword came up, twisting her wrists as she thrust for the face. That put the cutting edge uppermost, a strike at the vulnerable tendons of the inner wrist at the same time as the point menaced the eyes, motion smooth and fast with a *hunza* of exhaled breath.

The other's head turned, just enough to let the point of the *bokken* slide over the enameled metal of the flared helmet. The sword came down one-handed, the fisted right hand snapping aside to put it out of danger for an instant. Then both slapped onto the hilt and she cut from the side, looping up to slice at the younger woman's armpit. Swindapa bounced backward, in again; Marian was using minimal movements and counterattack against her partner's youthful speed and endurance. The Fiernan felt herself grinning as she fought despite the savage concentration of effort and will; this was as beautiful as a Star-Moon dance, in its way. That was how she'd seen it that first time, watching secretly at night as Marian performed *kata* with the sword on the deck of the *Eagle*. Dancing with the silver steel beneath the Moon . . .

There was a final clatter and crash of wood on wood, on steel armor, oak blurring in fast hard whipping arcs. Marian relaxed one leg, pivoted as she fell-stepped aside and snap-kicked the other on the back of a knee. That was hard to counter, wearing the weight of the armor; Swindapa went crashing on her back. Winded, she brought the sword up just a fractional second too late. Marian's came down in a flashing overarm stroke, left hand sliding down the back of the blade for an instant to add force, then clamping on to the hilt as the *bokken* came to rest across Swindapa's throat, motionless. Swindapa rolled her eyes to the side and met her partner's, grave and dark as she kept the crouched bent-legged posture for a further instant.

"I think that's pretty unambiguous," the Fiernan said.

"Sometimes I think you let me win, these days," Marian grumbled.

"Oh, I would, except that you might get hurt in a real fight if I did that," Swindapa said, grinning.

They knelt facing each other, laid down the blades and bent their foreheads to the ground between their hands, then sat back on their heels and emptied their minds, letting their breath go slow and deep. Marian said she used the image of a still pond to quiet her inwardness. That was hard for the Eagle People; they were always . . . busy . . . inside.

Swindapa listened to the Silent Song, the song that the stars danced to with their mother the Moon. Sometimes it was hard to hear it, but then you must try less, not more, and it came.

Voices murmured outside the canvas cubicle; Raupasha recognized King Kashtiliash's. Her hearing was still very sharp.

"You did not know, my brother?" he said in that bull rumble. Then Kenneth Hollard's voice, a murmur she couldn't make out.

"Among the Mitanni, a ruler must be perfect in body—at least, must have the use of all their limbs and senses. I grieve, too. She has served my House well, and she was brave and very fair—such another she-hawk as my Kat'ryn, with an honor I once did not believe a woman could hold."

Words I would much have given much to hear, Raupasha thought. *I have given much for them. I have given all I have, save my life—and that would be a little thing beside the cost.* Then: *No. I did what honor required. I must not count the cost. Ah, but that is hard!*

Hands touched her face, and she flinched an instant before steeling herself.

"The burn will heal faster with a light gauze covering," Justin Clemens said gently, putting down the mirror he had been holding for his patient.

Raupasha daughter of Shuttarna let her head fall back on the pillow; it still felt odd, shorn. *So is the fleece of all my hopes shorn and lost,* she thought. The words did not hurt much, no more than the dull background ache of her face and hand and side.

Clemens's hands were as gentle as his voice as he administered the ointment and laid the light covering on the left side of her face. The message of the mirror was burned into her, the thickened red scar tissue, the empty, sightless white eye.

"Will the healing . . . make the skin better?"

"Somewhat," Clemens said.

She turned her head—knowing she would have to learn to do that to see, with only her right eye—and watched his face. It held a compassion that hurt like fire, but also honesty.

"The scars will become less red, but the tissue will remain thick and rigid over about a third of your face."

Feather-light, his finger traced a line from one cheekbone across her eye to the forehead.

"Nor will the hair grow back here. I am very sorry, Princess, but all I can do is give you an ointment that will keep the damaged skin supple."

"Thank you," she said; he touched her shoulder once as he gathered his instruments.

"This will help you sleep," he said, and she felt the sting of an *injection* in her arm. A curtain seemed to fall between her and the pain, as if it was still happening but to someone else.

"My thanks again," she murmured, as he left on his rounds.

There are others who need his care more than I. Those with no eyes at all, or faces; those lacking limbs; those with worse woundings who yet could not die—it was not altogether a blessing, the healing art of the Island folk. It could save you for a life that was worse than death.

But at least I may weep alone. There was another murmur of voices outside, and Clemens saying something in a grudging tone.

Then the canvas door was pushed aside again, and she must be brave again. Then she saw who it was, and her hand made a fending gesture.

"No—" she said.

Kenneth Hollard came in and sat on the stool by her cot, catching the hand between hers. "Hello, Princess," he said calmly. His eyes did not waver . . .

Well, he is a warrior. He has seen worse. But not on the face of a woman who—I hoped—*he looked upon with the gaze of desire.*

"Hello, Lord Kenn'et," she said listlessly.

"Is the pain very bad?" he said, a trace of awkwardness in his voice. *This too must be endured . . .*

"No," she said.

"You—" he cleared his throat. "You did very well. You may have saved us all."

And I won his gratitude, when it is useless, she thought. Then, thrusting the bitterness away: *I would have given my life for his,* she thought. *What I had to give, I gave. Let it be enough. Let him remember me . . . perhaps name a daughter for me. It is enough.*

"Thank you," she said. "My father—and my foster father—would not be ashamed of me, I hope."

"Any man would be proud of such a daughter," he said. Then he took a deep breath, as if steeling himself for a difficult task: "And . . . any man would be proud of such a woman."

Her one gray eye sought his. *The medicine against pain is giving me dreams, as they warned me it might.*

"My lord?" she whispered. Then with a flash of anger her hand rose and lifted the gauze. "You saw me when I was fair—saw all of me, at the place of hot springs. Now *look* at me! I am a thing of horror—and princess no more."

"I have seen your face," he said. He leaned closer. "At least it isn't the face of a coward, like mine." She was struck wordless, and saw him force himself to go on. "Who wouldn't speak, because he was afraid . . . of politics, complications, of himself."

"Oh," she said. "This is a matter of honor."

"No, it's a matter of belated good sense," he said harshly, and squeezed her hand. "I faced the prospect of a life without you in it, Raupasha, and as for your kingdom, that was never more than a hindrance to me."

Now she did weep, as he bent forward to softly touch his lips to hers. "There it is, for what it's worth. If you spit in my face, I'll understand." A hint of his boyish grin. "Although I'd be very disappointed."

"Never," she said, her free hand going up to touch her lips and then his. The IV rattled as she moved. "Never in all the world."

"We're meeting him *here*?" Arnstein said incredulously.

"Yes," Odikweos replied, with that slight secret smile of his.

Walkeropolis had recovered with surprising speed from the *Emancipator*'s raid; the firefighting service seemed to be efficient, and they were already in the middle of so many construction projects that repairing damage just meant slowing the schedule on new buildings. He got a few glares as they rode downtown in Odikweos's chariot, and winced a bit at one long row of bodies laid out by the sidewalk to wait the corpse-wagon. Some were very small . . .

The slave market where they stopped was bustling, a huge complex of linked two-story buildings and courtyards, with doors and corridors color-coded for convenience. Ian worked his shoulders against the prickling feeling that went over them as they entered through polished oak doors and merchants bustled over to greet them.

"No, we will look ourselves. Do not trouble me more," Odikweos said, with an imperious gesture.

This place gives me the creeps, Ian thought.

Not least because it all seemed so *ordinary*. Sales were made in bulk and coffles marched off; men spat on their palms and slapped them together to mark a deal, as they might have for mules or sheep. Others looked at teeth or felt muscles, and some of the buyers had collars on their own necks, household stewards or workshop managers. Posters advertised skilled labor; stonemasons, bricklayers, seamstresses. Others offered to train raw slaves, and listed fees. There wasn't even much of a smell; Walker's hygiene regulations were in full force; otherwise, this crowded series of iron-barred pens would be a natural breeding ground for half a dozen different diseases. Fear and hopeless misery still sweated out of the dry whitewashed walls in a miasmic cloud he could taste.

It isn't as if Walker invented slavery here, he told himself.

That was true—every Achaean who could afford it had owned at least one to help around farm and house. In an economy without machinery, money, or a market for paid labor, it was the only alternative to doing everything yourself. And the palaces of the *wannaxakes* had imported hundreds of women from Asia Minor to make the fine cloth and perfumed oils that had been exported to pay for metals and grain. It wasn't any excuse for this, though.

The Achaeans *hadn't* based their whole economy on this sort of robotized forced labor. Slavery was a common institution, but societies based on slavery were rare. You had to develop elaborate control mechanisms to hold so many adult males in bondage; it just didn't pay, usually, except to mobilize labor for new uses or new lands.

A pair of green-uniformed guards went by, shotguns over their backs and billy clubs tapping against their boots; ex-slaves themselves. Walker had made it possible—not easy, but possible—for the ambitious to get manumission; that provided a safety valve and skimmed off natural leaders.

So he's a smart sociopathic scumbag.

He certainly hadn't expected John Martins to be here; all the reports agreed that he and his wife had been kidnapped by Walker back when he hijacked the *Yare*. They found the blacksmith telling two collarless men to lead away half a dozen with the iron rings around their necks.

"Hey, Professor," Martins said, holding out his hand. "Good to see you, man—I mean, like, it's a bummer you got to be here, but it's, like, maximum coolness for me."

Arnstein ignored the outstretched hand. Martins was in his late fifties and also tall and lanky, and balding on top. That was about the only point of resemblance; the other man's tie-dyed T-shirt and jeans and sandals, the tiny granny glasses on

the end of his nose and the ponytail behind . . . they'd followed
very different career paths in the sixties. His to San Diego and
ancient history, Martins up into the hills of northern California.
The hard ropy muscle that moved under his skin showed Martins kept up the trade he'd learned there.

"I didn't expect to find you buying slaves, John," he said
quietly.

Martins's hand clenched, and the sad russet-brown eyes
blinked. "You ain't been here in Mordor for ten years, man,"
he said, his voice equally soft. "I buy these guys so I can teach
'em and set 'em free, dude. And Barbs teaches the chicks.
We've got a good hundred people between us might have been
in the mines or the fucking arena without us, man!"

Arnstein felt a rush of shame. "Sorry," he said, holding out
his own hand. Martins's closed on it with careful strength.
"People change, you know."

"Yeah, man, I do," Martins said. He looked at Odikweos.
The Achaean nodded.

"These guards speak nothing but Achaean," he said. "They
are my men, also."

He turned and walked away.

Oh, yeah, Arnstein thought. *Yup, I've got plenty of chances
to escape—with six professional soldiers guarding me, and hundreds of miles of enemy territory between me and our forces,
and Mittler's goons longing to start pulling my toenails out—or
hold my head underwater, if they don't want marks. And me a
sixty-something desk jockey. Yup.*

"C'mon, man," Martins said.

They walked out into the cool sunlight. The men Martins
had bought and an equal number of young women sat in a
buckboard hitched to two mules; some of them looked stunned,
some sullen, some wistfully hopeful. The wagon took them out
of Walkeropolis to the northwest, up toward the harsh slopes
of Taygetos, then into a steepish narrow valley.

"Rivendell," Martins said proudly.

Rivendell, California, Arnstein thought. *There are places like
this up in the hills, or there were.*

He fought back the disorienting onset of post-Event-Syndrome once again; there were a half dozen low bungalow-style
adobe buildings with wood-pillared porches, a barn, footpaths,
a wooden water race turning a couple of small watermills, corrals and truck gardens . . . including one that looked very much
like a patch of genuine weed. A smell of baking bread, hot
iron, oil, and burning charcoal drifted down to them.

"Walker only let me out from under a little while ago," Martins said. "Till then I was, you know, working for the Man mostly. But I've been building this up for a while. Gotta have your own space here, man, or your head can get completely fucked up."

He pushed the small glasses back up his nose, a gesture that Arnstein copied without thinking of it, like a reflex yawn.

"So I got this place going. Sort of, like, a commune, you know? A couple of the guys I've taught stay on, and some of the chicks and their kids. The others out working on their own mostly chip in to pay us back, so we can do right by some more poor types. Gotta have the bread to pay off the orcs."

The wagon pulled up, and a swarm of children came running out to meet it. Martins handed out candied figs and hugs, but attended to business first. One by one the slaves knelt beside a small anvil, and Martins split the soft-iron rivets that closed their collars. Some of them wept and tried to kiss his feet; the balding Californian lifted them up and exchanged extravagant embraces instead, before a brawny young man and a woman in a long granny dress and headscarf led them away.

A hippie squire. Now I've seen everything, Arnstein thought, dazed, as he was brought inside to a big kitchen, all white-washed walls, copper pots and pans, and scrubbed-oak boards. The floor was brown tile, and one wall held a hand-painted mandala, hypnotic and beautiful.

"That's Barbs's work," Martins said, indicating it. "Groovy, hey?"

A comfortable-looking woman in her forties wearing an Achaean gown and a complex of painted scarves gave Arnstein a motherly hug. "Good to see an American again," she said, and pushed him down on a bench. "Hey, you don't get into my kitchen without eating."

She brought him a cup of hot herbal tea and a big bowl of . . .

"Granola?" he said. "This is really granola?"

"Sure, man—nuts, raisins, whole grains, natural sugars from honey," Martins said, blinking in surprise. "Keeps the minerals and fiber right. Ain't anyone making it on Nantucket? Hey, Barbs, we gotta lay on a big feed for the professor tonight. He's been having a pretty crappy trip; let's give him a good time before he has to go back to Sauronopolis."

The matronly woman in the long colored scarves nodded. "I'll get the barbeque going," she said. "We'll have the welcome-home party for the new folks at the same time." She bustled out.

Arnstein put a spoonful of the cereal in his mouth; the milk turned out to be fairly thick cream.

"Ah . . . John," he said, after a moment. "It *is* good to see you again. But why did Odikweos leave us together?"

"Oh, he ain't such a bad guy," Martins said. "You gotta take account of the state of the karmic evolutionary balance."

"Huh?" Arnstein heard himself say. *I will recover my mental balance. I really will.*

"Well, I mean, it stands to reason, man. See, everyone's going up or down the ladder, right? So back here in this cycle, most of the people haven't had as much time to get up or down the scale—so you don't get many people as good as say, Martin Luther King or Christ or the Buddha, and you don't get many as bad as, like, Nixon. Or Walker," he added with a grimace.

"Ah . . . that's logical," Arnstein said. "Ah . . . no offense, John, but you do realize you're still helping Walker?"

Martins laughed. "Hey, Professor, what do you think me and my guys make? We put on *horseshoes,* man, and repair plows, and make harrows. And we make ornamental stuff, wrought-iron grilles and gates. And yeah, I make swords and knives, like I did for the SCA and collectors back home. We make *good* swords; but these Achaeans, they aren't going to conquer nobody with swords, man."

Well, you've got a point, Arnstein thought, then felt something nudge his hand. He looked down.

Martins had pushed a small scrap of paper across to him. On it were a string of numbers and letters intermixed. He held it there long enough for the other man to read, then picked it up, produced a leather pouch, tapped out a brownish-green mass and rolled a cigarette with swift, deft fingers. That he lit from a candle on the table and took a long deep breath, holding it.

The acrid odor had been familiar enough once—Ian Arnstein had been on a California campus for thirty years by the late-nineties date of the Event, starting when the Vietnam War was just getting seriously under way. It had been a *long* time since he smelled it; or saw someone smoking anything, for that matter.

"Want a hit, boss?" Martins said.

"Ah . . . no, thanks. It reduces my IQ and makes me sleepy," Arnstein said. Then the complete sentence struck home. *"Boss?"*

Martins's eyes were almost the same shade as the remaining

russet-brown in his graying mustache. "Well, you've been running the Nantucket CIA, right, man?"

"Foreign Affairs Department," Arnstein said automatically. Then: "Wait a minute, you mean—"

"Like, totally. I've been working for you for years, man, years. Wow, outtasight—you're doing that secrecy shit so, like, you don't *know* I'm working for you, or even my code? Far *out*, man, like, fantastic!"

"Need to know," Ian said dazedly.

Doreen must be running him, he thought. *Wait a minute, that means he can tell her I'm alive? How does he get information out . . . no, I do* not *need to know that.*

"Well, a lot of people tell me stuff," Martins said proudly. "I mean, like heavy industrial shit, man—smiths stick together, and I trained a lot of the hot-pounders Walker used right back in the beginning. I got some *compadres* in Tartessos, too; worked with 'em back in Alba, or they came over here back when—we're pretty tight, some of 'em and me. We shed a lot of righteous sweat together, and you don't forget that."

"Wait a minute," Arnstein said slowly. "You mean to tell me that *Odikweos* knows you're an agent for Nantucket?"

Martins's long sheeplike face blushed under the weathered tan. "He, like, sort of figured it out," he said. "I don't know how—Mittler, Walker's tame Nasty—"

"Nazi," Arnstein correct absently.

"No, he's more like a Stalin type, seriously heavy authoritarian power trip, but he's plenty nasty, you know? Anyway, he's sniffed around, but he couldn't pin anything on me that the Man would listen to. He wanted to off me a long time ago, that guy."

Suddenly Martins's vague good humor collapsed; his face fell in on itself, looking every year of his age for once.

"Oh, man, you don't know what it's like, living here, you got no *idea*. I want out, man, I want to get Barbs and the kids and *blow* this place. Rilly, rilly bad. It's, like, Mordor here, just don't look as bad on the surface, but it's *worse* down deep. Rivendell, it's like an island in a sea of shit, man. I want to go *home*."

"I don't blame you," Arnstein said. "But . . ." His mind worked furiously. "I think we've got things to do first."

Well, keeping fit is a duty, Marian Alston thought, as she stripped off the armor and the sweat-sodden padding underneath. *I need the endurance and ability to think clearly under stress.* Plus the ability to use a sword with skill was a real military asset here and now. *No law saying I can't enjoy it.*

The practice yard bustled, shouts and *kia* and the thump and clatter of practice with *bokken* or the Empty Hand, personnel—mostly officers—getting in the time before the camp fully woke to the day's labor. It was just dawn, the light a twilit purple across the uneven ground and rocks and stumps; she'd never approved of getting too used to good footing and level ground. A steady firecracker ripple from the firing ranges told of others at work; a group of auxiliaries came by on the eastern beach, shambling exhausted beside their Marine instructors after a night exercise further down the long sandspit island.

McClintock says they're about as ready as they'll be without going through Camp Grant, she mused. *Oh, well, needs must when the devil drives.*

A lot of them had also stood around green with envy as the raiding party lined up to take the first installment of their prize money off the drumheads—part simple greed, part the prestige, status, *keuthes* of victory and plunder. Many of the Marines and Guard crewfolk felt that way, too; she'd seen one in line in a wheelchair with his leg in a cast, pushed by a friend with her arm in a sling, and they'd both been grinning ear to ear.

She doubted that any of the native-born Islanders would have been that cheerful. *It's not that they're any* braver *than Americans,* Alston thought. *They're . . . tougher? Harder-grained? They're certainly less likely to be . . . shocked . . . when bad things happen to them. Maybe* fatalistic *is the word I'm looking for.*

"What's on the agenda?" she asked Swindapa as the exercise-yard orderlies collected their armor, *bokken,* and sodden undergarments, handing them towels and harsh gray ration-issue bars of soap.

"It's 0545 now," the Fiernan said. "At 0700 you're supposed to meet those people Captain Reedy got out of the swamp. Then—"

"Fill me in while we walk, sugar."

The beach was blinding-white sand; it and the small wavelets were tinged pink by the sun rising over the water to the east, and the pine forest and marshland of the mainland beyond. The air smelled chill, damp, salt, and very fresh despite the thousands encamped near here. The doctors said the deep wells were producing abundant fresh water, and the composting latrines wouldn't contaminate it. More than enough water for freshwater showers, and some had been rigged here.

Not far away a long U-shape of prefabricated timbers ran down into the water, with smooth steel rollers inset. The *Farragut* was hauled out on it, kept upright with tree trunks braced against her upper sides, swarming with workers the way a dropped bannana would with ants. Most of the copper sheathing had come off her planks. Caulking hammers rang as oakum was pounded between her seams; new sections of planks showed yellow-brown against the weathered gray paint of the rest; tar heated pungent in buckets.

Gary Trudeau was there himself with his officers and chief engineer and the Seahaven people, directing the crews that had the damaged paddle bared to the bright new sun. With the protecting frame of timbers and metal gone you could see what the point-blank cannon shot could do; also how rod and cam angled each blade as it came down to strike the water or rise out of it. She remembered how proud Leaton had been of that . . .

"What's the word, Commander?"

"Well, the slipway works—no shifting now that the cradle arms are braced on the piles," Trudeau said. "Be a real *calisse de tabernac* if they moved with that much weight on 'em!"

Alston nodded soberly. The *Merrimac* was a lot heavier, and it was good in a way that they had a trial run first. A vagrant thought struck her: did the younger man swear in *patois* because it felt better, or to remind himself of the lost world of Aroostock County, Maine, and its expatriate *Quebecois*? There probably weren't a dozen other people in this whole world who'd grown up speaking French, and in another generation there wouldn't be a single one.

"The good news," the young officer went on, "is that there's nothing *major* wrong with her. No hull frames cracked, the diagonal bracing held. The bedding for the boilers and furnace is a lot better than I thought it might be."

He pointed to where a clangor of hammers sounded, like a legion of dwarves in a steel bucket.

"The funnel will be easy, and then she'll draw okay again. Best of all, we can arc-weld the sprung seams on the boiler pretty easy, once the generator's up."

"The bad news?"

"Ma'am, there are a *lot* of medium and small things wrong— we're going to have to replace all the blades on the port paddle, retrue the cams and rods, patch a quarter of the hull . . . a week."

"Fast as you can," Alston said. "I want that cannon and

ram to discourage any adventurous thoughts they have over in Tartessos City. And we'll need that slipway as soon as the *Merrimac* gets here."

She looked at her watch. "Now I've got to get on to those maroons."

"Maroons, ma'am?" Trudeau asked curiously.

She smiled, a slight baring of teeth. "Common phenomenon in slave societies, Mr. Trudeau. People who run away and form communities in swamps and forests and mountains, usually striking back at their former masters in raids."

"Ah," Trudeau said, his blue eyes lighting up in the long face, the Huron tinge in his ancestry showing in swarthy skin and high cheekbones. "Sort of instant, ready-mix, prefabricated guerillas, from our point of view."

"Exactly. And they can be *very* useful. Our good friend King Isketerol has been making himself a lot of enemies in his haste to build. An illustration of why slow and careful is better, sometimes."

Hetkdar, Zaumin's son, crouched behind a rock. It was cold, and he wore only a tunic of goatskin and rough hide shoes of the same material. He ignored the chill, as he ignored the lice in his bush of stiff black hair and the hunger that gnawed at his middle. If what the returned captive said was true—it sounded wild, but so many impossible things had happened in the years since he was a youngling. All of them had been *bad*, that was the problem. . . .

The open grassy valley below was on the northern side of the Dark Mountains, near the fringe of his tribe's traditional ranges, though not those of his own Ridge Runner clan. Now it was all that they had. The mountains directly to the south were high, with no passes that any but a Real Man could walk; that had kept the *Taratuz* away, for they were creatures of the flatlands. But one of their cursed-of-the-Bull roads was not far away to the east, with one of their twice-cursed stinking forts to guard it. The *Taratuz* could not find the Real Men in the hills, but the thrice-cursed *Adirak* to the north, who licked their piss, could, and would if bribed with weapons and meat.

I will eat the heart and testicles of their chief, the Bull hear me, he swore to himself.

Hetktdar looked around. Even he could see few of his men, which meant that no outlander could see any of them. Twenty-two, from the Ridge Runners, the Boulder Leapers, and one from the dead clan of the Spear Tossers—they had all been caught in a *Taratuz* ambush three years ago, and those who did not die went for slaves.

He shifted his grip on the Taratuz rifle that was his proudest possession—only three other men in the clan had one—and turned to glare at the ex-captive. The man was still dressed in a ragged *Taratuz* tunic of cloth, although he no longer had the fine curved steel sword he'd carried, of course; that rested safely at Hetktdar's side. He looked indecently well fed, too.

"Soon, my chief," the man said. "By the Bull I swear it."

Man? Hetkdar thought. *Eunuch. Woman.* No *real* man would let the *Taratuz* lead him away captive, to work in their fields and mines.

Then the captive pointed. "There! *There!* Did I not swear it?"

A buzzing drone came from the south, over the snowcapped tops of the mountains, echoing down the great slopes. The sun flashed on something there, bird-tiny. But it grew, and grew, until it was a fish-shape floating through the air, like a log in water. Hetkdar bared his teeth in hatred. So many new things, and all of them hurt the Real Men.

The great fish-shape came to a halt, hovering still. No wings beat about it. His eyes went wide as he saw men moving behind openings below the long hull; it was longer than long spearcast! The balloons of the *Taratuz* were nothing compared to this, for it moved like a boat in water, obedient to command. As he watched, ropes fell from its belly and men slid down those ropes. They knelt, in a posture he recognized from *Taratuz* war bands, their rifles ready. Hetkdar's eyes narrowed as he saw something protruding from the long house that ran beneath the belly of the airboat.

A cannon? he thought. No, for it seemed to be made up of smaller barrels, like a rifle—six of them, in a circle. *A weapon, though.*

He stood and walked toward the foreigners on the ground, the captive dogging his heels. The thing in the airboat moved a little. *A weapon,* he thought again. The strangers were properly wary; that was good. And if they had powers greater than the *Taratuz* . . .

He smiled broadly as the foreign chief squatted and held out a piece of smoked meat—proper manners, at least. The foreigner looked strange, with close-cut hair of a peculiar reddish-brown color; he was dressed all over in clothes the color of dry earth. That was good—perhaps the strangers had some notion of how to hide.

The stranger spoke. "He asks, do you fight the *Taratuz*?" the captive translated.

Hetkdar squatted in his turn, leaning on his grounded rifle as he would have on a spear.

"We fight the *Taratuz*?" he said scornfully. "As a hunter fights deer. They are blind; they are clumsy; they are deaf and fat and slow. Before they got the *rifles* we took their sheep, their cattle, their grain-food and bronze, their women, raiding almost to the walls of Tartessos City."

The foreigner nodded. "We have heard of this," he said. "We fight the *Taratuz* also. We have a gift for the Real Men."

Hetktdar leaned forward, quiveringly eager. The stranger smelled odd—almost like flowers. But . . .

"Rifles?" he said.

"Rifles," the stranger replied; Hetkdar needed no interpreter for that, since the word was much like the *Taratuz* one. "Rifles for all the warriors of your tribe. Plenty of ammunition, too."

"And in payment?" Hetkdar said, holding himself in.

"We want you to kill *Taratuz*."

A net came down from the airboat this time. In it were many long narrow boxes, and many small square ones. The chief of the Real Men leaped to his feet and howled, dancing and brandishing his rifle aloft. On the hillside his warriors stood likewise; the stranger blinked, and Hetkdar smiled at his astonishment.

The Real Men, with rifles, would kill *many Taratuz*.

CHAPTER TWENTY-SEVEN

April, 11 A.E.—Feather River Valley, California
December, 10 A.E.—Black Mountains, southern Iberia
January, 11 A.E.—Hattusas, Kingdom of Hatti-land
December, 10 A.E.—Cadiz Base, southern Iberia
December, 10 A.E.—Great River, southern Iberia
December, 10 A.E.—Off Tartessos City, southern Iberia
April, 11 A.E.—Feather River Valley, California

Cheers were coming from the riverside wall of the Hidden Fort. Dermentol son of Allakenal craned his neck to see what the fuss was about, over on the other side of town. He was bored with watch on the wall, and wished the regulars were back to do it.

All the men of the Hidden Fort were supposed to be fighting-men as well, but his work was with the engine of steam. He loved the machine, loved the smooth power of it, and the way it was *predictable*. With the eyes of his mind he could see the steam traveling through the pipes and *pushing*. None of the others understood it the way he did, and he was anxious for it. It was so powerful, but so vulnerable if the wrong thing was done.

Sometimes his wife complained that he loved it more than his children of flesh.

"I wonder what that is?" he said, and leaned over the parapet of the tower on which he stood.

"It's the ship from Homeland," someone shouted up from below. "It's come up the river, right up to us!"

Dermentol's eyes went wide. That would be tricky navigation for a keel so deep. He shook his head and peered eastward again.

An arm went around his throat, reaching from behind and to the right. For a moment he was too shocked to do anything, and in that moment the arm clamped his larynx in the crook of an elbow and squeezed it shut with brutal, unbearable force. Another hand came from the left and gripped his skull.

A voice hissed in his ear, in the Eagle People tongue: "*You shouldn't have hurt my dog, motherfucker.*"

The arms scissored across. He heard a crackling sound like a green stick breaking, and then heard nothing, ever again.

Peter Giernas lowered the body to the ground, ignoring the death stink, and looked casually behind him as a bored sentry might. Eddie Vergeraxsson climbed over the wall, then pulled up the long rope and unhitched the lariat-loop from the point of the palisade log. He was also in Tartessian military garb, and made a marginally more convincing Iberian than Giernas. Peter had shaved off his bright orange-yellow beard, but he couldn't do anything about his height, or the color of his eyes, or the short straight nose and general Baltic cast of his features.

They both went to the doorway on the top of the gate-tower. The sentry on the other side of the gateway had noticed them; he shouted something and waved. Giernas shouted something back and waved himself; it was just a little too far to see a man's face clearly if you looked down a bit.

"By the Blood Hag, I hope this works," Eddie said. "We'd never get away with it if their real fighting-men weren't mostly away chasing moonbeams."

Peter picked up the cloth satchel his fellow ranger handed him, and reached inside until he felt the toggle of the friction-primer. "I just hope Sue and Jaddi are okay."

The green winter landscape of the Guadalquivir Valley rolled by at twenty-five miles an hour; north and ahead lay the forested slopes of the Sierra Morena, the Black Mountains—white with snow on the summits, looking like shaggy white fur where it rested on the trees. Down here in the rolling plains it was much like a spring day back on Nantucket, just cold enough to make their sweaters—military pullovers with leather patches at the shoulders and elbows—comfortable.

It had been nearly a year since Marian Alston-Kurlelo had ridden in a motor-driven vehicle; more than ten years since she'd done so very often. She'd remembered how convenient and fast they were. The scent of burned hydrocarbons wasn't too bad when you'd grown accustomed to bilgewater at sea and streets that smelled of horse piss and dung by land, no matter how often they were swept and cleaned.

What she found she'd subliminally forgotten was how *loud*

internal combustion engines could be, in a way that even iron horseshoes on granite cobbles didn't quite match.

This one was louder than a car, of course. Most of it had started out as a gravel-hauling truck working for a Nantucket contractor. Leaton and his people had been working on it off and on as time allowed ever since; often as not adding wonderful gadgets and ingenious weapons that Marian then told them to strip off.

It had been like whacking puppies . . . but she'd yet to meet a Seahaven R&D type who really understood down in his gut why *KISS, Keep It Simple, Stupid*, was a governing principle.

Marian rode with her head and shoulders out of a hatch. The inch or so of camouflage-painted steel armor around the machine didn't make her feel invulnerable. It would stop rifle bullets or shrapnel. Cannonballs maybe; rocket warheads probably not. And if it went up, it would burn.

Swindapa's head came out of a nearby hatch, long hair blowing between the straps of a radio headset. "The ultralight reports—"

The little craft buzzed overhead, a plywood teardrop below a Rogallo fabric wing, with a tricycle of wire-spoked wheels beneath and a pusher-prop behind. Stub wings on either side held six-tube pods for light rockets; they were empty, and had a scorched look. The pilot waved, sunlight glinting on his goggles and crash helmet, scarf fluttering in the wind.

"—that they took out four more heliograph towers. The line's definitely broken in half a dozen places between here and Crossing, and between there and Tartessos."

Marian nodded. The chain of wooden towers flashing Morse-code light signals were almost as fast as telegraphs. Luckily, they were about as easy to cut, too.

"My congratulations, and then orders to refuel and keep company," she said.

The pilot didn't need to come here to report; that was reflex of a life where the only way to talk to someone was to get within shouting distance. And it was a valuable reminder that giving someone a uniform and a haircut, or even a lot of training, didn't make them over into a twentieth-century American.

Not that I should need a reminder, seeing as I sleep with the evidence every night. God knows I love her, but even after all these years, she's still weird sometimes.

"Halt," she said aloud.

The armored car slowed and came to a stop by the side of the road, engine ticking. The popping whine of heavy tires on the crushed rock of the roadway died out and left a silence loud by comparison. The two smaller Jeep Cherokees that'd been ranging ahead rolled to a stop as well, each to an opposite side of the road; they had armor panels, and Gatlings mounted on pintles. The gunners scanned outward, across rolling fields of grass and young wheat and dry corn stalks and occasional orchards or olive groves or copses of holm oak. Ahead—northward—there was a hamlet and a scatter of isolated houses with farm compounds around them.

The houses and village ahead had the dead quiet air of abandonment. Behind them, columns of smoke stained the sky, and scores of the huge black-winged Iberian vultures made circles that marked herds of slaughtered livestock. Swindapa winced slightly as her eyes followed Marian's.

Yeah, I know, sugar, the black woman thought. *Doing scorched-earth hurts, especially in country as pretty as this. But Isketerol can stop it anytime he wants. We're not here to conquer his country. We couldn't if we wanted to. All we want is for him to get out of our way.*

The crew of the car popped various hatches and came out, enjoying the fresh air and space; someone produced one of the foraged local hams and cut slabs of it to hand 'round. Marian took one and put it on a piece of dog biscuit, gnawing and taking an occasional swig from her canteen as she studied the map and waited. The earthy, salty taste of the acorn-fed and smoke-cured ham was so good that you forgot how vile hardtack was.

The rest of the Mechanized Battalion came up behind at last. The name was only partly ironic. After all, bicycles *were* mechanical transport . . . and about four times faster than foot infantry, on these fine roads the Tartessians had been kind enough to build. Watching seven hundred helmets bobbing along with rifles over their shoulders still brought a narrowing of the eyes that someone familiar with Marian knew for a smile. Another scatter of Cherokees and Hondas drew a brace of rifled siege cannon, heavy mortars, and trailers of fuel and supplies.

She fought down fierce envy for the two genuine Humvees she'd attached to Brigadier McClintock's HQ. *Fair is fair.* There were only three of those left in all the world.

"Major Stavrand," she said to the officer in charge.

"Commodore," he replied. "This is it, eh?"

He grinned enthusiastically. His white-blond hair, long narrow face and elongated build made him look like something

out of one of the gloomier Ingmar Bergman films. The Nordic
Death effect was spoiled only by his glasses, and the elastic
cord he wore to keep them on.

"Right over that ridge, and I think we've outpaced the news
of ouah arrival," Alston said. "Ride with me."

The troops put their bicycles on the kickstands and fanned
out, skirmishers moving forward until the thick bar of human
figures became a scattering across the rolling land. Stavrand
fastened his ten-speed to the rear deck of the car with a bungee
cord and perched on the turret, holding on to one of the welded
brackets and looking like a Stockholm-gargoyle rendering of
Alfred Nobel, or possibly the patron saint of demolitions.

The ultralights went by overhead with an insectile drone,
keeping an eye on the target and the countryside round about.
Marian waited until a signal flare went up before waving the
armored car forward. They crested the rise and halted.

Mmmm-hmmmm, she thought, as they halted in a vineyard
whose gnarled branches rose up from the earth like arthritic
black fingers. Yellow mustard flowers starred the grass between
the vines.

*Now for another bit of legal vandalism. Christ, but I hate
this business.*

The town lay in a valley that ran back up into the low mountains beyond; patches of woods thickened into outright forest
not far north of it. An earth-fill dam held back a considerable
lake north of the town, glinting blue with dead trees sticking
out of the water in spots. There were about three or four thousand people living inside the walls, she thought. It was all rawly
new, a gridwork of dusty streets and whitewashed adobe, save
where tall brick smokestacks marked smelters and forges. This
was a major center by Tartessian standards, their equivalent of
Irondale, working the minerals of the mountains behind and
forwarding the products to their capital.

"Major, I don't suppose . . . ?"

"I'm afraid not, Commodore," Stavrand said regretfully.
"See how the river runs? The flood'll go right past the town
when we blow it. Of course, that'll cut off their water . . .
mostly for waterpower, see how they ran the canal along the
contour to preserve the head? Quite well done."

An ultralight went by overhead, then turned into the wind
that blew out of the north and came in to land on the roadway.
Offhand skill flared the wing up to shed speed, and it came to
a rolling halt only ten yards from touchdown. The pilot vaulted
out and came running over, pushing back the goggles that kept

eyes from freezing or drying out and pulling off her helmet. She was small and slight—there was a 120-pound weight limit for pilots—and brown-skinned, with a broad face and a dense cap of raven hair so dark it had blue highlights.

Mmmmm-hmmmm, Alston remembered. *Lekkansu-born.* From one of the bands virtually annihilated by some uptime virus back in the Year 1; a few children had been bereft of even distant relatives to take them in, and ended up adopted on-Island.

"Ma'am, sir," she said, vaulting lightly up despite the heavy sheepskin flying suit and joining them on the deck of the turret. A glance at the map, and:

"Yeah, they've got fallback earthworks going up inside the gates, and they've just started putting up a berm to back the wall. Looks real crowded in there—lots of refugees, tents, and brushwood shelters in the streets and open spaces, ma'am."

"Thank you, Ensign Walters," Marian said.

"Ah, youth," Swindapa observed as the flyer bounded back to her little craft and vaulted one-handed into her seat; a couple of Marines swung it 'round into the wind.

Marian snorted. *This from someone who occasionally turns cartwheels in the street just for the fun of it?*

"Wait 'till you hit forty, 'dapa." She scanned the defenses. "Let's see . . ."

Curtain-wall of mud brick on a mound, wet moat, field of lillies.

Those were metal-tipped punji-sticks, a nasty low-tech version of barbed wire. It would be expensive to assault, but it was designed to keep out hillbilly raiders with clubs and bronze-headed spears. Nothing like the massive works around Tartessos City or some of their forts elsewhere; Isketerol had had too much to do to put that sort of thing around every town. Absurdly, there were still ducks swimming about the ring-ditch, occasionally dipping their heads and leaving twitching tails in the air as they fed.

"Right, let's give them a demonstration," Marian said.

The siege guns and mortars were ready within minutes, crews swarming antlike around them. The rocket launchers took a little longer, but the two-wheeled mounts were light enough to be towed by bicycle and manhandled around. The operators loaded six long, finned cylinders in each launcher's bundle of tubes and backed away, unreeling wire behind them.

"Driver, take us in to a thousand yards," she said.

The diesel pig-grunted in a cloud of black coal-oil fumes, and the car rolled forward again. The works that had been easy to dismiss through the binoculars grew larger as they neared. A cannon fired from the low square tower next to the gates, visible only by the flash and smoke.

Six-pounder, she estimated automatically—*brass smoothbore.* The light iron ball kicked up a plume of black dirt and dug a furrow through a cornfield not far to the left of the road.

"Pop the gate," she said quietly. "Then rake the parapet."

"Right, ma'am," the gunner said. "Ready—"

She slitted her eyes. The violent flash still made her throw up a palm in reflex, and everyone coughed at the bitter burned-zinc fumes. The rocket took off with a sound like a cat the size of a mountain vomiting, and drew a spreading cone of gray smoke toward the gate. At its head was a red spark. That turned into a globe of fire as it struck the ironbound gates of the town, and a vast hollow *whuddummmp* echoed back. A second later the turret Gatling cut loose with a long *braaaaaaapp*.

Motors whined, turning the turret and driving the machine gun; it blasted out ten rounds a second as the barrels vanished in a whirling blur, a continuous knife of red flame cutting through the fogbank that surrounded the war-car. Through it Marian could see the mud-brick parapets of the tower and wall disintegrating into powdered clay.

As if the car firing had been a signal, which it was, the two siege guns fired. They had no need to approach the wall; from a mile behind her the heavy shells went overhead with a grumbling rumble that rose in pitch as they passed. They were aimed for the town's metalworks, and she caught a glimpse of columns of dark smoke and pulverized building rising like instant poplars.

The crews leaped into action, running the muzzle-loading cannon forward again from the chocks behind the wheels, swabbing out the barrels, ramming down powder bags and shells. Before they were half-finished, the rocket-launcher operators spun the cranks of their field generators and pushed down the toggles that sent a brief pulse of current through the percussion caps.

Backblast scorched the hillside behind them in a sudden huge cloud that left crackling, blackened grass and crops behind it in a great wedge spreading out from the emplacement. Sixty trails of smoke and fire lifted from the katyushas in a rippling chorus of demon-screams—except for two that blew up not far from the launch tubes, and one that corkscrewed and landed uncomfortably close to the armored car, spattering its side with bits of metal and rock and dirt. Something rapped her helmet unpleasantly hard.

Memo to Leaton: "greatly improved reliability" doesn't mean "really reliable" yet, does it, now, Ron?

The rest slammed down on the wall to the left of the gate. It disappeared, in a boiling wall of rubble and dust and smoke that seemed to bear down on her like an avalanche. Enough of it reached them to set them coughing anew; Marian drank from her canteen and passed it to Swindapa, as the gunner and loader shared theirs in the turret and hull below. When the dust and smoke lifted, she shaped a soundless whistle. The sharp definite outlines of wall and mound and ditch had vanished. What was left was a lumpy ramp, leading from the open ground outside the town to a height about half what the defenses had been.

"Let's put up the parsley and see what happens," Marian said as a stunning silence fell leaving their ears ringing with the ceasing of the world-shattering noise.

Swindapa bent one of the whip aerials down and fastened a wreath of olive to it, and a white pennant beneath—local and Islander symbolism combined. The car rolled forward with a whine and crunch, stopping about ten yards short of the bridge that spanned the moat before the gate. Marion took up the microphone of a powered megaphone mounted on the turret— more psychological warfare—and spoke the phrases she'd memorized:

"SEND OUT YOUR LEADERS TO PARLEY! SEND OUT YOUR LEADERS OR BE DESTROYED!"

The harsh amplified sound echoed back from the surviving sections of wall, giving a blurring edge to it.

The gunner and loader worked the action of the rocket launcher—it opened inward, like a shotgun mounted sideways—and slipped home another of the heavy rounds. Then they waited; occasionally the turret tracked along the walls and the barrels of the Gatling whirled by way of warning and intimidation. Two ultralights buzzed overhead, circling the town and its vicinity.

Twenty minutes later Marian sighed and reached for the microphone to order another round of bombardment. Then Swindapa pointed:

"Look!"

Four Tartessians came climbing over the rubble of the gate and wall, waving green branches of their own. They had a white shield and a white flag on a pole as well, taking no chances. Two were youngish men in the green tunic and trousers and brown leather jerkin of Tartessian uniform; one of those was limping, and the other had a bandaged arm. The civilians were older, in shoulder-baring tunics, and sweating with fear from the way they wiped at their brows.

"Garrison commanders and mayor," she murmured. "All right, 'dapa, give them the word."

A harsh gabble of ancient Iberian; the wounded soldier spat in the roadway.

"He says King Isketerol will come with a great army and destroy your little band," Swindapa relayed.

Marian met the man's eyes and lifted a slow brow. Then she pointed to the ultralights.

"With those, we destroy your relay towers as we please. The highlanders and the bands of freed slaves are ambushing couriers on the roads. King Isketerol doesn't even know you've been attacked, and won't for days. By the time any force he sends could get here, we'll be gone . . . and your town will be destroyed."

"You will destroy it anyway!" the mayor burst out.

"But if you surrender, your people will live. Apart from your own lives, your King won't thank you for losing all those skilled men, as *well* as all the machinery and goods."

Marian climbed down from the turret, jumping to the ground and drawing her *katana. Hell of a way to treat good steel,* she thought, as she scratched a circle around the feet of the enemy leaders. The Tartessians flinched back from her. A reputation *was* useful now and then.

"Decide before you step out of that circle—life or death," she said, drawing her sword through a cleaning cloth and sheathing it over her shoulder in a single quick snapping movement.

A habit of reading history was useful too. . . .

The Tartessians went into a huddle, waving arms and yelling at each other; Swindapa came to stand by her side, translating bits into her ear now and then. At last they faced her, drawing themselves up and then going to their knees with bitter dignity.

"What are your terms?" they asked.

She kept an expression of distaste off her face; it was just the local custom, but she still didn't like seeing people kneel.

"All free citizens and their families to leave within two hours, taking only what they can carry. I'll allow carts for small children, nursing mothers, and the sick and old, but don't try my patience. Soldiers to be paroled on promise of staying out of the rest of this war."

So far Isketerol was sticking strictly to that, although the slash of indelible ink the Islanders put on each surrendered soldier's forehead—with a promise to shoot them out of hand if taken in arms again—might have something to do with it. The arrangement rested on solid mutual interest. Tartessos got to keep the men, who could work for now and fight again later, and the Islanders were spared the trouble of guarding and feeding prisoners. Since the alternative in cases like this where they *couldn't* take them back was killing them or cutting off their trigger fingers, she was profoundly glad Isketerol had gone along with it.

"Slaves to be freed, except those who wish to go with the rest of you."

A surprising number always did. *House niggers,* she thought, and then chided herself. A lot of them wouldn't have many options, particularly women with young children.

"Where are we to go? The highlanders are loose in the land; that is why so many have fled within our walls!" the mayor burst out. "If you drive us out defenseless, they will kill us all before tomorrow's sunset!"

OK, that's a valid point . . . and we did *arm the mountain men.*

"Twenty soldiers may keep their rifles, with ten rounds each," she said. "Men may keep a sword or spear, if they have it. You ought to be all right if you keep together and head straight for the Great River, that way." She pointed southwest. "That's my final word, so don't try wheedling."

She made herself watch as the citizens shuffled out of the gates, bent under bundles of their belongings—there would be a thick scatter of abandoned household goods all across the countryside, soon enough; the smart ones would have confined the loads to money, a change of clothing, and all the food they could carry. The curses thrown at her were easy enough to take; the sheer hopeless misery of sudden poverty wasn't, or the crying of the bewildered children trudging by holding on to their mothers' skirts.

If I can order it done, I can watch, she thought, her face like something carved from ebony. Swindapa wiped away a tear.

"And this bit isn't much more fun," Marian muttered, once the Tartessians were gone.

Like all the towns they'd seen, this one had a broad central square; she wasn't sure if that was old Tartessian custom or something Isketerol had imposed. Right now it was crowded with about five hundred people, mostly men in rough clothing, with a scattering of women. Some of the slaves looked gaunt and terrified, or bore the marks of shackle and lash, or the scars of working with hot metal and inadequate protection. Others still were just the usual work-roughened Bronze Age locals. All of them hung back from the frightening novelty of the armored car, which gave a useful circle of free space. Marian took a long breath and looked down on the sea of expectant bearded faces turned toward her and shouted:

"You are free!"

Swindapa turned it into Tartessian, working in smooth unison with her partner. Marian relied on trained lungpower; no need to terrify them more with the megaphone. Stunned silence, then cheers; they'd probably been expecting a change of masters at best . . . or perhaps rumors about the Day of Jubilee had reached this far. Marian grimaced at an almost physical bad taste in her mouth.

"We cannot take you with us," she went on; experience had shown that was one of the first questions asked.

If we tried, we'd slow ourselves down and the Tartessians might be able to mousetrap us.

"We will give everyone here a rifle and ammunition."

From the town armory; stolen goods are never sold at a loss, as the saying goes.

"You may take what you will from the houses and store-houses." More cheers at that; a lot of the poor bastards would get no further than the wine jars, and still be sobering up when the Tartessian army arrived. "But be quick, for we will destroy this town."

She pointed northward. "You may run for the mountains and the forests, or try to make your way south to our bases. Either way, move fast, for the Tartessians will send soldiers here soon, and we are not staying. My advice is to take weapons, clothing, food, and tools only, and to run far and fast."

The crowd cheered again and broke up, murmuring. Some were wandering around aimlessly, others heading for something long desired. A few thoughtful or timid ones were making for the gates, determined to catch up with their former masters.

Sighing, she dropped back into the turret. "Let's get to work."

"I'm thinkin' that ours was the first major battle in history where *both* sides retreated afterward," Patrick O'Rourke said quietly, warming his hands at the stove.

Doreen Arnstein gave a slight sardonic snort and kept writing. Kenneth Hollard cast him a quelling look.

"Not a funny joke, Pat," he said, hanging up his sheepskin parka and going over to look at the map wall.

It was snowing again outside the shutters of the ex-Hittite villa. He could feel the force of the icy wind out of the northern mountains. It came sweeping down and onto the high plateau of central Anatolia and driving drafty fingers in here, despite tapestries and rugs.

"Damn," he said softly. "But I wish he'd come on after the fight."

"Well, it's a bit close to the ragged edge we were, at the time."

"He was closer. All the intel says so, and I could *taste* it. And he wanted to, too, I could feel that as well. Every time he hit us—when he was personally in command, I mean—it was like getting whacked upside the head with a crowbar. Then he just turned around and walked away when he had us rocked back on our heels."

"It was the smart move," O'Rourke said. "As you say, he was run ragged by then . . . not least thanks to Princess Raupasha and the others."

"Yeah. You know what annoys me about Walker?"

"The complete evil of the man, is it?"

"No, Paddy. That's why I *hate* him. What *irritates* me is that if he wasn't such an armor-plated swine, he'd be a really valuable leader . . . and we need those, God knows we do."

"If only the fellah hadn't had his conscience surgically removed, the pity and the black shame of it. But I can't see him taking out his own garbage for the compost wagon, like the chief or the commodore."

"There is that," Hollard said, looking at the map again and trying to force his enemy's intentions out of it by sheer will. *Where? When? How?*

"It's a map, not an oracle, Brigadier sir," O'Rourke said. His voice grew a little dreamy. "By the way, have you been givin' any thought to what you'll do after the war?"

"Hmmmm," Hollard said. *I suppose I should*, he thought with surprise. *The Corps will be cut back drastically once we've won. Be a bit dull, drilling and the occasional skull-thumping expedition against some Sun People chief.*

"You know, I haven't, not really."

"Not thinking of settling down here, then? Or taking up the pioneering life back home?"

Kenneth favored him with another glare at the gentle teasing. "No," he said shortly. "Live here? Not if I can avoid it." *Not least because of the political complications.* "And I helped my brother out at harvesttime too often to have any illusions about farming." He grinned. "Why do you think I went into the Corps after the Alban War, Paddy, if it wasn't an easier way to make a living?"

"If you two gentlemen don't mind, we do have to *win* the war first . . ."

Doreen Arnstein was going over the papers at the head of the table, each pile arranged with her usual neatness and a cup of cocoa at hand; even near term her pregnancy didn't show much under the thick ankle-length wool robe. She spoke without looking up, her glasses on the end of her nose as she made a note in her small, precise hand.

And why is she smiling more? The offical reports were that Ian was alive and in Walkeropolis, no more. *She must know more than I do.* Which was exactly as it should be, of course.

Ken stayed in front of the map drawn on the plaster of the wall, looking at the pins and wondering how many of them corresponded to something real.

"God-*damn*, but I miss the *Emancipator*," he said. "We should never have risked her on a bombing run—far too useful shuffling high-priority stuff around."

A stamp-clash of feet and hands on wood and metal came from the corridor outside as the sentries brought their rifles to present arms in salute. The other Allied leaders trooped in; Tudhaliyas, *Tawannannas* Zuduhepa, Kashtiliash, and Kathryn . . . and Raupasha daughter of Shuttarna. He felt a chaotic mixture of anger, worry, and affection, and irritation at his own irrationality; fought them all down with an effort while everyone went through the necessary formalities.

She's walking better, he thought. The—*young woman,* not *"girl." Kathryn was right to ream me out about that*—was in the dark wolfskin jacket that had become something of a trademark, beating snow off it with her knitted cap, looking slim and dark and dashing.

Clemens said the left leg ought to recover full function, and the hand nearly so. Still a heavy limp, but less pain. *But the scar tissue will always be more sensitive to heat and cold, or to drying out.* It must have cost her considerably to come here through the weather outside.

He could see most of her face; the molded black-leather mask only covered the affected areas, a triangle from brow over the left eye and down to the corner of her mouth. That mouth turned up in a smile as she saw him, the lines of endurance melting to unaffected pleasure. He forced the silly grin back . . .

. . . *and yeah, it's logical to have mood swings after a trauma like that.* The problem was, how exactly did you convince someone you weren't just courting her out of a misplaced sense of personal honor? *Especially when you* are *a bit of a prig.*

Everyone sat, and also eagerly accepted the cups of hot cocoa an aide dealt out from the big pot warming over a spirit lamp in a corner of the big room.

Big market there after the war, he thought, half-amused at the sharp-nosed Yankee profiteer buried somewhere in his subconscious.

For that matter, Tudhaliyas and his queen were casting an occasional envious glance at the little tile stove. Even a Great King spent the winters here being miserably chilly when he was out of bed. Enough braziers to heat a fair-sized room also courted carbon monoxide poisoning, unless you left the windows wide open, which sort of defeated the purpose. Kenneth suspected that—presuming they beat Walker—Tudhaliyas would be moving heaven and earth to get an Islander engineer in to do a fixup on the palace. Which meant all his nobles would, too, and then . . .

"Let's get going," Doreen said.

Most of it was as boring as policy meetings always were; figures and estimates, troop dispositions and training, the endless question of how to keep the refugees fed; some of them had been moved all the way down to Carchemish to be within reach of grain barged up the Euphrates.

"So in the end," Tudhaliyas said, "What we have gained is a chance to do everything over again this coming year, with both sides stronger and my country a battleground once more."

"Better a battleground than spear-won land of the Achaeans," Zuduhepa said sharply.

Kashtiliash blinked, not quite used to a woman showing such outspokenness before a King. *Kathryn gets away with it,* Hollard thought. *But she's in a special category in his mind, I think.* He felt a moment's envy at the solid bond that was almost physically perceptible between the Babylonian and his sister. But then, they were both *solid* people; and they'd put in time and effort enough to earn it.

He wasn't looking forward to next year's campaign either. Raupasha didn't flinch when anyone looked at her any more, but God knew what another set of battles would do; he'd bribed her attendants to tell him about the nightmares and crying jags.

Doreen tapped the wooden handle of her steel-nib pen against the surface of a report. "We have gained time, which is the most precious thing of all," she said. "Remember, the war here in Hatti-land is only one front . . ."

The usual translation difficulties stopped them for a while, searching for a word for "sector."

". . . sector, division, *part*, then, of a larger struggle."

"So you say," Tudhaliyas said. "We fight Great Achaea, not Tartessos."

"As a matter of fact," Doreen said, smiling . . .

Smugly, Hollard decided. *But a* nice *smug, if you're on her side.*

". . . I've got something more concrete to tell you about the news from Tartessos."

"That was quick work," Marian Alston-Kurlelo said, looking at what was left of the *Merrimac.*

It was one of those mild, brilliant Andalusian winter days that gave her occasional daydreams of wangling a posting here after the war. Wind like spun silk caressed her face, and everything from the ship before her to the flamingos cruising like giant pink butterflies in the marshes had a fine-cut clarity.

"Four weeks and four days from the time we hauled her up on the slipway," the Seahaven supervisor said, wiping her hands on a greasy rag.

The gesture was one of Ron Leaton's trademarks, and engineers all over the Republic copied it, along with his air of abstracted competence. There were were worse role models, and most of the mechanics and engineers *had* come up through Seahaven or its spin-offs.

An entirely forgivable foible, Marian Alston-Kurlelo decided, walking through the construction-yard litter of timber, tools, and grinning workers slapping each other on the shoulders to view the craft from all sides.

The big merchantman had been cut down to the waterline. A sloping three-foot glacis surrounded the hull above that, solid oak beams a yard on a side covered by a bolted carapace of big interlocking steel plates three and a half inches thick. More steel covered the low deck, and a slope-sided central casement at midsection. That had three gunports a side, and a row of them in the cone-sectioned front and rear where a pivot-mounted gun could swivel around. A single thick smokestack rising from an armored collar, a couple of air-scoops and a low octagonal pilothouse with vision slits completed the picture topside, with a big bronze propeller at the stern.

It didn't give her the stab of pure pleasure a good sailing craft did; in fact, she still felt guilty at murdering something beautiful to make this. But it was . . . *solid workmanship,* she thought, taking a deep breath and inhaling the scents of drying paint, varnish, tar, timber, brass, iron, and whale-oil lubricating grease. *Satisfying. It'll do the job it's designed for.*

"Well," Gary Trudeau said. "At last I've seen something *less* seaworthy than my poor *Farragut.*"

Alston snorted slightly. "*Farragut* was supposedly designed to handle anything on salt water. This one was not *intended* for deep-ocean work, Mr. Trudeau," she said.

Victor Ortiz chuckled. "At least we know she can carry the weight; it came out from Alba in her hold."

A deep breath. "All right, let's get on with it."

Bosuns' pipes twittered, the Marine band played, and Swindapa stepped up to hand her a point-bottomed, jug-eared amphora of requisitioned Tartessian wine.

"I christen thee *Eades,*" she said, and threw the amphora.

It shattered on the reinforced ram that projected out just beyond the bows of the ironclad. Wine ran down armorplate and oak, red as blood. Everyone cheered; Marian smiled broadly, in a public display of emotion rather rare for her.

In fact, she was thinking of the original *Merrimac,* transformed into the ironclad *Virginia* by the Confederates for its meeting with the *Monitor* off Hampton Roads. How they'd have hated the thought of black-as-tar Marian Alston commanding something so like her; and how they'd have hated naming her after the engineer who'd designed the Federal gunboat fleets that stormed down the Mississippi and cut the Confederacy in half. Her father would have loved it.

I hope, somewhere, those bukra *ghosts can see this. While they roast in hell.*

Sledgehammers struck at the wedges and chocks. The timbers holding the *Eades* against the force of gravity gave way, and the steel rollers of the cradle rumbled and squealed as she began to move. The huge weight started slowly, then accelerated with terrifying speed. Waves of muddy water surged up in twin plumes on either side as the stern slid into the bay, then subsided as the ironclad shot out. A dozen thick cables secured to deep-driven tree trunks paid out and then came twanging-taut; the ship rocked and then settled.

Have to rearrange her ballast a bit, Marian thought, studying her trim with a critical eye.

"All right, let's get her boilers hot and see how she works," she said aloud.

"No," Isketerol of Tartessos said.

"Lord King—"

"Yes, they are destroying us bit by bit," Isketerol said.

He looked around at the war-captains and wisemen, their faces shocked or blank or calculating, mottled by the light filtering through the canvas of his tent. They were mostly men who'd come to power under him . . . and hence men he'd rewarded with grants of land and mines. Men with lands and mines in the provinces now being stripped and sacked by the *Amurrukan*. The tent stank of acrid sweat loaded with anger and fear; his guards were more than ceremonial, and their tension told it.

He grabbed patience with both hands and ran his finger across the map. "By the time news of their raids comes to us, they are already done," he said. "We used our light-signalers to react faster than the highlanders could. Now the *Amurrukan* do the same to us."

"Then we must meet their raiding forces with our own— forces larger than theirs."

Isketerol nodded. "Tell me how, Lord Miskelefol," he said. "They see us move by night or day, from the air. From the air their scouts report to their commander. And their forces move more quickly than ours." His fist hit the table. "On our own roads! By the time we react to what they are doing, they have finished it and are doing something else in another place. They lead us by the nose, and we take our marching orders from them! If we send out a column, they can avoid it . . . or bring together enough of their troops to smash it . . ."

Everyone winced; that had happened twice. He pointed out through the flap of the tent, to the long ranks of brushwood-and-earth shelters within the earthwork fortifications.

"We are too many for them to attack us here, and by our presence we guard the lands around Tartessos City. They cannot pass by without fighting this army."

"Then we should march out and crush them in one great battle!"

"Arucuttag . . . give me strength!" he snarled, making himself

stop short of asking the Hungry One to eat his supporter. "Their weapons are too much better than ours. If *we* attack *them*, they will slaughter us; that's why our invasion failed last year!"

He sighed. "We can only stand on the defensive; they cannot afford even a costly victory, much less a defeat, and if they attack us, we have the advantage. As long as the forts and cannon and rockets hold them away from this side of the Great River and Tartessos City, we are not defeated, because we have the core of the kingdom. From there, we can slip ships in and out. Time presses them in ways it does not do us. If we hold long enough, we may force them to accept our terms."

After so long on sailing ships, the little bridge of the *Eades* was a stifling closeness; stiflingly hot, too, with the boiler heat captured by thick oak timbers and steel-plate sheathing, and a throat-catching reek of sulfur from coal smoke. Engine throb shivered up through her feet with a slow heavy beat, tolling the movements of the big steam cylinders and the massive crankshaft driving the propeller—quieter than a diesel, beating like a great slow heart. The bridge sat like an octagonal lump at the forward edge of the casement; an eight-sided enclosure from her shoulders up, with vision slits at eye level, and an openwork basket where it protruded into the fighting compartment below. That stretched a hundred feet back, a single great slope-sided room, with only the armored sheath of the funnel in the middle and the crouching shapes of the guns to break it.

Hate to think what all this cost, she thought, peering out through the narrow horizontal opening ahead. The sea was a deep living blue, with an occasional whitecap impossibly pure against it. *Sweat wasted, acres of land not cleared, plows and harrows not made, factories not built, kids who didn't get an extra pair of shoes.* With any luck they wouldn't have to build anything like this again for a generation or two.

"Not exactly like old times, eh, Skipper?" Thomas Hiller said.

"Not exactly," she replied.

The *Eagle*'s old sailing master had lost his frigate in the Battle of the Pillars, as they were calling it now; that had given him a leg up over the other contestants for the XO's position. *And it's some compensation, I suppose,* she thought. Hiller had loved the brand-new clipper-frigate, almost as much as *Eagle*. He'd missed seagoing command, too, enough to leave his family on Nantucket. *Scratch crew all 'round . . . or picked, depending.*

Even the Black Gang were mostly volunteers under the direction of petty officers from *Farragut*, and she'd had to talk Victor Ortiz out of volunteering for *that*, with his burns barely healed.

Men, she thought. Then from a little ironic devil who lurked at the back of her consciousness: *Well,* you're *here, aren't you?*

"You should have delegated this, ma'am," Hiller said.

"You certainly should have," Swindapa said, looking up from the navigator's table.

"If I'm indispensable, I haven't been doing my job these ten years past," she said dryly. *So much for the awestruck obedience due the high commander.* "Helm—rudder amidships."

Swindapa gave an involuntary yawn. *And I'd forgotten how much trouble midnight feedings can be,* she thought. Her partner caught her eye and winked.

"She's still answering nicely," Hiller said.

They both made the instinctive beginnings of a gesture with their left hands—reaching out to touch a backstay and feel the forces channeled down from the rigging.

Hiller grinned: "Not enough experience in powercraft lately, Commodore. Either of us."

"How does she steer?" Marian asked the two sailors at the helm.

"Still just a touch heavy, ma'am," the CPO said. "Got to be careful to remember the lag and not overcorrect. This lady's heavyset."

Marian took a deep breath. "All right," she said. "Three days' shakedown and nothing new to fix is enough. This campaign has gone on far too long as it is. Let's go."

Ranger Sue Chau waited tensely; the smell of her own sweat came acrid as it soaked into the leather of her hunting shirt, mixed with the sour scent of old burned things on the gun deck of the ship whose crew had died. Jaditwara came rattling down the companionway, swearing in Fiernan, English, the Sun People language, and bits of the Cloud Shadow tongue picked up over the past year.

"They're all looking dead. The sails are still drawing and will if the wind doesn't change. Moon Woman receive our souls!"

"I sympathize," Sue said.

Jaditwara had some sailing experience; the Indians didn't know a bowline from a buttonhook. They'd towed the ship most of the way with the canoes, but the last approach had to look more natural. Sue squinted out through the gunport at the approaching dock and the enemy fort-town standing on its mound.

The jetty wasn't meant for seagoing ships; this *river* wasn't meant for seagoing ships. There were two of the flat-bottomed barges already at it, no place for the captured Tartessian vessel.

Oh, Jesus, Pete, don't get yourself killed, will you? Or you either, Eddie, even if you are a prick a lot of the time. Spring Indigo, where the hell *are you hiding, and can we get you out without anything hurting you or little Jared?*

Bright spring sunlight outside, incongruously cheerful and full of birdsong. The gates swinging open, people pouring down— brightly clad civilians, children . . .

"*Kakwa,*" Jaditwara murmured.

Their eyes met, and they went down the line of cannon, turning the elevating screws up two turns. The near-naked locals at the lanyards looked at them hopefully; once over their initial terror, they'd all immensely enjoyed firing the cannon off into the swamp. One lifted the lanyard enthusiastically and made to pull, to be met with frantic calls of *no! no!* in five languages; Sue remembered to toss her head instead of shaking it.

They backed off again; at least they knew enough not to stand *behind* the guns now. Sue swallowed something acid at the back of her throat. No way to tell now what would happen; she had to play it by ear with entirely too much that could go wrong at any moment. Was Pete's crazy plan too complicated, did it depend on too many things going right?

The crowd got near enough to notice the bodies in Tartessian uniform or sailor's slops draped about the deck or hanging limp over the rails. The ship drifted in . . .

Oh, thank You, Lord Jesus, Sue thought. The captured vessel was nudging in on the north side of the pier, its bow catching and stern swing 'round to ground hard on the mud—broadside still mostly trained on the fort. There was another frantic scramble as the two women ran down the line of guns, heaving at handspikes together; the locals were strong and willing, but they couldn't even *talk* to the Islanders, much less take directions.

The cries of alarm grew stronger; several Tartessians went pelting back up to the fort-town. And . . .

"Yes!" The gates swung open, and troops appeared there.

"Now, how long before they twig?" Sue muttered.

The civilians were milling around—scared of whatever had "killed" the crew, terrified by memories of the brief smallpox outbreak, a few of the bolder ones coming out onto the boards of the wharf. Troops forming up in the gates—

"Now!" Jaditwara cried and pulled the lanyard on her own gun; the hammer came down, flint sparked, and the twelve-pounder bellowed and leaped backward. At the other end of the line Sue repeated the action. Within a few seconds the Indians on the other four guns had done the same.

The crowd of civilians screamed and recoiled as the side of the ship shot out its long blades of flame and smoke. Many sensibly threw themselves flat as half a dozen cannonballs screamed by just above head height. Nearly all of them turned and fled pell-mell back up the gently sloping road toward the gates as the "dead" men on deck came alive, leaping over the ship's side with screeching war whoops. More tribesmen poured out of the hatchways, up from where they'd hidden uneasily in the darkness of the hold and orlop decks; an endless flood of stocky brown men in loincloths, waving captured rifles or swords or axes, their own obsidian-headed spears and darts, carved hardwood clubs.

The two Islander women waited an instant, as the south wind blew the gun smoke upriver. The broadside had struck on or around the gate, smashing lethal clouds of splinters out of the timbers of gate and towers, some of them falling short and going bounding and skipping up the roadway like monstrous lethal bowling balls, a couple whirring right through the packed soldiers at knee height. Sue swore softly at the results, then grabbed up her rifle as the other ranger dashed past.

The road up to the fort gates was a solid mass of people; surviving soldiers, fleeing farmers and artisans and their families, and the crowd of howling tribesfolk who outnumbered both. Sue hurdled a Tartessian woman curled protectively around a screaming toddler, shoved, cursed, and pushed; she and her companion were about halfway between the vanguard of their Indian allies and the last of them.

About the safest place to be, she thought, feeling her skin roughen at the thought of the cannon and rockets on the wall ahead. *Me, I don't have to prove a damned thing, I just want to win and live.*

The Indians pushed a screen of the townsfolk before them; more a matter of necessity than intent, but the effect was the same. Most of the Tartessians on the wall were civilian militiamen; the professionals among them mostly had family here as well. Reluctance to fire on their own, or to shut the gate in their faces, cost them crucial moments. By the time they tried, it was too late, and the gateway was full of a heaving mass of men who shot and stabbed, clubbed and slashed and throttled each other, trampling the dead and wounded beneath their feet. Those on the gate-towers couldn't shoot into the melee beneath; brave and foolish, most of them ran down to join it, where an alderwood club was as effective as a single-shot rifle.

Sue and her fellow ranger went in along the wall of the gate-tunnel, trying to force their way through the packed mass without getting caught up in it, kicking and shoving and using their rifle butts. A Tartessian saw her out of the corner of his eye and whipped his short broad chopping blade around in a reflex cut at someone obviously not of his people. Sue caught it on the stock of her rifle, grunting as the thick-shouldered power of the cut drove her into a half crouch; Jaditwara shot him in the face through the space Sue had vacated.

The report was deafening in the confined space, even over the snarling brabble of voices, screams of pain, clatter of metal and stone on each other and on wood. Sue dropped the damaged firearm and snatched out her blades, shouldering aside the falling body as she rose; stabbed another Iberian in the groin, and whipped the hammer end of her tomahawk down on a man's arm and felt the bones crack. The muzzle of Jaditwara's rifle came past her cheek again, and she ducked in reflex.

The Tartessian soldiers still on their feet held the whole struggling mass of humanity in the gateway like a cork in a bottle. But they were too mixed with their enemies and friends to keep it plugged for long. Like a champagne cork when thumbs have weakened it just enough, this one popped out all of a sudden. It spilled out into the open space that ran just inside the walls—and the Tartessians were suddenly in even more trouble than they had been a minute before. There were four or five Indians for each Iberian, and in the open they could take advantage of it.

Good, Sue thought, as the tribesmen poured into the fort-town and spread howling through the streets.

The more trouble they've got, the less attention they'll pay to two Islanders in buckskin. She stooped, picked up a dead man's rifle, and knelt in a corner between two buildings to load it while Jaditwara covered her.

"Let's go," she said. "Market square."

They moved out, trotting along the streets pressed as close to one side as they could, where the roofs—hopefully—hid them from the sight of anyone on the walls or defensive towers.

CHAPTER TWENTY-EIGHT

December, 10 A.E.—Off Tartessos City, southern Iberia
April, 11 A.E.—Feather River Valley, California
December, 10 A.E.—Off Tartessos City, southern Iberia
April, 11 A.E.—Feather River Valley, California
December, 10 A.E.—Cadiz Base, southern Iberia

"High tide in twenty minutes," Swindapa said quietly. "It's not going to get any deeper."

Marian nodded, looking out through the forward slit of the *Eades*'s bridge. The view was strange, a lot closer to the water than she was used to, but with no masts or spars to limit vision; merely the smooth gray-green slope of the casement's front section and the equally featureless front deck, awash whenever the knife bows dug in a little. The foam surged right up to the foot of the casement about every tenth wave, green and white against the painted steel, looking incongruously cool and refreshing in the stifling heat of the ship's interior.

"All ahead slow," she said. "Helm, mark your head."

"Two-seven-five, ma'am," the helmsman said.

"Keep her so," Marian replied.

Light and air came through the hatchway above; they had a deck lookout working. She waited patiently as the low shoreline came in sight, tasting the sweat on her lips. *Clear sky, steady good weather . . . it had better be.* No more Tartessian balloons, the ultralights had taken them down . . .

"Ms. Kurlelo-Alston, aerial scout reports?"

"Galleys massing just inside the harbor mouth," Swindapa replied. "No attempt to loft more balloons . . . wait. Launch trails reported!"

The lookout above cried out in the next instant, and came tumbling down the hatchway. The thick hatch itself fell with a doomsday *clung* next and then a *chunk* as it was dogged shut. The slit ahead seemed bright in the sudden gloom, and then a rippling cloud of red fire raced along the low sandy shoreline ahead. Trails of smoke climbed skyward . . .

"Incoming! All hands prepare for impact!" she called in a clear carrying voice.

Others took it up and repeated it. She found herself calling off the seconds as she waited, *one-one-thousand, two-one-thousand*. She'd gotten to *six* when the shrieking overhead turned to a whistling moan. The bridge crew slammed the covers on the vision slits closed and the last sunlight vanished, leaving only a lamplit gloom. The steady chuffing of the engine was the only sound before . . .

KUDDNNNGG.

The big ship shivered a little as the first rocket struck and burst, like a sharp blow with a hammer on a steel bucket. Then another hit, and another, building like a hailstorm on a tin roof, a roar of white noise that made her wince with its intensity. Hundreds more were landing in the water around, the dull heavy sounds of the explosions thudding against the iron-clad's hull.

Let too many come too close, and they might stave the planking; let a couple come right down the funnel, blowing their way through the wire baffles . . .

Silence fell, hard to realize for an instant while her ears still rang.

"Report by divisions!" she snapped, signaling the yeomen to open the vision slits. Fresh sea air came through like a hint of heaven to the damned.

"Three inches in the well—tight and dry, Commodore."

"Full steam, ma'am."

She hid a smile as cheers rang through the casement, and faintly up from the engine deck. Swindapa made a slight *phew!* face and mimed wiping her forehead, which made *gravitas* even harder.

"Silence fore and aft!" Marian called instead, and heard it echo down the chain of command.

The low shore was much closer now, the great drifting fog-bank left by the rockets' passage drifting away to the westward. An explosion pockmarked it as she watched—some of the missiles hanging fire and then going off together, propellant and bursting charges together.

I thought *we'd be okay,* she mused. The rockets carried simple gunpowder bombs, not shaped-charge warheads designed to punch a finger of superhot vapor through steel. They would have torn any wooden ship to burning splinters in seconds, but this lumbering knight-in-armor was relatively immune. . . . *On the other hand, I didn't know we'd be okay. Do Jesus, but I hate moments like that.*

She focused her binoculars. The entrance to the bay of Tartessos was fairly narrow, divided into two channels by a long narrow island. She could see the massive low-slung forts there now, scaling the land on either side like a dragon's armor. And the Tartessians had thoughtfully taken up the buoys that marked deeper water.

"Let's get down to it," she said.

Swindapa brought over the map and pinned it to the corkboard beside the wheel and compass binnacle. Hiller stayed glued to the vision slit, watching for the shading off of blue to green that would mark shoals—the *Eades* drew twenty-three feet. Marian focused all her attention on the task at hand.

She'd ignore the galleys coming out to defend their harbor as long as she could. They weren't as much threat as a mudbank, and what happened when those frail pine rowing boats met the ironclad would be unpleasant enough without dwelling on it beforehand.

The distant thud of ship's cannon boomed through the warm air, over toward the Feather River side of the Tartessian fort-town. Peter Giernas's lips skinned back from his teeth. A couple of the enemy were walking toward him along the fighting platform below the points of the palisade logs, looking over their shoulders in puzzlement.

"Go for it," he said.

Eddie reached over from his side of the door into the tower and pulled it open; it was a massive piece of carpentry, baulks pinned together and strapped with iron. A voice asked a question from within; Giernas jerked the toggle of the fuse free, waited until he heard the confirming hiss, then tossed the leather satchel in.

His partner slammed the door shut again. Giernas dropped a wooden wedge to the planks of the floor, heeled it home, then secured it with a stroke of his musket butt. The oncoming Tartessians *were* alarmed now, as the two men plastered themselves to the log wall on either side of the door and threw protective arms over their eyes. Then—

BADDUMP!

The door blasted out from between them, hinges ripped free, and pinwheeled through the approaching soldiers. Smoke and a red flash punched out after it, and erupted through the narrow firing slits that surrounded this level of the tower.

"Go, go, go!" Giernas shouted.

The two rangers plunged through into the interior, eyes watering and lungs coughing at the harsh reek of gunpowder. The trapdoor to the ground floor below was open, but the ladder was gone . . . too slow anyway. Giernas leaped upward, dropped through it, let his long legs absorb the impact as he was driven into a crouch, rolled forward with his rifle clutched to his stomach, and came up to one knee. The weapon came to his shoulder in the same movement, and he shot the stout gray-bearded man trying to open the door of the sally port between the shoulder blades. The Tartessian pitched forward against the wood and slid down it.

Lighter, Eddie bounced erect and kicked upward, his heel slamming into the chin of a Tartessian who'd come half-erect. Bone splintered; then they were both at the crank of the mechanism that raised the bar across these gates. Another couple of hundred Indian warriors were waiting, but they couldn't get in unless the portals opened.

Eddie jittered about. Pete studied it, Fimbulwinter-cold and methodical; Spring Indigo's fate depended on her man keeping a cool head, and so did his son's.

"Right," he said, pulling back an iron bar and tripping a pawl-catch. "Lay into it!"

They grabbed the bar and heaved; it was made for four men, and inertia fought them for long seconds. Giernas sucked air into his lungs, planted his feet, and pulled with all the strength that was in him—but carefully, carefully, how all the devils in Hell would laugh if he put his back out now!

A long moment when red throbbed before his eyes, and the mechanism went around with a *clank . . . clank . . . clank-clankclank*, spinning smoothly and easily as the counterweight swept up to the vertical and the gates swung open. Then he took up the bar, considered again, struck three wrecking blows, and jammed it deep through a shattered gear. Anyone who wanted to lower the gate now would have to cut cables and then *pull* it down past the tipping point.

"Let's go," Giernas said again. They shoved open the door leading inward into the settlement's perimeter street, darted out.

He didn't think the Tartessians around the gate would be paying much attention. Not when Indians in the guise of tribute-bearers brought out the weapons concealed in cloak and bundle and basket and attacked; nor when the ones skulking in field and grove ran howling to join them. He didn't think they could get the gate closed and barred again by unaided pushing, not before the warriors of the local tribes were inside . . . and from the sound of it, things weren't going well for them at the riverside gate either.

He and his comrade loped into the little settlement; they stopped for an instant to tear off their Tartessian jerkins and tunics and don buckskin. Getting stabbed in the back by a local who couldn't tell them from an Iberian was a worse risk than being shot by one of Isketerol's men who recognized an Islander.

"Jesus, Chaos and Old Night're loose here," he shouted, as they broke into the main square.

Awnings and goods lay tumbled and trampled; even now a few locals, some slaves and not a few warriors as well, were snatching things up. Their pen ripped apart, a herd of sheep ran about baaaing witlessly, adding a last touch of madness. The big blocky building with the tower seemed to be in Tartessian hands, someone getting them organized, and riflemen were shooting from the windows. Giernas filled his lungs:

"Indigo!" he shouted. Eddie took it up in unison with him. "Indigo!" *Christ, how are we going to find her in* this?

He saw a blond head across the square—Jaditwara, and Sue with her; they were shouting as well. His eyes flickered back and forth, eliminating the milling tumble and open only for the clue he sought, as he might blank out the forest for the outline of a deer's antlers.

A striped awning lay collapsed across a heap of vegetables, cabbages . . . It stirred, and a small brown form rose. She was naked to the waist, dressed in a local deerskin wrap . . . a baby slung behind her . . .

"*Indigo!*" he bawled.

Eddie clutched at his shoulder. "Take it smart, Pete!"

The other ranger brought his rifle to his shoulder and fired at the headquarters building. The two rangers across the square did so, too; the situation was shifting—he remembered school days, and a drop into a beaker that made crystals grow with dreamlike speed. Civilians caught in the attack fled; Indians went to ground behind tumbled wheelbarrows and carts or the corners of buildings. A few fired captured rifles at their foes, with scant hope of hitting anything; more waited.

Giernas left his rifle leaning against an adobe wall and sprinted out, jinking and turning, leaping tumbled goods. Spring

Indigo ran to meet him, young Jared's head swaying by hers. He met her, swept an arm around her, half carried her along with his body between hers and the enemy. Bullets chipped divots out of the ground at their feet.

Something struck him like a sledgehammer. He swung half around, and Spring Indigo cried out as much of his weight bore down on her. She staggered, then rallied and held him up; they hobbled back to safety, around the corner, where Eddie gave covering fire and the overhang of a roof sheltered them from the top of the tower.

"You're hurt—"

"Are you okay, is Jared—"

They looked at each other and smiled for one long instant; despite the shots and chaos and the baby's wailing. Then Giernas's face tensed and he crumpled back against the wall, one big hand clutching his thigh.

"Give me my rifle," he said, in a voice made curt by pain. "I'll . . . cover us. Take a look at it. Bandages in the haversack."

The Cloud Shadow people were hunters and warriors; she handed him the weapon before she knelt to rip the fabric open. Eddie kept his back to them, eyes never ceasing their movement. Giernas kept his on the square, thumbing back the hammer of his weapon, though even the gentle touch of his wife's fingers sent tendrils of cold fire reaching up into his groin and belly.

"The blood flows but it does not spurt," she said. "The bone is not broken and the bullet went through the big muscle of the thigh, high up, here. But it must be cleansed soon—dirty cloth carried into the wound, maybe."

"Just—"

The last two of their party ran up. "We'd better get out of here," Jaditwara gasped. "The palisade is burning."

Sue bent beside his leg; Spring Indigo sank back and gave Jared her breast.

"Good job, sister," Sue said. "I'll irrigate and sew later . . ."

"Later," Giernas agreed; he could feel the sweat pouring down his face; he forced the giddiness away. "Get me a stick or something. We've got to get this thing in hand."

Tunnnngg.

Everyone on the bridge of the *Eades* flinched involuntarily as another of the heavy cannonballs struck, the vicious whining *smmmmack* that followed was as unbearable as fingernails on slate. Beneath it went a crunching, grating sound that shivered up through the soles of their feet, the sound of a galley's light pine hull ground into pieces under the copper-sheathed oak of the ironclad's keel. The screams of the hundred-odd men in its crew were present only in thought.

The three portside broadside guns ran out, letting in a brief stab of light before they fired and added more to the choking cloud of smoke. Return fire smashed into the side; timbers groaned and buckled, and one burst in a spray of splinters. Corpsmen rushed forward to bandage and haul the wounded below; crewfolk scattered sand to keep the deck from growing slippery.

"Rudder amidships," Marian said.

Outside the slit the low roofs and seawall of Tartessos showed, rose-pink stone and whitewash and umber tile. There were fires along the docks now, and black pillars rising into the fading blue of the sky.

"Ma'am, two feet in the hold. We've got the pumps unplugged and we're gaining on it."

"Very well," she said.

Below the bridge there was a long grumbling thunder as the bow six-inch rifle was run out. Massive cranked arms opened the portlid and the muzzle came into view. She slitted her eyes against the long spear of flame; her numbed ears ignored the huge *thud* of its discharge, and she thought she could see the black speck of the shell in flight. The results when the hundred-and-fifty-pound steel forging struck and exploded were unmistakable; the stern of a docked ship vanished, to reappear as boards and timber falling out of the sky. The merchantman began to settle . . .

"Helm," she said. "Come right to one-four-zero."

"Command?" the helmsman said.

"Right, one-four-zero," she said, louder. *We'll all of us be just a bit less keen of hearing from now on.* "We've done enough. Time to go home."

Peter Giernas watched as Eddie and Jaditwara lifted Perks from the travois and carried him onto the captured ship.

"Pewks!" Jared cried, stretching out chubby arms. *"Pewks!"*

"Happier than he was to see me," Peter Giernas grumbled.

He lay back in the chair with his injured leg propped on a coil of thick rope; overhead a sail was stretched across the mizzen boom of the ship they'd renamed *Sea-Ranger,* giving a welcome shade. The big schooner was looking a lot neater . . . unlike the Tartessian settlement not far from the riverside;

about half of that had burned, including the whole circuit of the palisade. The massive black-oak logs still smoldered, and the great central pole had fallen in the night, like a whip of fire. The smell of burning mingled oddly with the spring freshness of the riverside greenery.

Chief Antelope came up the gangway behind the two Islanders carrying the dog. Perks's ears came up and his tongue lolled happily as they set him down beside his master; Spring Indigo kept a hand on her child, in case his prying fingers found the bandages irresistible. He'd already made his father howl with an unexpected grab, and there had to be *some* limit to the wolf-dog's forbearance.

"I greet you," Giernas said to the chief. He had some scorch marks himself, and a crusted cut on the ribs.

"I greet you," the tribesman said gravely, squatting on his hams.

The usual translation difficulties came next, but at last Giernas managed to grasp what the Indian was driving at.

"No," he said. "I don't think you should destroy the place completely. Make the people inside come out and give up, yes . . . you'll want hostages when their leader and his warriors get back."

And won't that be some homecoming, he thought with a trace of glee, looking down at his son and woman where they sat on the deck beside him.

"But if we don't," Antelope replied, "how can we . . . make things as they were? Maybe they'll build their Big House again!"

Giernas hesitated. This man wasn't really a friend; they couldn't even talk without skull-splitting effort. But they'd fought together—

"Things will never be as they were, here," he said. "Too much has changed already; the sickness, the horses, and other new things. Also . . . these strangers are not the last who will come."

"Your people?" Antelope said, with a trace of suspicion.

"Perhaps. Maybe later, to trade and hunt here. But if not mine . . ." He waved around at the ship. "My people know how to build these ships. Others have learned, and more will learn. You have a fine land here, but you are few and you lack . . . the arts that make for strength. Others will come, like the Tartessians—strong, hungry peoples, numerous and . . ."

He looked at Eddie, where he was standing at the rail with an arm around Jaditwara's waist.

". . . numerous and . . . heedless. You should be ready for them. To be ready, you need the Tartessians . . . what you can learn from them."

Chief Antelope's brows furrowed.

I hope that does you some good, he thought. Then the Indian spoke, and Giernas's sun-faded eyebrows shot up.

"You should stay. You could show us what we need; and your heart is good."

He flushed. *Well, that's flattering as hell,* he thought, and shook his head. "No, my friend; I have my own home and my own people to go to."

Shouts rose from the banks of the river. Giernas looked up, blinked, reached for his binoculars and swore softly as the motion jarred his injured leg. His first glance had been right; it *was* a standard Islander craft, a double-ended whaleboat of the type Guard frigates or large merchantmen carried, mounting a stubby lugsail. As he watched, that was struck and six oars a side flashed out and dipped in unison. They kept the mast up; besides Old Glory, it carried a white truce pennant.

Yup, that's the Guard, he thought, bewildered; blue sailor suits and flat caps, cutlasses and pistols. *And* they're *probably wondering what a Tartessian ship is doing flying our flag.* He looked up at the masthead; it was nice not to be the only one wondering what the hell was going on.

The whaleboat came alongside and an officer came up the companionway, looking around and then gaping at the burned-out Tartessian settlement.

"Permission to come aboard?" she asked. "Ensign Ellen Hanson, RNCGS *Winthrop.*"

"Permission granted," Giernas said, and returned her salute. "Lieutenant Peter Giernas, Ranger Service. Pardon me for not rising, Ensign, but a Tartie put a bullet through my leg day before yesterday."

"Then you don't know . . . the war with Tartessos is over, sir!"

"We've been a bit out of touch," Giernas said. He looked around and smiled grimly. "But yeah, we were under the impression it was over, too."

Marian Alston-Kurlelo rose as Isketerol entered the conference room of the tent. Not entirely by accident, a VCR was running on a table in one corner, showing a tape of Tartessos from overhead during the bombardment by the *Eades.* The way the Tartessian King had been shown into the harbor of Cadiz

Base past the ranked frigates, the ironclad, and the steam ram hadn't been accidental at all. The honor guard formed an alleyway to the tent and snapped to present arms. Their officer drew the tent flap aside:

"The King of Tartessos, ma'am, and his aide."

"Let them in out of the wet, by all means, Lieutenant."

Rain hissed down outside and dripped from the cloaks of the Iberian King and his young aide. . . .

No, that's his son—Sarsental, Alston decided, as they shed their sopping cloaks and the double flaps fell behind them. The cast-iron stove in the center of the room threw a grateful warmth, cutting the raw chill of the day. It was only an hour past noon, but already dim enough that the kerosene lantern swinging from the ridgepole of the tent was welcome.

His father looked dour, as if he hadn't been sleeping much; under a precocious gravity, Sarsental was taking everything in wide-eyed and eager, looking at her with awed interest, and at Swindapa. . . .

Do Jesus, the little bastard's undressing her in the twinkle of a mind's eye, Alston thought, amused. *Can't fault his eye for a fine fox, at least, or his brass.*

"Greetings," she said calmly. "Be welcome for the duration of this truce."

Swindapa brought four cups of cocoa from a pot on the stove and set them on the table, then sat herself and tapped a stack of file folders.

"I hope you do not mind that I brought my son," Isketerol said. "It is well for him to learn of these things."

"Not at all," Alston said. "As it turns out, it's fortunate that you did. Shall we to business?"

The youngster—he looked a little older than the sixteen years she knew he had—concealed surprise and outrage. Marian gave him a brief smile:

"We're not a ceremonious people," she said. "And I less than most of us."

"As polite as the blade of an ax," Isketerol agreed. "Well, it cuts what it's swung at, well enough . . ."

"I suppose you're here because of that," she said, nodding toward the screen. Silent shells burst along the docks of Tartessos City, and fires raged.

The lines grew deeper in Isketerol's face. "That, and the news that the territories south of the Pillars are in revolt." He sighed. "The fruit of much effort and work is being wasted."

Marian nodded. "I warned you of it, the last time we spoke," she said. "I also offered you terms."

Isketerol's teeth showed slightly, in what might have been a smile. "A King is the guardian of his people's honor, and their pride," he said. "I could not betray oaths and allies so easily."

"A good many people have died and towns have burned for the sake of that pride," she said grimly. *But it does argue he'll keep an agreement with us.* "Is it enough?"

The Iberian's fist clenched on the table. "You Islanders talk much of civilization—but it was you who made allies of the highlanders, who know only to burn and torture and kill."

Alston shook her head. "We *armed* them. We made no agreements or alliances."

"Ah," Isketerol said, thoughtful.

She could see the drift of those thoughts: *The Amurrukan will not seek to prevent me pacifying the wild tribes once more.*

"And you wouldn't have had so many problems with runaways and uprisings, if you hadn't had so many slaves who were ready to take any chance to strike back at you," she pointed out.

Isketerol shrugged: "Who would go down into the silver mines of the Black Mountains, who was not a slave in fear of the lash? Or work in the road gangs, or another man's fields? Not everyone can be a freeholder or master of his own workshop . . . but enough of that. I am ready to treat for terms." A wry gesture. "It is also the duty of a King to know when he must humble his pride, to preserve the kingdom's life."

Alston glanced at Sarsental. "Your father is a wise man," she said. Then to the King: "The terms will be harsher than last time," she said. "I'm here because the Republic sent me, and so are my sailors and Marines, but our allies . . ."

" . . . are here for loot," Isketerol nodded. "Yes. But my own people have suffered much; we can spare less."

Marian shrugged—he'd been the one to prolong the war—and slid a map across the table. It showed a chunk of coastline from Cadiz to Gibraltar shaded, and a similar patch on the northern coast of Morocco from Tangier to Ceuta.

"I thought you were not here for land," Isketerol said dryly; anger flickered in his eyes.

"That was the last time. Now we have thousands of refugees to care for. Some we'll send back to Nantucket; some can find employment in Alba; most we'll settle here in this strip around our bases, together with some of our own people and our allies—we'll give them all sixty-four acres and a mule. That'll make it easier for us to keep an eye on you. What we're demanding is a good deal less than the area we actually control now. And before you say that's intolerable, consider the alternatives."

Which is that your jury-rigged empire falls into its component pieces. And it wouldn't be nearly as easy to conquer it again as it was the first time.

Should we have held out until you were wrecked, damn the delay, to weaken a potential enemy in the long run? Oh, well, not my decision, thank you Lord Jesus.

"I agree," Isketerol said harshly.

They dickered through the terms of the war indemnity, access to supplies for the Republic's forces, temporary disarmament of the Tartessian fleet.

"And hostages," Isketerol said wearily at last. "I suppose you will want more."

"Not too many more," Marian said. "But hostages of weight. To begin with, your heir." She held up a hand. "For no more than five years, and he can visit home, and you him. He'll be treated with honor, I assure you—he can reside with the chief or with me, as you choose. And he'll get an excellent education."

Sarsental hid a start of alarm, then a dawning eagerness; he whispered urgently in his father's ear until silenced with a gesture. Isketerol rose and paced, hands knotted behind his back. At last he returned to the table.

"That is a bargain with several aspects," he said. A glance aside: "My son is wild to see the wonders of the fabled place. You hope to make him a friend . . . but you bribe *me* with the promise that he will truly learn things I only grasp as a man grasps shadows passing in the night. You are more subtle than I thought, Commodore."

Alston spread her pink-palmed hands and smiled slightly. "Blame the chief, and Doreen Arnstein."

"So." Isketerol's fingers rasped on the blue-black stubble of his chin. "Agreed—subject to a discussion of the details—on one condition." At Marian's arched brow, he went on: "Among the other hostages shall be my daughter Mettri; she has nine years. And she and Sarsental shall both study in due time at your . . . what is it called? OCS, yes. And the Oceanic University—they shall be free to take any course of study they will, as an Islander might . . ."

        *   *   **

Later that night Swindapa chuckled in her ear: "Sarsental, he would like to do that."

"He would," Marian said, sliding further down in the narrow bed. "So soft . . ."

A wailing cry interrupted her. "Oh, sweet suffering Lord Jesus, is that the *change me* or the *I'm hungry*?"

"Both, I think," Swindapa said, stretching luxuriously and lying back. "Your turn."

"How did we get from *maybe we'll keep him* to *it's your turn this feeding*?" Marian muttered, sliding out into the dank, dark chill of the HQ tent's bedroom.

A few sounds came from the great camp outside; a challenge-and-response, the rutch of boots on gravel, the endless lapping of the sea not far away. Marian hitched on her robe, sighed and went to the cradle.

"Both," she said.

She tossed the used diaper into the bin, secured the lid, pinned on the new, washed her hands and tested the temperature of the milk from the heater on the inside of her wrist.

The baby looked up at her through the dimness as she cradled the blanket-wrapped form against her with four infancies' worth of experience. She smiled down, and the infant responded with an enormous toothless grin, reaching for her and gurgling. Her heart turned over.

"All right, little'un," she crooned. He transferred his attention from her to the bottle eagerly, used to it by now. "Here you go."

Feeding, burping, and tucking-in over, the child went to sleep again with limp finality.

"That's a relief, after Heather," she said, sliding back into the bed. "*She* always wanted to stay up and play. Where was I?"

"*Aywo!* Cold hands!"

"The water's cold," Marian said reasonably. "You'd object a lot more if I hadn't washed them."

"Mmmmm. Did we . . . how's it go . . . *suck in* Isketerol with the hostage scheme, or did he *suck in* us?"

"That's 'sucker,' sugar, 'sucker him,' or 'take him in.' We'll find out in about ten years, I suspect . . ."

CHAPTER TWENTY-NINE

December, 10 A.E.—Nantucket Town, Republic of
*   Nantucket*
December, 10 A.E.—Rivendell, Kingdom of Great
*   Achaea*
February, 11 A.E.—Central Sicily, Kingdom of Great
*   Achaea*
February, 11 A.E.—Syracuse, Kingdom of Great Achaea
April, 11 A.E.—Central Anatolia, Kingdom of
*   Hatti-land*

"Why in the name of God didn't we deep-six this ridiculous so-called tradition right after the Event?" Jared Cofflin demanded.

"Because keeping it up made people feel better," Martha Cofflin said succinctly. "We *did* condense it. Hold still."

He did, as she stuck the white mustache to his upper lip. At least he wouldn't be sweating as much in this damned Santa suit when they got outside; late December in Nantucket was God-damned cold, Gulf Stream or no Gulf Stream. The Coast Guard tug was warm enough, with the boiler right below this miniature bridge. Not far away her skipper pulled on a lanyard, doing a creditable imitation of "Jingle Bells" in a series of cheery toots from the steam whistle.

The little side-wheeler swung in alongside the T-sectioned pier at the head of Old North Wharf. A huge crowd was waiting, big white snowflakes falling on fur caps and knitted toques, children held up to see or sitting on their parents' shoulders. More snow hung on rooftops, and made a white tracery of the rigging of sloop and schooner and square-rigger across the width of the harbor. Lanterns gleamed everywhere, soft flame light in the pearly fog, and hissing torches stood high; behind them the church spires and rooftops showed like outlines in a Currier & Ives print.

"Ho, ho, humbug," Cofflin muttered.

Back before the Event, the Christmas Stroll had just meant more work for then-Chief of Police Jared Cofflin. At least *that* hadn't changed. . . .

The crowd cheered as he shouldered his sack and walked down the gangplank. He waved back, grinning despite himself; it was mostly kids here, jumping up and down and yelling. He reached into the sack and scattered some of the little sacks of maple-sugar candy and precious chocolate, which at least kept the melee away from *him*. And there were things to celebrate besides getting through another year; the news from Tartessos was pretty damned good.

Amateur choirs struck up "Silent Night" as he walked up the wharf and up Main Street; it was anything but, though. The big covered market to his left where the old A&P had been was roaring, food stalls mainly, handing out eggnog and sausages in buns and grilled lobster tail on a stick and baked apples. A lot of mulled cider was going around, too, and these days cider had quite a kick. Main was pretty well clear of spectators except on the packed sidewalks and at every window and side street, but a big bunch of Fiernan dancers circled 'round him as he went up it; this was an important festival time for them, too, when Moon Woman danced the reluctant Sun back to warm the earth.

At least we persuaded the chariot boys not to sacrifice their horse, bull, and hound right here, he thought—and before the Alban War back home, they'd have given Sky Father a man, too, so the boss-god would be strong enough to chain the Wolf that would otherwise eat the sun and leave the world in eternal darkness.

They probably do *still do that over there, when nobody's looking, treaty or no treaty.*

At the head of Main he climbed the steps of the Pacific Bank. "Merry Christmas!" he called.

"Merry Christmas!" the thousands roared back—or versions of "Happy Solstice Festival" in a round dozen languages. The dancers went into a whirling, cartwheeling frenzy.

"Light 'em up!"

There were half a dozen big Christmas trees down the middle of the street, strung with an amazing assortment of ornaments pre-and post-Event; he rather liked the little carved painted horses that some of the Alban immigrants made. At his wave tapers were lit and touched to dozens of candles set on branches—and each tree had its own watcher with a bucket of water, now; those weren't electric lights. . . .

A sleigh pulled up at the steps, and he climbed in; Martha was already there. At least this year there was enough snow to *use* a sleigh; you couldn't always count on that. The team that pulled it was a pair of glossy hairy-hoofed giants, Brandt Farms' contribution to the festivities. Jared Cofflin resigned himself to ho-hoing his way 'round town as the horses took off in a silver jingle of bells and thump of platter-sized hooves on packed snow. The driver whistled under his breath as they drove, but at least it wasn't a carol.

Moving through the streets, the sleigh seemed to carry its own bubble of yellow light in a world of snow-streamers. Carolers and impromptu games of street hockey and people just moving about for the pleasure of it waved.

"Dispatch came in just now," Martha murmured in his ear. "Package from Marian and 'dapa, and the details on the text of the agreement with Tartessos. And a radio from Doreen in Hattusas . . . that's got some significant material in it. She wants authorization for a plan with some really radical potential . . ."

"Ho, ho," Jared said hollowly. Chief executives, policemen, and parents had something in common—they were always on call. "Let me have it."

When he got home at last it was a relief to sink into an armchair in his own living room, with the hideous fungus off his face, sensible clothes on, a fire crackling, and a glass of eggnog of his own at his elbow while he supervised the opening of presents and the smells from the kitchen made his nose twitch. His parents had always kept the day itself for going to church, and he and Martha had kept that up once they had a brood of their own.

Marian's two enjoyed their own presents; especially what their mothers had sent back from the Tartessian lands, a sack of precious oranges and lemons—those were expensive luxuries these days—parkas and gloves of beautifully tanned lynx skins, and a pair of olive-wood *bokken*. What brought the real squeals was a package of letters, though.

"Uncle Jared! We've got a *brother*! A real baby *brother*!"

"Ayup," he said, as they bounced around making plans for things they would do to and with him—you'd have thought the lad was eight, not a nursing infant.

And we've got a peace with Tartessos, thank God, he thought, closing his eyes for a second and thanking God indeed. There were entirely too many new names on the fresh stone slab down by the Town Building, but fewer than he'd feared.

Please, may we get rid of Walker without paying too much of

*a butcher's bill. Enough. It's Christmas; you can worry
tomorrow.*

"Did you get any letters, Uncle Jared?" they asked.

"Ayup," he said. "From your mothers, and from Aunt Doreen. But they were business."

"Like, let the revels begin!" John Martins said, and repeated
it in the gloriously ungrammatical Achaean. Ian Arnstein had
grown used to in the past few weeks and visits. Odikweos allowed it, as long as the guards were along.

It was chilly and rainy outside, rather than actually cold; but
the interior of Rivendell's main hall was warm and brilliantly
lit. Part of that was excellent lanterns; much of it was a half
dozen wrought-iron candelabra hanging by hand-forged chains
from the rafters. Those were elaborately carved, in varying
styles; the walls were done with murals that Barbara Martins
probably thought were Tolkienesque, but actually owed a good
deal more to Disney.

Tacky beyond words, Ian Arnstein thought, taking a pull at
the mulled wine. *Especially the big eyes.*

The ironwork wasn't, though. Not the candelabra, done in
the shape of phoenixlike birds holding the candles in their
beaks, nor the elaborate curvilinear dragons whose claws
clamped the roaring pine logs of the hearths on either side.
Floridly romantic, yes, but it had the integrity of a craftsman
who worked with a skill that let him precisely realize in the
real world the vision he saw alone with himself.

You took Martins a good deal more seriously, after you'd
seen his work, or seen *him* work. That seemed to apply to his
second, unauthorized occupation as well.

A roar went up from the dozen or so adults sitting down the
long table as the food came in—several turkeys bred up from
imports via Tartessos, and a small roast pig, with mounds of
bread and vegetables on the side. The strong good smell spilled
into the hall, mixing with the resin scent of the burning wood
and an undertone of damp dog and wool and silt from the
tumbling stream outside. A fresh warm scent of evergreen un-
derlay it, from the big fifteen-foot fir standing amid a pile of
presents in one corner.

All of the men here had the startling muscle definition that
Martins showed; it went with the trade. All were younger as
well, several much bulkier, but he didn't think any of them was
much stronger. An equal number of women sat among them,
and a round dozen children of toddler age and above tumbled

about on the flagstone floor amid the dogs. Martins had his son on his lap and a daughter beside him in the big chair at the head of the table; he and his wife seemed to have adopted a good many more—a good many even by Nantucket's post-Event standard—and his followers were breeding enthusiastically as well.

"Yeah, man," he said quietly to Arnstein. "Came in about an hour ago—didn't want to mention it, while, like, you-know-who was here. Don't want to tempt him to pile up any more bad karma, you know? Figure he's used to you staying over on visits by now."

Arnstein fought down trembling eagerness while he ate, the food sitting leaden on his stomach.

"Hey, you dudes gotta remember to eat your vegetables," Martins went on earnestly, looking down-table at his followers. "Natural fibers're essential to, like, cleaning out your impurities. Too bad we ain't got any brown rice."

The journeymen and apprentices looked a little bewildered. Vegetables were poverty foods here; the great nobles ate meat and some bread and fruit, and success was defined by how closely you could imitate them. They obediently shoveled down steamed cauliflower and broccoli with cheese sauce nonetheless.

If he suggested they paint themselves blue, they'd probably do that too, Ian thought whimsically. It was interesting to speculate on what the blacksmith subculture was going to be like here in a generation or two.

He managed to make himself wait until the ice cream was carried in—even then he couldn't resist snagging a bowl—and headed up the stairs. His anticipation was enough to overcome his usual revulsion at the long-bearded carved dwarves who upbore the balustrade. In his room he turned up the lanterns on the working table and took up the leather satchel tossed carelessly on the quilt—hidden in plain sight.

The heavy coarse paper of the envelope crackled around his fingers as he broke the seals. Within was a sheet written in a hand he recognized; for a moment he simply sat with the letter in his hand. Then he set it down and read:

"King's pawn to . . ."

He smiled. *Now,* there's *a cipher.* A substitution code, based on their favorite responses to the listed chess moves. Cryptographers back up in the twentieth could probably break it fairly easily, with their supercomputers and staffs of experts. Walker—or even Mittler? *I don't think so.*

Further inside the packet was another, and he lifted out the infinitely precious treasure; not forgetting to put his ice-cream bowl on the other side of the room and wash and carefully dry his hands first with the jug-basin-towel set provided.

"Oh, excellent," he said softly.

The watermark was perfect; mainly because it *was* Great Achaea's royal watermark, and that of the Temple of the Threefold Hekate. The handwriting was near-perfect, too; Walker's smooth hand with the little extra pressure on the "t," a very occasional splotch where too much pressure was applied. *Got a bit of buried anger there, Walker-me-lad, bubbling under that smooth exterior.* And Alice Hong's. *Slants backward. Ooooh, look at those spiky i's and the little horns on the w's. Classic. Got some unassimilated trauma lurking around there, don't you, you monstrous little bitch?*

"Well, come on now, Ian," he said. *Now I'm channeling Doreen. This place* is *driving me crazy.* "It's not really their writing, just a very very good imitation."

> Dear Will: Hi! Got to tell you, studmuffin, the *telestai* really have their testicles in a twist about the latest strategic-readjustment-of-forces. You said it; we need some victories. Or at least we need to throw someone out of the sled for the wolves . . . and *guess who* I think it should be? I've got some ideas about how, too, that you'll just love . . .

God, that was even her *style,* the giggling little-girl descriptions of how she planned to "operate" . . . did anyone really still use words like "wee-wee" for penis? The choice of words was perfect, worth all the effort and risk of getting samples. Walker's people had been pretty good about destroying documents with important *information.* They'd been much less careful about casual notes concerning nothing in particular. The Walker was good, too:

> Sic transit gloria His Krautness, babe. Heels have clicked for the last time; we'll get some *major* credit out of it, too. A King should always have at least one seriously unpopular minister around for occasions like this. It's a pity in a way, I wanted to keep our tame Kraut around a little longer, but on second thoughts it's time for him to go . . .

The date was in April . . . Yes, by God, April 1. That was the crowning touch.

"Of course, that means we have to have a victory about then for these to fit. Not a problem; if we don't by then, Odikweos won't move, nohow."

And he himself would die. Most probably exactly the way pseudo-Hong described in these precious pages. They'd been taken from real life, after all.

There were at least a hundred bodies around the gates, lying in the inevitable posture of the dead left on a battlefield—backs arched and limbs splayed as decay and gas build-up had their way with them. Brigadier McClintock grunted as he swung his binoculars back and forth. It was a common scene in Sicily, this February of the Year 11.

"What did they do, just charge right in?" he said.

"That's exactly what they did," Marian Alston-Kurlelo replied grimly, not taking her field glasses from her eyes.

The wind shifted and brought the gagging reek strongly down the road that wound up to the fort. She decided she was getting very sick of the smell of rotting human flesh combined with the bitter scents of burning. The damp freshness of the Sicilian upland winter and the bright sunlight through sky washed clean by yesterday's rain made it worse. Birds hopped and heaved and squabbled around the bodies; Walker must have given them this type of feast on a regular basis.

She shifted her attention to the countryside 'round about. *Not very Sicilian,* she thought.

Eagle had been through the Mediterranean several times before the Event, on training-show-the-flag voyages; a tall ship made great PR. Central Sicily in the twentieth was a wasteland of rock, scrubby maquis and scraggly crops, and the tumbled remains of worked-out mines. Makers of spaghetti Westerns used it as a good stand-in for Arizona, and it was full of crumbling gray villages where the only living things were ancient crones in black tottering along under huge bundles of brushwood. Or sitting and staring at you with hooded, bitter eyes.

Here it was a sea of branches, oak and hazelnut and pine shaggy on the sides of the hills, giving way to savannas of scattered trees and tall green grass on the flats. Some land had been cleared for contour-plowed fields of wheat and barley and clumps of fig and olive and soft fruits around the remains of a megaron-hall, an Achaean-style manor house; that was still smoldering, along with its outbuildings. She pointed a little further, to another collection of wrecked structures—most of those long, low-slung *ergastulae,* half-underground slave barracks surrounded by a fence of spiked bars and overlooked by the stump of a watchtower. Beside them was an ugly yellow gash on the side of the hill, pockmarked with the black mouths of tunnels, and a short thick smokestack.

"Sulfur mine," she said. "And see the collection of crosses around it?"

"Surely do," McClintock said tightly. "So the miners came up here and hit the fort after they'd finished off the overseers?"

"Overran the *latifundia* there first; probably a lot of the slaves from there joined them, and then they came helling up the road and tried to do the same here. The Achaeans were waiting for them, by then. Probably they were drunk . . . or just drunk on the prospect of getting their own back."

McClintock nodded tightly. Under Walker, the Achaeans had done their best to turn the whole island into a giant plantation, with gangs of slaves pumping out wheat and wool and cotton, sulfur and asphalt and timber for his projects. The process was far from complete, he'd had only a little more than half a decade, but it had gone a long way. They'd overrun a couple of labor camps that made even the mines look good.

"That fort would be expensive," he said after a moment. "Even with a good road, we'll have trouble getting enough artillery here and in range. They've got some of those . . . what are they called . . ."

"It's a rip-off of a French weapon called the Montigny Mitrailleuse—from the 1860s. A bunch of barrels clamped together, bullets in a plate you slide into the breech and fire with a crank. The Achaean word translates as *quickshooter.*"

"Those, yeah, in those bunkers around the perimeter. Mortars in the courtyards—see the craters on the hill slopes? No dead ground around here. Rocket launchers . . . Ma'am, it'll take a regular siege. I'd need at least a battalion, and, oh, six of the five-inch rifles . . . take a couple of weeks."

Marian nodded. "The problem is there are dozens of forts like this. That's why they built them in the first place, to nail down the countryside."

For that matter, there were a couple of pretty large areas where the Achaean settlers had come out on top against the slaves and natives, even with the Islanders providing weapons and backup. And Syracuse was still holding out.

So we can't sit down and blast the enemy out of every fortlet.

Not if we're going to pitch in and help the expeditionary force in the Middle East anytime soon.

"Well, what *do* we do, then, ma'am?"

She smiled grimly. The Islanders hadn't exactly taken over Great Achaea's Sicilian colony by landing and proclaiming liberation. They *had* turned it into a three-cornered exercise in massacre and countermassacre, as natives and slaves and Achaeans fought each other like crabs in a bucket. It reminded her of what she'd read about Haiti during the slave uprising there in the 1790s, years of terror and madness. However discouraging the Nantucketers' problems looked, she didn't think the other factions felt particularly victorious, either.

"I'm a hammer," she said. "I see problems as nails—even big, badass nails like that." A jerk of her chin at the fort. "The chief has a different approach. That's what I'm going to Syracuse for, to give it a try. And to see what they've been doing with the Fleet in my absence."

"I'm sorry, ma'am," Hiller said.

The longboat pitched easily, the crew leaning on their oars. The Great Harbor of Syracuse stretched around them, most of the shore swampy and noisy with duck and flamingos and spoonbills, adding a silty smell of marsh to the clean salt breeze. Water shone blue-purple, shading to emerald over shoal and sandbank. The Islander fleet was further away from the enemy guns, anchored in neat rows with a busy commerce of small craft and rafts shuttling back and forth to shore.

"We hit a mine, that's all I can say," Hiller went on. "Hit a couple, but the first two were duds. The third wasn't, and it blew a hole just back from the bows you could drive an oxcart through. It's a miracle we got most of the engine-room gang out."

Marian nodded; she knew what the words hid. The sudden inrush of water, like a wet avalanche down a hull with no interior bulkheads. The crew struggling up the ladders in darkness, with the roar of water and the toning sounds of the boilers' self-destruction all around them as cold sea met hot steel. . . .

"Lucky it was shallow and not many of their guns bore on it," he said.

"Not really luck; that's why they put the mines there."

In another history, during the eighth century before Christ, settlers from Corinth would have landed on the island they called Ortygia, and founded the city later known as Syracuse. Here it had been the seat of a local chief, until William Walker led Achaeans spearheaded by his rifle-armed troops here to conquer. The fortifications had probably started right away, and judging by the piles of stone were still going on. As she watched a ripple of smoke puffs ran along one of the slanting walls. Seconds later the dull flat *booommm* of heavy cannon came, and water began to gout skyward in columns of green and shattered white near the grounded ironclad. That was a small target, only the casement showing above the surface. Seconds later the ship's own broadside guns replied, their rifled barrels giving them a harder, sharper bark. Stone shattered where they struck and avalanched downward. Then the long forward six-inch gun fired, sending its heavy shell past the island and into the town proper.

"Eleven-inch Dalghrens," Hiller said. "We get ammunition and supplies to the *Eades* at night in small boats, and volunteers, and bring others out for rest. So far she's given as good as she's got, but eventually they'll pound her to pieces, since she can't move. Quicker, if they get that damned heavy mortar moved . . ."

Alston's eyes went to the civilan settlement around the head of the causeway. That was fortified as well, excellent low-slung works behind a deep moat and glacis. The Islander artillery on the heights of Epipolai beyond still bore on the city below, the distant slamming-door sound of its firing echoing across the water. Then came the long whistling fall, and another tall billow of pulverized adobe, timber, stone, and people. They were densely packed in there, too; Achaean colonists had fled here from all the province around. Crowds of Sicel natives and slave rebels sprawled near the orderly tent-rows and earthworks of the Republic's Marines.

"Not a problem, if . . . there," Alston said, looking down at her watch.

A rocket went up from the fortress on Ortygia, bursting green. The same signal came up from the Islander works ashore, and from the bridge of the *Farragut,* where she patrolled off the line of anchored frigates and transports.

"Head us in for the landing grounds, if you please, Mr. Hiller."

Her command tent wasn't big enough for the delegates this time; they met on a piece of sloping ground. They'd all agreed to come unarmed, trusting to Alston's reputation for keeping strictly to the terms of agreements. Nantucketer Marines separated the three parties, Achaeans and native Sicilians and uprisen slaves.

Although the Achaeans look like they need protecting from each other, Marian noted with cold amusement as dagger glances went back and forth. *Not really all Achaeans, either; lot of Walker's mercenaries are from all over.*

Walker's viceroy had been one of his original followers. Danny Rodriguez's body still hung from the gallows at the edge of camp, but he'd been dead when the Marines caught him, stabbed by a member of his hareem.

Even divided as they were, the Achaeans were a miracle of unity compared to the Sicels. The slaves were as numerous as both the other groups put together, but even less organized. Still, the month of fighting had thrown up some natural leaders . . .

"Greetings," she said.

An interpreter put that in Achaean, and all the respective groups had at least one person who could turn that into whatever.

"We are all come here under sign of truce to arrange an end to this war."

One of the Achaeans shot to his feet. "The King of Men will put an end to the war, and to you invaders!"

Alston put her hands on her webbing belt. "He hasn't shown much interest in doing so," she replied dryly. "His armies are in the Hittite lands, and his fleet is keeping to its bases, to defend his seat of power and his palace. He has abandoned you."

The Achaean snarled; he was wearing the remains of Walker's gray uniform. Some of the other Greeks around him nodded, though.

Ah. Doreen was right.

The problem with tying down a conquest by land grants was that it gave the settlers a vested interest. They'd fight to defend it, yes . . . but they'd also negotiate to defend it, if fighting didn't look too successful. These men had families and farms and homes to think of; and the first gruesome results of the uprising that had accompanied the Islander invasion were enough to make anyone thoughtful.

A Sicel chief rose next, a lean brown little man in a loincloth and cloak of goatskin, with long tangled black hair. His folk looked a lot like Tartessians, in a primitive sort of way, and spoke a language related to the Iberians'—about as close as Italian would be, would have been, to Spanish.

"Why should we talk peace when the invaders still stand on the Lady's holy soil? Let them get gone, or die." His eyes moved over to the slave rebels with whom he'd found himself in uneasy alliance. "The ones they have brought here, they can go, too."

Shouts and threats boiled free. Not many of the slaves had anywhere to go. Either their homes had been overrun by Walker's men, or they'd been sold by hostile neighbors not interested in seeing them back.

Marian waited a moment, then nodded. Swindapa picked up the powered megaphone and held the microphone near the output diaphragm. Feedback squeal stabbed into ears; forewarned, Marian kept her response to a slight flinch. Overhead the *Liberator* plowed the air in a slow circle, vastly more intimidating to eyes that didn't know how much of her bulk was fabric and gasbag.

"Silence!" she said into the quiet that followed.

A strong earthy smell came up the hill to her, and a reek of fear sweat. Most of these men had been fighting for weeks now, and going in terror of their lives—of seeing their womenfolk and children raped or burned alive before their eyes, as well. It showed; and their nerve wasn't what it might have been either.

"You—" She pointed to the Sicel. "Dakenterar. Your people are no longer numerous enough to hold this island by themselves. The Achaeans are as many as you, and their slaves twice as many."

Those were the proportions the Intelligence people had gotten from Foreign Affairs; the Arnsteins' numbers were pretty reliable. Of course, the whole population was a good deal smaller than it had been a month ago, but the reductions seemed to have been roughly similar all 'round.

"You Achaeans," she said. "If you continue to fight us, you can't hope to win. A few forts may hold out, but most of you will die; and even those who live will lose everything." She smiled unpleasantly. "We have a saying: *If you want to know the enemies in your household, count your slaves.*"

To the slaves: "You've won your freedom. Now is the time to see about winning new lives."

One of the rebels laughed. "Why not go on until the masters are *our* slaves?" he said, in Greek even she could tell was broken. So were his teeth, and stained brown. "Then we will have all their good things."

"Because you can't fight without us, and we won't help you do that—unless the Achaeans decide to fight to the death."

"Never will we betray our lord!"

That was the Achaean soldier who'd spoken first. Two of his

neighbors exchanged glances, then grabbed a leg each. Daggers flashed; Marian flung up a hand to hold the Marines back as the lethal brawl spread among the Achaeans. It was over quickly; three bodies lying limp, and another moaning and clutching a bleeding head.

Walker had sworn men who were personally loyal to *him*, but Achaea hadn't been a nation even before he came and vastly expanded it—the whole notion would be alien to these people. Only a few of the Kings and great nobles even thought of the Achaean lands as a unit at all. For the rest, local loyalties were to kin and place; and Walker hadn't had time to build up the sort of dynastic legitimacy that an established royal family here could call on. Another generation or two, and his system might have set down deep roots. . . .

But as it is, he hasn't. And oh, does that make a difference! Not while he's winning, but given a defeat, and an enemy on his soil . . . Plus his best troops were in Anatolia or Greece, not this backwater.

"Hear my word," she went on. "Here is my proposal. We are willing to let the Achaeans here live . . . so long as they promise to take no more part in this war and open their fortresses. They can keep their lands and goods as well."

That brought shouts of rage from the Sicels and slave rebels as well. She turned to them and made a soothing gesture; the Marines brought their rifles around to present the points of the bayonets.

"The lands of the King and the dead and those who don't live here, those are forfeit." Which would be a good two-thirds of the island. "Every slave who wants one can have a farm, or the tools of his trade; and so that nobody need fear his neighbor, let it be proclaimed that the taking of folk into slavery shall never be allowed here again. There will be land for you Sicels, too; not as much as you might want, but it's better than being hunted like game through the mountains or caught and sent to the mines, isn't it?"

The Sicel chiefs looked interested. They all came from the wildest parts of the mountains; the coastal tribes where most of the settlers were located had been wiped out long ago . . .

"But who shall till our fields?" a well-dressed Achaean asked in bewilderment. "If there are no slaves?"

Marian held up her hands and moved the fingers. "We have another saying: *He who does not work, does not eat.* You have your *machines* and the strength of your hands. For those who have more land than they can work, some of your former slaves might want to rent land, in return for tools and beasts and seed-grain. Or Sicels from the highlands, where making a living is so hard."

They weren't looking happy about that, but most of the bigger slaveowners had been absentees, or had died in the first explosive flare of the uprising because they and their retainers were so heavily outnumbered. The rest were farmers with moderate holdings or townsmen; Walker had handed out a lot of quarter sections, a hundred and sixty acres. That was riches by the standards of the Bronze Age, but he'd also had nineteenth-century farm equipment manufactured. A family could make a good living without killing themselves.

"More important—who shall *rule*?" another man asked.

Okay, let's see if we can get this across, she thought, and took a deep breath. "We don't wish to rule here. We suggest that each of your factions elect—get together and choose by show of hands"—none of these languages had a word for *vote,* but an assembly of the tribe's warriors was a familiar institution—"a man, a *consul.* The three *consuls* will rule, and each district should hold an assembly which—"

It took all day just to get the idea across. Probably the Sicilian Republic would dissolve in chaos as soon as the small Islander garrison departed—she was going to use a couple of battalions of Alban auxiliaries for that, as long as she needed Syracuse as a base.

Then again, it might not; and it would serve Nantucket's purpose either way.

Spring came late to the uplands of central Anatolia, but when it did it came with a rush. Kenneth Hollard inhaled deeply, taking in the scent of the flowering cherry trees and the fresh green of the grass underfoot; the breeze was from the south, carrying a kiss of warmth. It was good to walk freely, out of the fusty closeness of winter quarters, to air out the body and the soul.

Even better with a girl, he thought.

Raupasha's hand rested shyly in his. A dusting of the blossoms rested on her raven hair and the dark linen shoulders of her robe. He smiled down into the scarred, lovely face. Sabala sniffed at them, then raced off to make lunging snaps at butterflies.

"I did not dream a great warrior could be so . . . so *sweet,*" she said a bit breathlessly, after they broke the clinch and walked on.

I didn't dream I could be so goddamned horny *and not mind waiting . . . well, not mind it much,* he thought. And: *By God, an Islander upbringing gets you mileage here.* Men here didn't have much technique; they didn't really need it.

As if to confirm his thought, Raupasha went on: "It is so strange, this custom you have of men and women arranging their own marriages . . . doesn't it lead to much foolishness, as youth lacks the wisdom of age?"

He nodded. "We marry later than your folk, usually. But yes, about as much unhappiness as any other way . . . but we have a saying, that it's better to be ruled by your own mistakes than someone else's wisdom."

That shocked her a little; he could see her frown. "But . . . then, how can a man be sure his bride is a virgin? If she has gone about seeking a man on her own."

He chuckled gently. The question made complete sense, in her terms; for that matter, his own ancestors—unless they happened to be Fiernan Bohulugi, or Trobriand Islanders—would have agreed with it.

"We don't think more of virginity in a woman than in a man," he said. *Most of us, at least.* "And as for married women, people can either trust each other, or they can't."

"In that case," she said, halting again and putting her arms around his neck.

A few minutes later her fingers were scrabbling open the buckle of his webbing belt with desperate eagerness. He pulled the hem of her robe upward and she raised her arms to free it, gasping as his mouth sought a breast and they both sank toward the soft spring grass—

Arroooooooown. Arroooooown.

"Oh, God *dammit* to hell, what now?"

That was the charioteer's horn, the agreed signal of something important. Raupasha broke away, smoothing her hair and rumpled gown, flushed and smiling as they walked back toward the vehicle; he ground his teeth and walked carefully.

All winter to get over the trauma, and now that she has, *we get interrupted!*

A mounted Hittite messenger waited beside the chariot; his mount was lathered, and he sweat-stained and tired.

"Lord Kenn'et," he said, and extended a leather tube.

Kenneth broke the seal and tapped the paper out into his hands, unrolling it and reading quickly. Part of it was written in Akkadian, but in Roman letters. Raupasha's smile died as she looked at his face; hers was grave and waiting as he looked up.

"What news, lo-, Ken," she said. "Is Walker moving?"

"Yes," he said. His fist crumpled the paper. "But that's not the whole of it." Her brows went up. "Pharaoh has denounced the treaty with the Hittites. Evidently he thinks this would be a good time to get revenge for the Battle of Kadesh. A bit startling and a bit late, seeing that that was forty years ago, but . . ." He shrugged.

Raupasha blinked, turning from an eighteen-year-old in love to the ruler who'd commanded a chariot squadron behind enemy lines. For a moment her living eye was as blank as the molded leather one in the mask that covered the scarred part of her face.

"But how can we turn aside to the south, if Walker moves in from the west?"

"We can't," Hollard said grimly. "Tudhaliyas has called up his southern levies and vassals. They'll have to hold Pharaoh."

"But they are troops without firearms!"

He nodded. "Possibly the commodore can send help from Sicily."

"If not . . ."

"If not, Ramses may walk all the way to the walls of Hattusas."

"Or to the Euphrates, and cut us here off from Kar-Duniash, which is nearly as bad."

They looked at each other and stepped into the chariot. "Iridmi!" Raupasha called crisply. "To the camp—and do not spare the team."

CHAPTER THIRTY

April, 11 A.E.—Canaan, Kingdom of Egypt
April, 11 A.E.—Central Anatolia, Kingdom of
  Hatti-land
April, 11 A.E.—Canaan, Kingdom of Egypt
April, 11 A.E.—Eurotas Valley, Kingdom of Great
  Achaea
April, 11 A.E.—Damascus, Kingdom of Hatti-Land
April, 11 A.E.—Meggido, Kingdom of Egypt
April, 11 A.E.—Walkeropolis, Kingdom of Great
  Achaea
April, 11 A.E.—Meggido, Kingdom of Egypt
April, 11 A.E.—Achaean camp, western Anatolia

The cannon were keeping up well with the chariots; Pharaoh would be pleased.

Djehuty, Commander of the Brigade of Seth, was a little uncomfortable on horseback even after months of practice with the new saddle with stirrups; the son riding beside him had learned more quickly.

Still, there was no denying it was convenient. He turned his horse and rode back down along the track beside his units, with the standard-bearer, scribes, aides, and messengers behind him. The rutted track was deep in sand, like most of the coastal plain of Canaan . . . where it wasn't swamp mud or rocks. The infantry in their banded-linen corselets plodded along, their brown faces darker yet with dust and streaked with sweat under their striped headdresses of thick canvas. Round-topped rectangular shields were slung over their shoulders, bronze spear blades glinted in the bright sun. After them came a company of Nubians, Medjay mercenaries from far up the Nile. Djehuty frowned; the black men were slouching along in their usual style, in no order at all . . . although anyone who'd seen one of their screaming charges could forgive them that.

Then came one of the New Regiments; they wore only kilts

and pleated loin-guards, but there were leather bandoliers of papyrus cartridges at their right hips and muskets over their shoulders. Djehuty scowled slightly at the sight of them, despite the brave show they made with their feet moving in unison and the golden-fan standard carried before them on a long pole.

Their weapons are good, he acknowledged. "But will they stand in battle?" he asked himself. They were peasants, not *iw'yt,* not real soldiers, raised from childhood in the barracks.

After them came the cannon themselves, wrought with endless difficulty and expense. Djehuty's thick-muscled chest swelled with pride under his iron-scale armor at the number Pharaoh entrusted to him—a full dozen of the *twelve-pounders,* as they were called in the barbaric tongue of their inventors. Each was a bronze tube of a length equal to a very tall man's height, with little bronze cylinders cast on either side so that the guns could ride in their chariotlike mounts. Very much like a chariot, save that the pole rested on another two-wheeled cart, the *limber,* and that was hauled by six horses with the new collar harness that bore on their shoulders rather than their necks.

Better for the horses, he admitted grudgingly, passing on to the chariots. Those had changed in the last few years as well. Besides a compound bow and quiver on one side, there was a scabbard on the other for two double-barreled shotguns, and the crew was now three, like a Hittite war-cart—one being a loader for the warrior who captained the vehicle.

He reined in and took a swig from the goatskin water bottle at his saddle. It cut gratefully through the dust and thick phlegm in his mouth, and he spat to the side and drank again, since there were good springs nearby and no need to conserve every drop. Years of work, to make the Brigade of Seth the finest in Pharaoh's service, and then to integrate the new weapons.

To be good commanders, his father had told him, *we must love our army and our soldiers. But to win victories, we must be ready to kill the thing we love. When you attack, strike like a hammer and hold nothing back.*

"Stationed in Damnationville with no supplies," he said, a soldier's saying as old as the wars against the Hyksos.

"But sir, there are plenty of supplies," his son said.

Djehuty nodded. "There are now, boy," he said. "But imagine being stuck here on garrison duty for ten years."

The young man looked around. To their left was the sea, brighter somehow than that off the Delta. The road ran just inland of the coastal sand dunes; off to the right a line of hills made the horizon rise up in heights of blue and purple. Thickets of oak dotted the plain, and stretches of tall grass, still green with summer rain. Grain turned yellow in a few patches of cultivation, here and there a vineyard or olive grove, but the land was thinly peopled—had been since the long wars Pharaoh had waged early in his reign, nearly forty Nile floods ago.

And those did not go well, he remembered uneasily—he'd been a stripling then, but nobody who'd been at Kadesh was going to believe in the great Egyptian victory that the temple walls proclaimed.

A village of dun-colored huts with flat roofs stood in the middle distance, dim through the greater dust plume of the Egyptian host passing north. The dwellers and their stock were long gone; sensible peasants ran when armies passed by.

By the standards of the vile Asiatics, the hairy dwellers in Amurru, this was flat and fertile land. To an Egyptian, it was hard to tell the difference between this and the sterile red desert that lay east of the Nile.

"War and glory are only found in foreign lands," the younger man said stoutly.

"Well spoken, son," the commander said. He looked left; the Ark of Ra was sinking toward the waters. "Time to camp soon. And Pharaoh will summon the commanders to conference in the morning."

"My Kat'ryn . . ." Kashtiliash of Babylon said.

"Yeah, Kash?" she said, looking up from the washstand. Beads of water ran down the smooth-muscled shoulders, over breasts like lathe-turned wine cups. The pink nipples stiffened to the touch of the chill water, in the predawn cold.

He seated sword and revolver more firmly on his hips and took a deep breath. Holding his spear firm for the charge of a lion or boar was easier than this. Kathryn took up a towel and began to dry herself; uniform and helmet and weapons waited on a stand in the corner of the rammed-earth commanders' quarters.

"Kat'ryn, I have been months gone from the land of Kar-Duniash."

She nodded, suddenly slightly wary. "Yes . . . has anyone made trouble back home?"

"No," he snorted. "Nor will any, so long as they know I would come down the Euphrates with the New Troops and the cannon should a usurper arise; also my half brothers are here with us—and you know that is not chance. But . . . the Egyptians are moving, and they threaten our line of communications."

"You're worried about rebellion?" she said.

"I have no son of my Great Wife as yet," he said quietly. "My others are children. If I were cut off here . . ."

"You're going to pull the army out, Kash?" she asked steadily. Lamplight glinted in the alien blue eyes.

"No," he shook his head. "My word is good. But if our line to Babylon is threatened, I must send part of these troops to secure it. I *must*; the safety of my House and the realm require it."

She threw down the towel and came to him. "I understand," she said. A sudden lynx grin. "So, let's finish Walker first, and then it'll be Pharaoh's turn, eh?"

Ramses stood as erect as a granite monolith, wearing the military kilt and the drum-shaped red crown of war with the golden cobra rearing at his brows, waiting as still as the statue of a God. The officers knelt and bowed their heads to the carpet before him in the shade of the great striped canvas pavillion. There was a silence broken only by the clank of armor scales and creak of leather. Then the eunuch herald's voice rang like silver in the cool air of dawn:

"He is The Horus, Strong Bull, Beloved of Ma'at; He of the Two Goddesses, Protector of Khem who Subdues the Foreign Lands; the Golden Horus, Rich in Years, Great in Victories; He is King of Upper and Lower Egypt, Strong in Right; He is User-Ma'at-Ra, *Son of Ra; Ramses, Beloved of Amun."*

The officers bowed again to the living God, and Pharaoh made a quick gesture with one hand. The officers bowed once more and rose.

Djehuty came to his feet with the rest. Servants pulled a cover off a long table. It was covered by a shallow-sided box, and within the box was a model made of sand mixed with Nubian gum, smelling like a temple on a festival day. Its maker stood waiting.

The outland dog, Djehuty thought. Mek-Andrus the foreigner, the one who'd risen so high in Pharaoh's service. He wore Egyptian headdress and military kilt but foreign armor—a long tunic of linked iron rings. *Foreign dog. Disturber of custom.*

"The servants of Pharaoh will listen to this man, now Chief of Chariots," Ramses said. "So let it be written. So let it be done."

Djehuty bowed his head again. *If Pharaoh commands that I*

obey a baboon with a purple arse, I will obey, he thought. Mek-Andrus was obviously part Nubian, too, with skin the color of a barley loaf and a flat nose. *The will of Pharaoh is as the decrees of fate.*

The foreigner moved to the sand table and picked up a wooden pointer. "This is the ground on which we must fight," he said. His Egyptian was fluent, but it had a sharp nasal accent like nothing any of the Khemites had ever heard before. "As seen from far above."

All the officers had had the concept explained to them. Some were still looking blank-eyed: Djehuty nodded and looked down with keen interest. There was the straight north–south reach of the coast of Canaan, with the coastal plan narrowing to nothing where the inland hills ran almost to water's edge; a bay north of that, where a river into the sea. The river marked a long trough, between the hills and the mountains of Galilee to the north, and it was the easiest way from the sea inland to the big lake and the Jordan valley.

"The Hittites, the men of Kar-Duniash, the *mariyannu* of the Asiatic cities, the Armanaean tribes, and their allies are aproaching from the northeast, thirty-five thousand strong not counting their auxiliaries and camp followers, according to the latest reports."

The pointer traced a line down through Damascus, over the heights, along the shores of the Sea of Galilee, then northwest from Bet Shean.

"Of those, at least five thousand are infantry equipped with fire weapons, with thirty cannon, and four thousand chariots."

None of the Egyptian commanders stirred; there was a low mutter of sound as the Sherdana mercenary leader translated for his monoglot subordinates, their odd-looking helmets with the circle of feathers all around bending together.

"Favored of the Son of Ra," Djehuty said. "If we are here"—he pointed to a place half a day's march before the place where the coastal plain pinched out—"can they reach the sea and hold the passes over Carmel against us?"

Mek-Andrus nodded; he no longer smiled with such boorish frequency as he had when he first came to Egypt. "That is the question. They were here"—he tapped the place where the Jordan emerged from Galilee—"yesterday at sunset.

Another rustling. That left the enemy further from the plain of Jezreel than the Egyptians, but the path the northerners must cross was over flat land with supplies to hand; the Egyptian force must cross mountains.

"Thutmose did it," Mek-Andrus said. "If we take this pass"—his finger tapped—"as the Great One's predecessor did, we can be *here* and deployed to meet them before they expect us."

Thutmose . . . Djehuty thought. Then: *Ah.* One of the great Pharaohs of the previous dynasty, the one that had petered out when the Accursed of Amun, the Enemy, tried to throw down the worship of the Gods in favor of Atun.

His eyes narrowed as he watched Mek-Andrus. How did the outland dog know so much of Khem? Djehuty *knew* the barbarian didn't read the Egyptian script, so he couldn't have simply read the story off a temple wall the way a literate, civilized man might. The fire-weapons themselves weren't sorcery, just a recipe, like cooking—plain saltpeter and sulfur and charcoal, whatever the peasants might think. But there was something not quite canny about Mek-Andrus himself.

Yet the Gods have sent him to us. Without Mek-Andrus, the Hittites and Achaeans and other demon-begotten foreigners who knew not the Black Land or the Red would have had the new weapons all to their own. That would have been as bad as the time long ago when the Hyksos came with their chariots, before any Egyptian had seen a horse, and it had taken a long night of subjection and war to expel *them*.

"Who should take the vanguard?" Pharaoh asked.

Mek-Andrus bowed. "Let Pharaoh choose the commander who has both wisdom and bravery . . . and many cannon, so that they can hold off the enemy host until the whole army of Pharaoh is deployed."

Remote as jackal-headed Anubis deciding the fate of a soul in the afterworld, Pharaoh's eyes scanned his generals.

Djehuty fell on his face as the flail pointed to him. "Djehuty of the Brigade of Seth. The vanguard shall be yours. Prepare to move as soon as you may. You shall cross the pass and hold the ground for the rest of our armies. So let it be written! So let it be done!"

It was a great honor—and possibly the death sentence for the Brigade of Seth.

The courier threw back his head and drank, water running down his chin into the stubble and soaking into the filthy gray wool of his uniform tunic. The smithy was scorching, its thick adobe walls soaking up the heat of the two charcoal hearths, steam hissing as the hot shoe was plunged into the water. The man whose horse was being shod kept an eye on it even as he stuck the cup into the well bucket again; cooler out here . . . and even now, a certain magic clung to ironworking.

It had been a long ride overland from his landfall in Athens, even with good roads. The almond trees in the field across from the smithy and relay station were in bloom, their scent a breath of freshness amid the dust and dung of the roadside smithy. Soon he would be in Walkeropolis, where he could rest.

The saddlebags had the Wolf Lord's blazon on them. The death-fate laid on him if they were lost was gruesome.

The smith bent and lifted the right rear hoof between his knees, nails ready in his mouth. A slave girl came by just then, looking over her shoulder at the uniformed courier and letting her thin tunic draw tight against her buttocks. He smiled and worked the pump for her to fill her bucket.

Nevertheless, he was stern in his duty, shaking his head ruefully when she looked back at him from around the corner and rolled her eyes toward the stables. She made a face at him and walked off; he sighed and took the bridle of his horse as the smith's boy led it out. He swung back into the saddle and heeled his mount to the graveled verge of the road.

"Good intelligence can be worth an extra regiment," Marian Alston-Kurlelo said, returning Kenneth Hollard's salute and then taking his hand.

It was going on two years now since she'd ridden into Camp Grant and told him that he was going to Babylonia. *Grown a good deal.* Thirtysomething, but looking older and a bit thinner, and tired. *Done a good job.*

"It had better be worth a regiment," he said bluntly. "Because these two battalions are all I can spare, with the local levies. If we take any more from the northern front, we're fucked. Ma'am."

She chuckled, looking out over the vast sprawling chaos of the muster point where the hosts of the southern Hittite lands were gathered. Many of the assembled Hittites—and Syrians and Aramaeans and whatever—were still in hysterics from the *Liberator*'s visit; she'd sent the airship right back for another load of heavy weapons anyway. The dust and heat were already fearsome; even in April, the Damascus area was well into what felt like summer. The green oasis helped some, and the sight of the cedar-forested mountains to the westward.

Take me back to the River Jordan, she thought/quoted to herself. *It's about seventy-five miles thataway, south by southwest.*

"Most of the Egyptians will be old-style troops," she said reassuringly. "Doreen may be in her seventh month, but her spies are very mobile. Their rifle units won't be as good as the Tartessians, and they weren't as good as Walker's men in Sicily . . . and he's got all his best facing you."

Hollard nodded. "This is damned important, though, ma'am," he said. "A couple of crucial alliances depend on turning the Egyptians back."

"Awkward. I'd been hoping to bring my people in from Sicily directly in your support—invading Greece directly just now is out of the question, I'm afraid; I don't have the firepower or troops. Well, needs must when the devil drives; I'll handle the Egyptians if you can hold Walker. Good luck, Brigadier Hollard. Good hunting."

"And to you, Commodore," he said.

"I do not like the thought of cowering in a hole," Djehuty said.

The valley stretched out before him, land flat and marshy in spots, in others fertile enough even by an Egyptian's standards. Wheat and barley billowed in green waves with yellow streaks; the fallow plots between the fields were densely grown with weeds. Olive trees grew thick on the hills that rose on either side of the southeastward trend of the lowlands; orchards of fig and pomegranate and green leafy vineyards that would produce the famed Wine of the North stood around hamlets of dark mud brick. These lands were well peopled, a personal estate of Pharaoh and on a route that carried much trade from the north in times of peace.

"All the courage in the world won't stop a bullet," Mek-Andrus said. "A man in a hole—a *rifle pit*—can load and fire more easily, and still be protected from the enemy's bullets. They must stand and walk forward to attack; and the Divine Son of Ra has ordered us to defend."

Djehuty made a gesture of respect at the Pharaoh's name. "So he has," he said. *You purple-arsed baboon,* he thought to himself. Pharaoh was a living God, but a commander in the field was not always bound by his sovereign's orders—it was the objective that counted. And occasionally Egyptians had committed deicide. *No.* He thrust the thought from him. That was a counsel of desperation, and Ramses had been a good Pharaoh, strong and just.

"How do you advise that we deploy, then?" Djehuty said.

He looked back. Most of the Brigade of Seth were out, forming up in solid blocks.

"Let us keep the pass to our backs," the foreigner said.

"So—half of a circle?" Djehuty said, making a curving gesture.

"No, not today. That would disperse the fire of our guns. Instead—"

Mek-Andrus began to draw in the dirt with a bronze-tipped stick he carried. "Two *redoubts,* little square earth forts, on either end of a half circle whose side curves away from the enemy. That way they can give *enfilading fire.*"

"Please, O Favored of the Divine Horus, speak Egyptian; I plead my ignorance."

Mek-Andrus looked up sharply. Djehuty gave him a bland smile; let him see how a civilized man controlled his emotions.

The foreigner nodded. He held both hands out, fingers splayed, then crossed those fingers to make a checkerboard. "*Enfilading fire* means that the paths of the balls or grapeshot from the cannon cross each other, so," he said. "Instead of one path of destruction, they overlap and create a whole field where nothing can live."

The Egyptian's eyes went wide. He struggled within his head, imagining . . . *Those Nubians who tried to raid the fort,* he thought. A great wedge had been cut through their mass, as if sliced by the knife of a God. Within that triangle only shattered bone and splattered flesh had remained. In his mind's eye he overlapped that broad path of death with thirty more, and put Hittite charioteers in place of naked blacks with horn-tipped spears. His hand went of itself to the outlander's shoulder.

"I see your plan!" he exclaimed, smiling broadly. "It is a thing of beauty. And how shall we place the musketeers?"

Djehuty's son listened closely, waiting in silence until Mek-Andrus strode away. "Father and lord," he said hesitantly. "Is it possible that . . . some among us have been mistaken concerning the outlander?"

His father shook his head. "He knows much," he said. "But it is still a violation of *ma'at,* of the order of things, that an outlander should stand so close to the Great One. And to be granted a Royal woman as his wife! Not even the Great King of the Hittites was given such honor, when we were allied with them and at peace. No," he went on, dropping his voice. "The day will come when the foreign dog who knows not the Red Land or the Black will have taught us all he knows. On that day . . ."

Father and son smiled, their expressions like wolves peering into a mirror. Then Djehuty raised his voice: "Officers of Five Hundred. Attend me!"

Odd, Philowos thought, as he took the sealed folders from their leather casing. *There are six. Five is the standard number.*

The Assistant Underscribe (Ministry of Communications of Great Achaea, on loan to Walkeropolis-central from the *Mukenai* branch office) shrugged. There wasn't any regulation about it; and these were personal Royal correspondence. The King did as he willed, not as other men did.

"Come on, I haven't got all day," the courier said, standing there with an air of iron and horse sweat, letting in a little of the heat and white light of the street behind him. It was routine, but also somehow out of place in this world of quiet and rustling paper and well-bathed men.

"Thumbprint here," Philowos said.

The courier obeyed, and then slowly and laboriously wrote his name, tongue protruding from the corner of his mouth.

Good, Philowos thought.

A full literate *might* have noticed that the date partly concealed under the scribe's own thumb was that for tomorrow, not today. Not likely, but possible.

Philowos waited while the swaggering courier threw his saddlebags over his shoulder with the arrogance of a sword-bearing man and clanked away. Then he walked on into the corridor that led toward his own cubicle, pausing at a large ceramic container of water. Casually he twisted the bungstopper and filled himself a cup, gossiping a little with acquaintances passing by and leaving the dispatches waiting on a ledge. When he turned around they were gone.

His heart beat a little faster as he went on to his desk. Tomorrow the dispatches would be there, and a little chamois sack of sweet-sounding coins, the King's good *dinars*. No problem, no fuss . . . and the dating would be accurate.

"They come," the Medjay scout wheezed, pointing behind himself with his spear. His body was naked save for a gourd penis sheath and his skin shone like polished onyx with sweat. "Their scouts chased me, but I lost them in rough ground."

Djehuty nodded; the Nubian mercenaries in Pharaoh's host were recruited from desert nomads south of the great bend of the Nile—hunters, herders, and bandits. They could outrun horses, given time, loping along at their tireless long-legged trot. And they could track a ghost over naked rock, or hide in their own shadows. Djehuty knew it too well. His first command had been patrols against the Medjay along the southern frontier. You didn't forget waking up and finding a sentry with his throat cut and his genitals stuffed into his mouth, and nobody in camp any the wiser until the Ark of Ra lifted over the horizon. That was Medjay humor . . . but they were useful, no doubt of that, and true to their salt.

"Many?" he said.

"Many," the barbarian confirmed, opening and closing his hands rapidly. "As one of the True Folk runs"—that was their heathen name for themselves—"an hour's distance."

"Fetch my war harness," he said to his son. To a runner: "A message to the captains that the enemy approaches."

His chariot came up, the plumes on the team's heads nodding, and the Egyptian commander ducked into the leather shirt of iron scales. Sweat soaked the linen backing almost immediately; he lowered the helmet over his head and buckled the strap below his chin. The sunlight was painful on the bronze and gold that decked the light wicker and bentwood of the car, and the iron tires shrunk onto the wooden wheels. He climbed aboard, his son after him; the boy made a production of checking the priming on shotguns and pistols, but he was a good lad, conscientious. More eager than was sensible, but this would be his first real battle.

"Keep your head," his father warned, his voice gruff. "It's the cool-blooded man lives long on the threshing ground of battle."

"I'm not afraid, Father!" Sennedjem said. His voice started low but broke in a humiliating squeak halfway through. He flushed angrily; his mother had been Djehuty's first woman, a fair-skinned Libyan captive, and the boy's olive tan was a little lighter than most men of Lower Egypt.

"That's the problem, lad," Djehuty grinned. "You *should* be frightened." He turned his attention to the work of the day.

The signal fire on top of the bare-sloped hill to the southeast went out. "Soon now," Djehuty said.

Dust gave the chariots away. The Egyptian squinted; his vision had grown better for distant things in the last few years, worse for close work. *Chariot screen,* he thought. Thrown forward to keep the Egyptians from getting a close look at their enemy's force before they deployed for battle. Whoever commanded the enemy host was no fool. Now he must do the same. Without a close description of his position, the enemy commander would be handicapped.

"Forward!" he barked.

Well drilled, the squadrons fanned out before him. The driver clucked to his charges, touched their backs gently with the reins, and the willing beasts went forward. Walk, canter, trot; the dry hard ground hammered at his feet below the wicker floor of the war-cart. He compensated with an instinctive flexing of knees and balance, learned since childhood. The enemy grew closer swiftly with the combined speed of both chariot fleets, and he could feel his lips draw back in a grin of carnivore anticipation.

Syrians, he thought, as details became plain—spiked bronze helmets, horsehair plumes, long coats of brass scales rippling like the skins of serpents, curled black beards, and harsh beak-nosed faces. *Mariyannu* warriors of the northern cities, some rebellious vassals of Pharaoh, some from the Hittite domains or the ungoverned borderlands.

They came in straggling clumps and bands, by ones and twos, fighting as ever by town and by clan. He could see the drivers leaning forward, shouting to the horses in their uncouth gutturals, the fighters reaching for arrows to set to their bows.

"We'll show them our fire," he said.

A feather fan mounted on a yard-long handle stood in a holder at his side. He snatched it out and waved to left and right. The Egyptian formation curled smoothly forward on either hand. *Fast as ever,* he thought—the new harness let a team pull the heavier chariots without losing speed or agility. A drumming of hooves filled the air with thunder, a choking white dust curled up like the sandstorms of Sinai. The horses rocked into a gallop, nostrils flared and red, foam flecking their necks. The first arrows arched out, the bright sun winking off their points. Djehuty sneered: much too far for effective archery. Dust boiled up into the unmerciful sky, thick and acrid on his tongue.

"Amun! Amun! The Divine Horus!" the Egyptians roared. Savage war cries echoed back from the enemy.

"Gun!" he barked, holding out a hand. Check-patterned acacia wood slapped into it as Sennedjem put the weapon into his hand.

Thumping sounds smashed through the roar of hooves and thunder of wheels. Syrian chariots went over, and the high womanish screaming of wounded horses was added to the uproar. Djehuty crouched, raking back the hammers with his left palm and then leveling the weapon.

Now. An enemy chariot dashing forward out of the dust in a dangerously tight curve, one wheel off the ground. Close enough to see the wild-eyed glare of the warrior poised with a javelin in one hand. Bring the wedge at the front of the paired barrels to the notch at the back. It wasn't so different from using a bow; the body adjusting like a machine of balanced springs, but easier, easier, no effort of holding the draw. Squeeze the trigger, nothing jerky about the motion . . .

Whump. The metal-shod butt of the shotgun punished his shoulder. Flame and sulfur-stinking smoke vomited from the barrels, along with thirty lead balls. Those were invisible—strange to think of something moving too fast to see—but he shouted in exultation as he saw them strike home. The horses reared and screamed and tripped as the lead raked them, and the driver went over backward.

"Gun!" Djehuty roared, and Sennedjem snatched away the empty one and slapped the next into his father's grasp, then went to work biting open cartridges, hands swift on ramrod and priming horn. Djehuty fired again. "Gun!"

They plunged through the dust cloud and out into the open; the surviving Syrian chariots were in full retreat. Others lay broken, some with upturned wheels still spinning. A wounded Syrian warrior stumbled forward with a long spear held in both hands; Djehuty shot him at ten paces distance, and the bearded face splashed away from its understructure of pink bone. Some of the shot carved grooves of brightness through the green-coated bronze of the man's helmet. Out of the corner of his eye he was conscious of Sennedjem reloading the spent shotgun, priming the pans, and waiting poised.

"Pull up," Djehuty rasped. "Sound *rally*."

The driver brought the team to a halt. Sennedjem sheathed the shotgun and brought out a slender brass horn. Its call sounded shrill and urgent through the dull diminishing roar of the skirmish. Man after man heard it; the Captains of a Hundred brought their commands back into formation. Djehuty took the signal fan from its holder and waved it.

Meanwhile he looked to the northeast. More dust there, a low sullen cloud of it that caught the bright sunlight. He waited, and a rippling sparkle came from it, filling vision from side to side of the world ahead of them like stars on a night-bound sea.

"Father, what's *that*?" Sennedjem blurted; he was looking pale, but his eyes and mouth were steady. Djehuty clipped him across the side of the head for speaking without leave, but lightly.

"Light on spearheads, lad," he said grimly. "Now it begins."

The redoubt was a five-sided figure of earth berms; there were notches cut in the walls for the muzzles of the cannon, and obstacles made of wooden bars set with sharp iron blades in the ditches before it.

Djehuty waited atop the rampart for the enemy heralds, come for the usual parley, an attacker's inevitable demand for surrender after the first skirmish. They carried a green branch for peace, and a white cloth on a pole as well—evidently the same thing, by somebody else's customs. And flags, one with white stars on a blue ground, and red and white stripes. His eyes widened a little. He had heard of that flag. Another beside it had similar symbols, and cryptic glyphs, thus: R.O.N. COAST GUARD. He shivered a little, inwardly. What wizardry was woven into that cloth? A touch at his amulet stiffened him with knowledge of the favor of the Gods of Khem. Gilded eagles topped the staffs, not the double-headed version of the Hittites, but sculpted as if alive with their wings thrust behind them and their claws clutching arrows and olive branches. *So that is why the strangers from the far west are called the Eagle People,* he thought. It must be their protector-God.

"I am Djehuty, Commander of the Brigade of Seth in the army of Pharaoh, *User-Ma'at-Ra,* son of Ra, Ramses of the line of Ramses, the ruler of Upper and Lower Egypt," he barked. "Speak."

"Commodore Marian Alston-Kurlelo," the figure in the odd blue clothing said. He lifted off his helm. *No,* she, *by the Gods—the rumors speak truth. Odd, but we had a woman as Pharaoh once, and she led armies.* Djehuty's eyes went wider. The enemy commander was a Nubian; not part-blood like Mek-Andrus, but black as polished ebony. His eyes flicked to the others sitting their horses beside her. One was a woman, too, yellow-haired like some Achaeans; another was a man of no race he knew, with skin the color of amber and eyes slanted at the outer ends; the other two looked like Sherden from the north shore of the Middle Sea as far as their coloring went, although their hair was cropped close. A *Sudunu* stood uneasily by the foreign woman's stirrup; he stepped forward and bowed with one hand to his flowerpot hat to keep it from falling off.

"I shall interpret, noble Djehuty," he said uneasily; the Egyptian was fluent, but with the throaty accent of his people. Djehuty glared for a second. Byblos, Sidon, and the other coastal cities of Canaan south of Ugarit were vassals of Pharaoh; what was this treacherous dog doing aiding his enemies? *Sudunu* would do anything for wealth.

"Tell this woman that no foreigner goes armed in Pharaoh's dominions without his leave, on pain of death. If she and her rabble leave at once, I may be merciful."

The *Sudunu* began to speak in Akkadian, the Babylonian tongue. Djehuty could follow it a little; it was the tongue Kings used to write to each other, and not impossibly different from the language of the western Semites, which he did speak after a fashion. The interpreter was shading the meaning. That often happened, since such a man was eager to avoid offending anyone.

"Tell her exactly, as I told you—don't drip honey on it," he broke in.

The swarthy, scrawny man in the embroidered robe swallowed hard, and the black woman gave a slight, bleak smile.

"Lord Djehuty," the interpreter began. "Commodore—that is a rank, lord—Alston says that she is empowered by her . . . lord, the word she uses means ruler, I think—Ruler of an island across the River Ocean—and the Great King of the Hittites, and the Great King of Kar-Duniash, and their other allies, to demand the return of *George McAndrews*, a renegade of her people. If you will give us this man, the allied forces will return past the border of the Pharaoh Ramses's dominions, and peace may prevail."

Djehuty puzzled over the words for a moment before he realized that the name was Mek-Andrus.

"Barbarians make no demands of Pharaoh," he snapped. *Although I would send him to you dragged by the ankles behind my chariot, if the choice were mine.* "They beg for favors, or feel the flail of his wrath. Go, or die."

The coal-black face gave a slight nod. *No, not a Medjay,* Djehuty thought with an inner chill. They were fierce children, their *ka* plain on their faces. This one had discipline; doubly remarkable in a woman. And she showed no sign of fear, under the muzzles of his guns. *She must know what they can do. Mek-Andrus is of her people.*

If the stranger was a renegade from the service of his own King, much was explained. He schooled his own face.

"Pharaoh commands; as it is written, so shall it be done," he replied. "This parley is over. Depart his soil, at once, or the battle will commence."

* * *

BAAAAAAAMMMM.

The twelve-pounder leaped back, up the sloping ramp of dirt the gunners had shoveled behind it, then back down again into battery. Stripped to their loincloths, the crew threw themselves into action. Stinking smoke drifted about them, and the confused roaring noise of battle, but the men labored on, wet with sweat, their faces blackened by powder fumes until their eyes stared out like white flecks in black masks, burns on their limbs where they had brushed against the scorching bronze of the cannon.

These are men, Djehuty thought, slightly surprised. *More than that, they are men worthy to be called* iw'yt, *real soldiers.*

He wasn't sure about the warriors surging against his line, but whatever they were, they didn't discourage easily. He squinted through the thick smoke that stung his eyes, ignoring the dryness of his tongue—they were short of water, and he meant to make what he had last.

Here they came again, over ground covered with their dead. Swarms of them, sending a shower of javelins before them as they came closer.

BAAAAMMMM. BAAAAMMMM. The guns were firing more slowly now, conserving their ammunition. Grapeshot cut bloody swaths through the attackers, but they kept on. Dead men dropped improvised ladders of logs and sticks; others picked them up and came forward. Their cries grew into a deep bellowing; the first ranks dropped into the ditch around the redoubt, where the spiked barricades were covered with bodies. Others climbed up, standing on their shoulders to scramble up the sloping dirt or set up their scaling ladders. Only a few of them knew enough to cringe at the sound that came through shouts and cannonade—the sound of thumbs cocking back the hammers of their muskets.

"Now!" Djehuty shouted, swinging his fan downward.

All along the parapet, hundreds of musketeers stood up from their crouch and leveled their pieces downward into the press of attackers.

"Fire!"

A fresh fogbank of smoke drifted away, showing the ruin below—the muskets had been loaded with what Mek-Andrus called *buck and ball,* a musket ball and several smaller projectiles. The ditch was filled with shapes that heaved and moaned and screamed, and the smell was like a desecrated tomb. Djehuty winced; he was a hardy man and bred to war, but this . . .

this was something else. Not even the actions in the south had prepared him for it; the barbarians there were too undisciplined to keep charging into certain death as these men had.

"They run away, they run away, Father!" Sennedjem said.

Then, away in the gathering dusk, lights blinked like angry red eyes. Everyone in the little earth fort took cover. A long whistling screech came from overhead, and then the first explosion. The enemy cannon were better than the ones Mek-Andrus had taught the men of Khem to make; instead of firing just solid roundshot or grape, they could throw shells that exploded themselves—and throw them further. Djehuty dug his fingers into the earth, conscious mainly of the humiliation of it. He, Commander of the Brigade of Seth, whose ancestors had been nobles since the years when the Theban Pharaohs expelled the Hyksos, cowering in the dirt like a peasant! But the fire-weapons were no respecters of rank or person.

And they will shred my Brigade of Seth like meat beneath the cook's cleaver.

So Pharaoh had ordered . . . and it might be worth it, if it turned the course of the battle to come.

Earth shuddered under his belly and loins. He had a moment to think, and it froze him with his fingers crooked into the shifting clay. *Why only cannon?* From the reports and rumors, the newcomers had taught their allies to make muskets, too, and better ones than the Egyptians had. Yet all the infantry and chariots his brigade had met here were armed with the old weapons; some of them fashioned of iron rather than bronze, but still spear, sword, bow, javelin.

The barrage let up. He turned his head, and felt his liver freeze with fear. Sennedjem was lying limp and pale, his back covered in blood. Djehuty scrambled to him, ran hands across the blood-wet skin. Breath of life and pulse of blood, faint but still there. He prayed to the Gods of healing and clamped down; there, something within the wound. A spike of metal, still hot to the touch. He took it between thumb and forefinger, heedless of the sharp pain in his own flesh, and pulled. His other hand pressed across the wound while he roared for healers, bandages, wine, and resin to wash out the hurt. When they came he rose, forcing himself to look away and think as his son was borne to the rear.

"I don't like the smell of this," he muttered, and called for a runner. "Go to the commander of the northernmost brigade of Pharaoh's army," he said. *Who should be here and deploying behind us.* "Find why they delay, and return quickly. Say that we are hard-pressed."

"Ahhhh, not bad," William Walker said. "Fundamentally, life is pretty good."

He looked up at the tender green of the branches moving overhead, little sun-gleams flickering through them. Spring was nice. For one thing, it meant shuttling back and forth across the Aegean would be easier, without the winter storms to worry about. For another, he could finally get his hands on the Nantucketer bastards and deal with them once and for all. His grin turned wry.

Of course, they'll be expecting to deal with me, *won't they?*

He pushed the thought away, and worried about Sicily. *One thing at a time. We can take it back when we've made sure of the east.* Time for one last hunt and picnic with the family, even though the long gray-clad columns were swinging up from the coast.

There was a quiet bustle around him; he sat up and ate another dried apricot, savoring the sweetness. The glade was half an acre or so, more than enough for the hunter's camp— a platoon of the Royal Guards, a tent and the horse lines, a few servants. Two of the soldiers went by with another boar slung on a pole between them, a slight whiff of rank scent amid the spring wildflowers and pine and thyme. He grinned. Once upon a time he'd taken up hunting boar with spears because it gave you *mojo* among the wogs, something that a warrior-class man was just *expected* to do.

He hadn't really expected to start enjoying it. The hunting was excellent in this part of northwest Anatolia; the locals called it Seha River Land, and it had been Green Bursa in his birth-century. There were plenty of oak trees on the hills here, and acorns made for big, prolific wild pigs.

"Nothing like a day's hunt to give you an appetite," he said.

His son Harold flashed a grin at him; he'd been sneaking looks at the butt of the servant-toy kneeling beside Alice's folding canvas chair.

Just starting to get interested, Walker thought indulgently. *Have to get him a couple of experienced instructors in a while.* No son of *his* was going to have to suffer the sort of adolescent-male hell he'd gone through.

Hong was in what Walker thought of as her Safari Dominatrix costume: glossy boots, flared jodhpurs, belted bush jacket carrying revolver and hunting knife, and broad-brimmed hat with a leopardskin band. She took a tall glass of lemonade and playfully tickled the nude servant with the tassel of her riding crop.

Nude except for those body-piercing rings and the silver chains, Walker thought. He'd always thought the look sort of grotesque, but Hong was entitled to her own aesthetics.

"You know, your dear regent is seeing an *awful* lot of Arnstein," she said, then turned the handle of the crop into one of the chains and jerked sharply, shivering a little at the low shriek that followed.

Blue smoke drifted up from a hardwood fire, and a groom led horses by on their way to a downstream site on the little brook that gurgled through the meadow. The cooks were working hard by the hearths, and the smell made his belly rumble. Others set up the trestle tables and flared out the linen tablecloths. All the comforts of home now, and then some . . .

"I expected him to," Walker said. "Odi just likes finding out about things. That's one reason he's so useful. Sometimes you hardly remember he's a wog."

"You don't think he'll find out too *much* about Nantucket?"

"Oh, right, a *wannax* is going to go all mooney over town-meeting democracy." Walker chuckled. "No, he's much more likely to pick up valuable stuff from Arnstein. He'll be more to the dear professor's taste than any of *us.* Sanctimonious bastard."

Knives flashed as the barbeque was carved. Walker shoulder-rolled to his feet and strolled over with the others, snagging a roll as the hunting party and his guests—the Iraiina head of the Royal Guard, a couple of generals, some important local collaborators—gathered. There was the usual slight wait while the eagle-eyed kitchen steward checked nobody had made any unauthorized additions to the cuisine. Luckily the locals didn't know many good poisons—part of the reputation of Alice's cult was based on her uptime knowledge.

The first dish was a glazed loin of wild boar, stuffed with a filling of herbs, crumbs, and garlic.

"*Hot,*" Hong said, fanning her mouth and reaching for her wine cup. Then she fed morsels to the toy with her fork.

"Ah, you easterners never could handle real barbeque," Walker said, taking another slice. "We've finally got the chilies coming from the Lakonian estates, and the latest cook has some idea how to handle them."

He drank some himself; he'd also gotten the winemakers to understand that sweeter was not necessarily better. Day after tomorrow it would be back to campaign living, but tonight he could enjoy himself. The sun was setting behind blue hills to the west, casting low shadows as the meal wound down.

God, what's the proof on this stuff? Walker thought, as he spilled a little. *My nose is going numb already.*

The glass slipped from his hands. A sharp cry from Hong drew his eye. She was recoiling, bewildered. The toy had gripped the chain which spanned the rings in her nipples and wrenched it out. Blood spattered down her pale stomach, but her face was expressionless; then it broke into a dawning smile. She stood and ran three steps and fell facedown, her arms and legs beating a tattoo on the turf, like the wings of a beetle thrown on its back.

"Dad!" Harold cried. "I can't feel my hands! I can't—" He slapped himself, tears leaking down his face. "I can't—"

His words ended in a rush of vomit; Walker could smell how he fouled himself. His father tried to rise and go to him, but his hands slipped off the table despite the sudden and desperate fury that welled up and turned the world misty red. The generals and officers down the table were trying to rise as well, and falling, and moaning.

Walker looked at Hong. Her eyes were wide, and her hands clutched her stomach.

"Aconite," she whispered. "Chilies hid the taste—*ow!*"

The sun was falling . . . no, the light was falling, faster than the sun. Walker felt a pain in his gut, deep and strong, like a sword stab. He collapsed forward, all the huge strength of his body gone. Hong was shaking as she clutched at herself.

"It *hurts,* Will," she whimpered. "Make it stop, Will. Make it—"

The words were lost in retching and convulsions. Men were shouting and running, far away. Walker fumbled at the butt of his pistol, but there was no sensation in his hand. He had to get it out, find the cook, and kill—

Night fell, and he fell with it, endlessly.

CHAPTER THIRTY-ONE

April, 11 A.E.—Meggido, Kingdom of Egypt
May, 11 A.E.—Walkeropolis, Kingdom of Great Achaea
April, 11 A.E.—Meggido, Kingdom of Egypt

"**B**ack!" Djehuty snarled.

He smashed the pommel of the sword into the fleeing spearman's face, feeling bone crunch. Behind Djehuty, the men of his personal guard leveled their double-barreled shotguns, and the madness faded out of the faces of the soldiers who'd panicked. Those who still held their spears lowered them, and in the uncertain light of dawn he could see them shuffle their feet and drop their eyes.

"If you run from death, it follows you—and death runs fast," Djehuty said, his voice firm but not angry. "Remember that it is ruin to run from a fight, for you cannot fight and flee, but the pursuer can still strike at your naked back as he chases *you*. Return to your positions."

"Sir—" one said, desperate. "Lord, the thunderbolts strike us and we cannot strike back!"

"I know," Djehuty said. The bandage on one forearm reminded them that he ran the same dangers. "But they cannot take our position unless they send men forward to claim it, and those men you *can* strike." *Those of you who are still alive by then.* "Return to your companies! Fight the foe!"

He turned, stalking through rows of wounded men groaning on the rocky dirt, through shattered carts and dead horses— someone was skinning them for cooking, at least, and he must find who'd thought to organize parties to fill waterskins—and looked up the pass. Nobody; nobody but his reserves, and they were few enough.

If Pharaoh does not come, we will die here, he thought. Unless he withdrew now, leaving a rear guard . . . *No. We have lost too many of our draught beasts. I cannot save the cannon or the chariots.* A grim satisfaction: *I have done my part, and my men as well. If the plan fails, it is not our doing.*

Pharaoh's doing . . . he thrust the thought from him.

Then there *was* something in the pass: a messenger. A *mounted* messenger, plunging recklessly down the steep rocky way, leaning back with feet braced in the stirrups as his horse slid the final dozen yards almost in a sitting position. It hung its lathered head as the messenger drummed heels on its ribs and came over to him, wheezing as its flanks heaved like a bronzesmith's bellows. The man looked nearly as done-in as his horse, his face a mask of dust and sweat.

"Here," Djehuty said, passing over his waterskin.

The man sucked at it eagerly; the water was cut with one-fifth part of sour wine. "Lord," he gasped after a moment. "From Pharaoh."

He offered a scroll of papyrus; Djehuty touched it to his forehead in the gesture of respect and broke the seal to read eagerly; his eyes skipping easily over the cursive demotic script.

Enemy ships with many guns at the Gateway of the North, he read, and grunted as if shot in the belly. That was the fortress of Gaza, the anchor of the Royal Road up the coast. Only if it was securely held could even a single man return to Khem across the deserts of Sinai. *Troops armed with fire-weapons are landing and investing the fortress. Pharaoh marches to meet them. Hold your position at all hazards; you are the rear guard.*

Djehuty grunted again, as a man might when he had just been condemned to death. That was where the cream of the enemy forces had gone, right enough.

"Sir!" Another messenger, one of his own men, and on foot. "Sir, the enemy attack!"

Helmut Mittler felt himself sweat as he walked through the palace. There was panic in the streets of Walkeropolis, a few fires . . . not much, though.

My Security Battalions were ready, he thought with some satisfaction. And had Walker *really* believed he wouldn't find a way to monitor his correspondence?

The Americans had triumphed back home in the future, but it wasn't because they were better at espionage or covert operations or *dezinformatzia*. Even the stupid Russians had been better at that.

Now . . .

He took a deep breath. "Eumenes, Taltos, I'll go on alone from here."

The guards stationed down the long corridor bore the shoulder flashes of the regent's personal regiment, recruited from his ancestral estates in Ithaka. They stood like statues against the iridescent mosaics of the walls, no doubt ready to put down any challenge to their master's power.

Any challenge that can be met with brute force, Mittler thought. *Not that brute force is to be despised, but I think I've just demonstrated its limitations.* Odikweos would need him . . . and there would come a time when *he* didn't need Odikweos.

A last pair of guards firmly but courteously relieved him of his weapons and opened the tall doors with their wolfshead handles. The study within was one Walker had been fond of, with French doors overlooking a terrace, the gardens and the city he'd founded. *I will keep the name,* Mittler decided.

The . . . well, not exactly the regent anymore . . . was seated behind the desk. Two steel longswords rested on the subtly beautiful inlay; Mittler's brows rose, but he supposed there was some supersitious reason. At this stage of historical evolution such things were to be expected—the dialectic predicted them.

"My lord Regent," Mittler said. "I regret to report that rioters—doubtless in the pay of the conspirators—have eliminated the remaining family of our beloved fallen lord."

Some of the children had had to be dragged out of closets and from under beds. Regrettable, but given the dynastic beliefs of these people, necessary.

The Achaean nodded, his craggy features set and somber in the light of the single lamp. "Everything you say, my friend, is to the point," he said. "You are a man of swift wit, Lord Mittler. But you have never been a sailor."

"A sailor, my lord?"

"If you had, you would know that a rope is no stronger than its weakest part. So with a braided rope of thoughts. If the first strand is weak, all the others fail, be they braided with ever so much skill."

The French doors opened, and a tall man stepped in. He was in Achaean dress, but height and the glasses on his beak nose and the whole way he held himself shouted of the twentieth century.

"You," Mittler whispered.

"Me," Ian Arnstein said. He smiled unpleasantly. "The Jewboy. We *do* meet again, Herr Mittler. I understand that you enjoy chess . . . and so do I. Check, and mate."

Mittler felt blood running to his face, and rage made the

collar of his uniform tunic too tight. "*You*," he said. "I should have known—"

Odikweos lifted one of the swords and rapped it on the table. "You should not have assumed that because a man was born in this time, he was a fool. The King of Men, for all his cunning, also thought so," he said gently. "I have never made that mistake, even with women, slaves, or barbarians. A man who underestimates a foe is a fool indeed."

"You were in this with the Jew!"

The Achaean shook his head. "By no means. I was angry with my lord, and so I told this man. I told him also what I would do were my lord to fall; but I did not raise my hand against him. Nor did he slay my lord. *You* did, Lord Mittler. Thus when you die, my lord is avenged . . . and I am free of obligation, in the eyes of Gods and men. And Walker's handfast men are free to follow me, since their lord's sons died with him."

The noise from the city beyond was swelling. The crackle of small arms came loud, and the flat boom of cannon, and the screaming of many voices.

"That is the attack on the headquarters of your ministry," Odikweos said.

"You—" Mittler forced his anger down. "I will serve you well," he said. "You need me."

Odikweos laughed; it was a sound no man of the twentieth could have made, and entirely amused. "Serve me as you served the lord you betrayed?" he said. "No, Lord Mittler, I do not need you. I am not a foreigner who must rule the *telestai* of the Achaeans by putting them in constant fear. I am of the blood of Zeus; I am a man they can obey without cost to their honor. They have been at war and in a storm of change for near ten years. They will welcome one of their own—who holds the capital and the armies—and they will welcome a time of rest."

Arnstein crossed his arms and smiled again; Mittler wondered why he had ever thought the other man soft. The Achaean lord put the point of his sword under the blade of the other, near the hilt. With an expert flip of his thick wrist he flicked it up, to land at the German's feet. The steel sang with a discordant harmonic.

"Pick it up," Odikweos said, coming around the desk. He moved lightly despite the solid strength of his shoulders. "The talons of the Kindly Ones are on your neck, Mittler. My lord

Walker's ghost waits for your blood to be spilled in offering before he crosses Lethe."

Mittler picked up the sword. It felt heavy and awkward in his hand; for a brief instant he wondered how the same weight could be so graceful in Odikweos's grip.

The steel *kopesh* was lead-heavy in Djehuty's hand as he retreated another step; the ring of Egyptians grew smaller as they stood shoulder to shoulder around the standard. *For Khem*, he thought, and slashed backhand. The edge thudded into the rim of an Aramaean's shield, and the leather-covered wicker squeezed shut on the blade. The nomad shrieked with glee and wrenched, trying to tear the weapon from the Egyptian's hand. Djehuty's lips bared dry teeth as he smashed the boss of his own shield in the man's face, then braced a foot on his body to wrench the sickle-sword free. *For Sennedjem!* he thought, swinging it down. Distracted, he did not see the spearhead that punched into his side just below the short ribs. Bent over, wheezing, he saw the spearman staring incredulously at the way the bronze point had bent over double against the iron scales of his armor, then scream frustration and club the spear. Exhaustion weighed down his limbs as he struggled to turn, to bring up shield and blade. Something struck him again, he couldn't tell where, and the world went gray.

His last thought was that the earth tasted of salt from the blood that soaked it.

Bits of the formulae for addressing the Judge of the Dead flitted through Djehuty's head along with blinding pain as his eyelids fluttered open. But it was not jackal-headed Anubis who bent over him, but a foreigner with a cup of water. The Egyptian sucked it down gratefully before he thought to wonder at it.

Prisoner, he thought. *I must be a prisoner*. But he was not bound, and beneath him lay a folding cot with a canvas bed, not the hard ground. He turned his head carefully. He was under a great awning, amid rows of others. Sennedjem! His son lay not far away. Djehuty gasped relief to see his chest rising under a mummy's swath of bandages. But what was held in the clear glass bottle that was connected to his arm by a flexible tube?

Djehuty's eyes went wide when he realized that the same piece of sorceror's apparatus drained into his *own* arm. Gradually the fear died, and the pain in his head became less. When the foreigner's black commander came, he was able to stare back with something approaching dignity as she sat on a folding stool beside his cot.

She spoke, and the *Sudunu* interpreter relayed the words:

"You and your men fought very well."

Djehuty blinked, then nodded. "You deceived us very well. Ransom?" he went on without much hope.

She shook her head. "When the war is over, we will release all our prisoners."

Djehuty blinked again, this time in surprise. It would take a strong commander to deny victorious troops the plunder of victory, and the sale of prisoners was an important part of that. Even Pharaoh, the living God, might have difficulties. With an effort, he fought down bitterness against Ramses; what the Pharaoh decreed, must be done . . . even if it destroyed the Brigade of Seth at the word of the foreigner Mek-Andrus.

"Your king must be a ruler of great power," he said.

"We have no King," she said, and smiled slightly at his bafflement. "We come from . . . very far away. You might call us exiles."

"Your whole nation?" he said in bafflement.

"No," she said and explained: "Just one small island of us, and a ship. So we were stranded here and now."

"Ah," Djehuty said bitterly. "And with arts of war like none we know, you seek to carve out a great empire."

Long black fingers knotted into a fist on a trousered knee. "No. *Some* of us saw that they might become Kings here, with what they knew. The rest of us . . . must fight to enforce our law upon them."

"No King . . ." Djehuty frowned. "I find that hard to believe. Only a powerful King can make a people strong in war."

She shook her head. "That is not so, Djehuty of the Brigade of Seth. We have arts that your people do not, is that not so?" He nodded, reluctantly. "Well, not all of those arts are arts of war. We have found that one man's wisdom is not enough to steer a great nation, and how to . . . melt together the wisdom of many."

"I do not understand."

"Let me tell you," she said, "of a thing we call a *constitution*, which is a government of laws and not of men . . ."

When she rose with a promise to return and speak more, his head was whirling as badly as it had when the spear shaft clubbed him. He heard words in the foreign commander's language:

"*And that'll cause a lot more trouble than gunpowder, in the long run.*"

"Wait," he said. "One thing—what name will this battle be given? Surely it is a greater one than Kadesh, even."

Let the chronicles remember it, and with it the name of Djehuty. Chronicles that do not lie, like the ones that called Kadesh a victory for Ramses.

She turned, smiling wryly. "We will will name it from the hill that overlooks the battlefield," she said. "Har-Megiddo. Armaggedon, in our tongue."

CHAPTER THIRTY-TWO

May, 11 A.E.—Hattusas, Kingdom of Hatti-land
June, 11 A.E.—Babylon, Kingdom of Kar-Duniash
December, 10 A.E.—Tarim Basin, Central Asia
September, 11 A.E.—Nantucket Town, Republic of
  Nantucket
June, 11 A.E.—Ural River, Central Asia
September, 11 A.E.—Nantucket Town, Republic of
  Nantucket

*B*attalus Interruptus, Kenneth Hollard thought, dazed. *Here I've spent the last three years of my life getting ready to* defeat *Walker, and they just up and* kill *the bastard!*

He felt a surge of irritation, which died of shame when images from the last field hospital visit went through his head. Outside the command pavilion the sounds of the greatest block party of all time filtered in through the warm spring air. So did the smell of roasting meat; no more need to conserve every beast.

"No," Odikweos, King of Men, was saying.

"Excuse me?" Doreen Arnstein said sharply.

Her expression was sharp, but she hadn't let go of Ian Arnstein's hand since they sat down side by side at the head of the big table. He still looked a little stunned, after his first glimpse of his daughter.

"I said, *no*," Odikweos repeated, flashing a white smile through his grizzled beard. "Is this not your English word?" He tossed his head.

"No, I will not give up all the Wolf Lords . . . that is, the *eqwetai* of my former liege-lord. Those who needed slaying have been slain. The others are too useful to me; I shall confirm them in the most of their estates and titles, and their sons shall be Achaeans and serve *my* son. Nor will you attempt to slay them by stealth if you value my friendship. I will withdraw my troops from the Hittite lands; and since you hold it already, I will agree to make no moves against Sicily. Beyond that, *I* rule Great Achaea, and I shall make such changes there as seem good to me. We are not defeated suppliants in this war; we have decided to end it at our pleasure, for our own reasons."

Oh, please God, don't order me to invade Greece, Hollard thought.

Scratchy through the speaker, Jared Coffin's dry Yankee voice spoke:

"Something there. Let's thrash this out."

King Kashtiliash pulled at his curled beard. "I came here because of my treaty with you, to put down the threat of Walker," he said. "Now that threat is gone. I wish to go home, and settle my realm." A broad carnivore grin. "Since my realm now includes Canaan, the Egyptians having withdrawn from it."

Tudhaliyas stirred unhappily. Kashtiliash raised a soothing hand: "And my brother the One Sun of Hatti-land will doubtless have much to do. Now that he is the only monarch with the new weapons in these lands, who may easily sweep to the Achaean sea, put down the Kaska mountain tribes, and push his frontiers far to the north and east in the Caucasus and around Lake Van."

Tudhaliyas's long dark clean-shaven face began to smile; it looked a little unnatural on his gloomy countenance. "Oh, indeed," he said, rubbing his hands. Then he cocked a sharp eye at the other Great King: "Provided nobody encroaches on my domains of Karkemish and Ugarit."

"But of course," Kashtiliash purred, a rumble in his deep chest. "Although we should consult about these horse-tamer tribes they say are advancing against us through northern Elam, the . . ."

"Medes and Persians," Kathryn Hollard said. "And Saka and Scythians and whatnot."

"Yes, those. Perhaps we should divide those lands between us."

"Perhaps we should," Tudhaliyas said thoughtfully.

"Perhaps we should indeed," the *Seg Kallui* of Kar-Duniash said. "First thing *I'm* going to do, though, is visit Dr. Clemens and get the IUD removed. Please hold any wars for about ten months."

Everyone chuckled. Well, nearly everyone; Marian Alston just smiled slightly. "You're making a good start on getting back to managing your own affairs," she said. "Still, I think a general treaty all 'round would be a good idea—trade, that sort of thing."

"Ayup," Cofflin's voice said. They could hear a murmur in the background, as of someone speaking softly in his ear. "I've got some ideas on that . . ."

King Kashtiliash crouched to look down one of the avenues of the great model city atop the table. Justin Clemens and his wife Azzu-ena waited uncertainly amid a bustle of scribes, clerks, engineers Babylonian and Nantucketer, officers, and attendants. Outside the tent, the great sprawling construction camp on the west bank of the Euphrates was in full swing. Most of the streets and broad avenues were still only pegs and string, but thousands of laborers were already trenching the lines for sewers and water systems.

From the corner of his eye he could see a first section of sewer actually being built, an egg-shaped tunnel of fired brick set in asphalt mortar. Not far away rested lengths of ceramic water pipe, tubes ten feet long and a yard across, with walls four inches thick. The great petroleum-fired kilns added another tang to the air, under the massed stink of Babylon across the river.

"Ah, Justin Clemens son of Edgar!" the King said. Clemens bowed. "How goes your work?"

"Faster than I thought it could, King of the Four Quarters," Clemens said.

He walked to the edge of the model; it was twenty feet on a side, resting on thick planks and those on trestles. The city of dreams it showed was definitely Babylonian—marked with the terraced pyramids of ziggurats, the blocky shapes of palace and temple. The layout wasn't, though; a gridwork of avenue and street, with broad radial ways driving through from the center. Along the water side was a great brick wall and highway to contain floods, and three long-arch bridges crossed the broad Euphrates. There was no city wall; instead a quartet of low-slung forts bristling with cannon covered the landward approaches and commanded the river passage. Blue-painted canals brought water to parks and gardens as well.

Clemens pointed to his own project near the northeastern corner.

"The waterworks are going up quickly," he said. "The big pumps just arrived from Irondale in Alba, and a couple of Leaton's people. We should have enough clean water for the labor force within a week."

Kashtiliash nodded. His wife Kathryn looked up from the

other end of the table, making a quick note and handing it to a messenger.

"I want to get the sewer works functional as soon as possible too," she said. "If we can get the farmers using processed sludge rather than raw night soil, it'll cut dysentery in the villages around here by three-quarters."

"We need to put in village wells as well," Clemens noted quickly. "Sealed-tube wells with hand pumps."

"All in good time," Kashtiliash said. "There is work for my lifetime, and my sons'." He looked at his queen and grinned, and she returned the expression.

A shake of the leonine head. "But that is not what I wish to speak of, best of healers," he said. "Here, come."

He drew a cloth from a smaller table. The model there was of a complex of buildings, two-story blocks around courtyards; there were even models of tiny palm trees there.

"You wished to remain in the land of Kar-Duniash, did you not, Justin son of Edgar?"

Clemens nodded, a little wary. There was more good he could do here, and he thought it would be easier for him to adapt to this than Azzu-ena to Nantucket.

"Well, here you shall. It shall be called the *Clemens Teaching Hospital.*"

He stopped, grinning at the younger man. Clemens grew aware that his mouth was hanging open like a carp's. *Jesus, I thought we'd have a little clinic, build it up gradually . . .*

"King of the Four Quarters—I and my wife cannot run such an, an institution by ourselves."

Kashtiliash rumbled laughter under Kathryn's contralto chuckle.

"You won't have to," the queen said. "There's all those orderlies that the Coast Guard trained—remember, those slaves Kash's father gave us, and we freed? You did a fair bit of that yourself."

"And there will be other *Nantukhtar* doctors who will come," Kashtiliash said. "Even if they come only for a brace of years each, they will not find me niggardly. You yourself, Justin son of Edgar, I will double the wage you receive—and you will have this fine house, and I will add thereunto a thousand *iku* of well-watered land near the city by *kudurru*-grant."

Clemens felt a sharp pain in his ankle, where Azzu-ena had kicked him; outwardly she was the picture of demure modesty, with her shawl drawn over her head and held across her lower face with one hand.

"Ah," he said, bowing again, "The Bull of Marduk is generous!"

"And in this *hospital* you will not only cure the sick, but teach," Kashtiliash said, warming to his thoughts. "I have sent to your Island for copies of the books of healing—soon my own *printing press* will be at work, with men trained at Ur Base. You will take the sons—"

"And daughters," Azzu-ena and Kathryn said simultaneously.

"And daughters." Kashtiliash smiled fondly. "Of physicians and scribes and priests—thus their families will object less—as apprentices."

"And commoners, my Lord King," Clemens said, quietly but firmly.

"As you wish. And this is only the beginning! Near your *hospital* will grow over the years a great school of all learning—the lore of my folk, and the New Learning of yours. Such is called a *university*, is it not? Yes, it will take much gold, as much as many regiments of riflemen, but it will—"

He looked at the queen. "Remember that night on the terrace, beloved of the King's heart?"

"Yes," she said, smiling.

"I promised then that I would not leave my people in the dirt. And I will not!"

The great scarred hand closed unconsciously into a fist, and the dark hawk eyes flashed. Clemens cleared his throat.

"Ah, King of the Universe, I . . . my wife and I did plan to visit Nantucket before settling."

"Excellent," Kashtiliash said, all business once more. "You may arrange much of what we will need there. I will be visiting myself, and the *Seg Kallui*."

He laughed at Azzu-ena's start. "Yes, a conference of the Great Kings is to be called, wise lady, in Nantucket Town. Much thought has gone into the arrangements." A snort. "Not least, to ensure that the Great Kings are still Great Kings when they return—we have all agreed to move against any usurper, so there will be none such."

A boy's eagerness lit the King's face. "And I, I shall see the homeland of wonders myself!"

"Jesus, *that's* not going to fly again," Vicki Cofflin said.

She completed her limping walk around the staked-down dirigible. Or what was left of it. The hull had a perceptible kink in it, where broken frames and stringers creaked. Bits of the doped fabric that covered it fluttered tattered in the cold desert wind; large patches were bare, and she could see inside to the gasbags.

"Well, no," Alex Stoddard replied.

He didn't look as beaten-up as she—his right arm wasn't in a cast, for starters—but the bruises on his face had only begun to fade.

"None of the engines are functional, to start with," he went on, blinking at the sun and the alkaline dust blowing from the bare earth around them. "And going on from there. Still, she kept us alive, the *Emancipator.*"

"Which is a miracle," she said, looking at the riven rock that speared the sky not far to the north.

Wherever we are, it's a desert basin with some bloody enormous mountains around it.

"I thought we were all going to die when we headed for the moon after we dropped the emergency ballast," Stoddard said. "We must have hit twenty-five thousand feet, at least, the way the emergency valves spilled hydrogen. I passed out around twenty, I think."

Vicki grunted—it was more comfortable than talking, with a mouth bruised and cut inside on the edges of her own teeth—and looked over at the row of five graves not far away. They already looked timeworn, even though they'd only been there a few days. This eternal wind . . .

Which is why we stayed aloft so long. With no control, landing was extremely tricky. By the time they'd all become fully conscious again, it hadn't mattered how much further they drifted looking for a good spot.

"Heads up, ma'am! Delegation coming out from the oasis!"

The call came from the lookout in the observation post atop the hull. Vicki gave a quick glance around; nothing could hide the scrapes and broken bones, but everyone was as neat as possible . . . and more to the point, everyone had a rifle or pistol, and there were two functional Gatlings.

Plus the Shipwreck Kit, she thought—every Islander craft carried that, a set of how-to books and basic tools.

The locals came closer, a crowd of footmen with bronze-headed spears led by a brace of chariots and followed by a crowd of women and children. Vicki narrowed her eyes as she took them in.

Well, however far east we came, we aren't into Oriental country yet.

The man in the lead chariot was six-foot or so, in reddish-brown tunic and trousers and boots, with a falcon-headed bronze ax in one hand, knife and sword at his belt, compound bow and javelins racked in his war-car. His long beak-nosed face was about the same shade as hers, and his shoulder-length hair was a russet brown.

Ok, these look like Caucasoids, she thought—northern Europeans, at that; blonds, redheads, and brunettes all plentiful. Some were wearing what looked like tartan plaids, at that. She took in that, the plumed and bedizened horses drawing the chariots, the weapons . . .

"These bastards get around, don't they?" Alex said, echoing her thought.

"Get me the Number Three phrasebook from the Shipwreck Kit," she said.

That was the one titled: *Early Indo-European Languages—Useful Phrases.* She spoke the Sun People dialect of Alba; that ought to be a help.

"Hail," she said, when the chief's charioteer drew rein. *"Ekwos?"* she added, pointing to the horse . . .

"Osu, su-diwom," he said, and turned to take a clay goblet from an attendant. *"Poixesoine medhuos?"* he went on, holding it out to the strangers.

It was a long way home, and they'd need the locals' help. The surest way to get that was to make them offers they couldn't refuse.

They probably have some local enemies. Damn, I wonder what's happening at home?

The radio had been very thoroughly smashed. Not that news would make any difference *here*, but it would be nice to know . . .

"So, a new world," Doreen Arnstein said, laying Miriam down in her crib.

Ian leaned over his daughter, watching the infant-blue eyes blink into sleep. Outside the noise of the festivities was still a dull background roar under a clear autumn sky; the wine beat in his own ears, like his blood, or the sea. Through the window came the *pop* and multicolored starburst of fireworks. Their housekeeper Denditwara was in a rocking chair by the window, with her own newborn in her lap.

"It's a new world every time we produce one of these," Ian said, tucking the blanket up around his child.

"We?" Doreen said, raising a brow. "I seem to recall doing most of the work, myself."

"Details," he said loftily, as they turned down the stairs and he dodged her poking finger in his ribs.

They came out onto the little verandah, deep in shadow with only the whale-oil lights of the streetlamps. Up to the north there was a blaze of kerosene light and a sound of song from the old Congregational church, where a midnight service of thanksgiving was under way, Prelate Gomez presiding. Their friends were waiting for them, and David was deep in conversation with the Alston-Kurlelo and Cofflin children; he caught snatches of excited descriptions of Babylon and Hattusas and Mycenae. And a lament over the general uselessness of infant siblings, too . . .

"Glad I'm through making those speeches," Jared Cofflin grumbled.

"Glad we're through with the battles," Marian said. Swindapa squeezed her hand.

Several other pairs were coming up the road, away from Main Street. King Kashtiliash strode briskly, the embroidered robe of formality swirling around his muscular thighs like a warrior's cloak, the tall flowerpot hat spangled in gold sequins glittering in the lamplight; beside him Kathryn Hollard matched him stride for stride in robes more elaborate and just as gorgeously colored. Her brother followed, Raupasha at his side. Unlike the Babylonian monarch, she was frankly gawking as she peered about, clinging to her husband's arm. Isketerol of Tartessos brought up the rear; he was looking about him with a slight quirk to his lips, remembering, pointing out this or that to his son Sarsental. The boy goggled as openly as Raupasha much of the time, then remembered his dignity.

Odikweos of Great Achaea walked beside them with a sailor's roll to his stride, shrewd hazel eyes missing nothing.

"So this is the city that brought all the great kingdoms to their knees," he said, as they halted with the group about the steps of the Councilor for Foreign Affairs' house.

"Brought them together in peace, Your Majesty," Ian Arnstein said soothingly.

"Is there a difference?" Odikweos said; but he said it grinning. "Forgive my wayward son," he went on to Marian and Swindapa, bowing in courtly wise with a swirl of his cloak. "He found . . . ah . . ."

"Company more interesting than ours, and much prettier than his father," Alston finished for him. "We'd best be getting on to Guard House. I don't quite trust anyone else to do a moa leg properly—they go dry if'n you don't catch them just right. And the wine will have breathed, the steaks are sitting in the garlic marinade ready to go on the grill, and oysters are better chilled."

Swindapa leaned over to whisper in her ear and she laughed, an easy full-throated sound, as at an old family joke. Then she called: "Heather! Lucy!"

The children were eventually rounded up, to fall in behind the adults. They took the roundabout route to Guard House, which led them back into the crowds spilling up from Main Street; they dodged a conga line led by a couple of Marines in rumpled uniform, and including a Kassite warrior from the Babylonian Royal Guard, a piratical-looking scarred Achaean, a Tartessian in a saffron cloak followed by a nude redhead who was probably Fiernan and certainly the merrier for the bottle of screech she was waving in a free hand. The crowds about cheered them on, just as polyglot and nearly as carefree, in languages that rang with Semitic gutturals, the rapid-fire sinuosities of Greek, nasal Yankee twangs . . .

"Hard to believe it's over," Jared Cofflin said again.

"Over?" his wife replied. "It's barely beginning!"

Doreen Arnstein looked upwards. "Did you know," she said thoughtfully, "that time travel is mathematically identical to faster-than light travel? If one's possible, the other must be too. Someday . . ."

"Ayup," Jared nodded, in answer to both. "Mebbe." He looked around. "Mebbe this time we'll be able to avoid some of the old mistakes."

"Yes, we'll make new ones—all our own," Swindapa laughed.

"Undoubtedly," Ian Arnstein said. "At least they'll be new and interesting blunders. In the meantime . . . let's eat!"

Althea Walker, last scion of the House of the Wolf, turned in the saddle and looked behind her. The Carpathians had long since faded from view; all she could see from horseback was an infinity of grass that waved stirrup high on her horse, hissing in the long melancholy wind. Ahead was the line of a great river, marked by the green groves of trees vivid against the brown-tawny summer grass. She turned her mount away from the caravan and spurred it up a slight rise.

Here she could wave the mounted guards back a little, far enough that none could see the tears drying on her cheeks in the hot dry wind as she stared westward. It whipped strands of her blond hair around her face, sun-faded white against the brown tan.

Nothing to see except grass rippling like the sea, beneath the huge blue dome of heaven. Wagon after wagon creaked by, wheels jolting on the hard ground and canvas tilts fluttering in the dry hay-scented breeze; they and the herds of cattle and sheep and horses raised dust that hung overhead in a haze. They were important wagons, though; stuffed with machine tools and books, and the skills of those who rode in them or trudged along beside were crucial, too.

Mounted warriors formed a screen that stretched out to the edge of sight, sun blinking off their metal. Ohotolarix came trotting in from an inspection sweep, his horse taking the slope effortlessly despite a tall warrior's weight. Well, it was a son of Bastard, her father's quarter horse . . .

He saw the carved-stone set of her face, and the direction of her eyes.

"He shall be avenged," her father's handfast man said, laying his own hand on her shoulder for a moment.

Althea nodded. "But that wasn't what I was thinking of," she said.

He looked at the girl in surprise. "What, then?"

"That I won't make my father's mistakes. That I will not strike too soon, nor will I settle by the sea where the Islanders—" she spat to one side, into the tall grass—"can get at me."

Ohotolarix nodded. "Well, this Ferghanna place we're heading for is about as far from salt water as we could go," he said.

"Pete!"

It was Eddie, calling from the space he'd kept open in the basement taproom of the Brotherhood of Thieves. Treaty celebrations meant there was just barely room for three more at the end of the long table, now that the guitar-and-drums band on the tiny corner dais had folded up. A low roar of sound came out to meet them, along with smoke, the smell of roasting meat and frying fish and fresh bread and the smells of massed humanity; Spring Indigo flinched back a little as it died away and a song bellowed out:

> *Head the ship to homeward*
> *Shake out every sail*
> *Lithe leap the billows—merry sings the gale!*
> *Captain, work the reckoning*
> *How many knots a day?*

> *'Round the world—and home again*
> *That's the Island way!*

Peter Giernas touched her on one elbow, Sue on the other; she shifted Jared on her hip, smiled and headed in with them. A waiter eeled through the crowd, blinked in recognition, and half-shouted apologetically:

"I'm sorry, Captain Giernas—no dogs allowed!"

Perks was sticking close to his master's side, pressed against his thigh. At the words he looked up at the waiter, sensed his meaning and fixed him with a yellow-eyed glare, bristling and showing long wet teeth. Giernas made a precautionary grab for his ruff and smiled at the server.

"Don't worry," he said. "Perks here is fine, as long as I'm with him."

"Ah . . . oh, well, he's a war hero too, I suppose."

Heroes dime a dozen, Giernas thought, as they pushed the rest of the distance and squeezed in. He didn't mind the crowding—much. It wasn't as if he had to take it for long, after all. Eddie was grinning, a little the worse for beer but not drunk by any manner of means. The voices in the background went on, as the four of them settled in:

> *We've fought pirates from Achaea*
> *Bought tin 'mid Java seas*
> *Drunk beer in Anyang taverns*
> *In the shade of camphor trees!*
> *Across the Line and Gulf Stream*
> *'Round by Table Bay*
> *Everywhere—and home again*
> *That's the Island way!*

"Here," Eddie said. "Still hot."

The plates were heaped, with roast pork and crackling, potatoes, steamed new vegetables; there were hunks of good wheat bread hot from the oven dripping with butter, and honey for dipping. Spring Indigo nibbled a piece of the bread cautiously, then bit enthusiastically.

"This is better than bannock with bear fat!" she said.

"Hell of a lot better, honey." Giernas laughed and took a pull on the mug. "Well, people, I got through to the man at the Pacific Bank, and the prize's been condemned, right enough." He brought out a folded pice of paper from a pocket of his buckskin hunting shirt. "Here it is!"

When he read out the figures, Jaditwara's eyes went wide. Eddie let loose with a Zarthani war whoop, which didn't attract as much attention as it might have, not tonight. Giernas laughed long and loud himself; it was good to be young, a well-loved father and husband . . . and rich. Before the war, before the Expedition, he'd been a bachelor, content enough to rent a room over the Laughing Loon in Providence for the times he wasn't rangering around and camping under a tree. Now . . .

Now I'm not rich like Leaton or Brandt, he thought, diving into the roast pork and savoring the longed-for taste of fresh vegetables. *But I'm rich enough to be able to do what I want, eat my own mutton with my feet under my own table. And to look after my own folk without asking any man's leave to do it. That's a good feeling.*

"Medals are fine," he said aloud. "But gold is sort of a more *tangible* mark of the Republic's feelings. Speaking of which, you're going to have to show a little more respect from now on." He took out a pin with two small silver bars on it. "It's Ranger *Captain* Peter Giernas from now on."

"*Diawas Pithair!*" Eddie swore.

He and Jaditwara leaned over to slap him on the back and shoulder. Jared patted him, too, then went back to looking around, as alert as a cricket and fearless as a badger, beating time to the chanty with pudgy infant hands; a lot of others were doing that with beer mugs:

> *Nightly stands the North Star*
> *Higher on our bow*
> *Straight we run to homeward*
> *Our thoughts are in it now!*
> *A jolly time with friends on shore*
> *When we've drawn our pay;*
> *All about—and home again*
> *That's the Island way*
> *Oh, that's our Island way!*

The waiter came back with more beer, and a large meaty bone, rawly fresh. Giernas snaffled it off the tray before anyone else could try giving it to Perks—no sense in taking a chance of spoiling a happy occasion and the youngster certainly meant well—and handed it under the table without looking down himself. The wolf-dog's great murdering jaws took it; then slurping and cracking noises started to come from the floor by their feet. Perks wasn't what you'd call a finicky eater . . . but then, neither were a lot of the people here tonight. Spring Indigo was cutting up small pieces of her plateful and feeding them to Jared as she ate.

"Don't grovel too much," he said, swallowing and reaching for the mug again. "You three are lieutenants. I'm surprised the Council didn't take Prelate Gomez' job and give it to Spring Indigo here."

"Good to have gold and rank," Eddie nodded. "Now that I'm going to have a son to inherit my herds."

"Or a *daughter,* maybe," Jaditwara said sharply, looking at him with wry affection. "More to come, either way."

Eddie nodded, sobering a bit. "Oath-brother, Chief—Sue, Indigo, my oath-sisters—I will miss you."

"Hell, you planning on going further away than Long Island?" Giernas said. "That's not too far for a visit now and then."

The ex-Zarthani and the woman who'd been born to the Earth People looked at each other.

"New 'Sconset," Eddie began.

"By the Silver River," Jaditwara continued.

Buenos Aires, on the Rio de la Plata, Giernas thought. *Of course, no reason we should use the Lost Geezer names, now is there?*

"They're handing out land there," Eddie said. "Oath-brother, you wouldn't believe the land—*and* veterans are all getting a full section. So I'll . . ." he paused, yelped like a man who'd been kicked in the shin, ". . . *we'll* have two square miles together." He set his mug down with a thump. "But it means being very far away! I've half a mind—"

He cut off; Giernas was laughing again, and Sue and Spring Indigo along with him, laughing into his solemnity. Mercurial, his brows drew together in a scowl.

"Hell, Eddie," Giernas said at last. "What do you think I was about to try and talk you into? There's already a Ranger Captain here—they want another one down in New 'Sconset, to keep Hollard from falling over his thick Marine feet. They'll be needing Rangers; there's locals to deal with, not so many on the Pampas but lots up in the mountain country. Big stretch of unknown territory there! *And* scouting up along the coast . . ."

This time they all laughed; even Jared, happy because the adults were. Giernas wiped the plate with a heel of bread and belched comfortably, waving for a glass of applejack with his beer, and some of the cherry cobbler. Sue caught his eye and drooped the lid over one of hers; he put an arm around her shoulders, and one around Spring Indigo's waist. *Yeah, the night is young.*

"Land like you wouldn't believe," Eddie was enthusing. "Grazing fit for the Gods." He looked at Spring Indigo. "Like your people's country, oath-sister; tall grass to the horizon, but without the cold winters."

"My people are here," Indigo said, laying her head on Giernas's shoulder. "But it will be good to have broad plains about me."

"And to live by the sea," Jaditwara said. "And see the stars of the southlands—something to teach my daughters."

"Next-door ranches," Sue said. "And we can afford to develop 'em in style—no living in sod huts for twenty years while we slave to pay off loans."

"Good grazing and good hunting," Eddie went on. "I can see it now, my hall—oh, all right, Jaddi, *our* hall—broad fields golden for the harvest, pastures, the colts kicking their heels in the morning mist."

"A base," Giernas nodded. "Home, somewhere to rest in-between times."

The snowpeaks of the Andes floated before his mind's eye, and Iguassu falls, and the Amazon, and condors wheeling over the step-pyramids of Cerro Sechin. He raised his mug.

"Drink to it—to new beginnings!"

> *Oh, Tom will to his parents*
> *Jack will to his dear*
> *Jane to loves and children—*
> *Bob to steaks and beer!*
> *Vicki to the dancing room*
> *To hear the fiddles play;*
> *'Round the world—and home again*
> *That's the Island way.*
>
> *Oh, that's the Island way.*
>
> Everywhere—and home again
> *That's our Island way!*